WOLF WINTER

CLARE FRANCIS

WOLF WINTER

"Stephen King horror and
Ingmar Bergman darkness...
a galloping good read...
perfect for dark nights
in the dead of winter."
Washington Post Book World

"Espionage and treachery.
Plenty of action, intriguing politics,
sturdy heroics, chilling atmosphere."
Kirkus Reviews

"*Wolf Winter* has romance,
adventure, and suspense...
should become a bestseller...
Highly recommended."
Library Journal

WOLF WINTER

CLARE FRANCIS

AVON BOOKS ◆ NEW YORK

Originally published in 1987 in Great Britain by William Heinemann Ltd.

AVON BOOKS
A division of
The Hearst Corporation
105 Madison Avenue
New York, New York 10016

Copyright © 1987 by Clare Francis
Published by arrangement with William Morrow and Company, Inc.
Library of Congress Catalog Card Number: 87-24209
ISBN: 0-380-70689-X

First Avon Books Printing: April 1989

AVON TRADEMARK REG. U.S. PAT. OFF. AND IN OTHER COUNTRIES, MARCA
REGISTRADA, HECHO EN U.S.A.

Printed in the U.S.A.

K-R 10 9 8 7 6 5 4 3 2 1

FOR ROMA SCHAPIRO

My thanks to the many friends, old and new, here and in Norway, who helped me with the research for this book.

Contents

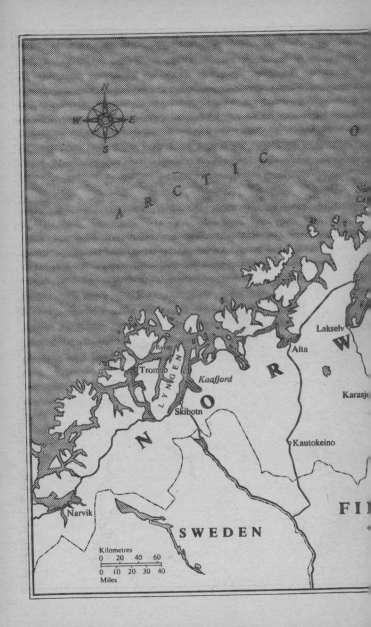

Prologue

North Norway, January 1945

The night was cold and brilliantly clear. You could see for miles: Peak after peak of ice mountains rose into the dome of the sky, jagged crystal teeth squeezed between the deep inroads of the jet-black fjords.

High in the mountains the near-full moon cast long shadows and lit the snow with transparent brilliance so that visibility was particularly good. Which was just as well for the two young men who were making a quick but properly cautious descent of the mountain known by the Lappish name of Goalsvarre.

At 4,230 feet the peak was not the highest in the Lyngen Alps—there were several higher, many of which were tantalizingly unclimbed—but Goalsvarre was close to the village of Lyngseidet and convenient for the bus and ferry ride back to Tromsø.

Most people, had they known of this expedition, would have considered it foolish. It was irresponsible enough to go mountaineering in the depths of a winter night, but to do so when the place was thick with Germans was asking for trouble.

But no one did know. And even if they had, the young men would have argued that winter was the best time to go mountaineering—the snow was firm and powdery—and that at sixty-nine degrees north, well within the Arctic Circle, the long hours of darkness at this time of year made night climbing more or less unavoidable.

And as for the Germans—well, the Occupation had lasted five years and if one waited for it to end one might wait forever.

The descent of the upper slopes went smoothly, and by seven in the morning they had regained their camp on a bluff below the main ridge and were eating a Spartan breakfast. They made desultory but contented conversation. It had been a good hard climb and they had done it in record time with the minimum of equipment.

Taking to their skis, they began the descent of the lower slopes. The moon was setting but the snow was vibrant with reflected starlight. Above the northern peaks the polar sky flickered with the ghostly radiance of the northern lights.

As always Hal led and Jan followed. They traveled in silence; there was no need to speak. It was enough to hear the soft hiss of the skis on the virgin snow and the resonant hush of the frosty air.

A frozen lake discharged into an equally frozen stream, its course discernible only by a slight depression in the thick snow. As the young men followed it downward, Lyngenfjord began to open out before them, a narrow black gash between the glistening mountains.

Hal gestured and they came to a stop.

From deep in the fjord rose a low hum. The two listened for a moment then skied on until they could see across the distant water to where Route 50, the German Army—built north-south highway, snaked its way tortuously down the far shore of the fjord. They paused again and stared, transfixed by the sight of a procession of glimmering pinpricks of light creeping slowly southward.

"Retreat?" Jan asked, unable to keep the excitement out of his voice.

"This far, anyway," Hal said cautiously.

"But surely they'll keep going. They're bound to."

"Well . . ." Hal said doubtfully. "It'll depend on the Russians."

"That's what I mean. The Russians'll chase them out!"

Hal was silent for a moment. "I hope so," he murmured finally.

The German 20th Mountain Army had been on the retreat from the Russian border for two months, dragging themselves across Finland and the top of Norway to this place, Lyngenfjord. During the retreat along the Arctic coast, the German

Army had been pursuing a ruthless scorched-earth policy, evacuating civilians, burning towns and villages, destroying livestock. For weeks evacuees had been arriving in Tromsø by coastal steamer, many of them to be sent farther south. Now more than a hundred thousand German soldiers of the 18th and 36th Mountain Corps were encamped at Lyngen.

Hal tried to imagine what this retreat must have cost the Germans, floundering first through the forests and lakeland of northern Finland, then across the vast emptiness of the high plateau until they reached this, the deeply indented coastline of northern Norway—and all in the depths of winter, on primitive roads that were often closed by avalanche and drift snow. And with the Russian Army on their heels.

It must surely rank as one of the most difficult retreats ever undertaken. Hal knew how impossible it was to move a heavily equipped army quickly, even in ideal conditions; at the age of twelve he'd had a taste for military history, and had read his way through a detailed account of the Napoleonic Wars. For a while he'd even wanted to be a soldier. But then at fourteen he'd discovered the glory of the mountains, and that had spoiled him for everything else.

Now he was almost eighteen and his old ambition to be a soldier had returned. Like every other boy of his age he wanted to get hold of a decent weapon and have a shot at the Germans and force them to get out of Norway.

But *would* the Russians come? There were rumors: It was said the Russians were already deep within the northernmost province of Norway, named Finnmark, and advancing fast on Lyngen. But Hal doubted it. No army would risk getting trapped on this coast, hemmed in by the fjords and open sea on one side and the mountains on the other.

No: The Russians would hold off. And the Germans, having abandoned Finnmark, would stay here at Lyngen until the bitter end.

"Come," he said to Jan, and they refastened their hoods and adjusted their gloves and set off once more.

As they continued downward the night retreated a little and the outlines of the mountains lost their sharpness and became soft and blue-tinged as the winter day, which would grow to no more than a dim twilight, glimmered slowly to life.

Lyngseidet came into view beneath them. Pausing, they looked down. The small village on the edge of Lyngenfjord was choked with German vehicles that hadn't been there the previous evening.

"Better keep clear," Hal said.

They turned away from the village and headed toward a pass through the mountains. This led to a smaller fjord called Kjosen, a finger of water that almost dissected the forty-mile-long Lyngen peninsula. A narrow snow-packed road led over the pass toward the Tromsø ferry. Even this road, though far from busy, had more traffic than usual.

Hal decided it would be risky to take the bus if it was running, which was doubtful. Their papers were in order, but with all this activity the guards at the checkpoints might be overzealous and ask questions about the unusual amounts of food and survival gear in their rucksacks. The guards were always on the lookout for young men fleeing over the mountains to Sweden to avoid *Arbeidstjenesten*—known as AT—the so-called "labor service" introduced by the Quisling government in a thinly disguised attempt to force Norwegians into the German Army.

Hal led the way down into the pass and, when it was safe to do so, on across the snow-packed road and up the opposite slope. Keeping high above the road and the checkpoints, they made their way along the mountainside, parallel to the road, until the pass was left behind and Kjosen Fjord lay below and to their left, a dark gash between the steep blue-lit slopes. Along the shore an occasional farm nestled darkly in the snow, the windows blacked out, the buildings dead-looking.

The hillside got steeper. Hal looked up, trying to remember the formation of the hidden upper slopes. There was a hanging glacier, he knew, and at least one deep snow-filled gully: avalanche country.

Finally they were forced to descend onto a gentler slope covered with sparse birch scrub. The road was now only a hundred yards away. Occasionally a German military vehicle sped past, throwing up clouds of snow, but, screened by the scrub, the two skiers remained unnoticed, striding along in the long sliding gait of practiced cross-country skiers.

A valley opened out to the right. They curved into its mouth to distance themselves from the road.

Suddenly Hal stopped dead so that Jan almost ran into him. Motionless, they listened. The air was very still. For several moments the silence was deep and unbroken. Then a muffled sound floated across the snow.

A human voice.

Hal stiffened. He saw them now: a group of skiers about half a mile away, coming straight for them on a reciprocal course. There were six of them, uniformly dressed in white parkas with rifles slung over their shoulders: a German patrol. And traveling fast.

Why ski troops should be down by this road Hal couldn't imagine, but they were. And there would be no escaping them.

It would be best to look casual and unconcerned when first seen. With a sigh of resignation and anger, Hal gestured to Jan and led the way forward again.

Just as it seemed the patrol must spot them, the leading soldier halted and trained his binoculars up the narrow side valley. He appeared to see something, for with a sudden movement he grabbed his rifle and put it to his shoulder. Then, just as abruptly, he lowered it again and, beckoning excitedly to his men, led the way into the valley, skiing briskly.

The opportunity was too good to miss. The moment the patrol was gone Hal and Jan thrust forward in a rapid kick-glide movement that was almost a run and crossed quickly behind the disappearing Germans.

As he ran Hal glanced sideways. The reason for the soldiers' excitement was now clear. High in the head of the valley were two black dots, plainly visible in the blue light. Men on skis. Climbing slowly up the steep slope at the head of the valley, like two ants on a white wall.

Reaching the comparative safety of a thick clump of birch at the far side of the valley mouth, the two young men paused.

Jan whispered: "Who can they be?"

Hal gave a shrug. The two figures couldn't be Lapps—the Lapps were miles inland on the plateau at this time of year—and they weren't likely to be mountaineers—it wasn't exactly a popular sport. They were probably AT evaders. Hal wished there was something they could do to help, but short of sidetracking the patrol and getting themselves arrested or shot in the process there was nothing to be done.

The Germans had now reached the head of the valley and were striking up a deep gully, climbing awkwardly and slowly. It was hard to be sure from such a distance, but to Hal's eyes the gully looked heavy with drifts, bulges, and hummocks of snow. Some distance above the gully was a steep snowfield with a thick cover of snow, smooth as a cake topping, which gleamed ice-blue in the late-morning twilight.

The gully looked tricky but it was nothing to the snowfield. That looked wildly unstable. Only fools or men untrained for these mountains would have chosen that route.

But the two black dots higher on the mountain knew their stuff all right, for they had bypassed the gully and were now making short work of a ridge well to the side of the pregnant snowfield. Soon they would reach the safety of the high mountains. Hal put up a silent cheer.

Halfway up the gully the soldiers were making heavy weather of their climb. They had slowed down visibly and the leader was stationary, as if undecided about the route ahead.

Suddenly the silence was broken by the distant sound of a shot, echoing once, faintly, through the valley.

Hal stiffened, thinking: They're mad.

There was a long and deathly silence.

Another shot rang out, reverberated once, feebly, and was quickly absorbed by the snow.

Jan gasped audibly.

A small puff of white had appeared at one side of the snowfield. Slowly, almost leisurely, more delicate puffballs ballooned out, like cannon smoke from a broadside.

The sound came seconds later, a low rumbling of distant thunder. Denser clouds blossomed out from the bottom of the snowfield, which lay curiously pristine and untouched in the center. Yet this was an illusion, for the whole face was in fact sliding, the bottom already voiding itself like some vast ponderous waterfall, a white cataract disgorging tons and tons of compacted snow into the gully beneath.

The surface of the snowfield cracked and heaved and segmented, and was slowly obscured by the billowing snow which rose up and outward in a vast cloud.

The six soldiers below seemed rooted to the spot. Then, as if at a signal, they moved at once, racing down the gully in jerky zigzags like insects fleeing a fire. Two figures collided and one fell. The others pressed on, their progress in the heavy snow painfully slow.

It was a race that couldn't be won. The avalanche poured remorselessly into the gully. Hal winced as the dense white cloud engulfed the first man and the next and the next, until four had been overcome. For a moment it seemed that the last two might escape—they appeared to be keeping ahead of the advancing wall—but then they too were enveloped in the rumbling cloud.

A German Army truck passed by on the road behind. It did not stop.

It was a full two minutes before the last thundering echo died away. A pall of blue cloud hung in the valley like morning mist.

Hal and Jan exchanged brief glances. They both knew what the other was thinking. Had the buried men been Norwegians they would have gone for help and tried to dig them out. But it was impossible to feel pity for Germans. It had been a long war and few families had suffered more than Hal's. In 1941 his elder brother had been lost at sea in a torpedoed cargo ship, and a year later his father had been deported to Germany.

Without a word they turned away.

Hal set off at a smart pace: the sooner they were clear of the scene the better. In the absence of anyone to blame, the Germans would doubtless arrest them.

Jan made an exclamation and, calling to Hal, gestured back up the valley. Following his gaze, Hal saw with surprise that the two fugitives had reappeared. Their tiny figures were heading downhill again, back into the valley.

Jan raised his eyebrows questioningly at Hal.

Hal thought for a long moment. "They might need help."

His words hung heavily on the air. If the men were wanted by the Germans, the risks would be considerable. The penalties ranged from deportation to internment in a forced-labor camp to a bullet in the head.

There was no discussion. Hal and Jan turned and skied into the valley. A short way up the valley they stopped and waited in the cover of a thicket of dwarf birch.

The figures had reached the lower slopes at the head of the valley. But instead of hurrying toward the valley mouth, they made a long traverse, heading for the vast pile of avalanched snow at the foot of the gully. Halting on top of the white burial mound, they went first one way then the other, as if searching for something.

After a while they seemed to find what they were seeking, for one moved across to the other and they both crouched in the snow. They remained in the same spot for some time, and Hal thought he could see them digging.

Finally, after a good five minutes, the two figures stood up, their task apparently completed, and began to ski down the valley.

Hal let them get quite close before emerging from the thicket.

The two men stopped dead. One slid an automatic weapon quickly off his shoulder.

Hal called a casual "Good morning."

There was a long silence, then: "Who are you?"

"Friends."

They murmured to each other then moved cautiously forward until the four of them stood face to face. The two were hooded and muffled, but Hal could see from their eyes that they were young, roughly his own age, he guessed.

Hal decided on the direct approach. "We saw what happened. We thought you might need help."

The taller of the two pulled the hood down from his mouth. "Help? You could say that. You could tell us how to get out of this place!"

"Where are you going?"

There was a pause while the tall one eyed Hal thoughtfully. He seemed to make up his mind. "North."

Hal blinked with a mixture of alarm and admiration. Only desperate men would try such a thing. The new German lines would be almost impenetrable. And even if they got through they'd have to run the gauntlet of the demolition squads before they could hope to reach the relative safety of the Russian lines.

"Not easy," Hal said.

The tall one gave a short harsh laugh, the sound uncomfortably loud in the silent valley. "Well, we know that, my friend!"

Hal flushed. Recovering quickly, he tried to think. "All I could do is direct you to a place where there are boats. Someone might be able to take you a few miles up the coast, past the lines. Though it's an awful risk."

The two exchanged glances. "We'll give it a try," said the second one. "Anything's better than freezing up there." He indicated the mountains.

"We need food, too," said the tall one. "As much as you can find." It was the request of someone accustomed to getting what he wanted.

"You're welcome to what we've got," Hal offered solemnly.

Another German vehicle passed along the distant road. Aware that both the fugitives had highly visible automatic weapons over their shoulders, Hal added urgently, "We must get away from here."

He led the way out of the valley and along the side of the fjord, keeping as high above the road as possible. Finally the narrow strip of lowland by the shore opened out into a wide flat plain and, hugging the edge of the mountain, they curved away from the road until safely out of view of passing vehicles. They stopped and made camp, waiting for the cover of the deepening afternoon twilight.

The two fugitives ate ravenously, consuming all of Hal and Jan's remaining rations. While they ate Hal examined them. They were both about eighteen, he guessed, twenty at the most. The taller one had a handsome face, with regular features, a thatch of thick yellow-blond hair, and vivid blue eyes. But what one noticed most was his taut energy: a sort of driving force that commanded attention. He talked in great bursts, as if his energy could barely be contained, and his eyes were charged with a restlessness that only fell away when he laughed; then he seemed exhilarated, almost euphoric.

His friend, who was dark with a pleasant round face, was altogether quieter, appearing strangely unaffected by the day's events.

They didn't offer an explanation of how they had arrived in Lyngen or where they had come from, and Hal didn't ask. But their accent was not a local one. It was from farther south, though Hal couldn't place it exactly.

It was Jan who asked: "Have you come far?"

The first one shot his friend a warning glance, but too late to prevent him from saying "Trondheim."

There was an awkward pause, then the conversation switched to the avalanche. The two strangers discussed it with great amusement, even pride. With a slight shock Hal suddenly realized that it was they and not the Germans who had fired the shots. He stared at them, slightly awestruck. Finally he asked: "You meant to start the avalanche?"

"Well, we didn't mean to, exactly. But we certainly caused it!" said the tall one. He gave a brittle laugh, his blue eyes sharp and shrewd, and Hal had the feeling that he had known exactly what he was doing with those shots. "We did well out of it too," he added. He patted the submachine gun propped against the rucksack beside him. "A Schmeisser," he said proudly. "Now we have one each."

"And ammo, and a knife, and new gloves, and goggles, and a warm fleece-lined cap!" his friend added, pulling article after article out of his rucksack.

"And look at this," the tall one boasted, producing a pair of field glasses, rubber-jacketed and overpainted with flaking white paint. "The Germans are very good at making binoculars. They make the best lenses in the world, did you know that?" He put the glasses to his eyes and twiddled with the focus. "Excellent!"

Hal wasn't so sure this booty was excellent at all. He murmured: "If they catch you with it . . ."

The tall one gave his short snorty laugh. "If we're caught, we're dead anyway!"

Hal wondered what they had done that was so serious. As if reading his thoughts, the tall one indicated his friend and said: "*He* beat up an officer, *I*"—he paused—"*I* executed one of their lot!" He said it with a bright mocking smile, as if he didn't care a damn, but his quick eyes darted straight to Hal's face, searching for a reaction.

There was a moment's silence. Hal was meant to be impressed, he realized, but he could only feel a stab of concern. When one of their number was killed the Germans always exacted terrible reprisals, executing dozens of civilians—sometimes even women and children.

The tall one sensed his dismay. "Sometimes these things have to be done," he said defensively. "We did everyone a favor, believe me. We're heroes back home. Or at least I hope so!" He laughed again. The sound was sharp and discordant in the silence. No one spoke. After a while the two strangers settled back in the snow and dozed. Hal and Jan kept watch until gathering clouds brought an early darkness. Waking the sleeping men, they packed up and set off again.

Luck was with them: the cloud thickened and they were able to travel fast across the flatlands with little fear of being seen.

Hal led them along the wide shore of Ullsfjord until they were safely past the checkpoint at the ferry link to Tromsø. Then he explained the way to the isolated settlement where they might find a boat.

"One favor," the tall one said to Hal.

"If I can."

"Your skis. You see, one of my bindings is almost off. I can't fix it without tools, but it wouldn't take a moment in a workshop. You don't mind, do you? I'll return them or at least repay you—I promise. Though I can't say when!"

Hal's face fell in the darkness. His skis were new. It had taken him two years to get hold of some seasoned spruce and hickory, and another year to persuade the local ski-maker to make the skis to Hal's own design: spruce upper with laminated hickory sole; narrow and very fast. They had proved to be everything Hal had hoped they would be, and more.

"You can't fix yours?" he asked, hoping for a miracle.

"Afraid not. And we've a long way to go."

Hal sighed inwardly and, wishing he didn't mind quite so much, bent down to remove his skis. He thrust them quickly into the other man's hand and took the damaged ones in exchange.

The tall one murmured to his friend in the darkness: "Yours all right, Petter?"

"Yes."

The four of them parted, shaking hands gravely in the darkness.

On impulse Hal said, "If for any reason you can't get away

and you find yourselves in Tromsø, ask for the Starheim house."

"Thanks," said the tall one in the distant tone of someone who never expects to have to take up an offer. And then the two of them were gone, and Hal and Jan turned back along the path to the ferry and the faint hope of a busride home.

Two days later the news flew around Tromsø: a boat had been stolen from Ullsfjord the previous night and gunfire had been heard in the fjord.

No one knew anything more. But in Hal's imagination it was only too horrifyingly obvious: the two boys had been captured and were already in gestapo headquarters in Tromsø. The memory of his father's incarceration in the gray forbidding building on Bankgata was still vivid in his mind. It was said that everyone thrown into its notorious cells talked in the end.

His friends on Ullsfjord would be betrayed and punished— probably executed.

But those fears were nothing to what he felt when he remembered that he'd told the two young men his family name. His *name*!

He couldn't believe what a fool he'd been. His mother, his sister, himself—they would all be taken and shot.

Two days passed with agonizing slowness. Then another day, and another. Still the gestapo did not come. Neither was there news of any arrests at Ullsfjord.

Gradually Hal began to hope. Perhaps, despite everything, the two boys had gotten away.

After a month he finally allowed himself to relax and, far from minding about the loss of his lovely new skis, he grew quite fond of the other pair. Not that they were of any use: quite apart from the damaged binding, one ski had a long crack down the length of the grain.

Had the fellow known about the crack when he suggested the swap? Probably. But in a strange way Hal didn't mind. In the same position he liked to think he would have had the nerve to do the same thing himself.

On examining the skis closely he saw that something had been carved into the tips then scratched out. From time to time he made desultory attempts to decipher the markings.

Then, several months after the German capitulation, when no harm could possibly come from knowing, he took a soft pencil and thin paper and did a rubbing.

Initials, faint but distinguishable.

R.B.

After that Hal put the skis in the cellar and forgot about them. Only now and again, when he was climbing in the Lyngen Alps or passing the insignificant valley off the Tromsø-Lyngseidet road, did he wonder about the skis' owner and whether he had gotten through.

He still liked to think that he had. But, on consideration, he thought not. The Russians had stopped short many miles to the northeast. It would have been an impossibly long journey across the devastation of Finnmark, and without supplies in the harshness of Arctic January.

No, the fellow probably hadn't made it. Hal was sorry.

PART ONE

February 1960

1

The major pulled up the hood of his parka and stepped out into the night. The cold snapped him awake as he'd hoped it would and, though his body was still warm from sleep, he stamped his feet and clasped his gloved hands to get his circulation moving.

He wandered idly away from the hut. It was four in the morning, but the dawn, such as it was, wouldn't come for a long time. Even then the day would be over almost before it had begun. What a godforsaken place this was! Too remote and lonely for his taste. Even the cold felt different—harsher, unforgiving, like the landscape.

The north had a sort of fascination, of course—he wouldn't be a good Norwegian if he didn't believe that—and on a night like this he had to admit that it had a stark, if severe, beauty.

The air was astonishingly clear. The outlines of the surrounding hills and distant mountains were hard-rimmed against the night sky. To one side the main body of the camp lay quiet, dark except for the perimeter lights and sentry posts, the huts clearly outlined against the soft reflections of the snow. Below, he could just make out the rough winter road from the Arctic coast running up the floor of the valley, a ribbon of white through the sparse birchwood. The road was, of course, quite devoid of traffic. It continued southward past the camp until, somewhere deep in the interior, it rose clear of hills and trees and disappeared into the wilderness of the plateau.

The major had never been on the plateau. On the rare occasions when he came up here to Finnmark he went straight to some garrison or military installation on the coast. It was such a distance—the best part of a thousand miles from Oslo to the Arctic coast of northern Norway—and travel was so difficult and time-consuming that, once his business was finished, he usually wasted no time in getting back.

He shivered and checked the time: 0410. Five minutes to the weather forecast and forty-five minutes to the time of departure. He stamped about for another minute then went back into the hut to see what was going on.

In the mess the two travelers and their driver were eating breakfast, talking quietly. The major did not join them. He was too tense to eat, and would anyway have felt out of place: the three had already formed themselves into a group, friendly but exclusive.

Instead the major asked shortly: "All right?"

Jan Johansen, the leader, looked up and smiled. "Fine." It was a reassuring smile and the major took comfort from it. The success of the venture lay with these men, yet the major was only too well aware of where the blame would fall if anything went wrong.

In the passageway a door banged. A staff sergeant appeared with a written forecast. Strong northerly winds and a sharp drop in temperature. The major passed it to Jan Johansen, who gave a slight dismissive shrug. The major, however, felt a twinge of concern: It didn't sound too good to him. He found himself wishing that Starheim were still around to discuss it.

Aware that he was hovering over the breakfasting men, the major went outside again. Two soldiers from the local battalion were loading the Land-Rover.

"Is that the lot?" the major asked.

"Apart from the skis."

The major inspected the gear. There didn't seem to be very much of it. "Has this been checked?" he asked.

The soldier nodded. "By Major Starheim."

"Starheim? Oh, you mean—yesterday?"

"No, about an hour ago."

The major hid his surprise. "I see." Starheim had left after the briefing the previous afternoon, giving every indication that he wouldn't be returning. Yet here he was again, unannounced. The major should have been annoyed—if it had been anyone else he would have been—but in truth he was rather relieved.

"Where is Starheim?" he asked.

"Gone skiing, Major."

This time the major blinked visibly. "When is he expected back?"

The soldier pointed up the hill behind the hut. "He just went up to the top. He said he wouldn't be long."

The major scanned the slope above. He couldn't imagine climbing it in less than half an hour. But then he was neither an Arctic explorer nor a mountaineer.

He sauntered off until he was clear of the lights and sounds of the hut. The night was swathed in silence. Nothing stirred save the wisps of snow drawn from the peaks by the hard cold breeze. It was difficult to believe that anything existed on the wind-scoured slopes. Yet he didn't doubt that Starheim was up there somewhere. The major pictured him moving silently and invisibly across the snow, a mountain man in his element. He tried to imagine himself like that: inured to cold and hardship, self-sufficient to the point of total independence, at home in the most desolate of places. But his imagination failed him, and he gave a sudden violent shiver.

Halvard Starheim stood high on the hill and looked down the length of the valley, toward the north and the distant mountains that stood above the Arctic fjords.

The air was cold, and it was going to get even colder. All the signs were there. The night was hard and clear. The surface of the snow, glowing luminously in the brilliant starlight, was powder dry. And now a wind had sprung up, as yet no more than a sharp breeze, but already frost cold against his skin.

He turned his face to it. Northerly. With perhaps a touch of east in it. Ice-bearing wind from the Arctic Ocean and the Pole beyond; a wind that was capable of taking the temperature down really low. Not a problem in itself—he and Jan had been through minus seventy degrees Fahrenheit overwintering in the Northwest Passage—but something to be borne in mind all the same.

He wished it were the only thing there was to worry about.

Over the Arctic horizon the northern lights shimmered in an iridescent curtain and, even as he watched, the aurora leapt outward until the sky was filled with a silvery radiance. Instinctively he thought: Radio contact will be bad. Then he remembered that there wasn't going to be any radio contact and he exhaled harshly, his breath vaporizing in a milky cloud.

He liked nothing about this expedition, as the major from military intelligence insisted on calling it. He disliked clandestine activities at the best of times. But most of all he disliked not having had a bigger say in the planning of it. Weather, ice, blizzard, terrain: he could deal with those. But this, with all its politics and subterfuge—this was distinctly tricky ground.

Sounds drifted up from the camp below. There were lights and movements outside the hut. Time was getting on. He pulled the drawstrings of his hood tighter over his face, checked his ski bindings, and looped his poles over his wrists.

Out of long habit he paused briefly for one last look around before setting off. Then he began a long traverse, the narrow skis hissing softly through the deep virgin snow, occasionally rasping noisily as they touched some unseen rock. Approaching a bank of what might have been soft drift, he prepared to turn. Pushing his uphill ski well out, he made a long sweeping telemark turn, then straightened again for the next long traverse.

As he dropped fast toward the hut he came onto hard crust and risked a jump turn, a difficult maneuver when wearing narrow cross-country skis and soft boots attached by the toe alone. But the turn went well and he allowed himself a moment of satisfaction.

He came to a neat stop on a knoll just above the hut and bent down to unfasten his skis. The quiet was disturbed by the sound of an engine whirring. The Land-Rover warming up. Fifteen minutes to go.

More sounds: the crunch of hard boots on snow. Hal looked up and saw a figure shrouded in a parka making his way carefully toward him. He recognized the man from military intelligence: Major Thrane.

Hal picked up his skis and went to meet him.

"How was it up there?" the major asked pleasantly.

"Oh—good."

"The weathermen seem to think it's going to get cold."

"I've no doubt they're right."

"But that won't be a problem?"

Hal suppressed a wry smile. Desk men always fretted about the wrong things. "No, not on its own," he replied.

The major nodded. "I wasn't expecting you back." His voice was friendly but curious.

"I thought I'd come and see them off. I hope that's all right."

"Of course," the major said quickly. "Glad you stayed."

They walked slowly toward the waiting vehicle.

The major cleared his throat and said a little awkwardly: "Last night I had the feeling you were still unhappy about something. Was I right?"

Hal hesitated. He often made the mistake of speaking too plainly. It was his greatest failing, at least as far as his career in the army was concerned. It had made him at least one enemy in high places. And he couldn't afford that at the moment.

The major waited expectantly. "Please feel free," he pressed. "Say what's on your mind."

Hal stopped and faced him. Thrane was in his early thirties, about the same age as Hal, with sharp watchful eyes suggesting a deep intelligence. "Well, if you really want to know," Hal said finally, "I don't like the idea at all."

"I see," Thrane said stiffly. "Well, I'm sorry about that." There was a pause. "Obviously if there'd been another way . . ."

"It *can't* be right to use civilians on a military operation."

"But it's *not* a military operation. It's an intelligence expedition."

Hal gave him a hard stare. "Come on."

The major conceded the point with a reluctant shrug. "Well—all right. Semimilitary, then." They began to walk again.

"In which case *I* should be going," Hal said.

"You know that's out of the question," Thrane said in a soft patient voice.

Hal gritted his teeth. Whether on exercise or one of his own expeditions he was used to being up there with his men. Staying behind went right against the grain.

Thrane murmured: "You're a serving officer. You know you can't be found—outside."

"Outside?" Hal echoed, shaking his head. Like all intelligence personnel, the major had a gift for euphemism. "You mean, it would be embarrassing if I were caught, but all right if *they* are?"

"They're civilians and more importantly Lapps—or part Lapp at least. They have a right to be there."

"They'll still be spies."

Thrane winced at Starheim's choice of word. "Hardly. In fact, no, definitely not! No one could call them that." He sounded quite hurt. "Besides, no one will ever know they were there." There was a finality to his words and he changed the subject briskly. "Now, about this cold—it isn't going to slow them down, is it?"

They came to a halt some yards from the Land-Rover. "Maybe. If it falls below minus forty."

"But they'll be able to keep going?"

"Difficult to say. Other things are more likely to slow them down—strong winds, heavy snow, a sudden thaw. It's not *just* the cold. But we've allowed for it. They've got time to spare." Hal added, almost to himself: "I'd be more worried about the other chap getting there on time, if I were you."

Someone was gently revving the Land-Rover's engine, so that clouds of vapor spewed out of the exhaust into the night air. Thrane murmured: "Well, one can only make plans and assume everyone will do his best to carry them through." He exhaled sharply, and added with sudden intensity: "Look, he's important to us, this man. Believe me. Otherwise we wouldn't be going to all this trouble."

Hal thought: I'd love to know why. But he didn't bother to ask. Secrecy was Thrane's stock in trade. Like the others, Hal had been briefed on the need-to-know principle. In his role as survival expert Hal had needed to know where Jan and Mattis were going, and that was about all. He'd been told nothing about the man that Jan and Mattis were to meet and bring back—not his name, age, language, or nationality, nor even his ability as a skier.

Hal disliked secrecy because in his experience it always led to misunderstandings and mistakes. On his own expeditions he always insisted on each man being fully aware of what he was doing and why.

A door opened. The soldier who was to be the driver for the first leg of the trip emerged from the hut and climbed into the vehicle.

While they waited for the others the major stamped his feet, making a full circle, and said in a conciliatory tone: "My God, I'd hate to be up on the plateau when the weather's bad. How on earth do you survive it?"

Hal gave a small smile. "We survive." People from the south always thought of the northern interior as empty and hostile, but then they had been fed on the richer diet of forests and pastures and couldn't see the plain beauty of simple things. The north might be relatively bleak, even harsh, but it certainly wasn't the barren uninteresting place people believed it to be.

"I first came up here in '45," Thrane was saying. "Helping to rebuild things. There was nothing left. I was posted to Alta. Hardly a house standing. At the time I wondered if people would ever bother to come back. But they did, of course." He shot Hal an apologetic glance. "But of course you come from this region, don't you?"

"Not quite. From Tromsø."

"Ah," the major grunted. "I read that somewhere." He added, almost accusingly: "It's impossible not to read about you nowadays. All the magazines and papers. Doesn't it bother you?"

"Not anymore." It wasn't quite true, but Hal didn't feel like going into that now.

"And you're planning another expedition, I suppose?"

"Yes."

"The North Pole again?"

"No."

The major wasn't going to be put off. "What sort of expedition, then?"

"A mountain."

"Ah." The major smiled. "A tall one no doubt."

A figure emerged from the hut. It was Mattis. Hal went to meet him, grinning broadly. "Okay?"

"Okay, Hal." They had known each other a long time. Mattis was a nomadic Lapp from a family that wintered in the middle of the plateau at Kautokeino and summered at Kåfjord, not far from Tromsø. He was also an ex-army cross-country ski champion. Like many nomadic Lapps he was small, barely a couple of inches over five feet, and characteristically bandy-legged. He was dressed in traditional winter costume, a *luhkka* of reindeer fur, reindeer-skin leggings, and *finnesko*, which are large grass-lined moccasins.

He climbed into the Land-Rover and laughed. "We'll be there too soon in this weather!" Hal didn't doubt it. Mattis had once skied ninety miles in twenty-four hours.

Hal wandered back toward the major, who immediately picked up the conversation again. "So where's this mountain?"

Hal took his time. "In the Himalayas."

"Not Everest!"

Hal tried not to feel annoyed at Thrane's astonishment. "Yes. The West Ridge."

"Ah. Is that difficult?"

"It's never been climbed."

Thrane nodded as if he'd known all along. "An army expedition?"

"No."

"Oh. I assumed—"

"The army gives me leave, that's all. And the odd piece of equipment when it wants something tested. I get no financial help." He was always explaining this. Outsiders seemed to believe that money for expeditions grew on government trees.

Thrane considered for a moment. "Tell me, I can understand doing the Northwest Passage—in the footsteps of Amundsen and all that—but why did you try for the Pole?"

This was a popular question. Hal pretended to consider his answer, although he knew it by heart. "Because I wanted to show that, if one was sufficiently well prepared, it was possible to travel fast and light to anywhere in the Arctic, even the North Pole."

"There were just the two of you, you and Johansen? And dogs?"

"Yes," Hal said patiently.

"But the supply plane didn't find you?"

"Well—something like that."

Their radio had packed up and, reaching a drop zone three days late, they'd found that the Canadian Air Force plane had been and gone, having dropped a few supplies blind. Though they'd managed to retrieve some of the scattered packages, they didn't have enough supplies to continue the attempt. Just a hundred miles from the Pole they'd been forced to turn back for Ellesmere Island.

But, then, you couldn't expect to win them all.

Jan appeared at last, much taller and looser-limbed than Mattis. He wore an entire outfit of reindeer skin, complete with leggings and *finnesko*, while on his head perched a stylish and gaily colored Lappish hat. Hal screwed up his face and laughed. "A real Lapp!"

"My grandmother would have been proud of me." Jan smiled and in the reflection of the lights it was possible to see in his features a hint of the high cheekbones, smooth skin, and dark eyes that mark so many Norwegians from within the Arctic Circle. Jan was a quarter Lapp and, unlike many, proud of it.

He glanced at the sky. "It's going to get cold, eh? But no snow, I think. So—nothing to slow us down."

Hal chuckled. Jan had a way of seeing the positive side of everything. During the winter of '54, when the two of them had been iced up in Prince Albert Sound in northern Canada and the blizzards had kept them hut-bound for three weeks, Jan's quiet optimism and ingrained good humor had never flagged. Hal had needed that; it counterbalanced his own darker, more impatient nature.

"Good firm going," Hal agreed. "The luck of the devil."

He pulled open the Land-Rover door. The two men stood for a moment, smiling at each other.

Hal indicated Mattis. "Have you warned him about all that chattering you do in your sleep?"

"No, but then he hasn't told me about his snoring."

It was an old joke, but they both grinned anyway, and a dozen memories of shared laughter echoed through Hal's mind. Memories, too, of the bad times, experiences they had survived together. It was as a team that he and Jan had developed Arctic travel and survival techniques.

Now, suddenly, they weren't a team anymore.

A wave of affection caught Hal and, overcoming his usual reserve, he reached out and embraced Jan awkwardly. Jan, after a momentary surprise, returned the embrace. The two men pulled back a little and patted each other's shoulders.

Hal said with forced cheerfulness: "See you, then."

Jan climbed in and Hal slammed the door. The engine roared. Jan gave a brief wave and then the Land-Rover was pulling away, its taillights weaving red traces across the astonishing clarity of the night.

Hal watched until long after the lights had disappeared. He felt depressed.

The major shuffled up. "Well, they seemed happy enough."

The two men made their way back to the hut.

"Incidentally," Thrane said, "will you be in contact with Johansen's wife?"

"I'll be seeing her. The day after tomorrow." A vision of Ragna swept into Hal's mind.

"She's been told some story, has she?"

"What? Oh, yes. That he's field-testing some new equipment for me."

"Good."

"Though I doubt she believes it."

Thrane ground to a halt. "What do you mean?"

"Well, she's not stupid." Hal pulled open the hut door and after a moment Thrane followed him into the warmth of the interior. "Jan can do field trials on his own doorstep, in the Lyngen Alps. He doesn't have to disappear into Finnmark for the best part of a week."

"Oh," the major said heavily. "Well—I trust she's discreet."

Hal thought of Ragna. She was many things: funny, bright, irreverent. And discreet: yes, that too.

In the mess there was coffee and a basic breakfast of rolls, cheese, and cold meat. The two men helped themselves and sat down.

Hal buttered a bread roll, and eyed Thrane across the table. He'd come across plenty of office men in his time, ambitious types who sat safely behind desks, determining other people's actions, taking the minimum of risk, and expending the larger part of their energies on plotting their own advancement. Certainly Thrane had all the polish and self-confidence of a man who expected early promotion.

Hal was irritated by him on principle. He asked suddenly: "What happens if anyone finds out about this operation? Like the Finns, for example."

A flicker of what could have been annoyance crossed the major's eyes, but he recovered well and said evenly: "Why should they?"

"That's not an answer."

"They won't find out," Thrane said firmly. "Anyway, that's our problem, not yours."

Hal persisted: "But these men have no protection if anything goes wrong."

"I don't see what you mean," Thrane said lightly. "The men are merely going into Finland to meet someone. They won't be breaking any laws. And they certainly won't be crossing any other borders, will they? There's nothing that can go wrong." He smiled soothingly. "Besides, they volunteered. They weren't forced to go."

"Not forced, maybe. But heavily persuaded!" As always when Hal showed his considerable anger, he instantly regretted it. He added more reasonably: "Well, that is my opinion."

Thrane eyed him tolerantly. "One has to be practical. There are certain jobs that have to be done. Gray areas which have to be covered. In an ideal world it wouldn't be like that, but as it is . . ." He trailed off.

Hal drained his coffee and got to his feet. "I have to go or I'll miss my transport."

The major stood up. "It's been a pleasure."

Hal searched for a hint of sarcasm, but there was none. He softened a little and gave the ghost of a smile. "You'll let me know?"

The major said smoothly: "But I won't know much, if anything at all, until it's over. I've no doubt you'll hear direct from Johansen before you hear from me."

A typically evasive reply. Hal thought crossly: I should have known.

Quickly, before he said something he might later regret, he turned on his heel and left.

Thrane wandered over to the window and watched Starheim stride off into the darkness toward the main part of the camp. It was a pity they had parted on less than amicable terms. Under different circumstances, the major felt sure, they would have hit it off. Starheim had a sort of prickly independence that Thrane always admired.

That independence was the trouble, of course. Starheim resented someone from Oslo telling him what to do. He was used to running his own show. No cloudy issues in Starheim's operations. Thrane doubted Starheim had appreciated his allusion to gray areas. Men like Starheim saw things in black and white, which was ideal for the front line or expeditions to the North Pole. But in the real world the areas of dark gray were just as vital, otherwise you lost the battle before it had begun. And Norway being where it was, there were plenty of gray areas to attend to.

Besides, the operation couldn't misfire. Starheim was overreacting.

Although it would be embarrassing if anyone found out. Starheim was right about that.

2

It is best known by its romantic name: the land of the midnight sun; and in midsummer it is indeed a land of continuous light and sudden, abundant fluorescence.

But it is also the land of the Dark Time, as the Lapps call it. For two months in midwinter the sun never rises above the horizon, and the day, such as it is, passes in a few brief hours of twilight. February is an improvement: The sun shows above the horizon for a brief hour or so with long periods of twilight on either side. The extra light is, of course, welcome, but it brings little relief to the inhabitants, for the winter is still tightening its grip and will not let go for another two months.

But this northern land within the Arctic Circle is two worlds. There is the coast, its fjords and attendant valleys successfully if sparsely inhabited; and there is the interior—which might as well be another planet.

The interior is mostly high plateau, or *vidde*, a great wilderness that reaches from the coastal mountains across northern Scandinavia to Russia, a stretch of tundra flowing into the wastes of the Siberian plain.

The plateau is not completely flat; its surface is covered by a maze of low hills and shallow valleys interspersed with small lakes. The land consists of moor and bog and to the inexperienced eye appears barren, especially in winter. But hidden under the snow are lichen and moss and berry-yielding plants, waiting to blossom thickly during the intense but brief summer. Toward Finland and Russia, the plateau falters and drops away to silent lakes or is cleaved by a deep-running river, and there dwarf birch and willow grow.

But now, in the depths of winter, everything is covered in ice and snow, and even the most adaptable of the plateau's inhabitants lie low.

For there *are* inhabitants: Arctic fox, ermine, wolverine, the rare lynx, wolf.

There are men, too. The nomadic Lapps have wintered on the plateau for centuries and made a living from this most unpromising of lands. For it is here that the reindeer come to scratch away at the wind-scoured snow to find the frozen lichen and moss that is their winter fodder. Their summer pastures on the coast, though less cold at this time of year, are covered by deep-drift snow which makes foraging impossible. The herds of reindeer, long domesticated by the Lapps, still range free, and the Lapps follow them on their migration to the winter pasture.

But the pastures cover hundreds of miles, the herds are widely scattered, and the Lapps are few. So to the traveler the wilderness appears featureless, a rolling desert of snow stretching into an endless distance, a hostile land where man is out of place.

And the traveler is wise to see it like this: the plateau is no place for people who don't know or understand it. On the vast unbroken plain the temperature has been known to drop to minus fifty or more. Animals, including man, can tolerate this sort of cold, but the wind is more difficult to survive. The long winters are punctuated by savage storms which drive heavy snow into the long fjords and steep mountains of the coast, then rise up onto the interior, where the winds tear unchecked across the bleak plateau, ripping at the snow cover and blowing it God knows where.

Yes, as everyone will tell you, it is the wind that is your enemy, for unless you have shelter the wind can freeze you to death.

From the army hut at Porsangmoen, the army Land-Rover headed inland, climbing steadily onto the high plateau. As the land became flatter the driver kept an eye on the marker posts, for the wind was blowing a fine drift across his path and the posts were his only reliable guide to the course of the road, the snow-packed surface of which was indistinguishable from the surrounding whiteness.

Eventually, after several hours, they came to the Lapp town of Karasjok, formerly the winter quarters of nomadic Lapps but now a permanent settlement and a spiritual center of Lapland. Perched in the middle of the plateau, it was the only real civilization for fifty miles.

On the outskirts of the settlement, by a single-story wooden house, the Land-Rover came to a halt. The two passengers got out and removed their gear. The vehicle disappeared in the direction it had come from.

The two men went into the house, unmistakably, a Lapp dwelling with its roughly built outhouses, sledging equipment, carcasses hanging from the eaves, and racks of drying reindeer skins. Inside, the men were given coffee, bread, and cheese. Half an hour later a rather battered truck drew up outside and an old Skolt—eastern—Lapp got out and entered the house. After further refreshments and some exchange of news the two men followed the Skolt Lapp back to his truck and, loading their gear, clambered in.

The truck set off. In the town—though *town* was a rather grand term for it—the road forked. One road turned left, to skirt the northern border of Finland for two hundred miles until, at the most easterly corner of Norway, it came to the Soviet border and an abrupt halt.

The battered truck did not take this turn, but took the right fork that led across the Karasjok River and, ten miles later, to the Finnish border.

The Skolt did not anticipate any problems at the border. The old man was a trader who went through about twice a month. Often the border guards waved him straight through. Only very occasionally did they glance at the contents of the vehicle or ask for identification.

This occasion was no exception. When the truck drew up at the frontier a guard strolled out and peered at the vehicle. The old man wound down the window. The guard saw the distinctive Skolt costume the old man wore and nodded in recognition. He did not bother to ask him where he was going or why; the Lapps were a law unto themselves and naturally secretive. Besides, apart from certain restrictions on goods, there was free passage between Norway and Finland. With a brief smile, the guard waved them through.

As he drove off again the old man started to talk, telling the younger men how his grandfather had remembered hearing from *his* grandfather about the days when there had been no such things as borders in the far north. Lapland and much of northern Scandinavia had been inhabited entirely by Lapps, and they had ranged freely across hundreds of miles of country. But then the land that had been theirs for thousands of years had been parceled out, becoming part of Norway, Sweden, Finland, or Russia. Slowly and inexorably the Lapps were driven farther north; many gave up their wanderings and settled by the coast to become farmer-fishermen, others became nonmigratory herders, many had their land taken from them.

The two younger men found the old man's curious eastern dialect difficult to understand and missed a word here and there, but they understood the underlying message well enough, and sympathized, not just because the Skolt was older and venerable but because among their own generation there was a growing awareness that one way or another the Lapps had lost out.

For mile after mile the road snaked across the lonely snow-swept plateau of northeastern Finland. Finally it descended toward the lowlands that stretch up from central Finland to Petsamo on the northern coast: a strange and unexpected region of primeval forests and silent frozen lakes.

The men could see from the snow flurries that the wind had freshened and that the temperature, already minus twenty, must still be dropping. But they were not concerned: one took the weather as one found it, and as the truck spun onward the snow was thick and firm beneath the wheels, the visibility was adequate, and they knew they were making good time.

It is two worlds, this northern province. There is the plateau, and there is the coast.

On the coast the winter is a miracle. The miracle is that the weather is not far, far worse. At this latitude the sea should, by the laws of nature, become ice-locked for months on end, and the land seized by a deep and unbearable cold which no summer could entirely thaw nor many creatures survive.

Yet animals and men survive pretty well. For the real miracle is the Gulf Stream, whose long arm reaches up the Norwegian coast from the south, keeping the sea ice-free and the air temperature bearable even in the depths of winter. The summer, when it arrives, comes quickly, so that oats grow as far north as North Cape, and thick forests grow in protected valleys.

The ice-free sea is used by sealers, whalers, travelers, and traders as an open all-season road to the Arctic. A blessing indeed.

But, as with many blessings, there's a dark side to it.

Norway is not the only country to rely on the Gulf Stream waters. There is also her vast neighbor to the east. Like a powerful genie trapped in a bottle, the Soviet Union has no year-round outlet to the Atlantic Ocean except through the bottleneck between Norway and the Arctic pack ice.

She guards these waters jealously and uses them continuously, sending the ships of her Northern Fleet out through the neck of the bottle into the Atlantic to cover her western flank.

And what a fleet it is. At this time, in 1960, it is growing rapidly; they say it will soon be the largest in the world. A massive collection of warships and submarines and auxiliaries, backed up by vast dockyard and technical facilities grouped around Murmansk and the Kola Peninsula. Murmansk: the only ice-free port in northern Russia, and, uncomfortably for everyone, very close to Norway, a NATO country.

They call the Kola Peninsula the most valuable piece of real estate on earth.

But it's the sea-lane that's beyond price.

And whoever controls Norway controls the sea-lane. Norway is the key. And, not to put too fine a point on it, she rather wishes she wasn't.

So the warming waters of the Gulf Stream are a blessing, but rather a curse, too.

Hal reached the boat in midafternoon as the twilight deepened. Across the water the peaks of the snow-covered island were hard and clear against the dark incandescent blue of the sky.

Almost home. He felt better already.

He ducked down the companionway to the engine compartment and, giving the Volvo Penta diesel a firm pat, bent down beside it. Releasing the valves, he gave it a few hand cranks to get the oil moving, sprayed it with Easy Start, then pressed the starter. The cold batteries turned the crank with agonizing slowness until with a loud splutter the diesel coughed once, twice, and chugged sluggishly into life.

Hal shook his head. The damned thing always did that—sounded like death, made his heart sink, and then proceeded to clatter away happily as if it were used every day.

He returned to the wheelhouse and waited for the engine to warm up a bit. Then, tightening the hood around his face, he stepped out onto the deck and went forward to let go the mooring.

The wind was fierce now. It blustered across the sound, solid and heavy with Arctic cold, sending sharp-ridged waves hissing against the hull. The cove, sheltered from most winds, was exposed to northerlies, and the deck pitched and jerked beneath his feet.

The mooring safely away, Hal made his way back into the wheelhouse and, slamming the door, pushed the engine into gear and pointed *Skorpa*'s nose out into the open water. It was three miles across the sound to the island, and in the clarity of the dying light he could already see the twinkle of Arne's lamp balanced on the rim of the far-off shore.

The diesel settled into a steady throb as *Skorpa* found the rhythm of the waves and surged forward. She was a good boat, *Skorpa*. A modern fishing cutter of thirty-five feet, she couldn't fail to be an improvement on the small gasoline-driven boat Hal had inherited from his father, which had specialized in spluttering to a halt halfway across the sound in the dead of night.

The snowy peaks of the island were clearly visible ahead, gleaming palely against the sky. Its lower outlines were indistinct though, merging into the mass of the islands that surrounded it. For the island was only one of a long chain of islands, rocky islets, and barren skerries that formed a massive natural barrier to the ocean beyond.

This particular island was twelve miles by five and its name was Revøy. Fox Island. Though Hal had discovered that it also had an ancient long-forgotten Lappish name—Gumpe Fuolo. Wolf Island.

Whether there had ever been foxes, let alone wolves, on the island Hal very much doubted. The only wildlife there now were hares and ptarmigan and, in the summer, eider and mallard ducks, oyster catchers, and sandpipers.

Skorpa buffeted her way into the short choppy sea until finally the island provided some lee and she rode more smoothly. It was four in the afternoon. The journey had taken almost twelve hours. First an army transport had taken Hal as far as Alta Fjord, then, after a two-hour wait, he'd caught a seaplane to Tromsø. Taking a ferry across Tromsø Sound—the new bridge connecting the island of Tromsø to the mainland was not yet open—he'd picked up the Land-Rover and driven the twenty miles to the cove where he kept *Skorpa*.

In just over twelve hours he would be leaving again. It was a lunatic way to live, but this was the only home he had and he felt a need to come here when he could, if only for a few hours.

The twin peaks of Revøy loomed higher. Nestling between them, deep in a valley, glimmered a soft golden light from an oil lamp placed in a window: the house. Down by the shore was the sharper whiter light of the hurricane lamp on the boathouse, its reflection glinting in the dark water. As he closed on the shore, Hal turned the boat westward until he caught the silhouette of the mooring buoy in the flickering reflection. Then he drove *Skorpa* straight up the path of light, ducking away at the last minute to turn a half-circle and bring the boat to a stop with her nose above the buoy.

As he secured the heavy chain there was a hail from Arne on the shore, and he returned a brief shout before going aft to stop the engine. As he lowered the dinghy into the water, a steady barking echoed across the water and he grinned to himself.

He jumped into the dinghy and rowed in long steady sweeps to the shore. Arne caught the boat and the two men pulled it well up the beach. A nose thrust itself into Hal's hand. Bamse. Hal took the dog's broad head in his hands and fondled it roughly, saying, "You devil! You old devil!"

The dog growled softly and thrust his weight against Hal's legs.

Arne grunted in the vague direction of the wind: "A north-easter. Cold."

"It's a lot colder up there."

"Ah, *there,*" Arne said, understanding immediately that he meant the plateau. "Ha! I don't doubt it." To Arne people who ventured on the plateau in winter were crazy. Nearly everyone—and certainly everyone Arne knew—lived on the coast. Only the Lapps belonged on the plateau.

Arne was sixty and looked eighty. A farmer-fisherman all his life, he had more lines on his face than a mosaic and his expression was fixed in a permanent frown. A widower for fifteen years, he lived alone a mile along the island shore, and looked after Hal's place when he was away, which was nearly all the time.

"I've lit the stove," Arne said. "And put something on the table."

"Thanks, Arne."

Arne took the hurricane lamp down from the side of the boathouse and extinguished it. They trudged up to the snow-covered track that was the only road. "I have to leave early in the morning," Hal said. "About five."

Arne nodded. "I'll come for the dog."

With a brief wave the two men parted. Hal started up the valley. Bamse danced around him like a young dog, which he wasn't anymore, then, remembering his dignity, scouted ahead, nose firmly to the snow, his limp less pronounced than usual, his tail wagging in a circle of pleasure.

The valley was two miles long and half a mile wide, its sides rising abruptly to the mountains on either side, giving it the name of Brattdal—steep valley. The valley floor rose quite steeply too, so that it was a brisk climb to the house.

As Hal left the sea behind, the hushed murmuring of the waves receded and he was met by the rushing of the wind swooping down from the mountains and hissing across the snow.

The house was hidden behind a slight hump in the valley floor, and it was not until he had been climbing for some minutes that it finally came into view. His stomach tightened with pleasure. He held his breath for a moment, savoring the powerful sense of homecoming.

The place always had this effect on him. Which was why he kept coming back.

The house was distinctive—some people called it extraordinary. It was the sort of house that wealthy nineteenth-century merchants built for themselves—in towns. A tall two-story wooden house embellished with high old-fashioned gables and ornately carved vergeboards and architraves, and fronted by a long veranda with fine latticed arches. It was a far cry from the simple functional dwellings that the fishermen built for themselves along the shore. Far from blending into its surroundings, the house sat proud and erect on the rising ground, like a grand old lady who, refusing to move with the times, still wore her most extravagant crinoline.

The light of the oil lamp burned large and gold in the window. Arne had lit the stoves well, and a wall of warmth met Hal as he entered the house.

A pungent scent of burning birchwood mingled with the elusive smell of age the house had always possessed. The paneled rooms, their wood darkened by time, reflected a soft glowing light. A familiar sense of peace and security settled over him.

He stoked up the stoves and checked the wood store. He put dried fish down for Bamse, who was still outside reestablishing his territory, then cut some cheese and bread from the supplies that Arne had left on the kitchen table. He took the food and sat in his favorite seat at the desk in the living room.

Most of his childhood had been spent at the family home in Tromsø, but Brattdal was his spiritual home, the home of endless summers and happy family holidays. It had never occurred to him that those days would end. But his sister had married and gone south, his brother had been lost at sea, and both his parents were dead.

The old rolltop desk had been his father's. Hal remembered him sitting here, late in the bright summer evenings, reading aloud from Egge or Hamsun. On the wall above was a photograph of his father taken in 1930 when he was thirty-three, a year older than Hal was now. Dressed formally in a three-piece suit and dark hat, he looked every inch the successful merchant he had become. Yet, if one looked carefully one could see a warmth in the eyes, hinting at the man beneath, the man who read extensively and spoke four languages and had great compassion for his fellow man.

His compassion had not been appreciated by the Nazis, however. They had objected to his attempts to save some young men from reprisal executions. At the end of the war his father had come back from the concentration camp alive—but only just. He died two years later. Hal's mother died of a tumor four years after that. He still missed them a lot.

Bamse scratched at the door. Hal let him in and cuffed him affectionately. Bamse was half Laphound and half husky, although his parentage was by no means certain. Hal accused him of having wolf blood. He had a long nose, a shaggy gray coat, white jowls, and sharp pointed ears. Normally Bamse stayed with Arne on Revoy, but occasionally, when no one was looking, Hal took him on training operations.

Bamse growled and, taking Hal's arm gently in his teeth, pulled at it.

"No time for games, you!"

Hal finished his meal, then, with a sigh, found the pile of mail that he had picked up in Tromsø. With Bamse at his feet, he began reading. There were letters concerning the new expedition, which, thankfully, he could hand over to the newly appointed expedition secretary. But there were others that could not be gotten rid of so easily: young climbers wanting advice on training, clubs wanting him to come and visit them, even a request from a group of Lapps asking him to support a Lapp rights movement.

He was curious about that one. Why had they written to him? He read the letter thoroughly. The Lapps wanted him to support their campaign for the reintroduction of the Lapp language in their schools and to protest the use of some of their land for a military training area.

Privately he sympathized on the language question. The Lapps' culture was dying and it was wrong for the government to force the Norwegian language on them. But it was a political issue and he couldn't possibly become involved in it.

As for protesting against a military training area—he gave a wry smile: that would be a quick way of getting fired.

In fact, he'd thought about leaving the army a lot recently—

though preferably not by getting fired. It had become increasingly obvious that something in his life would have to go, and the only part of his life he could spare was his military career. He'd only kept at it this long because the army was tolerant of his long absences, and he needed the pay. For years he'd plowed his earnings from lecture tours, books, and articles back into his expeditions, with the result that he was permanently broke.

He thought of the time it would take him to draft a suitably polite letter to the Lapps, and wished he had someone to deal with that sort of thing. He could do with a housekeeper, too. Arne was not exactly the most adventurous provisioner, and as for the cleaning, that probably hadn't been done in weeks.

On a sudden impulse he got up and threw open the doors of the cast-iron stove. The light leapt out and licked the paneling with flickering tongues of amber. It almost made the place seem lived in. Almost. The past rushed forward, and for a moment the room contained all the love and warmth of family evenings.

Would he grow old here? He hoped so. One day he would like to start a proper farm at Brattdal, and go fishing regularly, and write books during the long winters.

Hal stared thoughtfully at the flames. It would be no good on his own, though. He had been thinking about that a lot recently. When he looked at Jan and Ragna, so happy together, he couldn't help feeling a pang of envy.

In his twenties he'd carefully avoided long-term involvements. Looking back, he'd been rather too ruthless and single-minded about it. Then, four years ago, there'd been a serious girlfriend. He'd gone out with her for almost two years, he'd liked her a lot, but in the end something had held him back. A last urge to keep his freedom perhaps, or a feeling that she wasn't quite right—he wasn't sure. But whatever the reason, he had failed to write to her from the Polar expedition, and when he returned she had gone.

Since then there'd been others. There was a girl in Tromsø he saw quite regularly. She was pretty, cheerful, and very sweet, but . . . But what? He wasn't sure, that was the trouble. All he knew was that he didn't want her to come and live at Brattdal.

Now he was aware of time slipping away and a loneliness that crept up on him, reaching under his guard, troubling him even here, in this house, where he had always felt happy. The feeling had nothing to do with the exhilarating aloneness he felt on the Arctic ice or hanging on a rope from an ice wall. This was different—a forlorn kind of feeling, an ache of the spirit.

Bamse stirred briefly from his sleep and gave a loud yawn. Hal said: "You're no good to me!" Bamse lifted his head and stared at him.

Then Hal said affectionately, "Go to hell, you!"

Bamse yawned again and curled into a ball. He was a law unto himself, Bamse. That was why Hal liked him so much. He'd been a working dog most of his life and didn't have a lot of time for people—apart from Hal, of course. He'd belonged to a farmer over on Lyngen. Hal had found him one spring day, high in a valley, half dead, caught by the foreleg in a vicious steel leg-hold trap. His owner had wanted to shoot him. Hal had brought him back to Revøy.

Bamse was a good companion. But one shouldn't get too fond of a dog.

He closed the stove with a bang and, going into the front lobby, threw on a coat; bracing himself against the wind, he stepped outside onto the veranda. A new moon had risen, and in the transparency of the night he could see across the water to the promontory where the cove and *Skorpa*'s mooring lay, and beyond, to wide Ullsfjord and the jagged peaks of the Lyngen Alps. The view, though familiar, never lost its power to move him. Neither could he look at the Lyngen Alps without remembering that there were still a couple of good unclimbed peaks among them. He had marked them down for his retirement.

But for once his mind wasn't on the mountains. He was thinking of the wind.

Hal peered at the thermometer nailed by the door. Minus twelve: cold for the coast. It would be colder on the plateau—it was always colder on the plateau—maybe minus thirty, with another ten or fifteen degrees of windchill.

Jan and Mattis would be well into Finland by now, perhaps even as far as the lake. The weather wouldn't bother them;

there was no reason why it should. He thought: So why am I uneasy, then?

But he had no answer to that.

After some minutes he roused himself. Time was getting on. Tomorrow would be a busy day. Reluctantly he went back into the house to face the pile of unanswered mail.

3

Rolf Berg tore the paper out of the typewriter and stared blankly at his living-room wall. These articles were such a balancing act. Too much alarmist talk and people began to ignore what you said. Too little and you might as well not bother. He hadn't gotten the balance right on this one yet, not by a long chalk.

He focused on his latest acquisition: a painting by an up-and-coming Swedish artist. It was a remarkable piece of work. He felt a glow of satisfaction: he had been right to buy it. Quite apart from being a thing of beauty—and he very much liked having beautiful things around him—it would be a good investment.

He fed another piece of paper into the machine and typed his name at the top. He concentrated hard, turning more ideas over in his mind, but none of them gave him the attention-grabbing start he needed.

After a couple of minutes he exhaled noisily and decided, not for the first time, that fate hadn't intended him to be a journalist. Too much impatience. Too little self-discipline. As if to prove the point, his mind wandered. He remembered that he had a meeting later that evening, a meeting he was not looking forward to. He'd been hoping there might be some way of avoiding it. But there wasn't. He would just have to grit his teeth.

His mind then wandered to something far more pleasant: an Italian girl named Isabella, a warm vital piece of sunshine in the drabness of the Oslo winter, and very new—he'd only met her a couple of weeks ago; but then new relationships were the only kind he really enjoyed.

The blank paper stared up at him. Berg pushed himself out of his chair and strode over to the window. The outlook was bleak: an early darkness had settled over the quiet residential road and a veil of fine snowflakes whirled past the streetlamps, blurring the outlines of the apartment buildings opposite. A pedestrian walked cautiously along the icy pavement, his head bowed against the wind.

He forced himself back to the typewriter. He really had to get this piece done. It was important. The subject was nuclear weapons, and the issue was whether or not they should be allowed on Norwegian soil. He was reasonably confident that the Labor government would make the right decision, but a powerful article might just help to consolidate opinion.

He retrieved the screwed-up sheet from the floor and re-read it: *In 1958 Norwegian Air Force planes started carrying American Sidewinder missiles. Last year U.S. ground-to-air missiles, operated by American personnel, were installed on Norwegian soil. Next, if the U.S. have their way, these Nike missiles will carry nuclear warheads.*

The Soviet government have made it clear that they will be forced to draw only one conclusion from this progression of events—that Norway's intentions are aggressive. Putting ourselves in their place, can we blame them?

Berg shook his head. Wrong: far too pedantic and opinionated. Though the same could be said for most articles in the Norwegian press. He must think of something punchier. Finally it came to him and he wrote: *Norway is fast approaching a vital decision. Whether to step into the front line of the cold war.*

Not brilliant, but it got the point across.

For three hours he sweated away at the body of the article until he felt it struck the right note of balance and reason, giving the idea that he might have come down on either side if the evidence had justified it. He read it through once more, then put it to one side.

He would come back to the article later and give it a final polish before handing it in the next morning. But it had taken him much longer than he'd realized; it was almost five. Damn.

Now he'd hardly have time to see Isabella. He should have gotten down to work earlier.

He changed out of his Levi's into a pale-blue cashmere sweater and gray flannel slacks—both picked up on assignment in Paris—and wound a long white scarf around his neck.

Pulling on a cashmere coat he hurried out of the apartment to his car. There was a bit of traffic along the park, but then it eased and he was away: the Oslo working day finished at four and the rush hour was over. He stopped at a florist as it was closing and bought some roses. He loved gestures, however banal: anything that added amusement to life, which, if one wasn't careful, could be frighteningly serious.

A traffic light was turning red. He shoved his foot down and drove through it. Very un-Norwegian.

As he pulled up outside Isabella's apartment, he suddenly remembered that he hadn't phoned to say he was coming. But he'd told her he might drop in: she would probably have waited around just in case.

She hadn't: the doorbell remained frustratingly unanswered. He left the flowers standing up against her door and scribbled a note: *Where were you?*

As an afterthought he took off his tie and pushed it into the jaws of the mail box. He put a P.S. on the note: *For the rest of me dial 74 72 29.* Now she'd have to phone him. It would be a test. If she took it in the right spirit—lightly—she'd be okay. Okay to Berg meant fun while it lasted and no hard feelings afterward.

When he got back to the car it was only five-twenty. He didn't want to be early for his next appointment, so he decided to take the long route and use the time to get into the right mood.

Adjusting his mood wasn't easy. These meetings were always a strain. They'd been going on a long time—in fact, how long was it? He tried to think. A year. No, fourteen months. Good Lord.

It was beginning to feel like a life sentence.

He reached the suburb of Vinderen at five-forty. As usual, he parked some distance from the house and in a slightly different spot from the last time, to avoid being noticed by neighbors. It was all a bit cloak-and-dagger, but he rather liked that. It gave a frisson to the evening, and it needed it.

He waited in the car for fifteen minutes, smoking a cigarette, then, with a weary sigh, he got out and began to walk. The house was five minutes away. The evening was very cold, but pleasantly so. The snow had stopped and the air was dry and fresh against his skin. He rather enjoyed the climb through the avenue of tall pines, which sighed and moaned as the strong wind ripped at their tops. He should spend more time out of doors, he decided. One of these days he would go ski-touring again.

As he approached the house he paused for a moment, waiting in the shadows of the trees. As usual she was there before him, her car parked in the driveway and a light showing in the living-room window. As he watched, a light came on upstairs. He knew exactly which room that was.

He stood a moment longer under the firs then strode up to the back door and tapped with his fingers. After a while he heard the sound of her footsteps. The door swung open and she stood before him.

Fat, frumpy, fiftyish Sonja.

He smiled.

She gave the small laugh she always gave and stepped back to let him in. She closed the door and took his coat, and hovered expectantly.

He embraced her and managed a reasonably enthusiastic kiss, saying: "How's my girl?"

She looked embarrassed and pleased all at the same time. "I'm fine."

"You look well." What she looked, in fact, was her age.

"You too," she replied with a shy smile. She stared at him for a moment, then, replacing her spectacles carefully on her nose, said in a light voice: "I've got salmon tonight. I hope that's all right."

He followed her into the kitchen. The evening always followed a pattern. She would offer him a drink—Scotch, which she knew he preferred—and she would cook and they would chat in a general sort of way. After the meal they would go upstairs. That was the bit he quietly dreaded. In the beginning her body had had a perverse sort of attraction for him, but that had long worn off.

The evening was generally over quite early. He'd never had

to stay the night, thank God. The house was theirs only until ten-thirty, when its owner—a friend of hers—returned.

He sat down at the table and waited for her to pour his drink. He let her pour until the glass was almost full. She gave him a questioning look. "Hard day?"

"Very."

She went to the stove and rattled some pans about, talking in that smoothly reasonable way of hers, which he found rather irritating. At least he wasn't expected to reply until he'd finished his drink. He took the opportunity to eye her over the rim of his glass.

Her name was Sonja Bjornsen, and she worked for the Norwegian Intelligence Service, known as FO/E.

In the beginning it had been so easy—amazingly easy. He'd been doing an article about Norway's involvement with the CIA—an article doomed never to be published, of course. He'd been watching the offices of FO/E in an attempt to prove that the Intelligence Service did exist—a fact no one in authority would admit. She was among the people he'd seen leaving the building on Platous Gate. She'd looked just the right type: a spinster in a senior secretarial position. It had been a simple matter to follow her home. A week later, on her weekly visit to the cinema, he'd bumped into her—well, not quite accidentally.

After that things had progressed extremely satisfactorily. He'd had to take risks, of course, far greater risks than he'd ever taken before, but it had been worth it. She'd turned out to be a veritable gold mine, though it had taken him several months to realize just how valuable she was. In the last year he'd gotten two front-page exclusives on defense policy, in addition to a steady stream of pointers and hints which he'd built into nice little stories.

Yes, a gold mine.

Then she'd gotten promoted.

When she'd told him, he'd barely been able to conceal his delight. She'd been made queen bee: secretary to the Director.

But within a month his euphoria had faded. The lady had taken her new responsibilities very seriously indeed. Instead of dropping bigger and better morsels into his beak, she'd given him little more than crumbs. All he got nowadays was office gossip and interdepartmental politics.

He looked at her now with irritation. He was bored with having to make all this effort for nothing, he was bored with being patient. If she loved him so much, why on earth didn't she give him what he wanted?

She had stopped talking and was smiling gently. "I'm sorry, I'm chattering on. Poor Erik, you look shattered."

Yes, thought Berg, poor Erik. Poor Erik Leif.

Sonja always forgot how beautiful he was. It was odd to think of a man being beautiful, but there was really no other word to describe Erik. Whenever she opened the door to him, the sight of that face always gave her a small shock of pleasure. During the long days they were apart she thought about him a lot—even when she was working—yet her memory never quite did him justice.

Leaving the cooking for a moment, she sat down and prompted him to talk so that she could examine his features one by one. Straight nose, wide mouth, and blue eyes. But it was his hair that one noticed most of all—it was very thick and very blond. So many Norwegians were mousy-haired or pale blond, but Erik had really yellow hair.

He had stopped talking and was looking bored. She said hurriedly, "I'll get the food," and went to serve it.

She'd met him in a cinema queue. When she'd realized he knew exactly who she was she'd been rather alarmed, but as soon as he'd introduced himself properly everything had become clear. He was in the "other" department—the Security Service, known as FO/S.

She'd checked up on him of course. That was automatic. She'd phoned Anna, her opposite number in the Security Service, and Anna had confirmed that Erik Leif worked in FO/S. The hair color, height, and age had matched.

Which had left Sonja with just one concern: why someone as wonderful as Erik should be bothering with her. But he'd explained that as well. In fact, he'd been quite open about it, rather endearingly so.

What Erik wanted was a little inside knowledge.

And for a reason she could appreciate. Between their two departments there was some not-so-friendly rivalry which occasionally led to what was euphemistically called "difficulties." Erik wanted to cut through the ponderous interservice liaison machinery to, as he put it, help things along. Which really meant: to help his career along. Because Erik was ambitious. One only had to look at him to see that. But Sonja didn't mind; on the contrary, she loved being close to such drive. It made her feel young.

And so the affair had begun. She'd had a few short-lived affairs in her twenties, but nothing like this—nothing remotely like this. She'd had no idea she could feel so—powerfully. His body, the things he did to her—he was like an addiction. She couldn't help herself at all; she wanted more and more of him.

She didn't fool herself about their relationship, of course. She was perfectly aware that she was no beauty. In her youth she'd looked quite pleasant, many people had thought so, but in recent years she'd let herself go. There was an awful lot of weight in unsightly places. But looks weren't everything. In his own way Erik cared for her, she knew he did. He gave small signs of fondness now and again. He obviously respected her judgment. That was enough . . .

Their relationship was essentially a bargain, of course. The inside gossip in exchange for this time together. But she didn't mind the idea of a bargain. In fact, she rather preferred it; it gave her a sense of worth and self-respect, it gave the affair balance.

She chatted as she put the food on the plates. She always tried to accumulate a little store of amusing anecdotes and stories during the week, hoping they might interest and amuse him. She was careful to keep off certain subjects that bored him, though. Her invalid mother, for instance, with whom she lived. But then Sonja liked a rest from her too.

Sonja brought the meal to the table. "How's your drink?"

Without a word he drained his glass and held it out for a refill.

"Things must be bad," she said with a short laugh.

He shrugged. "Just rather a lot on at the moment."

"Really?"

His mind seemed to be elsewhere this evening. "What? Oh, there's a lot of maneuvering going on for the deputy's job, that's all. Which means that a lot of work is getting off-loaded onto us."

She was surprised. She'd thought the deputy's job at FO/S was filled. But maybe it hadn't been announced yet.

She began to eat. Erik halfheartedly pushed the food around on his plate.

"I hear the head of E Branch might be next," she said, smiling in expectation. He should be interested in this one. E was his own branch: Protective Security.

"I'd heard," he said shortly.

"Oh, have you? Tell me, what's the real story behind it?" And she paused with her fork halfway to her mouth to stare at his lovely face.

She was waiting for an answer. This sort of office gossip was always the trickiest part of the evening. He had to remember exactly what he'd told her the previous week—she had an excellent memory—and outline a plausible series of developments. Once or twice in the past he'd tripped up quite badly, and had a few adrenaline-charged moments extricating himself. But he usually managed pretty well. He liked to think he'd have made a good actor in another life.

"I think there was a row," he said.

"Oh?" She sounded surprised. He must be on the wrong track.

He said briskly: "But look, I really don't know. And to be honest, I'm not terribly interested. Office politics bore me to tears."

She dropped her eyes; the subject was over. She never pressed him.

She wasn't a stupid woman, Sonja. Just gullible. The Erik Leif deception had grown quite naturally. But the name hadn't come out of thin air—he wasn't that stupid. There was a real Erik Leif in FO/S, a low-ranking diplomatic protection officer whom Berg had come across some two years before when the man was guarding a visiting NATO minister.

After that Sonja had believed the lot. Everything they said about middle-aged spinsters was true: Age made them desperate, grateful, and blind. Sometimes he'd felt almost fond of her, in the way that ugly things have a curious and compelling fascination. But disenchantment had set in.

She cleared away the food and brought the coffee.

He thought: Last chance, Sonja.

Toying with his cup, he acquired a distant troubled look.

Sonja picked it up immediately: She was very quick on atmosphere. "Anything the matter?" she asked gently.

A slight hesitation. "Well . . ."

Her eyes blinked rapidly behind her spectacles. "What is it?"

Berg smiled fleetingly, then assumed a deep frown. "Something's come up, Sonja. I—" He broke off, apparently unable to continue.

She looked suitably alarmed.

"The thing is"—he took a deep breath—"I've got a new job."

Sonja froze. She knew it was bad news.

"It's a sort of promotion," he continued. "I'm heading a new team. It'll involve a lot of traveling at short notice. The team'll work very closely together. We'll have to keep in permanent contact with each other—in fact, the others'll need to know where I am at all times. So"—he stared her firmly in the eye—"it may not be possible for us to see each other very often . . . if at all."

She was staring, her face pale, her mouth slightly open. "But—surely—you'll have some free time." Her voice was gruff and uneven.

"I can't have a secret life, Sonja. And *you* are most definitely a secret."

"But surely there must be a way?" She was trying very hard to be brave.

"It's a permanent job."

She blinked a few times then gave a small quivery smile. "Well. We always knew it might come to this, didn't we? We mustn't complain, I suppose." Suddenly she pulled off her glasses and clamped a hand over her eyes. "Sorry . . ." she said with difficulty. "Sorry . . ."

He went around the table and, pulling her to her feet, let her cry against his shoulder. It was, after all, the least he could do.

After a long while she pulled away and, drying her eyes decisively, said: "Just such a surprise, that's all. I'm all right now. Really. Just such a surprise." They sat down again. He poured her a stiff drink. She took a gulp and asked with forced calmness: "I still don't understand. Why—what—tell me about the job."

Berg had planned his answer. "Well, we're troubleshooting really."

"Oh? What sort of trouble?"

"We think there may be a leak somewhere, and . . ." He shrugged. "We've got to sort it out."

"A leak?" Her tear-filled eyes sharpened.

"Maybe."

"Where?"

"If we knew *that* . . ."

"What sort of material's been leaked?"

This was developing in a promising direction. Taking it slowly, Berg frowned, as if considering whether to tell her. "We're not absolutely sure yet. But it seems to involve CIA-linked operations."

Horror leapt into Sonja's face. "Oh. *Oh*."

"I told you, it's only a whisper."

"But—we haven't been notified! Why haven't we been notified?"

Sonja was keen as a ferret when her curiosity was aroused. He'd have to go carefully. He said: "The leak seems to be from a Norwegian source and— Look, I've already said far too much. Even to you, Sonja."

"What're you saying?" she cried. "That the leak may come from *us*?"

"It's a possibility."

Behind the thick lenses Sonja's eyeballs were round as orbs. Berg felt as if he'd thrown a snowball and started an avalanche. She leaned across the table and said in a low urgent voice: "Erik, this is very serious. I—" She stopped abruptly and gave him an agonized look, as if she wanted to tell him more but couldn't.

Berg felt a frisson of interest. He prompted: "Yes?"

Her mind was hard at work. She said at last: "It just couldn't have come at a worse time."

Berg tried to decide whether she was playing games or not. In his experience women—even docile women like Sonja—were capable of almost anything when clutching on to a failing relationship. "Why's it a bad time?" he asked.

She hesitated for a long while, then shook her head decisively: she had decided not to talk. Instead she began to cry again.

He stood up.

She jumped to her feet, a panicky look on her face. "Wait! Please don't go yet. I couldn't bear it. I couldn't bear you to go just like that."

"Look, Sonja, it's best not to string things out, don't you think?"

"No, *no*! Please. *Please* . . ." She made a big effort to be calm. "Please. Whatever happens, I— Oh, I couldn't bear it. Erik, *please*. I can still be of help to you. I know I can."

He raised an eyebrow. "Oh?"

She stared at him for a moment, then came slowly and humbly toward him and, putting her arms around him, laid her head against his chest.

He longed to walk out, but his curiosity was pricked: he had to know.

He made the necessary mental adjustment to the idea of going to bed with Sonja one more time. Difficult, but it probably wouldn't kill him. He'd managed often enough before.

He began to stroke her hair.

Yes: if he concentrated very hard he might be able to make the incredible leap of the imagination needed to pretend that the plump body in his arms was that of Isabella.

Sixty miles inside Finland the truck came to a halt in the darkness beside a vast frozen lake. Here the three men unloaded the vehicle, removing rucksacks and skis, a bundle of birch poles, a roll of thick cloth, and several boxes of provisions. A short distance below the track, in a sheltered hollow among the trees bordering the lake, they made camp.

They built the curved birch poles into a domed tent frame and stretched the thick woolen cloth around it. They added a floor of birch twigs covered with reindeer skins and within twenty minutes the tent was completed.

It was a long time since either Jan or Mattis had erected a traditional Lapp tent, known as a *lavo*, but the old Skolt Lapp remembered the method well enough, although he himself hardly ever bothered nowadays. There was a perfectly good wooden hut ten miles up the lake that he normally used. But in this instance it was best to stay off the beaten track. The Skolt Lapp was well known in this region—indeed, he was related to several Lapp families hereabouts and belonged to the *siida,* or community, which had fishing rights on this section of Lake Inari—but the other two men were strangers and would attract attention.

The men retreated gratefully into the tent. The wind was blowing hard down the sixty-mile length of the lake; wind-torn clouds raced across the new moon, and to the north the stars had vanished behind an advancing mass of deeper darkness. Mattis lit the pressure stove—their only concession to modernity—and prepared a hot meal from dried fish and potatoes, followed by hard unleavened bread and cloudberry preserve with real butter, a delicacy in these parts. This was followed by coffee, and for the old man, a swig of aquavit.

The old man loved to talk and for a while the younger men listened politely, though it was hard to follow his rapid and mumbled dialect. He talked of prewar days, when his community had lived in the Petsamo region, an area trapped between east and west and the subject of eternal border disputes. Then it was Finnish; now it was Russian. Like many of his generation the old man wanted to return to his homeland. Yet he wasn't allowed to, and he still found it difficult to understand why.

He didn't like life here on Lake Inari; the fishing wasn't as good, the hunting was poor, and the Finnish settlers were hostile to the Lapps. What was the answer?

There was no answer and the younger men fell asleep, leaving the old man to have another slug of aquavit and contemplate the next day's fishing, and decide where on the frozen lake he would try his luck.

Eventually he too slept and the only sound was the insistent soughing of the wind as it blew the first swirls of snow against the side of the tent.

Sonja knew he was awake, but she didn't speak. At times like this it was best to leave him alone. Neither did she move, though as always she had a strong urge to touch him. She loved the texture of his hair, so rich and heavy; she liked to stroke his arm and feel the astonishing smoothness of his skin.

But she held back. Self-control was essential. Clever women never gave anything away, she knew that. They were careful not to show their feelings, careful not to make too many demands. And she'd been careful, so careful. And it had really paid off.

Until now.

What had gone wrong? She couldn't imagine. She had done nothing to upset him.

But then a part of her could imagine only too well what was wrong—he was bored with her. He was trying to get rid of her. The thought was agony.

This new job was just a pretext, she was certain of it. If he really wanted to go on seeing her he would find a way. After all, they'd managed this long without anyone finding out. Not a whisper of their relationship had ever gotten out into either department.

It was Erik who'd insisted on secrecy. He'd said it would damage his career. Deep down she suspected there was another reason—he was ashamed of her. She could see how some people might find the relationship ridiculous. They wouldn't understand, they wouldn't realize how dependent they were on each other.

Had been . . .

Torture.

She felt tears well up again, and held them back. So undignified, like that exhibition downstairs. What had she been thinking of, showing her feelings like that!

She'd been so happy with the way things were. In her twenties she'd expected too much—that had been her mistake. At thirty-five she'd still been waiting patiently for the right man, but suddenly there weren't any more available men, right or otherwise. It dawned on her that she'd been far too choosy.

Then Mother had gotten ill and Sonja had moved in with her and suddenly her social life had evaporated to a weekly trip to the cinema.

Now she was fifty and it was all far, far too late.

Erik stirred at her side. She held still, longing for him to speak, but he rolled away from her, breathing slowly and steadily. Outside, the wind sighed in the trees.

She thought: I'll do anything to keep him.

Erik rolled onto his back again and she held her breath.

His hand touched her arm and patted it.

A rush of love and longing surged through Sonja. She pressed herself against him. He swung his arm behind her neck and pulled her to him. With infinite slowness she stroked his arm and touched his hair, concentrating on each sensation so that she could store it carefully in her memory.

He murmured: "You know, Sonja, I'm really very fond of you."

She held still, eyes firmly closed, teeth gritted.

He sighed. "It's just that ... I'll be working all hours and ... I just won't have time." He added shortly: "This job's really important, you see."

Forcing her voice to be immensely reasonable she said: "I understand."

"Well, I'm not sure you do. It could be a big feather in my cap."

"Can I help at all?" Her words hung in the air.

He was silent for a moment. "Well ... I shouldn't think so." He sounded very doubtful. "Unless there's anything you think I should know about. I mean, anything sensitive that could be—well, easily jeopardized."

She knew exactly what she should tell him, but she wanted to be absolutely sure. She asked: "This leak—it might involve joint operations, you say?"

"Yes"—he sounded annoyed that she'd asked for elaboration—"anything involving operations with the NSA or CIA."

Still Sonja hesitated. There were joint operations with the U.S. National Security Agency and the CIA, certainly, but she had never given him details before. General policy decisions, details about intelligence-gathering installations—they had seemed completely harmless.

But never operations. And why should she now, when he was leaving her?

Erik bent over and kissed her, then, drawing back, looked down at her without speaking. In the dim light his expression seemed almost gentle. "You know," he murmured, "I *would* miss you."

"Don't leave me."

"Sonja, I—"

"You won't regret it."

"Well, I don't know. . . . Perhaps there might be a way."

"I can help, I really can, Erik."

A pause. "I'd begun to think you didn't want to help me anymore, Sonja."

"Oh, I do, I do, Erik. It was just that—it was so difficult deciding what was safe for you to know."

"Dear Sonja." Another pause. "Perhaps we could meet now and then . . ."

She let the words sink in slowly. Did he mean it? She wept openly, burying her head against his chest, and whispered in a sudden burst of honesty: "Erik, I can't help it, I do love you so."

He gave a short laugh. "Sonja, Sonja . . . I love you too."

And then, so that he would never live to regret those words and because she wanted to please him so much, she told him.

She was extremely careful *not* to give him the names of those involved or the precise location, but she told him the rest. About the two Lapps on their way to the border, about the meeting with the agent from Murmansk, the man who was buying his freedom with information from the Murmansk shipyards.

And then they made love again, and, overcome with relief, Sonja made a vow. That she would never disappoint him again.

4

Ragna Johansen stared at herself in the mirror and saw a cabbage. Not a bad-looking sort of cabbage, admittedly, but in the eyes of her former friends a distinct vegetable nonetheless. A woman who had thrown away her early promise for the vise-like grip of domesticity.

She'd given up nothing worth having, of course—but the idea amused her all the same, because in the old days the thought of being an ordinary housewife would have appalled her.

But then the old days hadn't been so brilliant. In fact, they'd been pretty awful.

She brushed her hair and held it in a bunch at the back of her neck. Tomorrow night she'd be seeing two friends from the old days—but good friends, not like the rest. Yet they'd still be curious to see what time and the north of Norway had done to her.

She eyed herself in the mirror, smiling in a self-mocking way. Not bad for almost thirty. There were faint laugh lines around the eyes, but her skin was good, her eyes clear. She'd always thought her eyes were her best feature, but it was her coloring that usually attracted attention. It had been a joke among her friends that one of her ancestors must have been a Greek or Italian sea captain. Both her parents had been fair-haired, but either her mother had had a lover—a distinct possibility—or the genes had skipped a few generations. Ragna's hair wasn't brown like many Norwegians', it was dark and glossy, and her skin had that smooth sheen that usually went with sun and olive oil.

She hovered over her meager assortment of makeup. Since living in Tromsø she had hardly bothered with it, but now she felt the need to look especially good—partly to bolster her confidence, and partly to show her friends that she hadn't entirely lost her sparkle.

She put on eye shadow, mascara, and lipstick, and clipped on some bright earrings. The effect made her pause; there were echoes of the past in that painted face. For a moment her confidence faltered; part of her suddenly didn't want to go to Oslo at all.

She'd been brought up in Oslo—if brought up was the right description; and there she'd spent some of the worst years of her life.

Her early childhood had been unsettled, disturbed, and disjointed. When she was fourteen her father, a writer and enthusiastic alcoholic, had left Ragna's stepmother—his fourth wife—and disappeared, leaving Ragna to be sent to her mother, a wild and unconventional poetess and former actress who lived with an eighteen-year-old laborer in two rooms overlooking Oslo harbor. At sixteen Ragna had run away with a film producer twice her age to become an actress, a career that led at the end of the war to Stockholm and leading roles in three low-budget films memorable only for their mildly shocking eroticism.

At nineteen she met her true Svengali, an avant-garde director, and made a film with him called *Chance*, which won prizes at two film festivals. She also made a baby with him, a little girl named Anne. There were several more films, and plenty of money. It was a golden time. It lasted—how long? Difficult to remember now. And hard to tell when it began to fall apart. But by the time she realized what was happening it was too late, and everything had turned sour . . . her lover, rotting and unproductive and ugly on hard drugs; herself, sunk in an uncreative unemployable mess; and then . . . Then little Anne. Even now her mind remained tightly sealed around the events of those dark days, unable to grasp completely that Anne had died from meningitis.

She called the years that followed the black time. She'd tried to escape in the only way she knew, by traveling a lot, and by surrounding herself with noisy people—lots of them—at parties, in communes, in fringe theater groups; never alone but always alone. There were men—too many of them—and the more they liked her, the greater and more barren was the emptiness around her.

Jan picked up the pieces. Why he'd done it she still wasn't sure. Jan: quiet, patient, and fathomless, a Norwegian of the sea and mountains—everything her artistic friends dismissed as faintly ridiculous and dangerously nonintellectual. But for her, a rock in an ocean of uncertainty. The marriage had been a success because it had given her things she had never had: stability, tranquillity, love, and a humdrum existence.

She exhaled sharply. Memories of the past still had the power to cause her pain. She turned firmly away from the mirror.

Outside, the glimmering twilight revealed a dark and stormy morning. Maddening. The flying boat would probably be delayed.

She finished her packing, throwing in some designer clothes she hadn't worn for years. They were a bit out of date now—fashions had changed, waists were disappearing, skirts getting shorter—but they would still wear well. And she'd included a smart dress. You never knew. She might get invited to dinner at Blom's, like in the old days.

There was a sound at the bedroom door. A small child tottered into the room, rubbing his eyes.

Ragna sighed. He was meant to have slept for another hour at least.

"Hello, you." She picked up her son and looked at him quizzically. His name was Kristian, known as Kris or Krisi, and he was almost two.

The child suddenly focused on her mouth and, frowning, prodded a finger at the unfamiliar lipstick.

Ragna smiled. "Funny, eh?"

Seeing that it was a joke, Krisi giggled. Then, ever curious, he looked around and saw the case on the bed. Ragna watched his face change. He knew very well what cases meant. They meant people—usually Jan—going away.

"I told you, darling," Ragna said calmly, "I'm going to Oslo for a few days. Not long." A small lie: she'd actually be away for ten days.

Krisi clung to her and began to whine. Ragna took him into the living room and tried to distract him with a few toys, but his arms stayed firmly locked around her neck. She loved him to pieces, of course, but he was just at the stage when he threw mighty rages, and from that point of view this short break wasn't coming a moment too soon.

Her mother-in-law, Sigrid Johansen, finally arrived. Ragna plopped a screaming Krisi into his grandmother's arms and went to collect her case. When she returned Krisi was quiet. The moment he caught sight of her he started crying again. Ragna pulled him onto her lap and gave him a cuddle.

Mrs. Johansen shook her head. "Going to Oslo alone. Such a long way." Mrs. Johansen had lived in Tromsø all her life. She didn't see the necessity for people to travel.

"Well, I have to go, I want to go. It's part of my new job, after all."

"But Jan away *too*," the older woman tutted.

"But if he hadn't been away he'd only have come with me to Oslo. So . . ."

"But why is he away? What's he doing?"

Ragna shrugged. "Trying out some new piece of equipment. I'm not sure what."

"Well, it's a pity," her mother-in-law said firmly. "What about the shop? Who's looking after that?"

"That runs itself." Jan had a sports shop in Tromsø which the small staff could run perfectly well on their own.

"Mmm. Well, I hope you're not taking on too much. With Kristian still so small."

Ragna ignored the implied criticism. She was looking forward to starting her new job. Expedition secretary: Everest West Ridge, 1963. The grandness of the title tickled her; it sounded better suited to a man of great distinction and mature years than to a former actress with little previous experience. But she was good at organization—the chaos of her early life had given her a mania for order; and she had a way with people. She was sure she'd make a success of it.

She went to collect her briefcase and paused at a window. The house stood among birch trees on the southern tip of the island of Tromsø, and looked down a wide sound toward Straumsfjord, with wonderful open views of mountains and water. On clear days at this time of year the whole scene was bathed in delicate pastels, the light so transparent you could see thirty miles or more.

Today, however, the weather was bad. Yet was it her imagination or had the blizzard eased a little? The wind sighed in the birches, and she could see its force in the swirl and bluster of the snowflakes, but the visibility seemed to have improved and the fjord was slowly emerging from the pall of darkness.

She gave a thought to Jan, somewhere up on the plateau. The weather might well be different up there; it often was, so they said. But even if it were blowing a blizzard he'd be perfectly at home. The harsher the conditions the more he seemed to like it.

The doorbell rang. The taxi. In the hall Sigrid Johansen and Krisi were waiting to say good bye. Ragna tried to make her farewell to Krisi as optimistic and firm as possible, but he howled all the same. She got into the taxi and waved with guilty relief.

It was five minutes to the center of Tromsø. The "Paris of the North," they called it. The boast always amused Ragna. It was a long time since Tromsø had been on the trade route to northern Russia, and even longer since the sea captains had brought the latest Paris fashions back for their wives. The place still had quite a few restaurants and night spots left over from the whaling boom, however, and for that Ragna was grateful. Compared to other Arctic towns, Tromsø was almost bustling.

The taxi dropped Ragna at the waterfront. The visibility had definitely improved, and she was relieved to see that the seaplane was already there, tethered a short distance off the quay.

The girl in the small airline office said a little reproachfully: "No, the plane won't be leaving late." She glanced at Ragna's ticket. "Oh, there was someone asking for you. Another passenger." The girl busied herself with the paperwork. "I believe it was Halvard Starheim."

Returning from a stroll along the quay, Hal came in and spotted her straightaway. You couldn't miss her. The dark hair, the way she stood, the well-cut clothes.

He made his way toward her, aware of a slight nervousness.

Turning, she spotted him and smiled broadly. Hal thought: I always forget how lovely she is.

Ragna declared: "Well! If it isn't my new boss."

Hal smiled a little uncertainly. He had the feeling he was being teased.

She said: "I thought you were already in Oslo."

"I had to stay on another day. Unexpectedly."

"Ah! On the same jaunt as Jan?"

The question caught him unawares. "No, I— It was something else."

She gave him a look of amused skepticism, and he thought: I'm a bad liar.

"You two are up to something," she said. "If I wasn't so nice, I'd be cross that you hadn't told me about it."

"Didn't Jan explain?"

"Well—he gave me some story or another. But I can always tell when he's skirting the truth. In fact, if you really want to know, I didn't believe a word of it!"

Because the subject needed changing and he couldn't think of anything else to say, he replied: "But you should always believe what your husband tells you."

She threw back her head and laughed uproariously. "Oh, Hal! You do make me laugh sometimes!"

He examined her face: What did she mean by it? He decided finally that she was making fun of him in a perfectly harmless way. Yet with Ragna he could never be absolutely sure, and for that reason she always made him feel slightly off-balance.

She laughed again. "With ideas like that you'll have to find yourself a very old-fashioned girl."

Hal made the effort to enter into the easy banter that was so characteristic of conversation with Ragna. "I've tried old-fashioned girls—but they always expect *me* to be old-fashioned and work regular hours and come home every night."

She was pleased with that. "Then you'll have to put your foot down."

"I'm too nice."

She cocked her head to one side and stared at him thoughtfully. "Yes," she said, "I think you probably are."

Hal looked away. She was teasing him again.

The passengers were called to the door: the Catalina was ready to leave. Hal picked up Ragna's hand luggage and led the way out. Darting flurries of snow crystals scythed across the quay and Ragna gave a small gasp. Hal took her arm and she leaned against him as they climbed down the steps to the waiting launch.

After a bumpy but mercifully short sea journey they reached the plane and climbed in. Ragna exclaimed: "I can never get used to the damned wind in this place. I don't think I was cut out for the north." They settled into their seats. She asked: "Doesn't it ever get you down? The wind, I mean?"

No one had ever asked him that before; they usually asked him about the cold. He considered the question carefully; he wanted to give her a proper answer. "The wind's just a part of it all—the terrain, the snow, the place. I can't separate the wind from the rest. So I don't feel strongly about it."

She shook her head. "You really love it, don't you?"

"What?"

"Oh, those wide-open spaces, pitting yourself against the elements and all that. I could never stand the isolation!"

"Well—I only love it for short periods. I'd hate it *all* the time. When I've a particular objective, something to aim for, then it's great. Everything becomes very simple and straightforward—it's just *you* and *it*, whatever *it* may be. And I never have time to feel isolated. Too much to do, too much burning ambition to achieve the objective." He was going to add that he'd felt lonelier in crowds than he'd ever felt in the middle of the ice, but that might lead the conversation into more personal areas, and he'd rather avoid that. He added: "But I'd go mad if I was in the middle of nowhere for too long. I need people, just like everyone else."

She gave him a sidelong look. "You surprise me. You always seem so—well, self-sufficient."

He smiled wryly. "Perhaps I'm not what I seem."

"A lamb in wolf's clothing?"

He shot her a quick questioning glance.

She wrinkled her nose and smiled. "No. Just a lamb."

She'd done it again: thrown him slightly. He decided that Ragna marched to a different and quicker drum.

"I can understand the attractions of simplicity, of course." She was nodding sagely now, a furrow of concentration between her brows, to show that she was giving his answers the serious consideration they deserved. "I think that's the part that Jan loves too." She added, with a snort of fond amusement: "You two are a real pair."

It was true and he smiled. "But you don't seem to mind," Hal said. "I mean, that Jan still wants to go on expeditions. That . . . well—"

"That he doesn't want to stay at home with me? No, why should I?"

"Most women would mind a lot."

"Well, I'm not most women."

Hal thought: I know that.

"I like him the way he is," Ragna continued. "Besides, he was already a mountaineer when I married him. He'd only be unhappy if I locked him up at home."

Hal pictured Jan and Ragna together and, though he tried hard to suppress it, was stabbed by the familiar pang of envy. Why didn't he have a marriage like that?

The Catalina revved its engines and taxied downwind, keeping in the lee of the shore. Finally it turned to face the buffeting wind and, engines rising to a scream, slowly accelerated, bumping and vibrating over the waves. Ragna held her breath and laughed. "I can never get used to this crazy business!"

With one last bump the plane rose into the air and, after seeming to hover motionless above the water, banked toward the south and gathered speed.

Ragna thought: Sometimes I don't know you at all.

She observed Hal covertly. He was pleasant-looking, with strong well-formed features, a long straight nose, and a rather nice expressive mouth. His hair was brown and short and slightly curly, the sort that's nice to touch. His eyes could be extraordinarily warm and kind when he let them, but most of the time they were dark and serious and shadowed by a frequent frown, giving him an absorbed intense look.

Beneath the serious manner Ragna suspected he was rather a honey, but in the four years she'd known him she'd never managed to get under his guard and there'd always been a slight awkwardness between them.

It was disappointing. Not only did Ragna pride herself on getting on with people but she liked to think she could strike up a spontaneous and open friendship with anyone she liked. However, Hal was a dark horse.

When she'd first met him she'd suspected that he was merely a man's man, one of that unattractive breed who secretly fear and dislike women. Certainly he was more at home discussing an expedition with his teammates than making small talk in a mixed gathering—though there were plenty of men like that, God only knew. But with Hal it was different. She'd noticed how other men looked up to him—mainly because of what he had achieved, of course, but also because he had that indefinable quality of leadership, a sort of iron resolve and detachment that men always admired. As far as the members of his expeditions were concerned, he could do no wrong.

Yet there was more to Hal than a simple man of action; something he kept in reserve, something he didn't choose to reveal to anybody. She tried to decide exactly what it was. A sensitivity maybe . . . Yes. And there was a passionate side to him, too. She suspected he was rather a romantic. Ah, that was it. And if he was a romantic he was vulnerable, and he wouldn't like that at all. No wonder he took such care to hide it.

Lots of women had tried to crack him, of course. They'd all failed.

She wondered what held him back. A broken love affair? A secret unrequited passion?

Something.

Yes. Sometimes she felt she hardly knew him at all.

She handed him a set of beautifully typed notes.

He was impressed: she had it all worked out. There was a diary of appointments with possible sponsors, plus a fallback list of companies and individuals who might be approached if the first list failed. Also a guest list for the press conference, due to be held on Wednesday morning. And he noticed that, despite earlier problems, she had been able to arrange a meeting with a senior government minister who might be able to push their case for a government grant.

"Well done," he said over the din of the engines. "But I

think we should try to see all these companies, even those on the backup list."

"Oh. But surely we should try the ones who are interested first." She indicated the main list.

Hal shook his head. "Believe me, getting a murmur of interest is one thing. Getting a firm commitment is quite another."

"You're wrong! You're established now. Everyone knows you. Everyone knows what you've *done*. They'll be glad to sponsor you!" She stabbed a finger in his direction and said: "You'll see if I'm not right!"

She made it sound so easy. But it never had been, and he couldn't see any reason why it should be now. He remembered all the times he'd had to sell himself and his ideas like some salesman trying to sell an unknown and unwanted commodity: no one had wanted to know.

When he'd first tried to get an expedition off the ground he'd known it would be tough, of course. This was a country where everyone—man, woman, and child—was something of a mountaineer and skier. A lot of people believed that, given the opportunity, they too could climb high mountains and traverse Arctic wastes. It was a hard job to convince them that you could climb higher and endure longer than they could. Though once they *were* convinced, and provided they knew and understood your motives, then they did give you their respect.

But respect didn't translate itself into cash. Norwegians, especially northerners, were generous and warm-hearted when times were hard. But they were also fiercely independent, self-sufficient, stubborn, and tight-fisted. They found it convenient to believe that, in some magical way, expeditions financed themselves.

Hal felt no bitterness. On the contrary, he understood their attitudes only too well. One only had to remember the rugged coast hidden beneath the thick cloud, the settlements and isolated farms clinging to the narrow band of fertile soil between mountains and sea, the hard-working women who ran them, and the men who went fishing winter and summer, gale or calm, to appreciate what a hard and tenuous life it still was for so many. In the past there had been terrible poverty, even famine. Now there was a growing prosperity, but memories were long, attitudes deep-seated, even in the wealthier south.

No, it wouldn't be easy. It never was.

Ragna was reading her own copy of the week's diary. He noticed there was a handwritten entry on her schedule that he hadn't remembered seeing on his. He checked: no, it wasn't there. He glanced back at the copy in her lap. He could see that the entry was for Thursday and that there was a time written to one side of it.

"What's that?" He pointed toward it.

She looked faintly defensive. "Oh. A meeting of mine. I just put it on there to remind me."

He leaned over and peered more closely. She made a slight movement as if to slide the papers away, then thought better of it.

He deciphered the handwriting and looked up at her in surprise. "The justice ministry? Why on earth are you going there?"

"Ah." She gave him a long appraising look as if she were making up her mind what to tell him. "Well, I'm going on behalf of some friends of mine really. It's a sort of favor."

"Oh?"

She shrugged and murmured something that he missed in the loud drumming of the engines.

He leaned his head closer to show he was waiting for her to repeat it.

A look of resignation came over her face. She said: "Some Lapp friends. They want me to go and . . ." She pursed her lips in annoyance, as if she'd been caught out in some way. "And . . . well, ask some questions for them, represent them if you like."

A small but powerful suspicion flew into Hal's mind. He hesitated, thinking he must surely be mistaken, but the suspicion had lodged too firmly to go away. Finally he had to ask: "It wouldn't by any chance be something to do with a military training area?"

Her eyes flashed darkly, and he knew he was right. His heart sank. "What sort of questions?"

"We want to know how the military can possibly lay claim to land which doesn't belong to them! And, if they insist on going through with this, how they expect to compensate the Lapps for the considerable disturbance to their herds. And a few things like that!"

"That's fighting talk, Ragna."

"Too right it is."

It was the actress in her, Hal decided: all zeal and big-heartedness. It was just a pity she'd chosen such a sensitive cause. Successive governments had been very good at closing their minds to Lapp rights, and he had a feeling they wouldn't take kindly to having objections forced down their throats.

He drew a deep breath. "Ragna, this is most"—he searched for the right word—"unfortunate."

"Oh? Why?" Her tone was defensive.

"It's a political matter. And we can't be involved in anything political."

"But it's me who's involved, and I happen to think this is important."

"Yes, but you're part of the expedition now. Your involvement would be misunderstood."

"By whom?"

"Government officials. Newspapers. You name it."

"But it's something I can do quite separately. I can use my unmarried name. I won't even mention the expedition." She added proudly: "You see, I can't let them down."

Hal sighed: "But why you, Ragna?"

"Why not?"

"Well, you're not a Lapp, for a start."

"But that's just the point! No one listens to them. They need someone like me, someone who can get them heard. Anyway," she added with a shrug, "Jan's a quarter Lapp."

"And what does he think about this?"

"He respects my point of view."

There was a long pause. Suddenly they hit some turbulence and the small plane bucketed and lurched. He saw that Ragna's knuckles were white on the seat arm.

Hal touched her wrist. "Okay?"

She gave a tiny nod, but her lips were set in a hard line, and her eyes were round and very dark. He wasn't sure if her anger and fear were directed at him or the plane.

Finally they flew into smoother air, and began a gentle descent to Bodø, where they would change to a DC-7C for the last two legs to Oslo.

Conversation became possible again. Hal prepared himself. He couldn't possibly leave this matter unresolved.

"Norway's a small country," he began, and immediately thought how horribly pompous that sounded, as if he were treating her like a fool. "I mean, everyone in government knows each other. People talk. There's no possibility of your association with this—*issue*—going unnoticed. The press—at least some of it—will sit up and take notice. People will find it strange, government officials won't be quite so helpful . . ."

"What are you saying exactly?" she asked stiffly.

"That—it would be an embarrassment to the expedition. And to me."

"But I can't just let them down."

"I wish you'd talked this over with me before."

"I didn't think I had to!"

"Well—yes, you had to. Everyone has to discuss things with everyone else. That's how a team works."

"This sounds like a lecture."

Hal dragged a hand across his forehead. The discussion was not going well. His instincts had failed him and he merely seemed to be antagonizing her. He said simply: "I'm sorry."

"You're forbidding me to go, is that it?"

For several moments he didn't answer. She wanted him to state things too baldly. "Well, I wouldn't have put it that way . . ."

"But it boils down to the same thing!"

There was a willfulness, a stubborn intransigence, in her, and he knew that one way or another she'd force the admission out of him. "All right," he said finally. "If you like."

A flush stole up her face and her lips narrowed. She turned away and stared doggedly out the window.

He had an urge to reach out and touch her arm, to show he regretted the incident. But something held him back and then the moment had passed.

The distance across the lake was eighteen miles, a journey of three or four hours in good conditions. The two men had planned to set out well before the first glimmering of dawn, but a fierce blizzard had kept them in their tent. There was no hurry. If necessary they could travel at night. One had to be adaptable. Only the foolish went out in minus thirty and a full gale unless absolutely necessary. It wasn't just that the visibility was down to less than five yards; it was the wind. Not only did it take energy to walk against it but it was energy one needed to maintain body heat and prevent one's extremities from freezing in the vicious windchill.

So the men waited and by midmorning their patience was rewarded. The wind began to moderate; the snow, though falling steadily, was not so dense; and Jan's pocket thermometer registered a small but distinct rise.

They ate a last meal of hot reindeer stew, cheese, and coffee, then donned their outer garments, rucksacks, and skis, plus an extra pair of skis which Jan strapped to his back. With a brief farewell to the old man, they made their way down to the lake. Then, using a compass bearing to guide them to their first landmark, an as yet invisible island some two miles out, they set off, settling into the long sliding lope of practiced cross-country skiers.

Jan kept his bearings by keeping the wind at an angle to his left cheek, only occasionally checking his compass. As soon as they had found and skirted the first island, they headed for the next islet another two miles away. Jan noticed that the wind was shifting slowly through north toward the west.

Once the men stopped to drink from the water flasks they kept close to their bodies. Dehydration was always a problem in intensely cold dry air.

Otherwise they kept going, thrusting through the soft snow in rhythmic strides, traveling surprisingly fast. The long, narrow wooden skis were light and flexible and bowed. The ends were polished and slid forward easily on the forward thrust, while the middle section, which only came into contact with the snow on the back thrust, was carefully waxed to make it sticky and permit no backsliding. The boots were light and soft, made of reindeer skin, and fastened to the skis by hide bindings at the toe, allowing the heel to rise on the stride. The Lapps needed no lessons in the art of skiing; they had been practicing it for more than three thousand years.

Another island reared up ahead, its side speckled with dwarf birch and dark patches of bare rock.

There were no more islands after that, and they headed out across a five-mile stretch of open lake toward a promontory as yet invisible on the opposite shore. Once there, they would follow the shoreline another six miles into a deep bay, and complete the crossing of the lake.

They would then stop at an isolated hut— if they could find it. The old man had told them that the *hytte* was situated a few hundred yards up a low fell leading off a tongue of the lake, but in the poor visibility and falling darkness they might well miss it. If they did, it would be unfortunate but not disastrous. They would merely dig themselves a snow hole for the night and, instead of enjoying a strong fire in the *hytte*, they would make do with the rather thinner warmth of the pressure stove.

Thereafter it was not far to their journey's end—in a straight line only six miles. The route would be relatively straightforward, taking them along a series of valleys and watercourses. But if the visibility was poor they would have to watch their distance: there was a border close by, a border they weren't intending to cross.

In the center of Lake Inari, meanwhile, the wind dropped away and the swirl of snow thinned to a few desultory flakes. From a cocoon of gray, the world slowly opened out before them. Dark specks showed in the whiteness ahead, hinting at rocky outcrops: the promontory. It was a welcome sight in the approaching night. Jan turned his head and raised his snow-crusted eyebrows to Mattis. The Lapp nodded back. They were both thinking the same thing: no cold discomfort in a claustrophobic snow cave after all; now they would find the hut and enjoy a relatively luxurious night.

5

As a newspaper story it was useless.

Berg pulled the sheet of notes out of the typewriter and read it through. A fantastic and explosive story—but no newspaper would touch it with a barge pole, not even if he veiled it so heavily as to be almost completely obscure. The Norwegian press, for all its self-righteous talk about freedom and rights, was desperately hidebound and law-abiding. Even his own paper, the *Sosialist Dagens Post*, which prided itself on its liberal roots, rarely printed anything controversial. All it did, as Berg knew only too well, was reinforce its readers' deeply entrenched opinions.

Well, there was more than one way of killing a cat. It was just a question of deciding which way.

He wandered restlessly around the apartment, thinking hard. He'd already sat on this for more than a day. He must do something soon or risk losing everything.

Trembling slightly, he lit a cigarette and inhaled deeply. This was the big one, the jackpot; no doubt about that. A coup. Beyond his wildest dreams. Beyond anything they had ever expected of him.

He calmed himself. He had to get it right. And right meant exposing the full extent of the CIA's involvement in Norway, so giving the lie to the idea that Norway was totally autonomous. Christ—what a balloon that was going to send up.

But exposing the truth wasn't going to be easy. He knew that the operation must be under the direct control of the CIA, simply because the third man, the man who was to be met at the Finno-Russian border, was an American agent. He had to be because Norway had no agents inside Russia—Norway had no agents anywhere.

He knew the truth all right—but how to convince the world?

And then there was the matter of Finland. The operation was being carried out on Finnish soil without that country's knowledge or consent. Handled correctly, that too would raise a monumental stink.

Berg could guess why the Finnish route had been chosen, of course. An operation on the Norwegian-Soviet border would have been far too difficult: the border was short and, Norway being a member of NATO, relatively well guarded. The Finnish border, on the other hand, was hundreds and hundreds of miles long and less heavily guarded, not only because Finland was neutral but because any Russian defectors who did manage to reach Finland were immediately handed back.

So—the possibility for double embarrassment.

Incredible. And as a bonus, the furor might just tip public opinion further against the nuclear-missile issue.

He stopped his pacing and sat down abruptly. He knew what had to be done. In fact, he'd known all along; he'd just put off the moment of decision, hoping there might be another way, a way that would leave him total control.

But that had been too much to ask for: sometimes one just had to take a backseat.

Besides, he was looking forward to seeing the look on Alex's face. He wouldn't have long to wait: he'd arranged to meet him for lunch.

It was eleven-thirty. Berg went into the bathroom, a brilliant box of a room lined with mirrors and sparkling starlike lights. The room had been featured in a leading home-design magazine. Berg kept a copy on the coffee table in the living room, open to the appropriate page.

This morning, however, the lighting assaulted his eyes and tinged his skin a rather unhealthy gray. He splashed cold water over his face and rubbed it dry. He looked up into the mirror. Lines, a hint of bags under the eyes: tired, older. Lack of sleep.

He ran an electric razor over his chin and combed his hair. Better.

Excitement churned in his stomach and his spirits rose again. He grinned broadly at his reflection and thought: *What a hell of a thing this is!*

Gathering a coat and his notes from the typewriter, he went out. The weather was vastly better: the sky was clear and the sun, making its brief midday appearance, made the snow sparkle and the buildings glow.

He drove slowly for once, letting the car pull itself up through the hilly suburbs to the restaurant on the high point of Holmenkollen. Berg hardly ever came here—he preferred Blom's or the Theatre Café—but Alex liked it. He said he liked it because of the spectacular view of the city, but Berg suspected he got a perverse amusement out of sitting among the other diners, who more often than not included diplomats and NATO personnel.

Alex was already there, by the window, his plump jovial figure beaming with goodwill. "This view!" he said immediately. "What a day to be up here! What a day! I never get tired of the view."

They went to the cold table and helped themselves from the unchanging selection of pickled and smoked fish, meat, and vegetables. Alex's plate was piled so high that slivers of pickled cabbage fell to the floor as he returned to the table.

Berg watched him stuff large mouthfuls into his already well-padded face. "Hungry?"

Alex smiled. "Always. It comes from starving as a child. Those memories never leave you. We used to boil up shoe leather, you know. And catch rats—those that survived the cold, of course. I was the champion rat catcher of Leningrad. Did I tell you that?"

"You told me."

"Ah. One forgets."

Berg thought: You never forget.

Alex took a mouthful so large that he had to leave his mouth open to chew it. Berg averted his eyes and took a small bite of pickled fish. He put down his fork—sometimes he despaired of the Norwegian mania for pickling everything—and began to give Alex some of the latest gossip.

Above the relentless grinding of his jaws, Alex was quietly absorbing every word. Berg had a reputation for knowing all the latest scandals and whispers, and for recounting them amusingly. And Alex, a GRU (Soviet military intelligence) officer with the Novosti Press Agency, was keener than most to keep abreast of events in the NATO community.

Berg finished with a little tale of a trade delegation visiting Sweden from a well-known Far Eastern industrial country and getting caught in a brothel, quite literally with their trousers down.

Alex laughed until he almost choked. His face scarlet, he held up his hand in protest. "Stop, stop!" he sobbed. "I can't bear it."

Berg watched him coolly. He suspected Alex would already have heard the story from his own sources, in which case he was putting on a good act.

Only the mention of dessert brought a halt to Alex's laughter. He collected a double helping of apple tart and cream from the cold table. Before plunging in, he asked: "Did you see that Polaris story in *Time* magazine?"

Berg nodded.

There was a pause. The two men exchanged glances.

It had been a jewel of a story, and it had been largely unearthed by Berg. It had concerned the secret building of a U.S. navigation station on the northwest coast of Norway, for use by Polaris submarines carrying nuclear weapons. The story had been cleverly disseminated by Alex. It had first appeared in an East German paper, and then been picked up by a Finnish left-wing daily. Variations of the story had subsequently appeared in other European papers until, finally, a Norwegian paper had plucked up enough courage to run a highly modified version of it.

The Norwegian government had squirmed and wriggled before finally admitting that a defense establishment was in the process of construction on the northwest coast. The affair had caused the government some embarrassment, particularly after the now-famous Bulganin Note of the previous year, in which the USSR had given Norway a strong warning of the consequences of NATO bases appearing on Norwegian soil.

"Mmm, the *Time* piece was all right," Berg said casually, "but it never made banner headlines in Tromsø."

Alex looked worried, then, as the joke dawned, laughed

heartily. "No banner headlines! Tromsø! You're cruel! Cruel! One day, one day!"

Berg smiled to himself. It was easy to make Alex laugh. One merely had to remember that his sense of humor was as subtle as a sledgehammer.

There was a short silence.

Alex spooned the last of the cream from his plate and sat back in his chair, focusing benevolently. "Well, what can this humble fellow journalist do for you today?"

"I wanted to sound you out on the official Soviet response to the presence of nuclear missiles on Norwegian soil."

Alex nodded slowly. This was the official reason for meeting openly—always openly—for lunch every few months or so. Many political journalists had professional relationships with Soviet officials and diplomats. No one thought anything of it.

If Alex remembered that Berg had asked him this question before, he didn't show it. "Sure. Sure," he said. "It's quite simple. The Soviet Union would take the arrival of nuclear weapons on Norwegian soil as a totally unprovoked act of aggression on the part of Norway against the Soviet Union." He threw a chocolate into his mouth and beamed. "Will that do?"

Berg didn't answer. A large party was entering the restaurant, a group of about twenty NATO personnel: Norwegian, American, and British naval and army officers. They walked rather stiffly and formally to a long table nearby.

Berg gave it a moment and murmured very quietly: "And how does the Soviet Union feel about clandestine activities by Norwegian agents on the Finnish-Soviet border?"

The chocolate chewing stopped. Berg felt a leap of pleasure; he had taken Alex totally by surprise.

"Ah," said Alex. "That's something else of course." He sucked at his teeth. "Now why would they be wanting to do such a thing?"

"To meet someone."

"Someone one knows?"

"Someone with valuable information; someone from Murmansk."

Alex swallowed abruptly. "Oh, dear, oh, dear. Now, what is one to make of that?"

"It hasn't even happened yet. But it's going to happen very soon. I have all the details."

Alex's jaw dropped open. "My friend, what can I say? You are really most—efficient." His eyes firmly on Berg, he jabbed a finger impatiently into his mouth in an attempt to dislodge some food stuck in his teeth. Then, giving his lips a brief wipe, he said breathlessly: "How will the world react to this, I wonder?"

"It depends on how quickly the story breaks."

"Yes, yes." Alex's eyes were shining greedily. His colleagues were very skillful at feeding information into the Western news system so that no one was ever quite sure where the original story came from.

"But what we need is some questions in the Storting," Berg said. "And quickly, to get the best out of it."

"Questions in the Storting? That's not so easy."

"Of course it is, Alex. Don't tell me you can't do it." Some members of the Norwegian parliament had affiliations with trade-union and other left-wing groups, in whose ranks were several converts to the cause.

"Perhaps you overestimate me," Alex said carefully. "Unfortunately I don't get to enjoy delightful meals like this with members of the Storting."

"But you know people who do."

Alex dropped his eyes. Berg raised a finger and wagged it at him. Then, taking the single typewritten sheet out of his pocket he passed it openly across the table.

Alex stared at the paper as if it would bite him. His face went a pale shade of yellow. Berg thought: He can't believe his luck. Alex's hand shook as he reached out and, with exaggerated care, picked up the paper and put it into his breast pocket. "You know, Rolf, these things should not be done this way. It is very dangerous—for *you*, I mean." As if to emphasize the point he swiveled his eyes in the direction of the NATO personnel.

Berg's face hardened. He didn't blame Alex for being nervous—he himself felt rather tense, though in a decidedly stimulating way. No, what he disliked was the road the conversation was taking. Unless he was mistaken, he was in for the set lecture.

Reading Berg's face, Alex looked as if he wished he could get out of it too.

"Rolf, listen," Alex began tentatively in a low whisper. "You are very valuable to us. Very, *very* valuable. Sometimes I don't think you realize just how important you are—not at all!" He made a gesture of exasperation.

Berg gave a heavy theatrical sigh. "Come *on*, Alex."

"But Rolf, things cannot continue like this."

"Why not?"

"It's asking for trouble."

"Nonsense. Unless you're about to defect, of course."

Alex raised an eyebrow and let that one pass. In his younger days he'd probably considered it several times. He persisted: "We should take basic precautions!"

"I'm no virgin, Alex. I can look after myself."

"But if you run risks long enough, you get caught."

Berg made a face. Bureaucrats to the last, Alex and his friends were longing to get him locked into the system. But Berg wanted no part of dead-letter boxes, clandestine meetings, and sordid financial arrangements. He wanted to do things his way or not at all.

"But at least let us look after you," Alex pleaded.

These attempts at entrapment were always childishly transparent. The Alexes of this world thought they could manipulate almost anyone with flattery, money, and gifts. That was because they judged people by their own standards.

Berg looked at the fat obsequious man before him, and thought: Does he really believe I'll swallow it? He laughed, and said: "Alex—come on! Can't you do better than that?"

Alex made a gesture of hurt surprise. "But we do want to take care of you. Anything you want. Just say!"

"I want nothing, Alex. Nothing. You know that, so why the hell do you keep asking?"

Alex sat back, momentarily defeated, and looked thoughtful. A sly, calculating expression came over his face, and he leaned forward again.

"An old friend was asking after you," he said meaningfully. "He's coming to Oslo soon. He was hoping to see you."

Berg's stomach tightened. "There's no one I want to see, Alex—"

"But this is your old comrade-in-arms," Alex interrupted smoothly. "He wants to see you for old times' sake."

A sudden anger came over Berg. "Don't, Alex."

Alex opened his hands in a gesture of incomprehension. "Don't what?"

"Don't go on. Do you understand?"

"Understand? My friend, I'm baffled! What harm can there be in meeting an old friend?"

A vision stole into Berg's mind, a vision of Nikolai Andreevitch, his uniform dirty and unkempt, his cap sitting jauntily on the back of his head, his face young yet faded by time and light, like the tints of an old photograph. Behind Niki was the camp just to the east of Murmansk, its outlines shaded in pale grays, like the snow, the mountains, the people. And somewhere in the foreground was the thin shadowy figure of himself: sick and cold and bitter because there was no war left to fight nor any home he wanted to return to.

He owed Niki a lot. He'd never begrudged the debt—but he'd repaid it many times over.

He didn't want to see Niki. What he did now he did because he wanted to.

"Piss off, Alex."

A conciliatory smile flickered across Alex's face. "Please—don't take offense. You are my friend. The last thing I want to do is upset you!"

Berg pushed back his chair. "Well, you can shut up then. And get busy." He waved his hand in the direction of the Russian's breast pocket. "I expect the works on this one, Alex. Don't screw it up, eh?"

He got up and walked abruptly away, almost bumping into two uniformed officers, one Norwegian, one American, maneuvering with loaded plates from the smorgasbord. Berg apologized. The two officers smiled and passed on, talking with the forced cheerfulness of military allies.

Press conferences were invented by sadists, Hal decided. The sort of people who liked bearbaiting. And today he was in the pit.

He took his seat behind a table at one end of the hotel conference room and faced the congregating journalists. Many smiled in his direction—though was it his imagination or were their smiles rather cool? Several came up and shook his hand with what seemed excessive politeness. Some just eyed him, like piranha.

He remembered with nostalgia the journalists he had met on his American lecture tour, and their energy, toughness, and openness. By comparison the Norwegian press was conservative and cautious, with a decidedly puritanical streak. Hal never quite knew what to expect from them, except that they seemed to make up their minds in advance.

Hal glanced down the room to the door where Ragna was crossing off the journalists' names on a list. She looked up and caught his eye and grinned, a cheerful sort of don't-you-worry grin. He smiled faintly back.

When everyone had arrived, the president of the Geographical Society rose and made an overlong and rather pompous introduction.

Then Hal was on his feet, outlining his plans for the expedition. He was aware of starting uncertainly, his voice sounding strangely flat and dead in his ears, but after a minute or two he got into his stride and when he sat down again twenty minutes later he felt confident he'd covered everything rather well.

The president invited questions.

A hand was raised and someone asked about the difficulties of high-altitude climbing. Hal described the training schedule planned for the run-up to the expedition, and how it would include oxygen-assisted and high-altitude ascents. Someone else asked about the food, another about team selection.

Then a woman Hal didn't recognize raised her hand and, after giving her name and newspaper, said: "Your previous experience is mainly in Arctic survival. Do you think you have sufficient experience for Everest?"

Hal resisted the temptation to give her a short sharp answer, and said reasonably: "I'm first and foremost a climber—"

"But you've never climbed at high altitude?"

This lady was definitely hostile. Hal felt his temper rising. "It's difficult to get to the Himalayas every day!" He let his anger subside a little. "I agree that I'm best known for my Arctic survival work, but climbing's my first skill. Those who understand mountaineering would consider Everest a natural progression for someone like myself."

The woman was silent. Another hand was raised. A man this time. "What is your motive for undertaking this expedition?"

"I explained. The fact that this ridge hasn't been climbed before. And it's a great challenge."

"But you've already navigated the Northwest Passage and tried for the Pole. Most people would find that more than sufficient. By adding Everest, your career begins to look like a quest for personal glory."

The anger swept over Hal in a red-hot wave. He'd never tried to hide his motives, yet here he was having to defend them. Only in your own country could you be made to feel guilty for your ambitions. He answered with elaborate care: "Some people work solely to survive, others for money. I, fortunately, work for personal satisfaction. I admit that that makes me a lucky man. As to the glory, well, I don't think such a remark deserves an answer. I do what I do because it's my life. It's in my nature to try for harder and harder things. How people interpret that is their own business."

The questioner stood his ground. "But is this expedition really necessary? Everest has already been climbed. And in these days of economic stringency, when the Norwegian people are striving hard under difficult circumstances, can the expense be justified?"

Ragna thought: Come on, Hal!

He'd started off far too modestly. He really wasn't the best person to sell himself; someone else needed to do it for him—and not the president of the Geographical Society, who was a hundred and five if he was a day and couldn't sell an orange to an Eskimo.

Anger had improved his delivery. The actress in her had applauded the last few answers: They had contained just the right amount of punch and dramatic effect.

Now, inexplicably, he was faltering again, sounding tired, almost apologetic.

She had a sudden thought. Hurriedly, she scribbled a note:

Tell them about rival American and Japanese expeditions. Other countries think expense IS justified.

Before she had a chance to change her mind, she made her way up to the table and placed the message in front of him. He paused, read it, looked vaguely puzzled, then nodded slightly. "There are several other expeditions lined up to try for Everest," he announced. "And at least one—an American team—is going to attempt the West Ridge the year after us."

Ragna willed him to go on and make the logical point, that if the challenge was worth it to other countries, why not to Norway?

But Hal was silent. Groaning inwardly, Ragna scanned the journalists' faces. Already she could imagine the sort of cautious moralistic articles that would appear: We think Starheim is courageous, but is his expedition soundly based?

People were looking restless. The president pushed back his chair, preparing to close the meeting.

As he came to his feet, a voice came from the other end of the room. "If I may . . ."

Heads swiveled. Ragna craned her head and saw a man detach himself from a group near the door. He came forward, a tall blond figure, immaculately dressed, with an easy confident walk.

On reaching the table he grinned broadly at Hal before turning to face the room.

"Well! I think we have been very privileged today to learn about the new plans of Halvard Starheim. We belong to a nation with a glorious tradition. We produced the two greatest names in polar exploration—Nansen, the first man to cross Greenland and tackle the Arctic ice; and Amundsen, the first man to reach the South Pole and sail the Northwest Passage. These men created a tradition of which we are justly proud. Thanks to Halvard Starheim that tradition is not only being continued but enhanced."

Ragna stared. Whoever this man was, she loved him!

"It's very easy to find reasons *not* to undertake great challenges," the stranger continued. "It is also very easy for other people to criticize"—

Ragna took a triumphant look at the sniping journalist.

—"but it takes a very special sort of man to set off into the unknown not just once but several times, to succeed in nearly every instance, and without the loss of a single man—and then be ready to undertake something even more challenging. Norway may be famous for polar exploration, but there is absolutely no reason why it shouldn't be famous for mountaineering too."

Hal was looking studiously at the table, a frown on his forehead, his lips clamped tightly together. But Ragna could see that he was pleased.

The speaker hadn't finished either. "We are a nation of individualists, proud of our self-sufficiency and independence, but also proud of our generosity to each other in times of hardship and need. Hal Starheim cannot mount this expedition on his own. He needs the help of the Norwegian people and, I'm sure you'll agree, he deserves it."

People were relaxing. The atmosphere had shifted. Even Hal seemed to have sensed it, and a ghost of a smile hovered on his lips.

The speaker glanced at Hal again. He had a fine, handsome face with vivid blue eyes. There was something very attractive in his smile, a sort of mischievous complicity.

"In 1954," he was saying, "I spent two weeks with Hal Starheim and his crew in Arctic Canada during their two-year journey through the Northwest Passage."

With surprise Ragna realized that this man must also know Jan.

"I went expecting to find a battered boat with an even more battered crew, but both the men and the boat looked ready to do the whole trip all over again. Spending that amount of time with someone in exceptionally tough conditions, you get a pretty good idea of what he's really like. Well, I can tell you that Hal Starheim is everything he seems to be. An inspiration to his men. And to us all." He paused for effect. "Join me now in wishing him every good fortune in his new venture."

Some got straight to their feet; others followed. The stranger approached Hal and, with elaborate formality, shook his hand and said loudly, "Good luck!" Then, unseen by everyone in the body of the room, he gave Hal a distinct wink. Ragna thought: What a character!

There was a spontaneous movement toward Hal, and one

by one people shook his hand. The room filled with the babble of easy conversation.

Ragna sagged with relief then shot to her feet as she remembered that she should be at the door handing out information to the departing journalists.

Later Ragna found Hal having a drink at the bar with the tall blond man.

Hal took her arm. "Ragna, my expedition secretary—Rolf Berg, from the *Dagens Post*. An old friend."

"So I gathered!" Ragna laughed.

They shook hands. His smile was just as attractive at close quarters, although she had the feeling he was well aware of the fact. He had very blue eyes, and a wide mouth, but it was his hair that one noticed. It was thick and unusually golden, and he wore it longer than was fashionable, to the collar.

A veritable Viking god, Ragna decided with a jaundiced eye. She had a long-standing suspicion of good-looking men.

"I'm delighted to see that Hal has a woman in the team," Rolf Berg was saying. "There are apt to be too many men on these things."

"I couldn't agree more," Ragna replied lightly. "But then he would have been mad not to have me. I was by far the best person for the job, you see."

Hal laughed: "Ragna's not one to be modest."

Berg looked amused.

"Thanks for what you did today," Ragna said more seriously. "I thought for a moment Hal was going to be eaten alive!"

Hal sighed audibly.

Berg gave a small dismissive shrug. "I was just saying that people get worried about success. They're nervous in case someone they admire turns out to be a fraud. They protect themselves by asking stupid questions. But wait and see," he said directly to Hal. "They'll end up by saying they thought it was a great idea all along." Berg flicked Ragna a sidelong glance. "Isn't that right?"

He had a way of making you feel you'd known him for years. Ragna liked that. "Of course!"

Hal said gravely: "I hope you're right."

"I am," Berg said. "Just like you're always right about the weather."

It was obviously an old joke, for they began to talk about the Northwest Passage and frosted eyebrows in minus fifty and falling fast. Masculine-reminiscence time; not Ragna's favorite sort of conversation. But Berg was an accomplished and amusing raconteur and, despite the irritation of knowing she might as well not be there, she found herself smiling at some of his more elaborate stories.

Someone came up to talk to Hal and the conversation ended. Berg looked disappointed.

Ragna asked him: "Are you going to cover this expedition too, Rolf Berg?"

He shook his head. "Can't stand heights."

"And you're going to let a little thing like that stop you?"

He bit his lip in mock shame. "Ah, I have a great weakness, you see. I'm a coward."

Ragna decided that, despite his good looks, Berg might be all right after all. She'd always had a soft spot for people who didn't take themselves too seriously.

"What about *you*?" Berg asked. "Are you going to Nepal?"

"Ah, no! One climber in the family's enough."

He looked puzzled.

"Jan, my husband, will be going."

"Your husband?"

Good Lord, thought Ragna, did he think I wasn't married?

"Yes," she replied. "Jan Johansen."

"Aah," he said very slowly. "I see."

"But there's nothing to see," Ragna said a little defensively. "I'm here in my own right."

"Of course." But he didn't look as convinced as Ragna would have liked. He drained his drink as if preparing to leave, then hesitated. "Didn't I hear your name yesterday? Weren't you lobbying the justice ministry on some Lapp issue?"

"Oh!" Ragna flicked an anxious glance in Hal's direction to see if he'd heard, but to her relief he was still talking. She looked back to Berg to find him regarding her curiously. Trying to laugh it off, she said: "I'm surprised you heard that. No one was meant to realize it was me, you see. I used my unmarried name."

At that moment Hal finished his conversation and turned back, looking from Ragna to Berg, waiting for them to continue their talk. If Berg noticed the warning signals emanating from Ragna's eyes he chose to ignore them.

"Well, even if people weren't meant to realize," he said, "they knew it was you, all right. As I heard it, you were objecting to the location of a military training area. Or have I got it wrong . . . ?"

He knew perfectly well he'd got it right. There was a stony silence. Ragna could feel Hal's eyes boring into her.

"Possibly," she said lamely. "But it's not something I discuss when I'm working."

Hal put his beer down on the bar. His mouth was set in a thin hard line. Ragna could feel the icy chill of his displeasure.

He said to Berg: "I'll see you, Rolf."

"We'll have that meal."

"Sunday."

"Sunday."

Without a word to Ragna, Hal turned on his heel and was gone. Berg raised an eyebrow.

Ragna took a deep breath and said coldly: "He wasn't meant to know about my visit to the ministry. It was strictly forbidden, you see."

"Then why did you go?"

"I couldn't let them down."

"Who?"

"The Lapps."

"Why?"

"Why? Because they're being trampled over and it's scandalous!"

Berg's mouth twitched with amusement, as if he found her answer touchingly naïve.

Ragna bristled. "Someone's got to stand up for them."

"But why you? Can't the Lapps represent themselves?"

"No! *Yes* . . . I mean . . ." She drew a breath and started again. "Jan's part Lapp. So I have a direct involvement."

"Ah. I'd forgotten. Of course." But the amusement was still there in his eyes. He said: "I'm sorry not to see Jan. Is he away?"

"Yes. On field trials."

Berg gave an elegant shiver, as if feeling the cold. "In this weather?"

"Oh, they'll be holed up in a tent somewhere, just like a pair of mountain Lapps. Living off dried reindeer and foul compo rations, happy as anything."

Berg looked at her strangely. "They're up north, are they?"

"Somewhere on the plateau, yes."

A slight pause. "Have they been there long?" His voice was very smooth.

It suddenly occurred to her that she shouldn't be talking about this. Yet the question was harmless. "Since early this week. Sunday."

Berg nodded, but his expression was curiously distant and thoughtful, as if his mind were already on other things.

The next moment he was saying a polite but brisk good-bye.

As he walked away Ragna made her judgment on Rolf Berg: charming, amusing—but tricky. Then, because she had met plenty of men like him before, she hardly gave him a second thought.

6

The position was a good one. They had made camp on sloping ground on the western side of the frozen lake. From here the two men could see across the snow-covered ice to the gully between the hills on the opposite side, and down to the southern end of the lake, which narrowed like the neck of a bottle. Anyone approaching from the southeast would use one of these routes.

But no one had come, not yet.

They had arrived two days before and dug themselves a snow hole in the lee of a rocky outcrop some way above the lake. Below, sparse scrub stretched down to desultory clumps of pine and birch, which obscured the immediate foreshore.

Now, as the short day began, Jan kept watch while Mattis slept. Misty cloud hung low over the valley, casting a flat shadowless light over the landscape. The temperature had risen slightly—it was no more than thirty below—and the wind had dropped away, leaving the air deathly still. In the silence the valley seemed completely devoid of life. Yet every now and then Jan swung his binoculars onto the slopes beneath to look for signs of wildlife. After an hour his patience was rewarded by the sight of an Arctic fox weaving stealthily through the scrub hunting for vole and shrew in their burrows beneath the snow.

Later Mattis awoke and, after lighting the paraffin stove, filled a pan with snow. While waiting for the water to heat, the two men sat in silence, looking out over the lake.

It was Mattis who gripped Jan's arm and pointed. Jan

squinted across the valley, then put the binoculars hastily to his eyes.

They were a long way off, farther up the lake on the opposite side, among the trees. Their form and gait were unmistakable.

Wolf.

Five of them, trotting fast, heads thrust forward—hunting, moving with purpose, as if following a strong scent or a well-trodden trail.

The two men watched closely, for wolves were a rare sight nowadays. Mattis was filled with regret, for if things had been different he might have used his rifle and there would have been two fewer wolves on the far shore, maybe even three. To the Lapp the wolf, the tireless stalker and killer of reindeer, could never be too rare.

But to Jan's eye the rarity of the animal gave it a certain beauty, and he felt no desire to kill. Though he remembered the winter of 1942, the coldest in living memory, when the wolves had come down from the *vidde* into some of the valleys in search of food, raiding farms and terrifying people. Then, despite the German ban on weapons, his father had taken his rifle from its hiding place and gone out to hunt them down.

People said that nothing like it had ever happened before, but Jan's Lapp grandmother had shaken her head and said there'd been other wolf winters far, far worse.

The wolves were almost level with them now, just half a mile away on the opposite shore. Suddenly the leader raised his nose to the air and the pack came to an abrupt halt.

Jan glanced questioningly at Mattis. "Us?"

"Not us," said the Lapp. "Too far away and no wind."

The animals remained motionless for several seconds then moved off again, though more slowly and with greater caution, their bodies closer to the ground, taking only a few steps at a time before stopping to sniff the air once more.

They had definitely scented something. Jan scanned the area immediately ahead of them, but could see nothing in the tangle of snow-heavy birch and willow.

"There!" Mattis's voice hissed at his shoulder.

Jan followed the Lapp's gaze to the southern end of the lake.

Then he saw it.

A gray speck against the stark whiteness: the distant figure of a man.

Jan jumped to his feet and, grabbing his rifle, put it to his shoulder and adjusted his sights. He hadn't much hope of hitting the pack leader at this range, but the sound of the shot might be enough to deter it from starting an attack.

The wolves were motionless: he held his fire.

The pack leader turned away, then twisted back again, nose to the scent, as if he couldn't make up his mind. This was repeated several times like a ritualistic dance. Keeping the leader firmly in his sights Jan steadied his finger against the trigger.

The leader sniffed the air once more, then turned for the last time and, with the pack on his heels, loped quickly away in the direction it had come from.

Slinging their rifles over their shoulders, the two men hastily packed away the cooking gear and placed it in the snow hole with the stores and bedding, sealing the entrance with snow.

Then, with a last look at the vanishing wolves, they skied down through the trees toward the man on the lake.

The three skiers converged across the snow-covered lid of the lake, the two at a fast gliding stride, the third at a slow plod. The stranger stopped dead in his tracks, apparently seeing the others for the first time.

Jan reached him first. Beneath the hood of a dirty white parka was a man of about thirty with a haggard face and eyes half closed with exhaustion. Offering the man water, Jan asked the question he had been told to ask.

He said in Norwegian: "Don't I know you? Aren't you Tor?"

The man was meant to answer: "No, that's my brother. I'm Alvar."

But the man said nothing, and there was silence except for the low rasping of his breath.

Jan repeated the question in Lapp and then in Finnish. The man said nothing but dropped his head and leaned heavily on his ski pole. Jan exchanged glances with Mattis and said: "Let's take him to the camp."

As they went to take the man's elbows he slowly buckled at the knees and collapsed into the snow.

Without discussion, Jan and Mattis started to revive him, one removing his skis while the other patted his cheeks. After a while the man opened his eyes and for the first time seemed to focus on his surroundings.

He spoke what was clearly a question. Jan frowned in alarm. He did not understand what had been said, but he certainly recognized the language: Russian.

There was a cold silence.

The man spoke again, this time in the only language that he correctly guessed they might have in common: English. "Where am I?"

"Finland."

A small flicker of what looked like relief passed over his face and he closed his eyes again. Then he stared at Jan and murmured: "Who are you?"

Jan paused before answering: "We're hunters, from near Karasjok."

"Please—you come to find my friend?"

Jan did not reply. This wasn't going according to plan at all. There was meant to be only one man, a man who spoke some Norwegian—enough to answer the set question at least. Now, suddenly, there was this other man, the wrong man: a Russian who spoke no Norwegian at all.

Finally Jan said, "What friend?"

With an effort the stranger sat up. "He comes to find you. I come with him. I have maps, skis . . . I want to come to West too. My friend said you meet us here. My friend try very much. But he is not good. The cold . . . too hard for us. We stop. Now he cannot come."

"What do you mean?"

"He is not good. He is sick."

Jan said roughly: "But what's wrong with him?"

"Very tired. *Very* tired. And bad foot. He hurt the foot."

Jan sighed. "But where is he? How far away is he? How far away?"

The man shrugged. "Two miles. Maybe more. Not so far."

Jan questioned the man for a long time, but there was nothing more to learn. He got angrily to his feet and stared blindly into the distance, furious with the stranger, furious with himself for not knowing what to do. The briefing had covered the possibility of a no-show, but it had covered nothing like this, nothing.

The decision was impossible, yet he had to make it.

Finally he decided: he and Mattis would accompany this man to the border. Then—then he would think again.

Hal slid a finger inside his collar and tugged at it. He never felt at ease in a suit and tie, and his new shoes were compressing his toes like pincers.

The austere office of the minister of cultural and scientific affairs was heated to the pitch of a sauna, and Hal's hands were slippery against the chair arms. The chair, a gleaming example of modern Scandinavian design made of bent steel tubes and shiny black leather, creaked loudly whenever he shifted in his seat.

Hal exchanged glances with Ragna, who gave him a small conspiratorial wink.

The minister, a severe bony-faced man in his sixties, was reading the proposal slowly, his elbows on the polished pine desk, his fingertips touching to form a perfect arch under his chin.

A fly walked sleepily up the treble-glazed window. Hal thought: The minister wouldn't approve of that.

Looking up, the minister's gaze went from Hal to Ragna, and he smiled. It was impossible to tell if this was a good sign. "I'm afraid cash is definitely out of the question," he said with an apologetic shake of the head. "It would be impossible to justify it to the taxpayer. But I'm sure something can be arranged on the matter of the equipment and stores. Although we *would* need to be certain that sufficient money had been raised to get the expedition off the ground."

"And then you'd be able to make an announcement?" Hal pressed.

"I would think that there's a reasonable possibility of that—once I have approval, of course."

Hal wondered if that meant a definite-yes or a maybe-yes.

Ragna asked ingenuously: "Does that mean yes?"

The minister blinked rapidly. "I would hope so."

Hal tried another tack. "When might this approval come through?"

"In two weeks—roughly."

Hal tried to hide his disappointment. Two more weeks of uncertainty; two weeks of lost momentum. "I see," he said tightly.

He was aware of Ragna shooting him a quick glance. She said sweetly to the minister: "Obviously our sponsors will be most encouraged by a generous government offer. The press will give it a lot of coverage—"

A flicker of alarm passed over the minister's face and he cut in hastily: "But it would be extremely premature to announce anything."

"Of course," agreed Ragna reasonably. "We wouldn't dream of it. However"—she sighed regretfully—"it will be difficult to prevent speculation."

"Oh? What speculation?"

"Well, everyone's expecting an announcement, obviously."

Clearly this was news to the minister. Hal tried not to look as though it were news to him too.

"I wasn't aware of this," said the minister.

"Oh? Weren't you?" asked Ragna with obvious surprise. "Well, only this morning the *Aftenpost*—and, indeed, the *Dagens Post*—were asking me how large a contribution the government would be making. They seemed to be expecting a substantial cash grant." She frowned suddenly, as if the consequences of this had only just occurred to her. "Rather unfortunate." A slight pause, then she added brightly: "Of course, once they hear about your offer I'm sure they'll realize it's most generous . . . as these things go." She repeated vaguely: "Once they hear."

Hal suddenly had to examine the view outside the window very seriously indeed.

The minister stared at Ragna with narrowed eyes as if grasping some elusive and not entirely pleasant interpretation of what she had just said. "Well," he murmured eventually, "let's hope they don't get the wrong idea."

Ragna nodded vehemently. "Quite."

The minister stood up and came around the desk with elaborate care, as if negotiating treacherous ground. He extended a hand to Hal. "I can say, in all sincerity, that it has been a great honor." To Ragna he added: "And—er—most illuminating."

Ragna gave him the benefit of her loveliest smile. "I knew you'd understand how important this was to us, Minister. And I assure you that I'll do my best with the newspapers."

She's overdone it this time, Hal thought, closing his eyes for a moment. Steeling himself, he risked a quick look at the minister.

A weak smile hovered uncertainly on the man's face. Then, held by Ragna's innocent and unblinking stare, he cocked his head to one side and conceded a wry grin. "Have you ever been in politics, Mrs. Johansen?"

My God, Hal thought, she's gotten away with it!

Hal waited until they were in the taxi before murmuring: "Ragna—sometimes."

"Sometimes what?"

"Was there a rumor?"

"No," said Ragna blithely, "not exactly. But he didn't know that, did he? So he'll make sure the papers get wind of the right story and appreciate which generous and farsighted minister arranged it. That way he'll come out of it smelling of roses. And by Monday morning everyone will know we're getting government support."

"Ragna—it was blackmail!"

"Nonsense. It was politics, like he said."

Hal shook his head. "I don't know . . . I don't know."

She patted his shoulder. "Hal, believe me, it's all for the best. We have to strike while the iron's hot."

The coverage had been astonishingly good, Hal had to admit. The expedition had made the front page of every paper and, apart from the odd cautionary remark, the response had been entirely favorable. Yet he didn't want a reputation for deviousness.

Sensing his doubt, Ragna said firmly: "Hal, listen, when I was an actress you either sat back and let your talents go unnoticed, or you kept yourself in the public eye and got lots of work. What I'm saying is that you have to *push* a little. We're not going to get good marks for being patient." She patted his arm. "Look at the money we've been promised already. Government support will put the seal on everything."

Hal couldn't deny Ragna's success so far. She had tied down an amazing number of sponsors in an incredibly short time. In fact, a few more promises and the expedition would be guaranteed. *Guaranteed.* The idea was so new for Hal that he could hardly adjust to it.

The taxi was approaching the apartment where Ragna was staying. "All right," he said finally. "But Ragna, do try not to ruffle people's feathers. We don't want to make enemies unnecessarily."

"Enemies! I thought the minister rather liked me!"

He tried to give her a reproving look, and failed.

She looked sorry and repentant and quite lovely all at the same time. "Don't think too badly of me," she said suddenly. "I always mean well."

"Mmm. Like with your Lapps." He hadn't quite forgiven her for going to the justice ministry behind his back.

"I said I was sorry. But I just couldn't let them down."

It was impossible to be cross with her. "I know," he said, and, on a sudden impulse, leaned over and gave her a peck on the cheek.

The taxi ground to a halt. He suddenly thought how nice it would be to take her to dinner. "Are you—"

She looked at her watch and exclaimed: "Good Lord! Is that the time?" She jumped out of the cab. Popping her head back inside, she declared: "I need extra time to get ready, you see!"

"Oh?"

She smiled impishly. "Got to look extra good. I'm going out with an old flame and I want him to be sick at what he's been missing all this time."

Hal was still smiling when the taxi drew up outside his hotel.

The men halted. They had come about two miles from the lake. The border lay just ahead, though it was impossible to be absolutely certain as to its position. There were no posts or fences; the landscape looked like any other stretch of snow-covered taiga. The only certainty was that ski troops regularly patrolled its far side and that beyond lay many, many miles of forbidden territory where interlopers—Russian, Lapp, or otherwise—risked instant arrest or worse.

Jan wrestled with indecision. The choice was impossible. Was it a trap? Was this man genuine?

Impossible. But then if he was going to be wrong whatever he did, he might as well try to save the man he had come to meet.

Torn with doubt yet keen to get the matter over and done with, he waved the others forward and the decision was made.

They were crossing the border.

The two Norwegians were uncomfortably aware that each stride was a step away from safety; a step, furthermore, that would have to be retraced. They were also acutely aware of the stillness and the growing clarity of the light and how conspicuous they must be, and how even the sleepiest patrol would be able to track them with ease.

Jan had wanted to leave Mattis at the lake, but according to their strange companion the sick man was too weak to ski, so Mattis had come after all, armed with a makeshift litter made of birchwood and padded with sleeping bags.

The Russian led the way, following his outward tracks, which were etched deeply into the snow.

Easy to follow.

For anyone.

Jan knew they must be approaching the Pasvik River, an area that would be heavily patrolled. Nervously he called a halt and questioned the Russian again. The man was adamant: his companion was very close now.

They continued through sparse woodland. With a cold sense of foreboding Jan noticed that the Russian's tiredness seemed to have mysteriously vanished and that his outward tracks were very straight for those of an exhausted man.

New doubts gnawed at his stomach. He thought of questioning the man again, but the Russian turned excitedly, indicating a point just ahead.

Motioning the others to halt, Jan went cautiously forward. As he approached the brow of a hillock he crouched low on his skis and peered over.

Below him was a slight hollow in which grew dwarf willow and low scrub. Under a gnarled bent willow something protruded from the snow. A sort of bundle. Covered in what looked like a dirty white anorak.

A man?

To one side of the bundle was a rucksack and a pair of skis, and to the other an area of well-trampled snow where people had walked in boots. He thought he could see a set of tracks leading into the hollow from the east in addition to the tracks coming out to the west. But that proved nothing: it was impossible to tell how many pairs of skis had used them.

He made a half-circle around the hollow, his ears straining, his eyes scanning every inch of terrain. Toward the river the trees were taller and denser: Anything could be hidden there.

Taking a last look around, he beckoned to the others and skied down into the hollow.

He went straight to the half-buried shape in the snow.

It was a man all right.

Removing his skis Jan knelt beside him and pulled the hood back from his face.

He stared. Realization came instantly. There could be no doubt: the eyes were only partially closed, the skin was marble-gray and strangely smooth, as if the man had never had a worry in his life. But he went through the motions all the same, feeling the pulse at the neck and wrist, lifting the eyelids to examine the pupils.

Jan put his fingers against the man's cheek. The skin yielded, not yet frozen by the air temperature, which was at least minus twenty. He hadn't been dead long then, probably less than half an hour.

A suspicion began to form in Jan's mind. He rolled the body on its back. Then he saw that he was right: the anorak and the snow beneath were stained brilliant pink; there was a large wound in his chest.

He examined the man's clothing and found the neat entry mark of a high-velocity bullet in his back.

Jan spun around and grabbed the Russian by the collar. "What happened! *What happened?*"

The Russian stared at the figure in the snow and his face crumpled in despair.

Jan shook him violently. *"What happened?"*

"At the river. They shoot at us. We escape in the night. We come back on our track and we walk close to the river. We travel all night. Then he cannot travel no more. . . ." He bowed his head.

"Why didn't you say?"

"I think you will not come. . . ."

Jan closed his eyes in exasperation.

Suddenly he became aware of the silence again. It seemed alive, as if some mysterious movement were taking place within it.

Gesturing to Mattis, he began to search the body.

They went hastily through the rucksack, then the anorak, shirt, and trousers. Because they knew only that the man was carrying something important but not what it was, they pocketed everything they could find: a map, a knife, a pistol, a bar of chocolate, a wallet, a pair of binoculars. They left the clothing with the remaining food.

Jan glanced at the dead man's face and paused. A distant memory stirred, so faint, so indistinct, that he shrugged it off. And *yet* . . .

He stared down at the empty gray features and tried to picture the face as it must have been . . .

The memory fluttered again, faint yet persistent. He tried to place it but failed. Yet there was no doubt: the features were vaguely familiar. Or maybe they reminded him of someone else?

There was a loud hiss. He spun around.

It was the Russian, standing on the hillock, gesticulating in the direction of the unseen river, a look of panic on his face.

Jan and Mattis exchanged glances. Hastily they refastened their skis and grabbed their poles. Mattis tapped Jan's arm. The Russian was leaving fast in the direction of the border, ducking and twisting away, poling off with rapid jerky arm movements, like a rabbit on the run.

Jan and Mattis did not follow him. Instinctively they made a fresh trail well to the north of their old track. They purposely chose difficult ground, through frozen marshland covered with myriad hummocks and waist-high scrub. They used other tricks, too, skirting even the smallest hills to avoid putting their profiles against the sky, keeping close to denser cover where it existed, forcing themselves to their limits, pushing forward in long thrusting strides, faster than their pursuers could ever achieve.

And they listened.

The endless landscape was shrouded in silence, a silence broken only by the steady swish of their skis and the sucking and panting of their breath.

Minutes passed. Jan made calculations. They must be within a mile of the border.

Softly now, softly.

The scrub was thinning. Ahead it petered out altogether and gave way to the openness of a frozen lake.

Jan conjured up the area map from his memory. The border—it must be on the far side of this lake.

Both men gave a sudden start and paused like animals scenting the wind.

A single sharp *crack!* floated on the air, muffled by distance and snow. Then again and again. *Crack! Crack!*

They listened for the last echoes, trying to gauge distance and direction.

Then they poled forward again, but swinging to the left, to skirt the terrible nakedness of the lake.

The silence pressed in, heavy and vibrant.

The horizon beckoned, the landscape opened out, wide and bare and naked around them.

They went on. They had no choice.

The border. So close, so close.

Even as Jan thought it, he froze in his stride and jerked his head up, his senses reaching out. He felt a moment of animal fear. His hand went to his rifle.

A movement. Away, away to the right.

The two men crouched and watched.

Suddenly they saw them.

A group of men, as yet tiny gray dots but approaching fast.

Jan and Mattis raced off again, instinctively arcing farther to the left to diverge even more from the patrol, creating distance.

But distance had little meaning, for there was no cover.

There was a muffled shout, a distant call. The two men's hearts lurched, but they did not turn.

A sudden *crack!* very loud, the bullet very close; then the echoing *thump!* of the detonation.

The two men sped on, their lungs rasping with pain.

More shots: *crack! crack! thump! thump!*

They were halfway around the lake. Ahead was a dip in the fold of the hills: freedom. So near.

Another volley of shots. But though Jan braced himself, his skin alive with fear, nothing came near. It occurred to him that the shots might be intended to miss . . .

More calls echoing feebly across the empty air.

The two men sped on. So *near*.

Another shout.

A new leap of fear. The sound came from the *left*.

Jan couldn't see them yet. Where were they?

He pressed on, the slow-burning terror pushing his aching limbs forward, forward.

There were no more shouts. For some moments there were no more shots either. Just the pounding of their hearts in their ears.

Then—*thud!*

A cry split the air. A moment of disbelief. The voice was his own, shrill and unrecognizable. The breath was knocked out of him. A terrible pain pierced his lungs.

He was not aware of falling, only of the burning pain and breathlessness, and a lightness in the head, like he was floating.

The snow pressed into his face. His mouth was liquid. A pink stain spread slowly across the whiteness. He coughed and cleared his mouth.

A part of his brain registered the *crack! crack!* of continuous shooting.

A cloudiness was creeping up on him. Fighting it back, he coughed and swallowed and tried to clear the choking in his throat. With a vast effort he called Mattis's name. His voice was infuriatingly faint.

There was no response. Silence. Even the shooting had stopped. He tried to turn his head. It was heavy, heavy. He twisted his body a little so that he could see past his feet.

He stared, blinked, refocused, and stared again.

For the first time he was overwhelmed by despair.

Mattis. He lay crumpled in the snow, his legs twisted under him, a ski protruding oddly into the air.

Struggling for breath Jan called again. Mattis remained infinitely still.

The cloud closed in again. The liquid rose inexorably in his throat; he fought for breath. He heard a gurgling sound. He knew he was drowning. His head was filled with a hot sweet roar.

One further moment of dim awareness . . . Voices murmuring, a sensation of hands turning him.

He made a last effort to open his eyes but saw nothing but shadows and the approach of a greater darkness.

7

Hal smiled. "You're not trying to get me drunk by any chance?"

"Drunk?" Berg looked at him in mock astonishment. "Hal, you're one of my oldest friends."

"So—no mercy for me."

They both laughed. They had dined at the Theatre Café. The meal had been good—no, thought Hal, excellent—with glorious food and a bottle of incredibly expensive French wine.

Now he accepted the glass of clear liquor that Rolf offered him and sat back on the sofa, feeling content.

The apartment was typically Rolf: very smart. Even the clutter of the work area looked well arranged and stylish. Most of the furniture was modern; Hal seemed to remember Rolf saying it was designed by Rastad and Rilling. Whatever, it was very striking. Around the living room were various pieces of exotica, presumably collected during Rolf's travels: a large Persian rug, an Eastern-style rattan chair, a Venetian mirror, jade ornaments, a Chinese vase filled with dried grasses. The heavy glass in Hal's hand was of finest Waterford crystal and the drink cupboard was well stocked with highly taxed spirits. A Bang and Olufsen hi-fi played Mozart in deep resonant tones.

Rolf lived well; Hal was pleased for him. He said with a smile: "I'm surprised you left such a pleasant life to come and see us in the Northwest Passage."

Rolf sat down in the opposite chair. "Anything for a good story."

"And it was, the way you wrote it."

He acknowledged the compliment with a nod, adding drily: "It was, of course, very sensible of you to let me write it."

Hal smiled. It was typical of Rolf to make an ambiguously arrogant remark.

"But you're sticking to political stuff nowadays?" Hal asked.

Rolf shrugged. "I seem to stir up the establishment satisfactorily. Better than anyone else anyway. The *Dagens Post* was a bit nervous to begin with—they'd hardly publish anything. But in the last year or so they've gotten much more daring. By their standards, of course."

"Where d'you get all your stories?"

Rolf threw back his head and laughed. "Hal! Only someone outside the business could ask a question like that! Journalists don't reveal their sources except on pain of death."

Hal grinned. "What a loyal lot you are."

"Actually the editor sometimes asks me the same question," Rolf said more seriously. "He says he hopes I'm not getting anything from 'irregular' sources. What he means by that I'm not certain. But I suspect he thinks that tip-offs from government officials and civil servants are irregular. In which case he's a fool. Where else would I get my information from, eh?" His eyes glittered with scornful amusement.

"Perhaps he worries about small details like breaking the law."

Rolf rolled his eyes. "Oh! Probably. We're so damned law-abiding that sometimes I think we're more self-righteously puritanical than even the Germans."

Hal hesitated, then ventured: "Some people—well, people in my line of work anyway—feel the *Dagens Post* does go a bit far. That it's unnecessarily antagonistic to the military. And blatantly antidefense."

Rolf corrected him. "No, no—anti-*NATO*. Which is quite different." He sat forward in his seat. "Surely you can see it would be disastrous to have nuclear weapons on Norwegian soil, Hal. If there was another war the Soviet Union would crush us like—like—glass"—he clenched his hand into a tight fist—"and they wouldn't wait for us to explain how we'd never actually meant to use the weapons."

"But surely it's right to be part of NATO."

"Why? *Why?* Far from saving us, it would merely make us a target. No, I think we should be neutral."

"We'd be a target anyway, Rolf. Our geography makes sure of that."

He shook his head. "War's all about submarines and long-range missiles nowadays. They won't bother with us unless we've let ourselves be turned into an American base."

"You're sounding anti-American, Rolf."

"Perhaps I am." His tone was light, but Hal knew he wasn't joking.

"I thought you enjoyed your time in America." Rolf had been there for a couple of years immediately after the war.

"I did. But that doesn't mean I want Norway to be America's pawn."

Time to talk about something else. This was a subject on which they'd never agree and Hal didn't want to spoil the evening. "D'you ever see any friends from your American days?"

"No."

There were certain subjects on which Rolf couldn't be drawn. His time in America was one. Their first meeting was another. They'd known each other properly for—how long? Six years. Since the Northwest Passage, when they'd been amazed to realize that they'd met once and so dramatically before. In all that time Rolf had given Hal only the scantest outline of those events. Rolf was a master at deflecting questions he didn't want to answer.

Hal knew that Rolf's wartime experiences had been very painful. He didn't want to reopen old wounds. And yet they were old friends. Wasn't friendship all about openness and trust?

The aquavit pushed any remaining doubts aside and Hal found himself saying: "You still owe me a pair of skis, you know. Yours were quite useless. We ended up using them for firewood."

A faint but unmistakable flicker of displeasure passed over Rolf's face. Getting up, he went to the sideboard to top up his drink. "Skis," he murmured, clunking bottles around. "I still haven't got a decent pair. But listen"—he turned and flashed a smile—"why don't we go trekking one of these days, eh? I'd really enjoy that."

"Good idea." Hal thought: He's done it again. But he wasn't going to be so easily deflected this time. Doggedly, he returned to the subject. "You never really told me what happened, Rolf. After you got away. You told me what happened to your friend. But that was all."

Rolf paused for a moment, then, picking up his glass and a full bottle of vodka, returned to the sofa. He placed the bottle on the coffee table in front of him and eyed it thoughtfully. Finally he said, "There's really not a lot to tell."

"But I'd like to hear it."

He considered for a moment. "It's hard for me to talk about it." He spoke slowly, his voice low and pensive. Suddenly he gave a short self-deprecating laugh. "You see, I hate the thought of other people knowing how—dreadful it was."

"You know it would never go any further."

Rolf stared at him for some time, his eyes sharp and startlingly blue over the rim of his glass. Finally he seemed to make up his mind.

"Well, it's not much of a story," he said, settling back in his seat. "We stole a boat that night, as you know. Naughty, but we didn't want to get your friends into trouble. The only problem was, someone must have reported us." He raised his eyebrows. "Charming, eh? Anyway, before we knew what had happened a gunboat came scooting around looking for us. We hid behind an island, among rocks. Bloody frightening, I can tell you. The rocks, I mean. Much worse than the gunboat. Anyway, the boat fired into the darkness for a while—to make themselves feel better, I suppose—then went away."

"So they never spotted you?"

"No."

"What happened after that?"

Berg took another gulp of his drink. "Did I never tell you any of this?"

Hal shook his head.

He gave a short bitter laugh. "Well, it was hilarious. Hilariously awful, that is. We ran up against a German death-and-destruction squad, slaughtering livestock and burning everything in sight. For several days we couldn't get past them. Then, when they finally left, there was no food. Nothing. We camped in the remains of a village. It was empty. Not a soul left. Not a scrap of bread. We began to starve. And freeze. God, the cold . . . Then we were incredibly lucky. We went hunting and shot a reindeer up in the hills. We got very excited. We thought we'd go on finding reindeer. We set off across the plateau . . ."

He clenched his lips together and stared at his drink. "But that was disaster. . . . There were no reindeer. We couldn't find the Lapps. When the meat we had with us was finished, that was it. . . . The cold was terrible—I can't tell you." He gave a small mirthless laugh. "But of course you would know. Anyway, I could see my toes freezing one by one. I was convinced I'd lose the lot of them. Petter did. The lot. Then he got sick—I never knew what was wrong with him. I suppose he just froze up slowly. Anyway, he couldn't move. He sort of gave up."

There was a pause. The Mozart had finished. The silence stretched out.

Berg looked up suddenly, his eyes hard and distant. "Then he died."

Hal felt the pain of it and sucked in his breath. "I'm sorry." For something else to say, he murmured: "Petter. I'd forgotten his name."

"If Petter *was* his name."

"Oh. I thought you knew him well."

"By then. Not before. But we stuck to first names so that we'd never get our families into trouble. For all I know he might have lied about his first name."

There was a haunted look in Rolf's face. Hal said: "But you don't blame yourself, surely? For his death."

"One always blames oneself."

Hal thought: What a burden to carry all these years. "What about you?" he asked. "What happened after that?"

"Mmm? Oh, somehow or another I made it back to the coast, to Alta Fjord. I thought I'd find the Russians there. But of course they never got that far. Still, I found some sea Lapps, thank God, and they fed me on fish. I survived." He shrugged. "So."

"Well, at least you escaped the Germans."

Berg gave a vague nod. "I told you it wasn't much of a story." Shrugging the subject off, he sat up abruptly and reached for the bottle of vodka. "Come on," he said with forced cheerfulness, "you're not keeping up with me."

"But I wasn't drinking vodka!"

"You are now."

It was a drinker's challenge, and Hal didn't drink, at least not in the Scandinavian way—that is, to oblivion. But there was something in Rolf's face, a loneliness, that made Hal want to keep him company.

"Rolf, you're a bad influence on me," Hal said affectionately. Knocking back the last of his drink, he held out his glass.

Berg poured the vodka and sat back. Thank God that was over and done with. He'd done rather well, he thought: almost faultless, in fact. Hal hadn't even asked what happened next.

Best to get onto something else though, just to be on the safe side. "You should have brought Mrs. Johansen along tonight," he said. "She's quite a character. No chance of your project being ignored while she's around."

"Yes, she's good news, isn't she?" Hal grinned like a rather amiable puppy, and Berg realized the drink had taken effect.

"Odd that she married Jan."

"How do you mean?"

"I would have thought they had little in common."

Hal gave him a slightly pitying look as if he had missed something blindingly obvious. "But they complement each other perfectly. It's because they're so different that it's such a success."

"Ah, I see." Berg said no more; he was a cynic on these matters. "Got a girl in your life, Hal?"

Hal made a rueful face. "Too busy to get serious."

And too honorable, thought Berg. Hal was the sort who'd want love and commitment before getting seriously involved. Not that Hal hadn't played the field until quite recently—once he'd actually pinched a girl from Berg, though Berg knew he hadn't realized it at the time: an extremely beautiful Swede who was very choosy about her men and had been much keener on Hal than she'd ever been on Berg. Berg hadn't felt the slightest rancor; he wasn't the possessive sort.

"Katya liked you a lot," Berg remarked.

"Ah." Hal gave a long slow smile of reminiscence. "She *was* lovely. But what about you, Rolf? Anyone special?"

Berg gave a short conspiratorial laugh. "There's always someone special."

"Until the next one turns up?" The disapproval was gentle and affectionate.

"Yes, until the next," Rolf admitted with a shrug.

The telephone rang. It was after ten. Isabella maybe. But more probably the office. Apologizing with a wave of the hand, he went to his desk to answer it.

A firm male voice said: "Is Major Starheim there?"

Berg glanced at Hal in surprise. "Yes. One moment."

Hal made an is-it-really-for-me face as he crossed the room. "I didn't think anyone knew I was here."

Berg thought: Nor did I.

Hal took the phone from Berg's hand. "Hello . . . Yes . . . Thrane! How—"

Berg went back to his chair and picked up his glass.

"What?"

Berg sipped his drink and stared at one of his best lithographs.

"No . . . *No* . . . My *God*!"

It was a cry of horror. Berg swiveled in his seat. Hal had crumpled onto a chair, his head bent, a hand clamped over his eyes.

Berg got rapidly to his feet and walked over.

Hal was groaning, like an animal in pain. Only his mouth was visible below the hand, twisted back in a ghastly grimace. The hand that held the phone was white at the knuckles.

Berg thought: Somebody's died.

Finally, after a long while, Hal spoke again, his voice rough and unsteady. "Yes. I'll come . . . What? . . . Yes, I'm leaving now." Slowly he replaced the phone. His face was deathly white.

Berg put a hand on his shoulder. "Hal? *Hal?*"

He rose awkwardly to his feet. Berg had never seen such an expression of blank despair. Hal shook his head slowly from side to side, his mouth open and moving soundlessly. Finally he cried out, a bitter cry of rage and anguish.

"*Hal!* What is it!"

The reply was a long time coming.

"Jan . . . *Jan.* And Mattis."

Berg turned the possibilities over in his mind. An appalling accident? An avalanche? A car smash? Or . . .

He took Hal by the shoulders. "I'm so very sorry. What happened?"

Hal didn't reply, but staggered toward the hall. Rolf followed him and helped him on with his coat.

"What happened?" Berg repeated.

Hal shook his head again, as if he didn't trust himself to speak. He reached for the door. At the last moment he paused and seemed to hear Berg's question for the first time. "They're . . . they're dead. Shot. But why? *Why?*" He searched Berg's face for the miraculous answer he knew he would never find.

It took a moment for the words to sink in.

Then it was Berg's turn to feel a jolt of horror, and he had to twist quickly away so that Hal wouldn't see the shock in his face.

Berg paced off along the dark quay, hands thrust angrily in his coat pockets, and came to a sudden halt. Spinning on his heel, he stamped back to Alex and said through clenched teeth: "But how could they have been escaping?"

"I know little more than you, my friend—just what was contained in the official protest," Alex replied. "The men were on the Soviet side of the border, heading for Finland. One assumes the guards thought they were common criminals—defectors to the West." He spoke with the weary regret of someone who half expects men to do foolish things. In the distance a large brightly lit ferry maneuvered into its berth. Alex watched it doggedly, as if it were his purpose for standing on the quay.

The man's nervousness was almost palpable. Berg thought angrily: The sod wants to be rid of me. As if to confirm it, Alex kept glancing over his shoulder, apparently obsessed by something at the far end of the quay.

"What the hell're you looking at? You weren't followed, were you, for God's sake?"

"No. No."

Berg felt helpless, as if he were drowning in mud. He exclaimed: "For Christ's sake, Alex."

Alex glanced over his shoulder again. "I told you. I know nothing."

"You're lying!"

The Russian looked miserable. "My friend, what can I say? I merely do what I'm told. That's all I ever do."

Berg succumbed to impotent rage; he had a strong desire to squeeze the life out of that big fat throat. "That's it then, Alex! No more meetings. No more cozy chats." He could hardly speak. "One of them was my *friend,* you bastard!"

"Friend?" Alex repeated vaguely. He was staring openly toward the square. Suddenly he stiffened and, gripping Berg by the arm, said in a voice heavy with relief: "Look, *I* cannot tell you much, but . . ." His eyes flicked to the right and with a small apologetic wave he sidled away.

For a moment Berg didn't understand, then he saw someone walking briskly toward him, someone Alex nodded to as he passed, and he realized this man had been sent to talk to him.

The man approached.

The feeble light from a nearby warehouse fell on his face.

Berg's stomach gave a violent twist of recognition.

Niki.

The Russian stood before him. The two men stared at each other for a moment.

Niki chuckled gently. "Fifteen years. You look just the same."

But *he* didn't. He looked quite different: plumper, affluent. He was beautifully dressed in a well-tailored double-breasted coat with deep lapels, a pale cashmere scarf, and fur hat.

But the intelligent knowing eyes were the same.

Berg suppressed a fierce anger: how dare they do this to him? How *dare* they?

And yet—Niki must know the truth of what had happened: Why else would he be here? And there was one thing Berg had to know: a question that gnawed at him continuously, like a wolf snapping at his heels. Now, without preliminaries, he spat it out. "Why did they die?"

"Ah. The Norwegians?" Niki's voice was a sigh of regret. "An unfortunate accident."

Berg made an effort to keep his voice calm. "How? Why?"

Niki drew a deep breath. "Believe me, it would have been infinitely preferable to have gotten the two of them alive. Then there would have been a proper trial and—well, shall we say we would have come out of it looking a little better."

"So what the hell went wrong?"

He made a wide gesture. "Rolf, the guards had orders to stop anyone trying to cross the border. They saw two men. They warned them. The warnings were not heeded. They shot them. It was regrettable. But it happened."

Some of the tension went out of Berg's body. "But why were they on the wrong side of the border! *Why?*"

Niki shrugged. "We'll never know. The point is, they were. It was their own doing."

Berg examined his face. His expression was unreadable. Berg said resentfully: "How do I know it's the truth?"

"You don't." His voice was sweetly reasonable. "But did I ever lie to you in the past, Rolf?"

Berg gave a small mirthless laugh that turned into a violent shiver. "That I certainly don't know."

Niki touched his arm. "Come. Walk. It's too cold to stand around." They began to walk toward the far end of the deserted commercial quay. "You must think positively, Rolf," the Russian said calmly. "Despite the—er—unfortunate aspects of the affair, it is already a major incident. It will strike a hard blow. I'm pretty sure it will bring this government down, you know."

"What?"

"Our official protest will be on the front pages of newspapers all over the world. Finland will be up in arms at the violation of her territory. In due course the CIA's involvement will be revealed, and then the government will have to answer for it. The incident will grow and grow. There's going to be an enormous row, Rolf."

The news charged around Berg's head. He felt as if he'd unleashed a mad tiger which had run amok. Yet Niki was too damned confident by half. There was one rather important aspect of the affair he seemed to have forgotten. Berg pointed out caustically: "Shooting two men in the back isn't going to endear you to the world."

Niki gestured with upturned hands. "We can't be blamed for shooting two foreign agents caught on our territory in the act of breaking every imaginable law. No, it is the country responsible for training and sending the agents who must bear the consequences. And that is Norway—in partnership with the CIA, of course."

Berg stared out across the black water toward the wide expanse of Oslo Fjord. Navigation lights gleamed and winked in strange rhythms like glowworms in a darkened garden.

"They weren't agents."

"What? Well—agents, spies; these are words. The men were recruited and trained. . . . They were paid. They were dressed as Lapps, I know. But even if they were Lapps it doesn't change the fact that they were agents going to meet a spy."

Berg shook his head. Niki didn't know everything after all. He said, "You're wrong."

Niki gave him a long stare. "Oh?"

"They were amateurs. It was a one-off. One was a Lapp called Mattis Hetta and the other was an explorer called Jan Johansen. Did you know that?"

Niki shook his head.

"Johansen's well known here, Niki. He was a climber, an explorer. No one will believe he was an agent. They'll think he crossed the border accidentally—innocently—and got ruthlessly shot in the back." He added sarcastically: "I assume it *was* in the back?"

"They'll know the men were recruited, Rolf, they'll know."

"They won't believe it! Johansen was Starheim's right-hand man. They did the Northwest Passage together. No one's going to believe he was a trained agent!"

Niki thought for a moment. "Why do you think they chose him, Rolf? Because he wasn't in the military, that's why. They wanted the whole episode to look innocent." He wagged his finger. "That's almost worse than sending a trained agent, don't you think?"

A chill wind whistled across the water. Niki looked across the wide basin to the dark high walls of ancient Akershus Fortress, behind which were the headquarters of the Norwegian

Defense Command. He stared for a moment, as if contemplating the vast array of NATO secrets it contained, then, waiting for Berg to fall into step beside him, began to wander back the way they had come.

Niki made a small exclamation. "But of course—you must have known him, this Johansen?" He raised a hand to forestall Berg's reply. "I've read all your articles, Rolf. I've followed your progress."

Berg pursed his lips in annoyance. He had the feeling Niki knew more about his life than he did himself.

Niki paused under a lamp. "Look, I'm sorry Johansen died." He shrugged to emphasize his regret. "But blame those who sent him." A speculative look came into his eyes. "Perhaps it was Starheim himself, eh? What do you think? Am I right?"

Berg hesitated, realizing with a slight shock that he was probably right.

Niki nodded knowingly. "But of course it was. Of course."

A hot anger came over Berg. There seemed no limit to Niki's probings, as if he were intent on reasserting his power over Berg. "Don't drag more people into this, you bastard! Don't spin your bloody webs." Making the most of his indignation, he thrust his face close to the Russian's. "In fact, I've had enough. Enough. I don't believe your accident story. I don't believe that the whole thing was bloody accidental. No more, Niki. I've had it."

He sensed Niki's alarm and felt a moment of vicious satisfaction.

"Had it, Rolf? In what way?"

Berg's confidence rose. "In the way that there'll be no more little meetings with Alex, Niki. Oh, I'll go on writing my stories, don't worry. But I'll never trust you with something like this again." Berg thought: They'll soon learn not to pressure me again. He felt a weight begin to lift from his shoulders.

"I'm sorry you feel badly about this, Rolf. After all that we've done for each other."

Berg almost laughed. "Stuff you, Niki."

The Russian dropped his eyes and inclined his head. "Rolf, may I explain one thing to you. May I explain that our actions in this matter were directed by one overriding consideration— our need to protect a vital asset. Now, when I talk of this asset

I am not speaking of the paltry secrets this spy was trying to trade. The man was of little importance—he had access to only minor classified information. But he is relevant to what I want to say, so I will tell you about him."

Niki started to walk again. Berg hesitated, not wanting to know, then, driven by a powerful curiosity, fell into step beside him.

"He was an electronics-design engineer in a Murmansk shipyard, working on submarines," Niki said. "Quite talented. Not in a top position. But still in a position of trust. Generous on our part considering he was foreign-born, a guest who had come to us at the end of the war."

Niki reached into his pocket and, bringing out a packet of cheroots, stuck one in his mouth. The elaborately elegant clothes, the cheroot, all seemed faintly ridiculous: He looked like a cheap gangster in a bad movie.

"So how did this guest repay us? Mmm?" Niki paused, sparking a lighter behind the shelter of his hand and drawing deeply until the cheroot end glowed red. "So how does he repay us? He decides he doesn't love the Soviet Union after all. In fact, he discovers his heart lies back home. He reestablishes his love of his homeland by passing oddments to the CIA through an agent in Kiev. Not a nice way to repay hospitality, was it? But we find out all about him, Rolf." His voice warmed. "In fact, we made good use of him. We used him to pass on a little nonsense from time to time. Everyone was happy. No problems. Then, suddenly, he makes this deal. He will escape in exchange for a package of information. We could have had the last laugh, of course, and fed him a marvelous bundle of nonsense to hand over on arrival." A pause. He added significantly: "But we couldn't let that happen, Rolf. We couldn't."

They were approaching the end of the quay and the Town Hall square, where small fishing boats came to sell their catches directly to the public. A short distance away, two lovers braved the cold on a bench, giggling loudly. The boy was saying: "It's warm under my coat! Come on, it's really warm!"

The two men turned back into the shadows. A taxi sped by on the main waterfront road.

"We couldn't do it, Rolf, we had to stop him. He was a Norwegian, you see. He had come over in 1945. He had traveled

across Finnmark—an epic journey of hardship and depriva-
tion, one gathers—to meet up with the Red Army near
Kirkenes."

Berg faltered and gave the Russian a sharp look.

"The soldiers took him in and fed him, though they had
little enough to offer him. The young man was grateful. He
joined the army for the last of the fight. He stayed on in Russia after the peace. He wanted to learn the language and complete his technical training. His new country was generous. He
was given every opportunity, every advantage. Nothing was
too much trouble—"

Berg felt slightly sick. He held up his hand, but there was
no stopping Niki.

"He had tuition," said the Russian, "a nice place to live. . . .
He was bright, you see, gifted."

Petter. He was talking about Petter.

Niki paused. "So you see, Rolf, when it came down to it we
couldn't let him go. He would have nailed you. Nailed you in
his first breath. Your name, your happy time with us—everything."

Berg broke into a hot sweat.

"So you see, he had to be stopped."

The realization hit Berg like a blow. "You mean—"

"Stopped from crossing the border. That's why the guards
had their orders."

"And—"

"Oh, he was stopped."

Berg stared blankly at the Russian.

"For you, Rolf. All for you. You see, *you're* our vital asset."

Then Berg knew. He'd never been free. And now he never
would be.

8

Sonja. He had to fix Sonja.

He found a phone booth near the harbor and called her apartment.

The number rang and rang. It was almost midnight; Sonja never stayed out late. And where was the sick mother? He felt his first pangs of alarm.

He kept trying, first from another phone booth, then from his apartment.

He must speak to her. Otherwise her imagination might make two and two into five.

Unpleasant possibilities seeped into his mind: that she already knew about the Soviet protest and had been called to her office for an emergency meeting; that she had told her colleagues about him; that at this very moment they were hearing about the second Erik Leif.

He built himself into a rage of indignation. Niki should have given him more time to protect himself!

He dialed Sonja's number continuously. Twice it was busy and his hopes rose. Then it didn't answer again and he realized someone else might be trying to call her too. The apartment became stifling and he went out again.

He found another phone booth. Should he try her office? No, that would be madness—or would it?

He dialed her apartment again.

It answered almost immediately.

Sonja's voice. "Hello."

He regained his breath.

"Hello?" she repeated.

"It's me. Where've you been?"

"Erik!" She sounded pleasantly surprised. "Oh, we went out to a cousin's at Drammen and the car wouldn't start on the way back. I've left Mother in Drammen and—"

"You've been out all day?"

"Yes—why?"

He felt limp. "I have to see you. *Now*. I'll be waiting at the university. Outside the administration building."

"What's wrong?" Her voice was low and panicky.

"I can't talk now. But look, if anyone else calls, do nothing, say nothing, until after you've spoken to me."

He hung up before she could argue, and drove straight to the university. The moment he arrived he wondered if he'd chosen the right place. The modern university buildings were set in open parkland and, apart from the traffic on the main road, it was very quiet. There was nowhere to hide.

He got a grip on himself: he was thinking like a marked man.

He parked around the side of a building and walked back to where he could watch the approach road.

She was late.

He waited, thinking furiously yet trying not to think.

Five minutes . . . ten. His mouth was dry, his skin cold. He forced himself to stay calm.

At last. Lights. Coming slowly. Hesitantly. Drawing in to the curb.

He gave it a moment, waiting in the shadows. No other lights appeared. No strange sounds.

He stepped out and went quickly over to the car. He opened the passenger door and got in.

She was looking frightened, her eyes round and white, her chest rising and falling like bellows. He realized: She knew.

He said immediately: "We were too late. We couldn't prevent it. The operation in Finland went wrong."

"I know," she cried. "They called me immediately after you did. But what happened?"

Berg realized: This thing could be turned to his advantage. For once he had all the facts at his fingertips. Putting a gentle hand on her shoulder, he gave her the outline of the story, carefully omitting details of the man from Murmansk.

Equally carefully, he managed to mention the names of the two Lapps. A small demonstration of his inside knowledge.

She looked miserable. "I can't believe it."

He examined her face, the tone of her voice.

He realized: She hadn't a single suspicion.

The relief was so great he could have laughed.

He should say something. He sighed aloud. "Given time we might have managed to stop it . . ." He shook his head. "I'm sorry."

"But why did it happen, Erik?" she asked imploringly. "What went wrong?"

"The Russians knew, that's what went wrong. They were tipped off by their friend in high places, whoever he is. The only good news, if you could call it that, is . . . well, we can't be sure . . . but the word is that the leak's from the American end after all."

She threw him an agonized look. "What I can't understand is why they were *shot*, Erik. *Why?*"

He looked her straight in the eye. "We'll probably never know."

She pushed up her glasses and rubbed her eyes fiercely. "Oh, Erik, what a mess! It's the worst thing that's ever happened." Her voice broke and he saw that she was near to tears. "I feel those men were our responsibility. I feel we've—failed them. Oh, dear, this is awful . . ." She found a handkerchief and blew her nose loudly.

"You mustn't blame yourself," he said briskly. "It really isn't your fault."

He leaned over and gave her a long hug.

"By the way . . ."

Drawing a long shuddering breath, she gave a sharp little nod to show she was listening.

He suddenly felt very confident.

He asked: "Was Starheim involved in this?"

It was morning, Hal realized. There were people in the streets, cars parking, defense staff entering the castle.

Thrane touched his arm. The two men made their way out

and into the back of the waiting car. The car threaded its way out of the Akershus compound and down toward the harbor, heading west.

A fine sleet fell, spinning in desultory yellow whorls around the streetlamps. A bus hissed past, its passengers gray and blank-faced behind the steamy windows.

Hal stared, unseeing. His anger was temporarily exhausted, burned out by the all-night meeting. All he felt now was a bottomless despair, a chilling hopelessness that engulfed him in a foglike apathy, dulling everything, even the pain.

The rush hour wasn't yet in full swing and in no time he recognized the street before hers, then, all too soon, the final corner.

The moment had almost come. Dread pulled at his stomach. Friday—the taxi ride, the hasty good-bye, the last sight of Ragna dashing into the apartment building—seemed so long ago. How long? He couldn't think.

They turned into the street.

The car slowed.

Hal said to the driver: "It's further along." Something caught his eye; he looked past the driver. There was a knot of people standing halfway up the street. As the car approached, some of them spread out in a fan. But it wasn't until the waiting group started peering excitedly in the direction of the car and aiming their cameras that Hal finally realized.

He exchanged glances with Thrane and said in horror: "What the hell—"

Thrane jumped forward and said to the driver: "Accelerate! Don't stop! Quickly. Back to Akershus."

Hal grabbed Thrane's arm. "No! No! We stop here! I'm getting out! D'you hear me?"

Thrane threw him a fierce look, seemed on the point of arguing, then gave a sudden nod. "Driver, stop as planned!"

The car accelerated then ground to a halt in front of the apartment building. Immediately the newsmen pressed in around the car. Faces were thrust against the windows.

Thrane pushed the door open and led the way out. As Hal followed there was a crackling of flashbulbs and a babble of voices. "Major Starheim—please, do you have any comments on the border incident?"

"Major Starheim, had Johansen been on one of these expeditions before?"

He ran up the steps. The voices cackled on, intrusive, hideous, bellowing Jan's and Mattis's names like so much public property.

"How do you feel about Johansen's and Hetta's deaths, Mr. Starheim?"

How did he feel?

He jerked around, ugly with rage, wanting to hit out at them.

Thrane hissed, "Don't!" and, grabbing his arm, pulled him inside the building. "You mustn't talk to them, you *mustn't*!"

"The bastards!"

Thrane led the way up the stairs. "They're just doing their job."

"They seem to know a hell of a lot!"

Thrane's head jerked up, and he paused in mid-stride. "Yes, they do, don't they?" He looked shaken.

Hal grabbed his arm. "How do they know?"

He shrugged. "Soviet sources."

"But the identities. How did they know *that*? Christ, this whole thing stinks!"

Thrane didn't reply but started up the stairs again.

They reached the second-floor apartment and rang the bell. The door was opened as far as the chain. Eventually they were let in by a woman wearing jeans and an artist's smock. The woman said: "She's ready. I hope you're going to keep the press away from her. They've been pestering us for hours."

The woman disappeared. Hal waited, his heart like lead.

There were murmuring voices, a door opened, the woman friend came out.

Then, in one fluid movement, with hardly a sound, Ragna was in the room.

She stood before them, very white and very still. Her clothes looked too big for her.

Hal stepped forward.

Tentatively he reached for her hand. In a small but distinct gesture of refusal, she pulled it away. She said in a flat monotone: "I don't want to talk. I just want to get home as soon as possible."

Hal dropped his hand awkwardly. "We've come to take you to the airport."

She waited passively, looking at the wall. Thrane picked up the suitcase that stood by the door. The woman friend took a handbag off a chair and hooked it over Ragna's arm, then embraced her strongly. The two women clung together for a moment, then pulled back. The woman friend turned away, crying gently.

The party made its way slowly out of the apartment and down the stairs. As they came into the hall Hal said: "The press are outside, I'm afraid. Just walk straight toward the car and ignore them completely."

She said nothing but he could see that she had understood.

Hal gripped her arm and, as Thrane opened the front door, led her out.

The pack was waiting.

A few flashbulbs popped. Some reporters looked as though they were about to speak. Hal looked daggers at them. They stood back in respectful silence.

Some decency at least.

But the moment Ragna bent her head to climb into the car, they closed in again.

"Major Starheim, did the men have orders to cross the Soviet border?"

"Please—could you tell us if the men were trained for this work?"

Hal followed Ragna into the car.

As he twisted into his seat one voice rose above the others.

"Major Starheim, could you confirm your part in the operation?"

Hal reached for the handle to pull the door closed.

The hectoring voice shrilled: "Major, can you confirm that you were involved in the operation? That you were in charge—"

Hal slammed the door shut. The car shot off.

The last words hung heavily in the silence. A vise seemed to close around Hal's heart.

Slowly, he turned to Ragna.

She was staring at him, a troubled look in those enormous dark eyes. As he met her gaze his eyes narrowed slightly, as if she had read something from his expression, something that confirmed her inner thoughts.

She dropped her eyes suddenly and looked away.

PART TWO

January 1963

9

Thrane crossed the hotel lobby and peered through the plate-glass window. Very dark; strong wind; snow swirling down the street. Tromsø by morning. He turned back to the taxi driver. "It doesn't look that bad."

"The boat won't be running."

"But are you sure? Can't we find out?" For the tenth time that morning Thrane wished he were on official business and had military transport at his disposal.

"The boats don't run in bad weather," the man said obstinately.

It was the first time Thrane had heard of a supply boat not running. He tried another tack. "Well, how *do* I get there then?"

Looking shifty, the driver pulled on his cigarette. He said suddenly: "He won't see you, you know."

Thrane looked at him in astonishment. "What?"

"Starheim. He won't see you. You'll be wasting your time."

Thrane relaxed. So that was it. "I'm not a journalist. I'm a friend of his. He'll see me."

"That's what the last one said. It didn't make any difference."

"Good Lord," Thrane commented, "they still bother him, do they?"

"Now and again. But they never have any success."

"Look," Thrane said patiently, "I'm an army officer, a former colleague of Starheim's." He took out his ID and passed it briefly in front of the man's face. "Believe me, he'll be happy to see me. Now, I'm told you can take me to the boat. So how about it?"

The man thought for a long time. Finally he made up his mind and, with a shrug, indicated grudgingly that Thrane might accompany him out to the car. But not without a last passing shot. "Well, don't blame me if he won't see you."

"How long will it take?" Thrane asked as they set off.

There was a long pause. "Depends."

Thrane gave up—he knew a brick wall when he saw one— and settled back in his seat. No doubt the fellow's intentions were good. Hal's name still had the power to arouse strong feelings and fierce loyalties. Hal's name, and that of Pasvik.

Pasvik.

Three years ago it had been nothing but a river that happened to flow along a border.

But international incidents need names, and so the Pasvik border incident had been born, or Pasvik for short. People would say: "After Pasvik." Or "In view of Pasvik." Or "If it hadn't been for Pasvik." A part of the nation's vocabulary.

Although to Thrane's secret relief it had been overshadowed a few months later by another event. The U-2 incident. That, too, had been a nasty shock to the country. The fact that U.S. spy planes had been using Norwegian bases was awkward enough, but for the Norwegian government to have to admit it hadn't been aware of the flights was a national humiliation.

At least the incident couldn't be laid at FO/E's door. Which made a change.

They came to a jetty. After a long wait, a ferry loomed out of the grayness and they drove on. It started across the main lead toward one of the larger islands. Thrane guessed the supply boat must leave from there.

The driver lit a cigarette and the car interior filled with smoke. Thrane got out for some fresh air. He had no problem finding it—it was forced down his throat by the buffeting wind.

The temperature was icy. He pulled up the collar of his jacket and walked to the boat's side. The sky had lightened a little. Looking up the lead to the north, Thrane could just make out the end of one island and the beginning of the next. If he'd gotten his geography right, Revoy must be just beyond that.

By screwing up his eyes he thought he could distinguish land in the right place: an indistinct shadow, a faint suggestion of darker gray in a slate-colored sea.

But then the weather closed in and everything blended into a dense twilight.

Hal scraped the snow aside and examined the base of the sapling. Quite dead. He sat back on his heels and looked thoughtfully at the blackened upper stems of the aspen. He decided, finally, that the topsoil must be too thin at this spot. He refused to accept Arne's prediction that the valley would never support anything but birch. Birch grew fairly easily; Hal wanted something different: a delicate varied woodland of rowan, aspen, bird cherry, and willow. This aspen hadn't survived, but he would plant another in a better place and make it grow, even if he had to wrap the entire plant in sackcloth every winter.

He hadn't been so stubborn about the shrubs near the house. He had admitted defeat over the lilac and flowering cherry killed by frost two winters ago. But a cluster of six young willows had taken well in the hollow to the west of the house, and he had walled in a plot where, in addition to the usual potatoes, carrots, and turnips, he had grown leeks, lettuce, and maize. Most farmers didn't bother with such difficult crops and stuck to root vegetables, cattle, hay, and fish, but Hal enjoyed the challenge of growing a wider variety of things.

His neighbors thought he was mad.

But from the moment he'd come to live permanently at Brattdal he'd wanted the place to be more than just a self-supporting farm. It gave him immense satisfaction to think he was creating something special, something beautiful and lasting. And why not? The mixed woodland, once established, would stop the wind howling down the valley and provide shelter for a whole range of plants and flowers. Slowly he would extend it, adding new shrubs and trees in fenced enclosures, until in the summer the whole valley would be ringed with greenery and color.

Most of the trees were coming along all right. Making the farm self-supporting was taking a little longer.

He cut down the dead aspen, checked the animal defenses

round the remaining saplings, and whistled for Bamse. The wind ripped the sound from his lips.

He looked up toward the head of the valley. The col was obscured by low cloud racing over the ridge and pouring down the slopes, like water flowing over a dam. He whistled again, and Bamse finally appeared, a small gray shape floundering through a patch of heavy drift, his nose close to the snow. Game was scarce, but Bamse never gave up hope.

Hal walked slowly down toward the house, stomping through the thick snow. The snow had come very early this year, with several exceptionally heavy falls since November. The temperature had been unusually low too, down to February levels over Christmas. Now, with the worst of the winter still to come, he was beginning to worry about the fodder. He had a variety of stock: a flock of thirty Steigar sheep, a dozen cows, and six goats. Normally he would let the goats out to forage during the short day, but the snow was too thick even for that.

The only animals that didn't need to live in the barn were the ten musk-oxen. Hal could see them now in the bottom pasture near the water's edge. These strange creatures were Hal's greatest experiment and his greatest success. Dark and primeval, with long low-curving horns and skirts of dense shaggy hair which brushed the ground, looking from a distance like small American buffalo with trailing coats, they weren't oxen at all, nor even cattle, but overgrown members of the goat-sheep family.

Once, a long time ago, they were thought to have ranged northern Scandinavia, but now they were found only in eastern Greenland and Arctic Canada. Hal had imported them specially.

It was impossible not to develop a liking for the beasts. Not only because they were thriving—for which Hal was extremely grateful—but because they were fiercely independent. One ram had charged him three times. The score was two escapes to Hal and one hit to the ram. The hit had taken the form of a powerful butt, a decidedly painful encounter which had left Hal with a two-inch scar on his backside.

The musk-oxen were a success. But there had been failures and a number of ventures that had fallen somewhere in be-

tween: an attempt to grow highly prized cloudberries had succeeded, only for the goats to knock down the fencing and
consume the entire crop; wild strawberries had flourished one
season and failed the next; an unusual strain of oats had failed
to ripen in the lower valley but managed to seed itself in a
couple of patches halfway up the hillside. You never knew
what would work, but it was a hell of a challenge to find out.

He paused just above the house and looked down the valley.
He often paused like this to contemplate the weather, the sky,
the light. The scene was never the same. Today the waters of
the wide sound were steel-gray, and the sky dark and streaked
with long strands of wind-torn cloud. Angry, cold weather.

But then in summer the days were long, the light continuous, the growth abundant. Infinite variety; he never tired of
the place.

Bamse caught him up at the door and they entered the
house together. The midday meal never varied: cheese, cold
meat, bread, bottled fruit or, if Arne had been to town recently, fresh fruit. Bamse had dried fish and, when Hal was
feeling generous, which was nearly all the time, a ration of
cheese. Hal took his main meal at six in the afternoon. The
evenings varied according to season. In winter he spent long
hours at his desk working on his research papers. He had two
projects in hand at present: a study of survival clothing for the
army, and a study for Oslo University of the feasibility of in-
troducing musk-oxen to Arctic Norway on a commercial scale.
In summer he tried to keep the written work to a minimum,
and spent the long daylight hours on the farm, or fishing, or
tinkering with *Skorpa*'s engine, or improving the farm buildings.

Recently he had started another project which took him into
the boathouse for hours at a time.

Now, as always, he spent a bare ten minutes eating before
going back to work. He never sat idle for long. Idleness led to
introspection, which never did any good. Life had to be lived
with the minimum of self-indulgence, and he arranged his
time accordingly.

He strode up to the barn and began to muck out the cattle.
He worked at a fast pace, shoveling the manure into a barrow
and carting it to a small silo for rotting down in the summer.

He worked fast and energetically, pushing himself hard so that his body would feel well used and dog-tired at the end of the day. It was the only way he could be sure of a good night's sleep.

After an hour the job was finished and, sweating well, he paused at the barn door to pull on his jacket and think about the remaining chores.

Something caught his eye. He became very still. A figure was climbing the path up to the house. And it wasn't Arne.

A sudden hot anger rose in Hal's throat. Strangers meant only one thing.

Bamse ran on ahead, growling. Hal strode down the hill, around the house, and emerged at the front, ready to repel boarders.

The approaching figure circled the growling Bamse warily, then looked up and waved. There was something familiar about him.

Recognition suddenly came.

Thrane.

Hal's first reaction was one of surprise and pleasure, quickly followed by vague alarm.

Thrane wouldn't have come all this way for a social call.

Nevertheless he managed a brief smile as Thrane strode up, panting hard. "Welcome," Hal said. "Not many people come to Revoy in January."

They shook hands. Thrane said: "I was just passing—if you could call it that. On my way back from Kirkenes. I would have let you know but—"

"I know. I'm not on the phone."

"I did try your neighbor. There was no reply."

"He's been in Tromsø."

Thrane sighed. "Wish I'd known. He might have given me a lift."

They turned toward the house.

"Quite a place you have here," Thrane said. "I didn't realize it was quite so—well, extensive."

"I added the large barn two years ago. There was only the *stabbur* before." Thrane admired the ornate wooden food store which stood just above the walled vegetable garden.

They climbed onto the veranda and Hal held the front door

open for him. "In fact, I am having a telephone installed. This summer. I already have electricity. It's made a lot of difference. Windup gramophones can lose their charm."

They hung up their coats and removed their boots. Thrane wandered into the hall. "What a beautiful place," he said admiringly.

"Thank you. Will you have some coffee?" Hal led the way into the kitchen and put the kettle on. Thrane sat down at the table.

Impatient with the niceties, Hal broached the subject that Thrane must surely have come about, saying: "Thanks for your last letter."

"I wish there'd been more to report."

"I was grateful for what you could tell me."

Silence. Hal waited expectantly, but despite the cue Thrane seemed happy to wait for the coffee to appear.

Had he come about something else then? Surely not.

The original FO/E inquiry into the Pasvik incident had taken place more than two years before. Not having been in FO/E, and, worse still, having resigned his commission, Hal had not been permitted to know the result. Thrane, technically sworn to secrecy, had taken quite a chance and dropped Hal enough pointers for him to build up a picture of the findings.

An accident, the inquiry had concluded. Resulting from misjudgment on the part of the two men, which had led them to cross the border.

The political judgments had been much more public, of course. There had been an outcry, rows in the National Assembly, endless recriminations in the press. When the U-2 incident occurred a few months later, it had seemed as if the government must surely resign. It had survived, in fact—just. But there had been a distinct shift in public opinion. Though still pro-NATO, the Norwegian people were no longer in favor of limitless cooperation with the U.S. and NATO. In a popular move, nuclear weapons had been banned from Norwegian soil.

Now, almost three years later, the fuss had died down. It was all over.

Except that Pasvik would never be over for Hal, because the doubts never went away.

And Thrane had doubts too, Hal was sure of it, although he never voiced them openly. That was why he kept the file open. That, Hal presumed, was why he was here.

Hal put the coffee on the table and sat down.

"I didn't come about that," Thrane said, reading his mind.

Hal shot him a questioning glance.

But Thrane wasn't ready to talk yet. He said conversationally: "I gather you still get unwelcome visitors."

"What? Oh, you mean journalists? Yes. Now and then. There was an American writing a book on the CIA. Came all the way up here. I didn't see him though. I don't see anybody. It's easier that way."

Thrane nodded. There was a slight pause. "How about the farming, then?" he asked pleasantly. "How's it going?"

Hal gave a wry laugh. "Nothing wrong with it that two more pairs of hands and endless money wouldn't cure."

"So how do you manage?"

"With difficulty. A place like this isn't really designed to be run single-handed. I manage with Arne's help, and a couple of students in the summer. But it's hard; I don't pretend it isn't."

They talked on for a while. Hal laid out a meal of smoked fish, smoked meat, cheese, jam, and bread.

"You're most kind," Thrane said, and looked as though he meant it. Hal began to wonder if he'd gotten it wrong and Thrane had come simply out of friendship. Yet they weren't close—impossible under the circumstances. Just united by events.

Thrane said: "Don't you find it hard here in the winter? It must be very lonely."

"I write a lot, I read, I listen to music. I go to Tromsø sometimes. Or friends come to visit me here." He gave a dry laugh. "I think it makes them feel adventurous."

Thrane buttered some bread and asked quietly: "But no more adventuring for you?"

Hal's heart squeezed uncomfortably. Time never softened that question. Especially when an American expedition was poised to conquer the West Ridge that very summer. His own expedition had been canceled immediately after Jan's death. Even if he'd had the heart to go ahead with it, which he hadn't, the project would have foundered: the sponsorship offers had evaporated into thin air.

He stood up and refilled the coffeepot. "No. No adventuring for me. I don't want it anymore."

Hal brought the refilled pot back to the table.

"How's Ragna Johansen?" Thrane asked. "I wrote to her some time ago, but she didn't reply."

Was this leading somewhere? Hal answered cautiously: "You mustn't mind her. She tears up letters from the military."

There was a pause. "But not letters about the proposed installation near Kåfjord?"

Hal looked up sharply. Now he had a very good idea of why Thrane had come. "Ah. Probably not," he agreed. "But then she feels very strongly about what's happening there."

Thrane frowned. "And—er—so do you, I gather."

Hal thought: Ah, now we have it. "I have no argument about the installation itself," he said evenly. "Just its location."

"But it's got to go somewhere, Starheim. If another valley were chosen, then another lot of people would object. Nowhere's perfect."

"Do you know the site at all, Thrane?"

"No-o-o," he conceded.

"Well then."

"What's so special about it? Tell me."

Hal eyed him sharply. Did Thrane really not know? Or was he feigning ignorance in order to probe Hal's stand on the issue?

Hal decided to give him the benefit of the doubt. "It's located several miles up the main valley of Kåfjord," he began. "And then a short distance up to the right, in the mountains bordering the plateau. I imagine it was chosen because of an old track that leads to a disused iron mine—easy to build up into an all-weather road, I suppose. But they didn't do their homework, Thrane!" He gave a small exclamation of disgust. "Planners behind desks! Doubtless they looked at a map and saw 'wilderness' and thought there couldn't be anything there. Well, I tell you, they're wrong. And if they'd bothered to consult the Lapps they would have found out. But they didn't. Oh, *no*."

Thrane had the resigned look of someone who was going to hear a lot more whether he wanted to or not.

"The Kåfjord Valley and the hills around it are the spring and summer pasture for two families of Lapps," Hal continued. "Their reindeer calve there. At calving time does are disturbed by the slightest thing—the smallest noise, other animals, certainly people. Imagine how it'll be when the road's being built—all those heavy trucks and all that terrible noise. And later there'll be the constant toing and froing of personnel." Hal shook his head. "It can't be right, Thrane. It can't. I'm not interested in what the installation is for, or why they want to build it in such a remote spot, but they really can't ignore the Lapps' rights. The people have been using that area for hundreds and hundreds of years."

Thrane stared at him thoughtfully. "Why this sudden interest? You were never interested in Lapp issues before, were you?"

He had a point. Hal conceded: "No . . . But then it was impossible for me to get involved in anything—controversial."

"But now it's all right? Could it be because"—he stared fiercely at his coffee cup—"because one of these Lapp families are cousins of Mattis Hetta?"

Ah, Hal thought, so he *has* done his homework. "That did make me more inclined to look into the matter, I suppose. But after that—it made no difference."

"Are you sure about that?"

Was he? In the sense that Thrane was suggesting, yes. Mattis was dead and gone. He wasn't trying to exact retribution from the military. He said: "I'm sure, Thrane."

"So why all this badgering of the authorities?"

That was very simple: a very persuasive woman named Ragna. But Hal didn't feel like telling Thrane about Ragna. He said: "I became more aware, that's all. Perhaps I'm more inclined to see the underdog's point of view nowadays."

Thrane gave a loud sigh. "You wrote to the minister of defense."

"And two other ministers. *And* the prime minister."

"And now Ragna Johansen is in touch with the press. Did you know that?"

"Yes."

"That sort of thing gets you noticed."

"Ah. Does it, now?"

Thrane looked unhappy. "Listen, I came here as a friend, not in an official capacity. Because I wanted you to—understand just what was involved. You must realize that this installation is not something that can be brought into question and discussed openly like a site for—well, a village hall. Not to put too fine a point on it, it's secret. If this matter becomes an issue—"

"It will, Thrane. It must."

Thrane's lips narrowed into a thin white line. "*If* it becomes an issue, then your opposition will be seen as—well, political."

Hal was silent for a moment. "I think I can live with that."

"The people of this country are still pro-NATO," Thrane said with exasperation. "They'll see your stand as anti-NATO. They won't like it. They won't understand it. You're going to lose yourself a lot of friends."

Hal laughed ironically. "I'm not sure I've got that many friends to lose."

Thrane leaned back in his seat and shook his head, as if Hal were already a lost cause. "You'll be marked as—"

"Yes?"

"Someone to keep an eye on."

"You mean I'll go on a list somewhere. Well—that's another sort of fame, I suppose!"

"They'll wonder who your friends are."

"Oh, will they?"

"You seem very well briefed on the exact location of this installation. Some people might regard the possession of that knowledge as rather unpatriotic. I don't suppose you'd care to tell me where you got it from?"

"Believe it or not, I don't know." Hal could look Thrane straight in the eye: it was the truth. "But I can't see that it matters one way or the other. It doesn't change the fact that the Lapps, who were here a helluva long time before *us*, are in danger of having their rights taken away."

The major shook his head. "If only it wasn't an installation, Hal."

There was a silence. Thrane was beaten and he knew it. Hal

felt a sudden sympathy for him; he had meant well. In a spirit of conciliation, Hal said brightly: "Have a drink!"

Thrane looked at his watch and said wearily: "No thanks, I've got to get to the jetty to meet the supply boat." He drained his coffee and stood up.

They walked in silence to the front lobby.

Hal said: "I appreciate your coming, you know."

Thrane leaned down to pull on his boots. "You can't win this one, Hal. It's a pity to lose your good name for nothing."

"My good name! I haven't got one!" Hal exclaimed, trying to keep the bitterness out of his voice.

"You're wrong!" Thrane said crossly. "Quite wrong."

But Hal knew he wasn't. People hadn't been able to turn their backs on him quickly enough. They'd crucified him once. They could do it again for all he cared. He didn't care a damn.

Buttoning his jacket Hal opened the door and stepped out into the cold. The wind had dropped a little, the cloud lifted off the sea. The view had opened out, revealing water, light, distant land.

Thrane joined him and, led by Bamse, they walked down the path toward the shore. Thrane was frowning, lost in thought. "Look," he said after a while, "there was something else. Though—" He stopped suddenly. "Can I trust you, Starheim? Absolutely? I must be sure it won't go any further."

Hal felt a leap of excitement. "Of course."

Thrane nodded as if he'd expected nothing less, and walked on again. "It may mean nothing, it may not tell us a lot, but— well, some very reliable information has come our way . . . about the third man."

Hal almost stopped in his tracks.

"Apparently he was a Norwegian by birth."

Hal absorbed the information greedily—and immediately felt a keen disappointment. He couldn't see how it was going to help.

Thrane continued: "As I say, it's probably neither here nor there. But for us it's a clue to his identity. There can't be that many Norwegians resident in the Soviet Union."

"Very few, I would have thought."

"They must have gone there at the end of the war," Thrane

went on. "We're checking the records to see who disappeared at that time. We're also working with a lawyer named Sorensen who specializes in tracing collaborators and Nazi war criminals. He's got an amazing set of files."

Hal almost stumbled, his mind far away. Eventually he said: "Thanks for telling me."

They reached the track. Thrane turned to face him. "There was a fourth man too, a Russian defector, trying to get out at the same time. They traveled together."

"And? What happened?"

"Both died. At or near the border. That's confirmed now."

For some reason Hal thought: Nobody left to talk. "Thanks for telling me," he said again. "You'll let me know? If there's anything else."

Thrane gave him a reproving stare, like a headmaster eyeing a wayward pupil. "I can't promise."

They shook hands and Thrane started along the shoreside track.

Bamse raced ahead of Thrane, making for a distant figure plodding steadily toward them. It was Arne. He and Thrane converged, greeted each other with a brief nod, and passed on their way.

As Hal waited for Arne, he turned Thrane's information over in his mind. It was maddening, but he couldn't see how it was going to help. Just as all the other things hadn't helped: retracing Jan and Mattis's route to the border, finding their camp, sifting through their gear, writing countless letters to intelligence experts.

And yet any piece of the jigsaw, however small, was better than nothing. Or was he wasting his time? Would there ever be a finished picture? And if so, would it show anything? Perhaps it had been exactly as they'd said—a stupid misjudgment, an accident.

Even if it had, even if there was no one to blame, it would be a relief to know.

The snow gleamed feebly. To the east the low cloud had parted in hard horizontal lines, as if cleaved by a knife, revealing gashes of pink light, like layers of a cake. For a moment the wavetops caught the faint color, but then the speckles of pink faded into the gray of approaching night.

Automatically Hal looked toward the Lyngen Alps, but they were already lost in a heavy band of darkness. When the visibility was poor like this he always missed the sight of their jagged peaks. He remembered what he'd told Thrane about not caring. It wasn't strictly true. There were still days when he hungered for the snow, for the bare simplicity of the old life.

But there wouldn't be any more expeditions. Because nothing was that simple anymore. Only, perhaps, his life here, at Brattdal.

Arne arrived. Not one to waste energy on conversation, he grunted a greeting and handed Hal the post.

Hal glanced quickly through it. Something from Oslo—official by the look of it—a couple of bills, a handwritten envelope which made his heart sink slightly. And—

Ah. A letter from Ragna.

He tore it open and, holding it close to his face, tried to read it. The light was bad, but Ragna's writing was worse.

. . . The journalist was a wash-out, he managed to make out. *I almost threw him in the snow! He only wanted to talk about you-know-what. Can you think of any other journalists we could try? And have you heard a single word from the ministry? They are* incredible! *Aslak and I should be back from Kautokeino on Tuesday night. I'll let you know how we get on. Though I'm sure the Lapps will be disappointed at the lack of progress. Can't blame them. I am!*

It was signed simply: *R*.

Underneath was: *P.S. I promise to take care of the Land-Rover. Nearly forgot—Wrote to that friend of yours, Rolf Berg. Good idea? Only met him that once, but he seemed all right.*

Arne was wandering off again, talking gruffly to Bamse. Hal considered for a moment, then called: "Arne, could you look after things tomorrow? And call Ragna Johansen to say I'll be down in the morning?"

Arne raised his eyebrows. "Tomorrow morning?"

"Yes."

"It's not Sunday."

Hal said heavily: "No, Arne, it's not Sunday. It's Wednesday. But could you tell her anyway?"

Back at the house Hal opened the rest of his mail, leaving the handwritten envelope until last. Eventually he tore it open. The paper smelled strongly of perfume.

It said: *Shall I come up on the weekend? I could bring food, music, books. Or why don't you come and stay here—there's a party at a friend's house. I'm on my own this weekend. I'd love to see you. Anna-Kristin.*

Hal pushed the letter to one side. He didn't want to deal with it, he didn't want to decide. In fact, he hadn't the first idea what he wanted where Anna-Kristin was concerned. He'd met her two months before. She was good-looking and vivacious and he enjoyed her company. But . . .

But he didn't want to pursue it any further.

He went to milk the cows. By the time he'd finished it was six. There were more chores to be done, but his mind kept going to the morning and his trip to Tromsø and Ragna and little Kris. Because Ragna had been away he hadn't made his usual Sunday visit, and he'd missed it. And he knew Krisi would have too.

He normally took the boy a small present. What could he take tomorrow?

He had a sudden thought. There was always the project in the boathouse—a rather large present he'd been planning to surprise Krisi with for some months.

Yes, why not? It was almost finished. It would be an awful sweat to get it finished by morning—he didn't dare think of what remained to be done. But it'd be worth it for the expression on the boy's face.

The chores would suffer, of course. He went through the pretense of wrestling with his conscience, then strode down to the water's edge. Throwing open the door to the boathouse, he lit the lamp and surveyed the beautiful sight before him.

Six hours should finish the job. Rolling up his sleeves, he set to work.

10

Ragna wiped the tears from her eyes and coughed until her lungs rasped with pain. The Lapps, who seemed totally immune to the choking wood smoke, glanced at her with good-hearted amusement.

The tepeelike tent, the *lavo*, was ten feet across and about as high, with a floor of birch twigs and, in the center, a ring of stones inside which a fire smoked profusely. Ragna eased herself away from the fire until her back was against the tent side. While the Lapps talked on in their singsong voices, she pulled a map out of her pocket and peered at it in the semidarkness, trying to work out exactly where they were.

She and Aslak had come up from the coast in the Land-Rover the previous day, driving up the long road into the interior, coming first into Finland and then, via a lesser road which was more of a track, back into Norway. It had been an awful journey, the visibility poor and the road covered in drifts. But finally they had arrived at the town of Kautokeino, perched in the middle of the plateau and, like Karasjok to the east, a traditional winter gathering place for nomadic Lapps.

They had expected to find the head of the Hetta family, Aslak's uncle Isak, at the wood-built family house. But only the women and children were there. The men, they were told, were away with the herd. After much uncertainty and some exasperation on Ragna's part—the Lapps were not known for their decisiveness—another relation of Aslak's had offered to take them to the herd.

Ragna had looked forward to the journey—she had never

been on the plateau in midwinter before—but when they set out early the next morning it had been dark and viciously cold with a strong wind blowing. Worse still, not having skied since the previous spring, she was rather unfit and had slowed the others down. Finally she had been allowed to ride on the reindeer-drawn sledge—a distinct improvement—but she had become almost rigid with cold. Her romantic image of the plateau in winter had rapidly faded.

After three hours they had finally gotten here.

But where was here? She made a guess and, putting her finger on the spot, showed the map to Isak. The old man peered at it, frowned deeply, and spoke to one of his sons in his own language. Then there was silence. Fighting back another spasm of coughing, Ragna asked Aslak: "What does he say?"

Aslak kept a straight face. "He says that maps are not very useful."

Ragna clamped her lips together. She tried another tack. "Could he show me the route the herd takes to the spring pasture?"

Aslak looked away, the two sons and the sledge driver sipped their drinks.

"Well?" Ragna demanded.

The old man turned to her. "The herd choose the way. I follow," he said in Norwegian.

"Yes, but—well, it would help tremendously if I knew your *route* into Kåfjord Valley. D'you see?" Her eyes burned so fiercely she had to bury them in her hands for a moment.

When she looked up the old man's eaglelike face was beaming at her and he was holding out a dish of food. She took the food, asking: "What will you do if they go ahead and build this thing? Can you take the herd somewhere else?"

Too late she remembered that Lapps—or at least remote mountain Lapps—did not deal in hypothesis; in their opinion it was completely pointless to consider something that had not actually occurred.

The old man was busying himself with his meal. Ragna had the feeling that the conversation, such as it was, was over. With a sigh of resignation, she peered at the contents of the dish. It was impossible to tell what it was. But it could only be reindeer, stewed or stewed. Oh, well, she *was* hungry.

She accepted a piece of hard bread. She'd heard about the Lapp bread and how it kept for over a year, and the moment her teeth came to grips with the stuff she knew it must be true. Barely pliable and slightly sweet, it tasted like old leather doused in syrup.

No one talked. Instead there were loud sucking and smacking noises as the Lapps got their mouths around some large bones. Through the gloom Ragna watched, fascinated yet slightly repelled, as they tore at the flesh with their teeth, chucked the bones outside to the waiting dogs, then sucked their fingers. Was it true that the mountain Lapps never washed? She couldn't believe it, yet a small suspicion remained. It was one of those things one longed to know but could never ask. Like whether they still practiced black magic and invoked the devil to put a hex on their enemies.

Old Isak said something in Lappish and, throwing back his head, gave a high-pitched cackle. The others joined in the laughter. Ragna smiled politely.

Whatever these people's customs, she was determined to respect them. Most Norwegians patronized the Lapps—laughing at their *yoiking*, the strange high-pitched, and to the Norwegian ear tuneless, singing; ignoring Lapp history and culture; branding the Lapps primitive, uneducated, and unreliable; even pointing out to foreigners that Lapps were "racially different, you know," as if that established their own superiority. Ragna never let comments like that go unchallenged and had earned herself a reputation for being outspoken and argumentative.

Nothing wrong with that. In fact, she was rather proud of it.

She peered at the stew and swallowed a few mouthfuls. It was watery and curiously tasteless. Gagging slightly, she put it hastily aside. The atmosphere was suffocating; she needed to get out. Pulling on her anorak, she dived for the flap, ducked outside, and drew in great gasps of freezing air.

Better. After a while she walked away from the tent, eyes half-closed against the wind, and stood looking at the great herd of reindeer scattered far across the wide landscape, hooves scraping at the snow, mouths pulling and chewing at the vegetation beneath.

She tried to estimate the size of the herd. That was another thing old Isak wouldn't tell her. It was too personal a question, Aslak had explained, like asking someone how much he had in the bank. She'd given an ironic laugh at that; she wouldn't mind telling Isak how much she had in the bank, because it was precisely nothing.

After a time Aslak came out to find her.

She said wearily: "Isak seems to think I'm prying. But I'm only trying to help."

"I know," he said. "Isak does appreciate it, believe me. It's just that old habits die hard."

"Well—there's not much point in staying. We might as well get back. Or am I hoping for too much?"

"Just wait for them to finish their meal."

They wandered back toward the tent and sat on the sledge, their backs to the wind, looking out across the plateau. "My aunt had ten children," Aslak told her. "Six of them were born up here in winter, in a tent just like this, in temperatures as low as minus thirty or forty."

Ragna shivered, pulling her hood closer around her face. It felt that cold now, though she knew it wasn't. "And they survived?" she asked.

"Seven out of ten did. Not bad for those days. But now my aunt stays in Kautokeino in the winter. Nearly all the women and children do."

"I don't blame them."

"No." There was a note of regret in his voice.

"Isn't it better that way?" Ragna asked.

He shrugged. "It's inevitable, that's all. Along with TV sets and snow-scooters. One of my aunt's neighbors already has a TV. Soon everyone'll have them. And the Sami will be that much closer to losing their identity."

Sami. It was the Lapps' preferred name for themselves. "The answer's to have the best of everything, isn't it?" Ragna suggested carefully. "To have TVs and snow-scooters, yet keep the culture and traditions . . ."

"But you can't do that while the Sami have no pride in themselves and take Norwegian-sounding names and allow Norwegian to be spoken in their schools. Not when all they get for trying to be good Norwegians is to be called *finnfaen*— peasants." He brushed some snow briskly, almost angrily, off his trousers. "You may find Isak hard to deal with, but at least he's a true Sami and unashamed of it."

"Of course!" she said hastily. "Really—I *admire* him for it!"

Aslak stood up. "I know. Here, give me that map of yours. I don't promise anything, but I'll see what I can do."

He went back into the tent, leaving Ragna to stare at the endless monotony of the plateau and to feel glad that she'd seen it in winter just this once—and to feel even more grateful that she wouldn't have to see it again.

It was late the next day when Ragna dropped Aslak at his home on Kåfjord and drove toward the ferry that would take her across Lyngenfjord. Once across the fjord she would have more driving and two more ferries to catch before reaching Tromsø. She was already dog-tired; by the time she got home she'd be dead.

And for what?

She hadn't gotten a great deal for her three days' hard traveling. Aslak had managed to draw her a line on the map, so she had a rough idea of the migration route, but she still didn't know how many reindeer were involved, just as she didn't know how many calves were born in the mountains above Kåfjord Valley each year. She could just imagine the men from the ministry seizing on her lack of facts with undisguised glee.

She drove dangerously fast along the side of Kåfjord, following the curve of the shore around into Lyngenfjord, only to see the ferry pulling away from the landing stage.

She swore aloud. And again, harshly. It would be at least an hour and a half before the next ferry. If she hadn't been so tired and if the roads hadn't been so snowed-up, she would have turned around and taken the much longer road route.

She parked at the landing stage and closed her eyes. Within seconds she was sound asleep.

Much later an insistent tapping woke her. She rolled her head around. A smiling face loomed at the window. She vaguely recognized a woman from Tromsø. Behind the woman was the local bus, blazing with lights, disgorging foot passengers for the ferry.

Ragna slid back the window and said without enthusiasm: "Hello."

"Going to Tromsø?" the woman asked brightly.

Well, she wasn't likely to be going anywhere else. "Er, yes," she admitted. "Why don't you join me?"

The woman, whose name was Karen—Ragna couldn't remember her other name—was not someone Ragna would normally go out of her way to talk to. But then that went for a lot of people in Tromsø. When Ragna had first arrived she'd thought how very friendly and open and uncomplicated the people were compared with down south. Now she saw them quite differently: as provincial, nosy, and opinionated.

It was the last three years that had lifted the wool from her eyes. After Jan's death people had reacted in one of two ways. Either they'd been too embarrassed to talk to her, or they'd positively swept her into their circle of friends, like some rare exhibit or trophy, and then debated the Pasvik incident right in front her, just as if she wasn't there. The arrogance of it!

But, then, what could you expect?

She was sounding jaundiced. She thought: But I *am*.

She managed a pale smile as the woman—*was* it Karen?—got into the passenger seat.

"This is Halvard Starheim's car, isn't it?" the woman asked.

"Yes."

"Ah," she said, managing to sound knowing and faintly surprised at the same time.

Ragna turned away and rolled her eyes in irritation. The whole of Tromsø had her and Hal virtually married off. It was that damned party line of Arne's. Everyone on the surrounding islands listened in, she knew they did. And to their simple minds, twice-weekly phone calls and regular Sunday visits meant only one thing.

Infuriating. Her relationship with Hal wasn't like that, and wasn't likely to become so.

"At one time I heard you were thinking of moving back to Oslo," Karen said in a chatty tone. "Did you change your mind?"

"Not exactly."

"Oh. So you're still thinking of going?"

"One of these days."

The ferry came into sight at last, its lights emerging from the gloom of the fjord.

"Well, I suppose Tromsø must seem very quiet compared to Oslo."

Ragna almost smiled. She could say that again.

"And I suppose having been an actress you like the theater and that sort of thing."

"Yes, I do, rather." What she liked was the idea of being in touch with the rest of the world, and the possibility that she might meet intelligent people and have interesting, amusing conversations: She loved the idea of feeling alive again.

"A bit of a change for your son. How old is he now?"

"Almost five." Ragna made a show of shivering. "Sorry it's so cold in here." She restarted the engine. With a bit of luck the noise might deter further conversation.

But no.

"Five's a lovely age," she said. "Kristian's his name, isn't it? Who does he take after?"

Ragna didn't answer for a moment. She didn't like speaking Jan's name to people she hardly knew. In fact, she had a complete phobia about it. She said: "No one in particular."

"Well, it'd be a pity to see you go. Your shop's been quite a thing for Tromsø."

The shop. The albatross around Ragna's neck. Just thinking about it made her feel depressed.

The woman continued: "We'd all be sorry to see it close."

"Oh, really?" Ragna replied, genuinely surprised.

"Yes, of course. Such wonderful clothes. Fashion's never gotten to Tromsø so quickly. Those sack dresses you had in— quite fantastic. So modern."

"Did you buy one?"

"Well—no," she said, adding hastily, "you didn't have anything in my size."

It seemed that most of Tromsø had failed to find anything in the right size: quantities of unsold sack dresses still littered the racks.

The ferry nudged against the landing stage at last and lowered its ramp. A van and a car drove off. A small group of foot passengers made for the waiting bus.

Ragna drove on and switched off the engine. As soon as the ferry was on its way, Karen started chattering again. Ragna realized she was a gossip of the first order, the sort who ac-

quired information like a sponge and dispensed it like a foun-
tain.

Ragna barely listened. The time dragged. The lights of
Lyngseidet seemed to get no closer at all.

Then a name sprang into the air, and Ragna woke up.

The woman had mentioned Hal.

"Sorry?" Ragna murmured.

"Oh, yes, he was there, at her party."

Hal going to parties? "Oh."

"She gives wonderful parties, of course."

She? Ragna felt a small pang of—she wasn't sure what.
"Does she really?"

"Oh, yes. She's made a lot of friends in no time at all."

"Sorry—who? I didn't catch the name."

"Anna-Kristin Dahl. I thought you must know her."

"No, I don't think so."

"Oh." There was a hint of relish in her voice. "She's such a
good friend of Halvard Starheim's, I thought . . ." She gave a
nervous laugh. "I thought you must know each other."

"Halvard leads his own life. There's no reason why I should
know all the people he knows."

"No, quite. Exactly so. No reason at all." Ragna was aware of
the woman trying to read her face in the darkness. "Such a
nice man," she rambled on. "And so is she, of course. They
seem to get on very well."

Oh, do they? Ragna thought with sudden fury. Why the hell
don't I know about this? Why hasn't Hal told me?

"I saw them at that recital last week. You know, the quartet
from Oslo. Bach, it was. And some Mozart. We should have
more music like that."

Recitals now. Ragna tried to bite back the question hovering
on her tongue but failed. "Oh?" she said in a casual voice. "I
must have missed that. When was it?"

"A week ago. Er—Wednesday, I think. Yes . . . Wednesday."
Now there was a triumphant note in her voice, as if she'd succeeded in catching Ragna out.

Which she had, damn her.

Hal had come to Tromsø without telling Ragna—twice.
He'd come without even phoning her. And he'd always said
that he hated coming to town.

Things had obviously changed, and rather abruptly, and he hadn't even had the decency to tell her. She felt distinctly put out about that.

Yet why should she mind? Did she mind? No, of course not. How could she? It was just that—what? She was used to knowing when he was coming to town. She was used to him visiting Krisi. Yes, that was what surprised her: that he hadn't come to see Krisi.

"And what about you, Ragna?" the woman said. "Anyone special in your life?"

Ragna gripped the wheel. "Me?" she said with a light laugh. "No. No time for all that." And she suppressed the rush of anguish and self-pity that swept over her.

She couldn't avoid driving past the shop. The windows were plastered with sale notices. Stopping for a moment, she peered at the racks visible in the display lights. They still looked jam-packed with clothes.

She drove on, feeling depressed. The shop had been a failure from the word go. She'd gotten a bit carried away with the fitting out and the stock levels, admittedly. But it was the Tromsø women who had defeated her: they just didn't buy.

And she'd been so certain it would work. As a sports shop it had been just one of three in the town, but as a clothes shop it had been the only high-fashion store for several hundred miles. You would have thought the women would have fallen over themselves to make use of it.

A few had, of course. But not enough. The outgoings were terribly high—and the income nearly always lower.

At the beginning she'd looked on the business as a welcome challenge, something that she could get her teeth into while she decided what to do with her life. Well, she'd decided what she wanted to do with her life—move to Oslo—but instead of selling the shop at a nice profit and setting herself up in a new life she was trapped here in a morass of debt.

It made her sick to think about it.

The house came into view at last. It was in darkness. Krisi was staying at his grandmother's.

Parking the Land-Rover, she slipped and slithered down the icy path. It needed clearing: yet another job to add to a long list that didn't get done.

She let herself in and turned on a few lights. There was a pile of mail neatly stacked on the hall table. Her mother-in-law must have been in.

Ragna took the mail into the kitchen and put the kettle on. She glanced through the envelopes. Her heart sank: one from the bank. She put it to the bottom of the pile.

Then an Oslo postmark. Curious, she opened the letter and glanced at the signature. Fred: one of Jan's old climbing friends. She thought: How sweet of him to write. Not all of Jan's friends had bothered to keep in touch. Losing your husband was only half of widowhood, she'd discovered: you also lost status and friends; you became an awkward reminder.

Fred asked after her and trusted she was well. He told her what he had been doing, and how he hoped to raise an expedition to K2 in two years' time.

The letter continued: *However we're still looking for a leader, someone the climbers will follow and someone the buckers will have faith in. There's only one person who fits those requirements, and that's Hal. We've been writing to him for months now. He said he wouldn't consider it, but don't you think he should? He's the only one we want . . .*

Ragna narrowed her lips; she had a very good idea of what was coming next.

. . . The point is—would you have a word with him? We feel certain he'll change his mind once he realizes how much people really want him. His exile is purely self-imposed, you know. I feel he's wasting his life unnecessarily, don't you?

Ragna slapped the letter down onto the table and, snatching a mug off the shelf, made herself a strong coffee. Impulsively she added a large dash of aquavit.

So, she was to persuade Hal to go off and make something more of his life, was she? That was rich. Hal was the one who was free as a bird, the one who could do just as he pleased. He didn't have to live on that bleak island. For some extraordinary reason he actually seemed to like it there. Well, lucky him. Doing what he wanted. Why should she try to persuade him to do something else?

No, if anyone's life was a waste it was hers.

She poured more aquavit into her coffee and, taking a long gulp, sat down, feeling empty and tired and hopeless.

She also felt ashamed. There had been a touch of envy in

that reaction of hers. Hal had talents that were in demand and she couldn't help wishing that she did too.

She thrust her head into her hands. It was this place that got her down. The place and the everlasting winter and the lack of money and the loneliness.

The loneliness.

The first year hadn't been so bad: her fierce determination had kept her going. That and the memories, the feeling that Jan was still somehow there, still loving her, still on her side . . .

But time had worn her down; time had cheated her, removing the warmth of the memories, leaving only emptiness. Now she tried not to think about Jan; she pushed him from her mind. She had learned to think of only one person apart from Kris: herself.

Now she was aware of life passing her by.

Tears dripped steadily through her hands into the coffee cup.

She kept thinking: I'm thirty-two. These are meant to be the best years of my life.

11

Sonja felt sad, of course. But she also felt reborn.

That day she had thrown the last funeral flowers into the rubbish and cleared out her mother's room. She'd packed away everything: ornaments, bed linen, even the curtains. Then she'd scrubbed the place from top to bottom.

She would give the room a new color scheme, she decided—pale pink perhaps: so fresh and young, and much more suitable to a spare room.

It would be nice to have people to stay, though she couldn't immediately think who. And of course she'd be able to entertain. Little supper parties, friends dropping in for coffee.

The possibilities opened out endlessly before her, though, like any prisoner suddenly released from a long sentence, she also found the new freedom a little frightening.

But she had no problem about what to do with the money. Mother, who'd always pleaded poverty, had had a surprising amount tucked away. Sonja, rather hurt by this deception, had spent the whole of the previous day in the shops, buying clothes. On her bed lay a wonderful black silk dress with a red jacket.

Passing the bed, she stroked the dress lovingly. By her standards it had been extremely expensive, but it had been worth every penny. She looked marvelous in it.

Seeing the time, she hurried to her desk to scribble a note. She wrote simply: *Dear One. Worst over. Feeling much recovered. Can't wait to see you. How about a holiday? Love.*

Popping it in an envelope, she carefully printed the name

Lundquist—a false name of their own invention—and the address on the front.

She'd already written to Erik twice in the last ten days. The first note had been simple but to the point: *Darling, Mother is dangerously ill. I have to be with her. Phone if you can.* The second had been stark: *Mother died this morning. Need you. Call as soon as possible.*

It was the first time she'd pressured him to call, but her need for him had been so great that she'd thrown caution to the winds.

Sadly, he hadn't called, which meant he must still be out of town. It had been a great disappointment.

She'd been very brave without him, of course. But she couldn't help imagining how much better it would have been with Erik at her side. She enacted little scenes in her mind all the time, scenes where she was being extraordinarily serene and composed, containing her grief with dignity while Erik looked on admiringly.

Maybe it wouldn't have been exactly like that, but the experience would have drawn them closer together, she knew it. However, there was no point in fretting over what might have been. She had the future to think about.

A future without Mother.

She couldn't help feeling a vast and rather wicked relief. She had loved Mother, of course she had. But the last two years had been a nightmare. Mother had said she'd rather die than go to a nursing home, so a nurse had had to come in daily, with Sonja taking over in the evenings. And Mother had become hysterical if Sonja tried to go out too often. Her meetings with Erik had been reduced to once every two or three weeks. Agony.

Now all sorts of delights opened out before her: bringing Erik here to dinner; having him stay all night; maybe even going on holiday together abroad. Why not? Yes, why not!

She almost laughed aloud.

She suddenly saw the time. Six. She mustn't be late. She flew to the bathroom, showered, brushed and lacquered her hair, and carefully applied some makeup.

Then she put on the black dress and red jacket. It looked so smart she almost burst with pleasure.

She left the apartment at six-forty, posted her letter to Erik, and got to the National Theatre in plenty of time to meet Elsa in the foyer.

It had been months since she'd been to a theater, and years—she couldn't remember how many—since she'd been to a first night. She'd forgotten how overwhelming it was: the bustle, the noise, the feeling of not quite belonging. She felt intimidated by the chattering people, the familiar yet strange faces of actors and politicians, the proximity of fashionable women in their gorgeous clothes. Then she remembered how smart she looked and realized she was being rather silly. She could hold up her head with the best of them.

She was a little disappointed to find their seats were in the upper circle, and right over to one side. But she was determined that nothing was going to spoil the evening. She concentrated hard on the play, a new-wave drama (so the program told her), full of long involved monologues about the agony of family relationships. She felt sure she must be getting a lot out of it.

During the intermission the crush in the bar was so great that they retreated into the auditorium and stood at the front of the circle, looking down on the audience slowly filtering back into the stalls below.

The bells sounded. The trickle of people turned into a steady flow. Elsa nudged Sonja and pointed to a woman in the moving stream below.

"Hildegard Lindman."

Sonja nodded. She knew the name. Hildegard Lindman was a famous actress who made films with a top Swedish director. Beautiful, expensively dressed, she was the sort of woman who quite naturally stood out from the crowd, even when one could see little more than the top of her head.

Sonja exchanged a quick grin with Elsa.

The actress seemed to be in a group of several people, all talking, their heads turned to each other, their hands moving expressively.

Beside her was a man with rich blond hair just like Erik's. The man reached out and put a hand on the actress's shoulder. Hildegard Lindman turned and smiled up at him so that Sonja could see her face. The smile was wide, warm, almost a smile of love. The man bent his head to hers and said something that made her laugh.

They stopped at the end of a row and waited for people to let them in.

Sonja caught her breath. The man's bent head, the obscured face—there was something shockingly familiar about him.

Suddenly she went very cold.

The man shuffled along the row, pulled down his seat, settled.

Then he took a sweeping look around the auditorium, his face raised, his expression languid and aloof.

Sonja gaped.

Erik.

The lights began to dim. Elsa whispered: "Come on!"

He had turned his head away. Sonja gripped the rail, waiting for another glimpse of that face—desperate to be sure yet horribly certain.

Elsa pulled at Sonja's sleeve. "The curtain's going up!"

Sonja dragged herself away and, following Elsa, stumbled back to her seat.

The rest of the play passed in a daze of babbling voices. The moment the final curtain dropped Sonja jumped to her feet, pushed her way past the row of applauding people, and ran for the stairs. She arrived in the main foyer and paused, breathless, to adjust her glasses. After a moment she decided the stairs would offer the best vantage point. She stationed herself halfway up and waited.

The applause died away, the doors opened, the foyer filled with people queuing for their coats. Sonja kept her eyes glued to the main exit from the stalls. After a time the stream of people thinned. She grew desperate. She couldn't believe she had missed them.

Suddenly it struck her: they would have gone backstage!

Or would they?

Miserable with indecision, she waited a little longer then went to claim her coat. Elsa rushed up to her. "What on earth's wrong, Sonja? Are you ill?"

Sonja pulled on her coat and, shaking her head, mumbled, "I have to go . . ."

Leaving the startled Elsa, she hurried around the side of the theater to the stage door. A group of five or six young people were hovering outside. Sonja retreated across the road to the porch of the Continental Hotel and waited.

Five minutes passed, ten. Now and then the odd person emerged: backstage people, she thought.

It was cold. Her feet began to freeze. She glanced nervously around, aware that she must look conspicuous. Yet she couldn't bring herself to leave.

At last more people appeared, people with loud, well-modulated voices and animated faces. Sonja recognized a couple of the actors from the play.

Then *she* was there. Hildegard Lindman. Standing in the doorway, swathed in fur, head turned, waiting for as yet invisible friends. Sonja stared, immobile.

A couple joined Hildegard Lindman and they strolled out onto the pavement. Beautiful people, totally at ease with themselves and the world.

Then *him*. Smiling, coming forward, taking the actress's elbow with easy familiarity.

Erik. There was no doubt.

Sonja pulled back into the shadow of the building, grimacing with humiliation and pain.

The party of four made off briskly toward the bare trees and snow-covered gardens of Eidsvolls Plass, the sound of their high brittle laughter echoing on the air.

Sonja crossed the street and followed, keeping close to the side of the theater in case they should turn around.

The foursome passed the statue of Ibsen and headed diagonally across the area in front of the theater. Sonja hesitated at the corner of the building.

There was a shout. Erik's party paused. Sonja ducked behind the wall, her heart hammering against her chest. She peeped out. Two men had joined the foursome. There was a short animated conversation, then loud good-byes. The two men were waving and walking toward Sonja, leaving the others to resume their walk.

Suddenly one of the two men stopped and shouted back: "Hey, Hildegard!"

The actress turned. Her companions stopped.

"Will you be in Stockholm for Ingmar's first showing?"

She called back: "Yes! Will you be there?"

"We hope so! Bye. Bye, Rolf!

Erik raised his hand and waved.

Sonja stared, not understanding.

The party set off across the gardens. Sonja followed at a safe distance. They walked briskly, purposefully, crossing the street on the north side of the square and heading into a building. A bright blue sign read: BLOM'S.

Erik led the way, holding the door open for the others, then they were gone.

Sonja halted, suddenly feeling deflated. What now? She couldn't wait here.

But she couldn't bring herself to leave either. She found a bench under the leafless trees and sank onto it.

How could he?

But he could, very well indeed. That was what hurt the most. He must have been doing this all along. Telling her he was away while he was actually with women like Hildegard Lindman.

And she knew why, of course. Because the Hildegard Lindmans of this world were beautiful and polished and desirable, and wanted him in return.

She'd always known there must be other women. She'd always known he was too wonderful to be true. Well, here was the proof. She shouldn't be surprised; she shouldn't mind.

Why then did she mind so much? The pain was so great that she actually hurt inside.

Tears slipped down her cheeks. She didn't try to wipe them away.

She suddenly remembered the notes she'd written, the pathetic heart-rending little notes. What must he have thought of them? He'd probably found them childish and overdramatic. Had he torn them up? Her stomach gave a lurch of humiliation and pain.

Had he ever cared?

She didn't want the answer to that. Standing up abruptly, she wiped the tears roughly from her cheeks. It was her own fault. It served her right. She'd gotten her just desserts. She should have faced this all along.

Time to go home.

She walked a few steps, then hesitated. Something held her back, and she tried to think what it was.

But of course she knew: burning curiosity. A need to know. Jealousy. Agony.

She walked up to the café at the far end of the gardens, opposite the Storting. They were about to close, but allowed her in for a coffee. She sat in a corner where she could just see the entrance to Blom's. Twenty minutes later the café turned out its lights and she left.

She walked back past Blom's on the opposite side of the road. It was ridiculous to wait: It was already after midnight. Yet she'd come this far—somehow a long cold wait didn't seem to matter much either way.

She waited on the bench, her toes like ice, her body numb.

After a time a taxi drew up in front of Blom's. Some people emerged from the restaurant and got in.

It wasn't Erik and his friends. But that was what they'd do. Order a taxi. And she'd be left like a fool, watching it drive off.

But then she'd need a taxi at this time of night anyway. With a groan she realized what she should have done right at the beginning. How much money had she? About a hundred kroner, she thought. Enough—maybe.

Running breathlessly to a taxi stand by the theater, certain that Erik must have chosen this moment to leave, she jumped into a taxi and told the driver to park just short of Blom's. Then she waited, miserable in case she had missed Erik, trying not to hear the remorselessly expensive click of the meter.

Forty-five minutes later a taxi swished past them and pulled up in front of Blom's.

Some people emerged from the restaurant.

Them.

Sonja felt slightly sick.

The foursome paused on the pavement, kissing each other's cheeks, gripping arms.

Then they split into two couples.

Erik and Hildegard Lindman got into the taxi.

Sonja leaned forward, clutching the front seat. "Follow that taxi!"

The driver threw her a strange look, but started off without a word.

They threaded their way through the narrow streets in the center of town, heading north, then west. Every time they approached a junction Sonja's heart froze in case the lights should turn red just at the wrong moment. One light turned amber as they sped toward it, but the driver kept going. Sonja breathed: "Thank you."

The driver snorted: "One second longer and I'd have had to stop."

Sonja got her bearings. The Royal Palace was to the left; they were heading along the north side of the park. Erik's taxi had drawn slightly ahead. Sonja said anxiously: "Don't let him get too far away."

"He's speeding," the driver said virtuously. "I'm not going to risk my license, you know!"

Sonja's heart sank. The other taxi was getting farther and farther away. At the corner of the park it turned left then right again and she lost sight of it. Then, as they came around the right turn, it came into view again.

Suddenly it slowed and turned off into a side street. Sonja gripped the seat again. It seemed an age before they reached the turn.

They entered the street. The other cab was there in front of them, stopped by the curb. Its back door was open. Erik was already on the pavement.

Sonja's driver braked. She realized with horror that he was going to stop, right there behind Erik's cab. She cried in his ear: "Go on! Go on!"

He hesitated, then accelerated. As they pulled out to overtake the stationary cab, she realized that Erik's white face was turning toward them. For a moment she couldn't take her eyes off him, mesmerized as if by a snake. Then, just as his eyes were about to lock onto hers, her heart gave an almighty thump and she came to her senses. She jerked her head down and pushed a shaking hand over her face.

She could almost feel Erik's eyes drilling into the back of her head. When they were past she scrabbled for her glasses, which had fallen onto the floor, and, jamming them back on her nose, twisted to look out the back window. Erik was walking casually across the pavement, his arm around Hildegard Lindman.

Sonja's shoulders sagged weakly.

The driver stopped. She got out and told him to wait. He grumbled about it not being "policy" to wait.

She thought: I don't think I can stand an argument! Then she realized that he was worried about the money. She thrust all she had into his hand.

The place was a newish apartment building, three stories high, set a little way back from the road. Expensive, she guessed. This was a very nice area.

She approached cautiously. Lights suddenly blinked on in two of the first-floor windows and she drew back a little.

Finding a courage she didn't think she had, she went up the short pathway to the main door. There were six apartments, each with their own bells and illuminated name cards. She thrust her face closer. EVVIND VORREN; PROF. HERMANN DAHLBERG, KAREN DAHLBERG; ROLF BERG; E. NETTUM . . .

She pulled back, then read the list again.

There was no Erik Leif.

She looked up again. The lights on the second floor continued to blaze while the rest of the building was in almost complete darkness.

The second floor. If there was any logic to the list of names, then that must belong to either the second or third name. Professor Dahlberg and his wife. Or Rolf Berg.

ROLF BERG. She kept staring at the card, remembering the man outside the theater, the shouted conversation, the last good-bye.

Rolf. He had called out: *Rolf*.

And it had been Erik who had waved back.

12

It was six when he set out. The morning was pitch black with occasional snow and a strong gusty wind. The temperature was about minus ten. The sensible thing, Hal knew, would be to change his plans and take *Skorpa*. But he had worked until past midnight to finish the job and he was loath to give up now.

It was tricky launching the boat from its makeshift trolley on his own, and in the end he had to float it off, getting water over one of his boots in the process. He pulled the boat's nose up onto the beach while he raised the gaff. The mainsail flogged furiously, creating a deafening clamor which shook the boat as if to death. Anxious to be off and put an end to the din, Hal raised the jib and, pushing the nose out, got ready to shove off.

Then he remembered Bamse and called impatiently: "Come, boy!"

Eventually a low skulking form slid unhappily toward him. Hal laughed. "Coward!" Bamse was not fond of the sea and even less fond of small boats. Eventually Hal had to grab the trembling dog and pull him into the boat by the collar. "Coward," he repeated, laughing again.

Hal poised himself with one foot in the boat and one in the water then shoved off hard, deftly swinging his body on board as he did so. Now came the difficult bit. As the westerly wind carried the boat away from the shore, Hal took the rudder from where it lay in the bottom of the boat and, lifting it outboard, attempted to slide it into the gudgeons on the sternpost. As he felt beneath the water for the lower gudgeon, a gust swooped off the land and filled the sails with a low booming sound. The rigging strained and creaked, and the little boat careered off downwind. Hal pushed the rudder around by brute force and the boat came up into the wind again, sails shaking and rattling, pausing bewildered in her forward charge.

At last the rudder pintles went home and, grabbing the tiller with one hand and pulling his padded gloves on with the other, Hal settled on his seat, found his course, and pulled in the sheets.

The boat surged forward and flew headlong into the darkness, the water hissing along her hull. The wind came pouncing off the land in great gusts and then, almost as quickly, fell away again in sudden lulls. As each icy blast bowled down onto the boat, she heeled, shivered slightly, then, gathering herself up, surged forward like a wild thing. The wind was coming from the west, off the outer islands, so that here, close under the shore, the sea was flat and there was hardly a wave to check the boat's headlong race.

Hal clung on to the tiller in sheer exhilaration. From time to time he crowed or laughed aloud. Bamse, curled under the center thwart in a tight ball of consternation, gave an occasional low whine.

"You don't know what you're missing, you old devil," Hal cried. "You should come up here!"

Hal patted the boat's side, sliding his glove over the glassy smoothness of the varnish. What a creature! He'd bought her for almost nothing from a fisherman on one of the outer islands. She was an eighteen-foot gaff-rigged fishing smack, built at the turn of the century for cod fishing off the Lofoten Islands. She was made of pine and spruce, clinker-built so that her planks overlapped, and had the sweeping lines, the high stem and stern, and the low freeboard of a miniature Viking ship. She had lain neglected in a boat shed for at least fifteen years. Hal had had to replace part of the keelson, recaulk all the seams, find a new mast, and remake all the rigging. He had also made a new removable rudder so that the boat could be beached. The only thing he had not attempted was the sail-making, and a new set of tan canvas sails had come from an old sailmaker in the Lofotens.

He had named the boat *Lillebjørn*. Little bear.

A squall came through, heeling the boat until she quivered, as if in fear. Hal sat out on the gunwale to keep her steady. Sleet drove down, obscuring the shore lights on either side of the sound. Hal pulled his hood more tightly around his face, ignored his freezing hands and feet, and peered into the gloom ahead.

He became aware of Bamse scrabbling about in the bottom of the boat. Spilling some wind from the sail, he sat inboard again. Bamse's shadowy form clawed its way desperately toward the stern. Hal realized what the panic was. The bilges were awash with water. Hal chuckled: "Oh, you miserable old devil! What a life, eh!"

It was the seams. He should have left the boat filled with water for at least a week, so that her planks took up moisture and swelled and closed the seams tight. But he hadn't, which didn't matter too much in itself, except that he'd forgotten to bring a bailer. He shrugged the problem off: if necessary he'd use his hands.

"Sorry, Bamse, you're going to get wet."

It was more than twenty miles to Ragna's on the southern tip of Tromsø Island, but it seemed no time before the sound opened out to the south and he was almost halfway there. It had taken two hours, which meant the little boat had been doing a good five knots.

Sheer bliss. Hal had quite forgotten how it felt to be content and carefree. In the old days he'd known nothing else. What was it they said? Youth was wasted on the young.

Determined to keep his mood, he ignored the increasing sluggishness of the boat. But finally there was no getting away from the considerable quantity of water sloshing backward and forward inside the boat.

"Bamse, where's the bailer, hey? Why didn't you remind me?"

From his refuge in the stern the dog gave a whine. Eventually Hal pulled off a damp boot and used it to bail. After fifteen minutes' hard work he'd made some impression and, leaving three or four inches of water in the bottom, returned gratefully to the tiller.

Buoyant again, the boat rushed on happily. Hal listened to the sound of the waves slap-slapping against her bow, the water swishing noisily down her sides, the wake gurgling behind. Around them, the first gray light of dawn crept up, gradually diffusing the darkness so that the boat, the sea, gained form and space.

It was two hours later that Ragna's house finally came into view. Hal sat on the aft thwart, his feet like blocks of ice, his hand frozen to the tiller. A bedraggled Bamse shivered at his side, his wolflike face a picture of misery. Despite constant bailing the water was well over the thwarts and almost lapping at the gunwale. Hal reckoned they had five minutes at best. He patted Bamse's head. "That's called timing, hey?"

The boat moved forward like a barge, solid and stately and exceedingly low in the water.

Ragna's next-door neighbor appeared in front of his house and stared. Hal waved graciously. The man waved slowly and hesitantly back, then stood motionless, as if glued to the spot. Hal understood: the arrival was beginning to look rather interesting to him too.

A delicate maneuver could no longer be avoided—a jibe, which was always a little tricky at the best of times. Hal moved himself across the boat, hauled on the mainsheet, and thrust the tiller over. Filled with a sudden wild excitement, he yelled: "Here we go!"

The little boat turned, the wind crept behind the mainsail and, with an almighty whack, slammed the sail across to the other side. Hal ducked to avoid the boom as it whistled over, then thrust his weight out onto the gunwale to hold the boat upright as she began to heel over. But as he struggled to balance the boat a gust of wind defeated him and the lee gunwale dipped under.

The shore was not far away; Hal could see sharp waves breaking on the shingle. But any remaining doubts about the outcome of events vanished as the water rose to his knees. There wasn't a hope. Hal giggled and, overcome by a ridiculous euphoria, kept the boat going as she slowly and majestically sailed under.

"Time for a swim, Bamse!" he shouted as the water—almost warm after the icy wind—rose rapidly to his chest.

Bamse, his nose high out of the water, was already striking

out for the shore. Hal attempted to swim the boat in, but she slowly capsized and lay dead and heavy in the water. Paddling around to the bow he got hold of the anchor warp and, with one end in his hand, swam to the shore.

"And what on earth do you think you're doing!" It was Ragna, hands on hips, looking very cross and very lovely.

Hal waded out of the water, like a dripping rat, and grinned. "Well, I thought I was having a sail!"

"You're mad! What's *this*, this—*thing*?" She jabbed a finger at the wallowing hull.

Hal began hauling the boat toward the shore. "It's a Lofoten fishing smack from the turn of the century—"

"No, I mean, what are you doing with it?"

"Well, I was going very fast."

Ragna sighed impatiently. "Really! You might have had more consideration. You've upset the whole of my morning! I only just got your message. Why didn't you call me yourself? As it is I've had to hang about and let Sigrid take Krisi to kindergarten and—"

Hal felt a keen disappointment. "Kris isn't here?"

"No, of course not!" she cried indignantly. "Really, Hal, sometimes!"

Hal smiled amiably. His spirits were too high to be quashed easily. Today he found her anger a distinct challenge.

"Well, if it's not convenient I shall call again another day. Good-bye," he said solemnly, adding in deep theatrical tones: "Back into the maelstrom!" He turned and walked back into the water, wading past the capsized boat until the sea was up to his shoulders.

"Come back!" Ragna screamed. "You're crazy!"

Hal continued until the water lapped his chin and the waves buffeted his head. This time it felt a lot colder. Just as he was beginning to think it wasn't such a good idea after all, he heard a loud shriek from the shore and turned to see Ragna hugging herself with laughter, staggering idiotically from side to side.

He thought triumphantly: Got you!

He prolonged the performance a little longer, standing upright and straight-faced as the waves broke over his head, until a large wave knocked him off his feet and he had to swim for it. She was still laughing as he righted the boat and beached it. She helped him bail it out and pull it up onto the shingle.

Seeing his chattering teeth and white skin, she declared: "Well, you'd better come and have a hot bath."

"Please—" Hal held up his dripping hands in mock politeness. "Don't feel under any obligation!"

"Ha!" She glared at him. "You might get pneumonia and then you'd be a real nuisance."

"You've such a kind heart!" They began to walk up to the house. Ragna snorted. "Kinder than you deserve."

Her mood, though abrasive, was improving. He gave her a sidelong glance, but she was looking thoughtfully ahead, a frown on her face.

"Look," she said abruptly. "I really do have lots to do today. I should be in town already."

"Of course. I've things to do myself. But first I'll have to borrow some clothes. You wouldn't have a little number in my size, would you?"

She said archly: "What did you have in mind?"

"Oh, one of those shapeless outfits will do. The ones like a sack with four slits in it that you sell for a fortune."

She ground to a halt, looking cross again. "You *are* in a funny mood today. What's the matter?"

"The matter?"

"All this smiling and joking. It's not like you."

Hal absorbed that one. She was right of course: he didn't find a lot to laugh about normally. "Well, I'm feeling rather happy today, that's all. Just came over me." His teeth clattered like castanets. He began to move off toward the house again.

But Ragna stood her ground. "What's happened?" she demanded.

Hal suddenly felt very sure of himself. "Happened? I sail miles in a sinking boat, almost drown, get sent back to the sea—all to visit you. And you ask me what happened?"

His tone, he suddenly realized, was breaking new ground: he was flirting with her, something that had never somehow been appropriate before.

She eyed him coolly and said in a flat voice: "I'll find some of Jan's old clothes for you."

Hal flinched inwardly and looked away. He thought: Ah, I got that message all right. It'd been as clear as a slap in the face. He turned and strode up to the house, his good humor evaporated.

He bathed quickly, rinsed out his salty clothes and wrung them hard. Opening the bathroom door he found some clothes neatly folded on the floor outside.

Jan's. He reached for them, an odd constricting sensation in his throat.

When he got downstairs Ragna was standing by the front door, coat on and keys in hand.

She pointed to the hall table. There was a large parceled box on it. She said levelly: "I'd forgotten—that's been sitting in a cupboard for ages. They sent it some time ago. The army, I mean." Her eyes slid to the parcel, then back to his. "Jan's things. Could you deal with them?"

She went out, calling over her shoulder: "Get rid of it all, will you?"

Ragna struggled into the house with two heavy bags of groceries. She called "Hey-ho," but there was no reply.

She dumped the groceries in the kitchen and went through into the living room. It was empty, but the coffee table was littered with sheets of paper and colored pencils. She bent over the table and looked at a large picture of a farmhouse in a valley surrounded by mountains, shaggy black-haired animals, and flowers. No prizes for guessing where that was.

She went to the window. There they were, in the very place she'd known they'd be. By the boat. She watched them for a moment, the man and the boy and the dog, huddled together in the twilight as thick as thieves.

She went outside and shouted: "Anyone hungry?"

They looked up, conferred with each other, and a faint "Yes!" floated across the air.

She prepared a hot meal of salmon and potatoes, with cheese and fresh green apples to follow. Krisi rushed in first, noisy, red-cheeked, and overflowing with excitement.

"Have you seen *Lillebjørn*, Mamma? Have you seen my boat?"

"Your boat?"

"Yes, *my* boat! My boat!"

Hal came in and, passing behind Krisi's chair, ruffled the boy's hair affectionately. She noticed that he was wearing his own clothes again.

"Ah! Before I forget!" His voice was bright—he was back in that extraordinary sunny mood of his. He came up to Ragna and she felt a moment's surprise as he took her by the shoulders and looked into her eyes. "We have an urgent request, Kris and I. A matter of great importance." His tone was ironic, his look roguish and amused. She thought: My God, you can be charming if you try!

Krisi was giggling furiously. "Of course," she said, rather looking forward to whatever he was about to say. "What is it?"

He narrowed his eyes. "It's my feet. They'd stay a lot drier if you could find me a bailer."

Krisi rolled off his chair, helpless with laughter. Hal smiled that quiet smile of his. Ragna sucked in a long breath before managing a pale smile. Her sense of humor was not in good shape today. "I'll see what I can find."

Recovering, Krisi jumped to his feet. "And Mamma, can we go to Brattdal on Saturday? *Please, please.* You promised. *Please.*"

Ragna made an indecisive face. They'd last been in the summer, in June, and Krisi had been badgering her ever since.

"One day soon, darling," she said vaguely, putting the food on the table.

"But I want to see the *mo'kusokse* again," Krisi whined.

Smiling at the mispronunciation, she said: "The musk-oxen won't go away, Krisi."

Hal said quietly: "I could come and pick up Kris on Saturday and have him back by six on Sunday. How about that?"

Ragna was taken aback. Hal had always asked the two of them before. Immediately she thought: It's that woman—she's changed everything.

She frowned at him. "I don't know. I'll think about it."

Hal and Krisi exchanged conspiratorial looks, and Ragna sighed audibly.

They ate in silence.

Then Ragna said: "I had a letter from Fred. He wants you to lead his expedition."

Hal made a face of affectionate exasperation. "They won't have any luck. I do wish they'd stop trying."

"He seemed to think I'd be able to persuade you. He wrote pages and pages."

He examined her face. "I'm sorry he bothered you. I'll write and tell him I'm definitely not interested." He added, almost to himself: "Although it might do me some good."

Ragna stared at him. His capacity to surprise her seemed limitless today. "Ah, so you might be tempted after all!" she said, hating the waspishness in her voice.

"Ragna—you're the one who's always telling me that I'm cut off at Brattdal."

Ragna opened her mouth to contradict him, but thought better of it. Standing up, she cleared the dishes away. "Well, you are, aren't you?" she said defensively.

There was a pause. Hal asked quietly: "What do you think? Should I consider going with Fred?"

"Don't ask me!" she said sharply. "What you do with your life is no affair of mine!"

The muscles in Hal's cheeks worked furiously, a sign she had learned to recognize. She thought wearily: Now I've gone and made him angry.

Hal said suddenly: "I must be going."

"Don't go!" wailed Kris. "Please don't go, Uncle Hal! Please don't go!"

"It's already dark, Krisi, and I have a long way to go."

Hal took him by the shoulders and, leaning forward, whispered in his ear. The child nodded violently and scampered off in the direction of the living room. "He's gone to finish his picture of Brattdal," Hal explained. "We need to have a quick talk." His voice was cool and his eyes had regained all their usual seriousness. "You never told me how your trip went."

She gave him a brief account of the journey to the plateau and what little she had learned about the migration route.

He listened, then said: "I should tell you that Major Thrane came to see me. You remember . . . ?"

She remembered him all right. Cool, clever, too smart by half: she hadn't liked him at all.

"He came to warn me off."

Ragna stared at him in amazement. "What do you mean?"

"He came to warn me off the Kåfjord protest."

"What a cheek!"

"He said I'd ruin my good name." Hal gave a short derisory laugh. "I told him I wasn't too bothered."

"Good Lord! What a nerve!" Ragna felt her blood pressure rising. "That's typical—thinking they can push you around."

"But Ragna, he did come as a friend. He thought he was doing me a favor."

"Huh!" Hal always put great store by friendship, as if friends could never let you down.

"He was quite curious to know where the information had come from. He seemed to think we must have fallen into bad company."

"He would."

"I told him I didn't know where the information was coming from."

"Which was the truth."

"Yes, but . . ." Hal was wearing his responsible expression, the one he kept for admonishing people. "Ragna, it's wrong—not knowing."

"I've told you, it's all aboveboard," she said emphatically. "Nothing illegal or sinister. I promise." It was best Hal didn't know about the Friends for Peace or one of its founder-members, an old acquaintance of hers who regularly phoned with little snippets of information. By any standards the group was left-wing, and she knew Hal wouldn't be very happy about that.

She said: "You're not going to take any notice, are you? Of Thrane's warning."

He gave her a thoughtful look. "No."

She smiled, suddenly pleased with him. "Good!"

He got to his feet, preparing to leave. "But what about this journalist you saw? Why wasn't he any good? Didn't he think it was a good enough story?"

"He thought it was 'too sensitive.' Ha! No guts!" To her mind, lack of guts was the worst sin of all. "But I'm sure Rolf Berg will be a better bet. By the way, I said in my letter to him that you were involved in the protest and would be—well—happy to give him an interview. I hope that was all right." She added: "Or is he an untouchable, like all the rest?"

She could have bitten her tongue off: a flicker of pain crossed his face. He was remembering the savaging some of the newspapers had given him three years before.

He said quietly: "No, of course I'll talk to Rolf. If he thinks it'll do some good." He was out of the room before she could soften the moment.

Her shoulders sagged; she had been unkind. In fact, she didn't like herself very much today.

They tramped down to the beach in the dim light, Hal with the bucket she had given him for a bailer, Krisi and Bamse dancing ahead amid whoops and shouts of joy.

"What about the Land-Rover?" Ragna asked.

"I'll pick it up sometime this weekend. Have you thought about Saturday?"

Ragna frowned. "Krisi's awfully young to go away. . . . And the weather . . ."

He exhaled harshly. "I'd look after him, you know that."

She didn't want Krisi to go away, and she wasn't quite sure why. "Well . . ."

"It'd give you a break," said Hal. "A chance to be on your own."

She thought: But I don't want to be on my own!

Suddenly she remembered the woman. "Will there be anyone else there?" she demanded.

"Only Arne." There was surprise in his voice.

"Ah. No—friends?"

He looked at her sharply. There was a long silence. She thought: So it's true!

He said finally: "No friends, Ragna. Just Kris and me."

He rigged the boat, carefully explaining the name and job of each rope to Kris. The child nodded furiously, as if memorizing every word. Ragna watched, feeling sad, though she wasn't sure why.

When the boat was ready they all helped push it into the water. Hal stowed something carefully under a seat. Ragna recognized the beastly army parcel.

Hal gave Ragna a firm impersonal kiss on the cheek, then swept Krisi up into his arms. The boy laughed as Hal held him high in the air. The two figures were etched black against the last of the glimmering light, a shadow play framed by the wide sweep of sky and mountains. Something about the scene made Ragna's heart give a curious twist.

The two silhouettes merged as the child sank gently into the man's arms and embraced him.

Ragna heard herself call: "Come on, you two!"

She and Krisi stood for a long time watching the boat sail clear of the land. After a while the little vessel tacked into a silver pool of reflected light. The sails, the man and dog in the stern, were ink-black against the pewter sea. The boat seemed to glide over the darkly glittering water, as if drawn by magic.

The boat passed through the pool of light and merged into the darkness.

Hal cut the cords that bound the parcel and took a deep breath.

He hadn't realized there'd be more.

Jan's personal belongings had been recovered from the Porsangmoen camp at the time of the incident. Following orders, Jan had left them there before setting out. A wallet, photographs of Ragna and Krisi, some money, a pocket diary with names and addresses.

Then there was the stuff they'd discovered at the camp by the lake. The hidden snow hole hadn't taken long to find—Hal had guessed where to look—and there they had found food, spare ammunition, and signs of a meal hastily abandoned.

It had never occurred to him that there'd be more.

He drew a deep breath and opened the outer packaging. Inside was a heavy cardboard box. He opened the lid.

A thick brown envelope lay on top. It was sealed. He slit it open. From deep within came the gleam of gold. He slid the contents into his hand.

A gold chain with a cross on it. A gold wedding ring.

He stared. This must have come back with the body. Why hadn't he known? Why hadn't they told him? But then he remembered: They had told Ragna.

He cradled the jewelry in his hand, a tightness in his throat.

Eventually he replaced it in the envelope and put it to one side. It would go to Kris when he was older.

Next there was a knife, the one Jan had always carried, a

Lapp knife, curved, with a distinctively carved horn sheath and a handle bound in leather. Jan had always kept it razor-sharp. He'd been able to skin and gut a hare in thirty seconds flat.

The knife, too, would go to Kris.

He saw to his surprise that there was another knife in the box. Hal picked it up curiously. He recognized the type—he'd seen dozens like it before. It was a dagger knife, straight and long with crossarms and a leather sheath designed to lace onto a belt. Even before he saw the swastika emblem stamped on the grip, he knew it was a standard German Army–issue dagger from the war.

Determined not to be caught unarmed or unprepared again, half the men in Norway had mementoes from the German surrender: daggers, pistols, rifles—even the occasional machine gun.

Yet Hal couldn't remember Jan having one.

He put it down on the floor and returned to the box.

Binoculars. Small lightweight ones with Polaroid filters for Alpine use. He knew them all right. He and Jan had each been presented with a pair by the manufacturers—ironically, a German company.

These joined the items to be kept for Krisi.

There was a pouch. Hal had last seen this at the final briefing at Porsangmoen. Then it had contained bank notes, he remembered. Norwegian kroner and Finnish marks. Not very many, just enough to buy food or transport if necessary.

The pouch was empty. That would be Thrane's lot, reclaiming their government-issue cash.

The Russians had kept the rifles and guns, he supposed, and they would have taken the maps, too, as so-called evidence. The clothing would probably have been destroyed.

Even as he thought it, he spotted a handkerchief, a pair of gloves. Good God, why had they put those in? He gulped awkwardly.

He reached hastily into the box for the last item and brought out a case containing another pair of binoculars.

He glanced over them but suddenly didn't have the stomach for any more. Getting hastily to his feet, he went outside for some fresh air. He stayed on the veranda for some time, staring into the distance.

When he returned he put the jewelry in a fresh envelope, wrote Kris's name on it and placed it in a drawer of the old rolltop desk, along with the hunting knife and the snow binoculars.

After some thought he added the gloves and handkerchief, although he wasn't sure they were the right sort of thing to pass on.

That left the dagger knife and the second set of binoculars.

He examined the binoculars. Zeiss 20 × 30's. Covered in flaking white paint, as though they had been adapted for military use.

Yes: There was a tiny swastika stamped on the body. And an engraved name: Schirmer. And some scratchings alongside: numbers and letters.

Perhaps the things had belonged to Mattis. But if so, Hal was sure he would have remembered seeing them.

He sat by the flickering light of the stove and let thoughts turn freely in his mind.

Some people might like to carry two knives, but why should anyone want to carry two sets of binoculars?

The explanation was probably obvious and mundane, yet he was curious.

He returned to his desk and wrote a letter to Mattis's family.

And just in case they couldn't help him, and because he never liked to leave any stone unturned, he also wrote a letter to Olso, to someone he knew at the Military Archives.

13

Berg carefully negotiated the doors of the *Sosialist Dagens Post* and made his way gently across the marble hallway. The elevator door was just closing. He thrust a shoulder in, the door jerked open, and he stepped inside.

A woman's voice said: "Morning."

Berg recognized a girl from the advertising department.

"You look terrible," the girl said, suppressing a giggle.

Berg narrowed his lips and turned away.

As soon as he reached the editorial floor he went to the men's room and stared at himself in the mirror. Eyes a bit red, a touch of puffiness underneath, skin a little mottled. But he still looked all right. Sour grapes on the girl's part.

But he should have gone easier on the wine. Judging by the ache in his head it must have been second-rate. He should have stuck to vodka or Scotch: You never went wrong with them.

He stood back and smoothed his hair and straightened his lapels. The problem was overtiredness and overwork. Nothing a good holiday wouldn't cure.

But the headache needed immediate attention. He fished in his pockets for an aspirin and, failing to find one, went across the floor to Ingrid, who always had a supply. Ingrid defended the editor from unwanted callers.

"Meeting in half an hour," Ingrid said, handing him the aspirin. "You don't look well," she added with a knowing look.

He made a face.

She wagged a finger at him. "You burn the candle at both ends."

He raised a tolerant eyebrow. "Is there any other way?"

She retorted: "Not for you, apparently!"

Taking a strong coffee from the machine, Berg wove his way through the modern furniture and tropical plants of the open-plan office to his desk in a far corner. With one foot he pushed a weeping fig across to hide the front of his desk—he didn't want social calls—and, washing the aspirin down with coffee, stared unenthusiastically at the mound of paper sitting in his in-tray.

The two prices of success: a hangover and a lot of mail.

Since he'd gotten his own by-line the mail had been coming in steadily. People holding strong opinions—and, this being Norway, there were plenty of them—seemed to feel it was their duty to express themselves at length. Most of it went straight to the editor of the correspondence page, but Berg couldn't afford not to glance through it first, just in case there was a tip-off.

The first mail had come with Pasvik, the next with the U-2 incident. Berg had nearly resigned over the U-2 story. The day after the Russians had announced the capture of Gary Powers, he had written a strong piece suggesting that the U.S. had been operating spy flights from their Norwegian bases for some considerable time, and without Norway's knowledge. The editor had been hysterical about publishing it, but when Berg had threatened to walk out, he'd run the story, though watered down.

Putting the mail off a little longer, Berg phoned his message service. Though message service was rather a grand title: it was in fact a grubby tobacconist's shop run by an Estonian. But appearances didn't matter: the Estonian had never met Berg, nor did he know Berg's real name, and only two people used the service—Alex and Sonja.

The Estonian answered almost immediately and Berg announced himself as Lundquist. The Estonian read out the latest message from Sonja.

Berg rang off with a sigh of irritation. Yet more family dramas. Why on earth Sonja wanted to saddle him with all this he couldn't imagine: he'd never even met her mother.

And a *holiday*. He pictured Sonja lying on a beach, large and whalelike, and gave a small snort of incredulity. An evening with Sonja was survivable, but a week would be a prison sentence.

He'd have to be careful about wriggling out of it though. Sonja was bound to be emotional at the moment. And emotion was one thing he couldn't cope with.

He'd have to phone her sometime, though. Tomorrow. Yes, if he had the time.

Lighting a cigarette, he drew on it deeply and, as the coffee and aspirin took effect, began to feel better.

Supported by a second coffee, Berg finally reached for the mail.

He opened envelopes steadily, glanced over the contents, and chucked them to one side. The usual stuff.

One letter made him pause. It was typewritten but headed with a handwritten *Dear Rolf* in a round feminine style. There was a Tromsø address. The letter was long and he had to flick through three pages to find the signature.

He felt an uncomfortable little twinge. Ragna Johansen.

What on earth could she want?

He stared at the name for a moment then went to the beginning and started to read.

It quickly dawned on him that she wanted a favor. He was vaguely flattered, yet also defensive. He didn't like having to put himself out.

But by the second page his natural skepticism had been overtaken by curiosity.

Kaafjord.

He read on then went back to the second page and reread it twice.

Kaafjord. Yes, he knew about that. Sonja had mentioned it when she'd been talking about security at installations and how new ones were to get extra protection. New ones like Kåfjord, she'd said.

She hadn't told him much about the installation itself or what its function would be, and he hadn't pressed her. He never did. With Sonja patience was the key.

She'd tell him eventually. She always did.

A number of secret installations had appeared in Norway in the last few years, and they generally fell into three categories: early-warning radar installations, NATO communications systems, or, most recently of all, a new navigation system for submarines.

This last category interested Berg most of all because the navigation system—Loran-C—didn't guide just any old submarines but Polaris subs carrying nuclear weapons. Norway being a nonnuclear nation, this was by any standards highly provocative stuff.

Now, if Kåfjord was anything to do with that . . .

But of course Ragna Johansen didn't know.

Ragna Johansen was interested in Kåfjord for a quite different reason. The Lapps.

Berg weighed the possibilities. Would it make a good story as it was? His instincts told him yes, though the Lapp issue was always a difficult one.

Mention of the Lapps brought out all sorts of guilts and neuroses in the Norwegian public. Quick to condemn racism abroad, Berg noted that his countrymen were considerably less vocal on matters close to home. This was because they'd persuaded themselves that the Lapps were well treated. The truth was somewhat less comfortable. Frequently regarded as inferior, primitive, and a little crazy, the Lapps had had a raw deal for a long time.

Nevertheless, when it came to protecting the Lapps against a U.S.-built and -financed installation, public opinion might well rally round. The underdog versus the American goliath. It might just work.

And then Berg could take a stab at the real target.

Who controls these installations? (The U.S.) *Who benefits from them?* (The U.S.) *How will they help Norway?* (They won't: They'll merely provoke the Soviet Union and intensify the cold war.)

Yes: the story had potential.

But he'd have to know what the installation was for.

That meant seeing Sonja sooner rather than later, which was a nuisance.

Glancing up, he saw Ingrid gesturing him toward the editor's office. Lighting another cigarette and searching half-heartedly around his desk for a pencil and notebook, he followed the rest of the staff into the meeting.

The editor, a nervous thin-faced sixty-year-old on the

wrong side of a heart attack, gestured Berg in and said immediately: "Something's come up that might interest you."

Berg sat down. "Oh?"

"A whisper. About an item that's about to appear in a British left-wing magazine—the *Examiner*. About Pasvik."

Berg's heart missed a small beat.

"Apparently a KGB man has defected to the British and told all. Including information about the third man at Pasvik."

Berg's stomach did a leap. He kept his face in a mask of passivity.

"Apparently the third man got as far as the border—might even have met Johansen and Hetta—but was shot also. And— listen to this—the report says this third man was a Norwegian, and that he'd been living in the USSR since the war."

There was a silence. Everyone looked at Berg. He raised his eyebrows. "Is the third man's identity known?"

"Er—no. It isn't."

Berg hid his relief behind a frown. "Is that all?"

The editor shuffled through the papers on his desk. "I think so." He reread his notes hurriedly. "Ah, wait . . ."

Berg drew on his cigarette, holding an expression of professional interest.

"Wait . . ."—the editor stumbled—"got it wrong. The defector to the British was a *GRU* man, not KGB."

If that was all . . . Berg breathed again and forced himself to think calmly. There really was nothing to worry about.

The editor looked at him. "So, what do you think?"

Berg thought quickly. There were so many different ways to play this. Eventually he said: "Well, it brings up all the same old questions that were never properly answered at the time of Pasvik, doesn't it? Like the extent of the CIA's involvement. And who planned the mission to the border. More to the point, it reveals an attempted cover-up, doesn't it? That idea put about by the government that the purpose of the mission was to meet a Soviet refugee." He gave a derisory laugh. "That's obviously nonsense. If this man was a Norwegian, then he must have been a full-fledged CIA agent all along."

The editor looked unhappy. "But this story's unsubstantiated. We can't get into the realms of—conjecture."

Conjecture. Berg liked that. "But this story's going to get

picked up all over the place. All the foreign press'll run it. We can't just ignore it."

The editor looked undecided. "Well . . ."

Berg was about to try a slightly different angle when someone said: "Aren't we missing something here?" It was the political editor. "Isn't there a story in how a Norwegian came to be living in the Soviet Union? I mean, I'd like to know how many arrived there at the end of the war. And, more to the point, how many might still be there against their will. Imprisoned, or whatever."

Another voice chimed in and Berg recognized a young staff reporter. "If you take it one step further, you wonder how many went to the Soviet Union and came back to Norway as model citizens, but with their loyalties ever so slightly adjusted."

Berg drew calmly on his cigarette. Somewhere deep inside he had a dreadful urge to laugh.

The editor was looking daggers at the young man who, because he was standing in for an absent superior, obviously wasn't fully familiar with editorial policy. Policy was never to be unpatriotic. Critical of government, yes. And, after centuries of domination by Denmark and Sweden, critical of foreign (which nowadays meant U.S.) influences, but this sort of suggestion smacked of stabbing oneself in the back.

The editor said icily: "We can't go off on wild tangents when we have no real facts. No, we'll keep this as a straight news piece. And short at that."

Berg wouldn't argue with that, he decided.

But the editor hadn't finished. He tapped his pencil thoughtfully on the desk. "Berg—you might just look into the idea of Norwegians kept in the Soviet Union against their will sometime. No hurry. That lawyer Sorensen—the one with all the stuff on collaborators and war criminals—he might be able to shed some light."

Berg looked doubtful, then, with a small dismissive shrug, nodded an okay. Better that he should do it than someone else. Far better.

The meeting moved on. Ideas came and went. When it was Berg's turn he put forward the Kaafjord story, carefully couching it in attractive nonalarmist terms—land rights, the future of reindeer herding as a whole, bureaucratic insensitivity.

When he'd finished the editor considered for several moments. Then, blowing out his cheeks, he slowly nodded.

Berg had gotten his story.

"Good morning."

Sonja looked up from her desk with such a start that her glasses slipped down her nose. It was Major Thrane. She hadn't heard him come in. He must have entered through the Director's office. She realized she was looking foolish, her mouth open, her glasses askew. She straightened her glasses and attempted a smile.

"I'm so sorry about your mother," Thrane said.

She put on a brave expression. "Sometimes these things are for the best." She added more brightly: "Have a good trip north?"

"Yes, thanks." He hovered, watching her carefully.

"Anything I can do for you?" she asked.

He pulled up a chair and sat beside the desk, leaning thoughtfully on his elbow. "I wanted your advice."

"Of course." Major Thrane was number two to the head of Security, a post he'd taken up three years before. He was one of the few people who were allowed unlimited access to information.

"We had a few chats during the security review, didn't we?"

Sonja was very still. She didn't want to talk about the review, she didn't want to talk about anything. She could hardly deal with the simplest things. Her mind had almost ground to a halt.

She managed: "Yes."

"Do you remember all the things we discussed? About new procedures?"

"Er . . . yes."

"Well, how do you think we're doing? Have we done enough?"

What was he getting at? She thought of the photocopier and felt rather cold until she remembered that he couldn't possibly know about that.

She said abruptly: "I would have thought so, but then I'm no expert."

Surprise flickered across Thrane's face. She realized her voice had sounded shrill and edgy. She thought: Get a hold, get a hold!

His expression changed to one of understanding, as if he'd momentarily forgotten the strain her mother's death must have put her under. He said pleasantly: "Well, you're not an expert maybe, but—well, you know better than anybody how things work around here."

She tried to summon up some interest in the subject. "Let me see . . . I think the regular screening's a good idea. And the more restricted access to information."

He nodded sagely. "We're thinking about more comprehensive screening for top personnel."

She thought: Why are you telling me all this? She moved some papers around her desk. "It can't do any harm."

"Mmm . . ." He pondered for a while. "Trouble is, it takes time and a great deal of money. And it may cause bad feeling." There was a pause. She looked up to find him staring at her. "I mean, how would you feel about having your life put under a microscope?"

"It would be a nuisance, I suppose. But I could hardly object."

Thrane did not reply, but rubbed his fingers slowly over his chin. Then, smiling abruptly, he got to his feet. "Well, thank you. You've been most helpful."

Sonja nodded a faint good-bye, and he was gone.

For several minutes she stared at the closed door, a dreadful aching feeling in the pit of her stomach.

What had all that been about? Did he know something?

The next moment she got a grip on herself. She was imagining things. Major Thrane often wandered about. He frequently dropped in on people and asked questions. It meant nothing.

She sat back, feeling weak, and rested her head on the back of her chair.

The buzzer sounded. She jumped again.

The Director. Ready for his meeting. She hurriedly patted her hair, picked up her pad, and went into his office.

It was a long departmental meeting. She surprised herself by managing quite normally. She took the minutes, typed them, and went to the photocopier in the secretarial office next to her own. Ten copies were needed.

She turned the dial to ten, put in the first page, and pressed the start button. The copies churned out. The machine fell silent.

She stared at the copier. One of the secretaries walked past her on the way to lunch. Then the office was empty.

Sonja swallowed nervously. She examined the first copy, decided it wasn't good enough, and, resetting the quantity dial to one, pressed the start button again. The extra copy came out.

She hesitated, not wanting to pick it up. Why was she doing this? There was no reason to, not anymore.

And yet . . . she wanted to keep the upper hand. She wanted to keep her bargaining power.

She wanted *him*.

The thought made her want to cry.

She decided: One last time. She'd do it just one last time.

She repeated the process for the second and third pages of the minutes. In each instance she examined the first copy, decided it wasn't good enough, and made an extra one.

She picked up the copies and the originals, collated and stapled them, entered the document and file number in the photocopy ledger along with the number of copies—she was careful to put down the correct number, which was three times eleven—and signed it.

Then she slipped three blank sheets of photocopying paper behind the sheaf of minutes.

Going to the shredder, she turned it on and carefully fed the three blank sheets into its jaws.

She made a neat entry in the destruction ledger: three substandard photocopies. And she added the document number and her signature.

Returning to her desk, she marked eight copies of the minutes for distribution and retained two plus the original for the files. The extra copy she slipped into her handbag.

Finally she took her shorthand notes to the shredder. Before feeding them in she read through them one last time, just to make sure she had missed nothing.

But no, she had understood it all perfectly. Every detail of Project Bluetail: the building of a new intelligence-gathering installation in the north.

Back at her desk, she got out her sandwiches and put them on the desk in front of her. She didn't eat. Instead she waited until the Director buzzed through to tell her he was going to lunch.

She gave it another minute then reached for the phone. First she called Anna, her opposite number in FO/S.

Anna was expecting her call. "I had a look at the file for you," she said immediately.

"I hope it was no problem."

"No! Like I said yesterday, he left us—let me see—six months ago. He's a security adviser for the railways now. I can tell you that all right. But why are you asking me, Sonja? I thought you knew him. You asked me about him before, didn't you?"

"Yes," Sonja said lightly. She'd rehearsed this bit. "I was just curious because he was talking so freely about 'work' and I thought for an awful moment he was still with you."

"No, no. He's not with us anymore," Anna said emphatically. "Besides, he was always a great one for security. Always went by the rules."

"You knew him well, then?"

"Well, a little. He was very quiet. I can't say I ever exchanged more than a few words with him."

"Oh? He seemed quite—outgoing—to me."

"Goodness, I must have missed something, then. He seemed mouselike to me. He was good at his job, such as it was. But he was never going to go far. That's why he left."

Sonja made herself laugh. "We have got the same man, haven't we, Anna?"

The other woman didn't laugh. Sonja realized she'd overdone it: one didn't joke about identities in the security services. Anna said: "Aged just over thirty, married, three children. Fair hair, six-two, round face, glasses, a bit thick around the middle. Bookish, a bit puritanical, I'd say; nondrinker, nonsmoker. How'm I doing?"

"Oh, that's Erik all right," Sonja lied. "Thanks, Anna."

The sick feeling returned to Sonja's stomach with a vengeance.

Trembling, she pulled open a drawer and took out a newspaper. She leafed through it until she came to an article on a center page.

The article was written by the owner of the second-floor apartment, the journalist named Rolf Berg.

She picked up the phone again and dialed the number she'd written on her jotter pad.

The number rang.

"Dagens Post," said a voice.

Sonja gripped the receiver more tightly. "Rolf Berg."

A pause, a click, background noise. The blood pounded around Sonja's head.

A *female* voice. "News."

"I wanted to speak to Rolf Berg."

"He's not around at the moment, I'm afraid. I'll just check. . . . No. Can't see him. Is there a message?"

"No, I—"

"Hang on! Hang on!" the female voice called. "He's just coming."

There was a clatter as the receiver was put down, the sound of voices, then—

"Berg."

Sonja held on tight, feeling weak.

"Hello? Hello?" A sigh of annoyance, then an aside: "There's no one here. Who was it, do you know?" A pause and a bored: "Hello . . . hello . . . hello."

Slowly, Sonja put the receiver back in its cradle. She'd heard enough.

It was him.

Shakily she got to her feet and went to the ladies' room. She doused her face with cold water, and again and again.

Finally she looked up into the mirror.

A reporter. All this time, a reporter.

And she'd told him everything.

A final door closed, a last set of high heels tapped down the corridor, and there was silence. Thrane waited a little longer, then strolled out of his office.

It was four-thirty in the afternoon—the Norwegian working day finished at four. The evening staff would already be on duty in the first-floor duty room. His own security men would have started their rounds. Apart from that, the building should be empty.

He locked his door and went toward the Director's offices. He stopped at the door of Sonja Bjornsen's office and knocked. After a moment he took a bunch of keys from his pocket and, finding the correct one, unlocked the door and went in.

Her desk was neat and tidy, with no papers on it. He checked the drawers, just in case, but there was nothing.

The files in daily use were kept in a special strong room to one side. He had collected the keys earlier, and now opened the door. He found the file he wanted, marked IG-FR 61: PROJECT BLUETAIL.

The minutes of the meeting held that morning had been filed in their correct place, on top. Thrane glanced through the three typewritten pages, then took careful note of the entry on the top of the document. This showed the number of copies that existed, and where they had gone. One plus ten: three in the files, eight distributed. Thrane noted the document number and, replacing the file, went through to the secretarial office next to Sonja Bjornsen's and looked at the photocopy ledger. He felt a moment of excitement. *Eleven* copies of each page! He checked the other photocopy entries for the day. Sixty-two in addition to Sonja's thirty-three. A total of ninety-five.

Kneeling, he unfastened the side of the photocopier and peered at the small meter inside. He compared its reading with the one from the day before and did the mental arithmetic.

Ninety-five. It tallied.

Next, he went to the shredder and examined the ledger there.

There was the entry: three spoiled photocopies. But had she really put them through? He opened the sack of shredded paper waiting for disposal, and taking an ultraviolet penlight from his pocket, shone it into the sack.

Several shreds of paper glowed back at him. He checked the ledger to see if any other spoiled photocopies had been shredded that day.

No. So the photocopying paper, which had been marked with ultraviolet-sensitive ink, must have been put through by Sonja.

He felt a pang of disappointment. He'd had such a strong instinct about this one.

He spent two hours checking that every copy made by the photocopier that day had gone to its proper destination. Then he returned to his office, puzzled but not defeated.

He would just have to put some extra thought into it. There had to be an explanation for the fact that five times in the last four months extra copies had been made on that machine. Extra copies that had been entered as spoiled copies and shredded.

In every case they had been signed for by Sonja Bjornsen.

14

The office of Lars Sorensen was a model of Scandinavian order and cleanliness: white walls, modern tubular furniture, and gleaming filing cabinets. Berg guessed no papers stayed unfiled in this place for long.

"So this is a general piece you're writing?" Sorensen asked. He was a thin-faced, sandy-haired man of about sixty, bounding with youthful energy, sharp-eyed, and, Berg suspected, even sharper-minded.

"I don't know if it'll make a story yet," Berg said. "I'm after background really."

"Oh, yes? What sort of background?"

Berg didn't answer but peered at the wall of cabinets. "You specialize in finding war criminals, I gather."

"Not in finding them, no. In accumulating evidence, yes. Evidence of crimes committed on Norwegian soil and against Norwegian citizens. Mind you, it's almost eighteen years since the war. Evidence isn't so easy to come by nowadays."

"Nor are war criminals, presumably."

The sharp eyes glittered. "Oh, I don't know about that. You'd be surprised how many are still hiding in the woodwork."

Berg said admiringly: "And you're ready to nail them."

Sorensen jumped to his feet with surprising agility. "Here, I'll show you."

He beckoned Berg into an adjacent room. Here the ranks of filing cabinets filled all the available wall space.

Sorensen began to talk with the enthusiasm of a dedicated specialist. "I have everything cross-referenced by victim's name, district, type of crime, and, of course, the criminal, where known. There is no serious crime of the Occupation that isn't here in these records, in some form or another." He added in a flat, unemotional voice: "My son was murdered by the gestapo, you see."

Berg was silent. He was staring at the sheer quantity of information. He'd had no idea the records would be so extensive.

"Look, each village, each town." Sorensen pulled open a drawer full of index cards categorized by place names. "I have a record of what happened in even the smallest village. I wrote to each *kommune* immediately after the war, you see, while people's memories were still fresh." He commented with pride: "It was a mammoth task."

Berg stared at the rows of place names. It occurred to him that somewhere deep in these files was a place and a name he knew very well indeed. The knowledge did not please him at all.

He said briskly: "I was actually interested in Norwegians who might have been detained in the Soviet Union at the end of the war. I don't know if that's your field . . ."

"But of course it is!" Sorensen exclaimed. "In fact, it's my main task nowadays."

Berg was incredulous. "Looking for Norwegians in *Russia*?"

"No, no. Missing persons generally."

Berg recovered his composure. It had been eighteen years. No reason to get rattled now.

He asked: "And are there any in the Soviet Union, do you think?"

Sorensen hesitated. "Why do you want to know, may I ask?"

Berg assumed a smile. "My paper's picked up a story about a Norwegian who lived happily in the Soviet Union for some years. We wondered how many others there might be."

The lawyer shook his head. "Ah, you have me there. Impossible to say for sure, I'm afraid. One can only guess. A boy might have been last seen near the Russian lines, or in a forced labor camp later overrun by the Russians. But even then—who can tell? The boy might not have got into Russian hands at all, but been killed by the Germans and put in an unmarked grave." He shook his head.

"So you don't have much luck with your missing persons?"

"Oh, I wouldn't say that," he replied firmly. "It depends on where and how the person disappeared. If the subject was in a camp I can often trace the person who last saw the subject alive. Surprisingly often I find someone who actually saw the subject die. Even that's a great comfort, you know."

"A comfort?"

"To the relatives."

"Ah."

"They rarely come to me expecting to find their sons alive. They just want to know the truth."

Berg flicked through the index cards in the open drawer. "So they come to you, the parents, and hire you to find their sons?"

"Yes. I do charge them a little, I have to—I give up a lot of commercial work for this. But I ask hardly anything. It gives me a lot of satisfaction, you see."

Berg said warmly: "I'm sure it does."

"I don't get so many requests nowadays, of course—"

A female voice called from an adjacent office. Sorensen hurried out, gesturing toward the cabinets. "Have a look if you want to. Please. Have a look around."

Berg stared fiercely at the rows of cabinets. He wished Sorensen hadn't issued the invitation. On the one hand he was drawn by a terrible curiosity, on the other, a strong desire to leave well alone.

He examined the drawer markers. The open drawer beside him was labeled HAR-HAU. Two cabinets farther along he saw POR-PU. The T's must be just beyond.

He took a step forward, then stopped, thinking hard.

Suddenly he relaxed and reached into his pockets, found a cigarette, and, lighting it, drew deeply. He must be mad even to consider looking. Why bother himself with all that? The information might be there—in fact, it probably was—but if so, it had been successfully buried for sixteen years or more. No one would find it now, not unless they were looking for it.

And why should they look?

Nobody was hiring Sorensen to search for *him*.

When Sorensen returned it was to find Berg flicking through the entries for BER-BOR with the slightly bored expression of someone who has seen quite enough.

Thrane stared at the blank sheet of paper on the desk in front of him, lost in thought. His assistant, a young man named Jensen, had given up trying to get anything out of him since arriving for work at seven-thirty.

"How much longer?" Thrane demanded suddenly.

"Any moment now," Jensen replied. It was the fourth time Thrane had asked in the last half hour.

"What the hell's taking them so long?"

"I'll go and see."

Five minutes later the internal phone rang and Jensen's voice said: "Got it!"

Thrane walked casually out of his office and down the stairs. But once in the basement he almost broke into a run. Passing the incinerator room he rapped on an adjacent door. Jensen let him into a large storeroom and jerked his head toward a tall brown paper sack. "The collection was a bit late today," he explained. "They were short-staffed."

Thrane cut open the neck of the sack and shone his ultraviolet penlight onto the contents. A few shreds of paper gleamed back at him. Thrane sagged with relief. At least they'd gotten the right sack. The roar of the incinerator could clearly be heard from next door: all the other sacks were already going up in smoke.

It took thirty minutes to pick out all the ultraviolet shreds. That was the easy bit. Spreading them out and examining both sides of the minute strips took much much longer.

The answer had come to Thrane at three in the morning. He'd realized it was the only way she could have done it. No record was kept of the amount of blank paper stored and used—a near-impossible task. But she'd had to use something. She'd had to be seen turning on the shredder and she'd had to be seen feeding paper into it.

Clever girl.

Thrane tried not to get excited too quickly, but halfway through the job he knew he was right. The feeling of triumph was glorious.

When the job was almost finished he left Jensen to it and ran upstairs. Within minutes he'd gotten the go-ahead to apply for a phone tap. It took an hour to get the application rubber-stamped and another two hours to get the tap in operation. He also put someone on to her office phone, although he knew he wasn't likely to get anything there.

He spent the rest of the afternoon in closed session with a tight-lipped Ekeland, head of Security, and a shocked and unbelieving Director. Thrane pressed for complete and immediate surveillance, but the Director delayed a final decision until he'd put it to an emergency meeting of the Security committee that evening. Thrane's argument for haste was overruled.

After that, everything seemed rather an anticlimax. Thrane worked out a detailed surveillance schedule with Ekeland, then went through Sonja's security file, only to find exactly what he'd expected to find—precisely nothing.

Finally he forced himself to face the fact that nothing much was going to happen at the moment. It would be a waiting game. In fact it might take weeks, even months, before they got what they needed. It wasn't just a question of proving that Sonja was removing information, it was a matter of establishing what she was doing with it. Who was she passing it to? Was it going directly to the Russians, or through an intermediary? Was she passing it knowingly to the Soviet Union?

Was she a fully trained agent, for God's sake?

As the full implications filtered into Thrane's mind he felt quite sick with anger.

Sonja had known almost everything. She was likely to be the greatest disaster to NATO security in living memory.

And the only proof he had was a few shreds of paper.

He began to fret again. He didn't know if he'd be able to survive a waiting game.

After everyone had gone home he sat down and went through Sonja's security file again with a fine-tooth comb.

Nothing. Everything desperately normal. Sonja led an exemplary life.

But a woman like Sonja Bjornsen didn't start spying just like that. There had to be something, there had to be.

There was, but it wasn't in the file.

His phone rang at 1845. It was Jensen. "The phone tap. The subject got a call at eighteen-thirty-four. A male who didn't give his name. They made a date for tonight. No time, no place given."

"Got the full script?"

"Yup. The man said: 'It's me. I've only just got back. Any chance of tonight?' She said: 'I don't know. It's very short notice.' He said: 'I'm away again this weekend. I can only manage tonight, that's the problem.' She said: 'I see.' He asked: 'Something the matter?' She said: 'I was so hoping to hear from you.' He said: 'I told you. I've been away. But I am sorry about your mother. Really. Now, how about tonight?' She said: 'I'll try. I can't promise. It'll be very difficult.' He said: 'Good. See you later, then.'" Jensen added: "She sounded distinctly cross with him."

"Get the tape up here as soon as possible."

"There was another call. The subject made it."

Thrane urged: "Yes."

"She called a woman named Monika. The subject asked if she could have the house for the evening. Monika wasn't at all keen and made a bit of a fuss. But our girl talked her into it. Monika's vacating the house between nineteen-thirty and twenty-one-thirty."

Thrane looked at his watch. Almost ten to seven. "Christ." He hesitated, remembering the Director's ruling.

To hell with it. He ordered: "Get someone around to her place. No, damn it—go yourself, Jensen. Fast."

An hour later Jensen called in.

"I've been here since nineteen-ten. She'd already gone. No lights, no sounds. Nothing."

Thrane groaned and buried his head in his hands.

Sonja was late arriving at the house in the pinewood. She saw with relief that Monika's car had gone.

There was no sign of Erik.

She let herself in. She hadn't brought food; there hadn't been time to buy any. Besides, she couldn't have eaten a thing. She'd remembered the Scotch though, and, pouring herself a glass, she took a sip.

Normally she didn't drink hard liquor, but tonight she didn't care what she was meant to do or not do. She needed it. She took a more substantial sip. It tasted good. So it should: it cost a great deal. In fact, liquor was taxed so heavily that a bottle was about the same price as a new dress. She stared at the amber liquid thoughtfully. Sometimes Erik drank half a bottle in an evening.

She gave herself a small shake. What was she doing sitting around drinking? Everything should seem as normal as possible. Finding some cheese in the refrigerator, she put it on the table, then, catching sight of herself in a mirror, hurried to the bathroom to tidy up. She did what she could with her hair, which wasn't a lot, and glanced at the overall effect. She stopped and stared at herself for a long time. Her face seemed quite different from before. Older, less attractive . . . defeated.

Tears sprang to her eyes. Turning hastily away, she returned to the kitchen and sat at the table, motionless.

After half an hour she heard a sound and stiffened, but it was only a car going to the next house.

He was very late.

Perhaps he wasn't coming.

The thought was agony and she could hardly bear to imagine it.

When the knock finally came, her heart hit her ribs with such a thump that for a moment she couldn't stand up.

Finally she went and opened the back door. He came in. She searched his face. She couldn't believe it: he looked just the same.

He gave her a quick kiss. His breath smelled of alcohol and stale cigarettes. She heard him say: "The traffic was bad."

He went straight into the kitchen and poured himself a large drink. He looked around. He seemed restless and distracted.

He spotted her drink. "Good Lord, Sonja, taken to hard liquor?"

"Yes."

"Oh, your mother. Of course. I am sorry." He came and put an arm around her shoulder.

"Didn't you get any of my notes?"

"I only got them today, I'm afraid." He gestured regret. "I really couldn't come till now."

She thought: Such lies. Why such dreadful lies?

He dropped his arm. "So, how are you bearing up?"

"I'm better now," she said eventually. "Managing quite well, really."

"Poor darling," he said briskly, swigging at his drink.

That was the total sum of his compassion, she realized. He wasn't going to ask another thing about her ordeal. He didn't care in the slightest.

But she wanted to be sure. She said: "I don't know why I told you that. It's not true. In fact, I haven't managed at all. I don't know if I'm managing even now."

He looked vaguely surprised. Sonja rarely complained about anything, and never about herself. His face assumed a mask of concern. "Oh, dear, how awful for you. Poor darling." His voice was cool, carefully establishing distance in case this marked the beginning of an emotional outburst.

She knew then that he really didn't care. Had she ever really believed he did?

He said: "How long have we got the house for?"

"Two hours at the most. No, much less now."

"Oh, what a pity."

There was relief in his voice. She knew why: because there wouldn't be time for lovemaking. The knowledge turned like a knife in a wound.

Her heart thumping, she asked: "How's work?"

He gave her a quick look. "Oh, all right. But I have to go away again this weekend." He sat down at the table.

"The department are sending you?"

He frowned. "Yes. Who else?"

"I don't know." She realized it was a stupid question: He was suspicious. She added quickly: "I thought you might have been seconded. There's quite a lot of secondment going on at the moment."

He was looking at her as if she were mad.

She sat down opposite, and burbled: "Where are you going, in fact?"

There was a pause. She never usually asked such bald questions. Eventually he answered: "To Kåfjord, actually. To have a look around the site of the new installation."

"Oh."

"Trying to protect FO/E's interests as usual. Though—also as usual—I'm not allowed to know what they are."

Sonja thought: My God, but you're brazen.

He raised his eyebrows, waiting for a response. That was what it had come to, Sonja realized: a prompt from him and a gush of information from her.

Suddenly Sonja wanted to kill him. She wanted to squeeze a trigger and dig a knife into his ribs and tear all that lovely thick hair out of his head.

She jumped to her feet and, going to the refrigerator, pretended to look inside. "I didn't have time to buy food."

She heard the snap of his lighter and the suck of his breath on a cigarette. "No matter."

In the shelter of the refrigerator door she closed her eyes, wanting to postpone whatever ghastly confrontation lay ahead. She dreaded challenging him.

She said, "We'll just have cheese, then, shall we?" and went to the cupboard to find some plates.

Suddenly she knew she couldn't face a confrontation. She couldn't face the arguments, the denials, the derision, the final scene when he would walk out. Because he would walk out, there was no doubt about that.

She could bear almost anything but that.

No, there wouldn't be a confrontation. The decision was a relief, an enormous weight off her shoulders. She felt almost happy now.

She dug in a drawer for some knives.

Of course she'd have to decide what to do eventually. She couldn't let things go on as before.

Suddenly it occurred to her—she could. Things could go on just as before—except for one thing.

The germ of an idea crept into her mind. At first she couldn't quite grasp it and, to give herself more time, said: "The cheese looks pretty old. D'you mind?"

He shrugged.

She put some of Monika's tomatoes on the table and a bowl containing some rather old fruit.

At last the idea came into focus and sharpened. She grabbed at it. Suddenly she knew what she was going to do.

She sat down rather abruptly.

Erik looked at her questioningly.

Rubbing a hand over her forehead, she said, "The drink— it's gone to my head." She added in a matter-of-fact tone: "So you're going to Kåfjord. We had a meeting about it only today."

"Ah." He displayed only the mildest interest.

Sonja thought of the minutes in her bag and tried to remember all the details of the installation. "It's something quite new," she said truthfully. "And very sensitive. So I'm not surprised they're sending you up there. Security will be quite a problem."

His eyes were like a cat's, blank but watchful. He was probably thinking how easy this was proving to be.

"And they really haven't told you anything about it?" she asked.

"Really."

She looked puzzled. "I don't know why, darling, with your—seniority. Anyway—Kåfjord is to be the first of a new navigation system. The system's called Delta. It's far more accurate than Loran-C. Apparently it can fix a submarine's position to within a few hundred yards."

"And Loran-C can't do that?"

She must get this right. "Not unless the sub's on the surface. And even then it isn't nearly so good. Only to within a mile or so."

"And Delta?"

"To within yards."

"When the subs are down?"

"Yes. Not too deep. But definitely down."

He appeared to be absorbing it all. He looked up suddenly. "But the site isn't on the coast."

"What? Oh—no," she agreed. She hadn't thought this far. He was waiting for an explanation. At last inspiration came. "It has to be installed high up, away from interference."

"Ah." Finally he nodded and said lightly: "Oh, well, all *I* have to do now is make it secure, don't I?"

He'd swallowed it. She felt weak. What a minefield lies were.

For a long while she sat limply, hardly hearing what he was saying.

Then she brightened up. Everything was going to be all right after all.

15

Skorpa plowed steadily across the sound, her bow cleaving the water into two neat white curls. The sky was transparently clear and, though the sun was well hidden behind the mountains, the light was unusually bright. Or so it seemed to Hal. He stood beside the wheelhouse, peering at the jetty ahead, screwing his eyes up against the electric white of the hills, suppressing a slight queasiness.

The hangover was no more than he deserved. Having been abstemious for weeks, he'd gotten involved in beer and aquavit with Arne, and hadn't remembered anything, including when to stop. A gold-medal performance. He wasn't feeling very proud of himself.

The jetty was drawing closer and he spotted two figures starting down it hand in hand: Ragna, in the bright-blue woolen jacket she often wore, and Kris, small and well wrapped at her side.

He waved. At first they didn't see, but then Kris pointed and, jumping up and down, waved back.

With more than his usual concentration Hal nudged *Skorpa* alongside. Ragna took the lines, looped them over the bollards, and strolled up. "Hiya," she called cheerfully. There was a warm glad-to-be-here smile on her face. Hal looked at her curiously. She looked exceptionally happy—something must have happened.

Ragna caught his look and answered with a small laughing shrug.

Climbing onto the jetty he kissed her dutifully on the cheek. "Are you all right?"

She made a face of mock surprise. "Yes—why?"

Something *had* happened. She'd sold the shop. She was moving to Oslo. She'd met a man. He hesitated, wanting to know yet unable to ask. Finally he murmured; "Nothing," and, leaning down, said a grave manly hello to Kris. "Where's your bag, young chap?"

"With Mummy!"

Ragna had gone to pick up a couple of holdalls. It seemed a lot of baggage for one small boy.

Hal took the bags from her. "I hope it's all right," she said, "but I thought I'd come too."

For a moment he didn't understand what she meant.

"It's probably the only good day we'll have for the rest of the winter," she explained. "It seemed a pity to waste it."

He took it in at last: she was coming to Brattdal. For a moment the suspicion entered his mind that perhaps she hadn't trusted him to look after Kris on his own.

"I could have managed."

"Oh, it wasn't that!" she exclaimed.

He still felt uncertain; she'd taken him completely by surprise. "There's nothing special to eat. And the stove's not lit in the other room. I wasn't expecting you . . ."

"That makes us quits then!"

"What?"

"On surprise visits. One each." With a smile she pressed the palm of her hand against his cheek. He turned quickly away. He wasn't as immune to her as he liked to think. Not yet.

He helped Kris onto the boat. Ragna made her own way on board. Her visit was obviously settled: he was pleased. It would give their new relationship a good start. She didn't know about this new relationship yet. But she soon would.

Hal had finally realized that waiting for a change of heart from Ragna was a hopeless cause. The sailing visit had revealed the situation very clearly—she was angry and impatient with him, she was irritated by his devotion, she wanted to go to Oslo to "escape"—and he was beginning to suspect she meant from *him*.

So he'd come to his decision. He would give up all ideas of winning Ragna. The two of them would become trusted old friends.

Hard, but not impossible, not if one was determined enough.

He'd already taken the first step: he'd asked Anna-Kristin to Brattdal for the following weekend.

As soon as they were under way he stood Kris on a box in the wheelhouse and pointed out the sights, because that was the way he had planned it. Ragna did not join them, but stayed on deck in the shelter of the wheelhouse, leaning against the window, tendrils of hair twisting and snaking around her face.

From the mainland jetty it was four miles across the sound to Revoy. The island gave a good lee and, once *Skorpa* was safely moored, the transfer to the dinghy was relatively easy. The only awkward moment came when Hal lifted Kris over *Skorpa*'s side and down into Ragna's waiting arms. Then, as he let go of the child, he lurched foolishly and grabbed for the rail.

"All right?" Ragna asked, swinging Kris down onto a seat in the dinghy.

"Nothing a hole in the head wouldn't cure."

She looked at him curiously. "You've been hitting the bottle!"

Hal grunted: "The bottle hit *me*." He forwent his usual athletic leap into the dinghy, and made his way carefully over the bulwark.

"Don't tell me you're a secret drinker!" She looked pleased at the idea.

"Not so secret," he said with a sheepish glance. He slid the oars into the crutches and began to pull toward the shore.

Ragna's eyes widened in surprise. "Oh . . . I see. A party."

"That would be rather an exaggeration." He gave a hard pull on the oars so that the dinghy creamed through the water.

She murmured, "The social whirl of Revøy, eh?" and settled back on her seat, watching him closely, her head tilted, her eyes half-closed.

Hal realized that her imagination was probably running away with her, but let it ride.

The dinghy crunched gently onto the shingle beach. Bamse met them with low barks and wild convolutions of his tail.

For fun, Hal had brought the tractor down for the short journey up the valley. But three people and two bags were going to be a problem in a one-seater.

"I can see that this expedition is man's stuff," Ragna said tactfully. "I'll walk."

"I can come back for you," Hal volunteered.

"No, it'll do me good." And she set off at a brisk walk.

Kris was wide-eyed and silent at the sight of the enormous tractor, whose rear tires towered high above him. Hal put the bags in a corner of the cab and started the engine. It fired with a roar. Kris screwed up his face. Hal climbed into the cab and pulled Kris up onto his knee and they set off, trundling and lurching up the hill. They caught up with Ragna, who stood to one side and waved as they passed.

Kris clung to Hal as the tractor took to the steepest part of the hill, its body rocking and jarring over the uneven surface of the hard-packed snow. Glancing down, Hal saw the boy's face alight with excitement, and he felt a sudden burst of happiness.

He thought: Why can't it always be like this?

Ragna came around the curve in the track and saw the tractor, empty of passengers, parked to one side of the house. Then the house itself came into view. She paused for a moment, head to one side, and took a fresh look at it. She'd forgotten how striking the place was. On her last visit in midsummer it had rained all day and the place had seemed as bleak and gray as the weather. But now, in the pale winter light, the mellow wood had a subtle warmth that was almost welcoming.

She walked on. Away to the right a number of shaggy long-haired creatures stood with their noses to the snow. The famous musk-oxen. To the left of the house were clusters of fragile saplings, and behind, a walled area. The much-prized vegetable garden. It all looked very ordered.

She reached the top of the path and paused to look at the house from close quarters. She'd forgotten how ornate the carvings and ornamentations were, and how pretty the veranda was, with its latticed arches. It was a ridiculous house for such a remote spot, of course. A monument to some over-blown nineteenth-century ego. Yet in a strange way it belonged here, like some grand dame lording it over her country estates.

If you felt like burying yourself alive, it was probably the perfect spot.

The front door opened and Hal and Kris and Bamse came out in a rush of shouts and barks. They were on their way to see the musk-oxen. Kris begged Ragna to join them, but she smiled a refusal and watched them dance off across the snow.

She strolled into the house. There'd been many changes since her last visit, she noticed: bright rugs on the pine floors; new curtains; old wooden farming tools and copper cooking utensils hung on the walls as ornaments; more furniture, most of it antique and rather beautiful; photographs, paintings, mementoes; and dozens and dozens of books arranged on shelves, in bookcases, and in high stacks on the floor.

Hal had been busy.

She peered at the photographs. Several of expeditions, a few of Jan and Hal in the old days, a series of formal poses from the last century, soft-focus family portraits from the 1930s.

On a long table under the window a large number of papers, books, and pamphlets were spread out. She peered at them. Research papers, notes, technical magazines, letters.

Her eyes focused on a letter that lay open on top of a pile. *My dearest Hal,* it said in large scrawling handwriting, *Just a quick note to say yes to next week. I've missed Brattdal very much. And you. It's good news that you'll be on the—*

On the what? Ragna flipped the letter over.

—telephone soon. Ragna blinked: he hadn't told her that.

The letter finished: *Are you interested in trekking on the plateau at Easter? Love, A-K.*

Ragna replaced the letter carefully in the position she had found it.

Anna-Kristin.

Coming to Brattdal. Going trekking.

Fine.

Not fine. She minded. Which was ridiculous. Why should she?

But she knew why. It was the feeling that Hal's life was bowling onward while hers was standing still.

Yet there was more to it, and she wasn't sure what it was. But she had a sudden acute feeling of loss.

Her good humor deflated, she halfheartedly continued her tour. The kitchen was simple and old-fashioned, with a large stone sink and scrubbed wood surfaces. The table had been laid with two places, complete with neatly folded napkins, and dishes of meat and cheese, conscientiously covered in muslin.

If she hadn't been so preoccupied, she would have thought the preparations rather touching.

Next to the kitchen was a storeroom, Spartan and with the musty smell of a room that is never used.

On the upper floor was the bathroom, such as it was, and three bedrooms. The main bedroom and the guest bedroom were at the front of the house on either side of a hallway. At the far end of the hall next to the bathroom was a room that connected with Hal's. This was obviously Kris's room, for the bed had been made and turned back, and his bag placed at the foot.

She went in. The window, decked with bright check curtains, overlooked the vegetable garden. She peered down and saw symmetrical rows of canes protruding from the snow. On the bedside table were some picture books—two of them brand new—a jug of water and a glass. On the center of the pillow lay a stuffed rag toy, a horse with one eye missing. It looked old and well loved.

The scene was very ordered and—what was the word—snug. It left her feeling vaguely excluded, almost as if she were an intruder.

The connecting door to Hal's room was open. She paused and, drawn by a glimpse of the view, walked in, aware that she really was an intruder now.

She went straight to the window. The view was magnificent. The valley walls and the falling ground created a frame for the expanse of dark glinting water that extended toward the shores of Ullsfjord. In the distance the Lyngen Alps rose in pink-tinged peaks, like icing on a giant cake.

I've missed Brattdal very much . . .

Ragna pursed her lips. She had, had she?

There was a distant sound. She put her face to the window.

She could just see the boys on the hillside. They were heading slowly back.

Turning to leave, she took a quick all-encompassing look at the room. Something made her pause. There were photographs by the bed. She recognized one of herself and Kris, another of Hal's family. But her eye was caught by a tiny picture stuck into the frame of the family portrait.

She padded silently over and peered at it.

It was a full-length color snapshot of a woman on skis, an extremely pretty woman in a sky-blue all-in-one ski outfit. Ragna wasn't quite sure what irritated her more—the woman's prettiness or the incredibly smart ski outfit.

The woman was laughing. She obviously liked a good time. Well—she'd be disappointed in Hal.

Or would she?

Perhaps Hal did give her a good time.

She gritted her teeth and hurried downstairs. When the others came in, noisy with chatter and stamping feet, they found her sitting thoughtfully at the window. Kris threw off his outdoor clothes and rushed up, ruddy-cheeked and bursting with life. It made her heart lift to see him so happy.

During lunch she observed Hal. He seemed very relaxed. She pictured him with the laughing woman, and thought: Sometimes I feel I don't know you at all.

After the meal they went out to enjoy the last of the afternoon light, climbing up the valley to one of the new plantations, where they examined the saplings and learned their names and guessed how tall they might grow. Later they climbed even higher, though Kris found the going difficult and hitched a lift on Hal's shoulders. The air was hard and fresh, crisp with the dry cold of winter. They found the tracks of a ptarmigan in the snow. Bamse, driven into an instant frenzy, floundered through the snow and disappeared over the ridge at a determined canter.

On the way back Kris insisted on Ragna seeing the muskoxen at close quarters. She had to admit they had a certain charm, with their thick black coats falling in shaggy fringes almost to the ground and their long old-man faces with the unexpected frosting of white around the muzzle, as if they'd just licked cream. But most of all she liked the way the thick black hair grew so suddenly and densely from the smooth forehead, rising in a high coiffure from a distinctive hairline. "They look as though they're wearing wigs." She laughed. Kris gave her a fierce look. "It's not pretend hair, Mamma!"

When the steely night-cold crept down from the mountain they headed home. The sky had a luminous radiance, all baby colors, pink and violet and silky blue, while beneath, the snow seemed transparent. Ragna had to admit it was lovely, magical almost. But the prospect of getting back to the warmth of the house was lovelier still.

Hal, with Kris on his shoulders, told the boy what his grandmother had told him: about the *huldrefolk*—the hidden people—who were meant to live in the valley, and of the trolls who had inhabited the mountains long ago and left giant footprints on the rocks, and of the ghosts, the *deildegasten*, who until recently had jumped out from behind rocks and frightened people to death. Then he laughed and said the ghosts had all been chased off by the musk-oxen, and Kris giggled with relief.

Later Hal cooked an early supper: halibut steamed with herbs, potatoes, carrots in butter, followed by Arctic cloudberries.

Afterward they played a game of happy families, but Kris, tired and difficult, made a fuss about losing, and Ragna hauled him upstairs to bed.

They had their customary bedtime hug. Tonight she looked down at him nestling contentedly on her lap and felt a sudden surge of emotion for this child of hers. It wasn't that she didn't love him all the time—of course she did—it was just that, coming on top of all her other worries, he sometimes wore her down.

She tickled his cheek and he made the funny little grunting sound he always made when he was content.

Hal came up as she was tucking him in. For a moment they stood at either side of the bed, looking down at the child. A happy family group, thought Ragna, except that this wasn't a family. Ragna said abruptly to Hal, "Why don't you read him a story?" and, kissing Kris firmly on both cheeks, walked briskly from the room.

It was half an hour before Hal came down. "Would you like a drink?" he asked. "I'm having a beer myself."

"The hair of the dog?"

He made a wry face. "Quite."

Ragna was about to refuse the drink when she suddenly thought: Why the hell not? And she had an aquavit.

They sat in the living room, on either side of the blazing stove, in long low armchairs with cushioned seats. The room was filled with the scent of pine. The light of the oil lamps made the wood gleam with a rich reddish hue, like mahogany.

The coziness suddenly irritated Ragna. "You know, if you get much more comfortable here you'll forget the outside world altogether."

Hal replied with a soft smile: "Ah. I don't forget the outside world, Ragna. I just do without it most of the time."

"But not all the time, I hear." It was out before she could stop it. A horrid shrewish remark.

He shot her a questioning glance.

Too late to back out now. She said lightly: "I heard you have a new friend."

Understanding came over his face, and he looked quickly away, frowning. She'd caught him by surprise. "Ragna—" he began, and closed his mouth abruptly. Finally he looked up again. "It means nothing. She's just—a casual friend."

"Oh, don't misunderstand me," she said hastily. "I don't mind what sort of friend she is. None of my business. It's just that I seem to have been the last to hear. And I think I mind about that."

"Yes . . . I'm sorry." But he looked curious rather than apologetic, and she found his steady stare rather disconcerting.

"At least it'll put paid to the rumors," she added.

"Rumors?"

Was he being slow on purpose? she wondered. She thought she caught a glint of mischief in his eye.

"You know what I mean," she said firmly.

He looked mystified. She felt sure it was just a ploy.

She resisted answering, then said in mock irritation: "Us."

"Oh—us!" he exclaimed, feigning surprise. "Now, why would they think that?"

He was definitely making fun of her; his eyes were full of laughter.

"Why?" she repeated drily. "It's that damned party line, that's why. They all listen in, I know they do."

"In which case you'd have thought they'd have gotten it right."

"Huh! You know what they're like around here."

"Pretty accurate, normally."

He was in an unusually gay mood. She couldn't work it out. "Not so accurate in this case," she pointed out.

"Well," he said easily, "perhaps they sensed the way I felt about you."

She was completely taken aback. He'd never talked like this before. She stared, for once speechless.

He got up. She realized he was coming over to her. She held her breath: she couldn't deal with this situation at all. He stood before her and put out his hand. "Want another drink?" he asked lightly.

She exhaled weakly, and handed him her glass.

He went to the corner cupboard where he kept the drinks. "Don't worry, Ragna. This isn't a declaration." He threw her a brief smile of reassurance.

She found her voice. "Oh."

He brought the drink and sat down again. "There was a time when I hoped we might become more than friends, but . . ." He shrugged. "That doesn't seem very realistic now, does it?"

Ragna didn't know what to say. Hal's presence—his devotion—had been part of her life for three years, something undiscussed and unquestioned. She'd gotten used to it, even reliant on it. Now here he was—what?—withdrawing it?

"You want to move to Oslo, you want lots of people around you," Hal went on. "And that desire is very strong in you, I can see that. Personally, I don't think crowds of people are ever the answer. But that's just me."

She said: "I could never live in a place like this, Hal."

He seemed to hold his breath. "I understand that. Well, now I do." He smiled so nicely that she wanted to hug him.

Hug him. She thought: That's the drink talking!

She said: "You've been very good to me."

"Good!" he exclaimed with a shudder. "I've just tried to be a friend, that's all. And because I wanted to be, Ragna. Because I admired and respected you. It wasn't just—because of Jan."

The drink gave her the courage to say something that had been unsaid for far too long. "I never blamed you, you know."

He stiffened visibly.

"Not for a moment," she said. "But I've never been sure you believed that."

He got up and, taking the poker, crouched in front of the stove and stoked the fire so that clouds of sparks flew up the chimney. He sat down again, frowning at the flames, then looked at her with sudden intensity. "I still blame myself for not having prevented it, and nothing will ever change that. Nothing. But my—feelings for you are quite separate."

She nodded, feeling strangely inadequate and oddly guilty. Hal would never forget about Pasvik—he didn't want to forget—whereas she couldn't wait to leave it far, far behind.

"I would have wanted us to be friends whatever had happened," Hal continued. "You do see that?"

She smiled, pleased.

"Anna-Kristin is something different," Hal went on, and Ragna's pleasure dimmed a little. "I—well, you know how it is—it's nice to have someone around now and then."

Nice? Ragna was sure it must be very nice indeed.

She imagined the woman here with Hal, and felt a small pang. Did they make love? Of course they did! What else would they do? She pictured Hal making love, and the picture was vivid, disturbingly so. He would be passionate—yes, very—but kind and gentle too.

She shifted restlessly in her chair, uncomfortably aware that she had not made love to anyone for three years. It suddenly seemed a very long time.

Hal was saying something. She made the effort to concentrate and realized they were still on the subject of Anna-Kristin.

"Our relationship isn't going to change. I would never ask her to come and live here, for instance. Not that she'd come anyway, I shouldn't think." He gave a brief self-deprecating smile. "I'm not perhaps the easiest person . . ."

She decided that he was probably right about not being easy, but that it was nothing to be ashamed of. Difficult people were generally far more interesting. She murmured: "It's just a matter of finding the right person at the right time."

They talked about choices then, choices between career and relationships, and how difficult they were to make. And how easy it was to make mistakes that could never be undone.

As they talked it seemed to Ragna that some barrier had lifted and there was a new bond of frankness and affection between them. Hal had yielded up something important to her. Trust, goodwill, but most of all his natural reticence, as if he'd decided to lay his most precious possession at the feet of their new friendship.

She was flattered. She was also intrigued—she'd never seen him so relaxed or expressive before. He seemed—unfettered. It suddenly occurred to her that he *was* unfettered—he was free of his feelings for her.

She should feel relieved. But she wasn't sure she did.

It was the drink. Or was it?

They talked for a long time and whenever he smiled—which was often—she thought how very nice he looked when he was happy, and how very attractive he looked when he was serious, and how very much she wanted to kiss that mouth of his.

Later he said: "You were so happy this morning. Has something happened?"

It all seemed a long time ago. "No. I was just determined to enjoy the day. I've been thinking that I don't perhaps"—she paused, searching for the right words—"live for the moment enough."

"Live for the moment?"

"Feel alive!"

He smiled.

She felt alive now—oh, yes. Her worries seemed far away—even the debts seemed unimportant. She'd never told Hal about those; she felt too ashamed.

Whatever was happening, he was aware of it too, because now and then he would smile at her for no particular reason, and she would hold his gaze and feel her heart move with excitement.

When it was really very late, she asked suddenly: "Do you think one should live for the moment?"

"It depends on whether you can live with the consequences."

"You're so wise!" she laughed.

"Ah, I'm good enough at the theory. It's life that doesn't follow the rules, damn it."

She could have stopped it a dozen times, but she didn't want to. She kept thinking: It won't do any harm. Life's too short. I've been so lonely. I need somebody—I want him—just for tonight. I want to feel really alive.

And then she couldn't have stopped it anyway. Some embers settled noisily on the grate, and as he leaned forward to throw fresh logs into the stove, she thought how fine his profile was and how much she wanted to touch his skin, and the next moment she knelt beside him and brushed his cheek lightly with her fingertips and sighed: "Oh, Hal."

Hell.

Nothing had changed at all! He'd never stopped hoping. He still loved her—he'd just gotten better at hiding it. Who'd he been trying to fool?

The flutter of her fingers almost paralyzed him with shock and exhilaration. The softness in her voice caught at his stomach.

Slowly—he made sure it was very slowly—he turned his face toward her and smiled a conspiratorial smile, as if her gesture had been the most natural thing in the world. Then he reached for her hand and pressed it against his cheek.

She knelt beside him on the rug, her face turned up to his, and he bent forward and brushed his lips against hers in the ghost of a kiss.

Then he smiled again because, whatever happened now, he mustn't frighten her away. And she responded with a small bewitching movement of her lips, and then they kissed—different kisses now: endless, deep, needful kisses, and Hal thought his heart would burst with wanting her.

Eventually he actually said it. "I want you."

She pulled back a little, and for a heart-stopping moment he thought she was retreating, but then she put her mouh to his ear and whispered softly about how important it was to stay friends afterward and not let this change anything, and was that all right with him? He agreed—he'd have agreed to *anything* right then. She asked again, was he sure? Of course he was sure—he was sure of everything. He even managed to make light of the moment by saying "What are friends for?"

They kissed once more, then Hal pulled her gently to her feet and, with a small step, made the first move toward the doorway. Her eyes dancing with dark excitement, she came into the fold of his arm and let him lead her to the stairs.

The silence seemed to roar in his ears. He couldn't believe what was happening.

He repeated: "What's the matter?"

"I'm sorry . . . I'm *sorry*."

"Ragna, what is it? Tell me, tell me."

"I can't explain. I just can't. I'm sorry."

They were standing by the bed in the darkness, their arms around each other. He hugged her tighter, feeling the wonderful warmth of her body against his, unable to believe she wasn't feeling that warmth too. But it was happening again: She was pushing gently against his chest, trying to escape. He was chilled by this incredible change around, this sudden appalling reversal. He held firm, unable to let her go.

"Ragna, Ragna, don't . . . don't do this."

"Hal, it wouldn't be any good. It wouldn't. I'm sorry—I'm *sorry*. It's all my fault. I should never have . . ." She moved in his arms, gently but insistently trying to free herself. "It wouldn't be— I mean, this isn't— Oh, *God* . . ."

A sudden rage overtook him. He gripped her roughly by the arms and almost shook her.

"Ragna, talk to me about this. Talk to me."

She gave a short sharp sigh that was almost a sob. "Hal, it just—wouldn't work."

"Why?" He tried to read her face in the darkness.

She was shaking her head miserably. "I don't know—I need time to think—"

"Ragna—we were talking about one night. Not a bloody lifetime. You were the one who wanted to live for the moment—remember?"

"But it wouldn't be like that, would it? I mean, it wouldn't be that simple."

He cried: "But I agreed to your rules, remember? I *agreed*."

"I know, I know. But—perhaps the rules were—no *good*."

He pushed her away. He was trembling with anger. "You wouldn't know what you wanted if you had the whole bloody world, Ragna. You've *never* known what you wanted. Christ . . ."

He sat down abruptly on the edge of the bed and put a hand to his forehead, completely lost for words.

"Oh, Hal . . ." She could hardly speak. He suspected she was crying, but he didn't terribly care. She said in a small voice: "I don't know what to say." With a small sigh she bent down to pick up her sweater where it had fallen on the floor.

He realized she was going.

Suppressing his anger, he said flatly: "Just tell me why."

A silence. She began to move toward the door. Finally she paused. "I don't know, Hal. I don't know."

And then she was gone.

He breathed: "Go to hell. Go to hell!" and threw himself on the bed.

16

There were good mornings, there were bad mornings. Thrane had no doubt which this one was, and not just because it was a Monday.

The *Sosialist Dagens Post* lay open on the desk in front of him. There was a news item on the front page. It announced that according to unconfirmed reports, the third man at Pasvik had been a Norwegian.

He cursed inwardly. How had they gotten the damn story?

Thrane's director had already had a word with the editor, who'd mumbled the usual rubbish about protecting his sources, then, as a softener, had dropped a hint that the source was foreign.

Thrane dismissed the idea. He knew who the source was: Sonja. He just couldn't prove it. Not yet.

After three days of around-the-clock surveillance, costing a lot of men and even more money, he had nothing that would survive in a courtroom.

Pushing the newspaper aside, he went through what little he did have.

Sonja went to work, she returned from work, she went shopping, she went to the cinema with a girlfriend on Saturday nights, she went for a walk, she talked on the phone to friends—all women—about the weather and the holiday she was planning in the Canaries.

The search of her apartment had revealed nothing out of the ordinary. Her bank account showed no outside earnings and her spending was modest, although she'd gone on a bit of a spree after the death of her mother, possibly in anticipation of an inheritance. The model of a quiet middle-aged woman.

But a woman with a secret lover.

He was the link man. He had to be. He was the only part of her life that didn't fit.

He'd give anything to know when she was due to meet the lover again. Thursday perhaps, if it was a regular weekly meeting. But he guessed not. The lover had said he was just back in town. It was possible he traveled a lot and their meetings were spasmodic.

So there was nothing for it but to keep the surveillance going and hope that the next meeting would be sooner rather than later.

In the meantime he could continue with the damage-assessment report. It was looking very black. Sonja wasn't just a deceiver; Sonja was a full-blown subversive.

He'd spent the first part of the weekend matching what Sonja had known to what had been leaked to the press. The connections were not always obvious. Sometimes a story would appear in the East German press first, sometimes in the Finnish, or Bulgarian, or Soviet, or French—agents of influence from many different countries were used to launch the stories. Yet the stories always did appear, and, in the case of NATO secrets, they appeared between five days and five weeks after Sonja had gained access to the information.

There was also the matter of Pasvik itself.

Sonja had been in the perfect position to leak that.

In which case he'd personally see to it that she got locked up for life.

Along with the mystery lover, of course.

Now all Thrane had to do was catch him. And her. Preferably together.

Restless, he left FO/E headquarters and went to the special-operations room they had set up in a safe house nearby. He'd already spent most of the weekend there in session with the Security committee and the Director, who was still shocked at the activities of his trusted secretary.

They'd examined the most recent secrets to which Sonja had had access. It was a depressing exercise. The minutes she'd so carefully copied just four days ago had covered the building of some highly sensitive COMINT installations for the U.S. National Security Agency.

If the Americans discovered that all the details of their new installations had gotten out . . .

It hardly bore thinking about.

Thrane went into the ops room and took a firsthand look at the surveillance team's latest report. It was just as they'd informed him first thing that morning: Sonja had gotten up at the usual time and gone to work.

Exciting stuff.

Then he called FO/S, to find out if their field operatives had noticed anything unusual around the installation sites in northern Norway. A long shot if there ever was one, but it was a case of leaving no stone unturned.

He hung around for a while, trying for the hundredth time to think of aspects of Sonja's life they might not have covered.

Finally, at eleven, when he was sure nothing was going to happen, he left to keep an appointment with Lars Sorensen, an appointment he'd made last week when his mind had been on other things—namely, the third man.

The lawyer was based near the town hall, in the center of town. Though it was freezing cold, Thrane decided to walk.

Oslo looked very gray at this time of year, the buildings dark and somber, piles of grimy snow deposited along the roadsides, the people unsmiling and with long-suffering expressions. Only the trams added light and color as they jangled gaily along.

The brisk walk did Thrane good, and he felt more cheerful as he climbed the stairs to Sorensen's office.

As always, Thrane was shown into Sorensen's inner sanctum precisely on time. The lawyer shook hands formally, and the two men sat down. Thrane couldn't help noticing that a single sheet of paper lay on the desk in front of Sorensen. It didn't look very promising.

"You've seen the *Dagens Post* this morning?" Thrane asked. "The report on the third man at Pasvik being a Norwegian. Well, that's our man."

Sorensen nodded. "I guessed as much."

"Well? Have you had any luck?"

Sorensen settled in his chair. "I have some rough figures for you. But first I'd like to tell you exactly how I've arrived at these figures so you'll understand how and why they must inevitably be imperfect."

"I see."

"In a country of only four million people with a highly regulated system like ours, missing people generally get noticed, although during and immediately after the war it all got very confused, as you can imagine." He paused. "My information on those who went missing comes from a wide range of sources—*kommunes*, population registers, central military records, regional police forces, and so on. It's relatively simple to find the total of all reported missing. But matching them to unnamed dead is much, much more difficult."

He stood up and wandered over to a filing cabinet. "Over the years I have obtained copies of all the Nazi records relating to Norway that I could beg, borrow, or steal from archives all over the world, from America to those behind the Iron Curtain." He opened a drawer and pulled out a file. "The Germans kept immaculate records for much of the time, as you know, and in many cases I've been able to match a dead concentration-camp victim to a missing Norwegian citizen. However, the gestapo here in occupied Norway were less orderly—not only because they were naturally more secretive but, more to the point, because they didn't always know the names of their victims."

He opened the file. "For example, here is an entry for Tromsø dated November twenty-third, 1942. Three men were shot early in the morning and put into an unmarked grave. Now"—he prodded the file—"these were not Tromsø men. It's probable they were three young men missing from the Bodø area since the previous August. Though why they were brought to Tromsø we don't know." He closed the file. "You see the problem?"

Thrane sighed: "I'm beginning to."

"Then there's the problem of those who died right at the beginning, resisting the German invasion, but whose bodies weren't identified. And those who went to fight with the Soviet Army and never returned—maybe they died, maybe they didn't. Needless to say, the Russians have not been forthcoming with figures or names. The only interest they've shown is in Nazi collaborators."

"So we have no way of knowing how many stayed on in Russia?"

"No."

"Do you think there were many?"

Sorensen shrugged. "Impossible to say. But there must have been a few. You know how it was. After four years of German occupation, the Russians seemed like angels to the people in Finnmark."

"So—where does all this leave us?"

"With a rather inaccurate picture, I'm afraid."

If Sorensen intended Thrane to feel discouraged, he was succeeding.

"The postwar records were quite useful, of course," Sorensen went on. "National-service records and so on. A surprising number of people turned up who'd been thought missing. There were a number who'd spent the war in Sweden and managed to evade registering with the authorities there. And of course there were some in Britain, in the army-in-exile. But— let's look at what you're interested in. The shortfall." He picked up the piece of paper. "Five hundred and sixty-five."

Thrane put a hand to his forehead and groaned aloud.

"We can discount a number on grounds of age. You said the man you were looking for was likely to be between thirty-three and fifty at the present time. So . . . that would leave four hundred and—let me see—forty-three."

There was a silence. Thrane stood up. "You've gone to a lot of trouble."

"But this is no good to you?"

"Not really. I'll come back to you when—if—I ever get any more information."

"The list will be here when you want it."

Sorensen walked him to the door of the outer office. "By the way, someone else was asking."

"What?"

"A journalist from the *Dagens Post.*"

"Oh."

"He was after background information. About how many Norwegians might have been detained in the Soviet Union against their will."

"Mmm." It was, he supposed, inevitable that they'd come snooping around. "But look, let me know if they start ferreting again, will you? And I'd rather they didn't get any figures or anything like that."

"Of course."

"In fact, I'd be grateful if you could keep me informed of any requests that might relate to this business in any way at all."

When Thrane had gone, Sorensen returned to his desk and picked up a letter that had been forwarded to him by the Military Archives. It was a request from Halvard Starheim for information on a German name and wartime identity number.

He had almost mentioned it to Thrane just now, but had thought better of it. On consideration, he was glad he'd said nothing. Though he had never met Starheim, he respected and admired him, and had sympathized with him over his unfortunate involvement in the Pasvik affair. He had no wish to bring the man to Thrane's attention unnecessarily.

Besides, the request was completely unrelated. There was no risk of having done the wrong thing.

Rolf Berg's nightmare goes like this:

The school gates loom up. The boy's father has him by the scruff of the neck and is hauling him up the path. The classroom windows are lined with the jeering faces of the boy's schoolmates. The boy is suffocating with humiliation. He wants to strike out and kill this man who is his father, this man whom he hates more than any person in the world. Most of all he wants to die.

The whole school is assembled. They turn to watch the boy being dragged to the headmaster's dais. Their eyes are filled with contempt.

The father deposits the boy in front of the headmaster and says shortly: "He won't run off again!" He turns on his heel and is gone.

The boy stands alone, burning with shame. This is worse than anything he can imagine. Worse even than the beating his father gave him that morning. *Please let me die.*

With a few gruff words the headmaster sends him to his place.

Now he must survive the day. Many of his schoolmates choose not to speak to him at all, but he can endure that. It is the jibes, the vicious whispers, that hurt.

"Traitor . . . Traitor . . . Informer . . . Murderer . . ."

They are talking about his father, of course. But the shame is as bad if not worse, because what they say is true, and there's nothing the boy can do about it.

Except hate. Hate his father with all his heart. Hate and plan revenge.

He is fifteen. Soon he'll be taller and stronger than his father. Then he'll kill him.

But the nightmare is static, claustrophobic. However hard he tries he can't move it forward in time. He remains fifteen. He is doomed to stand in front of the school forever. Their voices scream in his ears: "Informer . . . Nazi traitor . . ."

And he dies of shame. Again and again and again.

Berg woke with a start and looked around him.

A hotel room. Somewhere—Tromsø. He remembered now: the journey had taken all day.

Damn. He'd overslept.

He pushed the remnants of the dream from his mind and, sitting up, checked his watch. Eight. He stumbled into the bathroom and, splashing his face with cold water, tried to muster his thoughts.

He had phone calls to make—to the office, to people in Oslo, to Ragna Johansen.

He swore again. If Ragna Johansen went out to work, he would have missed her by now. Damn!

He showered and shaved quickly, feeling cross with the world and himself. Then he tried Ragna Johansen's number. No reply. She hadn't been there all weekend either. It would be just his luck if she was away. But unlikely, he decided—January wasn't a time to go visiting in these parts.

Going down to the dining room he had a quick breakfast of black coffee, half a roll, and two cigarettes, and returned to his room to try the office.

Nine was a bit early for a daily and it took quite a few minutes before the switchboard could find anyone to answer an extension, then several more minutes while a young journalist went to Berg's desk and checked it for messages.

None.

Then he called the Estonian tobacconist.

"One message," came the reply. "For Harri. It reads: 'Very interested in your latest. More detail would be useful.' That's it."

Alex.

Berg put the phone down.

Alex, wanting more information.

What a bloody cheek.

Still ... it meant Kåfjord was important. It meant that someone—which meant Niki—had considered it sufficiently important to want more.

Well, they'd have to be patient. Putting the request to the back of his mind, he set about getting hold of Ragna Johansen. He thought it might take a long time, but he'd forgotten how easy it was to find people in a town the size of Tromsø. The telephone operator not only knew whom he meant by Ragna Johansen but had a very definite idea of where to find her.

Ragna sat in the cubicle that served as her office and stared unseeing at the accounts ledger in front of her. She cradled her head in her hands and closed her eyes. From the front of the shop came the murmurings of customers' voices. The staff would be expecting her to give them a hand.

Leaning over, she pushed the door closed. She couldn't cope with customers today.

She shook her head slowly from side to side. The small voice was still there. And it kept saying the same thing over and over again.

What have I done?

Every time she remembered the events of Saturday night she felt sick. What a fool she'd been! He'd never forgive her. And she didn't blame him. She certainly wasn't feeling very proud of herself.

Sunday had been a terrible ordeal. He'd been as cold as ice. Polite, but chillingly distant. The day had passed with agonizing slowness.

What a mess.

If only she'd been able to explain. But she hadn't. Not at the time.

It was only later that she'd understood the stifling panic she'd felt at that awful moment in the bedroom. It was as if she were standing on the edge of an abyss of pleasure, about to enter an entrancing prison which, like a golden cage, would close around her and keep her trapped forever.

She'd realized quite suddenly that it would be impossible to have a casual affair with Hal. He was an all-or-nothing man. Whatever he'd pretended to agree to that night, it wouldn't have worked. He'd have expected all sorts of things from her—commitment, time, love. She couldn't live up to those kinds of obligations, not at the moment. Perhaps not ever.

She'd given commitment and love to Jan, and then he'd gone and—not been there anymore. She was no good at dealing with that.

She had a need for lighter things now: frivolity, laughter, the stimulation of different people, irresponsibility.

God—why had she let it happen?

Even as she thought it she knew the answer.

Loneliness: it wore you down and made a fool of you. It made you reach out blindly.

Oh, she'd wanted him badly enough. She'd wanted him far too much. That was the real trouble.

She clenched her fists at the still-vivid memory of him, at the touch, the feel of him, and sighed aloud. She knew—it would have been so good.

Yes: that was the real trouble.

And now he'd never understand. What must he think of her?

The telephone rang and she started violently.

She became aware of the office again, and the open ledger, and the sounds outside in the shop.

Pulling herself together, she answered with a brisk: "Yes?"

"Ragna Johansen?" came a strange voice. "I was beginning to think I'd never find you."

"Who is this?"

"Rolf Berg. You wrote to me."

Ragna tried to take it in. Rolf Berg. She heard herself blustering: "Oh, hello—*hello*. You read my letter? You're interested in the story, then?"

"Yes. In fact, I'm here in Tromsø. Can I come and see you?"

"Oh!" She thought quickly and groaned aloud. "I can't get away. Not until three or so."

"Ah." A slight disappointment in the voice. "Well—I can use the time to get some background, I expect."

"You could go and see one of my Lapps," she said quickly. "A nephew of one of the Kåfjord families."

"Yes." He sounded pleased. "That's exactly what I could do." She gave him Aslak's work address, and he rang off, saying: "I'll come to your shop at three, then."

Ragna went to a mirror and dragged a brush through her hair and put on some makeup, thinking: He's come all this way for my story! It was an exhilarating thought. Rolf Berg and his newspaper were influential, and the fact that he'd come to Tromsø showed that her judgment had been right all along. It *was* an important issue.

She could hardly concentrate on her work, which did nothing to endear her to the customers, who arrived in an unexpectedly steady stream from the late morning onward.

And then he arrived early, just when she was flustered and exasperated, trying to deal with a belligerent woman determined to squeeze into a dress two sizes too small for her.

Ragna came out of the changing rooms and he was there, standing by the door, looking surprisingly at ease in a women's dress shop. Ragna was suddenly aware of the scowl on her face, and her makeup which she hadn't retouched for hours, and her hair which had fallen over her eyes.

Undaunted, she pushed the hair back from her face and strode across to him, thinking: I'm going to impress you!

He shook her hand. "How are you?" His tone was intimate, as if they'd been friends for a long time.

"Fine!" she said briskly, taking in his confident stance, the immaculate grooming, the smart clothes. She'd forgotten what a sophisticated man he was.

"Give me five minutes, will you?" she said. "And then perhaps you'd like to come to my house. I've got all the papers there."

He gave her a long unhurried look and she sensed that those lazy blue eyes missed absolutely nothing. "Of course," he said.

She found him waiting outside. He held the door of her car open for her, a gesture that most men in Tromsø would think absurd, but which he carried off quite naturally.

As she drove, he told her about his visit to Aslak. He talked in a detached, almost bored, tone, but she guessed it was his normal manner. She took an occasional glance at him. He was a good-looking man, with that thick blond hair and long straight nose, although the face was harder than she remembered, with deeply etched lines on either side of the mouth and across the forehead. An interesting well-lived-in face, with experience—and probably the wrong sort—written all over it.

"I tried to find the reindeer-migration routes on the map," he said, "but Aslak wasn't sure."

"Oh, none of them can read maps," Ragna replied. "Because they never need them, you see."

"But he said you'd be able to show me?"

"Oh, yes!"

As soon as they got to the house Ragna put some logs in the stove and turned on all the lights so that the room looked welcoming. She prepared a tray of bilberry jam, bread, biscuits, coffee, and aquavit. On the way into the living room she paused in front of a mirror and checked her face.

She found him in front of a framed photograph of Krisi. He gave her an odd glance. "I'd forgotten."

She put the tray on the table. "He's almost five now. He spends the afternoons at a neighbor's house."

They sat at either side of the low table and she poured the coffee. He also accepted an aquavit, a large one, then lit a cigarette and drew on it deeply. He smoked like he drank, she noticed, with determination and long practice. That explained the slight bleariness of the eyes, and the hint of puffiness beneath; imperfections that saved his face from being too handsome, she decided.

She started in a businesslike way. "Right! Where would you like to start?"

Ignoring the question, he reached into his pocket and handed her a small package. "A little something for arriving out of the blue."

She opened it and found a box of handmade chocolates. "Well, you'll make me change my opinion of journalists yet!"

"Are we not in favor?"

"Ha! I think you're wonderful," she said emphatically. "Just as long as you're never allowed to ask the questions!"

He laughed suddenly, a nice deep laugh that transformed his face. She was rather pleased: she guessed that few people were clever or quick enough to make him laugh.

Unfolding a map, she showed him the position of the installation and the migration route of the Lapps who used the valley above Kåfjord.

"At this time of year they're way up on the plateau," she explained.

"Can we find them?"

She grinned impishly. "If you've several days to spare and some good skis."

"What about the installation site. Can we go there?"

"Yes. It's not that far."

"Could you fix it?" The question was asked charmingly, but she had the impression he was used to people doing exactly what he wanted.

She considered for a moment. "I would think so."

Then she showed him the correspondence she and Hal had had with the various government departments. He leafed through it, and asked casually: "How did you find out about the installation in the first place?"

"Ah." She wagged a finger at him. "You should know better than to ask for my sources."

He smiled, but his eyes were cool, and she thought: He doesn't like being ticked off.

"I just wanted to know how accurate your information was," he said.

She hadn't thought of that. She felt somewhat deflated. "Oh, I see. . . . Well, supposing I said I had friends with friends in the right places. Would that do?"

He didn't look entirely happy, but went on: "What about the function of the installation—do you know that?"

"No. Wish we did."

He drained his glass and, leaning forward, helped himself to another drink. He was making himself very much at home, she noticed, but she didn't mind that.

"A pity," he said. "It would be better to wage your campaign fully armed. If you knew the function of the installation, then you could suggest alternative sites and spike the military's guns—so to speak."

"Well, we just assumed it was a defense installation . . ."

"Ah, well, there are installations and installations."

He ran his fingers over his mouth, looking pensive. She noticed what beautiful hands he had.

Finally he gave a small shrug. "As far as I understand it, the place is more offensive than defensive."

"Oh. *Oh.*" She absorbed this startling new information. "So—it's all nonsense. What they've told me, I mean. About these places being essential for defense."

"Well . . . it depends on how you define defense."

"Do you know what this place is for, then?"

He shook his head and, changing the subject, said quickly: "Will you take me up to the site?" He gave her a slow winning smile. She thought: He's used that before.

But she wasn't going to be put off that easily. She demanded: "Why won't you tell me about the installation?"

A flicker of irritation passed over his face. "Because I honestly don't know." His tone was very soft, very reasonable, and very final. For some reason she was convinced he wasn't telling her everything.

He repeated lightly: "Come up to the site with me." He made it sound like an invitation to get to know him better.

She hesitated, wanting to press him on the unanswered question yet not wanting to alienate him. Finally she left it alone and said: "Yes, of course I'll take you. Wednesday would be the earliest, if I'm going to organize it properly." She gave a light laugh. "I'm no great skier, I'm afraid. But then every event needs a liability. We'd better have a guide though, in case the weather's bad. It's quite a trek up there. Aslak will be happy to come with us, I'm sure."

"How about Hal?"

Hal. Her heart thumped. A jumble of sensations tumbled into her mind, some exquisite, some painful, but all of them disturbing.

Rolf was watching her closely. He seemed to be reading her mind. She flushed and gave a noncommittal shrug.

He said: "It would be very good for the story if Hal came along. His name still means a lot—both to the editor and to the readers. Besides, I'd very much like to see him again."

Ragna pictured herself in the mountains with both Hal and Rolf Berg. It wasn't a very happy picture. But she couldn't see any way out of it. She nodded slowly. "I'll phone him."

"And tomorrow—can you suggest any more people I should see?"

"Certainly. I'll take you around, if you like."

"Please." He was getting to his feet, smiling that lazy smile of his. "I'm afraid I'll have to ask you to run me back now. I've arranged to have dinner with a local journalist."

Ragna was disappointed. She'd rather hoped he would stay for the evening.

"But how about dinner tomorrow?" he asked.

"Yes, that would be nice."

"Assuming I wouldn't be—er—keeping you?"

"Keeping me?"

"From the man in your life."

He was fishing. Was this a declaration of interest? She almost smiled: it was an intriguing thought.

She heard herself say: "I can spare the time."

Then for some reason she thought of Hal and felt incredibly guilty.

17

Thrane ordered a second search of her apartment, more to convince himself he was doing something useful than in the hope of finding anything concrete.

Immediately after they gained entry he was glad he'd come.

Things had changed. Sonja's high standards had slipped. The apartment had been scrupulously tidy before. Now there were clothes draped over the bedroom chairs, a mug of half-drunk coffee beside the bed, and a couple of dirty plates soaking in the sink.

Why the change of behavior? Was she worried about something? Did she know they were on to her?

Or, worst of all, had the lover flown, leaving her lovesick and forlorn? His heart sank at the prospect.

The four of them split up and searched different rooms. Thrane and Jensen chose the main bedroom. Wardrobe, dressing-table drawers, cupboard, bedside table, bed—a difficult one, this, they had to be careful to remake it in exactly the same way—light fixtures, curtains.

There was nothing. Thrane couldn't help feeling disappointed. One always lived in hope.

Through the hall to the kitchen. The other two were plowing their way through every pot, pan, screw-top jar, and cubbyhole.

Back into the hall. Cupboard with raincoat, light jackets, ski anorak. And on the top shelf a holdall and a handbag. Thrane went through the holdall, which was empty, then the handbag, which was empty too.

He closed the doors and turned away.

He ran a hand lightly over the antique table near the front door, and opened the single shallow drawer. Keys, tram tickets, a lipstick, pens, pencils, paper clips—unwanted items from a handbag, perhaps. And papers: a receipt from a plumber, a theater season guide, a letter, and, at the back, a thicker batch of papers.

He reached for the thicker papers, unfolded them, and almost choked with excitement.

The missing minutes.

It took him a second to work out what it meant.

It meant she hadn't passed them on yet! She hadn't made her contact!

He allowed himself a moment of triumph.

He gave the papers to Jensen to read, then, carefully replacing them in the same position, he slid the drawer closed.

Berg sat in the car beside Ragna and stifled a yawn. It had been a decidedly dull day. They had visited the Tromsø museum, where an expert on Lapp culture had explained at great length the significance of the reindeer-migration routes and how the various groups of Lapps laid claim to their pasturelands.

They had gone to one of the local newspapers only to discover that Lapp affairs hardly made local news at all. Neither the files nor the journalists had much to offer in the way of opinions or facts.

Then a local politician had made a brilliant job of simultaneously professing interest in the Kåfjord issue while backing off rapidly.

In fact, the only bright thing about the day had been Ragna herself. He took a glance at her now, as she drove back to the hotel. She was a good-looking woman; her profile, white in the reflection of the headlights, was quite enchanting. And she had the sort of wry humor that Berg liked. Yet he suspected that her sharp mind and vivid energy concealed a strong will. In the old days he'd liked women on the fiery side, but now he wasn't so sure. The more independent, the more difficult they were to deal with.

He realized he was already regarding an affair as a foregone conclusion.

He cast another look at her and knew he wasn't mistaken. If she wanted it, it would happen.

She caught his look and said: "Sorry it wasn't the most exciting afternoon."

He gave a dry chuckle. "Did I look that uninterested?"

"Yes," she said bluntly, and laughed.

They came into what passed for rush-hour traffic in Tromsø, a queue of three cars at a junction. He noticed that Ragna was tapping the wheel impatiently.

He said: "Do you enjoy living in Tromsø?"

"Enjoy? Well—I suppose so. . . . *No*," she corrected herself irritably. "What am I saying? No, I don't. Except when I'm in the mood for a quiet life. And that isn't very often!"

"I always understood Tromsø was full of life."

"Compared to where?" There was sarcasm in her voice.

"So why do you stay?"

The traffic started to move. Ragna shoved the car into gear. "Believe me, I'd like nothing better than to get away, but I've had trouble with the shop and I can't get rid of it."

"Ah." So he'd been right. Ragna wasn't the sort to stay in a place like this. He'd known she had too much style for a parochial town. He wondered why she had married Jan Johansen, and remembered wondering that once before, a long time ago.

"You used to be an actress, didn't you?" he asked.

She didn't answer straightaway, but concentrated on maneuvering into a parking space in front of the hotel. Finally she said lightly, "Way back, far too long ago."

"You don't talk about it?"

"Not often. It . . ." She hesitated and pushed out her lower lip. "It wasn't a good time for me."

"But that was your sort of world, surely. More than—" He gestured: here.

She pursed her lips, as if he'd uncovered some unwelcome truth.

"I'd like to hear about it over dinner," he said, and surprised himself by meaning it.

"I don't promise to talk about my past, but I'll take the dinner off you anyway." She said it with a casual shrug, but he thought she looked rather pleased.

"You're sure you don't have a lover?"

Her eyes flashed at him darkly, and he realized he'd touched a sensitive spot. She gave a light laugh, followed by a small shrug. "I'm sure."

He thought: I wonder why not.

He asked: "Do you have to go home first or—"

"My mother-in-law's there. She'll look after Krisi."

They got out of the car. "I suppose we'd better eat early," Berg said. "What time did you say we've got to start in the morning?"

"Five."

He grimaced. "Ouch! Usually I only see five when it's at the far end of the day."

She wasn't going to miss that one. "Mmm," she said, giving him an amused look. "It shows."

Berg smiled as he took her arm and led her into the hotel. He found himself looking forward to the evening.

He took her up to his room and offered her a drink from the two bottles he had there—normal social practice in a country where drink was prohibitively expensive. He poured himself a large Scotch, downed it in three, and felt himself come slowly alive.

He made a phone call to the office. Ingrid told him the editor wanted to know when he'd be free to go to Bonn to cover a defense story. Berg said hopefully never. Ingrid said she'd arrange it for Friday then, unless he wasn't going to be back from Tromsø in time.

Berg dropped the receiver into its cradle with a crash and swore under his breath.

Ragna said: "I've never seen a telephone glow before."

He almost snapped at her, but, seeing her good-natured smile, stopped himself in time. He took another drink and his anger melted away. It always did with the second drink. "It's my newspaper," he said. "Always asking the impossible."

"That's probably because you're too good at what you do. You should deliver a few dud stories." She wagged a finger at him. "But not yet!"

Berg took a shower while Ragna talked to her son on the phone. Then they went out, walking slowly through the brightly lit center of town, following the road that ran parallel to the waterfront. It was six. The restaurants were opening up, people were strolling along the snow-packed pavements talking, linking arms, laughing.

"Where shall we go?" he asked.

"Well, the food's pretty much the same everywhere. Fish. Or fish and potatoes."

Berg chuckled. "Don't tell me. Boiled."

"Or fried! But there is a place with a nice atmosphere. Nansen used to stay there before setting off on his Arctic expeditions. Or was it Amundsen? I always forget."

"Speaking of explorers, what about Hal? Shouldn't we have left a message at the hotel to tell him where we've gone?"

There was a silence. They stopped at a crossing. Berg noticed that a small frown had appeared on her forehead.

"He wasn't too sure when he'd get here," she said, avoiding his eyes. "He'll probably arrive too late. But yes, of course. We'll phone from the restaurant and leave a message."

She looked firmly ahead but he noticed that her lips were thin and tense and her eyes were narrow like a cat's. He thought: Now, I wonder what all that's about?

Hal realized he'd never make Tromsø in time for dinner. Everything had gone smoothly until late morning, when he made his last rounds and found a young musk-ox in the high pasture, lying in the snow, sick and weak. It was a one-hour job to rig up the tractor winch, haul the creature onto a litter, and bring it down to the barn. The animal was obviously in distress, but there was no way of telling what was wrong with it. All Hal could do was ask Arne to keep an eye on it.

Then, on a quick trip to pick up a batch of extra fodder from the supply boat, the tractor decided to get stuck in a drift. By the time he'd gotten it free, dropped the hay, and gotten back to the house, it was late in the afternoon. It would be a good three hours before he got to Tromsø. Ragna and Rolf would probably have finished dinner.

As he threw equipment into the trailer, a powerful image of Ragna sprang into his mind: Ragna across a candlelit dinner table, Ragna laughing, Ragna looking wonderful. He extended the scene to Ragna making love, and almost slammed his finger in the cab door.

He was about to set off when he realized he'd forgotten the

spare rucksack for Rolf and the compo rations. He ran down to the basement storeroom, angry at being so disorganized: he really had to get a grip.

When he returned, Bamse was waiting by the tractor, barking excitedly.

"If you think I'm taking you . . ."

Bamse wagged his tail furiously. Hal said crossly: "You'll be a nuisance, you old fool."

The dog whined and growled in a frenzy of happiness. With an exaggerated sigh of resignation, Hal gestured toward the open trailer and Bamse jumped up. "You'll need feeding, I suppose." He made one final dash into the house for some dried fish.

It was six and very dark by the time he'd ferried the equipment to *Skorpa* and had a last word with Arne. He pushed the engine to maximum revs for the journey across the sound, but it still took far too long. He unloaded at the jetty, took *Skorpa* to her mooring, and, collecting the Land-Rover, set off at a furious pace, throwing up clouds of snow on the road behind.

He was mad to be going at all, of course. He still couldn't think why he'd agreed. She'd taken him by surprise, that was the problem. When Arne had given him the message to call her, he'd imagined she wanted to talk, to explain—even—agony to think of it now—even to say that she'd made a dreadful mistake and would he forgive her.

Laughable.

Oh, she'd sounded sheepish and miserable all right—a couple of times she'd seemed on the point of saying something—but she'd managed to restrain herself without too much difficulty and keep to the subject of the call, which was to ask him to come to Kaafjord. And he'd heard himself agreeing because he was damned if he was going to show her how bloody hurt and angry he still was.

He was sounding bitter. He *was* bitter.

It would pass. He was determined that it should. He was not only going to survive this, he was going to emerge with total immunity to Ragna, so that she could never ever do that to him again.

From that point of view the trek wouldn't be a mistake after all. It would help the recovery process along. He couldn't help thinking that it would also be a perfect opportunity to show Ragna that he didn't give a damn.

Yes. He drew a childish satisfaction from the thought, and, giving a grim laugh, pushed his foot down. A moment later the Land-Rover bucked over a ramp of drift snow and swerved into the beginnings of a skid. The adrenaline kicked into his veins and, with a sense of perfect control, he steered carefully out of it.

As the car's speed dropped, a lot of his tension suddenly fell away.

He reviewed his earlier thoughts. They had been very childish. Scoring points off Ragna would achieve nothing except make himself look petty and foolish.

Far better to show nothing, reveal nothing, remain coolly polite; take things as they came. There'd be Rolf to talk to, news to catch up on. If he put his mind to it, he might enjoy the trip after all.

The new and as yet unopened bridge to Tromsø Island came into view, arching across the dark water toward the glittering lights of the town. It was eight-thirty. He might yet be in time to join Ragna and Rolf for dinner.

He pictured the candlelit table again, and saw her laughing her extraordinary laugh, a soft chuckle that came from somewhere deep in her throat; he saw her lips, moist and soft, and felt the warmth of her body and her powerful sensuality, and experienced a rush of feeling so strong that he gripped the wheel until his knuckles turned white.

He was the sort of man that she and her schoolgirl friends used to call a wolf. And in the old days she'd certainly had the sense to keep well away from the Rolfs of this world. But now? She didn't care: one had to live for the moment—wasn't she always saying that?—and at this particular moment she was enjoying herself.

There were two sides to Rolf Berg, she discovered. A serious side which expected a lot: well-informed opinions and quick answers. He was ruthlessly intolerant of sloppy thinking, and it was a challenge to pull herself up to his level. But the effort paid off: slowly her sluggish brain began to pick up and tune in to his thinking, until she was arguing with him, point for point. By the end of the meal they had talked their way through the politics and ethics of the cold war, the newly erected Berlin wall, and NATO defense strategy. She sensed that she had earned his approval. It pleased her; she guessed it wasn't something he gave very easily.

Their politics differed, of course: she was middle-of-the-road while he was left-wing and noticeably anti-American, but he was too sophisticated a man to be intolerant of someone else's opinions, and she had the feeling that he argued simply to exercise his considerable mind.

The other side of him was also challenging, but in a completely different way. He was sensual, charming, attractive, and spoiled. She guessed he'd had dozens of affairs: he had the slightly jaded air of someone who'd always gotten what he wanted and wished it wasn't quite so easy.

He produced a flow of amusing, sometimes provocative, conversation, sprinkled with anecdotes which she guessed he'd used a thousand times before; yet more than once she managed to cut through the polished delivery and throw him off-balance, and then he really came alive, laughing suddenly with obvious delight.

There was also a sense of uncertainty about him—even danger. Or did she mean excitement? Whatever, it was very attractive.

Ah, she thought: Am I thinking about him like that?

Yes, she was. It was impossible not to.

"You haven't told me about your acting days," he said over coffee.

"No, I haven't," she said with bright finality.

"Ah," he said, accepting her refusal calmly. "You may have a point. The past's only a millstone around one's neck, isn't it? Or at best irrelevant."

He signaled for the bill. When it arrived, he looked up suddenly and said: "I wonder what appened to Hal."

She felt a flutter of guilt. "The farm, the animals. Anything might have delayed him."

Rolf was giving her a long look. She thought: He knows.

He said softly: "You look—cross."

She laughed it off. "It's the idea of having to get up at four."

His eyes rested on her a moment longer, then he pushed back his chair and said abruptly: "Well, let's go and see Tromsø by night, then."

"What?"

"A nightclub. Doesn't everything start early around here?"

"Not that early. It's not even nine." Suddenly she had an idea. "There's only one thing that begins early." She led the way out to the car.

As he got in beside her he raised his eyebrows questioningly. She shook her head to show that the surprise, whatever it was, would be ruined by more explanation.

She drove up a winding road that led up the hill behind the town. When they reached the highest point on Tromsø Island she parked. They walked a short way to the brow of the hill and looked out.

There was no moon but the night was washed with diffused silver light. A sprinkling of stars shone dimly. A mist hung over the sea, soft, translucent, and so deep that it was impossible to see where the water ended and the sky began. To the north the mist rose toward the source of the silver glow—the northern lights, the aurora, which hung across the sky, brushed with soft colors, trembling and undulating like a vast crown of glistening thorns.

"There," she said.

He looked in silence.

She said: "I usually wave at them."

"What?"

"Wave at the lights. Up here they say you mustn't. It's meant to be very unlucky."

"So you do it to prove they're wrong."

"And because I can't stand superstition. But surely you'd heard of that superstition?"

"When I was a child I remember some old woman saying: Don't stay out late or the northern lights will take you."

"Did that frighten you?"

He thought for a moment. "The only thing that frightened me was the idea of being stuck in a small town for the rest of my life."

Ragna gave a short laugh, then realized that he was intensely serious. "Was it so bad? Where were you brought up?"

He didn't answer. Instead he shook his head in the direction of the panorama. "I'm afraid that I don't very much like beautiful places. They tend to depress me."

"Most people find them inspiring."

"Most people don't know what life's really about."

She laughed. "That's what I like about you. No false sentiment."

"Nothing false about me at all."

"Oh?" said Ragna archly. "In that case you're very unusual."

"Absolutely. I don't deny it." He shrugged, and she had the feeling he was only half joking.

He indicated the aurora. "It's caused by magnetism, you know. Electrons charging into the upper atmosphere at up to twelve hundred miles a second. The friction makes the atmosphere glow. Oxygen glows red and green. And I think it's nitrogen that produces the bluish purple."

"Oh, dear. That explanation rather lacks romance, doesn't it?"

She felt his eyes on her. He reached out and, turning her face to his, kissed her softly on the mouth. She was so surprised she didn't respond at first, then, just as she was about to kiss him firmly back, he pulled away.

She gave a short and rather nervous laugh, aware that he had thrown her off-balance. She rallied with: "Was that the missing romance, then?"

He laughed and they began to stroll back to the car. He put his arm around her shoulders. The gesture was oddly familiar, as if they'd known each other for years. Almost, Ragna couldn't help thinking, as if they were lovers.

Lovers. Ragna turned the idea over in her mind. As a distant prospect, it wasn't unattractive. No—she glanced up at him—not unattractive at all

"Perhaps they've already been and gone," suggested the waitress. "Do you want to order?"

Hal looked at the time. Nine. The waitress was right—he must have missed them. "No thanks," he said.

He paid for his beer and made for the door. A diner smiled at him as he approached and leaned out to touch his arm. "Off on another trip soon, eh?"

Hal looked at him blankly. He'd never met the man before in his life. With a brief shake of the head he passed quickly by. From the sound of the muttered exclamations behind, he'd obviously caused offense. To hell with it: he wasn't answerable to the public. He wasn't answerable to anyone anymore.

Nevertheless he was angry with himself as he walked briskly through the streets to Berg's hotel. The receptionist shot him a white toothy smile. She was sorry but Mr. Berg had not returned. Did he want to wait in the adjoining café?

Hal shook his head. Someone in the café was bound to want to talk to him and he wasn't in the mood for small talk.

He waited impatiently near the main door, then sat restlessly on a sofa by a large spiky tropical plant. There was nothing to read. He stood up again and wandered over to the window. Taxis and the occasional bus went past, their studded tires scrunching softly on the snow. A family party came in from the street, chattering loudly.

Hal felt his anger simmering up again.

He was about to turn away when a car swooped in to the curb. A woman was driving. She had rich dark hair. He recognized the car. Ragna.

She turned and, smiling, opened the door and climbed out. Rolf Berg appeared from the other side and came around. Taking Ragna's arm, he paused and put his mouth to her ear. With a wide smile she cocked her head slightly to one side so as to hear him better. They pulled back, laughing at some joke, and came toward the hotel doors.

Obviously Ragna was having no trouble enjoying herself. An unpleasant feeling spread through Hal's stomach.

He stood back and waited for them to come in.

Ragna was breathless and flushed, her eyes dark and sparkling. Seeing Hal she stopped with a tiny gasp and put a hand to her chest.

"Hal!" Her expression cleared and, coming up, she gave his arm a small hug then automatically offered him her cheek. He leaned down to kiss it. It was cool under his lips.

Rolf was smiling broadly. "Hal!"

Hal said: "We're very honored."

Rolf retorted: "I'll bet!"

Rolf had changed, Hal noticed; he looked tireder and

rather unfit. Or was it simply that they were both getting older.

Ragna said hastily: "We missed you at dinner."

"I was there just before nine," Hal said quietly.

"We must have only just missed you, then! What a pity!" A smile fluttered across her lips. She seemed flustered.

She chattered on. "We've just been to see some of the local sights."

"Tromsø by moonlight," Rolf said, with a touch of irony.

There was a short silence. Ragna made a show of looking at her watch. "Well, if we're really starting at five . . ."

"What are the arrangements?" Hal asked.

"Oh, didn't I tell you?"

"No. That's why I've been waiting."

She looked embarrassed. "Sorry—" She ran quickly through the morning's arrangements, her eyes darting everywhere except up to his face.

"We meet here, then," Hal agreed.

Rolf commented: "I hope you aren't going to be too talkative at five. It's not my best time of the day."

"Don't worry," Ragna said. "Our lips will be sealed."

She was having no trouble looking Rolf straight in the eye, Hal noticed, and very warmly at that. He remembered the two of them getting out of the car, the smiles, the extraordinary intimacy of their movements. His heart sank. She couldn't . . .

Hal said abruptly: "I'll see you to the car."

Ragna blinked at him.

He put a hand on her shoulder. It was a deliberately proprietorial gesture. Faint surprise registered on Rolf's face, followed by a mildly questioning look that went first to Ragna and then to Hal.

Hal stared back at Rolf and gave him his answer: Keep off.

A flicker of understanding crossed Rolf's face, he smiled faintly and said to Ragna: "Good-night, then." He leaned forward and kissed her lightly on the cheek.

Ragna murmured: "Thanks for the dinner."

Outside, Hal pulled open the car door and waited for Ragna to get in.

She hesitated by the door, on the point of saying something. He cut in: "Good-night, Ragna."

She said softly: "You've got somewhere to stay?" It was a polite inquiry, not an invitation.

"My friend's expecting me."

She caught his meaning and dropped her eyes.

As soon as she was in the car, he walked off, heading for Anna-Kristin's.

18

The route of the old mining track was just visible in the gray morning twilight, zigzagging its way up the side of the valley to the unseen plateau above. Hal led the way toward it, with Aslak at his shoulder and Rolf and Ragna following. Bamse raced ahead, nose to the ground.

They had driven up the rough road from Kåfjord and parked the Land-Rover beside the track. Now it was only three miles to the site as the crow flew, but the valley side was steep and the real distance, allowing for the snake of the track, was over four miles, and four tough uphill miles at that. Hal set a pace that wouldn't tire Ragna and Rolf, settling into an easy plodding rhythm that was echoed by Aslak, so that the rasp and fall of their skis merged into one.

They left the thin dark stubble of the birch scrub behind and started up the valley side. Around them hung the steep, near-vertical slopes of the mountains, steel-gray and wind-blasted where the snow had failed to find a grip on the hard, ridged gabbroid rock. On the track, however, the snow was thick and full, and Hal automatically looked around for signs of avalanche danger.

It grew noticeably colder. This side of the valley faced north and remained untouched by direct sunlight even in midsummer, for it was too steep to catch the low trajectory of the Arctic sun. Now, in the brief winter day, the twilight barely penetrated the thick cloud that hovered above the flat-topped mountains, and the hillside was cast with an oppressive gloom.

Hal reached a bend in the track and halted to allow the last two to catch up. Aslak stopped beside him and, rolling his eyes toward the sky, murmured: "Snow."

He could be right—the cloud was certainly heavy enough. With inexperienced people in the party there was a case for turning back, but something made him want to press on. He realized what it was: he didn't want to have to repeat the expedition another day.

The others were closer now. Their pace was almost leisurely. Clearly they didn't feel the need to hurry. They were too busy talking happily. As he watched, Ragna's head jerked back, and a shout of laughter rose up and was swallowed by the stillness.

Pressing his lips into a hard line, Hal gripped his ski poles and set off again. This time he went at his own pace, which no one but Bamse could match. It took a moment to find his rhythm, but then he experienced that extraordinary release that came from pushing himself hard, through and beyond the point of resistance, until his body slipped into the slow, effortless burn that could carry him for miles, even days.

After a while he came to a reluctant stop because he dared not lose sight of the others, who were already some way back. He saw with satisfaction that they seemed to be finding the climbing harder, for they had dropped into single file, their heads down and their bodies bent over.

No bright laughter now.

He surveyed the weather again. The cloud layer seemed to be lifting slightly—or was it his imagination? He looked down into the deep valley below. The visibility had definitely improved. It was possible to follow the line of the snow road back the way they had come, down the floor of the valley toward the fjord, six miles away. Immediately below him the parked Land-Rover looked toylike, even at this distance. The road went on up the valley, running alongside the frozen river, until it disappeared in the curve of the hills. But it only went for a few miles, he knew. After that it petered out into a foot trail as the valley rose rapidly onto the expanse of the plateau.

Aslak caught up. Finally the others drew nearer and Hal prepared to set off again. As he adjusted his gloves a tiny distant movement caught his eye, and he paused.

Something deep in the valley: a vehicle on the snow road, coming up from Kåfjord. Hal watched for a moment, wondering who on earth would be coming up here at this time of year. He looked questioningly at Aslak, who gave a small shrug. "Hunters?" the Lapp suggested without conviction.

There was the scrunch of approaching skis and a long feminine sigh.

"Goodness!" came Ragna's voice. "I'm not as fit as I ought to be!"

Hal pulled at his gloves again, harder. "There's still quite a way to go," he said. "Are you up to it?"

"Oh, yes!" she said hastily, her breath shooting out in white clouds which vaporized instantly in the frozen air. "I'm fine! It's just a few leg muscles I'd forgotten I had!"

"And how about you, Rolf? City life catching up with you?"

Rolf gave a wry smile. "Any moment now."

"Not on for a race to the top, then?"

"Ah . . ." Rolf made an exaggerated gesture of regret. "Another time."

Hal led off again slowly. A moment later a pair of skis caught up with his. It was Rolf. Hal smiled a welcome and the two men began to talk. After a while Hal found himself relaxing; Rolf had always been good company.

Men were so straightforward and uncomplicated. He thought: Why can't women be the same?

The path was getting steeper. Ragna concentrated on the climbing, trying not to fall too far behind the two men who, lost in conversation, were striding ahead with Aslak at their heels. She wasn't up to this, she decided: her boots were chafing, her legs were aching, and her skis were backsliding. Also, her hands and feet were freezing, while her body was raging hot. The correct thing to do was to remove a few layers of inner clothing, but she couldn't face the effort. She wasn't up to this!

It was all right for Hal. He was in his element; that was clear from the way he strode out, welcoming the challenge, relishing the steep climb. For some strange reason she'd never been trekking with Hal before. On holidays she'd always been with Jan or other friends, and then, when Krisi arrived, they'd kept to small excursions close to home.

Now she was glad that he'd come, very glad. She'd forgotten how eerily quiet it was up here, and how rapidly the weather could change, and how very easy it was to feel suddenly and unpleasantly alone.

Hal. Thinking of him she felt a renewed pang of—what? Remorse. Yes, and confusion. She did so wish they could talk.

Sometime later she looked up and realized Hal had slowed down, leaving the other two to go on ahead. He was waiting for her! She felt a leap of nervous excitement.

But on reaching him, panting hard, she found him staring intently through binoculars. Her breathless greeting went unacknowledged.

She realized he hadn't stopped for her at all. She adjusted to the idea with difficulty.

Following the line of his binoculars she saw he was looking downward. The valley floor was almost lost to view behind the bulge of the hillside, but it was just possible to see the Land-Rover, which showed as a tiny gray dot against the whiteness. Next to it, she noticed, was another vehicle, also stationary.

Was this what Hal was staring at?

There was a click as Hal replaced the binoculars in the pouch at his waist and, without a word, started off again, leaving her standing.

She hurried to catch up with him. "Whose car was that?" she gasped.

He was frowning. "What? I don't know."

She struggled to keep up. He was moving fast.

Finally she exclaimed in exasperation: "Hal . . . please."

"What?" He slowed down a little.

"Don't let there be bad feeling between us. I can't bear it."

He was silent. But she could sense the suppressed anger in his movements.

"Hal—"

"Ragna, I have absolutely no intention of discussing this now!"

Angry, Ragna stopped abruptly and let him pull away from her.

When she finally started off again she saw that Rolf was waiting for her.

"All right?" he asked.

"Apart from not enjoying myself very much, yes."

"It's not so far to the top."

They trudged on for a moment in silence. Ragna was glad to see that the track ahead was less steep; perhaps the worst of the climb was over.

Rolf, who didn't seem nearly so out of breath, said: "This story. Once I've written it, how will you use it?"

"How?" she panted. "I don't understand."

"How will you capitalize on it?"

"Oh." She hadn't thought about that. "I don't know. . . ." She trailed off, partly to catch her breath.

"You should go and see some members of parliament. Get pledges of support."

"Oh, I see. . . ." Suddenly she had to rest. She stopped, and Rolf waited with her, the two of them leaning on their poles.

She said "The problem is money. I don't have any. Certainly not for trips to Oslo, anyway."

"It wouldn't take more than a day or two."

"But the traveling—I don't have the fare. Anyway, which politicians would I go and see? And supposing they didn't want to see me?"

"I've a pretty good idea of who's likely to be sympathetic. I can get you the introductions. It would definitely help. So would another round of letters to ministers."

"Oh."

He heard the doubt in her voice. "Is that a problem?"

"Hal's the best one for letter writing."

"So?"

"I don't know if he'll—want to."

The blue eyes shot her a questioning glance. He said carefully: "Hal's a great asset to your campaign, you know."

She shivered; it was suddenly very cold. A keen wind seemed to have sprung up out of nowhere.

She murmured, "Yes, I know," and they set off again. With a sinking heart Ragna saw that there was another steep section ahead.

Behind, Kåfjord Valley seemed to drop away like a precipice. Ahead they glimpsed the sides of austere mountains and the beginnings of a shallow valley, a valley that led to the plateau.

Ragna was struck by a sense of desolation and emptiness.

Even Rolf was frowning and silent, and she guessed he was oppressed by it too.

God, he knew this place all right.

The plateau did not change. Still godforsaken, cold, empty. After all this time Berg had thought it wouldn't have the power to touch him, but the sights and sounds of the place triggered astonishingly powerful images in his mind.

He remembered the sound of the silence—he remembered that better than the howl of blizzards or the whine and rasp of wind-torn snow; better, even, than the endless drip-dripping in the snow cave. But he'd forgotten the incredible pervasiveness of it, and how its soft deathly absorbency enveloped everything. A permanent reminder that life and hope ended here.

For him it nearly had.

He couldn't remember the pain of the frostbite, though he knew it had been appalling, he could barely remember the sensation of hunger—but he did remember the cold. Oh, yes, he remembered that all right. It was the sort of cold that ate into you, seeping through flesh, then bones, and finally into your very guts. Given enough time it even consumed your hunger.

He was beginning to regret having come. At the same time he took a perverse satisfaction in being reminded of how appalling and precarious the other side of the coin of life could be.

Too much alcohol, too much good living, had made him soft. This was sharpening him up.

So was the cold. He felt it now, embedding itself in his cheeks, and paused to draw the hood of his anorak tighter around his face and up over his mouth.

Ragna did the same, sighing: "God—this place."

He thought: You should try it at minus fifty.

The ground was leveling off. The old mining track—if it was still there—was invisible beneath the snow. Hal led the way unhesitatingly up into the shallow valley until, after another twenty minutes, he finally stopped and dropped his rucksack onto the snow.

By the time Berg joined him, Hal was bent over a map with Aslak. The Lapp pointed to the head of the gently rising valley, where it divided into two passes between the surrounding hills. "We camp up there in the pass, away from the herd, so we make no sound that would disturb them. Down here"—he made a wide gesture that encompassed the body of the valley—"here the calves are born. The lichens, the grass, they are good in early May, you see. The air from the fjord, from the sea, is warm and the snow leaves early and everything grows well."

Berg pulled his hood back. "Where exactly will the installation be?"

Ragna panted up to the others and collapsed breathless on a rocky outcrop.

Hal pointed at the map. "If they're going to use the remains of the mining track then they'll probably site it around here, or over by the mine itself."

"Where is the mine?" Berg asked.

Hal pointed across the valley. Berg examined the various possibilities and decided that, though buildings might be located in the valley, the long cables that seemed to be an integral part of modern navigation systems would have to be suspended between two high peaks, possibly even across Kåfjord Valley itself.

"But why have it up here at all?" Ragna chimed in. "That's what I don't understand. Why not have it in a more accessible place?"

No one knew the answer to that except Berg, and he didn't speak.

Hal said: "We should eat."

Taking off their skis, they sat down on the rocky outcrop to drink coffee and eat sandwiches.

Berg asked Aslak: "Is there really no other valley where the reindeer could calve?"

The Lapp looked vaguely surprised that anyone should not know the answer to such a question. "The does were born here," he said. "Nearly all the herd were born here or very close to here. They do not know any other place. Their instincts bring them back."

"What would happen if you herded them into another valley?"

"If you herd reindeer you put them under stress. We'd lose

half the calves that way. Normally we just follow the reindeer, let them lead the way. We only herd them once a year for marking and slaughter."

"What about the miners when they were here? Didn't they disturb the reindeer?"

"It was long ago. But they came only in summer, when we were down in the low pastures." Aslak described the seasonal migrations, and the food needs of the reindeer at different times of the year.

Then he fell silent. Hal stood up suddenly and reached for his skis. He jerked his head toward the head of the valley. "I'm just going to take a look around."

They watched him pole off rapidly, then Aslak strolled across to his rucksack to find a cigarette and Ragna went to take photographs, leaving Berg to take a long look at the map. He realized it wasn't that far to the Finnish border. He worked it out on the scale: ten miles.

When Ragna returned, she peered over his shoulder. "Jan and I came trekking up here once. If you take the road right up to the end of Kåfjord Valley, then it's only a few miles until you're right on the plateau." She traced a route into a wide empty expanse of Finland. "There's a lovely icefall"—her finger hovered over the map—"here. And a couple of huts. I can't remember where. We went for three days."

"I thought you didn't like the plateau."

"But that was at Easter. It was sunny. And warm." She sank down beside him. "And I was fit! Not like *this*."

She hunched down, pulling her hood around her face, and said: "Well, what d'you think?"

"About what?"

"The story."

"Mmm. Promising."

"Surely you've enough."

"No."

"What else d'you need then?"

He stared into the distance. "The source of your information."

She hadn't been expecting that. "I can't!" she exclaimed. Then an idea seemed to come to her. She grasped his arm. "Although—well, we might be able to do a deal."

"Oh?" He looked down at her. She had the gleam of mischief in her eye.

"You could tell me what this place is going to be used for," she said.

She was a trier, he had to give her that. "And even supposing I could, what would you do with the information?"

"I'd use it to suggest another site. I'd use it to impress those politicians."

"Then you *are* coming to Oslo?"

"Maybe," she said meaningfully.

He considered. The information would help her campaign only if she handled it properly—that is, with discretion. Ragna was lots of good things, but not, he suspected, discreet.

Yet an idea was forming in his mind. He pushed it around for a moment, looking for pitfalls, assessing risks. He thought he saw a way of turning the situation to his advantage.

He might well give her the information. Not out of the goodness of his heart—in matters like this he didn't have any heart—but as a way to leak the information out into the press. It was far too risky for him to use the information himself— too many hard facts like that in his articles and the Security Service would soon start sniffing around—but if he gave it to Ragna and she bombarded the government with the information, it would soon leak out. Her lack of discretion would do the trick.

Then he could pick up the story and give it wider coverage.

One problem remained: how to let her have the information without implicating himself.

But he was beginning to see a way in which that too could be achieved

"Okay," he said, "tell me, then, what was your source?"

She hesitated. "Promise it won't go any further?"

Berg almost smiled. She was like a child. "Promise."

"All right," she said with due solemnity. "Well—some friends in Oslo told me. A group called Friends for Peace. They told me it was phoned to them anonymously."

Perfect. He asked: "And how did you get to know them?"

"From the old days. A writer friend of mine helped found the group. I've known him for years."

Even better.

She asked: "You know about the Friends, then?"

Berg knew them well. Left-wing intellectuals involved with the World Peace Movement, and with various antinuclear groups, and, more often than not, with the Communist party too. He had been careful to keep his distance from them.

"They're rather left-wing, of course," Ragna said, huddling down even farther out of the wind. "But their hearts are in the right place." She looked at him expectantly. "Well?"

It would work so long as he could trust her. *Could* he trust her?

Removing his glove, he touched her cheek. Her eyes widened, then, understanding that his gesture marked some important turning point, she returned his gaze with mischievous frankness, one eyebrow raised challengingly, a smile on her lips.

He decided. Careful that Aslak shouldn't overhear, he said softly: "You have to promise me one thing."

She nodded.

"You must never under any circumstances say how the information came to you. Because if you do, not only will my source realize I broke his trust, but no one will ever let me have any information again. Also, and more to the point, my source would get arrested."

Her expression was suitably serious. "I promise. Absolutely."

"Okay—" He drew a deep breath. "It's part of a new navigation system."

"Navigation." The disappointment showed on her face.

"Hold on, hold on," he said irritably, raising a hand to show that he hadn't finished. "The system has been designed with a very specific purpose in mind—to penetrate beneath the surface of the sea, up to ten yards down, to reach American Polaris submarines." He could see that she didn't understand the significance of this. He explained patiently: "Polaris submarines carry nuclear weapons—offensive nuclear weapons—and just two years ago Norway declared herself to be a strictly nonnuclear country."

Enlightenment dawned. "My God! I see."

"The system's called Delta. Not only will it give Polaris submarines their precise positions instantly—something they've never had before—but, because they won't have to come to the surface to find out where they are, they'll be able to obliterate Moscow without any fear of discovery. It gives the U.S. an immense advantage in the cold war."

She was taking it in.

"By the way, if it's anything like the Loran system it'll involve a massive array of long aerials which'll stretch from here"—he gestured toward the mountains—"probably all the way across Kåfjord Valley itself."

"And I can use all this?"

He chewed his lip thoughtfully, as if making up his mind. "Yes."

"Thank you, Rolf," she breathed reverently. "Thank you."

Berg gave a modest shrug and looked satisfied, which he was. It was all rather neat. Doubtless FO/S had been keeping an eye on Ragna for some time and knew all about her links with Friends for Peace. They would assume, reasonably, that she had gotten this new batch of information from her usual source.

And they would assume that Berg had gotten his information from Ragna.

Yes, all rather pleasing.

Before replacing his glove he rubbed his knuckles affectionately against Ragna's cheek.

Hal headed for the old mining camp on the far side of the mountain valley. It was a relief to be on his own, with only Bamse weaving irregular patterns in the snow ahead. His senses expanded toward the silence and the absolute stillness and the certain feeling that he was happy in places like this. The snow lay fresh and soft on the undulating ground, absorbing the faint hiss of his skis, so that the sound barely touched the vast silence.

Nansen had described the Arctic as a place "high under the heavens . . . the air was clear and life was simple. . . . Back to solitude—silence—greatness . . ."

That summed it up perfectly.

Hal broke into an energetic lope so that the backs of his skis rose in sharp little kicks at the end of each stride. He pushed hard, as if the exertion would obliterate unwanted thoughts.

When he reached the ruins of the mining camp and found there was nothing to see, he resigned himself to having to turn back.

It would have been nice to push on over the brow of the next hill—he always wanted to find out what was on the other side of things. But it was almost midday. The light would soon fade, making the downward journey tricky for Ragna and Rolf.

He enjoyed a last few moments of isolation, then started off. Instead of heading straight back, he decided to make a triangle that would take him down the near side of the valley, and then across the valley mouth at the point where the land began to fall steeply toward Kåfjord Valley.

He took the first leg at a slow plod, not wanting the excursion to be over too quickly. Before starting the final leg he paused to look out beyond the deep chasm of Kåfjord Valley to the mountains beyond, which were just emerging from the cloud. The weather would hold off all right.

His eyes swept across the vast panorama, dipped down toward Kåfjord Valley, and finally swung up to the three small black dots near the rocky outcrop.

It took a moment for his brain to absorb what his eyes had registered. Then he cranked his head back with a sudden jerk.

There had been a tiny anomaly, something out of place—

He redigested the visual information, trying to pinpoint the spot.

It had been something small, something moving, a shape that didn't quite fit . . .

Somewhere *there*. Near the top of the mining track, where it was steep and narrow.

Sensing the tension, Bamse whined at Hal's side.

Hal hushed him and, pulling the binoculars from its pouch, made a slow sweep.

He looked over the ground again and again. Nothing.

But there had been something.

Hooking the binoculars around his neck, he set off, heading for a point above the first zigzag of the track. The ground was hardly more than a slope yet; he had to go into a frantic kick-glide run to make speed.

Bamse went bounding ahead. Hal summoned him to heel with a sharp angry whistle.

At last he reached the point where the ground began to fall away more steeply and he could gain momentum. Even then he dug his poles in hard to gather speed and yet more speed, until he was careering headlong downhill toward the steep drop ahead. He almost came to grief on an unseen snow-covered rock—one ski skidded from under him, the other shot into the air, and he had to flail his arms in a desperate attempt to regain his balance. More by luck than design he landed on one ski and, with one final jerk of his arms, managed to find his footing.

His heart thumped with relief. He was out of practice.

The floor of Kåfjord Valley came into view below and finally the track itself, snaking away beneath him.

He halted and crouched down, very still, to watch.

Nothing. He felt a sharp disappointment.

Then suddenly—

There!

Movement.

A figure—a skier—on his way down the track, negotiating a bend.

Putting the binoculars hastily to his eyes, Hal examined the figure as it cruised out of the bend, accelerated down a straight, and then dropped from view.

He straightened up, frowning deeply.

He was still frowning when he returned to the others and led them slowly down the track, heading for home.

The figure had been wearing familiar kit.

White from head to toe. Except for the rifle, ammo belt, goggles.

But he'd recognized them, too.

Norwegian Army–issue, the lot of it.

19

Hal stood on the veranda and peered at the thermometer. Minus fifteen. And still dropping. The night was clear and cold. Stars carpeted the sky, but they shone palely, as if they, too, were dulled by the cold.

The wind was from the northeast. Everyone knew what that meant: a high pressure system over the Arctic and the risk of a big freeze.

It had been some time since they'd had a real northeaster—three years, in fact. Since the time of Pasvik. The high pressure hadn't properly established itself then and the freeze had only lasted a few days. But on the plateau it had dropped to minus forty.

Whenever he remembered the weather at that time an old torment returned, worrying at him like an aching tooth: that Jan might have died slowly. The picture was vivid and sickeningly familiar: Jan lying in a desolate windswept place, alone and bleeding, dying slowly, knowing he was dying, feeling the cold creep over him . . .

Hal shook himself free. There was no reason to think it had been like that. Yet the suspicion remained. He could only hope it wasn't true; he could only hope Jan had never realized what had hit him.

Turning abruptly, he went back into the house and closed the door firmly behind him.

It was seven. The end of a long day; the end of three long days since the trek.

Hal went and slumped by the stove. He was feeling very

low. First the sick musk-ox had died. The vet had come from Tromsø at great expense, only to declare that he had no idea what had caused the sickness. He had taken some blood and tissue samples for analysis, but hadn't been very hopeful. Hal had been upset; he was fond of the animals. It was almost like losing a family pet.

Then there'd been the extra work caused by the weather: feed to be doled out, constant mucking out because the barn was overcrowded, a musk-ox to be dug out of a drift, an injured goat to be dealt with.

As a result, the paperwork was piling up horribly. A report for the army on a new ski design was overdue. In his advisory capacity to a scientific expedition to Greenland, he had three equipment inventories to check over. Finally, as ever, there was the mail.

Rousing himself, he ate a quick meal, put on Beethoven's Fifth, and sat at his desk with a ration of aquavit to help things along.

He'd already opened some of the mail, and now flicked through it to remind himself of the contents. Putting the bills and business letters to one side, he reread a carefully handwritten and rather formal note from Mattis's family. They said that Mattis had never possessed a pair of binoculars of the type described. The only ones he had ever had were the ones given him on the Alpine expedition of 1951. They were sorry they could not be of further help. They sent kind regards.

Hal would pen a short note of thanks later.

He didn't need reminding who the next letter was from. No one else had handwriting like that. It was a large hasty scrawl, liberally sprinkled with punctuation that defied all known rules.

He reread the last sentence.

. . . *Hope you'll come on Sunday—Krisi wants to go tobogganing—would you??*

Sunday was tomorrow. He hadn't made a final decision about this yet, but he had the feeling the visit wouldn't be a good idea. Though the invitation was clearly a peace offering, he wasn't quite ready to make peace. He'd miss seeing Kris of course, but better to leave it another week and give things a chance to settle down.

And they would settle down, he was sure of it. Rolf had gone. He'd flown back to Oslo on Thursday with no plans to return. For Hal it had been a considerable relief. It was bad enough to be turned down by a woman like Ragna, but to watch another man win such obvious favor was like a slap in the face. The memory still made him wince.

But what really staggered Hal was that Ragna couldn't see what sort of man Rolf was. Rolf was an accomplished journalist, a warm and generous friend, but he was impossible where women were concerned.

Ragna surely had better judgment than to get mixed up with someone like that. It made him despair to think about it.

With difficulty, he forced himself to go back to the beginning of Ragna's note and concentrate on the main body of the message. It was dated Thursday A.M., the morning after the trek.

. . . Incredible information from my contact in Oslo—it's a navigation system called Delta—there'll be massive aerials, loads of maintenance men coming and going all day long—but, most incredible of all, it's for use by Polaris nuclear submarines—i.e., not defensive, but offensive—for use in a nuclear war!!! Would you write to the minister of defense and ask him how the Norwegian government can possibly allow it to be built on Norwegian soil???

Hal shook his head. Sometimes Ragna could be wildly unrealistic. He couldn't possibly ask that question. He couldn't even mention submarines. If he objected to the installation on anti-Polaris grounds, he'd be labeled even more of a subversive than he already was, and that would lead to a very quick cancellation of his army contracts. No contract, no money. It was very simple.

At the same time he must continue to help Aslak and his people, who, he never forgot, were also Mattis's people. Their rights were being overridden, and he couldn't let that go unchallenged.

He sighed harshly: "Ragna . . ." And, pulling out some paper, attempted to draft a letter to the defense minister that would make everyone happy.

Half an hour later he thought he'd achieved something that would further the Lapps' cause without, he hoped, putting himself in too subversive a light.

Though whether the watchdogs at FO/S, the Security Service, would see it that way was debatable. Doubtless he was already labeled a danger and had been given a file all to himself. Thrane hadn't said as much, of course, but Hal knew how the system worked. The U.S. insisted on rigid anti-Communist procedures where their interests were concerned.

As he typed the letter he thought of Thrane. He had the feeling the major wouldn't be at all happy when he heard about this latest lapse on Hal's part.

But he couldn't help that. He signed and sealed the letter, and put it ready on the ledge by the front door.

Then he sat and listened to the last magical strains of the symphony. The Fifth always cheered hm up. He put on some Mozart after that, because Mozart put him in a businesslike mood. Then he braced himself to start on the batch of unopened mail that Arne had brought up that afternoon.

There was a typewritten envelope from Oslo. He slit it open.

Bamse suddenly leapt up and, rushing to the door, barked furiously.

Hal heard Arne's distinctive stamp on the veranda outside and wondered what was bringing him out so late; he was usually in bed by nine.

Hal pulled the letter out of its envelope and glanced at it as he rose to his feet, intending to go and meet the old man at the door. He paused, staring at the letterhead.

"Cold," the old man remarked as he stamped the last of the snow from his feet and came in. "And it will get colder."

Hal hardly heard; he was too busy reading.

The letter was from a lawyer named L. J. Sorensen. He skimmed through the four paragraphs, then went back and read it again more slowly. The binoculars. This man had discovered whom they had originally belonged to.

The old man was hovering.

"One moment, Arne."

Nodding, the old man disappeared in the direction of the kitchen.

Hal read the letter a third time, rubbing his lip thoughtfully. Then he went to his desk and, pulling open the lowest drawer, started to search through it.

At last he found what he was looking for, an old dog-eared notebook, and flicked quickly through it. This was his diary from the early days, a record of all his early climbs and excursions.

He was trying to remind himself of what had been going on in the winter of 1944–45.

He saw that Jan and he had been on a couple of climbs. Yes: Blaamannen, Goalsvarre. But the knowledge didn't jog any other memories. If Jan had acquired a pair of German binoculars at that time, Hal certainly didn't remember it.

Arne returned, carrying a warm drink, and sat down by the stove.

Hal gave him a brief smile. "Sorry, Arne."

"There's a message."

Hal murmured absently: "Yes?"

"Ragna Johansen. She telephoned. She said she's sorry, but she won't be there tomorrow."

Hal looked up sharply. "Oh?"

"She's gone away."

Hal's throat went dry. "What? Where?" But even as Arne opened his mouth to reply, Hal knew.

"Oslo. She went to Oslo."

PART THREE

PART THREE

20

In the dream the cold was closing in on him. Berg opened his mouth to cry out, but no sound came. He tried to fight his way out of the blackness, but his arms were limp and useless and his legs heavy as lead. A weight seemed to press down on his body and he thought he'd never move again. He felt an immense surge of self-pity and impotent rage. He wanted to curl up and cry.

But Petter was shaking him by the shoulder, chivying him, calling out his name again and again. "Raf! Raf! You must get up! You must get up!"

The same words, over and over again, harsh and strident, invading his darkness when all he wanted was to be left alone.

The scene changed abruptly. He was being forced to move, hauled to his feet, but the effort was appalling and he cried out with the agony of it. When he tried to open his eyes a vicious whiteness assaulted them and sent an excruciating pain bursting inward on his brain.

Petter's voice again: "Come on! Come on, you son of the devil! Not much farther!"

The scene shifted. He was lying on the snow surrounded by reindeer, a vast herd that swarmed and stamped and snorted around him, their feet dancing closer and closer. He was overcome by terror: the animals were about to trample him, yet the stupid Lapps were doing nothing to prevent it. He tried to call out, but he was strapped down in some sort of sleigh and for some reason his mouth, like his limbs, would not move.

The panic rose in his throat.

Someone was shaking him again. Insistently.

This time he was really angry with Petter.

He moaned a long, loud "No-o-o!"

The sound of his voice came winging in from far away until it was suddenly very loud and very close.

He awoke with a violent start and looked straight into Ragna's face.

She was looking startled. "Are you all right?" she said. "I hated doing that, but you did ask me to wake you."

He took everything in—his bedroom, the gray light, Ragna bending over him—and flopped back on the pillow. He mumbled: "Okay."

He was aware of Ragna padding quietly out of the room. How had she gotten into the apartment? Of course: he had given her a key so she could come and wake him.

He reviewed the dream. It had been awful. It was that damned trek to Kåfjord—it had stirred up his memory.

He peered at the time: eleven.

He swung his legs out of bed, ignored the tiredness and the dull headache, and went straight into the shower. He ran it hot, then cold, and came out feeling more human.

Throwing on a robe, he followed the smell of breakfast to the living room and saw that Ragna had put out a steaming pot of coffee, squeezed orange juice, bread, cheese, and honey.

Very domestic. Not, therefore, to be encouraged.

As he sat down and poured his first cup of coffee she emerged from the kitchen. She was looking marvelous, he noticed. She'd obviously used the last few days to go shopping and have something new done to her hair.

She asked: "Did you get the article finished all right?"

He nodded. "At four." It'd been a stinker: a five-thousand-word piece on the Bonn Conference, and he'd only gotten back from Bonn at nine the previous evening.

She gave him an appraising look. "Feeling alive yet?"

He made a face. "Just about."

"In that case . . ." She advanced on him, put a hand on either side of his face, and gave him a forceful kiss. "That's a thank you!"

"Ah. It appeared, then?"

"You bet!" She passed him the *Dagens Post*. The editor had given his Kåfjord article a full inside page.

Berg said cautiously: "Well, we'll see what it produces. Don't hope for too much at this stage. But I'm sure this won't be lost on the man from the justice ministry. What time are you seeing him?"

She sat down at his feet. "Two."

"You'll go easy on him, won't you?"

She looked offended. "Well—I'm not going to hit him over the head if that's what you mean."

He smiled. He rather enjoyed teasing her.

She pretended to give him a fierce look. "You'll see—I'll have him eating out of my hand."

Berg said seriously: "He'll certainly sit up when he realizes you know what the installation's for. But be careful, won't you? I mean, don't say too much—just mention that you know what it's going to look like. And slip it in casually, as if it was common knowledge. Don't make a speech about it."

"I'll be careful." She had a grave expression, like a child trying to show how grown-up she was.

He sat forward on the edge of his chair and, reaching out, gently brushed his fingers against her hair. It was beautiful hair, dark, thick, and shining with color.

A tantalizing smile appeared on her lips. He leaned forward and kissed her. Her mouth was very soft. He thought: Tonight. We'll become lovers tonight.

His mood darkened suddenly: he remembered that he was due to meet Sonja that evening. He sighed peevishly. "Damn! I've just realized, we can't have dinner tonight." He thought for a moment. "But we could meet later, at about ten."

Ragna pursed her lips and looked at him through half-closed eyes, as if she were considering whether to accept. But he knew she would: Her laughing eyes gave her away.

That was what he liked about her: she made everything fun.

He gave her a lift to the apartment of some friends of his where he'd arranged for her to stay, then went on to the office.

As soon as he appeared, Ingrid said brightly: "Well? Wasn't Bonn exciting like I promised? Weren't you glad you went?"

He raised a sarcastic eyebrow and dropped the Bonn article on her desk with an exaggerated flourish.

The pile of mail in his in-tray was visible from halfway across the editorial floor. Flopping into his chair, he pushed the tray to one side and, lighting a cigarette, started leafing halfheartedly through the telephone messages. Contacts, minor politicians, pressure groups . . .

He remembered that he hadn't called his message service for some days, and immediately dialed the number of the Estonian tobacconist.

There was one message.

It was from Alex: *Contact me urgently.*

Berg replaced the phone, suppressing a vague feeling of alarm. He'd never had a message like that from Alex before.

He drew heavily on his cigarette, thinking hard, his mind skittering over possibilities, almost all of them unpleasant.

Leaving the office, he went to a public phone and, dredging his memory for the special number Alex had given him, dialed it.

It answered straightaway.

Berg said: "It's Harri."

A strange voice said, "Go to the Hotel Bristol, the Library Bar, in half an hour," and hung up without waiting for a reply.

Berg muttered contemptuously under his breath. Back to the cloak-and-dagger stuff. Yet as he walked briskly back to the office, his stomach was jittery, his mouth dry.

He arrived at the Hotel Bristol thirty-five minutes later.

Taking off his coat, he went straight across the main lobby, past the giant stuffed bear that glared out from a corner, and into the Library Bar. The bar was busy, most of the book-lined alcoves occupied by the writers and artists who liked to frequent the place. Berg recognized a couple of journalists he knew. Finally he saw Alex sitting in an alcove at the far end.

As Berg approached, Alex stood up and greeted him with a show of surprise, as if their meeting were accidental.

Berg played along with the pantomime and suggested a drink.

"Why not!" Alex exclaimed loudly, and ordered beer.

When the waiter had gone, Alex said in a low urgent voice: "There's a small—er—query, Rolf."

The fear rose in Berg's throat. "Oh?"

"The story you gave me. It's been looked into and—" Alex swallowed nervously and Berg noticed he was sweating.

Berg knew then: It was going to be bad.

"—we think there's something not quite—right with it, Rolf."

"What do you mean?"

"It doesn't fit with what we know, Rolf. Oh, there is a new navigation system. But we're pretty sure it's called Omega, not Delta. And the Omega installation is already under construction. But much farther south. At Aldra." He added unhappily: "We know this information is good, Rolf."

"But—perhaps the one at Kåfjord is a second site, part of a string."

Alex shook his head. "It doesn't work like that. Apparently a single installation is enough to cover the whole of the North Atlantic. It would make absolutely no sense to have a second. Also"—he took a deep breath—"the site itself, there at Kåfjord, would not be right. Surrounded by mountains, and with those tall Alps, the—er?" He searched for the name.

"Lyngen Alps."

"That's it—the Lyngen Alps. With them in the way, between the site and the sea . . . Technically, it isn't right, Rolf. They wouldn't put such an installation there."

There was an ugly pause.

Berg said harshly: "So what the hell's the place for, then?"

Alex raised his hands in a gesture of bewilderment. "We don't know."

"You seem to know everything else—"

Alex leaned a little closer. "Listen, Rolf, when I say we don't know, we don't know for sure. But when we first discovered that this site was to be developed, our people took a small guess at its function. They decided that, because of its location, it could only be something else."

"What else, for God's sake?"

Alex didn't like having to spell things out. He lowered his voice still further. "A monitoring station designed to pick up emissions from the upper atmosphere."

Berg rolled his eyes in exasperation; he wasn't in the mood to extract information by degrees. "What do you mean, emissions?"

Sensing Berg's anger, Alex said in a rush: "Well—signals from satellites. Our satellites—the Vostoks, the Luniks. The U.S. wouldn't miss an opportunity like that, would they? And apparently Norway is the obvious place, and this site, up in the mountains, is the ideal spot. Because—let me get this right—yes, something to do with other radio signals. Apparently it's essential to site such a place well away from interference."

A bell rang in Berg's mind. Sonja. She'd spoken of—what were her exact words?—needing to be away from radio interference.

She'd said it, but for the moment he couldn't work out how significant that was.

He said savagely: "But you don't know for sure."

"No," he conceded. "And of course we would very much like to know. But one thing, Rolf—" He shifted his considerable bulk in his seat and looked unhappy again. "Our people think it most unlikely to be a navigation system."

"I see," Berg said icily, suppressing his anger.

He gave it a moment, then said with a calmness he didn't feel: "So what does this mean, Alex?"

Alex made a feeble attempt to look reassuring. "Maybe nothing. Maybe nothing at all, Rolf."

They stared at each other. They both knew what it could mean. It could mean that they were on to him.

Berg found himself glancing around the bar, then jerked his head back. This was ridiculous. He was letting it get to him already.

He got to his feet and, in a halfhearted attempt to play out the pantomime, said brusquely: "Bump into you again soon, I hope."

He walked the length of the lobby, past the main entrance, and down the stairs to the men's toilets.

He needed time to think.

Locking himself in a cubicle, he sat down on the closed lavatory seat, lit a cigarette, and put his head in his hands.

Be calm, be calm. Think it out.

He went through it, step by step.

Sonja. Start with Sonja.

First: she might have made a genuine mistake.

Possible but unlikely. Her memory had never failed before.

When it came to her work, she was razor-sharp. She'd gotten the bit about the radio interference right, why should she get the rest wrong?

Second: the false information was a plant.

The thought made him ill. Yet it made no sense. They would never have planted such blatantly false information, for the very reason that it would be revealed for what it was.

Third . . .

He couldn't think of a third explanation. Except, perhaps, that Sonja had simply gone mad. It was possible. The death of her mother, her age . . . perhaps she was going through menopause.

He tried to remember the details of their last meeting: Had she behaved differently? She'd knocked back the booze a bit. And she'd been unusually jumpy. But that was easily explained by her mother's death. There was something else though. She hadn't seemed to mind about the lack of lovemaking; normally he'd have expected her to be more disappointed. Yes—that had been unusual.

But it was no good. He could think himself stupid without getting an inch nearer the truth.

He was sure of only one thing—that he was not going to the meeting with Sonja tonight. It would be madness. That house was a perfect trap. The thought was enough to make him shudder.

He forced himself to consider all the possible consequences, coolly, rationally.

Supposing they were on to him, then what was the worst and best he could expect.

The worst was simple: they already knew his identity and had enough evidence to convict him.

The best was also simple: they had no idea of who he was and no idea of how to find him.

The more he thought about it, the more optimistic he became. After all, he'd been very careful. It was very unlikely that they knew enough about him to have him under surveillance, and even if they'd been watching him he was sure he'd have spotted them. The only direct link was Sonja, and Sonja didn't even know his identity. There was no other way they could link this rubbish information to him.

Except—

Christ—

He jerked his head up.

Ragna.

The time. He thrust his watch face up to his eyes.

One-thirty.

Leaping to his feet, he shot out of the cubicle and ran up the stairs and across the lobby to the telephone booths.

He called the apartment. She had gone.

He waited until just before two, then called the office of the man at the justice ministry.

The secretary told him to hold, then Ragna's voice came on the line, a little breathless, rather surprised, saying: "Oh, it's you!"

And the relief flooded through him, cool and sweet.

Ragna ran a hand over her hair and stood back to take a critical look at herself in the mirror.

All right. More than all right.

Everything had come together perfectly: the striking aquamarine dress, slim and waistless and right up-to-date; the stranded jet necklace and matching earrings; the new shorter hairstyle, which hung smooth and sleek to just above her shoulders.

And her makeup was okay too. Dramatic, with strong color on her lips, because that was what suited her best.

She was dressed to kill. And kill she would. Mr. Rolf Berg. She grinned at the thought.

They were having dinner together after all. He'd managed to get out of his meeting and they were going to the Theatre Café.

Perfect.

She was filled with a childish euphoria. The moment she'd arrived in Oslo she'd known she'd done the right thing. It was as if she'd finally come home. She belonged in places like this—she always had—in cities, surrounded by energetic creative people, people like her—people who appreciated her. For the first time in three years she felt completely alive, and she'd forgotten how very good that feeling was.

When she thought how she'd dithered about coming! That

had been because of the money of course. But she'd managed to borrow some from her mother-in-law. Old Mrs. Johansen had been rather disapproving, which was no surprise. But really, what were families for?

The doorbell rang. Her throat was suddenly dry.

Rolf.

She hurried to the door and, swinging it open, gave a small exclamation of pleasure. "You're early!" she said warmly.

Berg paused for a moment on the threshold, his eyes hard and glittering. Then his expression softened and, stepping forward, he kissed her on the cheek. "You look stunning."

She laughed: "Thank you."

He led the way into the living room, and, going straight to the drinks trolley, helped himself to a large drink.

"No one else in?"

"No."

He began to pace up and down. "Are you all right here? Comfortable?"

"Yes."

"They look after you?"

She gave a small shrug. "Of course."

He seemed restless, almost preoccupied. She supposed he'd had a hard day. She made a mental note to ask him about it later, when he'd had a chance to relax.

He stopped abruptly and asked: "How did the meeting go?"

"Brilliantly!" She threw out her hands in an expansive gesture of delight. "He'd read your article. It'd made quite an impression on him, I think. Though he didn't admit it, of course. Anyway, he heard me out and promised that the minister would look into the matter of land rights and that he'd produce a full written answer to all my points." She added happily: "It was more than I expected."

"I'm sorry I had to call you like that."

She sat down on the sofa. Berg chose to stand by the fireplace. She noticed that his mouth was set in a hard tense line.

"Why didn't you want me to talk about Delta?" she prompted.

He looked down at her. "I discovered that the information was completely false. My source got it wrong. Someone had fed him a load of nonsense."

She tried to absorb it. "You mean—you mean, there's no Delta?"

He gave a shake of the head.

"It's not for Polaris submarines? It's not a navigation station?"

He said firmly: "No."

She gave a sigh of disappointment. This was a setback. "Then we're back to square one."

He sat down beside her. "Let's look on the bright side. There's no harm done." He gave her a quizzical mirthless smile. "Or is there?"

She blinked. "What do you mean?"

"You didn't tell anyone? You didn't use the information?"

"No. I haven't had the chance."

He looked relieved. "Good. Then everything's all right, then."

Ragna nodded vaguely.

Then she remembered.

Hal. Her note to Hal. She'd told him all about it. And she'd asked him to write that letter to the defense ministry.

She looked at Rolf uneasily. She had the feeling he wouldn't be pleased.

Perhaps she needn't tell him.

But that was silly. It would be far better to get it out in the open. And straightaway.

She was opening her mouth to speak when Rolf said: "It's a good thing we found out in time. You see, someone's out to get me. Trying to make me look stupid. You might even say he tried to set me up." He fixed her with those intense blue eyes of his. "It would have been extremely embarrassing if the information had been traced back to me. But it can't now, can it?"

"No." That was true enough. Hal didn't know it came from Rolf.

He seemed partially reassured and went to refill his glass.

Ragna thought frantically. Would Hal have written that letter yet? She pictured him alone at Brattdal, doubly angry and hurt now that she had left Tromsø; she couldn't imagine he'd be in the mood to do her a favor. But she decided to phone Arne first thing in the morning and leave an urgent message, just in case.

Yes: No sense in alarming Rolf unnecessarily. If Hal hadn't written the letter, then Rolf never need know.

If Hal had . . . Well, she'd cross that bridge when she came to it.

Rolf was draining his glass. "Let's go to dinner."

Pushing everything out of her mind, she smiled at him. "Lovely."

He glanced at his watch, frowned momentarily, then led her to the door.

Eight-ten. There was a sinking feeling in Thrane's stomach.

He took another look at the luminous dial of his watch and groaned inwardly.

He had been overconfident. And now he was paying the price.

It had all looked so promising: the sudden break in routine, the shopping for dinner, the drive to the love nest in the pinewoods, and then . . .

Nothing.

But Sonja had been expecting her lover, no doubt about that.

Thanks to the Norwegian custom of never drawing downstairs curtains, Thrane and his team had had a perfect grandstand view from the pinewood.

They had watched her preparing dinner, laying the table, looking at her watch, peering out the window, pacing nervously back and forth.

Now, after two hours, she was sitting at the kitchen table. She had long since stopped peering out the window.

He put the binoculars back to his eyes and focused carefully on the brightly lit interior. She was sitting motionless, her back to him, a drink at her elbow which she hadn't touched for some time. He wondered how a woman like Sonja could sit for so long, doing nothing.

Almost as he thought it, she jumped to her feet and disappeared from view. He picked her up again as she crossed an adjacent window, then lost her again. Making his way softly through the pines, he skirted the house until he found her in the living room.

She was on the phone, dialing rapidly.

She held the receiver to her ear without speaking. After a time she jiggled the cradle and dialed again.

Thrane thought: I'd give anything to know that number.

She waited for about a minute then crashed the phone down and buried her head in her hands. A handkerchief appeared and was clamped over her eyes.

Sonja had been stood up.

Thrane felt the full weight of his disappointment.

There was always a chance that the lover might turn up another time, but somehow Thrane didn't think so. He had the nasty feeling that something rather final and irreversible had occurred.

No evidence for that, of course, just his intuition and the way Sonja was hunched forward, rocking visibly, crying her silly eyes out.

He dropped the binoculars and waited.

An hour later Sonja finally emerged and made her way to her car. She drove off slowly. Thrane and his men followed in two cars.

At first Sonja seemed to be heading straight for home, but then she turned east, and Thrane felt a flicker of interest.

For a while he thought Sonja was on to him, for she suddenly accelerated and shot across a junction. But then she slowed, hovering close to the pavement, and pulled over to the side. Thrane overtook and risked a quick glance.

She had her head in her hands again.

He pulled over and waited. After five minutes she moved off, turned right, then right again. Back the way she had come.

Sonja had changed her mind.

She was going home after all.

Ragna looked across the restaurant table at Rolf Berg and thought: He'd be the perfect lover.

He was talking seriously, about politics. She had a suitable expression of interest on her face, but she was really picturing his naked body—cool, hard, smooth—and imagining the way he'd make love—with immense skill and experience. He'd know exactly how to give pleasure to a woman, how to build that pleasure up slowly, and then wait until just the right moment . . .

A delicious warmth spread through her and, suppressing a smile, she dropped her eyes for fear that her lascivious thoughts should show in her face.

He had stopped speaking. When she glanced up, he was looking quizzically at her. "Did I say something funny?"

"No. Do go on." Recovering her serious face, she asked him a question about the trend toward socialism.

He gave her an odd amused stare, as if he wasn't quite sure if she was serious, then began to answer.

Ragna watched him again, and decided he would be the perfect lover not only in bed but out of it as well. He would treat lovemaking as a simple pleasure between two people, something to be enjoyed, with no stifling obligations on either side. He wouldn't expect her to be around all the time. He wouldn't be cross if she had her own life. He would understand her need for freedom. Certainly he would never talk about *love*.

She pictured her life once she'd moved to Oslo. She'd get a small apartment, put Krisi into a local kindergarten, find herself a job, and see Rolf twice or three times a week. They'd go to the theater a lot, dine out in restaurants like this; she'd get to meet his friends, who, she felt sure, would be just her sort of people: artists, writers, actors.

She became aware that he was silent again. From the expression of mild amusement on his face she knew he'd seen through her question on socialist trends. His earlier preoccupation had obviously passed.

"Oslo suits you," he said. "You sould move here."

Ragna made a wry face. "I know!" She looked around the restaurant. "I love it all." The Theatre Café rippled with conversation and laughter and continuous movement. The spacious room looked like the interior of a Renoir café: all dark wood and soft golden lights and turn-of-the-century decor. Up in the gallery the pianist smoothed light melodies out of a grand piano.

"I love it all," she repeated. "The only problem is, what would I do? Look at me. I'm not qualified for anything."

"I'm looking at you." And he was. It was a frank expression of interest. She grinned and a look of complete understanding passed between them.

"Ah—if looks were everything!"

He burst out laughing. It was a wonderful deep laugh and she found herself thinking: I could love that laugh.

The bill arrived. He said: "But really, you'll have no trouble getting work. You're very unusual. Most important"—he touched her hand softly and thoughtfully—"you have life in you. That's a very rare and beautiful quality." He added firmly: "But, then, I'm not telling you anything you didn't already know."

He caught a waiter's attention and handed him the money. "But it's all wrong, you know."

"What is?"

"That you should be alone."

Ragna's heart lurched. "Ha! Don't give me sympathy," she said, putting on a bright voice. "I'm not used to it. I dissolve into a jelly!"

He gave her a gentle look. "You must have been very unhappy."

On the verge of feeling sorry for herself, Ragna covered the moment with a harsh, rather unnatural laugh. "Stop it, you'll have me crying in a moment!"

"I apologize."

"I should hope so! If you go on like that I'll run out on you!"

He liked that, and grinned. "Oh, no, don't run away, Ragna. Don't do that, whatever you do." He got up and held out a hand to her. "Let's go home instead, shall we?"

Home.

It was all decided, then. She felt a delicious suffocating anticipation.

She had had one brief moment of doubt.

They had walked into his apartment and he had pulled her gently toward him and started to kiss her. His lips were soft and teasing, brushing across hers, exploring the shape of her mouth, then pulling back a little to start again. She responded, opening her mouth under his, moving closer, pressing her body against his.

He kissed her more deeply then, and she felt that delicious warmth again, more powerful now, and her body responded, growing warmer still . . .

He pulled away and took a step toward the bedroom and stood, gently tugging at her hand, waiting for her to follow him in.

It was then that she looked at him and felt a flicker of doubt. His face: it was an impenetrable mask—his eyes hard and glittering, his expression empty of warmth or feeling. A sudden chill came over her, and she hesitated.

He seemed to sense her doubt, for, with obvious effort, he broke out of his mood and smiled.

Yet there was something bleak and lonely about that smile. Still she hesitated, searching his face, thinking: I don't know you at all!

Then he stepped closer and exclaimed: "Oh, Ragna, don't say you're going to run away after all!" And he laughed so charmingly and with such sudden warmth that she couldn't help laughing too, and her doubts dropped away, and all her need for him came back in a rush.

This time he didn't stop kissing her, not until they were standing by the bed and he was slipping her dress off, and even then his lips moved quickly back onto hers.

She felt shy, a little nervous. It had been such a very long time. She was aware of trembling slightly.

He pulled her gently down onto the bed. His mouth moved down her body, his lips pulling at her skin, probing, licking, exploring, until she couldn't have stopped even if she'd wanted to. He left no pleasure untried. He took her over completely, guiding her hands, whispering his demands, until he carried her over and beyond the last restraints.

And then she didn't want him to stop ever again.

Berg had thought that nothing could relieve the deep sense of unease that had nagged at him all day, but he was wrong. She did, for a while.

He'd also thought that no woman had the power to really excite him anymore, but he was wrong about that too. For a while.

She was shy at first, almost as if she were inexperienced, and it suddenly occurred to him that she hadn't had a lover since her husband had died.

The thought was strangely arousing. So too was her curious

mixture of reticence and sensuality. She seemed uncertain, even nervous; he felt her tremble. He had the urge to re-awaken her, to see her lose control and cry out and beg him to satisfy her.

He took it slowly, gently, one step at a time, finding each sensitive point, touching, licking, kissing, closing his mind to everything but the sensation of her.

Then, quite suddenly, her reticence vanished and her movements were urgent, demanding, knowing. He felt vaguely disappointed, even let down. Had the shyness been a pretense?

Pushing the thought from his mind, he concentrated on taking his own pleasure, losing himself in the sensations of his own body. He whispered a demand; she hesitated slightly, then obeyed. He whispered a second demand, adding soft words of affection, and she did that too. And then he knew there was almost nothing she wouldn't do for him, and he abandoned himself to the rapacious hunger of his senses that, much as he fed it, was never satisfied.

When it was over, Berg fought off the sense of emptiness and futility that he dreaded, but it crept up on him surreptitiously, pulling him down and down, until he thought bitterly: Why does it always have to be like this?

Ragna stirred beside him, soft and acquiescent and slightly damp from their lovemaking. He thought: She wasn't different after all. He felt disappointed, even slightly resentful.

Yet he hadn't had enough of her, not by a long way.

There was also the matter of the Delta business. She wouldn't break his trust, he knew that. At the same time it would be best to keep an eye on her until this little problem with Sonja had sorted itself out.

Sonja.

He'd had her on his mind all evening.

Tonight he'd failed to show up, but that was no solution. He had to know the truth. He had to find out if they were on to him.

The question was: how?

21

Lars Sorensen's meeting had overrun and he got back to his office at five with the prospect of at least an hour's paperwork ahead of him.

He went in through the side door that led directly into his private office. To his surprise his secretary popped her head around the door, though she usually left at four.

"There's someone waiting for you," she said. "It's Halvard Starheim. I suggested an appointment, but he wanted to wait."

Sorensen blinked, adjusted to the news, and, feeling a mixture of pleasure and curiosity, headed for the outer office.

The man who rose to his feet and shook Sorensen's hand looked just like his photographs, except taller, more impressive, with a fierce gaze from dark intense eyes.

Sorensen said warmly: "I hope you haven't been waiting long."

Starheim shook his head briefly, as if such trivialities were unimportant. "I would have made an appointment except I came to Oslo at short notice." His expression was serious, contained, yet he seemed full of suppressed impatience.

Sorensen invited him to sit. He noticed that Starheim carefully tweaked up the legs of his formal gray suit and adjusted his shirt cuffs. The clothes seemed incongruous on a man with such an athletic frame and work-hardened hands.

"You received my letter?" Sorensen asked.

"Yes. I was amazed."

"Amazed?"

"That you could discover so much."

Sorensen shrugged it off. "It's not so hard. The National Archives have some information, stuff which relates directly to the Occupation. But they're not geared up to individual requests like yours, which is why they pass them on to me."

"You're certain about this Schirmer, though?"

"Oh, yes. Wait a moment, please." Sorensen went into the inner office and returned with the file containing Starheim's original request.

"Now, let me see," he said. "You gave me the name Schirmer and the markings Three/GJR two-eighteen. Etched on a pair of binoculars, you said. Well, it's very simple. GJR stands for *Gebirgsjäger*—mountain troops. Three was for Third Battalion. And two-eighteen for the Two hundred eighteenth Regiment. Now, the Two hundred eighteenth Regiment was part of the Seventh Division, at least toward the end of the war. It had been converted from the One hundred ninety-ninth Infantry Division—"

Catching Starheim's expression, he said: "Sorry, I'll try to keep it simple. The Seventh Division was part of the Eighteenth Mountain Corps. Now, the Eighteenth Corps had been on the Russian Front at Kestenga, but during 'Northern Light,' the German retreat of the winter of 1944 to '45, they drove back through Finland and into Norway as far as Lyngen, arriving between November of '44 and January of '45."

Furrows of concentration appeared on Starheim's brow.

"So much for the regiment," Sorensen continued. "Now, this man Schirmer. That was simple too. I merely contacted the German Military Archives at Breisgau in the Black Forest, and they looked him up under Two hundred eighteenth Regiment, and there he was. A lieutenant, full name: Hans Schirmer. But, then, I'd guessed he'd be an officer."

"Why?"

"Having his name on the binoculars. It meant that they had to be his own property. And only officers carried their own binoculars. The name was properly engraved, I take it, rather than scratched on?"

"Yes."

"There! That's what I thought."

Starheim had been listening restlessly, tapping the tips of

his fingers together. Now he prompted: "But this Schirmer died?"

"Indeed."

"Do you have a date?"

"Yes—didn't I give that to you?"

"You said January 1945."

"In fact, he was reported deceased on——" Sorensen referred to the papers in front of him. "Yes, on January twenty-first, 1945."

"Where was that? And how did he die?"

Sorensen shook his head. "I can't say. And it would be difficult to find out. Although . . ." He did his thinking aloud. "It's unlikely he died in action, not on that date. There was no fighting going on at the time. Not at Lyngen, anyway. It's possible that he was injured at some earlier date, at the Russian front for instance, and invalided to a military hospital."

"But he died in Norway?"

"No, we can't be sure of that. Is it important?"

Starheim gave a harsh sigh. "I don't know."

There was a pause. The lawyer asked: "Can you tell me why you need this information?"

Starheim's dark eyes gave Sorensen a hard appraising stare, as if trying to make up his mind about him. Then he shook his head, a sudden sharp movement. "It's rather complicated. I can't really explain. Except . . ." He frowned deeply. "It's a personal matter, something that goes back a long way."

Sorensen said: "I understand." Although he wasn't sure he did. So-called personal matters usually concerned the unfortunate by-products of war, such as sexual liaisons with the enemy. Only this week a Norwegian woman had decided after all these years to try to find her German soldier lover, to tell him his son was nearly fifteen.

Obviously this didn't fall into that sort of category. Sorensen was rather intrigued.

Starheim asked: "Look, is there any way to find out where and how this soldier died?"

Sorensen hesitated. It was a tall order. It was a job for researchers, who would need to go through archives in Breisgau and Bonn. It might even be necessary to contact some of Schirmer's old comrades. The job could take anywhere from a day to a week. Even then, they might not come up with the answers. He blew out his cheeks. "I can't promise anything. And it would take a lot of time."

"If it's a question of money I'll be glad to pay," Starheim said firmly.

"Well—"

"Please. Will you put it in hand for me? If there's the slightest chance."

Sorensen understood: this really was important. He made up his mind. "All right. I'll see what can be done without incurring too much expense. If there's a problem, I'll come back to you. Are you in Oslo for long?"

Starheim hesitated: "I'm not sure. Two days. Maybe three."

"Where can I find you?"

"I'm staying with a climbing friend for a couple of days, then returning to Tromsø." He gave Sorensen the telephone numbers, and explained about leaving messages with Arne.

The lawyer stood up and led the way to the door. "Are you off on any expeditions?" he asked pleasantly.

There was a short silence. The frown on Starheim's face had deepened visibly. He clearly wasn't one for small talk.

Then they both spoke at once. Sorensen said, "Well, I suppose you're too busy—" just as Starheim rallied himself to say, "No, not at present."

They paused on the threshold.

Starheim forced a smile, as if realizing how distant and forbidding he must seem. "Thank you. I appreciate it very much." He hesitated. "Of course—this thing, it might be nothing . . ."

Sorensen nodded. "You don't have to explain. I understand. Sometimes one just has to find out, one way or the other."

It was bitterly cold. The streets were empty of taxis, and Hal couldn't remember which route the trams took. He jammed a hat on his head, wound his scarf tighter around his neck, and began the long walk along the icy pavements.

He thought about Sorensen and what he'd told him. He thought even more about what he hadn't been able to tell him, and felt a momentary despair. It wasn't that he held out much hope of getting useful answers, he was just tired of uncertainty. Uncertainty wore you down. He sometimes thought it was worse than bad news itself.

And there was quite enough bad news to be going on with.

He had reached some important decisions in the last few days, decisions that were extremely painful but necessary.

Brattdal would have to go. As a working farm, at least. He'd been crazy to think he could run it on his own. He could always hire a farmhand of course—though it was unlikely anyone would want to come and live in such an isolated spot—but the cost would be high and the whole operation would become even more unprofitable than it already was. One thing was certain, he couldn't go on trading on Arne's generosity.

Neither could he go on living there alone. He'd been trying to prove something that wasn't worth proving: that he didn't need anyone. It wasn't true. He did need people, and, more particularly, he needed a woman in his life. He'd been hoping that person would be Ragna. But he'd been wasting his time; she hadn't been worth waiting for.

Now he had an urge to make up for lost time, to cast off the past and rejoin the human race, preferably in large numbers.

For a moment he remembered all the work—the vegetable plot, the animals, the musk-oxen—and felt a crushing sense of futility. But he forced himself out of it. Regrets were useless. The chapter was closed.

He arrived at the Hotel Bristol at six-fifteen and came face to face with his partners in the other major decision he had made. Fred; and another old climbing friend, Carl.

Carl's grin stretched from ear to ear and he shook Hal's hand so hard that Hal pulled it away with a theatrical wince.

"Hal! Hal!" Carl cried. "This is wonderful news! Wonderful!"

"I haven't promised yet."

Carl winked, to show that it was only a matter of time. "You'll be with us, I know you will!"

Hal thought: He's right. And the idea cheered him. He slipped out of his coat. "How long before the meeting?"

Fred glanced at his watch. "Ten minutes." Fred had set up a meeting with a wealthy shipowner interested in financing the expedition.

Leaving Carl and Fred in the lobby, Hal went to a phone booth and called Arne's number seven hundred miles away.

The Tromsø operator gave the two long and one short ring that was the code for Arne to answer. After a pause Arne's voice sounded down the line. Hal could almost hear the neighbors picking up their phones to listen in.

"A calf's sick," Arne began. Hal knew immediately: a muskox, and his heart sank.

They discussed it briefly. The animal had sores around its mouth, but its general weakness suggested the same infection as before. Until the vet's report came through there was nothing that could be done.

"Ragna Johansen called," Arne continued, and Hal couldn't stop his stomach from doing a small hop.

He said: "Oh?"

"She wanted to speak to you urgently. I told her you were in Oslo. She wanted to contact you, but I said I wasn't sure where you were."

Hal felt a savage delight: that would keep her guessing. Good old Arne.

"I have a telephone number. She said it was very urgent." Hal wrote the number in his notebook. "Thanks, Arne."

"You'll be back soon?"

"Soon, Arne."

Hal went back to the lobby to join Carl and Fred. They started to walk into the main lounge. Carl was saying "I told you, Hal, didn't I, about the Geographical Society?" when Hal suddenly stopped in his tracks.

Reaching for his notebook he found the phone number Arne had just dictated to him and, leafing through his combined diary-address book, compared it with one he had there.

It matched.

The number was Rolf's.

For a moment he stared at the page, then, snapping the notebook shut, he clapped Fred on the shoulder and said firmly: "After the meeting, my friends, we are going to have a reunion party."

Berg came out of the phone booth, looked briefly up and down, and walked off, suppressing the urge to hurry.

The *Dagens Post* office was only fifty yards away, just around the corner in Akersgata. He had plenty of time. He picked his way across the mound of hard-packed snow by the curb, crossed the road, and walked briskly along the street and around the corner into the brightly lit entrance.

Nodding to the night porter, he strolled up the first flight of stairs until he was out of sight. Then he accelerated, passing the editorial floor at a smart trot.

A door led onto the roof. He extricated the key from the small glass-fronted box marked IN CASE OF FIRE and, unlocking the door, went out.

The roof of the *Dagens Post* building was flat and covered with a thick layer of crusty snow. He crossed it rapidly, following the tracks he had made half an hour earlier on his reconnaissance. The next roof, being considerably lower and steeply pitched at the sides, was trickier, but it was fronted by a parapet and, once he had lowered himself gingerly down onto the flat ridge and climbed down the incline on the fixed metal rungs than ran down one side, there was an easy path along the wide snow-filled gutter.

This was the last building on the block, and he approached the corner cautiously, at a stoop. Crouching behind the parapet, he raised his head over the edge and took a long look.

He was above a square called Aschehougs Plass, which was actually a small triangle formed by the junction of three streets. In the center of the triangle was the phone booth he'd just used.

It was eleven thirty-nine. He had made it from the phone booth in under five minutes.

From beneath his padded anorak he pulled out a small pair of binoculars and began to search the scene below. He could see straight up the main street that led off to the west, and up the narrow street that came in at a diagonal to form the triangle. By sticking his head over the parapet he could also see the street immediately beneath him that went eastward. There was only one blind spot: the south side of the square, which was hidden by a protruding building.

A tram jangled along below, turned into the square, and disappeared up the narrow street that ran off at the diagonal.

Otherwise nothing. A pedestrian, the occasional car, the sudden whooping shout of an unseen merrymaker.

His mouth was a little dry, his stomach tense. He calmed himself; whatever happened he would be safe up here.

The streets fell quieter. He could feel the cold biting into his hands. Beneath his padded clothing, sweat was cooling fast on his skin.

He put the binoculars back to his eyes and made a slow sweep from the top of one street, down into the triangle, up the next street, and down again.

Nothing.

Only ten minutes to go.

If she came.

She would, he was sure she would. She had been angry of course, her voice ice-cold and reproachful, but he knew Sonja: obedient, loyal, curious. She would come.

But the question was: would anyone else?

He sat up.

A car. A car in the narrow street was stopping at the curb. Its lights died. No one got out.

Berg's hands shook slightly as he grasped the binoculars.

Watchers.

He felt a moment of childish triumph.

An instant later he uttered a sigh of disgust.

A door of the car had opened, a woman had emerged. Waving to the driver, she walked off. The car lights flashed on again and it pulled away.

Berg's shoulders sagged and he sucked in a long breath.

Time passed. Another tram appeared and rounded the square, the rasp and rattle of its wheels unnaturally loud in the frozen air. Berg blew on his aching hands and tried to suppress a sense of foreboding. Supposing nothing happened? Supposing Sonja wasn't followed? Then he'd be no wiser than before. He almost *wanted* to catch the watchers in the act. It was uncertainty that really frightened him.

Suddenly he spotted Sonja's ancient Volvo.

He jammed the binoculars to his eyes. The car was coming hesitantly into the square from the main street. It slowed, stopped, then started off again. Typical Sonja. Wondering whether she dare park in a restricted area.

She disappeared for a moment, lost to view in the blind spot. Then she reappeared, still driving indecisively.

Finally she seemed to make up her mind. Rounding the square, the Volvo headed back onto the main street and pulled over to the curb. The lights were switched off. Sonja remained inside.

Berg swept the binoculars back and forth.

He couldn't believe it. Nothing.

Unless—

There.

This time he didn't allow himself to get excited. Another car had drawn up some distance farther up the main street, too far away to see clearly. But it looked dark-colored, maybe even black, and fast. Its sidelights were on, but then they too died. No one got out.

Back to Sonja. She too was waiting.

The minutes ticked slowly by. No one moved.

Eventually, the door of Sonja's car opened and she emerged. Pulling her coat closer around her, she picked her way across the icy road to the center of the triangle. She looked up the narrow street, then began to pace slowly back and forth. He could almost sense her agitation.

He swung the binoculars back to the parked car. Nothing.

Sonja left the triangle and, wandering over to the beginning of the narrow street, began to pace up and down again.

Berg suddenly realized that if the occupants of the car *were* watchers, they couldn't possibly see Sonja from there.

Which meant there were others. Somewhere.

He looked hard, but couldn't spot them.

Another five minutes passed. Sonja was still at the far corner of the square. She had stopped pacing and was standing still. Then, suddenly, she was on the move again, but fast this time, recklessly half walking, half running across the street.

She had given up on him. Doubtless she was in tears.

Suddenly he held very still.

She wasn't heading for the Volvo. She was coming straight for *him.*

He watched in vague horror as she drew nearer and, turning onto the street below, crossed the road and marched along the side of the *Dagens Post* building. He craned over the edge of the parapet.

She had the determined stride of someone who knew exactly where she was going.

Crouching low, he ran along behind the parapet until he reached the end of the roof, then peered over again. She was rounding the corner of the *Dagens Post* building.

Ignoring the fact that he might be horribly visible from the street, he scrambled up the metal rungs onto the ridge and levered himself up to the roof of the newspaper building.

He ran lightly through the snow to the front of the building. Crouching, he pushed his head over the edge of the coping.

He froze with disbelief.

She was there, just short of the entrance to the *Dagens Post*, standing still. Then she began to walk forward again, hesitantly, looking over her shoulder, as if she hadn't finally made up her mind what to do.

Where was she going?

But he knew. He knew with dreadful certainty even before she got there, so that when she reached the *Dagens Post* building and stopped again it was like a rerun film, a nightmare he'd already enacted in his mind.

He ran at a crouch to the corner and looked back toward the square. His stomach jolted savagely.

They were there. Out in the open.

Two of them.

The first walking briskly down the side of the newspaper building. The other coming more slowly from the direction of the parked car.

He jerked back to Sonja, as yet invisible to the approaching watchers.

She was still there. Standing. Looking up at the building.

Indecisive.

He felt a small spark of hope.

She was looking around. Turning her back on the newspaper building. Bending her head. He focused the binoculars. She was searching her handbag.

He looked back. One watcher strolled up to a tram stop and tried hard to look as though he were waiting for the last tram, though it had long gone. The other was immediately below Berg, and rounding the corner. The watcher, seeing Sonja stationary before him, did the only thing he could, which was to keep walking and go straight past her.

Sonja was still standing there, her head swiveling between the newspaper entrance and the corner.

Finally she made a few tentative steps.

Back the way she'd come.

She took another few steps, looked back over her shoulder, almost hesitated again, then, head down, quickened her pace.

She was heading back toward the square.

The relief washed over Berg in a hot wave.

He watched her walk briskly around the corner, down the street, and across to the triangle.

But it wasn't over; she was going into the phone booth.

The watcher who'd been waiting at the tram stop had retreated toward the black car.

Sonja stayed in the booth for several minutes. Berg had the ghastly feeling he knew exactly what number she was calling. His own.

At last she came out of the booth, slamming the door behind her, and made for her car.

The lights came on, the Volvo pulled away and disappeared.

A second later the dark car came into view doing a U-turn, and went off in the same direction.

Berg sat on the freezing roof for a long time, vicious with rage, trying to absorb the awful truth.

Sonja knew who he was.

Sonja knew.

How? *How?* He racked his brains.

No—forget how. That wasn't important now.

Much more important: did anyone else know?

Them. The watchers. Did they know?

If so they'd already be tapping his phone, watching silently, biding their time, waiting. . . . He felt violated and enraged. His mind lurched toward nightmare visions of captivity.

With a vast effort he pushed the images aside.

He clutched at a single powerful thought.

They couldn't have evidence. Not hard evidence. They couldn't prove he'd used the information for anything but his journalism. It suddenly occurred to him that they couldn't even prove he'd received the information in the first place.

They only had Sonja's word for it.

And it was possible they didn't even have that. Yet.

He progressed the idea. Suppose Sonja hadn't talked. Suppose they knew nothing about him. Then they'd be doing exactly what they'd done tonight: watching Sonja like a hawk, hoping she would lead them to him.

He became excited by the idea. It made perfect sense. If they had been on to him, they would have been watching him tonight in the same way they'd watched Sonja. Yet there had been no sign of a second surveillance team. He would have spotted it, he knew he would have. And if his phone had been tapped, there would have been a giveaway, a click or something.

The more he thought about it, the more convinced he became that Sonja hadn't yet blabbed.

As long as the watchers hadn't read too much into that determined walk of hers to the entrance of the *Dagens Post*, as long as they didn't realize the significance of that pause in front of the building, then he might just be all right.

Now—how to stay all right . . .

A thought came into his mind. He grasped at it, turned it over in his mind, warmed to it, and felt the beginnings of hope.

Three hours later he sat in a parked car with Niki.

Niki was tapping his fingers on the wheel, staring across the icy waters of Oslo Fjord. They had driven out on the Drammen road, past Fornebu Airport, to the end of a road of quietly affluent houses set in thick woodland. A snow-covered jetty, redundant until the spring, stretched out into solid ice. In the ice-free channel beyond, the lights of a small vessel glided across the fjord.

Around them few lights showed; there was silence.

In the faint silvery light, Niki was looking unhappy. He said stiffly: "Who is this woman?"

"Her name's Sonja Bjornsen. She works in the defense ministry."

Niki's head snapped around. "What? You're not serious—"

"But I told you, she's totally unimportant. She's nothing but a ledger clerk. I stupidly thought she had access to important stuff. But she doesn't. Would you believe it, but she works in accounts! I just got it wrong, that's all." Berg gave a small shiver. "Not only did I get it wrong, but she gives a whole new meaning to 'Hell has no fury.'"

"And she could really blow you?"

Berg gave Niki a long haggard look. "Yes, I'm afraid so. What's more, the timing couldn't be worse. I'm just on the point of getting some wonderful stuff, Niki." He paused for effect. "I've been working on this for a long time. If I lose it now it'll be a bloody tragedy." He gave a bleak laugh. "Quite apart from the fact that I don't want to go to prison."

The Russian said impatiently: "We wouldn't let that happen. We'd take you out."

A prison by any other name.

There was a silence. Niki was clearly in the throes of an inner struggle. "You don't know what you're asking, Rolf. It's—" He shook his head. "It's much more difficult than you might imagine."

"But possible?"

"Possible," he agreed, "but crazy. This woman works for the defense ministry. It's going to get noticed. They'll look into her life—"

"And find nothing."

"How do you know that?"

"I've made sure."

"Rolf, Rolf . . ." Niki sighed with exasperation. "Things aren't done this way. Maybe defectors, our own people who've sold out. But this . . . I mean, if suspicion came our way . . ."

Berg said, a touch irritably, "Surely you can deal with all that."

Niki's mouth was set in a stubborn line. "Better to take you out, Rolf. We could do it now. Tonight."

He had to be joking. It was so ludicrous Berg almost laughed.

He realized he was going to have to spell a few things out. He said gravely: "Niki, look at the choices. They are—well, blindingly simple. Either you protect me and my principal supplier and I get this fantastic new stuff for you and you earn yourself a fat promotion. Or . . . I get blown and my contact with me and you never get another foreign posting in your whole life."

Niki looked upset, which was just what Berg had intended. He was thinking of life in a backwater of the GRU without the foreign perks, the nice Moscow apartment and the pass to the foreign-currency shops. He started tapping the wheel again. "This information your contact's producing—you say it's good."

"I said so, and it is."

Niki hated having to ask, but he overcame his reluctance. "Well? Give me an idea!"

Berg had prepared this; he had simply chosen what he imagined Niki would most like in the world. "NATO's 1964 strategy for northern Europe."

The Russian froze for a moment, then licked his lips. His eyes glinted hungrily. "Rolf, you never fail to amaze me."

"Good. Well, now amaze *me*. Give me what I need."

There was a pause. The Russian looked away, his face contorted with thought. Then he sighed gently, a sigh of resignation, and gave an almost imperceptible nod.

Berg realized it was all settled. He felt a rush of relief.

"You're certain they're not on to you already?" Niki asked.

"Certain," Berg lied.

"Good. But you should go away for a while. Somewhere out of town—abroad maybe—and don't tell anybody where you're going."

"How long for?"

He considered. "A week—I don't know. But keep in touch. We'll let you know when to come back."

As they drove back toward town Berg considered where to go. Sweden? Finland? No, too far away to keep in touch easily. There were things he still needed to keep an eye on.

Then, suddenly, he had it. He knew exactly where to go.

22

Sonja Bjornsen sat by the telephone in her living room, fighting down a bad case of nerves. She glanced at the clock: it was past seven.

Now.

She reached for the phone, hesitated, and pulled back.

She took a walk around the room and sat down again. She wanted a clear head, but lack of sleep had fuddled her brain. She'd gotten to bed at one, dozed fitfully for three hours, then woken, gripped by a single obsessive thought: that she had to contact Erik.

Time and again she imagined the moment when he answered the phone. The confirmation that he was indeed Rolf Berg, the stunned silence when he realized who she was, the denial that he was Erik, the pretense that there was some mistake. Then the realization that she had caught him out, the grudging admission, and, finally, the agreement to meet.

And this time he'd turn up. He'd have to.

Sonja squirmed with a mixture of anticipation and misery. Why had he failed to turn up a second time? Why hadn't he phoned to explain? What on earth was going on? Underlying all her fears was the suspicion that something dreadful had happened—though she couldn't make up her mind what.

Perhaps it was that stupid Delta story she'd given him. He'd discovered it wasn't true; he'd been made to look a fool and he was angry with her. Yes, that must be it. She could kick herself. Why had she made it up? Why had she been so stupid?

She had tried to call him last night from the phone booth—

it had been easy to call then, when she was hurt and angry. But he hadn't been at home. And they'd said he wasn't in his office. Now she regretted not having marched into the *Dagens Post* building; the staff might well have been able to tell her where he was and she could have avoided the necessity for this.

It had to be done.

She made herself sit down calmly. Rehearsing her words over and over again, she lifted the phone and carefully dialed his home number.

The number rang. She gripped the receiver.

It went on ringing. . . . Her hopes began to fall. He wasn't going to be in.

Then, suddenly, it answered.

"Hello?" A woman's voice.

Sonja held her breath.

"Hello?"

Slowly, Sonja replaced the receiver.

She exhaled sharply. She should have known! Probably Hildegard Lindman. Or another. He probably had dozens of them. The thought cut her like a knife. Damn him!

Sharp bitter tears sprang to her eyes. She didn't mean to cry, but somehow she couldn't prevent it and the tears fell in a steady stream.

A moment later she pressed her lips together, blew her nose, and stood up purposefully. This was no way to carry on. Crying was the first step on the long slippery slope to depression and despair. She'd spent twenty years learning how to avoid it.

The smooth balm of self-control spread over her.

She noted the time. She must leave for the office; life must go on as normal. She would call Rolf Berg at the *Dagens Post* during the morning.

Before leaving she put on makeup and examined herself critically in the mirror. She'd lost some weight, something she'd always longed to do, yet she wasn't sure it suited her. Her face looked lined: older.

At the front door she paused, a faint memory nagging at her. There was something she should have remembered and hadn't. She searched her foggy mind in growing frustration until, suddenly, it came back to her. She pulled open the drawer of the hall table and found the sheaf of photocopies. It had been very careless of her to leave them there, just lying around. Quickly, she took them into the living room, placed them in the grate, and, putting a match to them, watched them burn until there was nothing but ashes.

The journey to the office was so familiar that she made it without thinking: first the commuter train, then the tram, finally the quarter-mile walk. Only when she arrived at Platous Gate did she force herself to consider the day ahead.

She showed her pass and walked toward the elevator, her head down, trying to concentrate. There was the weekly departmental meeting at nine, she remembered. Then two further meetings scheduled for later in the day. She would be taking the minutes: somehow she mustn't let the tiredness affect her work.

The elevator started up, disgorging people on its way. The doors opened at her floor, she walked out.

Someone approached her. It was Major Thrane. She managed a small polite smile. She realized he was going to speak to her.

"Sonja, could I borrow you for a moment? Before you go to your office?" He gestured that they were to go in the other direction.

She blinked. "Er . . . yes. Of course."

He led the way along the passage to the stairs and started down them. A small alarm sounded in Sonja's mind, she almost spoke, but something about the major's brisk manner made her hesitate.

They continued downward to the basement, then along a passage. Sonja wasn't familiar with this part of the building. She tried to remember what it was used for. Whatever, she couldn't imagine what Thrane could possibly want with her down here.

Thrane stopped outside a door and, opening it, stood aside for her to go in.

She stepped over the threshold, taking in the bare walls, the metal chairs, the windowless room, the people waiting for her.

Then, in the next instant, she realized.

It was all over.

She glanced at Thrane. His eyes confirmed it.

It was all over.

Before her sat the head of Security. To his right were two of his staff, one of whom had a notepad and tape recorder ready on the table before him.

Thrane rubbed a hand over his eyes. He was tired, which wasn't surprising since he'd had three hours' sleep in the last twenty-four. It was almost one. He'd been interrogating Sonja Bjornsen for four hours. The head of Security had left as soon as Sonja had made her first admission, which had been within five minutes. Now only Thrane and a colleague remained.

Sonja sat opposite them, a plate of sandwiches untouched on the table in front of her. She was ashen-faced, yet oddly composed, as if she didn't believe she had done a great deal of harm.

Thrane found her calmness infuriating. He had the urge to shake the life out of her, to force the silly woman to understand what she'd done. He couldn't be absolutely certain how bad the damage was, not until he went through everything with her, item by item. But she'd made the most important admission.

She had been passing information, and she had been doing it for some time.

As she'd talked he'd gotten the nasty feeling that the final cost was going to be heavy.

And they hadn't even discussed Pasvik.

He was purposely keeping that until later.

He switched on the tape recorder once more, throwing the switch across with a loud snap. His colleague leaned over his pad.

"Right," he said sharply. "So let's go back to the beginning again. Did you honestly never suspect him?"

"No. Not until very recently, like I told you."

"Yet you checked up on him? Right at the beginning."

"Yes."

"So you had a suspicion?"

"No. It was just a sensible thing to do. To check."

"What about his appetite for information. Didn't that make you suspicious?"

"It seemed natural to chat. Departmental gossip."

"Gossip? But it wasn't gossip, was it, Sonja? It was hard information."

She was silent.

"And you expect me to believe you never suspected him? That you never realized he wasn't Erik Leif?"

"I told you. I had no idea until recently."

Thrane took a deep breath. "Okay, so what finally made you suspicious?"

The eyes slid away. "I don't know . . . lots of things. Small mistakes. Things he should have known and didn't. His secretiveness."

"So you checked up on him more thoroughly?"

"Yes."

"And discovered the truth?"

She nodded.

"Then why in hell didn't you come to me?"

She licked her lips nervously. "I wanted to be sure. I— " A look of what might have been pain flickered across her face.

"You wanted to protect him?"

"No."

"Then what?"

"I wanted to—talk to him. I felt sure there must be a reason, an explanation. I was sure he'd tell me about it."

"What sort of explanation did you think there could be?" Thrane asked in disbelief.

She replied levelly: "You're wrong about him, you know. He didn't pass anything on to a—a third party. I mean he wasn't a"—she tripped over the word as if it were distasteful to her— "a spy."

"How do you know?"

"I just—know. He . . . couldn't have been." She put a hand to her eyes.

Thrane wanted to exclaim: You've been completely fooled, you stupid woman! Instead, he pushed back his chair with an angry shove and took a walk around the room, still incredulous that such a sensible woman could have deceived herself so thoroughly. She had sold her country down the river, for what?

Not ideology. Not money, not immortality.

No, for what she called love. A furtive sordid once-a-month

whiff of it; an infrequent roll in the hay with a virile young lover.

It was staggering—no, pathetic—that sex could reduce a woman to such complete gullibility.

Returning to the table, he said: "And you've never had the chance to confront him?"

She shook her head.

"So what made him run for it?"

She looked startled. "What do you mean?"

"Disappear. Vanish. Run for it."

Doubt and alarm crossed her face. "He hasn't disappeared," she said.

"He failed to turn up not once but twice. A fairly clear indication, I would have thought." Thrane didn't add that the second time had all the signs of a setup. As if the lover and his friends were checking up on Sonja, to find out if she was under surveillance. Well, they had checked up, and now, presumably, they knew. Which was why Thrane had decided to bring Sonja in.

"What other explanation could there be?" he prompted.

She was about to speak, then changed her mind, her mouth moving soundlessly. Finally she took a deep breath and said in a rush: "I gave him some false information, stuff I made up— and I think he may have found out. It's the only thing I can think of."

Thrane thought he must have misheard. "What do you mean—false information? What are you talking about?"

"It—concerned Project Bluetail, the installation at Kåfjord. He wanted—" She broke off.

Wanted to know all about it, thought Thrane savagely.

"He asked about it," Sonja continued carefully. "I told him it was a new type of navigation system. A system which could be used by submarines when submerged. I even gave the system a name—a made-up name. I said it was called Delta."

"Delta? But why did you tell him all this?"

"Because—I knew he wasn't who he said he was. I couldn't tell him anything—true."

Thrane was puzzled. "But I thought—I thought . . ." He suddenly felt a leap of triumph. "You've lied to me!" His words went pouncing across the table. "You said a few moments ago that you never had the chance to confront him!"

She blanched. He had caught her out. "I—I was angry and upset. I needed time to think. To work out how to tackle him. In the meantime I didn't want him to have anything—useful. So I told him lies."

"And warned him off in the process!"

"No, I'm sure I didn't!" she said with unexpected intensity. "I'm sure he'll come back!"

Thrane stared at her. There was something very peculiar here. It just didn't make sense. She was too certain. "Why?" he asked quietly.

She shook her head. Clearly she wasn't going to answer. He returned to the subject they'd already covered several times.

"Surely you must have gotten some clues as to who he might be?"

The slightest hesitation. "No."

There it was again, something furtive. Something to hide.

"You tried to phone him last night, you said. After he stood you up."

"Yes."

"At your friend Monika's house, at the place you normally met."

She nodded. "I thought I might have gotten the meeting place wrong. That he was waiting there."

"I don't believe you. I think you know how to contact him directly. We'll check, you know. On whether you really did call your friend's house."

She dropped her eyes. He thought: Ah, she doesn't like that!

He tried again. "So, you don't know who he is," he said, letting the sarcasm show in his voice. "He must have let something slip though, about where he lived, what he did, how he amused himself. After all, this"—he flicked his fingers across his notes—"is not very much, is it? Tallish, thick blond hair, blue eyes, early thirties. I mean, that's half of Oslo!"

Her face had gone blank. The shutters were down. She had closed off again.

Thrane thought: Right. You've had your chance. Now we do it the other way.

"Okay, Sonja. Let's go through it item by item, complete with dates, documents, and all the details. I have a list of events to help jog your memory. But we'll start with something you'll have no trouble in remembering. Pasvik."

"You're wrong!" Sonja was so appalled that she repeated it twice, her voice tearful and shrill like a child's. With an effort she calmed down and said more reasonably: "You're wrong. He never knew the location, he never knew the names. I didn't tell him. I *never* told him things like that! He wasn't responsible for . . ." She couldn't bring herself to say anything but, "this."

"But you told him the rest, didn't you?"

"I . . ." She stopped abruptly, torn between a desire to tell the truth and the lurking fear that in telling it she might step into some awful trap.

"I told him there was an operation on," she began slowly. "I told him that we were meeting a man near the border—"

"Were you specific?"

She tried to remember: What *had* she said? "I said the meeting was to be in the Inari region. But I was no more specific than that. Really."

"And?"

It was such a long time ago. She racked her brains. "I told him the third man had done a deal with us. Information in exchange for freedom."

"Go on."

"I can't remember."

"I think you can."

She buried her head in her hands and cast her mind back to the evening when Erik had almost left her, the pain of it and the relief when he'd changed his mind. What *had* she told him? . . . That one of the men was a survival expert. Yes, she remembered telling him that. And she had the feeling she'd told him the other was a Lapp. And that the third man came from Murmansk. Not so much, but if she told Thrane he'd jump on it and draw those dreadful conclusions again. And he'd be wrong.

Whatever Erik-Rolf was—overambitious, manipulative—he was nothing more sinister than a journalist. He may have used the information to further his career, but he couldn't possibly be responsible for the catastrophe at Pasvik.

She decided to stay silent. Because Thrane would never *ever* understand, not unless she told him the truth about Rolf, and she wasn't going to do that. When she'd first denied knowing Erik's real identity she hadn't been sure why she'd done it. She'd only been certain that it was the right thing to do.

But now she understood why she must go on lying. It was essential to prevent this ghastly thing from growing. She must keep her hand pressed over the hole in the dam or the poisonous water would gush out and drown everything, everybody—her whole world. The moment she told them Rolf's name they would go and arrest him, and she'd lose any chance of seeing him again.

Aaah. The thought stabbed at her.

Avoiding Thrane's hard unyielding stare, she said: "I told him nothing else about Pasvik. Nothing."

"I don't believe you."

She didn't reply.

"I believe you told him everything. I believe he was a Soviet agent, and that you told him everything, Sonja. And that he acted on that information, just as he's acted on all the information you've given him. What's more, I think that in the last week he somehow got wind of trouble and skipped it. Disappeared. Left the country. Leaving you, Sonja, to face the music. All on your own. A real friend, eh?"

"You're wrong."

"Why, Sonja?"

"I just know." She felt the beginnings of desperation. This continuous badgering was wearing her down. But he'd never stop, she knew that; these awful questions would just go on and on.

The germ of an idea came into Sonja's mind and she snatched at it. She realized it would give her the two things she desperately needed—time, and an opportunity to see Rolf. The idea blossomed and consolidated. She said to Thrane: "Look—perhaps there's a solution, a way I can prove he's—not what you think. A way you can find out who he is. Let me go on as if nothing had happened. Let me continue at work, let me go home each evening. Then I'm sure he'll contact me again."

"You're sure? Why are you sure?"

Sonja realized she would have to lie again. One lie seemed to lead inexorably to another. "Because he's done this before. Not turned up."

"You didn't tell me that!"

"Oh . . . well, it's true. But you see, he always comes back again."

Looking unconvinced, Thrane hesitated, as if on the point of challenging her, then seemed to think better of it. "So," he said finally, "let me get this absolutely right. You'd be prepared to entrap him for us?"

The bluntness of it took Sonja back. But he was right: it would be entrapment. Could she do it? She imagined the scene: Erik-Rolf coming to a meeting place, responding reluctantly to her quiet questions, becoming faintly concerned, and finally, in a crushing moment of realization, staring at her in surprise and horror. The vision was bittersweet.

She whispered, "Yes, I'd do it," and felt tears prick her eyes. "But only—" She gathered her courage in both hands. "Only if you give me a chance to talk to him. In private. For some time. Hours, I mean. I must have that!"

Thrane shifted in his seat, full of suppressed rage. He finally spluttered: "This isn't a game we're playing for your gratification, you know!"

She said quietly: "It would have to be a condition of the—arrangement. You'd have to promise." The tears poured down her cheeks, falling in a steady stream onto the table.

A succession of expressions crossed Thrane's face—frustration, disapproval, then thoughtfulness, as if he were giving the idea serious consideration after all.

He got up and paced the room for a while, then, pausing beside her, said with a harsh ironic laugh: "How do I know you won't just tip him off?"

"You have my word."

There was a silence. She looked up to see his face contorted by a black derisive smile. "Your *word*, Sonja?"

"Yes."

Eventually he dropped back into his seat, looking weary, and said with a heavy sigh: "I'll think about it." He raised an admonishing finger at her. "But only when we've been through everything, and I mean everything, item by item." He shuffled his papers. "Now, where were we?"

She knew the answer. And her heart sank.

Pasvik.

Thrane faced the Director and told him: "She will not budge!"

"But she knows his identity?"

Thrane said emphatically: "I'm sure of it! Or at least how to find him, which boils down to the same thing."

"This deal she's offered, it's quite attractive." The Director was a believer in expediency.

"I don't know . . ."

"Well, she hasn't asked for much, has she? I mean, most people in her position would ask for a deal on the sentence."

"Well, we certainly couldn't promise her that."

The Director was grim-faced. "That bad?"

"Pasvik, I'm sure of it. Though she swears she never gave him the exact location or the names of our men. But it has to be her. It all fits."

"Our priorities are quite simple," the Director said firmly. "The first is to find out where the stuff was going. The second is to get proof, and I mean hard evidence, against both Sonja and her contact. This deal she's offering would give us both. So—I think we should agree." He spotted Thrane's frown. "Why not?"

"I'm certain the bird has flown."

"But it must be worth a try."

"I'd rather wear her down and get it out of her directly. She knows, damn it!"

The Director retorted: "But an allegation isn't enough, is it? You know perfectly well that we have to catch the contact accepting information or, even better, passing it. It's useless just having his name!" He considered for a moment. "We'll give Sonja two weeks."

Thrane knew a decision when he heard one.

It was eight at night. He went back to his office and arranged for the surveillance cover on Sonja to be increased so that there would never be less than three men watching her at any one time. Then he went and told her that the deal was on and she was free to go home.

He retired to his office, tired and dejected. This exercise was a waste of time, he was sure of it. The lover had flown, and the knowledge was driving him mad. He couldn't help thinking that if he'd only gotten on to Sonja sooner—just a week sooner—then the lover would have walked straight into his arms.

Jensen came in. "There're a couple of things you should look at before you go."

Go? Did Jensen mean home? Thrane hadn't even considered the possibility. Home, like sleep, seemed to belong to another life.

Jensen placed two sheets of paper in front of him.

Thrane rubbed the tiredness out of his eyes and focused. The top sheet was a surveillance report from FO/S. *Location: Kåfjord Valley. Future site of Top Sec ELINT PROJECT BLUE-TAIL* . . .

Thrane skipped to the body of the report. A party had been observed climbing up to the site and taking photographs. The party had consisted of four persons on skis, plus a gray dog resembling a wolf. (FO/S was nothing if not pedantic, Thrane noted.) The party had arrived by Land-Rover, later identified as belonging to—Thrane sighed aloud as he read it—Halvard Starheim.

So. Hal hadn't taken the slightest notice of his advice. Some people never learned, however often they were told. Thrane was disappointed: he'd thought Starheim would have known better. Well, from now on Starheim was on his own. Thrane felt under no further obligation to help or defend him.

He turned to the second sheet and realized angrily that this also concerned Starheim. It was a copy of a letter from Starheim to the defense ministry. He read impatiently. The usual thing. Lapp rights. Historical associations. Disturbance to the reindeer. Size of the installation.

Size?

Thrane read with more concentration.

. . . *this Delta navigation system, with its long aerials and maintenance requirements, is likely to cause considerable disturbance.*

Thrane clutched a hand to his forehead and stared, horrified.

Take your time, take your time. . . . Think.

Delta. Delta system.

Sonja.

Sonja had mentioned the name Delta. She'd told him she'd made it up.

Hell—

Think. Think.

But however hard he thought, there was no escape from it. Delta. *Delta.*

Sonja had made it up for the benefit of her lover. She'd *invented* it.

So where in God's name had Hal gotten it from?

For a moment Thrane rested his head in his hands, then he said quietly to Jensen: "Neither of us will be going home tonight, I'm afraid. Get on the phone. Tromsø police first. Find out if Hal Starheim's at home on Revøy."

23

Hal let himself into Fred's apartment and saw that the debris of the party was still strewn around the living room: dirty glasses, beer bottles, and an empty bottle of aquavit.

Hal dropped his coat onto a chair and, flopping down on the sofa, closed his eyes. He'd felt worse, but he couldn't remember when. The headache was the sort that pummeled the back of your eyeballs and stultified your brain. He rubbed his aching temples and wished for the hundredth time that he'd never suggested a party.

At nine that morning when he'd gone out to a meeting at the Geographical Society he'd still felt drunk—the party hadn't finished until four—but by midday the hangover had set in with a vengeance. Now, late in the afternoon, he was still suffering.

He was disgusted with himself. Why had he done it? He'd known perfectly well that he'd regret it. He'd always hated the whole sordid business of drinking Norwegian-style, not knowing—or caring—when to stop, forcing the drink down as if there were no tomorrow.

Well, this was tomorrow, and the hangover was a stinker. It served him right.

Eventually he roused himself and, after clearing away the glasses and bottles, went to Fred's desk to work on a draft proposal for the K2 expedition.

Finally at six he decided on some hair of the dog. Aquavit. He drank it like medicine, his nose crinkled up, his eyes closed. After a time he felt a little better, which was more than he deserved, and, turning on the radio news, let the distant voice of the newscaster wash over him.

De Gaulle had vetoed Great Britain from membership of the Common Market; at a Communist congress in East Berlin the Chinese had attacked Khrushchev for withdrawing Soviet missiles from Cuba; and the U.S. and Britain had affirmed their determination to build a NATO Polaris submarine force.

On the home front, the freeze continued . . .

Hal pricked up his ears.

Oslo temperature: minus twenty. In the north there had been heavy overnight snow, with exceptionally low temperatures—Tromsø, minus eighteen; Kautokeino, minus forty. Outlook: unchanged.

Hal snapped the radio off and went to the dark window. The outer panes of the double-glazed window were frosted with glittering white lace. Beyond, the snow-drenched trees and snow-decked roofs of the suburban landscape gleamed palely beneath a night sky that was hard and brittle.

Hal thought of Brattdal and the recent snow and the exceptional cold, and was immediately haunted by visions of Arne struggling with drifts, broken-down tractors, and sick animals. What a fool he'd been to leave! He should have known something like this would happen. It was almost February: just the time for difficulties and disasters.

Well, he'd get back as soon as possible. Yes—tomorrow.

In the meantime, Arne should be phoning at any moment. Hal glanced at his watch, suddenly impatient for news.

While he waited he went through the pretense of convincing himself he wasn't going to have another drink, then weakened and poured a beer.

Normally he never drank on his own, but Fred wouldn't be back for another half hour or so, and he needed the company. He was overcome by a deep despondency. Oslo and its mass of people always depressed him; he had the feeling people could live and die here without anyone noticing. And here he was, about to give up Brattdal to live in Oslo for months at a time while he organized this expedition.

Give up Brattdal . . . The thought was very painful. Like stabbing a friend in the back.

The phone rang. He answered it hastily.

Arne's voice sounded a long way off. But his words were immediate. Three more musk-oxen were sick, with great swellings and sores around their mouths. The vet had phoned to say he thought it might be contagious ecthyma, a viral infection common in sheep and goats, in which case the only hope was to segregate the sick animals. Arne had tried to get the sick animals down to the lower pasture, which was fenced, but he had been defeated by the heavy snow. With the temperature as it was, the old man expected the affected animals to die that night. However, he was going back immediately to see if there was any more he could do.

For a moment Hal couldn't speak. Finally he said weakly: "I'll be back as soon as I can, Arne. Tomorrow, the first plane."

"One more thing," Arne said. "It's getting colder."

The instant Arne hung up, Hal called the airport. The first flight north was at six-forty the next morning. He packed his bag immediately, then lay back on the bed, filled with a restless aching despair.

All futile: the musk-oxen, the farm, the new trees, Ragna, the ridiculous search for the owner of the binoculars. His life. Yes, that too. A bloody waste of time.

The phone jangled in the living room. One of Fred's friends, no doubt. He considered leaving it unanswered but thought better of it.

"Halvard Starheim?" a voice said. "It's Sorensen. You're in luck."

Hal thought: I am?

"I've got something for you. It's very unusual to get this sort of thing so quickly. But we have my good friend Christina at the Breisgau Archives to thank. She's a bright girl, good at following her nose and taking a few well-chosen short cuts."

Hal realized what he was getting around to. "You've found out how the soldier died?"

"Yes. Christina found his family, or at least his brother, still living in the same town—Mühldorf—in Bavaria. Getting the original address was the hardest part—she had to go to the Bonn Archives with his name and regiment. But once she had Mühldorf it was simple. She got a local telephone directory and started phoning people in the town who had the name

Schirmer." He added with a triumphant chuckle, "Very lucky."

Hal controlled himself with difficulty. "And?"

"He died at a military hospital in Lyngseidet of injuries received in an accident. Apparently—according to the brother, that is—it was an avalanche."

Hal didn't speak. After a moment Sørensen added: "I hope that gives you the information you wanted. I'll have to charge you for some of Christina's time, I'm afraid. I hope that's all right. . . . Hello? . . . Hello? . . . Are you still there?"

Hal finally murmured, "Charge me anything you like," and rang off.

Ragna let herself into Rolf's apartment, deposited the groceries in the kitchen, and ran a bath. She sank into it, topped it off with more hot water, and lay back, letting the heat soothe her.

The day had been frantic, trying to cram two days' appointments into one, but in the end it had gone extremely well. Three months ago when she'd tried to interest the press in the Kåfjord issue they had been mildly attentive but distinctly unhelpful. Defense stories made them nervous, but security matters frightened them to death. Rolf's article had changed all that; suddenly the Kåfjord Lapps were news and everyone wanted to interview her. The foreign press, too. It had been Rolf's idea to get them involved.

It had been a long time since the press had wanted to take Ragna's photograph. In her far-off Swedish filming days she'd become quite well known—people had come to recognize her in the street—but she hadn't given a damn about the press then; she'd been arrogant enough to sweep past photographers in dark glasses. Not now. Now she took the trouble to get the pictures right. With Aslak's help she'd found a young Lapp at the university who was vaguely related to a Kåfjord family, and had persuaded him to become a full-fledged Kåfjord Lapp for the day—a slight realignment of the facts that was justified, she felt, by the need to strike while the iron was hot.

And so the campaign was bearing fruit: a respected senior politician had promised to take the matter up in the Storting.

And she'd received the detailed letter she'd been promised from the justice ministry—without the answers she wanted, of course, but it was a start.

Ideally she needed more time in Oslo, but she'd have to manage the follow-up from Tromsø. Rolf was flying north first thing the next morning and wanted her to go with him. Since he'd offered to help out with her ticket, she couldn't afford to miss the opportunity.

She smiled to herself. Whom was she fooling? She'd have gone with him anyway.

The thought of him filled her with wonderfully impure thoughts and she sank lower into the bath and closed her eyes. As a lover he'd been perfect, just as she'd known he would be. Confident, knowing, generous; taking her body into long-forgotten areas of delight. He was a very sensual man.

At the same time he maintained tht iron detachment of his. But she liked that—he put no pressures on her, asked nothing of her except what she was extremely happy to give.

The only thing she found unsettling about him was his moods. He had the ability to leap from cool to warm in one breathtaking moment. The previous night he'd come back very late, at four in the morning. She hadn't asked him where he'd been—she wasn't going to fall into that old trap—but she hadn't been able to ignore his tense preoccupied mood.

At first nothing she'd said seemed to reach him, and he'd lain there at her side, awake and restless. Then, for no apparent reason, he'd moved over and started to make love to her with such haste and intensity that he'd taken her by surprise. She'd called softly, "Hey, wait for me!" and he'd paused and, sinking his head against her shoulder, had murmured, "Ragna—I need you, I need you very much." It was the only time he'd ever shown anything approaching emotion. She'd felt a sudden wave of tenderness and, taking his face in her hands, had kissed him softly, over and over again. Afterward, when they lay apart, she was aware that he had drawn the shutter over his emotions again, and that she was once more excluded from his thoughts.

She was careful to remain detached too, of course—it was an essential part of her newly established freedom—yet she was left with a curious sense of loss. She didn't love him, she didn't want to love him, yet she couldn't help feeling that their relationship was lacking in some vital way.

She sat up suddenly and jumped out of the bath. It was almost seven. Rolf had said he'd be back at eight. She must hurry. She needed to get herself ready, phone Krisi to tell him she'd be returning the next day, and cook supper. She also needed to pack because there wouldn't be time in the morning.

She put on a loose sweater and jeans and brushed her hair. She didn't bother with makeup; she was quite satisfied with her face as it was.

She got through to Tromsø just as her mother-in-law was putting Krisi to bed. Krisi was tired and grumpy and, apart from telling her that the sea at the bottom of the garden was so icy that people were walking on it, she couldn't get much out of him. But he sounded pleased that she was coming home.

She put down the phone and felt a small pang of love and remorse. She missed Krisi. Sometimes he drove her mad, sometimes she wondered if she'd been born with a short measure of maternal instinct, sometimes she . . .

It was painful to progress the thought, and she paused.

Sometimes she resented him—no, not him, she could never resent him, but she resented his emotional hold on her. Was it that she was terrified of losing him, too?

In her brave new mood she could almost admit to that possibility.

Perhaps the problem was that she loved him too much.

She hurried into the kitchen and started making dinner. Cooking wasn't her favorite pastime, but she tackled the preparations with something like enthusiasm. She'd spent a lot on the food—cantaloupe melon, fillet steak, peppers and spices for a sauce, French cheese and a gateau to follow. It was the sort of sophisticated meal she imagined Rolf would like.

After cutting and decorating the melon, she carried it through into the living room with the cutlery and glasses, and laid the table.

The doorbell rang.

She looked at the time. Seven-thirty. Rolf without his key? No, he wasn't the sort to forget. A friend dropping by perhaps. It crossed her mind that it might even be a female friend. Well, she was a big girl: she could handle that.

Ragna went to the door, glancing in a mirror as she passed. She opened the door and swung it wide.

She gaped, astonished.

Hal.

Trying to recover, she made one or two ineffectual attempts to speak, and finally managed a weak "Hello, Hal."

His face was ice-cold. "Where's Rolf?"

"He'll be back at about eight."

He half turned away, looked at his watch, hovered indecisively, then came across the threshold. "I'll wait."

She closed the door and followed him into the living room, saying: "I hadn't realized you were coming down to Oslo too, otherwise we could have traveled together . . ." It was the wrong approach; she was burbling, sounding guilty. She started again. "When did you come down?"

Ignoring the question, Hal strode to the side, began to unscrew a bottle of aquavit, changed his mind, and poured himself a mineral water. As he took a gulp, he looked around, his eyes sweeping over the table laid for two. His face seemed to harden and for a moment she thought he was going to speak, but then he went to the window and stared resolutely out into the darkness. He was wearing a smart gray suit, Ragna noticed. She couldn't help thinking how well it looked on him.

The silence stretched out. She found it disconcerting, like an accusation. Searching for something to say, she said brightly: "Have you seen the coverage we've been getting?"

He didn't move; his profile was unyielding. She realized he had no intention of making conversation. It occurred to her that he was doing it on purpose, to make her feel uncomfortable. And what was more, he was succeeding.

Suddenly she remembered—the message, the need to speak to him about the mixed-up information.

In a small burst of indignation she demanded: "Didn't Arne tell you to phone me?"

"What?"

"To call me. It was urgent."

"Oh . . ." Without turning from the window, he gave a small confirmatory nod.

"Well?" Ragna made the effort to suppress her annoyance, and explained levelly: "It was about Kåfjord. The installation. Unfortunately I was given the wrong information. It's not going to be a Delta navigation system at all. The place has nothing to do with it, apparently."

He showed no interest. Suddenly she was angry: he was sulking like a spoiled child. "Did you use the information?" she demanded. "Did you write to the defense ministry?"

He half turned, frowning. "I may have."

"Well, *did* you?"

"Yes. I mentioned the name of the system. And the fact that it would have quite a few aerials."

Her heart sank. Rolf would not be pleased. In fact, he'd be very angry. Rolf was not one to suffer fools gladly. He'd want to know why she hadn't mentioned it before. He'd be furious because it was too late to cover himself. Quite rightly, he'd put all the blame on her.

She groaned and sank down onto the sofa. "Oh, Lord . . . Look, Hal, could you write to them and explain? Explain that you've made a mistake and now realize it isn't going to be a Delta installation. I know it's a lot to ask, but it *is* important—"

"Ragna, I'm not going to discuss this now." He turned and looked at her at last, and there was a deep well of coldness in his eyes.

"But it's important!"

"I couldn't care less at the moment."

Her mouth dropped open; he was treating her like an idiot. Overcome by a sudden fury, she jumped to her feet. "Why have you come, Hal? Why do you want to see Rolf?"

He looked away again, his lips set in a thin determined line. She was almost speechless with exasperation.

"Really, Hal! This is ridiculous! Whatever you have to say to Rolf you can say to me!"

He glanced back at her, raising an eyebrow. "Oh? Why should that be?"

"Well . . . presumably this concerns me in some way."

He gave her a crushing look. "You flatter yourself, Ragna. Believe me, you are the very *last* subject I would bother to discuss with Rolf."

She didn't believe him. "Really?" she asked sarcastically. "Then why are you so angry? Why are you here?"

He shot away from the window in a sudden startling movement and came and stood in front of her, full of suppressed anger.

"What I discuss with Rolf is my business, Ragna. But I can assure you that women have never loomed large in our conversation. With Rolf's voracious appetite, it would be too tedious and time-consuming to go through his conquests."

Ragna spluttered: "My God! You're behaving like a jealous child, Hal!"

He'd begun to turn away. Now he spun back, his eyes glittering with anger. "Jealous! You've got it wrong, Ragna. There's never been any jealousy between Rolf and me. We've shared women in the past, you see! Or at least passed them on. Doubtless we'll do it again. It hardly merits discussion." Ragna retreated under the downpour of his words. He laughed mirthlessly. "Besides—this doesn't qualify as sharing, does it? Since you weren't mine in the first place. No, Ragna, it really doesn't bother me! And I'm sure it doesn't bother Rolf!"

She gasped aloud and felt the heat rush into her face. She couldn't speak.

Hal was gathering himself for another broadside. She braced herself.

"If you want to make a fool of yourself, that's your business, Ragna. But I'd rather not know or hear about it."

"How dare you! I'm not making a fool of myself."

"With Rolf you are! He—eats women up, then spits them out when he's finished with them. Usually it happens so fast they hardly know what's going on."

"So what?"

He stared at her, astonished.

"Who said I wanted it to last?" Ragna cried. "In fact it's rather nice knowing it won't. Then I can enjoy it for exactly what it is. An affair. Nothing more, nothing less. I don't want commitment and marriage. I just want—fun." She stabbed a finger at him. "And God alone knows, I need it!"

He was very still. "So . . . fun makes it all right?"

Ragna growled: "You men and your double standards! You think nothing of sleeping around when it suits you. I'm free and over twenty-one, and there's been nobody in my life for a long time. So what's the problem?"

"The problem?" His jaw muscles worked furiously. "What about feelings, Ragna. What about caring and small things like that?"

"I can't handle all that."

"You can't handle it—"

"That's right."

"Ha! So I see!"

"But that's what *you* wanted, Hal, and I couldn't . . . couldn't . . ."

He closed his eyes for a moment in disbelief. "What did I want?"

"A—deep relationship."

"Since when?"

"Oh, always!"

Hal colored slightly.

She almost retreated then, but her anger pulled her inexorably forward. "You expected things of me! You wanted me to be there and bury myself at Revøy. . . . I wasn't ready for all that. . . . I'm not ready for it now!"

"No," he said with sudden calm. "You're absolutely right. That is not in dispute, Ragna." Without another word he turned on his heel and went back to the window.

Ragna breathed, "Oh, shit!" and sank down on the sofa. To her disgust she felt tears well up and fall hotly down her cheeks. She lowered her head and arched her hands over her eyes, determined he shouldn't see her cry.

She thought: I don't need to feel guilty. I don't have to care about what he thinks.

But even as she thought it she knew that she did care.

From the window Hal said flatly: "Ragna, whatever happens, Krisi's very important to me. I'd hate not to see him anymore."

She managed a gruff "Of course."

There was a pause. Through the arch of her hands she saw his feet come into view. She masked her eyes still further. A handkerchief was thrust in front of her nose.

She hesitated, then took it with a firm "Thanks." The feet withdrew a little. She blew her nose and said simply and quietly: "I'm sorry, Hal. I—I'd hate to lose you as a friend." She looked up.

He stared down at her for a long time before saying with a deep weary sigh: "You haven't lost me, Ragna. But—you can hardly expect it to be the same."

Ragna thought: But I want it to be the same. As a small conciliatory gesture, she offered: "I'm going back to Tromsø tomorrow."

He said: "So am I. All my damned animals are sick."

"What? Oh, no. Oh, Hal, I'm so sorry." She jumped to her feet. "Not the musk-oxen?" She could see from his face that it was. She couldn't bear it. Her heart went out to him. "Oh, Hal . . ."

He gave a dismissive shrug. "I've decided to give the place up anyway. So it makes no difference . . ."

Ragna reached for his hand and clasped it. "You can't."

"Oh, can't I?" He gave a bitter laugh, but his expression was grave and he carefully avoided her eyes.

She squeezed his hand. "Hal, if there's anything I can do—"

A voice said: "Well, well!"

Ragna jumped, Hal dropped her hand.

Rolf stood in the doorway. He walked easily across to Hal, a grin on his face. "You old devil! I didn't know you were in Oslo!"

Hal smiled back. The two men began to talk.

Ragna retreated into the kitchen and, pouring herself a generous glass of wine, began to chuck ingredients into a saucepan. After a moment she stopped abruptly, sank onto a stool, and, leaning her head on her hands, closed her eyes.

Berg watched Hal's face carefully. He could see that this wasn't a social call. Pouring himself a large Scotch, he sat down and asked: "So what brings you to Oslo, Hal?"

Hal dropped into the opposite chair. "Oh, business. Climbing business mainly."

"Nothing I can help with?"

"Not really. Thanks anyway."

They talked for a while. Hal was tense. Berg had the feeling he wanted to broach some subject but hadn't yet found the right moment.

Eventually they lapsed into silence.

Hal drew a deep breath. "An extraordinary thing happened. I thought you might be interested."

Here it came.

"It's the most remarkable—well, coincidence."

Berg didn't like coincidences; they smelled of trouble. Neither did he like the cold watchfulness in Hal's eyes. "Oh, yes?" he said amiably.

"A friend of mine has a pair of old binoculars. The other day he told me about them. It's quite a story. In fact, Rolf, it's extraordinary"—he shook his head at how extraordinary it was—"but I think that at one time the binoculars might have belonged to you. To you—or to your friend Petter."

With difficulty Berg held an expression of polite interest.

"Petter?" he asked smoothly. "I'm sorry, I'm not quite with you."

"The fellow with you at Lyngen all those years ago. The one you went north with."

Berg played for time. He said: "Ah, poor mysterious Petter. Of course. . . . And—er—there might be a connection?"

"Yes. This friend of mine bought these binoculars some years ago. They're German, dating from the war. They had a name and serial number on them and, being a curious sort of person, he traced the original owner. He discovered they'd belonged to a soldier who died. He died, Rolf, in January 1945, at Lyngen. We"—he indicated the two of them—"saw him die. In that avalanche, Rolf."

Berg's mind was racing. Binoculars? The avalanche? Petter? Christ, what was the connection? And what did Hal know about them? In a flash of vicious anger Berg realized Hal had been digging around behind his back.

Hal said: "I thought maybe the binoculars might have been the ones you or Petter acquired that day."

This required caution. Berg gave an indifferent shrug. "God God, I've no idea. What an extraordinary thing. Where did this friend of yours find the binoculars?"

"He bought them from some Lapps up on the plateau. They didn't say where they'd found them, and at the time my friend didn't think to ask. But I immediately thought of you and Petter. I mean, you were up on the plateau, weren't you? And Petter died there, didn't he?"

Berg hesitated slightly. "Yes."

"So maybe the Lapps found them at the place where he died. I thought you'd want to know."

Berg blew his lips out and looked incredulous, which he was. "Well, what an extraordinary thing."

"Unless they were yours, of course."

"Who can tell? Maybe they were."

Berg could have kicked himself. That was a stupid slip and Hal was straight onto it. "You both had a pair, then?" he asked in surprise. "I mean, you dug *two* pairs out of the snow that day?"

"No. Just the one pair. But I honestly can't remember who ended up with them."

"So you don't know what happened to them?"

His tone was calm but persistent. Suddenly Berg knew: Hal was on to something.

Berg tried to think: Where *had* those binoculars gotten to? He knew where his own gear had ended up, and it certainly wasn't on the plateau. But these binoculars, which were undoubtedly Petter's—perhaps something had happened to them. Perhaps Petter had dropped the damned things. He tried desperately to remember, and couldn't. He had the nasty feeling it was very important.

He stalled. "But there were several soldiers in that avalanche. Presumably they all had binoculars."

"Apparently not. Only two of them at most. This pair belonged to the young lieutenant in charge of the patrol we saw that day."

You've got it all worked out, haven't you? Berg thought savagely.

The question was: why?

Berg went into the attack. "This friend of yours, when did he buy them?"

"Oh . . . about three years ago."

"Who is he?"

Hal frowned. "He lives up in Alta. A fisherman."

He was lying, Berg was certain of it. Time to nip this thing in the bud. "Well, if he can't shed any more light on it . . ." He shrugged to show that he was losing interest in the subject. "All this was a very long time ago, wasn't it? And I certainly can't remember. For all I know, the Lapps who rescued me might have taken them."

Hal searched his face, then, frowning, sank back in his chair and stared moodily into the fireplace.

Berg gave it a minute before asking: "Now, why don't you tell me what this is really about?"

Hal's eyes locked back onto his and gave him a long appraising stare. Berg prompted gently: "Journalists can always smell a story, Hal."

Hal looked thoughtful. He said carefully: "Really—there's nothing more to it. I just thought you'd be interested. I thought you might like to find the spot where your friend died. To tell his family. And get him buried properly."

Berg quickly adjusted to the new tangent and realized with a shock that this was a clumsy ineffectual attempt to trick him.

Grimly triumphant, Berg replied: "Family? But I told you before, Hal, I never knew Petter's name. I have no idea where his family came from."

Hal gave a slow nod. "Ah. I'd forgotten."

Berg thought: Like hell.

Hal stood up. "I must be going."

Berg got slowly to his feet and fixed Hal with one of his best smiles. "Wish I'd been able to help, but there we are." He added: "But won't you stay for dinner? Ragna and I would love it if you did. I'm sure the food will stretch."

With satisfaction, Berg saw Hal stiffen at "Ragna and I."

"No thanks." Hal made for the door. "I've an early start in the morning."

"Oh?"

"I'm going back north."

"Perhaps we'll see you on the plane, then."

Hal frowned with surprise. "What?"

"Ragna and I are going to Tromsø in the morning as well."

Berg followed him into the hall and opened the front door. After some hesitation, Hal asked: "You're doing more on the Kåfjord Lapps, then?"

Ragna came out of the kitchen, wiping her hands on a towel. Berg looped an arm around her shoulders and pulled her toward him. "No. I'm just taking a bit of a break. I thought I'd help Ragna put the shop and the house on the market."

Hal looked at Ragna, then back at Rolf. A small spark of mutual hostility flashed between the two men. Hal gave a perfunctory nod and left, pulling the door sharply behind him.

Berg spun on his heel and went to the drinks tray for a large refill. He had to think.

He became aware that Ragna was talking about musk-oxen and Hal having a bad time. He wished she'd shut up. He flung her a fierce glance and she got the hint, saying briskly: "Dinner'll be in ten minutes if that's okay."

He made an effort to be civil. "Could you make it twenty?" Barely waiting for her nod, he headed for the shower.

He plunged under the water, running it alternately hot and cold, occasionally reaching out to the adjacent shelf for a gulp of his whiskey.

What had it all meant? What did Hal know? How the hell had those binoculars turned up?

He turned the possibilities over and over in his mind. Hal might have been telling the truth, the things might have been found on the plateau, the Lapps might have sold them . . .

But that would have been *too* much of a coincidence.

No, there had to be a reason for Hal's terrierlike interest.

He swore with exasperation. It would help if he could remember whether Petter had still had those damn binoculars in Petsamo. But his memory wouldn't deliver.

He went over scenes and images from Petsamo, magnifying and distorting them, trying to see beyond the dirty clothing and windburned face that was his lasting image of Petter. Trying to look to his waist, to the belted anorak, to the rifle and ammo . . .

Suddenly he went very cold. Leaving the water running, he stepped out of the shower and stood naked and dripping, staring blankly at his blurred image in the steamed-up mirror.

He remembered.

He remembered going hunting with a group of soldiers from one of the camps surrounding Petsamo—crazy harddrinking lunatics from Kirov. He remembered Petter showing them how to stalk hare, climbing a low hill, crawling onto a ridge, sweeping the landscape for signs of game. In this vision, which grew ever more vivid, he saw, quite clearly, a picture of Petter.

He had the white-painted binoculars in his hands.

In Petsamo, behind the Russian lines.

His mind raced through the implications.

The binoculars could not possibly have been lost on the plateau. They'd never been found by any Lapps.

Hal had been lying.

The water drummed noisily on the floor of the shower, the steam billowed out.

But there was worse—much worse.

The binoculars could only have turned up in one way.

He sank down onto the edge of the bathtub.

Pasvik. At Pasvik. With Petter.

The full implications came winging into his mind.

They must know Petter was the third man. They must know that Berg had lied about Petter's death.

They must know that Berg had been in Russia too.

Which meant—

Standing up, Berg reached into the shower and turned off the water. Slowly, methodically, he toweled himself dry and pulled on some clothes.

They. He was thinking of a "they." Perhaps there was no "they." Perhaps it was just Hal.

Just Hal.

He nursed the idea. After a while he made a small exclamation of triumph.

Of course it was Hal alone. Hal had no ties with the military anymore. If the Security Service had been on to Berg, they would never have let Hal come and warn him off.

No, somehow or other Hal had gotten hold of these damn binoculars and worked things out for himself. Quite on his own.

He thought of his forthcoming trip to Tromsø and suddenly the problem didn't seem so insurmountable after all.

24

The driver peered anxiously through the windshield and slowed to a crawl. A wall of fog loomed up and enveloped the taxi in a dense gray cloud that the headlights failed to penetrate.

Hal chafed with impatience. At this rate he was going to miss his plane.

"One can always tell how cold it is by the fog in this valley," said the driver. "Believe me, it's cold. But we're almost out of it now."

And then miraculously they were, and the road ahead was brilliant white in the headlights, and he car picked up speed, the wheels making a drumming sound on the hard-packed surface.

When they finally turned off to the airport it was six-twenty. Hal relaxed a little. Twenty minutes; he'd make it after all.

He sat forward in his seat and showed an envelope to the driver. "I need this letter delivered to a house over in Kolsas as soon as possible. Can you do it?" He also flourished a hundred-kroner note. This seemed to catch the driver's eye better than the letter, and he gave a grunt of agreement.

They drew up outside Departures. Hal reminded the driver, "Drop that letter as soon as possible, won't you?" and sprinted for the check-in desk.

Thrusting his ticket forward he said to the girl: "I'm not too late, am I?"

The girl glanced up, a professional glazed expression on her face, then, with a flash of recognition, gave a nervous smile. "Ah. Mr. Starheim. Could you wait one moment please?"

"But the flight," Hal said impatiently. "Am I all right or not?"

She looked mildly apologetic and gestured to one side. Following her gaze, Hal became aware of someone standing close by.

Thrane. Thrane?

"Starheim." He gave a brief nod of greeting. "I need to talk to you."

Hal replied firmly: "Look, another time, Thrane. I've got to get this flight."

"This won't wait."

"It's got to, I'm afraid."

Thrane slowly shook his head. "The next flight. Possibly."

Hal felt his temper rising. If this was just another ticking-off . . .

He was about to argue, but something about Thrane's expression made him pause. His anger gave way to curiosity. Perhaps there had been developments . . .

He asked: "It really can't wait?"

"No."

Hal rebooked himself on the next flight and followed Thrane across the concourse and down a long corridor. He suddenly noticed that two men had fallen in behind them. So—it was just as he'd first thought: This was to be a ticking-off! His anger rose again.

Thrane led the way into a conference room with a long table surrounded by plastic chairs.

"They belong to you?" Hal demanded, indicating the silent followers.

Thrane closed the door. "Yes, but they stay outside."

Hal sat at the table, tense and angry. "So! I have the distinct impression that this isn't going to be a friendly chat."

"Starheim, if I was following the rules I'd have you down at Mollergata with the OP making a formal statement. As it is I'm giving you the chance to cooperate like this—informally."

"It sounds pretty formal to me."

Thrane narrowed his lips and sat opposite. "Very well. I won't beat about the bush. You have quoted certain information in a recent letter to the defense ministry, information concerning the site at Kaafjord. You said the installation was to be a navigation system called Delta. Now I must know where you got that information from."

Hal thought quickly. It was Ragna. Ragna had put it in that scrawled note: . . . *from my contact in Oslo* . . .

Then last night she had said that the information was no good after all. She'd seemed rather upset that he'd used it. She'd asked him to write to the ministry to correct it. What else had she said? He hadn't really been listening.

He said: "Look, Thrane, I have only used the information in that letter. And I have no intention of using it further. And I certainly wouldn't give it to the press or anything like that. So you really don't have to worry about the security risk."

"But where did you get it from?"

Hal had rather suspected Thrane was going to stay on that tack. "Ah. That I really don't know."

"Don't know?"

"Really. I have no idea."

"Or you won't say!" retorted Thrane in a burst of anger. He got to his feet and strode to the window. Returning, he leaned forward with both hands on the table. "Let me get this right," he said. "Am I to understand that you intend to protect your source?"

Hoping he could live with a slight distortion of the facts, Hal said unhappily: "The truth is that I honestly do not know the source."

"This information came out of thin air, then, did it?" Thrane exclaimed with heavy sarcasm. He sat down again and gave Hal a long appraising stare. "How long have we known each other?"

"Three years."

He said with quiet bemusement: "In all that time I've always felt sure that you and I—shared a common purpose, that we—stuck out for what was right, cut through the nonsense— cared about the truth, damn it. But now—now you're forcing me to think I must have been wrong all this time." He gave a small gesture of amazement. "Have I been wrong?"

Hal shook his head and said with a heavy sigh: "No, Thrane. You're not wrong."

Thrane cheered up a little. "So?"

Hal made a face. "It's difficult. . . . A matter of trust."

"Ah." That was something Thrane could understand. "Well, I think you'll find your loyalties are misguided. Listen—I'm going to stick my neck out a million miles and tell you that the information you were given, this Delta thing, leads straight back to an enemy of Norway. A traitor, Hal. Someone who's caused the most appalling damage. Do you understand what I'm saying? D'you see—there's a direct connection between this information and the traitor."

Hal looked into his face and saw that it was true.

"Now . . ." Thrane said with heavy emphasis. "I've trusted you. Trust *me* now. Tell me—where did this Delta information come from?"

Hal tried to absorb the full implications of what Thrane had said. His instinct was to help Thrane all he could, yet he couldn't bring himself to drop Ragna in the dirt without talking to her first. He heard himself being sucked into a lie. "All I can tell you is that the information came from Oslo. It was phoned through. . . ."

There was a heavy silence. Thrane's face was a mask of cold fury. "I don't believe you," he said eventually. "What's more, I think you're deliberately hiding the truth. You don't seem to realize what's involved here!" He hunched forward over the table and pointed a finger. "Or perhaps you do. In which case I can only draw one conclusion. That you're deliberately being obstructive."

The conclusion was right, of course. Hal saw now that this was one fence that could never be sat on. He said: "Okay. The truth is that I personally don't know, and you'll have to take my word on that. But what I will do is try and find out."

Thrane searched his face and seemed to make up his mind that he was telling the truth. He relaxed a little. "Ragna Johansen wouldn't by any chance be the one who can tell you?"

Ragna might well have been a fool, but Hal didn't want Thrane judging her in advance. Hating the lie, he said: "No."

Thrane looked doubtful but let it pass. "This'll mean letting you go."

Hal realized with a slight shock that Thrane had seriously been thinking of locking him up.

"No one knows about this security leak yet, Hal. If it got out I'd be crucified."

Hal began to appreciate just how far Thrane had stuck his neck out. "It won't go any further. I promise."

Thrane stood up. "Look, this thing's very urgent. How soon can you find out?"

Hal pushed back his chair and joined Thrane by the door. "I'm not sure. A day—maybe two. I'll do my best." A disquieting image of Ragna arguing fiercely for the right to protect her source popped into his mind. Ragna was a girl for sticking to her guns; he had the unpleasant feeling that nothing was going to shift her.

As if sensing his doubts, Thrane gripped his arm. "Hal, this leak's been going a long time. Over three years." There was a message in Thrane's eyes: Hal was intended to read something significant into what he had just said.

Three years. There was only one thing he could possibly mean. Hal's stomach gave an ugly lurch, and he stared at Thrane, his heart racing with savage excitement.

Thrane gave a quick nod. "There's a direct connection, Hal. Whoever your informant is, there's a *direct* connection. *Now* d'you see why it's so important?"

It was the longest weekend of Sonja's life. They spirited her away for six hours' interrogation each day, then returned her home in the evenings in a state of exhaustion and despair.

Yet she'd stuck to her story; she'd never altered a word.

But now was the hardest part: going through the pretense of going to work again. And she was going to be late. She was never late. Yet she saw that her lateness was just another symptom of the terrifying disintegration of her life. Like the sleepless nights, the growing despair, the chilling loneliness.

It was a quarter to eight when she hurried out of the apartment and along the road. The lighting was poor and she peered intently at the slippery pavement ahead. Suddenly she was on top of some ice and her boot was skidding out from under her. With a loud gasp she tottered backward, wheeling her arms, and just managed to regain her balance.

Flushing hot and cold, she paused for a moment to regain her breath.

She wondered what the watcher was making of it. He was there somewhere, she knew he was. Someone from FO/S. Or would he come from the security section of FO/E itself? She didn't look back.

Now she could see that the pavement was gleaming with ice. She went slowly. After all, she thought wearily, what did it matter if she was late? There would be nothing for her to do. She wouldn't be allowed near her office, she wouldn't be allowed to talk to anyone. She would be put in an empty room again, in disgrace. The disgrace depressed her more than anything, more, even, than the growing realization that she would be punished.

She'd been thinking about the punishment. What would they do to her? When they discovered that no real harm had been done they wouldn't try to send her to prison. Surely not. They couldn't. She hadn't done anything really terrible. No, she'd surely get away with summary dismissal, which wasn't so bad. Not *so* bad. Yet she was haunted by the fear of losing her pension; it was all she had. Could they really be so cruel? But she knew they could and, if Thrane had any say in it, they would.

No job, no security. No Erik.

Unbearable.

She almost lost her footing again, gasped, and found herself on the brink of tears. Sometimes she just couldn't take it all in. She felt as if she were being sucked down and down into a quagmire.

Only one thing could save her. Finding Erik. He would tell them, he would explain.

Finding Erik . . .

They'd let her keep a telephone at the office, of course, in case he called. But he wouldn't. She knew that now. She would have to contact him.

As she neared the end of the road a train drew out of the station nearby. It would be ten minutes until the next.

That made up her mind for her.

There was a phone booth on the far side of the station, on a filling-station forecourt. She crossed over the bridge, went up to the main road, and, reaching for the change she had ready in her coat pocket, stepped into the booth.

There: she was committed now.

She could imagine Thrane's questions. Who were you calling? Why didn't you make the call from home? It was him, wasn't it?

She hadn't worked out what she would say to that yet. She didn't call from home, of course, because the line was tapped. Closing her mind to the consequences, she began to dial. Clamping the receiver to her ear, she made a silent prayer: Please let it answer. Please.

It began to ring. It rang on and on, drilling rhythmically into her head, until there was no possibility of a reply.

He was away. On an assignment. Or staying overnight with a woman. Or . . .

She hung up. She'd slip out and try his office later. The other journalists would know where he was. In Paris or Berlin or . . . She'd find him, somehow.

Even as she thought it, she couldn't shake off a small but persistent suspicion that she would never see him again.

She made her way back across the bridge to join the group of heavily muffled foot-stamping passengers gathering on the platform. When the train finally arrived it was very crowded and Sonja found herself crushed between two tall men in the center of a compartment.

The train gathered speed, rocking and grining over the rails. Someone was saying: "It's the coldest winter since '46, so they say." A voice replied: "No, '42. It was '42, the really bad one."

Holding tight to a post, Sonja let herself be rocked by the press of swaying bodies and, momentarily lulled, closed her eyes. Immediately the worries that had obsessed her during the long night returned: how to lure Erik-Rolf to a meeting, what to say when she finally confronted him . . . the need to see the expression of horror and—yes—respect on his face as he realized that she'd outsmarted him. She thought: Is that all I want—revenge?

No . . . yes . . . she wasn't sure. She wasn't even sure she wanted him to be caught. She could warn him, prevent him from incriminating himself, give him time to wriggle his way out of it. Was she capable of doing that? What a sacrifice! Was she that brave and unselfish? She couldn't believe she was. But the knowledge that she had it in her power was extraordinarily precious, and she savored it.

At the same time she relived other nightmares: the chilling accusations Thrane had made in that icy voice of his. At first she'd drawn comfort from the certainty that he was wrong. He was mad, mad to try to blame her for Pasvik—how dare he? But as the time had passed, tiny doubts and uncertainties had burrowed into her mind, and eaten away at her confidence, until the idea had acquired shape and substance.

Please. Let Rolf Berg be in his office today.

The train grated to a stop, restarted, and stopped again, winding its way through the western suburbs toward central Oslo. Gathering speed downhill, it dived into an underground section. The sudden inrush of air buffeted Sonja's ears, the crush seemed worse. A man's shoulder pressed hard against her face. Pushing against him, she stepped back and tilted her face upward to get some air. Suddenly she realized she was standing on what could only be someone's foot. Hastily shifting her weight, she said "Sorry" and glanced around.

A face turned away with a jerk. She looked down. The foot could only have belonged to the owner of the averted face, a man wearing a black coat and black Astrakhan hat with earflaps.

She murmured another "Sorry" in his direction, but he turned his back and the apology was lost against the broad bulk of his coat.

Finally the train clattered to the end of the line at the National Theatre and disgorged its passengers. Letting the crowd go ahead, Sonja plodded wearily up the stairs to street level. She thought of walking all the way to Platous Gate, but the freezing air was knife-sharp against her cheeks and she couldn't face it. Changing direction, she went and joined the long line at the tram stop on Stortings Gata.

As she waited she looked across to the National Theatre, and back to the dark façade of the Theatre Café, and felt a sudden piercing longing. It took a moment for her to understand: it was a longing for all the good times she'd never had—would never have —for close friendships and easy comradeship; for the gaiety and passion that seemed an integral part of brightly lit places; for all the things that seemed to belong, quite naturally, to more beautiful people; for everything that she had touched in Erik . . .

A tram ground to a clanking halt. Sonja let herself be carried forward by the jostling crowd. She was about to step on board when, filled to capacity, the tram closed its doors. The unlucky passengers fell back stoically, saving their energies for the next attempt.

She turned her eyes back to the façade of the Theatre Café and to the bright neon lights of Stortings Gata beyond.

She thought suddenly: They'll lock me away and I'll never see any of it again. And with that thought she realized that she had made room for the possibility of going to prison, even for the idea that she might have done something very terrible after all.

A tram appeared at the top of the street. People began to maneuver gently for position, shouldering forward surreptitiously.

A vision of Erik walking gaily toward Blom's restaurant flashed into Sonja's mind—Erik with that woman on his arm, admired, indulged, getting what he wanted, and she suddenly thought: Why should he have it all?

Leksand had been with FO/S for two years and had his sights on early promotion. Surveillance was important, he realized, and he appreciated that it had to be carried out punctiliously, but it could be incredibly dull. Standing around in hedges and sitting in cars didn't make full use of a bright mind like his.

Of course it wasn't so bad when one was on the move, tailing a subject. But in this case the tail wasn't much of a challenge—the whole team knew exactly where the subject was going. To FO/E headquarters on Platous Gate.

Nevertheless the team consisted of three men on foot and two in a car. Heavy numbers by any standards. But, then, if the subject worked at FO/E she was bound to be important.

Leksand stood in the tram queue and, as the line shortened, maneuvered gently around the outside so that he was behind her and slightly to one side, with two people in between. At the briefing they'd said that she knew of the surveillance, but that she must be watched for attempted contacts.

That meant getting reasonably close. She might pass a note

or a package. She might whisper. And if she was going to do any of those things she would do it in a crowd.

He moved himself farther forward until he was to one side of her, with one man in between. He glanced sideways at her. Her gloved hands were in front of her, her eyes staring intently across the street.

He followed her gaze. Nothing to see.

He looked back.

A tram came into sight at the top of the street, jangling loudly around a corner.

The subject continued to stare into the distance.

What a noise these trams make, Leksand thought: Why don't they oil them or something?

The tram was coming fast. People craned forward to see how full it was. Its tall narrow carriages vibrated heavily over some unevenness in the track; the headlights quivered angrily, holding their fierce gaze like an animal with prey in its sights.

Sonja was still thinking about Erik-Rolf, but now she was thinking that she'd probably get all the blame and he'd escape, because he was clever and she was not. In no time he'd be back with his women, sitting in Blom's or the Theatre Café, while she was locked away in some dreadful place. She thought with sudden resentment: Why should he get away with it?

In a surge of bitterness she decided she'd not only trap and incriminate him but she'd give Thrane every ounce of evidence she could.

Immediately she was struck with shame and self-loathing. How vindictive she was! How low she'd sunk! She lowered her head.

God help me, I love him so. I love him so.

The tram began to brake with an ugly grating sound. People shuffled forward. Sonja felt someone come up behind her.

A sudden weariness came over her. For an instant she closed her eyes.

The tram was ten feet away, still braking hard . . .

The person behind was very close. Sonja turned her head slightly and saw a pair of staring eyes topped by an Astrakhan hat.

She frowned with vague recognition and instinctively made to move away.

It was then that she felt hands grip her waist.

What was he doing? Her instincts screamed violently, she sucked in her breath to cry out, she flung back a hand to grab at him.

Then it came. A powerful punishing jab in the back, a solid push. She felt an incredible surprise, a vast disbelief, a great leap of panic.

She felt her body arch, her stomach jerk forward—

Then her whole *body* was falling.

Dreadful heart-stopping fear surged into her brain. Images of childhood flashed before her . . . falling from the apple tree, falling fast, the ground rushing up, her mother's scream . . .

The ground was rushing up now, ground cleaved by a shiny metal rail.

She thrust her hands forward, landed heavily, bumped her head with a sickening crack, felt the breath hiss out of her, fought for air.

A deafening grinding and screeching enveloped her.

Sick fear tore at her stomach.

Move. She had to move. It wasn't too late.

She pushed up with her hands, turned her head a fraction, and in one appalling moment of realization knew—

It was too late for everything.

She opened her mouth to scream, but no sound came.

A bundle shot forward. It looked like someone's coat. It took an instant for Leksand to realize.

Her.

Everything happened slowly at breathtaking speed. The woman fell spread-eagled across the track. The tram wheels screamed. The driver's face contorted with horror. Leksand stared aghast, wondering if the tram could ever be stopped in time, willing it to brake harder. But despite the screeching of locked wheels, the heavy beast had a sickening momentum and Leksand knew that nothing could stop it.

The woman's head came up and turned slightly just as the deflector bar hit her. Leksand felt a moment of hope—the bar must push her aside—but the hope died instantly as he realized the deflector bar was riding over her, and over and over. It happened with such slowness that Leksand had a last unreasoned urge to shout: Move!

He saw an arm come up, her head fall back, and then she was right under the tram and the near-side wheel was rolling onto her.

The tram finally halted, its front wheels astride the body.

Leksand closed his eyes. Women screamed. Men gasped. Leksand reopened his eyes to see the driver shouting soundlessly.

The crowd shrank back. Women were still screaming. Men's voices were loud and ugly. The driver was spewing. Someone moved away, bumping Leksand's shoulder, his face blank as he elbowed past.

Leksand suddenly came to his senses and looked quickly about him. What should he be doing? Where should he be looking? God—could he have prevented this?

He ran forward to look at the woman. Her head was sticking out, a wheel over her neck, blood pouring from her mouth, a garish look of pop-eyed surprise on her purple face. Completely dead.

He spun back to look at the crowd. Horrified faces, staring, covering their eyes. Toward the back, one of his colleagues, his eyes round with disbelief.

Quieter now. People moving farther back. The hushed murmur of stunned voices, the occasional sounds of weeping.

Leksand felt the urge to talk to someone, to say how dreadful it was, to share the horror, but he forced himself to think. Everything he'd learned in his training seemed to have vanished from his mind.

Be observant. Look around you. Don't miss the obvious. Photograph the scene in your mind. Remember everything, everybody. What was out of place? What was so normal that it was abnormal?

He went back over it—the tram, the bundle shooting forward.

Shooting forward.

It came to him in a flash.

She'd been pushed.

He felt a moment's elation at his own cleverness. Then, in the next instant, bitter self-reproach at his stupidity. He hadn't seen the one thing he should have seen—who had done it. And now he was too late—the crowd had moved back, people had shifted.

He searched the crowd, examining each face.

No one looked suspicious, everyone looked suspicious.

He turned, doing a complete circle. A larger crowd was forming on the pavement, along the street, their gray faces contorted with horror.

A small memory pulled at him.

Right at the beginning, a bumped shoulder, someone moving off, someone with a blank face.

A *blank* face?

Who the hell would be unaffected after something like that?

Then he moved fast, diving out of the crowd, half running, half walking, searching desperately for—what?

Hat. A dark hat with earflaps. Heavy face. Over six feet tall.

He skidded to a halt on a corner. To his left paths crossed the dark tree-studded square, to his right the pavements of Stortings Gata ran alongside well-lit shop fronts.

Nothing.

He forced himself to stand still and keep looking both ways. The bastard couldn't have gotten that far.

He began to lose hope.

Then—there! Across the square, walking briskly toward a corner. Was it him?

Leksand started off at a cautious walk, then, realizing that he had committed himself, ran gently across the square. The hat disappeared around the corner. Leksand accelerated, bolting across the street, dipping out of the way of an approaching car, slipping once on ice, and then, reaching the corner, grinding to a halt.

There. Not far away, going strong, black Astrakhan-type hat on bullnecked head.

Leksand fell in behind.

Black Hat looked around, eyes missing nothing. Leksand quickly looked down at the pavement and thought: He's a pro. He felt a small leap of triumph—he *must* have gotten the right man.

Black Hat crossed the street. Leksand did not. Coming to a junction Black Hat turned a corner, looking over his shoulder as he did so.

Leksand carried on, head down, eyeballs swiveled so far to the side that it hurt. Beyond the junction, Leksand crossed the road and doubled back, trying to ignore the possibility that he might come face to face with his man.

He peered around the corner.

Black Hat was still walking.

Oh no he wasn't.

He was getting into a car.

Automatically, Leksand looked for the license number.

Too far away to see.

There was a risk of being spotted, but, ignoring it, Leksand dived out from behind the corner and ran toward the car, weaving his way through pedestrians, fighting to keep his footing on the treacherous surface, keeping an eye on that license plate.

The car pulled out.

Leksand stared hard at the number.

The car roared off and disappeared. Leksand pulled out his notepad and wrote the number down.

Then he hurried to a telephone. The longed-for promotion might come sooner than he'd hoped.

He'd been briefed on that number some time ago.

Unless he was very much mistaken, the car belonged to a Bulgarian import-export company.

25

It was official: it was the coldest winter in twenty years.

The high pressure system over the Arctic Sea had deepened. The nights were long and cloudless and the frosts exceptionally hard. At high altitudes the air was incredibly clear, while in the valleys the air was so still that thick mists formed, plunging everything into a white gloom. At night the mists froze, covering everything with hoarfrost and decorating branches and twigs with fine webs of white lace.

Trains no longer ran on time; some trains no longer ran at all where lines, brittle with cold, had fragmented under load. In the inner reaches of the fjords, fishing boats were frozen in. Wildlife perished, domestic animals sheltered, and in Oslo twenty people a day were admitted to hospitals with bones broken on icy pavements. No one stayed out longer than they had to. People compared it to 1942, when, so it was said, the cold was so intense that your nose was at risk of dropping off—but this was recognized as a bit of an exaggeration.

In the north no one bothered to exaggerate; they were too busy trying to get on with their lives. On the coast, where the temperature was minus twenty, the men sailed for the Lofoten banks to go cod fishing because they always did in February, while the women stayed home and ran the snow-locked farms because that was what they always did at this time of year.

Up on the plateau, where it was minus forty, life for the Lapps was a little harder than usual—water stored inside their tents froze overnight and had to be remelted every morning, food had to be thawed, and extra peat and wood found for the fires. But with two thousand years' accumulated knowledge, the fierce weather meant no more than a bit of extra work, and in conditions that would defeat most other people, babies continued to be born, meals cooked, and the herd watched.

And it was getting colder . . .

Each night the frost bit more deeply into the earth, each day the ice in the fjords crept farther out from the shore.

The country gritted its teeth and waited for a respite.

But it isn't the cold that's the real enemy—it's the wind. At present the wind was faint, no more than a frozen whisper, but its touch was like a whiplash.

Hal climbed steadily up the side of the valley, the dry snow squeaking gently under his skis. When he'd gained sufficient height he continued along the side of the slope, skirting the herd, until he was to the west and downwind of them. Then he closed in.

A coward's approach.

The herd stood in the blue light, watching him curiously. Only six remained out of the original ten. They stood pressed close together, shoulder to shoulder, heads low, in a solid black mass of shaggy hair and thin legs.

When he was five yards away he stopped. Checking that Arne was in position to the right and Bamse well away in the rear, he swung the .22 up to his shoulder.

Scenting danger the musk-oxen stamped around, snorting anxiously, their black eyes glaring and fearful. Yet they didn't run. They had become too trusting for that.

Hal thought bitterly: trust misplaced.

He looked for the mother and calf, but the other musk-oxen, in the age-old instinct of the herd, had surrounded them.

Nothing for it, then.

Slipping off the safety catch he sighted carefully on the wide shoulder of the large bull. Yet he was forced to pause—there was a lump in his throat, he could hardly see—and he had to close his eyes for a moment.

Opening them again, he sighted and, before there was time to hesitate, squeezed hard.

A faint thud as the silenced shot found its target, and the beast crumpled soundlessly into the snow, its great head lolling to one side. The other musk-oxen skittered sideways in alarm, then paused to eye their fallen leader.

The mother was clear of the others now, the calf at her side. Hal sighted quickly and felled the mother. The calf screamed and brayed. Clamping his teeth, Hal took the calf hurriedly, but he knew even before he saw the fallen creature kicking and jerking that he'd made a mess of it. Cursing himself, he poled quickly over and, trying to ignore the eye-rolling terror of the young animal, finished the job.

The remaining three musk-oxen were bolting. Arne took one, the unsilenced shot cracking loudly across the valley. Bamse blocked the other two and wheeled them back. Hal dropped the first as it cantered toward him. The last, a barren cow, paused, breath steaming from her nostrils, eyes wild with fear. Raising his rifle for the last time, Hal took it through the chest. The beast crumpled, knees first, into the snow.

The valley was silent, the snow stained butcher-red.

Hal dropped his rifle and stood, staring at the slaughterhouse. A deep ache constricted his chest, his throat was dry. After a time Bamse crept up and sat beside him.

The roar of the tractor split the silence. Arne drove up and, turning, reversed the trailer up to the bull.

Shivering himself to life, Hal wiped some iciness from his cheeks and, hoisting the rifle over his shoulder, skied down to the tractor. Wordlessly, the two men tied ropes to the creature's hind legs, hooked up to the winch, and hauled the dead bulk up the ramp onto the trailer, ready for its short journey to the makeshift dump where the frozen carcasses of the other four animals lay covered in snow.

As Hal took the second load he noticed the supply boat running close along the shore below. Normally it dropped the mail and supplies at the other end of the island, then passed much farther offshore. Today he guessed there must have been a special delivery for himself or Arne which the boat would have dropped at the cove just beyond Arne's place. Hal waved to Arne riding on the footplate and, catching his eye, pointed toward the boat. The old man nodded.

On the third trip they loaded the carcasses of the mother and her calf. The calf's forehead, nostrils, eyelids, and mouth were covered in puffy yellow-red swellings. The animal could only have had a short time to live. The mother, on the other hand, seemed unaffected. Then Arne pulled back the animal's lip and Hal saw the burgeoning nodules inside the mouth.

Hal drove down to the dump in a mood of black despair, and it wasn't until Arne leaned in from the footplate and touched him on the arm that he realized the old man was trying to attract his attention. Arne pointed down the hill.

Then Hal saw. Three figures. At the side of the house, making their way up the hill toward them. The light was dim and the figures heavily muffled, but Kris's small figure was unmistakable. Suppressing a rage, Hal slammed the tractor to a halt, killed the engine, and jumped out.

Aware of the carcasses in the trailer and his own blood-smeared overalls, he shouted down to them: "Stay there! Don't move!" Tearing off his gloves, he climbed out of the loose white army overalls which covered his anorak.

Rolf and Ragna stopped obediently, but little Kris ran forward, puffing and panting up the hill. Ragna shouted after him, but the boy kept coming.

Kicking the bloodstained overalls away, Hal hurried down to meet him and, sweeping him up in his arms, planted a rough kiss on the boy's nose.

Kris recoiled. "Ouch! Your face is all prickly."

"Haven't shaved."

"Ughh! You're no good for kissing!" And wrinkling up his nose, the boy giggled, his little face breaking into an impish grin. Hal's heart twisted with love and he hugged the boy hard against him.

Then, with Kris in his arms, he strode down to the others, his mood darkening.

"What are you doing here?" he demanded fiercely.

Rolf said firmly: "I thought you might need an extra pair of hands."

Ragna pulled the tightly wound scarf down from her mouth. "We came to see if we could help, Hal."

Hal didn't know what to make of this kindness—if kindness it was. "Why didn't you call, for God's sake! I could have told you not to waste your time!" Then to Ragna: "And Kris—why bring him?"

Kris wriggled in Hal's arms, and Hal could feel the boy's hurt and bewilderment.

"We did phone," Rolf cut in smoothly, "but there was never any answer. So we thought we'd better come over, just in case. The skipper of the supply boat seemed to think you had an epidemic on your hands."

"All the more reason not to come."

Ragna asked fearfully: "The musk-oxen—is there any hope . . . ?"

Aware that Kris was soaking up every word, Hal shot her a warning look. But it was too late. In the way of all children, Kris understood immediately that the news was bad and buried his head against Hal's shoulder.

Hal shot Ragna an accusing look.

Ragna whispered: "I just couldn't leave him behind—really."

"Well, you should have! This is no place for a child!"

Kris began to cry. Hal groaned. Putting a hand on the boy's cheek, he said softly: "It's nothing to do with you, Kris. You know I love having you here. But it's the animals. They're sick, you see."

There was a short silence. Then a snuffly "Will they get better?"

He couldn't bring himself to tell the whole truth. "Some of them will. But some of them won't, Krisi."

Rolf said briskly: "Why don't you tell me what I can do? Shall I go and help up there?" He indicated the tractor with Arne waiting beside it.

Without answering, Hal dropped Kris onto his feet and said to Ragna: "Take him down to the house and be sure to keep him inside." He leaned down and whispered to the child: "Will you and Mummy warm up the house and make some food for us?"

A small nod and, looking a little happier, Kris took Ragna's hand to walk down to the house.

Hal called after them: "Leave your boots outside the house—you'll see a box there- -and wash your hands carefully."

Ragna mouthed an "Okay" over her shoulder.

"Is this thing dangerous to people, then?" Rolf asked as they climbed the hill. He didn't sound quite so willing to help all of a sudden.

Hal retrieved his overalls from the snow. "Highly unlikely. But until we get the final vet's report I'm not taking any risks."

"Tell me what I can do, then."

Hal wanted to say: Not a lot. He resented this unexpected intrusion, as if Rolf's arrival had violated Brattdal in some way. More than that, he resented Rolf himself. He suspected Rolf had not been telling him the truth. Now he felt a division between them, an unspoken chasm of distrust.

Yet why be churlish? This was a stinking job, and another hand would get the job finished sooner.

He said with heavy humor: "Want some practice at shooting sitting ducks?" He gave a mirthless laugh. "Or rather, penned sheep. Can't miss."

Rolf shot him a sideways glance. "Why don't you take a break? The old man and I can deal with it."

They reached the tractor. Hal pulled his overalls and gloves and swung himself rapidly up into the cab. Suddenly he was too tired to be angry anymore. "No. With three of us the job'll be done that much quicker."

As Hal fired the engine he was aware of Rolf's eyes on him, hard and cold and watchful. Then he knew that for Rolf, also, their conversation in Oslo was neither finished nor forgotten.

Ragna had done her best with what she had found: dried fish, onions, carrots, potatoes, flour, milk, cheese—but no herbs. She tasted the finished pie and made a face. What she could have achieved with parsley and thyme . . .

She found herself examining the kitchen critically, rearranging it in her mind, installing jars of dried herbs and spices, stocking cupboards with tins of unusual vegetables and fruits, and rice, pasta, and preserves.

Then she remembered. Hal was giving the place up. Had he really meant it? Could he ever bring himself to leave? She pictured the kitchen devoid of warmth and clutter, the house silent and deserted, the cold slowly penetrating the empty rooms. She couldn't help feeling it would be a dreadful pity. All that hard work of Hal's, all that passion and determination. No one else could have done so much in such a short time.

But now he was bitter and defeated. She hated to see him like that. Hal of all people, who'd never given up anything in his life.

Kris charged into the room and cried: "I can't find Lilli." Ragna gave a small sigh. Kris had been very difficult since her return from Oslo, throwing tantrums, demanding attention, and generally trying to wind her up. Making an effort, she asked kindly: "Who's Lilli?"

"Lilli! Lilli!" he repeated with a stamp of the foot, as if she should know.

"Really, Kris," she retorted, chopping vegetables energetically. "You insisted on coming, so now you have to make do. I don't have time to find this Lilli, whoever he is."

"I want Lilli. I want Uncle Hal! I want Uncle Hal!"

"Well, you know he can't come now. He's busy."

There was a silence. She looked around. Kris's face was contorted with misery, and he was taking a deep gulp of air, ready to bellow.

With a sigh of fond exasperation she went over and knelt down and put her arms around him. The bellow, when it finally came, deafened her.

"Oh, Kris!" she cried.

He was inconsolably unhappy, screaming and beating his fists against her chest. She tried to hold on to him, but he fought his way free and stood before her, his face red and tear-streaked, his small body shaking with fury. "I hate you! I hate you!"

She held out her arms to him but he ran off, sobbing wildly, and stamped loudly up the stairs.

She felt bemused. What had happened to her lovely boy? Where had her easy acquiescent child gone? She thought guiltily: It's my fault, I've been neglecting him. And she realized it was true. First there'd been the distractions of the shop, then the sudden trip south, then the arrival of Rolf. Worst of all, only that morning Kris had glimpsed Rolf leaving her bedroom. She felt terribly guilty about that.

And now, on top of everything, there was the loss of the beloved musk-oxen.

She stiffened: gunshots sounded from up the hill.

Abandoning the food, she ran quickly up the stairs and found Kris in the small end room, lying curled up on the bed, his body shuddering to the spasms of deep sobs. As she approached, something outside the window caught her eye. In the gathering darkness, beyond the far wall of the white-clad vegetable garden, the snow had been heaped into a large circle. In the center was an amorphous mass of black. Black animal bodies. A figure clad in overalls was adding the bodies of sheep to the sorry pile.

She realized then: Kris had looked out and seen the gruesome burial ground.

The shots continued to echo down the valley.

She whispered, "Oh, Kris," and, lying down beside him, put her arms around him and hugged him tight. "Oh, poor, poor darling. Poor darling."

At last the distant shots ceased. After a time the sobs, too, subsided.

She said: "I'll help you find Lilli if you like."

He said nothing but, reaching for something that had been buried in his arms, he pulled it out: a battered rag horse. Of course—why hadn't she remembered? She said: "Hello, Lilli."

The animal disappeared into his arms again, the warm little body snuggled closer, then a small unsteady voice asked slowly: "Is Uncle Hal cross with me?"

Ragna squeezed him to her. "No. He's not cross with you, darling, not in the slightest. He's just ... upset ... about other things. He still loves you just as much as ever. Honestly."

There was a pause while this was absorbed, then: "Why do things get ill?"

"Because—well, just now and again a nasty little bug comes along which the animals can't fight against and then ... very occasionally they die. Like now."

Another pause. "Is that why Daddy died?"

Ragna tried to adjust to the astonishing switch. "What?"

"Did bugs make Daddy dead?"

"No, darling. Daddy died in an accident, like I told you."

"What's an accident mean?"

"It's—something that happens suddenly. So suddenly you know nothing about it. It never hurts you, it's too quick. It just—happens."

A long pause this time. "Like falling over and bumping your head?"

"That kind of thing."

"Did Daddy fall over and bump his head?"

She closed her eyes. "Like that, but worse."

Silence. She felt him relax against her. She savored the peace, gently stroking his hair, enjoying the warmth of his dear body against hers, thinking: Beautiful child, I love you so.

He moved again. She prepared herself for another question.

"Uncle Hal—is he going to die too?"

She gave the ghost of a laugh. "No, darling. Absolutely not." Sensing he was unconvinced, she added: "Promise."

"I don't want Uncle Hal to die."

"No, darling. He won't. Honestly."

She stroked his cheek and kissed his forehead. The strength of his love for Hal had always left her with a mild feeling of exclusion and—yes, if she was honest—resentment. It had given Hal a claim on her that she didn't want him to have. But now she was glad, glad that Kris had a man like Hal to love and admire.

She kissed the small forehead over and over again, glowing in the warmth of her love for him.

A voice broke the silence. "Oh, there you are."

Ragna looked up with a start.

Rolf stood outside the open door. She hadn't heard him come up the stairs. He said briskly: "I'm going down to the old man's house to find the telephone." He shook his head with irritation. "Why Hal doesn't have one beats me."

"Are the others coming in?"

"In a while. But tell me, will you? Where the hell does Hal keep his drink? I can't find it anywhere."

"In the corner cupboard. In the living room."

"And towels—I need a good wash. It was like a slaughterhouse up there. All blood and guts . . ." He gave a shudder. "I got covered. . . . I've washed most of it off, but . . ."

Appalled, Ragna looked down at Kris. His eyes were wide open; he had taken it all in. His face slowly crumpled, and, clutching at her, he began to cry again.

Ragna shot Rolf a horrified glance, but he was staring at Kris, a frown of annoyance on his face. "The towels?" he prompted finally.

Controlling her anger with difficulty, Ragna managed: "The cupboard by the bathroom."

As she quieted Kris down again she heard water running in the bathroom, then footsteps as he went downstairs. Finally a door banged; he was gone.

The silence blossomed out. Ragna settled her head back on the pillow. Interesting how small things could be so revealing. He obviously didn't care for children at all. What was more, he wasn't even prepared to pretend he liked Krisi for her sake.

It didn't surprise her. It just made her wonder. Why had he come back to Tromsø? An interest in her welfare? It was flattering to think so, yet a part of her couldn't quite believe it. For that matter, why had he been so insistent on coming here to Brattdal? She couldn't believe he was that concerned about Hal's welfare either. Were he and Hal still bosom friends? It didn't seem so.

No: There was something strange going on. She couldn't work it out at all.

Krisi sniffed. She dried his eyes and blew his nose and read him a story.

Sounds rose from the kitchen.

Were the others back? She remembered the pie and groaned; she hadn't even put it in the oven. "Come on, darling," she murmured to Kris and, picking him up, carried him down to the kitchen.

Hal was there, stripped to the waist, bending over the sink up to his elbows in soap and water. The muscles of his back were strong and firm. A vivid memory of embracing that back, that body, leapt into Ragna's mind; she remembered the smoothness of his skin and the hardness of his body and the gentleness of his touch. The memories affected her oddly, almost as if . . .

Half turning, Hal said: "You wouldn't pass me the towel, would you? Has Rolf gone down to the phone?"

"About half an hour ago." Sitting Kris on the table, she found a towel hanging beside the stove and passed it to Hal. He started to dry himself vigorously, then, spotting Kris's downcast face, went and sat down in front of him.

"Hello, old chap . . ."

Leaving the two of them talking in low voices, Ragna went to the stove and, sprinkling some grated cheese across the top of the pie, slid it into the oven, and chopped more vegetables.

Behind her the murmur of voices ceased. She turned to see Kris scampering happily out of the room. Hal came and stood before her. "I need to talk to you, Ragna."

He had missed a smear of soap above one eyebrow. Taking a corner of the towel he still held in his hand she dabbed at it, suppressing the urge to smooth away the deep frown from between his eyebrows.

His mouth twitched slightly. Firmly, he pulled her hand away. "Listen, this is important. I have to ask you something—something which is absolutely vital. I can't explain why—and it may not be easy for you to believe how important it really is, but . . ." He chewed at his lip, searching for the words. "Sometimes things have to be taken on trust, don't they? And I'm asking you to believe that this is vital. . . ."

Ragna couldn't think what he was working around to, but she had a nasty feeling it would be something awkward. "Go on."

"That information about the installation—being a navigation system called Delta and being used for Polaris submarines—Ragna, please tell me where it came from."

Ragna's heart sank. She had so wanted to avoid more difficulties between them. But this was the one thing she could never tell him. She'd promised. She'd sworn faithfully. With a soft groan she said: "I can't tell you that."

"Ragna—I wouldn't ask if it wasn't important."

She gripped his arm lightly, wanting him to understand—what?—that she would have helped if she could have.

Reaching for her hand he grasped it and squeezed it hard against his chest. "I'm asking you this one thing, Ragna, as I've never asked you for anything before. Trust me, please."

"Hal—I promised. And *that* was a matter of trust. I wish I could, but . . ." She shook her head.

"One day I'll explain why—"

She unfastened her eyes from his, extricated her hand, and leaned back against the counter, her silence giving him his answer.

"Ragna!" He rubbed a hand savagely across his eyes. Finally he gave a deep sigh and said gently: "It's not for my sake that I ask. It's for Jan's, Ragna. For his sake."

She looked up, startled. "I don't understand."

"I can't say any more. But, believe me, it's true."

What was he trying to say? That this concerned Jan in some way? How could it? She bristled with indignation. How dare he use Jan's name like this? What a cheap tactic!

She said coldly: "Please don't bring his name into this."

"But it directly concerns him, Ragna!"

She thought angrily: Ah! Got it now! It was Hal's army contacts. They were behind this—trying to discover her source, trying to stop any more information from getting out. And Hal had invented this imaginary connection with Jan in order to twist her arm. Doubtless he would tell her it was all to do with Soviet agents and national security.

She wanted to say: Well, pull the other one!

"I can't reveal my source," she said coldly. "So there's nothing to discuss."

The effect of her statement was quite different from the one she'd expected. Instead of arguing, he slumped visibly, and suddenly looked very tired. He murmured, almost to himself: "If only . . ." Then, shaking his head, he sat back on the edge of the table, looking defeated.

She felt a twinge of doubt. Cheap tactics and manipulation had never been Hal's style; would he really have stooped so low? And Jan's name—Hal of all people would never use it lightly. She began to wonder if she hadn't been too hasty.

"It really concerns Jan?" she asked tentatively.

He looked up, his expression open, his gaze direct, and said simply: "I wouldn't lie to you."

And she realized instantly that it was true.

She gave a long sigh. She knew then that she would have to choose.

The long walk down the hill had been a complete waste of time.

No Alex. No message from Alex.

The previous day Berg had called from Bodø airport on the journey up from Oslo, then twice from Ragna's, and now a fourth time, from the old man's house, but there had been nothing.

Berg stalked angrily away from the old man's place.

Could Alex be away? No: Alex never went away. He was a desk and drink man, far too lazy to set foot out of Oslo. Perhaps, then, something had gone wrong with the contact system.

But someone had always answered that special phone number in the past. Always.

Head down, Berg walked rapidly along the track, then, still going fast, struck up the hill toward Brattdal.

He decided to give Alex's special number one more try the following day. If it still didn't answer he'd call the Novosti switchboard and leave a message for Alex from "Harri." It wouldn't do any harm just this once. But even as he thought it he wasn't so sure. These remote islands had primitive telephone systems. Doubtless the operator listened in on every call. Well, he'd just have to be careful, that was all.

He climbed rapidly and, nearing the brow of a hill, caught a glimpse of a light from the house. The silence was deafening, the mountains tall and somber in the last of the twilight. It was so cold his breath was freezing around his nostrils. He thought: This was the last place God made.

Yet, he reminded himself, it had its advantages. No one knew he was here and no one would think of looking for him here—his newspaper thought he was taking a few days' vacation in Denmark. And if he wanted to get out, there was the seaplane twice a day and Bardufoss airport and the Finnish border a matter of hours away.

The house loomed large, a single light glowing in a front window. Berg considered the evening ahead. He must broach that unfinished business with Hal, find out what the hell he knew. But how to tackle it? Casually, he decided, just as if he'd been thinking about it and was curious to know more about the extraordinary appearance of the binoculars. Then, once he'd gotten Hal talking, he'd simply trip him up. It shouldn't be too difficult. Hal was a bad liar.

He climbed the steps to the veranda, hot under his thick clothing, impatient for a drink. He took off his boots and, opening the door, paused abruptly. The murmur of voices was coming from the kitchen.

Moving with care, he closed the door silently behind him, left his jacket and boots in the lobby, and padded up the passage toward the kitchen. He stopped short of the open door and listened.

The voices ceased. The silence stretched out.

He thought: Pity.

But he remained motionless, listening hard, just in case.

Ragna agonized. Jan . . . it concerned Jan. Yet she'd made a promise to Rolf—a strict promise. He'd been adamant about the importance of keeping it. If she broke the promise he'd be beside himself with anger. He would accuse her of ruining his career. She'd never see him again—though the prospect wasn't quite as upsetting as she'd previously imagined.

Perhaps she could hint at Rolf's involvement without actually giving him away, simply by referring Hal to Rolf. But the thought of the ensuing row made her feel quite weak.

There was an alternative, of course. To tell Hal and make him swear not to mention a word to Rolf. As long as they both kept quiet, then Rolf would never know.

It was the coward's way out. It was very attractive.

She made her decision and, instinctively moving closer to Hal so they wouldn't be overheard, opened her mouth to speak.

Suddenly there was a sound, so slight it was no more than a break in the silence. She paused and looked questioningly at Hal. He gripped her arm and sent warning signals with his eyes. She closed her mouth.

They looked around. There was a pause.

Silently Rolf appeared in the doorway.

* * *

Hal and Ragna. Hal gripping Ragna's arm. Yet again. They seemed to make a habit of touching each other when he wasn't around.

They looked startled and guilty, like two children caught stealing sweets. But what really interested Berg was the look of defiance that flashed briefly across Ragna's face.

He thought savagely: now what have *you* been up to, my love?

And he knew then: he could no longer trust her.

26

Thrane sat in the hot seat and thought fleetingly: Now I know how it feels. Being on the wrong side of an interrogation was uncomfortable enough, but facing people whose minds were quite made up was distinctly unpleasant.

He had been asked to give what the Director called "a full account." By any other name it was a carpeting. On the opposite side of the table sat the Director flanked by the Deputy Director and Thrane's immediate boss, Ekeland, the head of Security.

The Director gave him a look of disbelief. "So you actually told Starheim. You told him there was a major leak?"

"Indirectly—yes."

"Didn't it occur to you that you were breaching security?"

"Yes."

"Good God—why did you do it, then?"

"I had to find out where he'd gotten that Delta idea from, I had to give him a reason to tell me—or rather, to find out for me. I trusted him. I still do."

"But he hasn't come up with any information."

"Not yet. But I'm sure he will."

The Director dropped his eyes. "And you still believe your trust is well placed, even after what's happened?"

Thrane said tightly: "Yes."

Ekeland leaned forward and tapped the table. "It was an extremely serious and unjustified breach of security." Thrane thought: Now, that statement gives a whole new meaning to departmental loyalty. "And," Ekeland continued, "we must face the possibility that this breach led directly to Sonja Bjornsen's death."

"You can't say that!" Thrane exclaimed. "The opposition were already on to Sonja. They were already watching her."

"We don't know that at all, Thrane," said the Director in the slightly exasperated tone of someone going over old ground. "There's no hard evidence, is there?"

"There's the fact that her lover failed to show not once but twice, and the second time had all the signs of a setup."

No one looked convinced. The Director rubbed his forehead.

Ekeland said: "Now I'd like to play devil's advocate for a minute and see where it gets us." He made a show of rearranging his notes. Thrane thought: I know where it's going to get us—to you smelling of roses, and Starheim in deep trouble.

"Now, we have the following. . . . *Fact*"—he tapped a finger on the table—"you, Thrane, let it be known that we are on to a major leak in high places. *Fact*—two days later, Sonja Bjornsen gets pushed under a tram—"

"But you can't connect the two things just like that!" Thrane exclaimed. "There are absolutely no grounds—"

"Please." Ekeland interjected in the patronizing tone of a headmaster addressing a difficult pupil. "We've taken note of what you have to say. Now, if you would let me continue? *Next* . . . we have Sonja Bjornsen's assurances that she never revealed the names of those involved in the Pasvik affair. If we believe her we must ask ourselves, who did have this information? Who could have passed it on?"

"No one need have passed it on," Thrane argued. "It's possible that either or both of the men were interrogated before they were shot, and volunteered their names in the process."

"Possible," Ekeland conceded. "But unlikely. The Russians may have overreacted at Pasvik, but I don't think anyone believes they actually interrogated the men then executed them in cold blood. Besides, the Soviet protest came only hours after the event. They could hardly have had time for interrogations. It's much more reasonable to assume that the Soviets knew the names in advance, don't you think?"

There was a silence. Thrane shook his head. Ekeland returned to his notes. "Next . . . the exact location of the Pasvik operation. That was obviously leaked—"

Thrane interrupted wearily: "Not obviously. They might have followed the third man to the border. They might have been watching him for months beforehand. We can't possibly be sure that they knew the exact location in advance."

Ekeland and the Director exchanged glances, one skeptical, the other troubled.

Ekeland continued with the air of someone who's been interrupted unnecessarily. "Next . . . you tell Starheim that the third man was a Norwegian. And very shortly afterward this gets into the press. Not of direct importance, but still interesting, you must agree."

Thrane sank back into his chair and crossed his arms.

"*Next* . . . Starheim writes all these anti-NATO letters to various government departments and politicians. He's seen up at the installation site, snooping, taking photographs. *Finally*"— he paused for effect—"we have this Delta business. Which reveals a direct link from Sonja Bjornsen through her contact to Starheim." He pushed away his notes in the self-satisfied way of someone who's proven his point.

Thrane gave a short incredulous laugh. What could he say? Ekeland needed a scapegoat and, now that he'd found one, he obviously wasn't going to get deflected by the facts. "If you seriously believe that Starheim is working with the Russians, then you're"—he was going to say "completely mad" but settled on—"mistaken!"

Ekeland conceded: "It's possible he doesn't have *direct* links. . . . He may just be in contact with a front organization— a political group, a peace group, or whatever. But then he must know what these groups are all about. He must know they have strong Soviet links. He's been trained in all that, for God's sake!"

The Director gave a loud sigh. "The whole thing may be much more straightforward than all this. He's a man of strong principle, isn't he? Well, he may simply have decided his principles are more in accord with another country's. Who knows? Anyway, the point is, all these—facts—lead back to him. We must follow the thing up."

There was a heavy silence. Thrane decided it would be a waste of breath to start arguing again.

The Deputy Director said: "We should mount a surveillance."

Thrane exclaimed: "What—on Revøy!"

"Well—intercept the mail, tap the telephone."

"He uses a party line in a neighbor's house. Rather public for sending messages to the Russians, don't you think?" Thrane murmured.

The Director flung him an icy look. "We've got to cover it, Thrane. We can't afford any more blunders. We've made quite enough in this affair as it is."

"I agree," Thrane replied with sudden relish. "And our greatest blunder was to let Sonja Bjornsen go. If we'd locked her up I'm certain she'd have blabbed and led us to the lover. And then we'd have been able to expel half the Soviet Embassy instead of a single Bulgarian heavy!"

The Director suddenly looked tired and worn. Thrane imagined the sort of pressure he was under, with both the Cabinet and the Americans at his throat. But that was no excuse; the man had to face facts.

Ekeland looked uncomfortable, but then he'd never liked hearing the truth. "Certainly I think we can give up the idea of finding the contact," he said carefully. "Which means we should concentrate on finding the knave in our own pack. We should bring Starheim straight in for questioning. It's too late for surveillance."

"But then you ruin our only hope," Thrane cried.

Three pairs of eyes regarded him with guarded interest.

Thrane continued: "Okay, I admit there's a connection between Starheim and Sonja—though I'll bet anything you like it's a very tortuous one. But let's concentrate on that connection. Let's find out what it *is*—"

"I agree," said Ekeland.

"In which case let's leave Starheim to come back to us with that information he promised. Remember, he's the only one who *can* find the connection."

"You're assuming he's prepared to find out. You're assuming he's not withholding the information."

"That's right! That's exactly what I'm assuming!" Thrane

said, holding his temper with difficulty. "If we have to put the tabs on Starheim, okay—I suppose we must. But don't let's bring him in and ruin our only chance of getting the people behind all this. Who knows, we might catch the lover after all."

"On the other hand, we might just succeed in sending the whole lot to ground," said Ekeland.

"What are you suggesting?" Thrane asked darkly. "That Starheim is merely going to tip them off?"

"Directly or indirectly, it must be a possibility."

Thrane gave him a condescending look. "Well, in that case he would have done it already, wouldn't he? And they—whoever they are—would have hopped it two days ago, so we wouldn't have a hope of finding them anyway, would we? Which just goes to prove we have nothing to lose by trusting Starheim. In fact, we have everything to gain."

Ekeland looked as though he'd been made to appear stupid, which he had.

The Director considered. "All right," he said wearily. "But I want some hard information from Starheim within two days."

Nikolai Andreevitch Yurasov stared at the heavy polished door and knew what real fear was like. Fear was imagining life without diplomatic privileges, fear was demotion and a poky little apartment in an outer suburb of Moscow.

Fear was waiting to see the Navigator.

This nightmare had haunted him all his working life; the terror that only a senior GRU officer can know when, after twenty years' service—which meant twenty years' patient and, as Yurasov used to congratulate himself on, highly skillful maneuvering through the minefield of GRU politics—he suddenly blows it.

He still couldn't believe it. Agent 173—*his* protégé—had taken him for a ride and done it so effortlessly that even now the memory of it made Yurasov want to weep.

The question for Yurasov was: could he survive it? Did he have enough friends at the Aquarium? Enough people to put in a good word for him? Enough people to remind the First Deputy of all the wonderful stuff he'd pulled in over the years?

He stared straight at the solid bulk of the polished mahogany door and felt extremely unsure of the answers to these questions. The only certain thing was that there'd be no champagne sitting on the Navigator's desk, not like the time when 173 had started coming up with pure gold, and Yurasov had basked in the glory of having recruited him, and the Navigator had beamed with delight at having probably the most important agent in Europe under his control. Congratulations had come directly from the First Deputy.

No, there definitely wouldn't be any champagne—but would there be a syringe? They always sedated you before evacuation. He knew the procedure well enough: he'd helped evacuate plenty of his colleagues over the years.

When he thought about the nasty events of the last few days, which he did constantly, he could almost feel the needle in his arm. The news about the woman had been the worst, because then he'd known precisely what lay in store for him.

The woman Rolf had identified as a threat, the woman he had dismissed so lightly as a nobody, far from being an accounts clerk, had been—he still blanched at the thought—personal secretary to the Director of FO/E.

And he—Nikolai Andreevitch—had stuck his neck out and obtained authorization for his Bulgarian neighbors to take care of her. Provocation was too mild a word for what he had done. Norwegian Intelligence would never forgive such a thing. You didn't suddenly go and beat your fencing opponent around the head with a blunt instrument. Because then he got angry and refused to play by the rules—rules that the GRU had learned to use to enormous advantage.

Of course it wouldn't have been so bad if the truth had never come to light. After all, middle-aged women did occasionally fall under trams.

But had his Bulgarian friends used tact and skill and finesse? Had they used their eyes? Had they used their minute brains?

Of course not. Although the surveillance must have stood out a mile, although a blindfolded child would have spotted it, they'd managed to avoid the use of either their limited vision or their pea-sized brains.

Moreover, just to ensure complete disaster, they had been seen in the act. Seen, followed, and identified.

The disaster was total. Yurasov, even from his viewpoint, could see nothing to ameliorate it. Sweat trickled from his temples. His mouth was dry. He couldn't think. He resigned himself to the inevitable; it would be the syringe. No more foreign postings, no more well-cut clothes, no more surreptitious meetings with Valya, a colleague's wife he was rather in love with.

And all because Rolf had tricked him.

He'd kill him if he ever got hold of him. Rolf had wanted it both ways, and Yurasov had been too trusting to see. Rolf had used him, manipulated Yurasov's need for success—and he had fallen right into the trap.

The minutes ticked by. No sound permeated the two-foot-thick reinforced concrete walls of the embassy basement. No voices, no sound of ringing telephones, could be heard through the heavily soundproofed door of the Navigator's office. Only a faint hum filtering down from the air-conditioning vents.

Yurasov thought about Rolf and how he could cheerfully murder him.

But of course Rolf would survive. He would be allowed—no, encouraged—to remain *in situ* as a valuable agent of influence, writing his articles, traveling the world, acting the playboy-journalist. The man who had it all. The thought cut Nikolai Andreevitch to the quick. Why the hell *should* he have it all!

An idea sprang into his mind, a ridiculous idea for revenge, whereby Rolf would have to skip the country and go and live in Moscow, condemned to spend the rest of his life in a seedy apartment, suffocated by ugliness and mediocrity. Yurasov savored the idea—it would be the perfect irony—but then, with a weary sigh, he pushed the idea aside. This wasn't the time to indulge in such luxurious thoughts.

He must concentrate on more important matters—saving himself.

A shaft of light. The heavy door swung open on silent hinges. Nikolai Andreevitch's heart catapulted into his mouth and he shook as he'd never shaken before.

He got to his feet and forced himself to walk smoothly across the thick carpet into the room.

The Navigator sat behind his massive desk, his hands on the polished wood, palms down, his face unreadable. To Yurasov's surprise no one else was present, nor, he quickly noticed, was there any sign of a syringe. He allowed himself a small flutter of hope.

The Navigator said: "The Center has ordered your recall."

The flutter of hope died. Yurasov closed his eyes and felt sick. There was no doubt then: it was evacuation.

"However, this order will not be executed immediately." Yurasov looked up at the Navigator in surprise. "Not until the matter of One-seventy-three is settled."

Yurasov stuttered: "I'm most grateful, Comrade Colonel."

"Save your breath. You will be staying merely to help salvage this calamitous situation."

"Of course, Comrade Colonel."

"The Center are talking of pulling One-seventy-three out."

Through his misery Yurasov almost laughed.

"They are convinced he must be blown." The Navigator leaned forward urgently. "But is he blown, Yurasov? *Is* he?"

Yurasov pulled himself together. "There is no evidence for it, Comrade Colonel. He reported no surveillance. He seemed convinced that he was clear—"

"Exactly. Now—if we can show this, if we can show he's not even burned, then it will be clear that our action in protecting him was fully justified. And then . . ."

He didn't need to say more. Yurasov was way ahead of him. "So, Comrade Colonel," Yurasov said carefully, "we give One-seventy-three every indication that it is safe to become operational again?"

"That is so. I appreciate that he may not be so—er—forthcoming. But as an agent of influence he would still be extremely valuable, and the situation would be immeasurably—improved."

Improved? For Yurasov it could mean salvation. And when he looked into the Navigator's eyes he knew that he, too, was thinking of his own skin.

"We must give him every support," the Navigator continued, "every encouragement to return to normal as soon as possible. Reassure him, give him whatever he wants."

"We will have to be cautious, Comrade Colonel," Yurasov said unhappily. "He does not respond well to control."

"I wasn't suggesting pressure, merely encouragement."

Yurasov made a show of nodding at the wiseness of the Navigator's words. Then, because it was something that really had to be discussed, he ventured: "What if he *is* blown, Comrade Colonel?"

The Navigator didn't want to hear about that. He said gruffly: "Then we pull him out. Evacuate him."

"He wouldn't come willingly, Comrade Colonel. I feel he'd rather do anything than come over to us."

The Navigator was alarmed. "You didn't put that in your reports!"

"No, Comrade Colonel, no," Yurasov said hastily. "It was only a suspicion, no more. I thought it wisest—"

"Yes, yes." The Navigator relaxed a little. Such observations did not look good on a report.

"But I am sure I did not misread these suspicions of mine," continued Yurasov. "He regards retirement in Moscow as an unacceptable option. As I think I've indicated to you in the past, Comrade Colonel, One-seventy-three is without scruples, without true principles. I believe he would do a deal with the Norwegians rather than come over."

"That must not happen!"

Yurasov understood the Navigator's fears only too well: The colonel was terrified of a second scandal coming quickly after the first. It would mean certain disgrace for him as well.

"Then we would evacuate by force if necessary?"

The Navigator gave him a strange look, as if suspecting the motives behind the question. "If necessary."

Yurasov's vision of Rolf living out his days in a dreary Moscow apartment suddenly didn't seem so far-fetched after all.

"But first we must try to reactivate him," the Navigator said firmly.

"By all means, Comrade Colonel."

"And if he should manage to produce something useful, so much the better. You understand me?"

A pipe dream, thought Yurasov. He was convinced the woman had been 173's only source. But he certainly wasn't going to say so now. Instead he said firmly: "Indeed, Comrade Colonel."

The Navigator rubbed a hand harshly across his eyes. "So! We must restore communication."

Yurasov blinked. "Er—communication? Is it in need of restoration, Comrade Colonel?"

"Yes. The line to Savin's people has been left unmanned. A precautionary measure."

Yurasov couldn't believe it. How could the Navigator have been so foolish? Despite Yurasov's many and detailed reports, the Navigator obviously hadn't understood Rolf's nature. Rolf would not take the lack of contact well. Yurasov could picture his frustration and anger. He might even misunderstand the silence—take it as a warning. It was too uncomfortable to contemplate.

Yurasov said unsteadily: "Ah . . . I imagine that will have been very—er—unsettling for One-seventy-three. How soon will the line be manned again, Comrade Colonel?"

"Within a day."

"Er—not sooner, Comrade Colonel?"

The Navigator regarded him coolly. "Savin has been evacuated. Another precaution. Also, the safe house was vacated. Time is needed to set things up again."

"Of course, Comrade Colonel."

"I want you to compose a message for One-seventy-three. So that he knows you are still around and with his best interests at heart. But you yourself will remain here in the Residency."

Yurasov stood up to attention. "Yes, Comrade Colonel." He walked quickly out of the room before his legs gave out from under him.

Outside, three of his colleagues stared at him in surprise, as if they hadn't expected to see him again.

Yurasov managed a brave self-confident smile.

But he knew perfectly well it was only a reprieve.

Lars Sorensen had spent a whole evening searching his files, and had come in this morning—Sunday—just to have another look. But it was no good. Starheim was going to be disappointed. No German had been murdered in Trondheim during the period in question. It was inconceivable that such an event could have gone unrecorded, if only because of the terrible reprisals the Germans had always exacted when one of their own men was killed.

He'd looked at the files on other towns in the region of North Trondelag, just in case, but nothing had fit.

Starheim's note had been specific enough: The killing had taken place sometime in the autumn or early winter of 1944–45 in Trondheim. Two young men had been involved and had gone on the run, one whose Christian name was (probably) Petter, aged about eighteen at the time. The other's name was Rolf Berg.

Sorensen had raised his eyebrows when he'd read that second name. *Dagens Post*. His first reaction was to think it couldn't possibly be the journalist, but Starheim's footnote had confirmed it, and added: *That's why it is so very important to keep this confidential.*

Sorensen took the point. At the same time it made the whole thing rather intriguing.

Which was why Sorensen was loath to admit he was beaten. This sort of challenge was right up his street.

But now he must think about giving up for the day; his daughter and grandchildren were coming for lunch and he mustn't be late.

He paused a moment longer, leaning an elbow on the desk and chewing thoughtfully on his knuckle.

On an impulse he riffled through his address book, looking for a half-remembered name. Not finding it, he went to the back section, where all the names were cross-referenced by places, and found what he was looking for. Many useful names were recorded in the large red book, people who had been helpful in the past or might be in the future, people he had barely met as well as those he knew well.

The man he was calling had been mayor of Trondheim from 1940 to 1942. After the preliminary greetings, the former mayor sounded a little insulted at Sorensen's question. A murdered German in the winter of 1944–45? Of course not. He would have remembered, he would have known, it would have been on record.

A German who'd died for any reason at that time? Well, that was a tall order. Ordinary soldiers, troops always on the move. . . . He couldn't possibly know what Germans might have died. But he'd think about it and call back if he came up with anything.

Sorensen hesitated on the brink of asking him if he knew Rolf Berg, but decided that even someone as pedantic as the former mayor would put two and two together, and that wouldn't do. Sorensen thanked him and said good-bye.

Next Sorensen called a journalist who'd once interviewed him about his work, a man who worked on a Trondheim daily newspaper. The man was out.

Giving up for the moment, Sorensen went home to lunch, ate too much of his wife's excellent fruit pie, dandled his grandchildren on his knee, had a snooze, and finally caught up with the journalist early in the evening.

It was difficult to ask for information without being able to give anything in return, especially when the request involved Rolf Berg, whose name the journalist would undoubtedly know. But he eased the way with "I'd tell you all about it if I could, but I can't, and that's that. But when and if I am free to do so, believe me, you will be the first to know." The journalist gave a wry laugh, because Sorensen had spun him the same line before, but agreed instantly because once not so long ago Sorensen *had* come back to him with a good story.

It was the next morning, just after eleven o'clock, when the Trondheim journalist called back.

There was no trace of anyone named Rolf Berg in Trondheim.

Not in the school registers, not in the *Folkeregister*—the local population register.

Rolf Berg had never lived in Trondheim.

But far from being discouraged by the discovery, Sorensen's interest quickened. This warranted a completely different approach.

During his brief lunch break he went to work, starting with the Oslo telephone directory. Of course it was possible Mr. Berg wouldn't be listed, but in Norway's informal open society only one or two really famous people found it necessary to be ex-directory.

Berg, Rolf. There were three entries under that name. He took a guess at the one with the most expensive address, then, to check it, phoned the *Dagens Post* and, saying he was a lawyer trying to deliver Rolf Berg an important letter, asked the personnel department to confirm the address, which they did. An important letter . . . it was near the truth. He always was—well—near.

Next he called a man named Willy Minge. Minge's son had vanished during the war. Sorensen had helped to establish what had happened to the boy—he'd ben shot and his body dumped in a fjord. But Minge had been grateful to know.

Minge was a policeman, a sergeant of many years' seniority, in the Kripos, the criminal police, based at the central police station on Mollergata.

Minge greeted him warmly, then, when the pleasantries were over, asked helpfully: "Now, what can I do for you?"

Sorensen told him, adding: "I know this is a little—out of the ordinary. But it's not for any nefarious purpose, I assure you, Willy. It goes back to the war." He purposely left it vague, hoping that Minge would put a purely humanitarian interpretation on his interest.

"There is no way it would ever . . . er . . ." Minge's question hung in the air.

"Be traced back? Oh, no!" Sorensen declared. Minge was nearing retirement. Understandably, he didn't want to blot his copybook.

"Just checking!" he said cheerfully. "Give me an hour."

In fact it was twenty-five minutes.

Rolf Berg had a driver's license issued in his name at the address given in the phone book. Minge read through the details—the date and place of issue, the date of expiration. Then—and Sorensen stiffened—the date and place of birth.

Bergen. Rolf Berg had been born on April 5, 1927, in Bergen.

Sorensen got it all down and thanked Minge profusely.

Sorensen became aware of the time. His lunch break was over; he should be studying a difficult case that was going to court next week. But because he could never bear to conceive a plan without immediately putting it into action, he picked up the telephone again.

Sigi was a rambunctious lady at the local office of the *Folkeregister*, the register where births, marriages, deaths, and current and former addresses— it was compulsory to notify a move of house—were recorded. Sorensen had been carrying on a mild flirtation with Sigi for twelve years, mainly over the telephone. Now they spent a couple of minutes asking fondly after each other, exchanging news and inquiring into the health of their respective grandchildren. Then he made his request.

It would be a simple matter to find out, she assured him. After all, he was only requesting what was a matter of public record.

He hung up thinking what a nice woman she was, and got down to work. He thought she was an even nicer woman when she called back at two-thirty.

Rolf Berg had been born on April 5, 1927, in Bergen. He had gone to school in Bergen until 1937. Then his family had moved. But not to Trondheim.

Sigi's voice said clearly: "His family emigrated to the United States."

Sorensen was surprised. "America? But with him? With Rolf?"

"Oh, yes," she replied.

He began to thank Sigi for her help when she lowered her voice. "Because it's you, and I thought you might be interested, I looked back through his past addresses."

He dropped his voice to a whisper. "Ah."

"His card goes back to 1947—he's moved twice in that time, both times in the Oslo area. Before that—before 1947, that is—he was in America. He reapplied for—and got—a Norwegian passport."

"You mean—he was in America throughout the war?"

"Looks like it."

Sorensen thanked her and rang off, his mind racing. There was some mistake here. Starheim must have gotten his facts wrong—and yet . . . His letter had been so definite.

If Starheim wasn't mistaken, then . . .

Well, it was really very simple. Then, in January 1945, Rolf Berg had been in two places at once.

Sorensen tried to suppress a growing excitement. He loved a good mystery.

He thought hard, then decided that, despite Starheim's request for confidentiality, he would throw a little caution to the winds.

He made another call. A cool female voice informed him

that Major Thrane was not available and was not likely to be available for some considerable time. When pressed, she admitted it could be a matter of days. Sorensen left a message because there was nothing else he could do.

Some minutes later, as he sat drumming his fingers on the desk and wondering where else he might get the information, his secretary announced that Major Thrane was on the line.

So—not so unavailable after all.

"Is it a quick one?" Thrane asked impatiently, and Sorensen could hear the tension in his voice.

Sorensen made his request.

There was a hesitation on the other end of the line and Sorensen guessed Thrane was fighting his natural curiosity. Finally he said abruptly, "I'll get someone to call you," and rang off.

The call came shortly after. The crisp young male voice identified himself as Jensen, Thrane's assistant, and announced that he had the information he'd requested.

Sorensen knew what the young man had open in front of him. A military-service file. Every male over the age of seventeen had one. "Yes . . . date and place of birth, Bergen, April fifth, 1927. Height six foot one, weight a hundred fifty pounds. Hair blond, eyes blue, no distinguishing features." A pause. "Oh, he did no military service. Exempted because of war service."

"War service?"

"With U.S. Bomber Command. Posted missing October 1944." Papers rustled as the file was searched. "Mmm. That's all. Presumably he was shot down or something. But his parachute obviously worked okay. Is that what you wanted?"

"Yes. It doesn't say where he went missing, does it?"

"No. But a bomber . . . Over Germany perhaps?"

"Yes. I would think you're probably right. Thank you so much."

For ten minutes Sorensen sat staring into space. Then he decided.

The way did not lie forward, but back the way he had come.

27

A faint rushing sound; a murmuring, soft but sinister. At first Berg couldn't work out what it was. Then he realized: the wind. He shivered slightly. This place . . .

He was sitting alone in the living room, a drink in his hand. Hal was outside doing some final chores or whatever conscientious farmers did. Overhead, floorboards creaked as Ragna moved about on her way to bed.

The three of them had eaten together. It had not been the happiest of meals. Hal had looked as though he were about to put a gun to his own head, Ragna had seemed guilt-ridden, as if the animals' disease were her own fault, and Berg's attempts at conversation had met with limited response.

The back door slammed, there was a stamping of feet and a scuffle of paws. The scruffy mongrel came trotting into the room. Sighting Berg it halted and growled, its hackles raised, its head down. It looked like a wolf. Berg met its eyes and stared it out. The dog backed away and sloped off. He and dogs understood each other perfectly: complete and instant dislike.

Hal came in, a wild unhappy expression on his face. Doubtless he had been tormenting himself by looking at dead animals again. He hesitated for a moment then came and threw himself down in the opposite chair.

"Have a proper drink," Berg said lazily. "You look as though you need one." Hal shook his head, but Berg got up and poured him one anyway. At first Hal waved it away, then, with an abrupt change of heart, he took it.

Berg sat down again. "This is a hell of a blow for you. Will you be able to replace the musk-oxen?"

Hal stared into the open stove. "I won't bother."

"Oh?"

"I won't keep animals at all."

"That bad?"

"I'd already decided. Before."

"Ah . . . Why?"

Hal made a dismissive gesture. "The place is uneconomic."

There was a silence.

Berg murmured: "I'm sorry."

Hal's jaw muscles worked furiously. He looked up suddenly. "Why did you come, Rolf?"

"Ragna was concerned—"

"I'm not talking about Ragna," he interrupted. "Why did *you* come, Rolf?"

Berg eyed him over the rim of his glass.

"Was there something bothering you?" Hal pressed. "Something you wanted to discuss?"

Berg wasn't quite ready for a head-on collision. "Discuss?" he asked innocently. "On the Kåfjord story, you mean?"

Hal uncoiled himself from the chair like a spring and shot past Berg to the far side of the room. The sound of a drawer opening and shutting, and Hal came back and stood in front of him.

He was holding an object in his hand. A pair of field glasses, faded white, wartime German Army issue. "You didn't by any chance want to discuss these, did you?"

Berg thought: I'm hardly likely to admit it, am I? He raised an eyebrow and, taking the binoculars, examined them casually. "No. Why on earth should I—" He gave a short laugh. "Hal—I can see you're obsessed with some idea about these things, something which concerns me. So why don't you tell me about it?"

"You recognize them?"

As if to humor him, Berg turned the binoculars over in his hands and looked at them more closely. "I can't say I remember them. But if you say they're the ones . . ." He smiled ingenuously.

Hal glared at him, clearly in the throes of some inner struggle.

Berg asked reasonably: "Look, Hal—there's obviously something on your mind. Why don't you spit it out?"

The words, when they finally came, flowed quickly and smoothly, and Berg realized Hal had rehearsed them.

"They were found with Jan at Pasvik, Rolf! These binoculars were returned with his effects! But they weren't his. They didn't belong to him. He acquired them. How do you explain that? Mmm? How do you think that happened? When Jan left for Pasvik he had one pair of binoculars with him, a pair I knew very well. When he died he had two pairs, Rolf. *Two*. He also had an extra knife. How do you think that happened? Where do you think these extra things came from?" He stood over Berg, quivering with deep controlled anger.

Berg forced his face into an expression of mild astonishment while he absorbed the information. It was bad, no doubt about that. At the same time it was a curious relief to have discovered, at long last, what Hal knew.

He was about to shrug it off when Hal cut in: "Oh, and don't give me that rubbish about some Lapps finding them. Don't even try giving me that!"

"But that was what you told me, Hal."

"I—didn't want to cloud the issue."

"You mean you didn't trust me enough to tell me the truth?"

"I didn't want you to know it concerned Pasvik."

"I see. So what's the reason for telling me now?"

"The facts don't fit. They don't fit with what you told me."

"Ah. Is that another way of saying I lied to you?"

A pause. "Possibly. Yes."

Berg gave a small mirthless chuckle. "Now, why do you think I'd do that, Hal?"

A cautious expression came over Hal's face. He retreated back to his chair and eyed Berg for a long moment. "I think that the third man was your friend Petter."

It had to be a guess, pure and simple. He couldn't possibly know for sure. Berg said levelly: "But Petter's dead."

"Now. But he wasn't then."

Berg sighed like a parent dealing with a naughty child. "A

pair of binoculars, and you jump to these incredible conclusions?"

"They can't be so incredible, otherwise you wouldn't be here."

"What do you mean?"

"I mean you didn't come here out of the kindness of your heart, Rolf."

"I came because we're friends. I came because Ragna was worried."

"Don't give me that either."

"What?"

"That you came out of regard for Ragna."

"I'm very fond of Ragna."

"I don't think so."

Berg opened his mouth to argue, then shrugged and let it pass. He realized that his silence was an answer in itself.

Hal persisted: "You still haven't answered my question. How did these binoculars come to be with Jan's stuff?"

Enough was enough: it was time to get indignant. "Okay, Hal. If you're determined to believe there's something sinister in all this, then please yourself. But I strongly object to being cast as the villain. How the hell can I explain completely inexplicable things? How the hell should I know how the damned binoculars got there?"

"Suggest something. Put my mind at rest."

"I take exception to being called a liar."

Hal's eyes were hard as ice. "Try, Rolf. Try to put my mind at rest."

Berg replied heavily: "Petter died on the plateau, Hal."

"Is that all you're offering me?"

"Yes. I don't see any damn reason why I should offer you more."

"You don't? What about Jan and Mattis?" Hal stabbed a finger at him. "I think they died because of your friend."

He gave a sigh of disbelief. "Christ, what next?"

"I think it was a setup."

"You're obsessed with Pasvik," Berg scoffed. "You just haven't learned to live with your own guilt, Hal. Grow up. Two men died. You sent them. So—tough."

Hal, instead of rising to the bait, went on remorselessly: "I think your friend is the key to the whole thing, Rolf. I don't think he died on the plateau. I think he went to live in Russia. What's more, I think you know what his name was. I think you've always known."

Berg got slowly to his feet. "Hal—really. I think you're rather tired and overwrought."

Hal stood up. He said deliberately: "And I think you're a liar, Rolf."

"Oh, no!" Berg corrected him with sudden viciousness. "Let's get this right! You're not saying I'm a liar—what you're saying is much, *much* worse than that, isn't it, Hal?"

Hal looked away. Berg scented the advantage. "You've gone mad with this idea of yours, Hal. You're trying to find scapegoats, even after all this time. Well, if you want a scapegoat, then I suggest you look a little closer to home."

There was an ugly pause. Hal said quietly: "I'll find out the truth, Rolf. One way or the other."

"And if you don't?"

"I'll keep trying."

Berg felt a sudden upwelling of bitterness. What had he done to deserve this wolf at his heels? Hal wouldn't give up. He'd keep at it, darting in, snapping away at the flesh until he pulled Berg to earth.

He thought viciously: God damn you! Why the hell do you have to get in my way?

Ragna pulled back into the shadows of the staircase, her mind racing.

Rolf's voice was suddenly much closer. He was making for the door.

Hastily Ragna picked up the skirt of her nightdress and tip-toed upstairs, keeping to the edge of the treads, praying no loud creak would alert Rolf to her presence. She got back into her room and, closing the door softly, slid into bed.

She lay rigid, thinking hard, trying to make sense of what she'd heard. Pasvik. Why was everyone suddenly talking about Pasvik? First Hal with his mention of Jan, then—this.

It was like a nightmare that one pushed to the back of one's mind, almost banished, only for it to pop up again, as vivid and ugly as ever.

Accusations. Talk of scapegoats and lies. Lies?

She felt confused and angry. She also felt betrayed. Why had she been excluded from all this? What was it they knew that they couldn't or wouldn't tell her?

And Rolf—was this why he had been so keen to come to Brattdal?

She had to know what was going on. She would demand an explanation from Rolf.

But even as she thought it she knew she wouldn't. She wouldn't dare. For one thing he probably wouldn't tell her the truth; for another—the realization came to her suddenly—she was frightened of him.

She adjusted to the idea. Yes . . . hidden behind that easy manipulative charm was something cold and hard, something pitiless . . .

A sound outside the door. She stiffened. There was a soft click as the doorknob turned.

Rolf.

Her heart sank. She didn't want to share a bed with Rolf tonight. Not here at Brattdal . . . perhaps not anywhere.

He approached.

She made herself relax and breathe more deeply as if she were asleep. Ridiculous to be in this state. After all, it was only Rolf—Rolf, her lover.

There was the sound of undressing, of rustling clothes, then his weight sank onto the other side of the bed, the quilt moved slightly, and he got in.

He settled himself then lay still. He didn't touch her. She felt a vast relief. After a time his breathing steadied into a soft rhythm.

She lay awake for a long time, going over what she had heard, trying to make sense of it all, trying to decide what she should do.

An image of Hal sprang into her mind. *I wouldn't lie to you, Ragna.*

She felt a fluttering of relief. She knew then what she had to do.

She stayed absolutely still for several minutes, listening to the rhythm of Rolf's breathing and the sounds beyond. Apart from the soughing of the wind in the eaves, the house was silent. Faint starlight filtered in through the unshuttered window.

With infinite slowness she began to move, first a leg, then an arm. Eventually she had her body on the edge of the bed. She paused motionless. The breathing from the far side of the bed continued.

Gently, she pushed back the quilt and swung her legs to the floor. Bit by bit she moved her weight onto her feet, aware of the mattress lifting behind her.

She froze. Something had changed. The breathing had stopped.

She half turned.

A sudden movement. She gave a start.

His voice, shockingly loud in the silence of the night. "Where are you going?"

She expelled her breath with a slight laugh. "Oh, you gave me a shock!" She stood up. "To the bathroom. I was trying not to wake you."

His hand found her wrist and gripped it hard. "Come straight back, won't you?"

Her heart thumping against her ribs, she crossed the room and went out, closing the door behind her. She paused, her eyes screwed up against the light burning at the far end of the passage, outside Kris's room.

Facing her was Hal's door. It was closed. She turned away and padded up the passage to Kris's room. She looked in through the open door. He was sleeping soundly. The connecting door to Hal's room was closed. She hovered uncertainly. Was there time? She imagined creeping through, waking Hal, explaining why she'd come, telling him what he wanted to know, having to repeat it, having to elaborate . . .

Losing her courage she hurried into the bathroom and splashed her face with water. She came out and hesitated again.

Was there time?

She thought of Rolf, waiting. Waiting and listening.

Reluctantly she went back down the passage and into her room.

She climbed into bed. He lay still at her side yet she sensed that he was wide awake. With a feeling of hopelessness, knowing she would never sleep, she closed her eyes.

He shifted, the bed shook slightly. His hand reached across and touched her. Her eyes flew open, she tensed. He moved closer. His lips found her mouth, his hand began to explore her body.

She said with a small laugh: "Oh, Rolf, I'm tired."

He raised his head, searching her face in the faint light.

"Tired, or—is there something the matter, Ragna?"

There was something chilling in his voice.

"The matter? No, of course not."

"Good . . ." He moved across her. "Good . . ." His mouth touched hers and then moved down onto her body, his lips beginning their soft skillful exploration . . .

Her body responded—she couldn't prevent it, she wasn't entirely sure she wanted to—but her heart was lonely, lonely and cold.

It was hopeless. He was never going to sleep tonight.

Hal snapped on the bedside light and reached for a book. He read a few pages then realized he hadn't taken in a word. He put the book back on the table and looked at the time. Two.

With a sigh he turned off the light again. The darkness slowly gave way to soft starlight, and the familiar shapes of the room formed themselves into soft shadows. Outside, the wind whispered against the front of the house, gentle but insistent, as if gathering its strength.

It was an east wind. The fishermen likened it to the Russian bear because it snapped coldly at their heels, blowing them out to sea. For Hal it merely darkened his already cold mood.

He was certain Rolf was lying. He felt it—he knew it. Why otherwise hadn't he admitted the possibility of a connection between Pasvik and the man Petter? If Petter had really died on the plateau, surely Rolf would have gotten Petter's full name and address from him as he lay dying, so as to inform the family? Yes . . . yes.

It just didn't fit.

A creak. He half listened. The house always creaked after the stoves were turned down for the night or when the wind came up or when the place was full of people.

He tried to avoid thinking about the occupant of the room opposite. Or was it occupants plural?

Curiously he felt no anger at the thought of Ragna with Rolf, just a dull ache, like the familiar twinge of an old wound.

The only thing that concerned him was the questions Rolf had avoided answering. He realized with dismay that Rolf had succeeded in outmaneuvering him yet again, slipping agilely past awkward questions then turning the tables on him.

Another creak. A distinctive one. In the passage.

He raised his head. Kris looking for Ragna? Someone going to the bathroom?

He'd heard someone moving about before, but much earlier.

Another sound—a rustling. Then a slight metallic noise. He sat bolt upright, his senses reaching out into the darkness.

A click. A doorknob. *His* doorknob.

He felt a leap of fear.

. . . Rolf?

Christ.

Hal rolled out of the bed, landed lightly on his feet, and went softly into the shadows of the wardrobe.

The door was resisting, but then gave suddenly, with a slight sound.

He peered around the wardrobe.

The door was open, a figure was silhouetted against the light from the passage, then it was entering the room, closing the door behind it.

A figure in a long pale nightdress.

Hal exhaled with relief.

Ragna.

She began to creep across the room.

He stepped out from behind the wardrobe.

She gave a loud gasp and, staggering backward, almost fell.

"It's all right," he said hurriedly. "It's me."

She put a hand to her chest and, leaning back against the wall, let out a long sigh.

"All right?" he asked.

She was shivering violently. He took her by the arm, guided her across to the bed, and made her sit down.

"Here." He pulled the down quilt up around her shoulders.

She seemed to come to her senses. She looked quickly at the door, then turned back to him. Her skin was translucent, almost ghostly in the pale light; her eyes glistened softly. She seemed unreal.

She whispered: "Would you tell me, please, what's going on?" Her voice was thick and rough, and it struck him that she had been crying. She went on: "I overheard you talking down there. About Pasvik. You were arguing. Why?"

He considered how much he could safely tell her. Choosing his words carefully, he said: "I think Rolf may—know something—something that might help—explain what happened. But for some reason he won't tell me."

"Why not?"

"I don't know."

"You mean—he's purposely not telling you?"

Hal hesitated. "It's possible. I don't know."

She stared at him for a moment, searching his face; then, with a faint nod of acceptance, looked down at her hands so that her face was hidden in shadow.

"Hal . . . I've been thinking about what you asked me. About the installation, and that Delta thing." She spoke with an effort.

Hal held still. "Yes?"

The words came slowly. "It was Rolf."

"What?"

"He told me the place was going to be a Delta navigation station for Polaris submarines."

It took a moment for Hal to understand.

Rolf.

The knowledge hit him like a punch in the stomach. Yet at the same time he had the strange sensation of having known all along. A cold anger swept over him, closely followed by a feeling of bitter satisfaction.

Got you, Rolf! Got you! There was no escape now. Let him try and wriggle out of this one!

With a sudden shock he understood more. The Delta information . . . Thrane had spelled it out. It was a direct link to Pasvik.

That made two links. *Two.*

Rolf was more than a liar, Rolf was . . .

But he hesitated. He couldn't quite grasp the enormity of what Rolf might be.

"Now will you tell me," Ragna was whispering. "Tell me what it all means?"

With difficulty he focused on what she had asked. Tell her? What would he tell her? That Rolf was connected with Pasvik? That Rolf was somehow mixed up in her husband's death?

How could he tell her that? He could never tell her that.

He suddenly felt protective, tender. Putting an arm around her, he pulled her gently against him. "I don't know. Honestly."

"But—surely . . ."

"Ragna. I don't know."

She was silent, as if she understood that it was necessary to lie to her.

More realizations flowed into Hal's mind, took shape, hardened . . . Chilling realizations. Instinctively he squeezed Ragna's shoulder.

She stirred. "Don't tell Rolf I told you, will you? Will you?"

"No. I promise."

"I must get back now."

"Don't."

She escaped his arm and stood up. "No, better if I do."

Hal couldn't bear it. "Go and sleep with Kris!"

She paused for an instant then shook her head. She took a step toward the door, then on a sudden impulse turned back and embraced him quickly, pressing her cheek against his. The next moment she was gliding soundlessly across the room and opening the door. She didn't look back.

The young man raised the rifle to his shoulder. It felt very light, almost toylike, as if it were made of wood. He pressed himself against the wall and sighted on the door of the house across the road. He waited. Whatever happened he mustn't take his eyes off that door.

Then in the next flash of awareness he found himself facing the opposite way, not concentrating at all. He looked for the door he was meant to be watching, but in some curious way it had become obscured by low snow-covered trees. He tried to move but found himself floundering in deep snow. In a burst of frustration he fought his way out and along the wall until the house came into view once more.

He was almost too late. The door was opening.

In a panic he fumbled for the rifle which had inexplicably fallen into the snow. It was even lighter than before and seemed to have shrunk.

The man he was going to kill was already walking down the path. He tried to sight on him but the man was walking too fast, and however hard he tried, the rifle barrel would not catch up with the moving figure.

A woman appeared in the doorway. Everything slowed down. The man on the path stopped and turned questioningly to the woman. The woman was saying something.

Here the picture was exceptionally vivid.

His sights settled on the center of the man's broad round back, halfway between the shoulders and just below the bull-like head with its ridiculous hat.

Bull-like. An animal. A beast to be slaughtered.

Now. He must do it *now.*

His hand was limp and ineffective. He couldn't press the trigger, he couldn't shoot.

The woman stepped backward into the shadow of the doorway. The man on the path turned toward him again.

Ah. Now he could do it. It had been the woman's fault, it'd been the woman who'd prevented him!

He sighted with fresh concentration.

The man was approaching the gate.

Now.

He squeezed, the trigger gave under the pressure, the gun fired—*he'd done it!*

Or had he?

No sound—just silence. He looked down at the rifle in his hand—it had turned into a wooden toy pistol. Yet the man had fallen. Yes—*definitely.* He was lying crumpled in the snow.

He'd done it! He felt a wild elation coupled with a vast relief, as if some terrible blight had been removed from his life and nothing could prevent him from being happy forever.

Laughing, he turned his head to Petter, but Petter had disappeared.

Suddenly he was lying facedown in the snow although he'd been standing just a moment before.

Then—his throat filled with horror—he couldn't move, his

limbs were like lead. A terrible weight was pressing him down into the snow. *Someone was standing on his back.*

He tried to look around. A hard object struck him a vicious blow on the head. There was no pain, just a memory of pain. But he felt the searing sickening humiliation all right, *that* was always real; the agonizing shame tore at his guts. To his disgust he couldn't stop himself from crying, just like he had as a child, loudly and pathetically, whining hideously through his tears.

Finally he was able to turn his head.

His father stood over him, a long leather strap in his hand.

The young man cried: *"But I just killed you!"*

His father gave a low chuckle and, his face contorting with pleasure, raised the strap.

A vicious blinding rage swept over the boy in a red-hot sea and he knew then he would kill him with his bare hands.

Maddeningly the vision faded. He almost choked with frustration. He wanted to finish it, finish it once and for all!

A strange sound impinged, coming from far, far away.

Somewhere in his unconsciousness he realized that the sound was pulling him toward reality, that if he concentrated on it he would wake. He clutched at the possibility and, fighting his way out of the darkness, rose and rose toward the light. Finally he pulled himself into consciousness with a jerk.

He opened his eyes.

Ghastly. He hadn't had a dream like that since—

Suddenly he remembered the strange sound.

He spun his head on the pillow.

She wasn't there.

He sat up, his ears straining. He went back over the memory of the sound, trying to pin it down. A creaking floorboard?

Yes! Ragna creeping off. Sneaking off. Behind his back.

To Hal? It could only be to Hal!

Well, he'd soon put a stop to that.

He was about to swing his legs to the floor when it came again—the sound. A creak. Someone moving in the passage. He paused, as tense as a spring.

The door opened. He leaned back on one elbow.

She came in, a tall slim figure in a nightgown, closing the

door behind her. She began to creep toward the bed, then, seeing him, uttered a small exclamation.

He said nothing.

"You're awake," she breathed nervously, getting into bed. "I went to see Kris. He had a bad dream."

She really expected him to believe that?

Berg said nothing. There was no point.

She was lying, he knew she was lying.

He lay back, thinking hard.

28

Sorensen was woken by pins and needles in his right leg. Apart from a faint slit of light under the door, it was pitch dark and he had to peer at the luminous hands of his watch to establish that it was morning.

He swung his legs stiffly to the floor and decided it was high time he got a longer couch; this wasn't the first time he'd spent an uncomfortable night in the office.

He went to the men's room for a quick wash and a scrape at the stubble on his chin. It was seven. He had an hour before the staff arrived.

Another hour to find—what?

The previous evening he'd spent five hours looking through his files, interrupted only by the brief appearance of his wife bearing sandwiches. At two he'd finally given up.

He'd established that during the winter in question there had been the odd skirmish between Germans and partisans, between mountain patrols and young men escaping labor service; but actual murder? He'd looked through every major town, including Bergen, and every smaller town as well, looking for evidence, but apart from the usual gestapo activity— the sudden arrests, the indiscriminate cruelty—nothing had fit.

It had gotten him nowhere.

And yet, and yet . . .

He couldn't let it go. He itched to speak to Starheim, to see if he could clarify the matter. He'd tried the Tromsø number twice the previous evening but had gotten no reply. Now he tried again. There was a lot of clicking on the line and operators saying they were trying to connect him and finally a distant voice which informed him that the line was engaged and would he try again later, please?

Sorensen sat back. A small but persistent thought had been ticking away in the back of his mind and now he gave it some air. It was a possibility so faint that he might normally have ignored it. But the mystery of Rolf Berg's military career was too absorbing to leave alone.

He glanced at his watch. Seven-thirty. He could spare another half hour, then he really must do some work on that new case. There was an important meeting on it later in the morning.

At the risk of irritating the former mayor of Trondheim, he called him again.

The mayor told him he hadn't been able to think of any other German deaths that winter, murder or otherwise.

Sorensen put to him his new question: had there been two young men in trouble around that time? In trouble for any reason at all, either with the Germans or the local police.

He almost added their first names, but decided against it.

There was a long pause on the other end of the line, a grunt, then a hesitant "Well . . . there were quite a few who went into the mountains, you know, to avoid labor service."

"Yes, of course. But what about more specific sorts of trouble? They'd have been about eighteen."

"What kind of trouble? You mean murdering a German?"

"No, forget that. I must have gotten that wrong. Forget that completely."

"Ah." Another pause. "Mmm. Well, I'll have to think about it."

Sorensen was used to being patient. "Of course. In the meantime I might try the police. But thank you anyway. I appreciate it very much."

"Wait—" The mayor's voice was slightly resentful. He wanted to be the one to help Sorensen, not the police. "Let me think . . ." A silence, until Sorensen began to wonder if they had been cut off. "There *was* something," he said finally. "A boy. And his friend."

"Yes?"

"They disappeared that autumn."

"What was the story?"

"Well . . . the boy's father was a collaborator. The boy had a tough time of it. This is a small town and in school—well, I'd imagine he wasn't allowed to forget it."

"What was his name?"

"The father—his name was Carl Blakstad."

Sorensen wondered if he had this Blakstad on file. He prompted: "And the boy, what was his name?"

A pause. "Mmm . . . You must give me a moment to remember. It's seventeen—eighteen—years ago now."

"The boy—did he get into any sort of trouble?"

"There was a rumor, a whisper . . . most people didn't believe it, some people did believe it but kept quiet to protect the boy."

"Yes?"

"Well . . . it was suggested that the boy had come back and killed his father."

"Killed him?"

"Shot him. Coming out of his house one day. No one was too sorry, believe me. The man was a bully. Quite well educated—a lawyer, I think—but with a nasty streak, very nasty. Anyway, he was shot. The Germans never found out who the killer was—but then they never made much of an effort with collaborators. Besides, I can't imagine he was that much use to them. I mean, everyone knew he was a collaborator so everyone kept well clear of him."

"But it was the boy—it was the boy who came back and did it, you say?"

"Ah, now I wouldn't like to state that for a fact. If memory serves me, he disappeared some weeks before the shooting. If he did come back—well, there was never any evidence for it. Only rumor. Though you know how people are—they do have a way of getting it right . . ."

"What happened to the boy?"

"Afterwards? Can't say. He disappeared."

"He was never seen again?"

"Never. Nor was his friend."

"Ah—what was *his* name?"

"That I remember. Axelsen. His name was Petter Axelsen."

Petter. Sorensen felt a small frisson of excitement. "And Blakstad—you still don't remember his name?"

"Hang on . . . let me think. . . . Ah, wait . . . Something—ah! Yes, I think it was Roar. But he was known as Raf, I don't know why. Yes—that's what it was—Raf Blakstad."

The moment he rang off Sorensen hurried into the records room and went to one of the cross-index files. WAR CRIMINALS: DEAD. No Blakstad there. Not surprising. Although the index contained the names of many collaborators, they were people who had committed serious crimes of betrayal leading to arrests and deaths. Blakstad obviously hadn't qualified.

He tried the voluminous missing-persons files.

Blakstad . . .

His fingers hurried over the cards, impatient for the prize.

There.

Blakstad, Roar. Official list of missing persons: Trondheim *Folkeregister.* Registered missing, June 1945. Certified missing, June 1946. Last seen, September 1944.

There was nothing else on the card. No sightings. No information from the Red Cross.

And no inquiries from the family.

He slammed the drawer shut and went to the drawer above, with the A's.

Yes, the other one was there too.

Axelsen, Petter. But the Axelsen family *had* inquired, because there was a Red Cross reference.

Sounds came from the outer office. His secretary put her head around the door with a cheery "Good day!"

It was eight. He tried the Tromsø number again. After several minutes a rough elderly voice answered and said abruptly that he would take a message. Sorensen remembered: Starheim had told him the phone was away from his house.

He considered what he should say in the message. Then decided he would put as much into it as possible. Why not? He began to dictate. The line crackled and faded, a tenuous seven-hundred-mile link to the icy north. The voice of the old man repeated the message back to him, word for word, and rang off with the promise that he would pass it on within the hour.

Sorensen forced himself back to his desk, to the enormously fat file whose contents he must fully absorb before the ten-thirty meeting. But try as he might, he could not concentrate.

He kept thinking about Rolf Berg. Was he on the right track? Could Berg really be the same man as Raf Blakstad?

If so, one could understand the fellow wanting to change his name—anyone would if he'd had a collaborator for a father. In Norway people had long memories for that sort of thing.

Yes, a change of name was understandable.

But if the two men were the same, it wasn't just his name he'd changed—it was his entire identity. And he hadn't chosen a false identity either; he'd acquired a real one.

Now the question was: how on earth had he managed to do a difficult thing like that?

Berg let himself silently out of the bedroom and listened hard. An occasional sound, faint and muffled, rose from the kitchen below.

He padded softly up to the child's room and peered in. A dark head was visible on the pillow.

Downstairs a chair scraped, a voice murmured.

Hal. Talking to himself. Or to the dog.

Berg forced himself to wait. His patience was quickly rewarded. Below, a door opened and closed, then there was silence.

He went to a back window and looked out into the darkness. A well-wrapped figure, dull gray against the paler luminosity of the snow, was stomping up to the barn with the dog at its heels.

No time to lose. Berg went swiftly into the child's room. As he approached the bed the child popped his head up, blinking sleepily.

"Hello, Kris," Berg said, trying to sound friendly. "Mummy's having a lie-in. But she asked me to take you for a walk."

The child looked suspicious.

"We're going to see Arne," Berg said firmly. "Don't worry, we'll be back in time for breakfast."

The child rubbed his eyes and sat up. Grabbing some clothes off a chair, Berg thrust them at him. The child didn't move.

"Come on now," Berg said coaxingly. "Mummy wants you to go straightaway."

With excruciating slowness the child began to move. Berg waited impatiently while he puffed and panted out of his pajamas and battled with vests and sweaters and socks and quilted dungarees. It was all taking too long. With a sigh of exasperation, Berg stood the child on the bed and finished the job with brutal efficiency.

As the last sweater was pulled forcibly over Kris's head, his lower lip began to tremble. "I want to stay with my mummy."

"I told you. She's asleep and doesn't want to be woken up."

"Can't I go with Uncle Hal?"

"He's out with the animals. He asked especially if we'd go down to Arne's for him, to see if there were any messages. He said it was quite important."

The child almost looked convinced. Making the most of it, Berg led him quickly downstairs. Pulling on boots, anoraks, gloves, and hats took more precious minutes, but then at last the two of them were ready.

Berg hurried out the front door, pulling the child so fast behind him that Kris's feet barely touched the snow. The wind scythed into Berg's unprotected face and he lowered his head defensively. Glancing back he saw that the light in the right-hand bedroom had come on. Ragna was awake. She would discover Kris had gone and assume he was with Hal. She wouldn't realize her mistake until Hal returned, which, with a bit of luck, wouldn't be for some time. Then she'd do her mother-hen bit and run around looking for Kris.

One thing she wouldn't do was sit down and have a cozy chat with Hal about Berg.

Kris. His small but comforting insurance policy. He tightened his grip on the boy's hand.

The path became steeper and icier. Berg skidded. As he jerked his arm to regain his balance he pulled Kris off his feet. The child fell facedown into the snow. Berg picked him up, dusted the worst of the snow off his face, and started down the hill again. The child whimpered and whined, tottered a few steps, then ground to a halt, crying: "I don't want to go! I want to go back to my mummy!"

Berg swore under his breath. He wasn't in the mood to deal with a spoiled child. But he made a supreme effort and said cheerfully: "Come along, there's a good boy. We promised Uncle Hal, remember?"

The child moved forward again, but reluctantly, sniveling loudly. The old man's house seemed a long way off; the wind was vicious and sharp, freezing Berg's face and creeping down his neck. He might have been able to stand it if the child's thin voice hadn't risen to a high-pitched wail. A terrible fury rose in Berg's gullet. It was all he could do to stop himself from shouting at the child.

Finally, shivering with rage, he hoisted Kris roughly into the air and, gritting his teeth, sat him on his shoulders. The child quieted down.

Suddenly he was alert: something moved in the darkness ahead. A dumpy figure. Coming toward them, head down, stomping heavily through the snow.

The old man.

They drew level. "I'm just going to use the phone," Berg said.

Kris whined and, wriggling hard, reached his arms out to Arne.

Quickly, before the old man could say anything, Berg moved off fast, saying loudly for the old man's benefit: "It's all right, Krisi. No need to be afraid of the dark!" The child struggled, drumming his feet against Berg's chest, and burst into violent sobs. Berg could feel the old man staring into his back.

Berg hissed "Shut up!" through clenched teeth and pinned the child's ankles hard against his chest.

After a while Berg risked a backward glance. The old man had continued his journey.

The noise from the child subsided, and there was only the

rhythmic rumble of the waves on the foreshore and the hiss of the wind.

At last they reached the old man's small single-story house. Berg stamped inside and let the boy down. The child pulled himself free and, running into the kitchen, slammed the door behind him. Berg made straight for the living room and the telephone.

He lifted the receiver, listened, and swore under his breath. There were voices on the line, talking slowly and incomprehensibly in heavy dialect. "What the hell—?"

Christ—a party line. He hadn't realized that the previous evening.

Berg dropped the receiver in its cradle and waited, picking it up again from time to time. The conversation dragged on. Finally he let his impatience rip. "Get off the line! There are people waiting!"

The voices paused, then, to Berg's disbelief, resumed their maddening drone as if nothing had happened. They were doing it on purpose. Berg was incredulous yet not that surprised: it was the sort of behavior one would expect from northern peasants.

Finally the droning voices exchanged interminably slow good-byes and ceased. Berg jiggled the telephone rest until the operator finally answered. He gave her the emergency number in Oslo, thinking: At last.

After what seemed a long time the connection was made and the number rang. Berg waited tensely.

The ringing went on and on, a long lonely sound. It wasn't going to answer.

He jabbed at the rest again while he leafed rapidly through his address book. He muttered: "Come on! Come on!" The operator finally came back, a condescending tone in her voice, as if she were doing him a favor. Making an effort to sound polite, Berg gave her the number of the Novosti office.

Not quite eight. Was it too early for them?

It answered: a woman's voice. Berg asked for Alex.

There was a pause, then: "He does not work here."

Berg's stomach gave an ugly lurch. "What do you mean?"

"He has been transferred. Is there someone else you wish to speak to?"

"*Transferred?* Where's he gone?"

"Another posting. Thank you for your inquiry." The line clicked and Berg realized she had hung up. How could they do this to him? But he knew: they could do it all right.

Okay, he thought savagely, if that was the way they wanted to play it.

Going to the back of his address book, to the list of embassies and consulates he kept there, he found another number.

He jiggled the cradle. Nothing. He tried again. Where the hell was the operator? He kept jiggling the phone.

"Yes?" the operator said coldly.

She took an age to connect him, only to announce that the number was busy. She said she'd try again in a few minutes if he liked.

He vacillated—was it wise to make the call at all?

He heard himself asking her to try again.

While he waited he lit a cigarette and wandered around the house. The tour didn't take long: there were four small rooms and, behind a fifth door, dark steps leading down to a cellar, which he didn't bother to investigate. In the kitchen the boy was sitting at the table, chewing on a piece of bread.

"All right?" Berg smiled.

The boy looked up at him with large round eyes, his lower lip drooping resentfully.

The telephone jangled a sort of code: two long rings and one short. It must be for him.

Berg strode into the living room and snatched up the phone.

The operator announced that she was putting him through. A cool male voice replied.

Even as Berg asked for Niki he had a premonition, a sudden chilling certainty, of what he'd hear, so that the words, when they came, were like an echo.

"Second Secretary Yurasov is on leave. Did you wish to be connected to the third trade secretary?"

Berg tried to understand what this meant, and failed.

The voice said: "Hello? Hello?"

Berg almost hung up, but something made him pause. He said harshly: "I have a message. That Harri called. Harri called. Okay?" Hastily replacing the receiver, he sat for a long time, staring at the wall.

He constructed a theory. Niki and his colleagues must have found out about Sonja. They must have discovered Sonja was no clerk. But surely it couldn't matter that much? Not when his safety was at stake. Surely he was more important than Sonja any day.

So he'd lied to them—so what? That wasn't any reason to freeze him out.

Crass idiots.

But then he had another thought: Perhaps the silence was a warning. A warning to keep away for a while.

That pulled him up short.

There was only one thing they could possibly want to warn him about, only one thing that could possibly have happened.

Sonja hadn't been dealt with after all. Sonja had talked . . .

The fear crept up on him, chipping away at his confidence. He knew then that he must get away from this place. It was beginning to feel more like a trap than a bolt-hole.

He swept into the kitchen. Seeing him, the child jumped up and ran into the corner.

Berg tightened his lips. "Come on, old fellow. We're leaving."

The phone rang in the other room.

Berg hesitated.

He recognized the sequence: two long and one short.

Turning abruptly on his heel he went back into the living room and said into the telephone: "Yes?"

"Is Major Starheim there?"

"No."

A pause. "But he's there on Revøy?"

"Yes."

"Can I leave a message, then? It's Major Thrane here."

A small shiver of alarm went up Berg's spine. Thrane? He knew that name. He said calmly: "By all means."

"Who am I speaking to?" The voice was suddenly wary.

Berg put on the semblance of a northern accent. "A friend of Arne's."

"Ah." The voice relaxed a little. "Well, could you tell Starheim that I am desperate for that information he promised me. Could he please call my office as soon as possible?"

"I will tell him."

"Tell him it's even more important than before."

"Right-o."

"And . . ." A hesitation. "Tell him—tell him I'm doing all I can on this end."

Berg dropped the receiver slowly into its cradle, feeling very cold.

Thrane—he had placed the name.

Sonja had mentioned it several times.

Major Thrane was at FO/E. Major Thrane was in counterintelligence.

. . . *desperate for that information.* Berg thought: I bet he is!

So Hal hadn't been on his own after all. Hal was working with FO/E.

The realization flooded over Berg in an ice-cold wave.

Immediately following it came the reassuring thought that Hal hadn't yet delivered his information.

He moved fast then, running into the hall, searching shelves, pulling open cupboards and rummaging in corners. Nothing.

But there had to be at least one.

He tried the kitchen next, ignoring the child as he looked wildly around. Ah! He let out a small exclamation of triumph.

There behind the door. Set on brackets on the wall. A rifle, a Lee Enfield .303. He took it down and felt along the tops of cupboards and yanked open drawers until he found the ammo. He loaded his pockets with clips and, grasping the rifle in one hand, reached for the cowering boy.

"Come on! We're going back to Mummy!"

Thrane paced the room impatiently.

Would Starheim get the message all right? More to the point, would Starheim have the information? Had he had time to find out?

There was nothing to do but wait and see.

But time was running out. One more day, then— Then both of them would have had it.

The door opened; someone entered without knocking. Only one person did that: Ekeland.

The Security head was wearing the grave expression he reserved for moments of extreme self-importance. Thrane had a sudden sinking feeling.

Ekeland began: "It may interest you to know that a Russian is boarding an Aeroflot flight for Moscow at this very moment. A member of the Novosti staff in Oslo. Name of Aleksander Savin. Heavily escorted, heavily sedated."

"Savin?" The name rang a bell.

"GRU, according to FO/S."

"Could he be—"

Ekeland was already shaking his head. "Not unless she lied to us. He isn't blond-haired or blue-eyed. And he had a heavy Russian accent."

Thrane wasn't too disappointed. He'd hardly expected Sonja's lover to be a fully accredited Russian.

But why was this boy being sent home in disgrace? He must have been involved in a screw-up, and there was only one screw-up it could be. Sonja's death.

Developing the idea, he said aloud: "I bet this fellow arranged Sonja's death without permission. Or without realizing her importance. Without knowing how badly we'd take it."

"That's purely conjectural. No facts," said Ekeland.

Thrane couldn't argue with that one. Damn, damn. Thrane felt the connections unraveling and slithering away from him like snakes in the grass.

"The timing could be significant, don't you think?" Ekeland remarked with heavy emphasis, and Thrane realized he was going to squeeze every ounce out of his point, whatever it was. "One might think there was a tip-off involved."

"Purely conjectural. No facts," replied Thrane facetiously.

Ekeland licked his lips, savoring some as yet undisclosed gem. "Not when we put it together with the telephone call which was made from the island of Revøy yesterday . . ."

Thrane tensed himself.

". . . The call was made to an Oslo number. We traced it. The number belongs to an apartment which is frequently visited by Soviet citizens. According to FO/S it is in fact a safe house." Ekeland paused for effect. "One of the most frequent visitors to the apartment was a member of the Novosti staff."

Thrane closed his eyes.

Ekeland finished triumphantly: "This member of the Novosti staff was, so FO/S tell us, the assistant to one Aleksander Savin."

It took a moment for Thrane to take it in, then he sank into a chair, empty of all emotion except a deep sense of bafflement.

Incredible.

Starheim. Of all people . . .

After a time Thrane glanced up at Ekeland and said in a weary voice: "Okay. You were right. I was wrong—God, *was* I. . . . But let me go up there, will you? Let me go to Tromsø. I want to be the one to bring him in."

29

The goats at least were still alive. Hal had no idea whether he really cared or not. He closed the barn door and, pulling his hood up over his mouth, started back to the house.

The wind surged up the hill, kicking up hard snow particles which pattered against his clothing. Bamse trotted down the path ahead, head low, ears flat, dead on target for home.

Hal went in through the back door. Ragna was at the stove, cooking.

She gave a wan smile. "Hello. I thought you might like a good breakfast." Her eyes had shadows under them, he noticed, and her wonderful skin was slightly blotchy.

"Thanks." He took off his anorak and boots.

"Are the others behind you?" she asked, returning to the stove.

"The others?"

She gave him her full attention. "Kris. Rolf."

"No. They're not with me."

She stared at him.

Suddenly Hal understood. "You mean they're not here?"

She shook her head wordlessly, fear and alarm spreading across her face.

"You're sure?"

"Yes!"

Shaking with anger, Hal grabbed his anorak and boots and, running to the front door, shot out into the darkness, yelling: *"Kr-i-s!"* Hopping along the veranda, pulling on his boots, he kept shouting Kris's name at the top of his voice.

After a time he stopped, straining to hear beyond the rushing wind, trying to pick out sounds in the silence beneath.

Nothing. He shouted again.

A sound floated above the hissing gusts. A hail, a shout of greeting.

Hal recognized Arne's distinctive call. He yelled: "Have you seen Kris?"

"Yes," came back on the wind.

Hal thought: Thank God! He went down to meet Arne on the path. The old man panted: "They're at my place. The boy and—him."

Hal's relief gave way to suspicion. Why? What possible reason could Rolf have for taking Kris?

Spotting Ragna hovering anxiously on the veranda, Hal shouted the news to her. She disappeared back into the house. He found her in the kitchen, looking very thoughtful. She said to Hal: "But why would he want to take Kris down to Arne's?"

"I don't know. Perhaps Kris wanted to go."

She looked unconvinced.

He had a need to reassure her at any cost. "Perhaps they both woke early and wanted something to do."

Ragna said firmly: "Will you go and get him for me, please?"

He nodded. "I'll go now," he said, and headed for the door.

Arne called him back. "A message. Important." Hal took the piece of crumpled paper and, striding off, took a quick glance at it.

Halfway down the hall he ground to a halt. He skimmed over the words, then went back to the beginning and read them again, carefully.

When he had finished he stared blankly at the paper, thoughts flying off at tangents, realizations building, hardening . . .

Then it came to him.

Rolf worked for the other side.

The conclusion came directly, forcibly, like a punch in the stomach.

Yet it was such an appallingly final judgment that he forced himself to stop and go through it all over again. Slipping into the living room, he sat weakly at his desk, taking each thought slowly and logically.

The man he knew as Rolf Berg could not possibly be Rolf Berg; in the winter of 1944–45 the real Rolf Berg was a U.S. Air Force flyer who had been shot down in a bomber somewhere over Europe.

Meanwhile, the young man who had killed a collaborator in Trondheim, the young man who had run north with a companion named Petter Axelsen—this young man had not been Rolf Berg, but someone named Blakstad. And he had vanished, never to be seen again.

Was it the same person? Was Rolf really this Blakstad?

If so, he had managed to take on the identity of another man. But how? How does a man acquire a whole new identity?

But then Hal could guess the answer to that: with help from his friends. And there could be no doubt as to who his friends were.

In 1945, when Hal had sent him on his way after the avalanche, Rolf had been heading northeast. But instead of getting no farther than Alta, as he'd told Hal, he'd obviously kept going.

There could be no doubt: Rolf worked for the other side. But how far had his treachery gone?

Hal remembered Thrane's words.

A direct connection to Pasvik.

And Petter, the third man.

He knew then: there was no limit to Rolf's treachery. Rolf had betrayed Jan. Rolf had betrayed them all.

Another equally unwelcome thought came into his mind: he was the only one who knew.

He had to remedy that, and quickly. He had to let Thrane know. But how? He agonized over it for a moment, then, hearing the murmur of Ragna's voice, went back into the kitchen.

Ragna and Arne looked up, startled. Ragna said in alarm: "Is anything wrong? I thought you'd gone—"

Hal almost said something, but, thinking better of it, shook his head and beckoned Arne into the living room. He scribbled a note, folded it, and put it into the old man's hand. "Listen, Arne. I want you to take the tractor and go down to your place. Tell Rolf that breakfast is ready and that we're all wait-ing for him and Kris, and that they're to use the tractor. Un-derstand? But as soon as they've gone I want you to get on the phone. Call Major Thrane—I've written the number on the top here. It's urgent, Arne. Whatever happens you must make the call. But be sure the tractor's safely gone before you do it."

The old man frowned deeply, as though he didn't like the sound of the idea at all.

Hal explained: "Arne, I'd do it myself except—I don't think Rolf would be happy to leave me alone with the telephone. Do you see?"

This caused a flash of amazement, then one of indignation, to cross the old man's face; for the first time he seemed to understand the nature of the problem. He nodded his agree-ment.

Hal went to the lobby to collect Arne's jacket, glancing out the front door as he did so. Dim gray light, rushing wind; nobody.

Ignoring Ragna's questioning stare, he led Arne through the kitchen and up to the tractor shed at the side of the barn. When the tractor was started and Arne was perched on the seat ready to go, Hal shouted over the engine noise: "If you can't find Thrane, then get his superior, d'you understand? Just hang on until you get the right person."

Arne nodded and, putting the tractor into gear, started off down the hill.

Ragna was waiting for Hal at the back door. "What's going on?" she cried.

He couldn't begin to explain. Instead he said: "Arne's gone to fetch Kris and Rolf. I couldn't go after all—there's some-thing I have to do." He backed into the hall. "I'll explain later . . ."

She set her lips, he thought she was about to argue, but then she retorted, with a sharp sigh: "All right!"

Hal left her and, running down the stairs to the cellar, went to the gun cupboard. He took out his Walther, loaded it, and slipped it into a pocket, along with four spare clips of am-munition.

He let himself out by the cellar door which led directly off the stairs, and emerged into the gray wind-whipped morning.

Stationing himself by the corner of the house, he watched the track leading up from the shore and settled down to wait.

Berg strode doggedly along the track, the child silent and cowed on his shoulders. A phalanx of white-topped waves marched across the sound and pounded onto the pebble beach, breaking like thunder. The wind was scorching in off the sea, buffeting him, dragging at his hood, pulling tears from his half-closed eyes.

He paused suddenly. A sound rose above the rumbling of the surf. An engine . . .

He saw it then, coming over a slight rise in the ground. The tractor. Instinctively, he felt for the rifle at his shoulder.

The child began to fidget with excitement. He let the boy down but held firmly on to his collar. Then he waited, his body turned a little sideways so that the rifle wasn't immediately visible from the approaching vehicle.

Hal. It had to be. Berg felt the tension spring through his body.

It wasn't until the tractor was slowing to make a half-circle and come up alongside them that Berg realized his mistake. It was the old man. He exhaled gently.

The old man brought the vehicle to a halt beside them, climbed down, and, raising his voice to be heard above the rattle of the engine and the thunder of the surf, shouted: "You're to take the tractor. Breakfast is ready." He didn't wait for an answer but turned away, only to do a double take that almost jerked his head off his neck. His eyes fixed on a point just above Berg's shoulder. Berg realized: He had seen the protruding rifle barrel. The old man frowned, moved his lips soundlessly, then, clamping his mouth firmly shut, turned abruptly and stomped off in the direction of his house.

Frowning, Berg watched him go for a moment before lifting the boy into the cab and climbing up after him. Grasping the boy in his lap, he thrust the tractor into gear and started off. His foot rested lightly on the throttle; he didn't want to go too fast. He was too busy thinking.

The tractor pulled up and over a slight incline. Berg glanced behind; the old man was out of sight. Berg took his foot off the throttle. The tractor rolled to a halt. He pulled on the hand brake and had another think.

Why had the old man said nothing? He must have realized it was his own rifle.

Worrying. Very worrying.

He came to a decision.

Sitting the boy in the driver's seat he stopped the engine and jumped down. The boy began to fret. "Stay there! D'you hear?" Berg tried to imagine the boy's worst fears. "Otherwise you won't see your mummy again for a long time, d'you understand?"

The child's face creased up in horror and he shrank back into his seat. Berg turned on his heel and began to run back down the track. With the wind behind him and only the rifle to carry, he made good time despite the cumbersome snow boots on his feet. Soon he was over the rise and going downhill. Rounding a slight bend, the house came into view.

There was no cover and the snow on either side of the track was thick and soft; he had no choice but to stay on the hard-packed road and hope he wasn't seen. He pounded on, breathing hard, sweating beneath his thick clothing.

A last spurt and he was there. He ran softly up the few steps to the door and paused to catch his breath. Gently he turned the doorknob and slipped inside, closing the door swiftly behind him.

Silence. Only the rattling and murmuring of the wind. He listened hard.

A sound. More than just a sound—a voice. Berg's heart hit his ribs.

He moved out of the tiny lobby into the hall, tiptoeing awkwardly over the resonant wooden floor.

The voice again. From the living room.

The telephone.

Berg moved up to the door and listened.

Silence again. Then: "Yes? I want Major Thrane. No . . . I see. . . . When, then?"

Berg felt a surge of relief—it wasn't too late. The relief was quickly replaced by grim anger.

Taking the rifle in both hands he stepped forward into the room.

*   *   *

Why hadn't they arrived? Hal looked at his watch and worked it out again. Ten minutes at the very most for Arne to get there, five minutes for the others to pull on their outdoor clothes, then ten minutes for them to drive back. Thirty minutes at the most.

But it had been forty.

He considered his original plan again: wait for Berg and Kris to enter the house, creep in behind them, and, using the momentary surprise, pull Kris safely to one side before challenging Rolf—or not challenging him. He hadn't made up his mind about that.

Now the whole plan was hopelessly irrelevant anyway.

He chafed and fretted, and finally could bear it no longer. Leaving his cold perch at the side of the house, he strode around to the front and collected his skis from the veranda. He thought of going in to reassure Ragna, but decided against it. She'd only get worried, and he wanted to spare her that.

He poled away, gathering speed down the slope. He realized Bamse was on his tail and halted abruptly.

"No—stay, boy. Stay. Look after Ragna. D'you hear? *Stay*." The dog hovered reluctantly, hoping for a change of heart, but, receiving an angry hiss from his master, knew an order when he heard one. With a reproachful look he sloped back toward the house.

Leaving the track, Hal made for the valley wall and, maintaining as much height as possible, kept to the hillside, following it toward the sea, around the curve of the valley mouth until he was running parallel to the shore. All the time he kept an eye on the track on the foreshore below, but there was nothing.

Later the hillside lost some of its steepness and he had to lose height in order to maintain speed. He calculated that he would come down onto the track long before he reached Arne's.

He rounded a bulge in the hillside. A stretch of track opened out before him. He spotted the tractor immediately. He frowned. Now, what on earth was it doing there?

He headed straight for it, dropping fast, his skis rasping and kicking over the protruding stony surface of a scree.

As he approached he looked for signs of life, but there were none. Yet the tractor was facing Brattdal—Rolf must have been on his way back when it had stopped. Had the tractor broken down? Had he gone back to Arne's for help? Had he—

Trying not to speculate, he pressed forward, forcing the last ounce of speed out of his skis.

Almost there.

Something in the tractor caught his eye—a pale blob behind the windshield, a small shape . . .

It looked like—

Dropping onto the track, he skated the last few yards.

A small face—

It *was*. Kris.

He shouted. The small figure jumped up and, as Hal came to a halt, leapt into his arms. Kris clung to him tightly, like a small limpet. Hal squeezed him and patted his head.

"It's all right now. It's all right. Everything's going to be all right." Then he asked: "Where's Rolf?"

The boy was silent. Hal pulled back and looked down at him. "Where's Rolf, Kris?"

The boy's mouth pulled down. He seemed on the point of tears.

"Krisi—where is he?"

"Went."

A tear spilled onto the boy's cheek. Hal wiped it away with his glove. "And he left you here?"

"We—were—coming for breakfast—an' he just went away!"

"Where?"

"Back."

"To Arne's?"

A nod.

"Why? Was there a reason?"

Kris's lip trembled. This was a question he couldn't answer. Hal tried another tack. "Perhaps he'd forgotten something and had to rush back for it?"

"He—just went." Reliving the fear and indignation, Kris began to sob quietly.

"It's all right. Promise."

Gently untwining Kris's arms, Hal popped him back into the

cab and slid his skis in behind him. Then he went and started the engine. It fired first time. Not a breakdown, then.

He considered what to do. He would have liked to take Kris back to Brattdal, but he was filled with a deep sense of urgency and foreboding. Why had Rolf gone back? Had something made him suspicious? Had he guessed Arne might be going to use the phone?

He decided—he must go to Arne's.

With Kris on his lap, still hugging him tight, he turned the tractor around and drove flat-out for Arne's, the vehicle clattering and jumping over the uneven snow. At last the house came into view.

Hal stopped well short of it. He decided to leave the boy in the tractor, at least for the moment. Doing his best to reassure Kris, he climbed down and walked the last few yards to the house.

Everything looked normal; the door was closed, everything was in its place. Yet he felt horribly conspicuous, almost as if he were being watched.

He climbed the steps to the door. As he reached for the doorknob the door rattled suddenly and he hesitated. But it was only the wind.

Reaching into his pocket he gripped the pistol and entered. The wind leapt past him, sending whorls of scurrying snow into the lobby, causing the row of coats to shiver and stir.

He shut the door quickly, and listened.

There was no sound. Only the wind hissing angrily against the closed door behind him.

He called tentatively: "Arne? Rolf?"

He stepped into the hall. Nothing. He went toward the kitchen. The door was wide open. He peered in. Empty. He turned toward the living room.

The door was ajar. He stopped abruptly.

Had there been a sound? A faint knock?

He called again: "Arne? Are you there?"

Silence. His mouth was dry; he licked his lips.

He approached the living room. He pulled the gun from his pocket. Reaching out with his free hand, he pushed at the door with his fingertips. It swung open.

For an instant he thought the room was empty. Then his eyes traveled downward and his heart stopped.

Someone lay sprawled on the floor, the upper half of his body hidden by the table.

Arne.

Hal raced over and knelt beside him. The old man's face was turned away; Hal leaned across.

The mouth was open, slack and sagging, and stained red-black with fast-congealing blood from the stream that had drained from his body and formed a dark pool on the floor. The eyes were half-open and unblinking.

Automatically, Hal put a finger on the jugular. Nothing.

He sat back on his heels, fighting down outrage and grief.

A sound. Abruptly his mind cleared; he was suddenly aware that he hadn't been listening. He looked over his shoulder. No one. Yet the bastard couldn't be far away. He glanced back at Arne's body and his anger hardened.

He tightened his grip on the pistol and stood up.

His senses reached out into the vibrant silence of the house, and then beyond, to the murmuring wind.

A gust hit the house with a low whooshing sound. Wood creaked under pressure. The gust subsided. Hal crouched forward a little, his weight on the balls of his feet, gun hand forward, his finger lightly on the trigger: old training remembered.

He stepped out into the hall, sweeping it rapidly with his eyes. He ran lightly to the kitchen door, paused, listened, then put an eye around.

Still nothing.

He sprang inside, pushing the door back as he did so.

Quite empty.

The bedroom next. The door was closed. He flung it open, took cover, then cautiously looked in. Nothing. He checked the room more thoroughly, then went back into the hall.

Only the lavatory and the cellar to go. They, too, revealed nothing.

Where the hell had he gone, then?

He had to be outside.

Outside—

Kris.

He prayed: *Dear God, don't let anything have happened to Kris.*
Racing for the front door, he flung it open.

The tractor stood there. The cab was empty.

His heart sank.

He looked rapidly about. There was nobody in sight, no-body racing down the track, no sound above the muffled crash of the surf.

No Kris.

He felt a surge of ferocious rage and launched himself down the steps.

The bastard couldn't have gotten far.

A sound. He ground to a halt a few paces from the steps, and crouched, his senses taut.

Direction—left. He swept the hillside above.

Again, a sound. Much closer.

Where from? He got it at last: from the side of the house.

He ran to the front wall and, keeping close in, approached the corner.

Then he heard—a sniffle. A child's sniffle.

He put his head around the corner.

Kris! *Kris.*

The child stood there, small, white-faced, and very still.

Hal let out an exclamation of joy and relief and stepped forward.

The boy pulled back, his expression changing, contorting. Almost like horror. . . . For a split second Hal stared at him, uncomprehending.

Then three things happened in quick succession. There was a sound from a completely different direction; he caught a fast-moving blur on the periphery of his vision; and his mind found time to log the fact that this moving object was the cause of Kris's terror.

Last—and far, far too late—came his reaction.

He tried to twist his body, to yank his head around, to throw his arm up and protect his head. But even as he contorted his body and raised his arm and jerked his head reflexively to one side, he knew it was too late. Something was swooping viciously and inexorably toward him. He felt a split second of frustration and rage.

The blow, when it came, caught him on the side of the

head, a massive sickening blow that exploded inside his brain. He had the impression of falling—but forever, as if from a great height. A screeching filled his ears, then everything closed in around him and he sank into a sea of blackness and nausea.

Agonizing pain brought him around. A violent stabbing pain that screamed through every nerve ending, like a blunt knife jabbing at an open wound. He opened his eyes, saw nothing, and tried again. One eye registered snow very close up, the other a dense reddish veil. He put a hand to his face to push the blood away, but however hard he tried, his right eye continued to transmit an impenetrable red fuzz.

His self-defensive instincts took over. He reached out, moving his hand over the surface of the snow, searching for the pistol. No pistol. He turned his head a little.

His good eye saw a foot. Rolf's foot.

He tried to lift his head and instantly regretted it as his brain did several appallingly painful circuits of his skull.

When the nausea subsided he opened an eye again.

Rolf stood above him, looking down the barrel of a .303.

Hal felt a brief moment of disgust at his own stupidity. In the next moment he was working out the odds of grabbing Rolf's foot and pulling it from under him, of snatching the rifle, of feigning unconsciousness then jumping at him.

"Don't do it." Rolf's voice was very smooth and very sure. He added: "We want Kris to be safe, don't we?"

And then Hal remembered the boy and knew that he could never endanger Kris's safety, and he groaned with bitter defeat.

"Get up." Rolf had stepped backward and lowered his rifle to chest height.

"Not—sure—I—can. . . ." Hal's tongue felt large and swollen in his mouth.

"Get up."

Very slowly, Hal raised his head and rolled onto one elbow. The nausea welled up and he deposited the meager contents of his stomach onto the snow. When the spasms had passed, Rolf's voice repeated: "Get up!"

Finally Hal staggered to his feet. He still couldn't see out of one eye.

"Into the house."

Through his dim half-vision Hal saw that Kris was close by. He reached for him, but Rolf stepped smartly around and dropped a protective hand on Kris's shoulder. "I'll look after this young fellow. Won't I? We're chums, aren't we?"

Kris stared at him, round-eyed.

Clutching his head, Hal staggered off, leaning against the wall for support. The pain was overwhelming. Finally he made the steps. Rolf gestured him through the hall toward the living room.

Remembering Arne's body, Hal hissed: "Not the child!"

"Of course." Rolf's tone was approving. "Into the kitchen, Kris. And stay there, there's a good boy." He propelled the boy toward the door. Kris walked stiffly, as if in a dream. He did not look back.

Hal made his way into the living room and sank onto a chair, cradling his head in his hands. His good eye registered Arne's foot protruding from behind the table.

"You didn't—" Hal's voice came out as a dull, barely audible croak. He took another breath. "You didn't have to kill him, you bastard."

"He was trying to deliver your message, Hal. I couldn't let him do that."

"But you didn't have to kill him."

"But *he* was trying to kill *me*." His voice was sweetly reasonable. "What else could I do?"

It was a lie, but then that was probably the case for everything Rolf said.

"Tell me, Rolf . . . One thing." Hal peered up at him through the veil of red. "Why? Why—all this?"

There was a long pause, and Hal thought he wasn't going to answer. But finally he said: "They gave me a name, a new life, Hal."

"Christ—is that all?"

"All? You try living with a name that's—filth." The bitterness broke through into his voice.

"I don't understand."

"My father. He was a collaborator. I killed him."

"You could have changed your name."

"But it wouldn't have altered the fact that I was his son, that

I'd killed him, would it?" He shifted his weight, suddenly rest-less, and waved the rifle toward Arne. "Move him!"

"But is a name worth all this, for God's sake?"

Rolf gave a cold derisory laugh. "You don't seem to under-stand, Hal. It's not just a name now. I'm highly valued. You might even say, exceptionally important."

"You're not important any bloody longer."

"Ah—I think I am. I know I am." He said it with calm un-derstated pride.

The boast was chilling. Hal knew then that Rolf's conceit was boundless.

He also knew, with sudden certainty, that Rolf was going to kill him.

Hal said: "Thrane already knows—about you."

Rolf shook his head. "I don't think so. Now, come on"—he jerked his head at the body—"I want him down in the cellar."

"Listen to me—Thrane *knows*."

A flash of anger. "Don't give me that, Hal!" he said viciously. "He doesn't. Because you haven't had time to tell him. Now, get that body into the cellar!"

Rolf retreated to the other side of the room as Hal made his way unsteadily across to Arne and, taking the body by the an-kles, began to drag it toward the door. Hal tried not to look at Arne's lolling head bump-bumping over the floor into the hall.

The exertion made him feel faint and he had to stop. After a moment Rolf gave him a prod. Outside the cellar door he lowered one of Arne's legs to open the door. Steps led down-ward into pitch darkness.

Rolf ordered: "Turn on the light!"

"I don't know where it is."

"Find it!"

Hal knew where the switch was: inside, tucked up behind the doorframe. He made a show of searching for it, then gave a single shake of his aching head.

"Go on down!" Rolf said through narrowed lips.

This was the real Rolf, Hal thought fleetingly. No charm now.

Hal retreated down the steps, pulling the deadweight of Arne's body after him. His head felt as though it would crack open at any moment. A single light suddenly blazed on above his head; Rolf had found the switch. Too much to hope that he wouldn't.

Hal pulled the body beside a stack of storage crates and sank onto one knee, exhausted and vaguely nauseated again. Rolf was coming slowly down the steps into the pool of light.

Hal panted: "Are you going to kill me now?"

"What would you do in my place, Hal?"

Still crouching, Hal felt around the concrete floor with his left hand, looking for something—anything. "It's true—what you said—about Thrane. He doesn't know about you."

Rolf paused on the second-to-last step, looking curious. "Ah."

"But the researcher knows about you, Rolf. The one who found out about your early life."

Rolf cocked his head to one side, listening hard.

"He's someone who works closely with Thrane. He'll have reported this by now. To Thrane himself . . ."

For the first time Hal felt that he'd gotten Rolf's full attention. He went on talking, working his hand up the stack of shallow wooden crates as he did so. Each crate had wide ventilation openings in the sides. Holding Rolf's eyes, he began to ease his hand into one of them.

He said: "The man's an expert on missing persons. He uncovered your identity straightaway. He knows you're really Blakstad . . ." His hand closed over a rough oval object the size of a large egg: a potato.

". . . He also knows that Blakstad disappeared in the direction of the Russians . . ." He tried to withdraw his hand: It stuck. He shifted his grip on the potato.

". . . and that you acquired the Berg identity. He'll realize you must have had help . . ." His hand jammed again; he pulled hard. Gradually it began to scrape through, then came out suddenly, like a cork. His body swayed.

Rolf's eyes darted suspiciously.

Hal put his right hand to his head as if he'd just had a fit of dizziness, and slowly got to his feet. "You're finished, Rolf."

"I prefer to think not." The handsome face hardened. He brought the rifle up under his arm.

Fear leapt into Hal's throat. He thought: *He's going to do it now.*

Hurriedly, he flicked the potato at Rolf's head. A look of surprise came into Rolf's eyes, he gave a start, the potato missed him, and the rifle went off with a deafening *boom!* that filled the room.

Hal gathered himself to spring for the single naked bulb, but even as he uncoiled himself he saw Rolf recover, hastily operate he bolt, and swing the rifle back onto him. He froze.

Rolf's mouth set hard. His trigger hand seemed to tighten.

Hal shouted: "I can prove it!"

A pause. "What?"

"That they know about you!"

He hissed: "Prove it, then."

Straightening up, Hal reached slowly into his jacket and pulled out the note that Arne had brought up the hill first thing that morning. He held it out, then, seeing Rolf wasn't going to come and get it, threw it at his feet.

Keeping his eyes on Hal, Rolf picked up the note and unfolded it with one hand. He held it up to the light and began to read, flicking his eyes back to Hal as he did so.

Suddenly the note took all his attention. "Sorensen . . ." He looked shocked, his mouth turned down into an ugly grimace, the rifle barrel dropped slightly.

This time Hal didn't hesitate. He sprang for the light and, taking a wild swipe at it, smashed the bulb. His momentum carried him on through the sudden darkness. He threw up a hand just in time to break his fall against the wall.

There was another *boom,* the explosion so close that Hal flinched, instantly deafened. It was only as he pushed himself off the wall that he felt a burning sensation in his cheek. He launched himself forward, reached out, hoping to grab a foot or a leg. There was a scuffling sound, as if Rolf had momentarily lost his footing. The bastard was close, *close.* Wildly searching for contact, Hal dived forward again. His foot met concrete, he pitched forward and landed sprawled on a lower step.

He staggered up. Dimly—so dimly—he saw an outline, a silhouette against the light filtering down from the hall above. The indistinct form was scrabbling up the steps, trying to gain height and distance.

For a split second Hal thought it was hopeless—the dark shape was moving so fast. But then his good eye seemed to see a leg, a foot, not *so* far away. Summoning his energy, he made one last leap. His hand caught a boot, he reached—stretched—for the ankle, touched it, grappled for it, gripped—gripped harder as Rolf tried to jerk it away. Rolling onto his side to gain leverage, Hal gave an almighty heave.

With wild, vicious kicks Rolf tried to pull his foot free. Hal held on with grim determination, trying to reach forward and upward and get a grip on another part of Rolf—an arm, the rifle, anything. In his determination he never saw the other boot shooting toward him. He knew nothing until the heavy savage kick smashed into his nose with a sickening crunch. He yelped with shock and pain and fell back against the wall.

Then, unbelievably, his head took off again as the rifle butt swung into his skull. A deep *thud*, a vicious pain in his temple, and he was spiraling downward. He saw stars, the ringing sound in his ear became a roar, and he pitched backward into the darkness.

Berg approached cautiously, rifle at the ready, and peered at Hal's crumpled body in the dim light. Blood was streaming from the cheek and nose; the head was bent at an odd angle. It occurred to him that Hal might be dead after all. Crouching, he felt for a pulse at the wrist.

A distant sound came from above: a faint whooshing. He jerked his head up, listening hard. The wind?

He longed to go and find out, he longed to get away, yet he had to be sure about Hal. He felt for the pulse again. Nothing. He tried the neck, jabbing his fingers impatiently into the flesh, searching for the jugular. Nothing. Then—he moved his fingers again—yes: a faint throb. He cursed under his breath. Now he'd have to finish the job.

He stood up and operated the rifle bolt. The ejected shell clattered noisily onto the floor.

The silence closed in again. He aimed the rifle, prepared to fire, then hesitated, his mouth dry. He didn't want to have to do this. Damn Hal!

He gripped the rifle once more. A sound broke the silence. Berg gave a violent start. It had come from above: a loud rattle. The wind again? The child? Or—God forbid—Ragna?

For a split second he hovered indecisively, his finger on the trigger, then, turning abruptly, sprinted up the steps. At the top he ground to a halt and paused, his ears straining. Eventually the rattle sounded again. He located its source—the front door—and, striding through the lobby, flung it open.

No one. He exhaled sharply.

He closed the door and, returning to the hall, paused at the cellar steps. He should go down and finish Hal, yet he resented the necessity. Then it occurred to him that there *was* no necessity: Hal would die anyway. In this cold, with those injuries, he'd last no more than a few hours. And there was no risk of his being rescued: It would be days, maybe weeks, before anyone came.

By that time Berg would be long gone.

With relief he pulled the cellar door shut, turned the heavy lock, and tested the door with his shoulder. Then he headed for the kitchen to deal with the child.

30

Ragna peered out the window into the murk. Still no sign of them. Bamse sat patiently on the veranda, ears up, nose to the wind. Why were they taking so long? Kris would be starving by now. So would Hal, wherever *he* had gotten to. And the ham and eggs were rapidly congealing in the oven.

The more she thought about it, the more she could have kicked herself for not having gone with Arne. How much better that would have been! Then, if Rolf had been busy on the phone, she could have given Kris—and everyone else—breakfast down there.

As it was she was waiting here uselessly, missing Kris, missing that funny little face of his. The moment his small figure appeared over the rise she would run down the hill and scoop him up and almost squeeze the breath out of him.

And where was Hal? Why hadn't he told her where he was going? And why had he looked secretive?

It occurred to her that he might have gone down to Arne's to join the others—perhaps even to challenge Rolf, as he had last night. They might argue again. She had an unpleasant thought. What if in the heat of things Hal gave her away and revealed what she'd told him last night?

The fear she'd felt the previous night returned and she gave a slight shudder. She sensed that Rolf, for all his cool exterior, had a temper, well controlled but fierce. He was impatient and intolerant of anything that got in his way. Ambition and achievement were everything. With sudden insight she realized he was no different from the so-called friends she'd known in the black time, the people who'd pulled her down, the ones she'd run away from. Did she really want to be part of that again?

She sighed sharply. What a muddle!

Straining her eyes, she peered out into the dark gray morning once more. Where was Hal? If he were here she'd know what to do. If he were here she'd feel—safe.

She strode into the kitchen and looked at the clock. She decided to give Hal another ten minutes, then she'd battle her way down to Arne's. She poured a cup of coffee and switched on the radio.

The news came on. She listened with half an ear. A Bulgarian diplomat was being expelled from Norway for activities inconsistent with his diplomatic status. The big freeze continued. Strong winds in the north were causing severe drifting and several villages were cut off. A woman had been killed under a tram in Oslo. She had been named as Sonja Bjornsen, a civil servant in the defense ministry.

The voice droned on. At one point Ragna thought she heard something outside and turned the volume down. Had there been a sound? She thought of going to the front window, but decided it would be unlucky to go again so soon—it would be asking for them *not* to be there.

She listened hard. Wood creaked. Outside, a whooshing sound that reverberated around the house. She gave a contemptuous laugh. Of course! It was that dreadful wind; it fairly howled up this valley. Well, it had almost caught her out—but not quite. With the satisfied air of someone who isn't so easily fooled, she reached for the radio and, turning the volume up again, let the newscaster's voice fill the room.

Berg strode up the hill, panting hard. Coming within sight of the house he paused for breath.

The tractor had damn well failed to start, so he'd had to make the journey on foot. He'd spent the first part of the trip cursing and raging at his appalling luck. To be blown, after all he'd done—it was incredible. He couldn't believe it. Nor could he believe that the damage couldn't somehow be repaired.

But it couldn't. He knew that. The note that Hal had shown him, the message from Sorensen, it had been genuine, he was convinced of it. Sorensen was on to him.

Then, as he'd turned away from the shore to plow up the hill, he'd realized he owed Hal a debt of thanks. Hal had warned him; Hal had saved him from arrest. He thought bitterly: Good old Hal. Reliable to the end.

He continued toward the house.

As he started up the last slope he looked up and saw the dog.

It was standing in front of the steps, head down, ears flat, hackles raised. Berg tried staring it out, but realized that, on this occasion, it wasn't going to work. The dog bared its fangs and growled ominously. The creature could obviously smell something—blood? Berg looked anxiously down at his clothing then up at the windows of the house.

No blood. No sign of Ragna.

He considered for a moment.

"Here, boy." He stepped closer. The dog's growl rose to a fierce roar.

He went down on his haunches. "Come on, boy. You know me."

The dog snarled and snapped on empty air.

With rising anger Berg realized the animal meant business. He cursed. If Ragna hadn't been within earshot he would simply have blown the damned thing's head off.

"It's all right, boy," he said in a friendly voice. "I'm not going to hurt you." He gave the animal a wide grin and wandered innocently off toward the vegetable garden. He glanced over his shoulder. The beast was following, its head down, its teeth bared.

He headed for the corner, intending to go up the side of the house and around the back, but the dog suddenly accelerated and, overtaking him, stationed itself in his path.

Berg sighed deeply. "I see." He slipped Hal's pistol out of his pocket and held it out for the dog to see. "Come and get a mouthful of this, boy."

A long low growl sounded in the dog's throat. The animal began to advance, but very slowly, placing each paw in front of the last with infinite care, as if walking on ice. Berg goaded it. "Come on, boy. Come on. Let's have you! Let's have you!" Finally the dog could bear it no longer and poised itself to spring. As it leapt forward Berg stepped neatly to one side, swung his arm high, and brought the pistol butt savagely down. It hit the dog's head an ineffective glancing blow. The dog landed heavily, a little off-balance, then, recovering, twisted its body around for another attack.

But the animal wasn't so quick this time—perhaps the blow had made some impact after all. As the creature came in again Berg crouched well down and threw his left forearm up in front of his face. The dog took the bait just as Berg knew it would. Sighting the forearm, it adjusted its stride, opened its jaws, and was about to embed its teeth in his arm when, too late, it saw his right arm coming winging down. It made a desperate attempt to escape the trap, reopening its jaws, contorting its body to one side, but Berg had the trajectory right this time. The pistol met the animal's skull with a satisfying crack, and the dog fell.

Berg stood up and glanced over his shoulder. Still no Ragna. Lucky. He looked down at the prostrate animal. It was rolling its eyes and floundering its legs. Slipping the rifle off his shoulder Berg raised the butt high in the air.

Just as he threw his weight into a long downward thrust there was a sound.

From the house. Reflexively, he tried to pull up, to reverse the momentum of the blow, but it was too late to stop it altogether. His weight carried the butt down onto the animal's head, though not heavily.

Ducking quickly, Berg glanced around, listening hard.

Nothing. False alarm. No one in sight. Lucky. He grabbed the animal's back legs and dragged it rapidly up the side of the house and under the wall. He glanced back. There were a few blood stains on the snow, but they wouldn't be visible from the door.

The dog was still twitching. It was more dead than alive. He didn't have time to deal with it properly. He murmured derisively, "Sorry, old chap," and, straightening his anorak, walked quickly around the front of the house toward the veranda.

A movement. Ragna came out of the house, tying her hood, preparing to go somewhere. Seeing him, she started visibly and pulled the hood down from her mouth. "Where did you come from?" she shouted over the wind.

"Oh, I came up another way."

"Where are the others? Where's Kris?"

Berg strolled up the steps. "They're fine. They've gone off on an expedition."

"*What?*"

"Hal thought it might take Kris's mind off the musk-oxen. They've gone to look at some rare birds or something."

"Hal's down there?"

"Oh, yes."

This seemed to reassure her. Then she frowned again. "An expedition in this weather? And what about breakfast? I've got it waiting for them!"

"They've had some. At Arne's. But I wouldn't say no. I could eat a horse."

She sighed sharply. "I don't understand. Hal *knew* I wanted Kris back here. He knew I'd made a hot breakfast!" There was a fretful worried tone in her voice. For the first time her eyes focused on the rifle slung over his shoulder.

Berg took her arm and guided her into the house. The smell of food made his mouth water. "The problem was Kris," he explained gently. "He was starving. Arne offered him some bread and cheese and he gulped it down. Hal decided he may as well eat too."

Ragna turned and said accusingly: "Why did you take Kris with you this morning? Why did you take him without telling me?"

Berg unslung the rifle and propped it up in a corner. "You were asleep, my love, and Hal was off somewhere, up at the barn. Kris was bored stiff. I thought he might enjoy the walk down to Arne's. And he did."

She was halfway there, wanting to believe him yet not quite convinced.

He pushed the hood back from her face and, stroking her cheek, said cheerfully: "Honestly, we had a wonderful time. He's a great little boy."

The pride showed in her face and she gave a ghost of a smile. Berg thought: almost there.

"Now can I eat some of that breakfast?" he asked charmingly. "Then we'll talk about the rest of the day."

He ate nearly everything: four out of five eggs and three slices of ham. Ragna poured him another coffee and sat down expectantly. "Well?" she asked. "You wanted to talk about the rest of the day?"

"Yes. I have to get back to Oslo. The office is frantic. They need me to go to Washington tomorrow. I have to leave straightaway, I'm afraid."

"Oh." Ragna hid an immediate sense of relief. It would be a good thing. Rolf was a disturbing influence. He didn't belong up here. Neither did she want him up here—not at the moment, at least. Not until she understood what the problem with Hal was all about.

Rolf continued: "Hal's offered me the fishing boat."

Ragna was surprised. "*Skorpa?* But—what? Take it on your own?"

He looked a little offended. "It's not far across the sound. I think I can manage. Hal's letting me have the Land-Rover too. That reminds me . . ." Abandoning a last mouthful he shot rapidly to his feet and began to hunt around. "Where does Hal keep the keys?"

"In the hall, I think. On the table there."

Berg went off and reappeared with a bunch of keys. He searched through them. He seemed to find the ones he wanted, for he chucked them in the air and, catching them with a neat swipe of the hand, slid them into his pocket. He was full of suppressed energy, she noticed, a sort of nervous impatience, as if he could hardly wait to leave.

"One thing," he said. "Could you come out to *Skorpa* with me? Apparently the engine won't start unless there are two of us. There's some sort of a problem. Hal explained it all to me."

"Me? But—it's so windy. I couldn't possibly. I can't row."

Leaning over the table, he took a piece of bread, wiped the last remnants of egg from his plate, and popped the morsel into his mouth. "But I'll row on the way out. And on the way back you'll be going downwind. It'll be easy. Honestly—the wind'll blow you straight to the shore."

Ragna was appalled. The sea terrified her. "I *couldn't*."

"You must!" His eyes flashed with sudden anger. "Otherwise I'll be stuck here."

"But—why can't Hal do all this?"

He gave her a long look, as if deciding whether to tell her

something. "Listen." He sat on the edge of the table. "To be perfectly honest, Hal and I are not exactly the best of friends at present." He shrugged it off as mildly ridiculous. "And—well, I think he'd rather avoid my company on the trip. He's got some wild idea that I know something—" he paused, choosing his words carefully, "on a matter that he's obsessed with. . . ."

"Pasvik."

His brilliant eyes flashed darkly. "Oh. You know?" His expression became more veiled, more thoughtful. "What did Hal tell you?"

Why had she said that? Why? "Oh, nothing really. Only that he thought you might know something. . . . He didn't say what."

"I see." He gave her an odd look, and she could see he was unconvinced.

She murmured: "He just can't let the subject go. He's never been able to—leave it alone." She added hurriedly: "But it's all a waste of time, of course. I know that. I mean, there's no more to find out, is there?" Standing up abruptly, she took his plate to the sink. She could feel his eyes boring into her back.

Hurriedly she returned to the subject of the journey. "But if you take *Skorpa* we won't have a boat. We'll be stuck here."

"What? Oh, Hal said he'd put you on the supply boat tomorrow."

"But that takes hours, and it goes miles."

"He said he'd arrange for it to call in at the end of its round."

She sighed. "And what about the Land-Rover?"

"I'm to leave that at Bardufoss airport. He'll pick it up next week."

He seemed to have it all worked out. She had no more energy to argue.

If only she didn't have to do this beastly rowing.

She tried one last suggestion. "Can't we wait for Hal to come back—just to get *Skorpa*'s engine started, I mean?"

There was a pause. Rolf's attention seemed to have wandered for a moment. He was staring thoughtfully out the window. "No," he said suddenly, "they'll be gone for some time."

"I don't think I can do this!" gasped Ragna as she tried to stand up in the little boat, fighting to keep her balance as it bucked and yawed at *Skorpa*'s side.

"I'll give you a heave!" Rolf chucked his bag onto *Skorpa*'s deck and, turning back, took Ragna's wrists and hoisted her over the gunwale. She landed awkwardly and stumbled against the wheelhouse.

And to think she had to go through all this again. She was already soaked to the knees from helping to launch the dinghy through the surf. She found her feet and, feeling *Skorpa* pitching under her, held tight to the rail.

Rolf went aft to tie the dinghy onto the stern and, returning, went straight into the wheelhouse. Shivering with cold Ragna looked in through the open door. Rolf was searching impatiently for something.

He demanded: "How do the electrics turn on?"

"I don't know."

"There must be a master switch. Surely you've seen where Hal turns it on?"

"No. Didn't he tell you where it was?"

Rolf didn't reply but disappeared down the companionway. A minute later he reappeared and twiddled one of the switches by the wheel. A red light came on. He disappeared again. Ragna waited to be told what to do.

There was a loud sluggish whirring as the engine turned over. The whirring went on and on, then stopped. Ragna looked down the hatch. Rolf was crouched beside the engine, his face very grim.

Suddenly Ragna remembered something. "He usually sprays something into the middle of the engine when it's cold."

"What?"

She shrugged. "I'm not sure what the stuff is. Spray. In a can. Something to get it going."

Rolf hunted around. Ragna looked toward the shore, and thought longingly of Brattdal and the others.

Rolf stood up, holding a can of Easy Start for her inspection.

"That's it."

He went to work then, opening up levers on the top of the engine. He seemed to know what he was doing.

After a time he shouted: "Turn the starter, will you?"

She looked at the instrument panel and, recognizing a large

black switch she had seen Hal use, turned it. The whirring began again, but this time it sounded distinctly brighter. Rolf dashed up and waggled the throttle back and forth. The engine coughed once, twice, Rolf dived down the hatch again, then slowly, painfully, the engine chug-chugged into life.

Ragna sighed with relief. Thank God! Now she could think about starting back.

Rolf reappeared and played with the throttle until the revs settled to a satisfactory level.

She rebuttoned her hood. "I'll go back now."

"Sure." He went to fetch the dinghy.

After a moment she went out onto the side deck and looked aft to see how he was getting on. He was walking back toward her, empty-handed. Why hadn't he gotten the dinghy?

He came up to her. "The dinghy's gone!"

"Gone?"

"The rope was rotten. It's blown away."

The full implications of what he had said struck her. "What— Oh, God! But I must get ashore. How am I going to get ashore? You *must* put me ashore!"

"But how?"

"At Arne's. At the other end of the island. *Anywhere.*"

He made a show of looking at his watch. "There aren't any landing places for miles."

"There's the cove where the supply boat landed us!"

"Have you seen the surf?" he said derisively. "I'm sorry, it's impossible. Look, Kris'll be fine with Hal. It's best you come with me. Then you can take the supply boat back in the morning and go and fetch Kris yourself."

"No—"

"I tell you. There's no other way." His lips were tight with determination. "Really."

She felt a momentous helplessness. She gave him a pleading look but he turned away and, lowering his head against the wind, made his way carefully up to the bow. Then she realized: He was preparing to leave.

She couldn't bear it.

Clutching the rail for support she made her way forward along the pitching deck. Rolf was unwinding chain from a fastening post. She shouted, "Rolf!" but the wind whipped the words from her lips. She ran the last few feet and lurched into him.

"Please—"

With a great heave he threw the chain and the bright red marker buoy over the bow and turned away. She clutched his arm and yelled, "Rolf, please get me back somehow."

Pausing for an instant, he gave her a disapproving look, as if he couldn't believe she would make such a fuss. "Don't be hysterical, Ragna. You'll see Kris tomorrow. It's not that long to wait, surely." His tone was final. He pulled his arm free and hurried into the wheelhouse.

Ragna stood motionless, grasping the rail, overcome by a dreadful suspicion.

He'd done it on purpose. He'd let the dinghy go on purpose!

The boat pitched into a wave and almost jerked her off her feet.

Slowly, unsteadily, she made her way down the length of the deck to the stern, and stared toward the empty shore.

"The number is out of order."

Sörensen put the phone down and stared crossly into space. No wonder Starheim hadn't called him back.

But what was he to do now?

For once he was finding it almost impossible to come to a decision. If it had been a legal problem, a matter of weighing up this factor against that, he could have dealt with it—his work, after all, consisted of nothing but problems. But this was different: this was a moral dilemma.

Should he break Starheim's trust and honor the assurance he had made to Thrane? Or should he stay quiet and risk allowing a serious matter to go uninvestigated? Because the more he thought about it, the more certain he was that it must be serious. A man might go some lengths to hide his past—but not that far.

One thing was sure: whatever he did he was going to break one of the two promises he had made.

If only he'd been able to talk to Starheim.

His secretary put her head around the door and said: "The taxi's waiting."

He frowned. "What for?"

She gave him a look of affectionate rebuke. "You've forgotten! You have a meeting at the fishermen's cooperative."

He groaned and made a face. "Two minutes. Just give me two minutes."

Suddenly he made up his mind. It was a matter of conscience, and such matters could not be allowed to rest. May the Lord strike him down if he was doing the wrong thing, but do it he must. He reached for the phone.

31

A long black tunnel yawned before Hal, sucking him down, floating him along a stream of unconsciousness to a place where there was no more pain. He yielded to it, allowing it to rock him gently along.

Yet something nagged at him, a single persistent thought that darted out of his conscious mind and wouldn't let him rest. He pushed it away, but the thought returned, more insistent than ever.

With a vast effort he tried to isolate the thought. Finally it came to him: unless he woke up he was going to die. Dying itself didn't seem so important, but there was some vital reason why he mustn't die, though he couldn't work out what it was.

Inch by inch, he fought his way out of the tunnel, until, with a last effort, the darkness released him and consciousness returned in a sudden rush of pain.

He opened his eyes. Blackness. He listened, but all he could hear was a loud ringing in his ears. He moved his hand and felt the rough concrete floor. He wasn't dead yet.

He moved his head. Terrible. He moved again, raising himself onto hands and knees, feeling his way along the floor until he reached the wall.

Forcing himself to sit up, he took an inventory of the damage. His right cheek, deeply scored and still wet with blood. His nose, a bloody swollen mess. And his skull—God only knew. As far as he could make out, the rifle butt had struck him twice, once behind the right ear—which accounted for the high-pitched ringing—and a second time on the left temple.

But it was his eyes that really worried him—they registered nothing. Not even a suggestion of light. Maybe it was just dark.

A sudden panic overtook him. How long had he been lying there? Hours? A few seconds? Rolf might be on his way back to finish him off. And Kris—where was *he*?

Pulling himself up, he felt his way along the cold walls of the cellar, bumping into crates, tripping over something large and soft. He felt down: Arne's body. He must be going the wrong way. He was about to turn back when something made him pause.

A tiny sliver of gray. Light. He blinked; the image was very blurred. Then he realized: He could see with his left eye but not his right. Still—better than nothing. He worked out where the light must be coming from—the loading door high up in a side wall.

He felt his way back along the wall until his foot met a step. He climbed until he came to the door. He felt for the latch and lifted it. Solid. He pulled at the small handle, but the door was firm as rock and, he seemed to remember, about as thick.

The loading door. It was the only other way out.

Slowly, carefully, he felt his way back down the steps and across the room to the sliver of light. The door was set well up in the wall. How to reach it? He felt for a pile of crates and dragged them across. The effort made his head throb with deep-seated pain.

He climbed up, feeling unsteady, and ran his hands over the rough wooden surface of the door. No handle—a bar. He gripped it. It refused to budge. He struck it with the heel of his hand. It seemed to shift—or was it his imagination? He gave it another shove, then, overwhelmed by dizziness, clutched at it for support.

Recovering, he had another go. This time it gave. Sweating, he pulled it open. His left eye registered a flood of gray light, his right eye, darkness.

Turning back into the cellar he rooted around among the crates and storage racks until he found an iron bar. Tucking it into his belt he climbed up and through the door, out into the snow. For a moment he lay on the soft whiteness, regaining his breath, then clambered up the bank.

He made for the front of the house. To his surprise he saw that the tractor was still parked where he had left it. Was Rolf still in the house, then?

He couldn't work it out. Retreating, he went around to the other side of the house and, pulling himself up the wall, risked a quick look in through the lighted window of the living room. No one. He did the same at the kitchen and bedroom windows.

Nothing for it but the front, then.

He approached the door cautiously and turned the handle. It was locked. It was never locked. He rattled it, then put his shoulder to it. Nothing budged except his brain, which did a couple of sickening circuits of his head.

Using the iron bar he hacked at the door, then levered the bar in between the door and the frame and put all his weight behind it. Finally there was a sound of splintering wood and the lock gave.

"Kris—"

Silence.

He went into the kitchen, the living room, then the rest of the house. Nothing. He almost wept.

"Kris—"

Silence.

He called again and again, thinking: Dear God, *please*.

He stood in the hall, shoulders sagging, momentarily defeated.

Then he heard it: a faint baleful cry.

The kitchen. But—

He hurried back.

It came again. . . . From behind the door. Hal swung it closed.

The boy stood there—alive, *safe*.

Hal's throat constricted; he couldn't speak. He reached out his arms.

Kris stared at him, opened his mouth, and screamed, a long ear-splitting sound.

Hal scooped the child into his arms, carried him to a chair, and pulled him down onto his lap by the still-warm stove. He held him tight and rocked him and stroked his hair and murmured soft words until the screaming stopped.

Eventually he stole a look at him. The child's face was blank with shock, his eyes staring vacantly downward, his body stiff. Hal wondered what terrors the boy had lived through.

"Kris. I'm here." Hal rubbed the circulation back into the boy's hands. "You're all right now! Come on!" Nothing. He added much louder: "Hey! Wake up!"

The child blinked, his gaze sharpened. His eyes locked onto Hal's face and grew round with horror again.

Hal put a hand to his face and realized: It was his face that was the culprit. "Come and help me wash."

Sitting the child on the draining board, Hal washed his face rigorously, and flinched violently when he touched his nose. It hurt like hell, especially when the loose bone moved. He put disinfectant on his cheek, so that that too hurt like hell. Drying off, he asked: "Better?" From Kris's expression he guessed not.

He hugged him again. "Sorry I look so horrible, but I'm the same inside!" He smiled to show it was a bit of a joke.

Carrying the boy, he went into the living room and picked up the phone. He jiggled the cradle. Dead. He looked for loose wires, but couldn't see any. Then he peered out the window and, even with one bad eye, saw plenty. Cables drooped uselessly from the post.

He found a clock: It was three in the afternoon.

"Come on. We'll go and find Mummy." He instantly regretted the words. Perhaps they wouldn't find Mummy. In fact, why hadn't Ragna come looking for them hours ago?

He hunted rapidly through the kitchen. Arne's .303 had gone, but unless he was going to be very unlucky there should still be an old Webley revolver and a box of ammunition hidden on top of the dresser. Reaching up, his hand touched the cold metal of the gun and he pulled it down triumphantly. It was about time something went his way. But then he corrected himself: Something *had* gone his way—he had found Kris, and that had been the most important thing of all.

Loading the weapon, he stuffed it in his pocket with a handful of spare rounds. He cut bread, spread it with butter and jam, and gave some to Kris with a glass of evaporated milk. He ate and drank, too, though chewing was painful. The food made him feel a lot better.

Wrapping Kris in a thick down jacket of Arne's, he hoisted the boy on his back and prepared to leave. "All right?" No answer, but the arms encircling his neck gave an answering squeeze.

He made straight for the tractor and, sitting Kris down, tried it. The engine gave a couple of feeble turns and died: The battery was flat. He tried the hand crank. And again, and again. Nothing. He opened the engine casing.

He could see nothing wrong. He tried cranking it one more time without success.

With resignation, he settled Kris on his back once more and set off on foot, bending into the force of the wind. The wind had shifted even farther to the east, he vaguely noticed, and was ice-cold. The surf crashed loudly onto the beach, retreating across the pebbles with a powerful sucking and clattering noise.

As he crested the rise in the track his eyes automatically went to the point just off the shore where *Skorpa* lay at her mooring. But he couldn't make her out; he couldn't make anything out in the general blur.

He walked on and tried to focus again without success.

It wasn't until he was almost at the boathouse that he finally got a clear if one-sided view of the mooring. His stride faltered. He looked again. But he wasn't mistaken—she wasn't there.

He groaned inwardly: Of course! What else would Rolf have done but take the boat? He scanned the sound and the distant fjord for sight of her, but the gathering darkness pressed down grayly on a gray white-flecked sea, so that, to his cloudy vision, color and detail were indistinguishable.

Wearily, he began the long climb up the hill to Brattdal. His head throbbed viciously; he felt nauseated again. He plodded on, closing his mind to everything but the need to reach the house. Finally it came into view, its lights shining into the dusk, calm, almost as if nothing had changed.

Hal climbed the steps up to the veranda and walked straight in.

The silence was very deep.

Kris said: "Where's Mummy?"

Hal had a strong feeling that she wasn't going to be there. But he said cheerfully: "I'll have a look for her."

Leaving Kris in the kitchen he searched the house. Rolf's things had gone. But Ragna's bag, her clothes, her toothbrush, were still there. His heart filled with dread.

He searched the rest of the house before returning to the boy. He tried to think of something to say. "I think Mummy's had to go, Kris. Back to the mainland. To—see to things." He trailed off. "I think we should go to the mainland too, don't you?"

Kris began to cry inconsolably. Hal put an arm around him. Turning his good ear toward the hall, he kept listening. For what he wasn't sure.

Suddenly he went cold.

Bamse.

He leapt up. "Just got to take a quick look outside."

Kris's face was a picture of despair.

Hal pleaded, "It's the animals, Kris. I've got to go and see to the animals!" and left before the child had time to speak.

He went out and whistled long and hard. Nothing. He climbed the hill to the barn, whistling as he went. On opening the barn door he was met by hysterical bleating and bellowing from the animals. No Bamse. He hoisted several days' supply of feed into the goats' stall and split the sacks open. The goats couldn't believe their luck. He did the same for the cattle, checked their water, and went outside again.

He scanned the darkening valley, and whistled long and loud.

He strained to hear an answering bark, but there was no sound, just the rustling of the snow as it was lifted and sifted by the wind.

Ragna. Bamse. He felt a flicker of hope. It might be significant that both of them had disappeared. Ragna might have gone to get help and taken Bamse with her. But how? If she'd gone overland to the nearest farm she'd have had to pass Arne's place, and she wouldn't have done that without searching for Kris. And the boat—Ragna could never have gotten Bamse on board by herself.

The hope died.

No: Ragna and Rolf had gone with *Skorpa*. And Bamse?

He decided on a quick circuit of the house. Skirting to the north and east he searched for signs of fresh tracks, but in the somber ebbing light the snow had lost all contrast and even Bamse's favorite well-worn paths were hardly visible. He came around the front of the house well below the veranda, still whistling, scanning the gray valley walls, just in case the familiar wolflike figure should come loping into view. Giving the last corner a wide berth, he went to the vegetable garden and peered over he wall.

Nothing. He headed back toward the front of the house. He stopped. Something caught his eye; something on the snow just in front of him. He crouched down to see better. Marks: dark splotches—stains—on well-trodden snow. And from here a width of smoothed snow led away toward the side of the house, as if someting had been dragged over it.

He followed the swath.

Then he spotted it—a dark shape close under the wall of the house, hidden in the deep shadow of a lighted window.

He couldn't make out what it was. He approached cautiously, creasing up his good eye, forcing himself to see.

At two yards he saw.

And stopped. Not wanting to go on. Not wanting to be right.

Dear Lord.

He cried aloud: *"No—"* And it was a cry of despair.

He moved the last few steps, dropped to his knees, and ran his hands over the coarse fur. For an instant he felt a wild euphoria: The flesh was pliable and slightly warm. Inside the deep rib cage the heart still fluttered.

But then his searching hands found the indentation in the top of the skull, and the euphoria died, and he felt a wild and savage anger, because however he ran his fingers over the indentation, however he tried to pretend it wasn't deep, the thing was a bloody great cavity—a sickeningly deep hole—and in his heart he knew that terrible damage like that could never ever be undone.

With infinite care he picked the dog up, moved him into the shaft of light from the window, and laid him in a soft bed of fresh snow. Gently he felt over the fine intelligent head again, still hoping that the furrow would be less of a bloody cavity—but it was still there, deep and savage, and his throat constricted with grief and pain. He pulled back the eyelids and saw the dead unresponsive eyes and, putting a hand to the powerful chest, felt the shallowness of the breathing.

He laid his head against the dog's and stroked the long back, feeling the richness of the fur, murmuring, "Silly old fool. Silly old fool," and tears fell hotly across his nose and onto Bamse's ear.

Then, his cheek still pressed against the warm head, he pulled the revolver from his pocket, cocked it, and held it hard against the back of Bamse's head.

With a sharp intake of breath, he jerked his head abruptly away and squeezed the trigger.

The Aeroflot advertising manager lay on the sofa, bored and frustrated. He'd read all the newspapers and the book he'd brought with him was unreadable.

The safe house, an apartment in the Frogner region of Oslo, was as still as the grave and just as depressing. The manager—a lieutenant in the GRU—went to the window and looked out. An old woman shuffled carefully along the icy pavement, a delivery man unloaded a large box from a van, a car trundled past. He sighed. He had another four hours of this, and only some sandwiches and the occasional coffee to break the monotony. And monotonous it would be. Nothing, unfortunately, was likely to happen. It never did on his shift.

The phone rang.

He jumped violently and stared at the instrument as if it had gone mad.

Then, pulling himself together, he sat down beside it and marshaled his thoughts.

He started the tape recorder and lifted the receiver. "Hello?"

"It's Harri—where the hell have you been?"

"I was hoping you'd call."

The voice floated in from a great distance. "Well, you don't have a very good way of showing it, you bastard!"

The young GRU man raised his eyebrows; this was going to require tact. "There was a slight logistical problem, that is all," he said. "The telephone line had a fault."

"A fault? Well, why the hell didn't you fix it?"

Ignoring the question, the advertising manager said smoothly: "How are you? Is everything well?"

"No, it bloody isn't. Things are very—unwell."

The Russian absorbed this. "Oh? I'm sorry to hear that. Are you ill?"

"Yes."

"And there's nothing that can be done?"

"Nothing, you sod."

"Do you need anything?"

"Yes—a holiday. And soon."

"You can't come back to the office first?"

"No!" The voice was tight with anger.

"I see." The GRU man thought fast. He had instructions for this eventuality, but he must remember them precisely. "Do you want help with tickets?"

"Not yet. But I will."

"That will be no problem."

"I want to go on a real vacation. To South America or some-where like that."

"Of course. How nice."

"That can be arranged?" The hostility had gone.

"Most certainly. Just as soon as you decide where you want to go."

A pause. "I thought I'd go and see some relatives first. A cousin on my mother's side."

The advertising manager felt relief. Harri had just made things a lot easier for everyone. He had chosen to go to Helsinki.

"You'll phone me when you arrive?"

"Will you be there, you sod?"

"Someone'll be here. All the time."

"And from my cousin's I want to go straight on vacation— understand?"

"Of course. Oh—and Harri?"

"Yes."

"A special friend sent his very warmest regards."

"Stuff him."

The phone went dead.

The advertising manager exhaled sharply. He had the feeling his superior would be extremely disappointed to hear about this. The news that the subject was making for Helsinki would, on the other hand, provide some solace. It was only a six-hour busride from Helsinki to Leningrad. Tourists made the trip all the time. The Winter Palace and the Hermitage were great attractions.

The operator said: "There seems to be a fault on the line."

"A fault?" Ragna clutched her forehead in disbelief. "But when will it be repaired?"

"Out there? It could be weeks."

Ragna rang off and put her head in both hands. This was getting more dreadful by the moment. If she allowed her imagination full rein, it seemed so dreadful she could hardly bear it.

Kris. Hal. What had happened to them? Were they all right? Had they really gone on an expedition?

Had Rolf lied? Had he let the dinghy go on purpose? If so, why?

She was sitting in her living room, but it seemed strangely unfamiliar, as if an enormous amount of time had passed since she'd last seen it. One of Kris's toys lay on the floor. The sight of it made her want to cry.

If only she'd stayed at Brattdal. If only she'd gone down to Arne's. If only Hal had come back.

Hal. She felt a powerful need of him, a sudden longing for him. Why wasn't he here?

Rolf's voice sounded from the hall. "Still no reply?"

She didn't answer.

He put his head around the door. "Come and help, would you?"

She rose, thinking: Anything. Anything to humor him. Anything to get rid of him. She rose and followed him into the hall.

She found him pulling clothes out of the coat cupboard and throwing them onto the floor. "What on earth are you looking for?"

"Warm clothes. Rucksacks. Oh, and I'll need skis and boots just in case the car gets stuck. I suppose you've got some?" He stood back, waiting for her to sort out the clothes, as if such task were too menial for him.

"The road to Bardufoss isn't that bad!"

"We're not going to Bardufoss."

Ragna stared at him. "We?"

"We. I need you to come along."

"What? But where to?"

"Finland."

Ragna gaped. It was miles to the border, but that was nothing to the distance beyond it. And the road. It ran high over the plateau for miles and miles. In this weather it might well be closed. And where could he possibly be aiming for? It was at least twenty-four hours to any real sort of civilization.

She managed: "But why?"

He whirled past her into the kitchen and threw open some cupboards. "We'd better take food. Collect some tins, would you?"

He headed back for the door but she blocked his way and demanded: "Why?"

"Just got to, and that's all there is to it, sweet one." He chucked her under the chin and smiled that charming empty smile of his.

She thought: I'm going to scream. "But where in Finland, for God's sake?"

He moved past her into the hall. "Helsinki, probably."

"That's at least two days. I can't be away that long! You'll have to go on your own. I'm sorry. Rolf, do you hear me? You'll have to go on your own!"

He shook his head. "No, I'm afraid I need you. To help with the driving."

The argument had a nightmarish quality to it, like when you try to tell some vital truth and no one listens. She made an effort to sound sweetly reasonable. "Look. Suppose I find someone else to go with you. Someone—"

"No."

"Rolf, this is ridiculous!"

He turned on her, his blue eyes very hard and very cold.

'What's ridiculous, my love, is wasting time when we should be on our way!"

A shudder ran down Ragna's spine. She thought: I don't know this man at all.

He grasped her chin in one hand, his fingers pinching her cheeks. "Now, the quicker we leave the quicker you'll be back. Eh?"

He turned away and bent down to stuff some clothes into the holdall that he had brought in from the car.

Sticking out of the top was the long barrel of the hunting rifle.

Shaking slightly, Ragna went into the kitchen and began taking food off the shelves.

Hal made Kris sit down in the stern and covered him with a piece of canvas. He shouted over the crash of the surf: "Keep wrapped up!" Checking that his rucksack was well wedged under the helmsman's seat where it wouldn't get wet, he prepared to launch.

It was not going to be easy, not when the waves had a clear seven-mile run from Lyngen and were steep and short as small walls, and almost as hard; not when it was full night and pitch dark and he still felt rough as hell.

He hoisted the mainsail, which flogged viciously, hell-bent on self-destruction, then the foresail. He checked that the rudder was ready to hand, and the tiller. Then, putting all his weight into it, he hauled the boat down the shingle into the water. The water lapped coldly against his boots, then, with the next heave, to his knees; finally, as he floated her off, a large wave broke against his legs, soaking him to the groin. The boat's bow rose and fell pistonlike in the breaking surf.

Gripping the gunwale to keep the boat's nose into the wind, Hal worked his way down toward the stern. Reaching the stern he grabbed the rudder from inside the boat and tried to guide the pintles into their sockets, but every time they were almost home the breaking surf bounced the rudder out of alignment.

Cursing silently, he tried again, only to feel a wave skew the bow off to one side. A second wave caught her; he heard it

break into the boat. He waded forward and hauled the bow
back into the wind again. As he returned to the stern he saw
the pale oval of Kris's face peering over the gunwale. He
shouted: "It's all right, we'll be off soon!" The face disap
peared.

This time he held the rudder rigidly in alignment by
brute force and guided the pintles into place. The rudder
dropped home. At last. He jammed the tiller into the rud
derhead, then, pushing the boat out as far as he could be
fore the waves broke over his legs, he let the bow fall away
until it pointed straight out to sea. As the sails caught scent
of the wind and *Lillebjørn* made her first tentative lunges at
the waves, Hal hoisted himself over the gunwale and dropped
headfirst into the boat, scrabbling to hoist his dripping legs in
after him.

He pulled himself up, grabbed for the tiller, and hauled in
on the mainsheet. The sail filled and *Lillebjørn* responded with
a sudden forward surge, setting herself resolutely at the
waves. Her bow rose to the first, but the wave was too steep
for her and its breaking crest foamed in over the port bow
pouring heavy torrents over the triangular foredeck and down
into the boat.

The boat picked herself up, shook the last of the water
off her deck, and, straining at the bit, pointed herself at the
next wave. This time she had a little more speed and Hal was
able to nudge her bow up into the fast-approaching wave so
that she took it cleanly, cleaving its breaking crest neatly
in two.

Two more steep breaking seas advanced on them—one of
them curved into a hissing crest into the boat—but *Lillebjørn*
battled her way through, and then at last they were through
the worst and into the regular pattern of the longer deep
water waves. Hal got his bearings on the faint lights on the
opposite shore and altered course. He sheeted in the little
foresail, trimmed the mainsail to the beam wind, and felt
Lillebjørn rocket forward, quivering at her freedom.

Now it was the sheer boat speed that made the going wet:
sheets of spray rose into the air and flew back over the bow
and into the boat. Hal reached for his newly acquired pump,
checking Kris as he did so. The boy seemed quiet enough, and

fairly dry: he was above the level of the slopping bilges, and had curled himself into a ball and pulled the canvas over his head.

Hal pumped energetically until the sound of sloshing water subsided, then took a rest. He wiped some stickiness from his eyes. It dawned on him that it was blood. He felt his head; he was bleeding from the bruise on his temple. He ignored it, but the blood continued to dribble sluggishly down his face. Unwinding the strip of toweling from his neck, he pushed back his hood and wrapped it several times around his head.

His neck now felt very cold. But the sensation was soon eclipsed by the coldness of his body as the piercing wind penetrated his waterproofs and, finding his sodden clothes, tried to freeze them onto his body. His hands ached with cold, then throbbed, then began to lose all feeling. He slipped them inside his jacket one at a time in an attempt to keep the circulation going.

Halfway. Lethargy crept over him; he wanted to sleep.

He came to with a start and grabbed the tiller with both hands. Not a moment too soon, as a violent squall blasted down from the distant mountains, wailing like a demon, throwing *Lillebjørn* over on her beam ends. Hal quickly eased the sheet, spilling wind from the main. Slowly—heart-stoppingly slowly—*Lillebjørn* tottered up again, as if recovering from a blow, and, gathering herself, cannoned forward into the blackness, her half-filled sails flogging violently, her shrouds humming, her mast shaking so hard that the whole boat vibrated. Hal clung on, holding her steady because there was nothing else he could do.

Almost as quickly as the squall had struck, it was past, and the shore lights, blotted out by the racing cloud, slowly reappeared. *Lillebjørn* resumed her upright posture and slowed, settling herself sedately in the water like a ruffled seabird.

Hal relaxed and focused his good eye on the shore again. With only one eye it was hard to judge distance, but he guessed it was no more than two miles away. Less than half an hour.

He fell into the numb mindlessness induced by sea and intense cold and, hunching his body over the tiller and keeping his back to the wind, stared blankly into the darkness, steering over the waves by feel and instinct. The only time he moved was to check Kris, curled motionless at his feet. Otherwise he remained immobile, instinctively trying to conserve his body heat. It was an impossible hope, and after a while he began to shiver uncontrollably.

He blinked himself into concentration. The shore lights were much closer now and the sea was already calmer as *Lillebjørn* came into the lee of the land. He blinked again: some of the shore lights were moving. Then he realized. Headlights. A car.

The lights slowed and stopped at a point dead ahead of *Lillebjørn*'s bows. Could it be the Land-Rover? Rolf would have the Land-Rover by now; he knew that because the keys had been missing from the hall at Brattdal.

But why would Rolf come back?

Perhaps it was another car. A strange car. His hopes rose. If so, it would be a godsend. He prayed to the unknown vehicle: Don't go away.

Using the lights of a nearby farmhouse to guide him, he looked for the jetty. Then he realized that the strange vehicle was parked on or near the jetty, and that all he had to do was head for its lights.

The wind, deflected by the land, went fluky and dropped. *Lillebjørn*'s speed slowed to a gentle dribble. Hal chafed with frustration.

He watched the car: it still had its lights on. Something showed in the beam—a mast, a superstructure. A craft alongside the jetty.

Skorpa.

A small gust caught *Lillebjørn*'s sails. She shot forward; the jetty was drawing closer. Hal saw a figure climb down onto *Skorpa*'s deck. Who? The nearby farmer, curious to know why *Skorpa* hadn't been left at her mooring? Yet that was impossible: No one around here—and certainly not a humble farmer—had a car.

Rolf? Why would he bother?

Hal gave up trying to make sense of it. Instead he reached a stiff hand under the seat and into his rucksack. After a moment he found the revolver and pushed it inside his jacket.

The wind seemed to have abandoned him again. He willed it back. It must have heard him, for after a couple of false starts it came swooping in along the land, catching him unprepared. He retrimmed the sails and *Lillebjørn* surged forward again.

Skorpa loomed up in front of him. He saw now that there was more than one person on board. A hope sprang into his mind: Ragna. She'd managed to get help. They were on the point of setting out for Revoy. How wonderful that would be!

Yet some instinct made him keep out of the beam of the headlights and make for the far end of the jetty, where it was dark. Once there, he rounded up and, bringing *Lillebjørn* neatly alongside the wooden piles, lunged for the main halyard and let go. The mainsail dropped into the boat with a loud clatter. Kris's face appeared from under the canvas. Hal whispered: "Stay there!"

A dark figure silhouetted by the headlights was visible advancing along the jetty toward them. Taking the revolver from his jacket, Hal tried to cock it. He swore under his breath: his damn fingers were too cold!

Fumbling, he put both hands to it and finally heard the hammer click back.

The beam of a torch sprang out of the darkness onto *Lillebjørn*'s mast. The torch holder came to a halt above him.

"Identify yourself." The voice was not Rolf's.

Hal felt a momentous relief. He dropped his gun hand down by his side and stood up, saying weakly: "My name is Halvard Starheim and I need some help."

There was a pause. The dark figure said: "Come up here."

Hal didn't need any encouragement. At the same time he didn't want the gun to go off and frighten everyone. Bending down into the shadows he managed to uncock the revolver and stick it back inside his jacket. He made *Lillebjørn* fast on a long line, then climbed up onto the jetty and said urgenty: "Is there anyone on *Skorpa*? On the fishing boat?"

The torch flashed full into his face. The voice said cautiously: "No."

It had been too much to hope for. Hal said to the shadowy figure: "Listen—it's a miracle you're here, whoever you are. There's an emergency. It's too complicated to explain, but first

I must get to a telephone, then I must get into Tromsø. Can you take me? I can't tell you how important—"

"Herr Starheim," the voice interrupted heavily. "I am Sergeant Christiansen of the Tromsø police. You have to come with me."

"The police?" Hal echoed. Then, realizing what he was hearing, he laughed with stupid relief. "Oh, thank God! Ragna—Ragna's told you! That's why you're here. She told you."

A pause. "We are here because you are required to come to Tromsø."

Hal's relief evaporated. "You haven't heard from Ragna Johansen?"

"Come!"

"You don't understand!" Hal said in frustration. "Listen— something very terrible's happened, a—" He almost said that a man was dead, but stopped himself in time; the sergeant would probably arrest him for murder. "A woman's missing. We have *got* to get to a telephone. The borders—the airports—they must be watched. I have to—" He tried to clear the fog in his brain. "I have to contact Thrane. Yes—Thrane, and—"

"You must come with me," the heavy voice repeated.

"What do you mean?" He couldn't believe what he was hearing.

"I have orders. You are to come to Tromsø."

"Why?"

The plodding voice repeated: "You are to come with me to Tromsø."

"And if I refuse?"

"I am a police officer, Herr Starheim. These are strict orders. You would be best not to argue."

"But there's a woman in danger of her life! We have to go and look for her, for God's sake!"

"You will be able to make the appropriate representations at the station. But now you must—"

Hal knew what came next: *Come with me!* Visions of long hours shut in a police station with dozens of Sergeant Christiansens flashed through his mind. Like hell he'd come!

A second figure was walking toward them, coming from the

direction of *Skorpa*. Another bovine representative of the Tromsø police force, no doubt.

Hal said hastily: "I've got to get the child first."

"The child?"

"In the boat." Before the sergeant could object, Hal swung himself down over the edge of the jetty. The sergeant stepped forward to have a look and, failing to see the boat, which had floated clear on her long line, shuffled closer to the edge.

That was his mistake. Hal, still hanging on the side of the jetty, reached up, grasped the sergeant's ankle, and in one powerful movement yanked his leg outward and downward. The officer tottered, windmilling his arms, then fell forward. He must have been a heavy man for he hit the water with a resounding splash.

His partner arrived at a rush.

"He's fallen in the water," Hal said helpfully.

"What? Oh!" The second officer sounded young, dazed, and not entirely sure of what he should do.

Heavy splashing noises sounded nearby: the sergeant was obviously something of a swimmer, though winter bathing was probably quite new to him. Hal called reassuringly to the young officer on the jetty: "I'll go and get him."

A pull on the long line brought *Lillebjørn* gliding in alongside the jetty. Hal jumped lightly in. The splashing sounds were slowly and breathlessly approaching.

Untying the mooring line, Hal pushed off and hoisted the mainsail. There was a cry from the jetty. Hal shouted back: "I'd climb down and help him out if I were you."

Another cry. Hal did not answer. He pulled in the mainsheet, the wind caught the sail, and *Lillebjørn* shot off into the enveloping darkness.

32

Thrane got stiffly out of the car, stretched painfully, and walked into Tromsø police headquarters.

The journey from Oslo had been one long delay: a missed seaplane connection at Bodø, a transfer to a Bardufoss-bound turboprop that had required two hours' repair before takeoff, and finally, a slow tortuous drive over the snow-swept road to Tromsø.

Seven hours in all. But he should be grateful: getting anywhere in the northern winter was a miracle.

Now he must deal with the local police. From previous experience he guessed that they would be a little defensive, a touch suspicious, and that some diplomacy and tact would be required on his part.

But he was wrong: the Tromsø police chief was immediately and unreservedly cooperative. This, Thrane soon realized, was because he was in a state of shock. Not only had one of his officers been thrown in the sea but he'd been chucked in by a man who until the previous day had been Tromsø's very own local hero.

But that wasn't all. According to the Security Service's man-on-the-spot, a fellow named Krog, three phone calls had been made from Revøy that morning: one to the same Oslo number as on the previous day; the second to the Novosti Press Agency, asking for Aleksander Savin by name; and the third—God, it seemed incredible—to the Soviet Embassy.

Now it was Thrane's turn to be stupefied. Here was proof, if more proof were needed, that Starheim was with the other side. Yet the whole thing was beyond belief: how could Starheim have deceived him on such a massive scale? How could Thrane have been so wrong about the man?

Yet a part of him still couldn't help thinking: I don't believe it.

Thrane was given a desk, complete with a list of messages. Most of them demanded that he call Ekeland. One, however, was an urgent request to call Lars Sorensen.

He put them all aside. They could wait for a while.

He had only one priority now: find Starheim.

Krog said: "The Fortress approved a special watch on the borders and airports about an hour ago. It should be in effect by now. For backup, a couple of MP units are being called in."

"Yes, but isn't our man at sea?"

"He can't get far in a small boat," Krog pointed out. "Not in this weather anyway. And we've put a guard on his fishing boat, the *Skorpa*."

"What about other people's fishing boats? He might well borrow one of those."

"Around here something like that would be missed pretty quickly. What is definitely missing, though, is his Land-Rover. He might well have hidden it somewhere."

Thrane got up and looked at the wall map, thinking hard. "Okay. Let's ask our friends for some road blocks. One just north of Kåfjord, and one to the south—they'll know where best to put them."

He considered: That would cover the north-south road. There was already a watch at Bardufoss airport and the road over the border to Finland. That left—what? With mountains on one side and sea on the other, not much. Unless you were a magician.

Or Halvard Starheim.

He couldn't help thinking that Starheim was the one man who would be able to find another way. What Thrane had to work out was: which way?

He had a sudden thought and stabbed a finger at Tromsø Island. "We should keep a watch on the Johansen woman's house too. He might well go there." Turning back to Krog, he added: "D'you think our friends will be able to manage all this?"

Krog shrugged.

Thrane said: "Well, we can but find out."

The Land-Rover ground to a halt. Pulling on the hand brake, Rolf said, "You drive," and started to move across.

She realized that she was to be the one to get out and walk around to the other side. As she got down she was met by a sharp blast of icy air which whipped the hood off her head.

She climbed into the other side and, adjusting the seat, started off. The headlights reached out ahead, illuminating the brilliance of the road and the gleam of the mountains, accentuating the blackness of Lyngenfjord as it widened darkly to the left. Suddenly the car swerved and shook, buffeted by a powerful gust. Ragna slowed down.

"Only the wind," said Rolf. "Keep going!" His voice was tight, and a little condescending.

Ragna bristled. Yes—why not drive dangerously? With a bit of luck they might have an accident. She pressed her foot down. The wheels spun then took a grip. The Land-Rover accelerated, jolting over small drifts and bumps of snow. The speed rose to fifty then sixty.

A corner loomed up, unexpectedly tight. Ragna's heart went into her mouth, she turned the wheel, the Land-Rover seemed to hover on the brink of leaving the road, then, with no more than a slight skid, they were around the turn.

She slowed down, her heart beating against her chest. It was no good, she didn't have the nerve to have an accident. She wanted to get back to Krisi and Hal in one piece.

The road swung to the right, into the mouth of Skibotn Valley, and then curved left to cross the frozen river. Ahead was a fork in the road. Straight on, the highway continued along the sides of the fjords for hundreds of miles, all the way around the Arctic coast. Right, however, was the turn for Finland and the long bleak road over the plateau.

The last time she'd come this way had also been in the Land-Rover—but with Hal driving and Rolf in the seat behind—and then they'd gone straight on, heading farther along Lyngenfjord, making for the next valley—Kåfjord—and the installation site. The trip seemed a very long time ago now. But she had a clear memory of Hal at the wheel, silent, thin-lipped, his profile full of unspoken reproach, and her heart squeezed painfully. She had behaved badly toward him. And now she felt as though she had failed him, let him down in some vital way.

She slowed at the junction. Rolf took a long look around, glancing over his shoulder and peering carefully through the windshield. Then he gestured—right.

Ragna turned the wheel, her heart sinking at the thought of the long hard drive ahead.

Hal pulled a glove off with his teeth and put a hand down to the boy's face. The skin was cold, though quite how cold he couldn't tell.

The boat yawed across a wave. Hastily regloving his hand, Hal pulled her back on course. They were heading southward, running down the mainland shore with the wind on the port quarter and going fast —too fast—carrying too much sail, so that *Lillebjørn* surged and yawed about, rolling heavily in the following seas, threatening to broach in the strong gusts. He knew he should reef her down, but he kept putting it off, loath to waste valuable time, reluctant to undertake what might be a tricky maneuver.

He got his bearings. They were approaching the northern tip of Tromsø Island. He reckoned they still had another eight miles to go. At this speed, an hour and a half.

Forever.

The lights on the mainland shore were tantalizingly close. It would be a simple matter to beach the boat and knock on a farmhouse door. The people would be helpful and generous. Unfortunately they'd also be exceedingly curious. They'd want to know how he'd acquired a squashed nose and a bloody face and a blind eye and a permanent headache. They'd insist on fetching help in the form of doctors and policemen.

He considered the alternative—to carry on. It was blowing intensely—a full gale he guessed—and the wind was cold and hard as a sledgehammer. In summer this kind of sailing would have been exhilarating. In February, soaked to the skin, it was a grim matter of survival.

His body temperature was well down, he knew that from the loss of feeling in his feet and hands, the pain in his joints, and the sluggishness of his brain. It crept up on you, a frozen brain. If you weren't careful the thought processes became so slow that the brain couldn't appreciate the danger it was in— and then of course it was too late to do anything about it.

Somehow he must keep alert, and certainly awake. He remembered hearing of a fisherman shipwrecked in midwinter on one of the outer islands who'd rubbed tobacco into his eyes to keep himself awake, and therefore alive. But Hal had no tobacco, and he could think of nothing that would have a similarly irritant effect.

To exercise his brain, he tried to work out yet again why the hell the Tromsø police had come looking for him in that decidedly belligerent fashion. He kept coming up with a single answer.

Thrane. It could only be Thrane. But why? What had happened to make Thrane decide that Hal was an enemy of the people?

Hal had been under the impression that they'd trusted each other. And they had—hadn't they? So much so that they'd made a deal, or so he'd thought.

So what had gone so terribly wrong?

Hal decided: As soon as he got ashore he'd try to contact Thrane on the phone and talk to him. Persuade him to start looking for the right man before it was too late. On the other hand, he mustn't fall into the trap of trusting Thrane too much. Thrane may well try to entice him into another meeting with the Tromsø police, and that had to be avoided at all costs.

He needed Thrane—but he wasn't quite sure if Thrane was still on his side.

Where the hell did that leave him?

Nowhere.

He leaned down to touch the boy again. Was it his imagination, or was the child becoming hypothermic? He hadn't uttered a sound since they'd made their hasty retreat from the jetty. Hal couldn't decide whether he was half frozen to death or deeply asleep.

Without warning, a violent downdraft dropped out of the sky and hit *Lillebjørn* with a heart-stopping roar. The boat leapt forward like a frightened animal. Hal tried desperately to hold her, but her rolling became more violent until she took a wild lurch to leeward, shooting her nose toward the shore, then flipped back and took an equally wild roll the other way, then back to leeward again, this time broaching uncontrollably, pressed hard over, her boom hitting the water with a mighty hiss, her lee gunwale almost under, her mainsail flogging thunderously.

Fighting to bring her back, Hal clambered up the steeply sloping seat, forced his weight up onto the windward gunwale, and pulled the tiller even harder toward him. At last he felt her respond, her nose dipped away, the lights of Tromsø reappeared over the bow, she came upright, the squall died away, and Hal dropped back inboard, shaky with relief.

It took him a moment to realize that Kris's pale face had appeared from under the canvas.

"Kris?" he called above the rushing wind. "Are you all right? Kris?"

A faint yes floated up. The boy settled again, pushing himself farther under the seat. Hal tucked the canvas in around his body.

"We'll go on, shall we, Kris? We'll go home to Tromsø. Would you like that?"

"Yes."

It was decided, then. It was the only place Hal really wanted to go anyway. He had a vision of Ragna watching and waiting for them, a slim figure standing in a lighted window, the room behind suffused with warmth and soft beds and hot food.

Then he had another vision. The house was cold and dark and empty. And it was this picture that stayed firmly in his mind.

Thrane leafed through the transcripts of the calls. There was the one to the safe house in Oslo—a no-reply. Then the one to the Novosti Press Agency, asking for Savin by name. The caller—he still couldn't quite bring himself to think of him as Starheim—hadn't had much luck there. Then the one to the embassy. No joy there either. And he'd left a message saying that "Harri" had called.

It seemed as though his Russian comrades didn't want to know.

No wonder Starheim was trying to run for it.

There'd also been Thrane's own call, which had been answered by the anonymous friend of the old man. That was an odd one. Thrane remembered the voice: very cool, strangely smooth for a fisherman-farmer from such wild parts, and, unless he was mistaken, young. He mused on that as he flicked back through earlier transcripts.

He sat up abruptly. There had also been a call from Sorensen. Good God. He glanced at the date and time. That morning. Early.

He read quickly through the message that Sorensen had dictated to Arne, tried hard to understand what it meant, failed, and read it through again.

Rolf Berg—he knew that name all right. He should. Rolf Berg was a leading journalist on the *Dagens Post.* Left-wing, anti-NATO, usually antigovernment, someone who could always be relied on to stir things up.

More to the point, he was the writer of the piece on the Kaafjord installation.

Now why, oh why, did Starheim want to dig into Berg's wartime activities? They'd worked together on the Lapp story, so presumably Starheim knew and approved of the fellow. So why should he be interested in his past? It was not as if there was anything remarkable about Berg's story: he'd emigrated to the U.S., joined the air force, and got shot down.

And then there was this second person, Blakstad, first name Roar. What did he have to do with anything? The man had disappeared back in 1945, along with one Petter Axelsen.

Disappeared . . . Thrane was interested in people who had disappeared.

Lars Sorensen had been trying to contact Thrane. Was it to do with this? And if so, was it connected to Starheim's activities? He couldn't immediately think how. Yet he noticed that a small knot of excitement had formed in his stomach. You never knew; in this business you never knew at all.

He reached for the telephone and asked for Sorensen's office number. While he was waiting Krog put his head around the door. "Sergeant Christiansen's here."

Thrane looked mystified.

"The swimming policeman," Krog explained.

Thrane nodded and gestured Krog to bring him in.

As Sorensen's number began to ring, a well-built broad-faced police sergeant came stiffly into the room and sat down. He looked pink and well scrubbed, as if he'd just had a hot bath.

Sorensen's office number rang and rang without a reply. Realizing it was well after office hours, Thrane asked Krog to try the lawyer's home number, then turned his attention to Sergeant Christiansen.

"Stop for a moment!"

Ragna put on the brakes and brought the Land-Rover to a halt. Removing her gloves she squeezed her hands together and blew on them hard. The heat, though on full, was barely adequate.

Rolf got out to refuel from the spare cans in the back. They had come about twenty miles from the coast at Skibotn, up through the long valley, slowly gaining height, rising above the tree line, until the towering mountains had diminished and fallen behind and the road had emerged onto the high undulating plateau.

Ragna gave a sudden shiver. Stationary like this, the bleakness really hit you. Wind-whipped snow swirled and danced in the lights, the road, visible only by its marker posts, stretched forward into an endless distance, and she was struck by a sense of appalling emptiness.

Then she remembered the border. They must be very close.

She reached for the map Rolf had been using and tried to read it in the reflection of the dashboard lights.

Rolf opened her door, letting in a blast of frozen air. "I'll drive," he commanded. As Ragna moved across she saw Rolf take something from the back and slide it down beside him.

The rifle.

All Ragna's helpless terrors returned. Not trusting herself to speak, she folded the map away and stared rigidly ahead.

Rolf jammed the car into gear and they moved off.

They came over a slight rise and there before them was a cluster of bright lights.

The border. Rolf had known exactly where it was.

As they drove toward it Rolf shifted tensely. She noticed he was biting his lip, pulling roughly at it with his teeth. He was very nervous. Dread sucked at her stomach.

A heavily muffled figure strolled out of the customs post and stood waiting for them.

Rolf stopped short of the barrier so that the guard had to walk toward them. A second guard came out and, after examining their license plate, went back into the guardhouse. Through the brightly lit window Ragna saw him consulting a clipboard.

Rolf had wound down his window, letting in a blast of cold air. The first guard leaned down and asked for his driver's license. Rolf reached one hand over into the back and felt around in his rucksack. Ragna noticed that he kept his eyes firmly on the guard.

The second guard reemerged and called to the first. The first looked up, hesitated, then strolled back. The two men went into a huddle, glancing in the Land-Rover's direction.

A movement. A third guard appeared from the guardhouse and stationed himself behind the barrier. He had a large automatic weapon in his hand.

Ragna was instantly alert. She'd never heard of three guards on a border post before.

Rolf, too, had noticed. He had stiffened visibly, his expression fierce and livid.

The first guard broke away and came back to Rolf's window. Peering closely at Rolf's face he said: "You'd better come inside. This may take a moment."

The slightest pause, then Rolf said casually: "Okay."

The first guard stood back a little, the second returned to the guardhouse and could be seen lifting a telephone, the third remained behind the barrier, the weapon in his hands. Rolf leaned forward, as if to turn off the idling engine.

Then everything happened at once. Rolf jammed the car into gear, it shot backward, Ragna was thrown forward against the dashboard, hit her head and cried out. The car rocketed backward, weaving wildly from side to side, the engine screaming. Ragna thrust out a hand, grabbed the door handle, and clung on. The first guard was gesticulating and shouting soundlessly. The third guard dropped into a crouch and leveled his gun at them.

Only when she heard a distant *crack! crack!* over the shriek of the engine did Ragna realize they were actually being shot at.

She screamed and ducked her head between her knees.

A sudden swerve knocked her sideways. She was dimly aware of the car skidding to a halt, of Rolf winding viciously on the wheel, of the car shooting forward and accelerating.

They were heading back the way they had come.

Hal picked Kris up in his arms and started toward the house. He felt exceedingly despondent. There was a snow-reflected glow from the porch light at the front, but the rest of the house was in complete darkness, the windows staring blackly across the water.

Hal gripped the child more tightly. Yet again no Mummy.

Trying to think positively, Hal thought of what they *would* find. A telephone, fires waiting to be lit, some food, and, with a bit of luck, Ragna's car. In which case he would drive Kris over to his grandmother's.

He trudged heavily up the side of the house, praying that the front door would be open. Ragna sometimes locked it, though few people bothered around here.

The corner of the house loomed ahead. He strode toward it, nearing the pool of light.

As he stepped out he froze in mid-stride.

On the road, a dark gleam. Metal. He focused his good eye. A car. Parked on the road.

Very slowly, very quietly, Hal retreated, one step at a time, sliding back into the shadows.

He leaned back against the wall.

He should have guessed.

A sound. From the front of the house. Lowering Kris, Hal risked putting his eye to the corner.

A dark figure. At a window. A police officer. Nose to the glass and peering in.

Kris pulled at his sleeve. "Where's Mummy? Where's my mummy?"

Hal shushed him with a rapid shake of the head and a gloved hand over the boy's mouth. The boy's eyes popped with surprise. Hal risked another quick look around the corner.

The officer had stopped looking in the window and was wandering slowly toward the door. He didn't appear to have heard Kris's voice.

The officer stopped under the porch and rapped loudly on the front door. As he waited he suddenly glanced in Hal's direction.

Hal jerked his head back. The silence stretched out.

Hal considered walking straight out and trying to explain. Perhaps the man would listen.

Then again, perhaps he wouldn't.

He couldn't risk it.

Footsteps crunched on crisp snow. Distinctly at first, then growing fainter.

Hal dared another look. The officer was walking away down the path toward the car. A door slammed. Hal waited. The car started up, its engine idling. The engine note remained low. Then Hal realized: The car wasn't going anywhere. They were merely keeping warm while they watched and waited. For him.

He thought longingly of the garage on the other side of the house and Ragna's car, which was very probably inside.

He put his head down to Kris's ear and whispered: "We've got to play hide and seek for a minute. Then we'll go to Granny's." Time for the unpalatable truth. "Mummy's not here, you see."

The boy was getting used to bad news. His face showed nothing.

Keeping to the shadows, Hal made his way back down the garden and helped Kris over the wattle fence into the next property. Five minutes later the two of them emerged onto the road some three hundred yards beyond the watching car.

Ignoring his throbbing head, Hal hitched the boy onto his back and set off at a brisk walk. It was twenty minutes to Sigrid Johansen's house, maybe more.

He was painfully aware that time was racing away, time that Rolf would be using to the fullest.

Ragna clung to the door handle as the Land-Rover tore back toward Skibotn at breathtaking speed.

This was what bad dreams were made of, except that in this nightmare she wasn't allowed to wake up. She'd had a wild hope that the Land-Rover would skid and turn over, but it stayed firmly upright. She'd prayed that they would run out of gas. But between wild lurches of the vehicle she'd managed to get a look at the faintly illuminated gauge and seen that it was still half full.

Approaching the junction at Skibotn she thought Rolf might slow down, but, the road having fewer drifts, he merely accelerated. And turned right.

To the north.

Ragna's heart sank still further. Away from Tromsø. She couldn't bear it.

In rising panic she considered escape—throwing open the door and rolling out—but at this speed the snowbank at the roadside would be harder than concrete. Perhaps if she begged—pleaded—he'd stop and let her out. She'd promise anything if she thought it'd do some good.

Then it occurred to her: perhaps if she made a nuisance of herself he'd stop and throw her out anyway.

She examined the idea: she'd have to make a really terrible nuisance of herself if it was to have any chance of working. It took a long time for her to screw up her courage. The road had turned right on its ten-mile detour into the deep indentation of Kåfjord before she blurted: "Let me out!"

He flicked a glance at her and, without replying, turned his attention back to the road.

She raised her voice. "Just stop and let me out!"

"Shut up, Ragna. I need you." His profile was implacable in the reflection of the lights.

"I'll scream! I'll scream and shout and scratch your face and kick and yell until you let me out!"

He didn't answer.

She'd never screamed in her life—never really screamed. She didn't know if she could do it. But she'd damn well try. She filled her lungs and opened her mouth.

Then out of the corner of her eye she saw Rolf move, so quickly that the scream died on her lips, and in one reflex action she pushed herself against the door.

But he wasn't reaching for her at all—he was diving for the dashboard. She realized: He'd switched off the lights. The road ahead had disappeared, swallowed up into the surrounding snow.

"What—"

He kept looking out his side window. Then she understood. He had seen other lights—a cluster of them. On the far side of the gash of black water that was Kåfjord. Beams of light, stationary.

A group of parked cars?

Her spirits leapt. The police! The border guards must have alerted the authorities. And the police had blocked the road! No need to scream now.

As she watched, a pair of lights detached themselves from the cluster and began to move along the opposite shore. She could see both the rear and front lights of the vehicle as it ran parallel to them.

Perhaps this too was a police car. Yes—why not? In which case they would meet it on the road—they couldn't avoid meeting it—for both of them were converging on the top of the fjord. She allowed herself to hope.

Then the doubts came. Why, if this car could so easily be a police car, was Rolf driving like a maniac toward it?

The Land-Rover gave an almighty bump. Ragna almost hit the roof. She cried out. Rolf swerved to avoid something. The car seemed to be off the road—there was a terrible jolting and juddering—Rolf fought the wheel, then they were on a smoother surface again.

Clinging on tightly, bracing herself for the crash that might come at any moment, she tried closing her eyes, but that only made her sick. Looking ahead was no better. Road markers loomed up and whooshed past with terrifying speed. Desperate, she finally fastened her eyes on the headlights across the black water.

The beam of gold was moving steadily along the steep-sided northern shore. But slowly, so slowly. Barely keeping pace.

Rolf was still racing, hunched forward over the wheel, peering intently through the windshield.

Yet the two cars must still meet.

Or must they?

Suddenly Ragna realized why Rolf was racing.

He was racing for a prize. The prize was the road at the

head of the fjord. The turn that led up the valley and into the mountains, past the installation site and up to the plateau. A road that led nowhere, a road no one would bother to search—the perfect place to hide.

In her mind Ragna egged the distant car on, willed it forward, compelled the driver to look across the expanse of water and see the unlit vehicle racing him to the top of the fjord.

But after a time it was clear that the lights were slowly, inexorably falling behind.

Rolf was winning.

As the water narrowed between the converging mountains, and the head of the fjord drew nearer, her hopes died. Even the night glow seemed to have intensified, to make the road markers more visible. Rolf wouldn't make a mistake now.

As they neared the head of the fjord the road curved into the valley mouth. The Land-Rover went into the bend fast, lurched and skidded, and for a moment Ragna thought they'd crash after all. But Rolf fought the wheel, the vehicle swerved from side to side and straightened up; he regained control. Ragna suppressed her disappointment.

They came to the frozen river that emptied out of the valley; they flew over the bridge. There, just ahead, was the turn.

Ragna looked for the headlights on the northern shore. They were closer—but not close enough.

She resigned herself: there was no chance now.

Rolf slowed a little, turned up the valley road, and accelerated again. The Land-Rover bumped noisily as it hit roughly compacted snow.

Aslak's house was half a mile along on the left. Ragna stared longingly toward the golden ornamental lights hanging in its uncurtained windows, hoping against hope that Aslak might be looking out.

They swept past. Twisting, she peered back through the plastic rear window, but the house was lost in the dense snow cloud whirled up by the wheels.

She looked ahead. Ahead was nothing but darkness.

To her disgust, she began to cry.

Aslak Hetta pressed his nose to the window. He was peering out because he always peered out whenever he heard something on the road. It was his business to know what went on in Kåfjord Valley. Hunters out of season, reindeer poachers, officials snooping: you never knew.

This time his curiosity was fully roused.

No lights. Who was mad enough to drive around with no lights?

And the vehicle—a Land-Rover. Just like Hal's. He was sure of it: he'd seen its silhouette against the snow; and the lights of the house had for a moment reflected on its high gray metal sides. Yet Hal wouldn't drive past without stopping to see him—it was inconceivable.

Much more worrying, what possible reason could Hal have for wanting to go up into the valley on a night like this? It was freezing, the coldest night for years. No one in their right mind was out.

Could it have been someone else? He dismissed the idea: a few people lived higher up the valley, but none of them had a car. And no one else in the entire area had a Land-Rover.

Hal. It had to be.

He couldn't understand it.

After a few minutes' thought, he pulled on an anorak, snow boots, gloves, and hat, and, calling to his mother, went out.

33

The police chief admitted: "Nothing, I'm afraid." He shifted in his seat and looked uncomfortable and faintly resentful, as if the whole business had been invented by Thrane to make his life difficult.

"So he's disappeared?" Thrane tried to sound calm.

"We sent a car up from the south. And one down from the road block at Kåfjord." The police chief shrugged. "No sign."

"But a Land-Rover can't disappear."

"No. Either he stopped somewhere or—"

"Yes?"

"We missed him."

There wasn't a lot one could say to that. Getting up, Thrane said as pleasantly as possible: "Thank you. I'd be grateful if you'd keep me informed."

He found Krog outside their makeshift office. Krog nodded toward the half-open door of an adjoining interview room and raised his eyebrows doubtfully. "He says he's got more."

Thrane strode in. The swimming sergeant sat hunched over a sheet of paper, scribbling hard. Seeing Thrane, he said earnestly: "I think I've got it now." He gathered himself to talk at some length. Thrane sighed inwardly—the sergeant was not the most succinct of speakers. "I definitely remember," the sergeant began, "that he seemed to think I must have heard from this Ragna Johansen. Then, when I said I hadn't, he talked about having to look for a missing woman. I think that maybe"—he paused to lay proper stress on his words—"maybe he was talking of the same person. I mean, this Ragna Johansen. Meaning—she was the missing woman."

"Yes, possibly," Thrane cut in restlessly. From the corner of his eye he saw Krog signaling from the door.

"And he definitely said that something terrible had happened, though he gave no indication of what it might be—"

"Quite." Thrane looked longingly toward the door. Krog had disappeared. "Sergeant, I have to go now. Please—do continue to write it all down. It's most useful." He turned rapidly away.

"One thing—" The sergeant jumped to his feet and pursued him into the corridor.

Thrane paused impatiently. "Yes?"

The sergeant hesitated awkwardly, eager to please yet rather sheepish, as if he'd been caught napping. "Er, he seemed to have hurt himself."

Thrane stared. "What?"

"It's hard to be sure. It was so dark. I only had a torch . . ."

"Yes?"

"Well, his face seemed very swollen up . . . Around the nose and eyes. Now, I wouldn't normally have mentioned it—I mean I don't actually know Starheim, except from photographs and you can never tell from those, can you? And it was so dark, of course—and for all I knew he always looked that . . . Except, well, what makes me think that he was hurt as opposed to just looking odd was his nose—it was sort of bent. And his eyes seemed a bit swollen. And there were streaks. Down one side of his face. At the time I thought it was just dirt, you know. But now I come to think about it, well, maybe it was blood." He put a hand to his head. "Coming from somewhere here."

There was an electric pause.

Thrane tried to make sense of it, tried to place it in the already muddled scheme of things, but failed. It was just another piece that didn't fit. A terrible event. A missing person—presumably Ragna Johansen. And now this.

Violence on Revøy? A struggle? But who with? With Ragna Johansen? A lovers' tiff? Hardly. Someone like Starheim didn't get hurt easily, and never, surely, by a woman. But if not her, then who?

He felt a mixture of excitement and despair. All these things meant something—he *felt* it, he *knew* it. Vital threads there, waiting to be grasped and drawn together. Yet maddeningly elusive.

Krog, hovering, touched his arm and gestured him into the privacy of the office. "I've just spoken to the border guard," he said. "There were *two* people in the Land-Rover! One was a woman."

Ragna Johansen. "And the man? Was it Starheim?"

Krog's eyes betrayed his excitement. "The guard didn't think so. He said he'd have recognized him. No, this man was fair-haired. Very blond. He was positive about that."

Thrane thought: Of course. That was how Starheim had gotten the Land-Rover up to the border so fast. It hadn't been him at all.

Thrane sat at the desk and plunged his head into his hands.

An idea burst into his mind. For a moment he put it to one side and looked at other possibilities—he looked at the love angle, the idea of Fair Hair and Hal being in a fight over Ragna. But then why the escape from the border guards? No, it made no sense. Fair Hair had to be involved in something else—perhaps he was an activist, an associate of Ragna's who wanted to keep the source of the Delta story secret. Perhaps—

He kept coming back to the single burning idea that he'd first leapt at. He turned it over, examined it from every angle, let it rest a moment, worried at it again.

It was possible.

A direct link to Sonja's lover. Perhaps even—

No, that would be too much to hope for. Or would it?

He sat up suddenly and barked at the waiting Krog: "Did we try Sorensen again?"

Krog made a face that said the matter had temporarily slipped his mind, and reached for the phone.

As Krog made the connection Thrane flipped quickly back through the transcripts of the calls from Revøy. The memory of a cool voice saying "No, this is a friend of his" froze in his mind.

He let an unjustified excitement grip him.

When Sorensen came on the line, Thrane said without preamble: "Tell me what you were digging up for Starheim. And tell me why."

He listened carefully, taking notes. He felt a sudden stab of interest. "You mean—Blakstad and Berg are probably the same man?"

Sorensen started to go through all the suppositions and maybes and who-can-tells, but there was no doubt about what he was saying. Yes. In which case—

He suddenly realized what else Sorensen was saying. He interrupted: "You've *met* Berg?"

Sorensen affirmed it. Then, in an agony of suspense, Thrane asked: "Tell me, Sorensen—what exactly does he looks like?"

But he knew. Even before Sorensen described the thick blond hair, the sharp blue eyes, the looks, Thrane knew.

He rang off in a state of euphoria, and banged his fist down on the desk, shouting aloud: "Got you! Got you, you bastard!"

Then he remembered that the only thing he'd actually gotten was his identity.

"Krog! Find out if anyone knows where Rolf Berg is. Find out if he's come up here recently. Find out if he could possibly be here now."

In furious self-reproach, he added: "We've been fools, Krog. Complete fools. We've been after the wrong bloody man!"

Sigrid Johansen's house stood on a quiet road of neat well-spaced houses in a birchwood near the Tromsø museum. Hal paused well short of it and took a good look, which involved turning his good eye toward the subject and squinting hard.

No police car. Not in the road at least.

Hitching Kris higher on his back he continued, straining for sounds of approaching cars. The high-pitched ringing in his right ear was back—it seemed to get worse with exercise—but he could make out the sound of the wind harrying at the snow and moaning in the trees above, and the soft *pluff!* of some snow sliding from a roof onto a path below, and the rasp of his own breath. No car engines.

But getting closer, he saw there *was* a car. An empty car parked at the side of the house.

He stared hard, not quite believing his luck. He strode forward, anxious to get a better look—but there was no doubt: the car was Ragna's. For a wild moment he thought that

Ragna might be there in the house, that she had recently arrived, but then he realized the car had been parked for some time: its windows and roof were white with frost.

He hurried the last few yards up the path and rapped impatiently on the door.

He heard a sound from inside: a door opening, footsteps. Fru Johansen opened the door and, taking one look at the two of them, clamped a hand over her mouth and let out a loud cry of horror.

Hal stepped quickly past her. "Where's Ragna? Have you heard from her?"

Sigrid Johansen shook her head, still staring over the firmly clamped hand.

"You haven't seen her?"

Another shake of the head.

Hal absorbed his disappointment. It had been too much to hope for.

Sigrid Johansen started to moan, "Oh, dear! Oh, *dear*!"

The woman was overreacting; Hal did wish she wouldn't. But then as he swung Kris off his back and down onto the floor he glanced up into a mirror. Then he understood. Through his fuzzy monocular vision he saw a strange, oddly familiar face that didn't seem to belong to him at all.

Eyes puffed up like a boxer's, a bloody swollen nose, and a deep angry groove across his cheek which didn't look as though it were going to heal too well.

He dropped his eyes and turned away. It was only a face.

Sigrid, having recovered herself, was clucking over Kris, removing his anorak, rubbing his hands.

Hal carried the silent child into a bedroom, laid him gently on a bed, and, removing his shoes, examined his feet and hands for signs of cold damage. The toes and fingers were cold but gratifyingly pink. Sigrid brought a mug of warm cocoa and, when the child had downed it, they dressed him in pajamas and covered him with a down comforter. The child snuggled down under the thick quilt and gave a small sigh.

His grandmother said: "I'll get him something to eat, poor love."

"Too late," Hal murmured. The child's eyes had closed; he was almost asleep.

Hal watched him for a while, leaning down to put his fingers against the smooth velvety cheek, touching the fingers that protruded from under the quilt, wanting to be certain the warmth was slowly returning to his body. When he was satisfied, he returned to the hall.

Sigrid was hovering, itching to question him.

Hal said abruptly: "I can't explain." And thought: I'm always saying that nowadays.

"At least let me bathe your face," she said, wringing her hands.

He brushed the idea aside with a gesture. "No, I've got to—"

He thought: What—phone? Phone Thrane?

Yes.

He went to the telephone and sank onto a chair. He was feeling unsteady and slightly sick and far too hot. It was the sudden almost unhealthy warmth of the house. He pulled off his anorak and boots and exercised his toes. His body, having been aching with damp and cold, was now clammy with half-dried sea water.

To make matters worse his head was aching again, with a vicious viselike pain. Gingerly he ran his fingers over the swelling on his temple, then around to the other side of his head, to the lump behind his ear. Feeling it, he wasn't surprised it had knocked the hell out of his eye as well as his head.

He pulled himself together. Where was he? Yes—Thrane.

As he lifted the phone Sigrid reappeared, and before he could protest she stuck a warm cloth against his cheek and, tut-tutting in mild admonition, started to bathe the wound. "This needs proper attention," she announced, dabbing cautiously. "You must see a doctor. Before anything else. Do you hear me?"

"Can't."

"But you *must*." She spoke sternly in the tone of a woman used to men's childish ways.

The operator wasn't answering. Hal muttered angrily: "Come on! Come on!"

Sigrid Johansen tut-tutted again. "You don't change. Jan wasn't any better. Always the same. Always in trouble. Like the time the two of you went climbing and came back covered in cuts and bruises from head to toe." She sighed harshly. "You never change. I guessed something was wrong when Aslak called. I got a feeling. And I should know by now—I'm never wrong."

"Aslak?" Hal gently pushed her hand away.

"He called. Not long ago. He thought he'd seen you."

Abandoning the telephone, Hal sat up. "What do you mean?"

"He saw your car. Or he thought it was your car. The Land-Rover. Going up Kåfjord Valley. In the dark. Of course it couldn't have been you. But I knew all the same: Something was wrong."

He gripped her arm. "What else did he say?"

"I—" She swallowed, intimidated by the intensity of his interest. "Well—only that he had gone specially to a neighbor's house to telephone because he thought it was so strange. Now what *was* it that was so strange? Yes—that you hadn't stopped. And . . . there was something else." She shook her head with the effort of remembering. "Ah, yes. He said the car had no lights on. He was anxious to check with you, but he couldn't get through to Revøy. And you weren't at Ragna's. So—he called me."

Hal reached for his anorak and boots and started to haul them on again.

She cried: "Where are you going?"

"Look after Kris, won't you? When he wakes up he'll be worried about his mother."

"Where is Ragna?"

He swept up some keys from the table. "Are these her car keys?"

"Yes, but—"

Hal made for the door.

"Where *is* Ragna?"

He called over his shoulder. "I don't know."

Her voice came floating after him. "But Aslak wasn't sure it was your car! He couldn't see . . ."

Then she saved her breath. Hal was already running to Ragna's car and pulling open the door.

Even with the headlights full on it was hard to follow the road. Berg craned forward, searching for the marker posts on either side. Though the word *post* was too generous for the thin birch saplings sticking out of the snow.

They were high, well above the tree line and still climbing. As they'd gotten higher the wind had become stronger until now it was blasting straight at them, driving the snow in a moving carpet across their path. The whole surface was shifting like sand over a desert, creeping and whirling and eddying first one way then the other, so that Berg had nothing to fix his eyes on. Increasingly he was having to blink and refocus to make sure his eyes weren't playing tricks on him.

But he wasn't worried: he hadn't missed the road yet.

The engine droned on, solid and reliable. Good old Hal. Only Hal would have the perfect vehicle for the job, and beautifully maintained; only Hal would have a car with plenty of spare fuel, two powerful hand torches, a number of large-scale maps, a compass on the dashboard, and a spare on the shelf.

Even as he thought it the engine strained, the Land-Rover slowed, and he felt a lurch of alarm.

His eyes flipped to the fuel gauge. All right. Yet the car was moving sluggishly. It seemed to be gliding over a sea of snow, a sea that was slowly rising to engulf them. He broke into a cold sweat. Beside him he saw Ragna stiffen and reach for the handgrip.

There wasn't a road marker in sight.

He halted and, opening the window, peered out. Needle-sharp snow stung his face. He drew back and closed the window. Grabbing the torches he handed one to Ragna. "Look for a marker!"

He shone his torch through the window, sweeping it back and forth.

Ragna's voice said dully: "There."

He leaned over and peered out through her window. A sapling showed in her torch beam. "Good girl!"

They'd left the road, that was all.

Leaning down to the transmission casing, he engaged the four-wheel drive and, putting the car into gear, slowly let out the clutch. The engine whined, the wheels bit, the car began to move. Then the wheels spun and they stopped.

He eased off the power and tried again. He tried reverse,

hen forward, then reverse. He bit back bitter rage. The car was digging itself deeper and deeper into whatever constrained it.

"Goddamn!" He hit the wheel with his fist.

He calmed himself and tried the door. It would barely open. There was snow up to the sill. They were in a deep drift.

Closing the door he thrust an open hand toward Ragna. 'The map," he demanded.

She didn't respond; she'd been silent for some time, ever since her last threat to make his life impossible unless he let her out. She was no fool: she'd realized it was pointless to make those sorts of demands when there was quite simply nowhere to go.

Finally she reached for the map and passed it over.

"And find something for us to eat, will you?"

Leaving the engine idling and the heater full on, he settled down with a torch. They had passed the offshoot to the mining road and the installation site some half an hour ago. At roughly fifteen miles an hour, that must put them very near to the top of the navigable track.

So—getting stuck had probably lost them very little.

The top of the track ran along the edge of a frozen lake and ended at a hut. A hut that would be used by Lapps, summer trekkers, and occasional hunters—but used very rarely, he suspected, and certainly not at this time of year, even by Lapps.

The hut would be uninhabited but not, he hoped, empty of fuel. Huts were so few and so isolated that the Lapps usually left a supply of wood—sometimes even food—in them in case they should get stranded.

The hut could be no more than a mile away, probably less. And from the hut it was only six miles to the border.

Ragna had unwrapped some food and was halfheartedly tearing at a piece of bread with her teeth.

Berg reached into her lap and found bread and a hunk of cheese. He chewed on them hungrily.

He said: "There's a hut up ahead. It's not far."

She didn't answer. He looked across and realized she was crying silently.

Berg was disappointed in her; he thought she had mor guts than this. "Ragna," he said reasonably, "it's not far to th border. It's only seven miles."

"But there's nothing on the other side! *Nothing!*"

"Not true," he said patiently. "Look." He flicked the torc onto the map again. "There's another hut over the border Then a third. Then we can get back onto the main road an get a lift. Simple."

"But it's miles. Days. And in this—we'll freeze to death."

"It's only thirty miles. And I don't think we'll freeze. We'v got all the gear. And the huts'll have food. Though it'll proba bly be dried reindeer meat."

"It's impossible. We'll never make it." Her voice broke.

"There's just a bit of wind, that's all."

She turned and laid her hand on his arm, her eyes larg and tearful in the dim glow of the lights. "Why do I have t come too? Just tell me why."

He thought: You have to come because I can't bear to b alone. He said aloud: "Because you've been over this trail. Yo know it."

She turned away in exasperation. "That was in spring When it was warm. And light."

"You'll recognize the trail once you see it."

"But I won't, I won't! And this weather—I've never bee out in anything like this. I don't know what to do!"

"You're worrying too much. I've been on the plateau before And in worse conditions than this." He wasn't sure about th worse conditions, but since nothing could be as bad as bein short of food and fuel and proper clothing, it didn't seem par ticularly relevant. Besides, nothing was going to prevent hin from getting over that border. The border was a new life i America . . . or maybe Australia—he hadn't thought of tha

Ragna said in a rough low voice: "Rolf. Can you—will you— tell me—about—" With an effort she finally got it out. "Kris Is he really all right?"

The reminder was unwelcome. Berg felt a twinge of some thing approaching guilt. If things had gone to plan the chil would have been released by now. As it was Berg wouldn't b able to get near a phone for at least twenty-four hours, mayb more.

But he'd left the child in the kitchen, hadn't he? There was food, water, wood for the stove. He gave Ragna a brief reassuring smile. "Of course he's all right."

Ragna closed her eyes with relief. Then she asked: "And the others?"

"I have to admit I sent them off on a wild-goose chase. So they'll have gotten rather cross and tired. But otherwise fine, I should think."

She dropped her head back on the seat and sighed audibly. After a while she asked dully: "I suppose you won't tell me why on earth you have to get over the border."

"Come on," he said, ignoring the question. "We've got a lot of gear to sort out."

"If you've done anything wrong the Finns'll hand you back."

"Ah. That's where you're mistaken. They won't, you see. Come on, let's start on this gear."

When it was done, when they had packed all they could reasonably carry into their rucksacks, Berg leaned forward and turned off the engine, then the lights. The darkness enveloped them.

For a moment they were both still, gripped by the insistent rat-tatting of hard-grained snow blasting against the windshield.

Beyond, Berg heard another sound, a sound that rose and fell and rose again: the roar, the hiss, the ebbing fall of the wind as it tore unchecked across the wilderness. Berg heard it and remembered: It was the loneliest sound in the world.

Anyone else and Aslak might have suggested waiting for the weather. But not Hal. He wasn't someone you offered advice to, not even when he was planning to go up onto the plateau in the midst of a howling winter night; not even when he was injured.

So Aslak methodically assembled a reindeer-skin jacket, leggings, woolen undergarments, goggles, gloves, and a rucksack. Hal was a lot taller than Aslak, but a bit of improvisation and a quick visit by Aslak's mother to a neighbor down the road—a Norwegian and therefore tall—and Hal had the overtrousers he lacked.

Boots were a problem though. All too small, and the neighbor wouldn't part with his. It was decided that Hal should keep his existing boots for skiing, damp though they were and carry a soft pair of oversized *finnesko* with a sedge-grass lining to warm his feet during the stopovers. Aslak's wife replaced his damp socks with dry woolen ones that more or less fit after some energetic stretching.

Aslak also lent Hal his best sheath knife—a mountain Lapp's proudest possession; a compass—a curiosity he never himself used; and a newly acquired rifle, which in truth he disliked anyway.

He thought it impolite to comment on the handgun that Hal had tucked inside his belt.

Aslak had no map to offer, but Hal found a rudimentary map in Ragna's car, and the two men inspected it, examining the high terrain that spread out from the head of the valley marking the huts such as they were, and examining trails, of which there were only two.

There were six pairs of skis to choose from. Aslak offered Hal his best pair and adjusted the bindings for him. His mother packed a mixture of fresh, dried, and preserved food and a bottle of fresh water. She also stung Hal's wounds with strong disinfectant and bound his head tightly in a bandage.

Hal spent the last fifteen minutes writing a letter. Aslak noticed how low he bent over the paper, and how he screwed up his eyes and paused frequently to rub his forehead.

Finally Hal folded the paper and addressed it.

"This needs to go to the police, Aslak. Give me a couple of hours then go and telephone from next door and say you have a message from me. They'll turn up pretty quick." He stood up and snorted with grim amusement. "They're looking for *me*, Aslak!"

Aslak blinked. This was hard to believe. It occurred to him that Hal might be affected by the bump on his head. He said gravely: "You shouldn't go alone. You're not well."

"Just deliver the letter, Aslak."

"I should go with you," Aslak repeated.

Hal tapped the letter. "It's more important that you get this to the police so that they can mount a watch on the Finnish side. Just in case I miss them, Aslak. D'you see?"

Aslak didn't see at all. Hal's earlier explanation had been

ess than clear. He persisted: "When I've delivered it I'll come after you."

Hal shook his head. "You'll never track me in the drift, Aslak. It'd be hopeless . . ." He considered again and finally conceded: "All right. Two days, Aslak. Come for me after two days."

Berg had that sick feeling he always got when things went wrong.

They had lost the track. And visibility was dropping all the time.

It had been all right in the beginning when the wind was just blowing—the driving snow had frequently subsided into flurries that scurried idly around his feet, so that once his eyes had become accustomed to the faint light he'd been able to see a short way ahead and pick out the next marker.

He'd used a system. He'd leave Ragna at a marker and, using the compass as a guide and the wind direction as a double check, he'd ski forward until he found the next marker. Then he'd signal with his torch and wait for Ragna to catch up. That way they never lost the track.

But after a time the wind didn't just blow, it blasted out of the air, and everything disappeared—snow, sky, dimension. Grains of snow bombarded his goggles and fought their way into his hood and up his nose; he could hardly see; sometimes he could hardly breathe.

And the markers had disappeared.

One lull, another . . . But then there were no more lulls, and the gusts blended into one continuous gust, and the wind rose from a hiss to a shriek, and the swirling whiteness closed in on him, impenetrable as a wall.

He stopped and turned his back to the wind. He shone the torch on the compass. Which way had he been going? Due east? No, slightly south of east. He worked out the reciprocal and began to plod back toward the place where Ragna should be.

How far had he come from the last marker? Twenty yards? Fifty? He flashed his torch regularly. The beam leapt back at him, deflected by a vortex of whiteness.

No answering flicker came out of the darkness.

The sick feeling got worse.

He peered at the compass again to check his bearing an
went a bit farther. He shouted. And again. Louder an
louder, until he heard himself scream her name.

The ghastly wind screamed silently back at him.

He stopped and shouted again, forcing all his rage into th
cry. Panting, he waited, waited for something—anything.

Underneath the shrieking wind was absolute silence.

He found it impossible to grasp the fact that he might wa
and wait forever and there would never be an answering cry

He shouted again: *"Ragna!"*

The wind pulled the sound from his lips and sucked it int
the darkness.

34

She caught a glimpse of it as the weather closed in. It was no more than a dark smudge, a suggestion of shape against the snow. Ahead and to the left.

Now the smudge had disappeared. Everything had disappeared in the swirling murk. Including Rolf.

So she waited, because it seemed the only thing she could do.

At first the cold was almost bearable, then it became painful; finally it was paralyzing. She stood with her back to the wind, shoulders hunched, not moving, not able to move as the cold held her in a viselike grip. She felt as if she were slowly freezing to death. And part of her thought: I am.

With enormous effort she twisted her head around and, screwing her eyes up against the sand-blasting snow, tried to peer into the darkness. But it was impossible; Rolf might be shining his torch two yards away and she'd never see it.

She felt her mind seizing up. She had the urge to sit down—her rucksack felt incredibly heavy—but even her slow-moving brain knew that it would be disastrous; she might never get up again.

A gust buffeted her. She swayed, almost overbalanced from her skis, and came to with a start. She'd been half-asleep. Whatever happened, she mustn't close her eyes.

But Hal did sleep in the open—how? He dug himself a snow cave, she remembered, and her heart sank. She hadn't the first idea of how to make one. The job probably required a shovel, and that she certainly didn't have.

She had to decide: stay or move.

If she stayed much longer she'd be unable to move even if she wanted to. And what was the point anyway? Rolf had been gone a long time, and she had the feeling he wasn't coming back.

She had no choice, then: She must move. But where to? Back to the Land-Rover? Hopeless: she'd never find the track; she'd get lost in minutes.

Toward the dark shadow, then? In her mind the vague amorphous blotch had grown into something solid and three-dimensional: a hut. She came to her decision: she would try for the hut.

Forbidding herself to move until she had a clear idea of where she was going, she tried to picture the hut's position in her mind. How far away had the thing been? She wasn't very good at distance. Thirty yards? And in which direction? Off to the left at about forty-five degrees, she seemed to remember. But at forty-five degrees to what—the wind? Or the track?

Forget the track—she couldn't even see it.

Clinging to the image of the hut—she'd persuaded herself it definitely was a hut—she turned stiffly into the wind, head bent forward, hand shielding her eyes, trying to get her bearings. She turned until the wind hit the side of her hood at roughly the right angle, then set off, plodding one ski heavily in front of the other.

She couldn't see much, and soon gave up trying, keeping her head bent well over, her eyes half-closed against the rush of icy air. Her body was stiff and unresponsive; she had to lean hard on her poles and goad her legs into action.

Her skis slithered and slipped on hard crust. Then she hit uneven ground: one ski dipped and met an obstruction. A hummock—maybe. She climbed over the hump, hit soft snow, climbed out of that, met more hummocks.

The rough ground continued for some time. She imagined it was frozen bogland on the shores of the lake. She vaguely remembered the lake from the trek with Jan all those years ago. She even had a distant memory of a hut, though she couldn't remember exactly where it had been. On the shore of the lake? Or set back?

She stopped abruptly. How far had she come? She hadn't been calculating. She should have counted her strides or something. She recalled the map and tried to work out how far she might have come.

Doggedly she set off again. After some time she realized the snow was smooth under her skis. Fumbling in her pocket she managed to find the torch. Its light was very dim. Crouching, she brushed at the snow with her glove until she got through to the surface beneath. It was rock-hard. Ice.

Was it the lake?

She carried on a short way. The surface was still smooth. Crouching, she dug again. Still rock-hard. She tried to clear a larger space but it instantly silted with drift snow. Using both hands she cleared it again and quickly rubbed her glove over the surface. Slippery.

The lake.

She had an image of a vast boundless lake on which it was possible to become *really* lost.

Quickly, not thinking about angles and distances, she turned around until she had the wind on the other cheek, then headed straight back to the shore.

After a while the ground rose abruptly in front of her—the shore. She climbed up with relief. The ground was uneven again, though not so rough as before.

She stopped. Where now? Right? Left? Was she back in the same place or farther up the shore? She didn't know.

The wind bullied and chivied at her mercilessly. Her nose, her cheeks, felt dead. She attempted to pull her headwarmer higher over her face, but inside its heavy glove her hand was stiff as wood. She felt a moment of despair. All she'd achieved was to get herself twice as cold and twice as lost as before. Leaving the track had been a terrible mistake. Rolf had probably found the hut, gone back to collect her, and, finding her gone, given up.

She cried a little. The tears froze on her lashes.

Then, because there was nothing else to do, she set off again, blundering about wildly, becoming more and more disoriented. The wind seemed to come from one way then the other, as if it were circling. Then she realized: *She* was circling.

Savagely she pulled herself together.

Stop. Start again. Try to make zigzags in one direction—

downwind; try to cover the ground methodically, working your way along between lake and track.

Being methodical made her feel better. It concentrated her mind and stopped her from thinking about the cold in her feet and hands, and the fear in her heart.

Her ski hit an obstruction. A hummock probably. She tried to lift the ski over, but however high she lifted it, it wasn't high enough. She kicked out in sudden frustration. The ski hit something and bounced off. She raised her head and peered at the obstruction, whatever it was.

A great shadow loomed in front of her. She stared, blinking hard. She reached out. She patted the blackness with her gloved hand. Solid. Flat.

She pressed both hands against it, giggling with astonishment.

It was the hut! *The hut!*

Leaning hard against the rough wood to make sure it didn't go away, feeling a hysterical relief, she worked her way along the wall, around the corner, on to the next corner, until finally she found the door.

She pushed the latch. It wouldn't move. Locked? She tried again. It yielded with a snap; it had been frozen. She pulled at the door; it, too, was stiff. She threw her weight into it, the door flew open, and she almost fell off her skis.

She gave a ragged laugh, halfway to a sob, and said aloud: "Dear God—thank you!"

She leaned down to loosen her bindings and stiffened.

A sound. A faint cry carried by the wind and whipped away. A voice, calling what might have been her name.

She listened hard. The sound came again. Pulling down her headwarmer she took a deep breath, opened her mouth—and faltered, the shout unspoken.

Why should she call to him?

She could leave him out there—leave him to freeze.

The idea gave her a glorious feeling of power, a savage satisfaction.

The sound came again, faint but with a shrill note to it, almost like a cry for help. She listened coolly. The cry sounded again and again. She stepped out of her skis and, going into the hut, slammed the door behind her. She stood in the pitch darkness, eyes closed, and pushed the sounds out of her mind.

They seemed to float on the air. She started to move, her boots making gratifyingly loud sounds on the wooden floor; she felt for the torch in her pocket, shone it around the dark walls. But the echoes of the voice lingered and intensified. And she knew that however hard she tried, they would never go away.

With weary resignation, she reopened the door and called into the darkness.

The car came to a halt.

Hal took it calmly. It was a miracle that the thing had gotten this far; it wasn't designed for mountain roads. But then a snow tractor wouldn't have been much good either. Conditions had deteriorated rapidly, visibility was almost zero, and there was bad drifting.

He would have to wait the storm out.

He examined the car mileage and put a mental mark on the map. He reckoned he was about three miles short of the end of the track.

Pulling on his anorak he got out and flashed a torch on the snow immediately in front of the car. The surface shifted and oscillated around his feet. If there had been tire tracks they had long gone.

Without straying too far from the car headlights he went forward, sweeping the torch back and forth. At one point he bent down and examined what might have been a faint furrow. Inconclusive.

He returned to the car.

He had a choice: either to spend the night in the car, which, metal box that it was, would soon be reduced by the wind to the temperature of a deep freeze, or to make himself a shelter in the lee of the car, where, despite the wind, he should be warmer.

The inside of the car won, mainly because the prospect of building a proper shelter was too wearing—never an excuse he'd allowed himself before—but he was desperately tired and the urge to sleep was overwhelming. However, he did force himself to make hot soup on the miniature pressure stove, and to eat two large sandwiches.

He prepared to sleep. He put his damp boots into his sleeping bag in the hope that his body heat might dry them out a little. He opened a downwind window for ventilation. Then, removing his outer clothing, he climbed into his sleeping bag and lay down on the backseat, pulling the hood of the bag up until only his mouth and nose were exposed.

He thought of Rolf and Ragna. Where were they waiting the storm out? In the Land-Rover? Or in the hut by the lake? Was Ragna safe? Had she gone willingly or had Rolf forced her? He must surely have forced her; she'd never have gone otherwise. If he'd hurt her—

He didn't know which was worse, imagining Ragna hurt or picturing her terrified. And terrified she would be—she must have realized exactly what sort of a man Rolf was by now.

He just hoped she didn't know everything. He'd give anything to save her that.

Ragna . . . Ragna . . .

Before he could think any further, he sank headlong into a deep sleep.

Thrane was trying to be patient, but it was hard. He said into the telephone: "Three *hours*?"

The local CO confirmed: "Three hours. We'll try to do better of course."

"God help me!" Thrane exclaimed under his breath.

The CO had sharp ears. "You could try Him, of course," he said frostily, "but in the meantime we'll do what we can, shall we?"

Thrane had asked for that. He apologized: "Sorry, I know you'll do your best."

He rang off, thinking uncharitably that the Russians, if they ever decided to invade, were unlikely to give three hours' notice.

All he wanted was five or six men to go up onto the plateau. But his hopes of hot pursuit were turning cold. The army was insisting on sending their best men—crack mountain troops from the *Fallskjermjegeren*. One would have thought such people would be easy to find inside the Arctic Circle. But apparently not. Not in the middle of the night in the middle of a blizzard, at any rate.

Yet he was being unfair. Everything took time up here—three hours wasn't bad to get troops into a truck, fully briefed, and up the long road to the top of Kåfjord. Besides, even if by some stroke of magic the troops got up there immediately, it'd probably be too late. From Starheim's note it seemed certain Berg was heading for the border; and the Finnish side of the border was one place the troops could not go. Pasvik had put paid to that.

Which put the matter in the hands of the government. But it would have to indulge in some pretty fancy footwork if it was going to persuade the Finns to arrest Berg. Had Berg been a thief or a murderer it would have been simple—the Finns would have cooperated instantly. But a spy? Finland had spent seventeen years trying to establish a stable nonaggressive relationship with her vast Soviet neighbor and, by treading the marshy ground between open friendship and strict military neutrality, had begun to succeed, even managing to win a measure of trust.

Considering the Soviet Union trusted no one, this was quite an achievement.

But so keen were the Finns to build up the relationship that where an issue like this was concerned they would go to almost any lengths to avoid giving offense. And catching a Soviet spy and handing him over to a NATO country would certainly give offense—lots of it.

Thrane foresaw the scenario. Finland would carefully consider Norway's request for assistance—and consider it and consider it, and go on considering it until it was all far too late and Berg had been spirited away.

In other words they would do nothing—and who could blame them?

Which left Thrane with his hands tied firmly behind his back.

Sick with frustration, he went to the window and stared out. Wind-driven snow flickered through the beams of the streetlamps and traced whirling spirals past the window. The streets were empty; it was very late. In the parking area beneath, police cars stood white-covered on the upwind side, as if bombarded by a paint sprayer.

Was this storm a help? Was it delaying Berg? He liked to think so. Time was his only hope.

Behind him, a door opened. Thinking it was Krog he

sighed: "How the hell can we get some people up onto that plateau fast?"

But it wasn't Krog, it was the police chief. He considered the question. "I can only think of the Lapps," he suggested cautiously. "I don't know whether they'd agree to do it, but you can always ask."

Perhaps he had a point. Not only did the Lapps know the plateau but they weren't subject to frontier restrictions. "Who? Which ones?" Thrane asked. "This Aslak Hetta?"

The chief shrugged. "Maybe."

"Well, d'you know anyone else?"

"Not really. You'd need mountain Lapps, but all the mountain Lapps are up on the central plateau at this time of year."

"We'll ask Aslak Hetta, then. He should know the right people, shouldn't he?"

The chief looked doubtful. "He might suggest a few names. But the Lapps are a strange lot. You never know where you are with them. They promise one thing and do another. I've rarely gotten a straight answer out of them. Or any answer, for that matter."

Thrane wasn't too surprised; the man didn't exactly invite confidence.

The chief was frowning doubtfully. "But even if you could get them to agree, what would they do once they were up there?"

Thrane tried to look as though he'd thought the thing through in detail, which he hadn't. "They could find Starheim," he said finally.

"And then?"

Thrane pulled a face and said truthfully: "Then I'm not too sure."

"Wake up!"

Ragna huddled farther down into her sleeping bag.

Someone was shaking her shoulder; the sleeping bag was pulled back from her face. The voice repeated stridently: "Wake up!"

She opened an eye. The scene came rushing toward her, nightmarish in its familiarity: the dim oil lamp, the leaping flames of the open stove, the unpacked gear, the remains of the meal.

And Rolf.

Looming over her, his face in shadow. He said sharply: "Come on! It's time to go." He went to his rucksack and, dropping onto one knee, began to pack hastily.

Ragna blinked herself awake. It felt like the middle of the night. Then she realized—it was. The small window by the door registered ebony black. The aroma of the meal still hung in the air.

She had been dreaming. The dream crowded back into her mind, vivid and ugly. She had been lying on a bed in a room full of people. For some reason she had been overcome by complete helplessness, unable to move. Across the room she had seen her little girl—her first beloved baby—lying on a bed. At first the child seemed well, but then Ragna had realized that she was still and pale, gasping for breath—ill, the life slipping out of her. And not one of the crowd of people had noticed; no one was even looking in the baby's direction. Only Ragna could see, and she was paralyzed by some dreadful lack of will, held down by her own inability to act. As she watched, the child closed her eyes and became utterly still. And Ragna screamed in silent agony because the child had died alone. Without even a hand to hold, without soft words of love . . .

The scene shifted to encompass Kris. He was there, standing at the edge of the crowd. Healthy, thank God: eyes bright, cheeks pink. Yet he too was alone! As she watched he seemed to become aware of it for the first time, and looked around, lost, anxious, betrayed. She couldn't bear the sight of it—it tore at her heart. She watched him look for her—he didn't see her—he called, he became upset, then frantic. Finally he crumpled with despair.

Krisi! Krisi! It was unbearable.

Then Jan—he was there too.

Except he was lying in the snow, lying covered in snow, so that she had to scrape the whiteness away from his body. She uncovered his face. She didn't touch it. It was so cold, so very cold, the skin blue and waxen. So cold.

Even as the dream memory faded and she lay watching Rolf pack his bag, the sense of despair and helplessness suffocated her. She felt as if she were being carried along by a flood of terrifying events over which she had no control. All she wanted to do was close her eyes and shut it out.

"Come on, Ragna!"

She murmured: "I'm not going with you."

"Oh yes you are." He didn't even look up. "The storm's passed. It's a lovely night. There's even a bit of a moon. Ideal."

"You don't need me."

"Ragna—I need you! Come on. Hurry!"

No, she thought, this is where it all stops. She lay still.

After a moment Rolf's head spun around. There was an electric silence; he crouched motionless like a cat, then sprang rapidly over to her.

She braced herself.

He hovered, his anger reaching out to her. Then he exhaled long and hard. His hand came gently down and stroked her hair. "Ragna," he said in a coaxing voice, "I do need you."

"Nothing will make me come with you."

He pulled his hand away. "But I can't let you go back," he said tightly. "Not yet. You'd tell Hal, you see, and he'd tell his friends and unfortunately they'd believe him. And then they might try to snatch me out of Finland. I can't let that happen, Ragna."

Ragna persisted: "You can't make me come with you."

There was a pause. He said in a rough low voice: "Ragna, don't force me . . ."

"You can always put a gun to my head, of course."

"Ragna . . ." His voice rose with exasperation. "Why do you make me . . . ? Why can't you. . . ?" He sighed. "All right. *All right.* I'll spell it out for you. If you come with me, I promise to let you go the minute we get down into Finland. But if you refuse"—he shook his head as if it were all very painful to him—"then I'll have to lock you up here to ensure that you can't leave. And since there isn't much food or fuel left, that won't be ideal, will it? Which do you prefer?"

"To stay."

His anger was almost tangible; it leapt across the silence. "You'll only be making it worse for the others!" he declared.

She looked up at him, her heart thudding against her chest. "The others? What do you mean?"

He said: "I had to lock them up."

She sat up, her throat suddenly dry, not believing what she was hearing. "Not *Kris?*"

"I had to do it for his own good. I didn't want him to wander outside into the cold." He made it sound the most reasonable thing in the world. "He'll be all right, don't worry. He's in the kitchen with food and water and all that he needs."

"The others?"

"The others are in the cellar."

"Locked there? Away from Kris?"

"Yes. It was the only way."

Alone! He'd left Kris *alone!* Ragna gaped at him.

"Now do you see?" he said quietly. "If you come with me they'll be free within a day, perhaps sooner. If you don't . . ."

For a long while she couldn't speak.

Then, galvanized by dread, she swung her legs out of the sleeping bag and wordlessly began to dress.

From the depths of sleep Hal's brain was trying to tell him something. He managed to shut the message out for a while, but it chivied at him until he finally awoke. His senses came reluctantly, slowly to life and reported coldness, tiredness, and absolute silence, in that order.

One of these sensations bothered him. It took him a moment to work out which.

Finally he had it: the silence.

He opened an eye. The insides of the windows were covered with ice. He sat up and tried to scratch some away, then forced the door open. Its frozen hinges creaked loudly in the silence.

He looked out. Stars. Stillness. The storm was over.

Perfect traveling weather. It was four in the morning.

Climbing out of the bag, he tried the car's starter. The thing turned feebly once, then gave up. He wasn't too surprised: Batteries never worked in the cold.

Then he moved fast, pulling on his outer clothing, repacking his gear, chewing at some bread and dried fish, taking a long swig of water from the water bottle, lacing his boots, and waxing his skis.

Allowing for windchill, he guessed it was about forty below. The greatest problem of traveling fast in these temperatures was not frostbite but overheating—the sweat drew heat from the body and destroyed the insulation of the clothing. The trick was to wear several layers of loose clothing with a windproof outer and, nuisance though it was, to stop and remove an inner layer when necessary.

At the moment he was purposely a little underdressed and therefore cold, because he didn't want to have to stop.

He stuck the torch inside his outer clothing along with the water bottle and the pistol, and pulled the drawstring of his hood tight so that only his eyes were showing. Then he fastened his skis, hoisted his rucksack and rifle onto his shoulders, and set off.

The first quarter hour was hard going—his muscles were cold and he was bothered by dizziness. But he pressed on, climbing the slight gradient, forcing himself forward, until at last the warmth spread into his veins and he began to move more easily.

Despite his blurred one-sided vision he could see that the visibility was good. A new moon hung in a dark sky, outlining the low rolling hills and casting faint shadows on the undulations of the shallow valleys beneath.

He judged his speed by long experience and marked off the distance on the map in his head, checking his estimate against the lie of the land.

After two and a half miles he spotted the Land-Rover.

It was up to its axles in drift snow.

He went over it quickly—empty—then looked for tracks.

Nothing. Which meant the car had been abandoned while the storm was still blowing.

He hurried on. The hut was clearly visible about a quarter of a mile ahead.

He stopped abruptly. A wisp of vapor came from the chimney, rising palely against the black sky before arcing downward as it condensed and froze. He dropped into a crouch. No window on this side, not that he could see anyway.

Slipping the rifle off his shoulder, he approached softly, coming under the cover of the hut wall. He made his way cautiously to the corner and peered around. He made out what seemed like fresh tracks in the snow, going off to the southeast.

Taking no chances, he ducked under the window and took a closer look. Yes—two sets of tracks converging into one. Heading for the border.

Still taking no chances he removed his skis and, quietly un-latching the hut door, burst in at the crouch, rifle at the ready.

Empty. He searched it anyway.

The remains of a meal. A fire that was still red with heat. He poked at the embers. It had been fueled fairly recently, an hour ago—ninety minutes at the outside. His spirits rose. They were only a few miles ahead—seven, eight miles at the most. Over the border. But that didn't worry him—they still faced at least twenty miles of wilderness before they reached so much as a road. Plenty of opportunity for him to catch them.

Pausing only to drink, he prepared to leave. As he hastily refastened his skis, a nasty cold sweat hit him, and he leaned shakily against the wall of the hut. He fought it for a minute or so, then was violently sick.

As soon as it was over he set off, closing his mind to the sickness, thinking only of the weather, praying that the conditions would hold.

This time when the heavy door swung open on its silent hinges Yurasov felt strangely calm. The long-postponed evacuation would come almost as a relief.

The Navigator sat behind his desk, looking tired and battle-worn, as if he'd been up all night fighting for his military life, which Yurasov suspected he had. "You are to report to the Center today. You leave on the early flight."

Yurasov nodded. So—at last. He'd been expecting the final summons ever since he'd heard that 173 was making a run for it. "Then—I'm no longer needed, Comrade Colonel?"

"No." The Navigator reached for the button under the top of his desk.

Yurasov couldn't bear to leave without knowing. He dared to ask quickly: "Is the matter of One-seventy-three concluded, then, Comrade Colonel?"

The Navigator paused with his hand on the button and eyed him thoughtfully. Then, as if they were two rats in a sinking ship, he said in a sudden bout of confidence: "Our friend One-seventy-three has been creating a great deal of activity."

"Yes, Comrade Colonel?"

"The Norwegians are on to him—if they weren't already." He gave Yurasov a vaguely reproachful look. "They have asked the Finns to search for him and to hold him pending the issue of a warrant for his arrest."

Yurasov closed his eyes.

"Apparently he is making his way over the border on skis."

Yurasov's heart sank even further. Berg had only gotten that far! Well, he'd no chance of getting to Helsinki, then, let alone Moscow; the Finns and Norwegians were bound to get him first. In which case the Center would be robbed of its final prize, the propaganda victory.

And Yurasov would be robbed of his last chance of saving himself from the poky little apartment in the Moscow suburbs.

Reading his mind, the Navigator murmured: "Don't give up all hope, Yurasov. We may yet get to him first." He pressed the button. The side door swung open. Three comrades entered, one of them bearing a metal bowl containing the syringe.

But even without the sedative Yurasov went quietly. He was drawing comfort from the Navigator's last words and the hope that Rolf might yet end his days safely buttoned up in Moscow.

35

Berg plodded steadily forward and came to a decision. He would have to abandon Ragna. He would have preferred not to abandon her at all, of course—a promise was a promise—but she was holding him back, and he couldn't afford to waste any more of this wonderful weather.

It was eleven in the morning; the blue light was at its most intense and vivid and, though the temperature was very low, the air was clear. They should have covered a good twenty-five miles by now. Instead it was a pathetic fifteen. But for Ragna he would have had a good chance of reaching the road that night. He'd been ridiculously patient—but not any longer.

There should be a hut of some sort about five miles ahead, the only one for miles. It was the logical place to leave Ragna. She'd manage. At heart she was a tough girl. But not so tough that it wouldn't take her at least twenty-four hours to get to the road, or, if the weather deteriorated, a great deal longer. The trip back over the border would be no faster. Either way, he'd have enough time to get clear.

He looked over his shoulder. Ragna had stopped yet again to fiddle with a troublesome binding. He waited, gritting his teeth with exasperation. If he had any sense he'd leave her now, this minute, and she could make her own way to the hut.

But, impressed at his own generosity, he waited. He hadn't forgotten the way she'd guided him to the hut last night. He was suitably grateful. And he knew that she'd tried very hard

to keep up—tried too hard, in fact, and exhausted herself i
the process. Perhaps it had been a mistake to tell her about th
child; it had made her frantic.

He waited. But this, he decided, was definitely the la
time.

"Come on!" His call was absorbed by the hungry silence,
silence that was vibrant, alive, as if something menacing wer
taking place within it.

At last Ragna stood up and started forward again. Behin
her Berg noticed that the horizon was less distinct, and tha
some of the blue had gone out of the light.

A change—he should have known!

Seized by a new sense of urgency, he started off again, mc
mentarily forgetting Ragna, searching the landscape, lookin
for landmarks. Ahead, a large hill rose to his right, an
beyond it another. According to the map the hut should be o
the far side of that second hill. The landscape was distinctiv
enough for him to be fairly confident. Not like earlier in th
day when the light had been dim and the rolling terrain espe
cially deceptive, and they had turned south too soon and al
most lost themselves in a valley that hooked back over th
border.

The blue was fading fast. Everything was turning a monoto
nous gray-white. Only a scattering of stunted birch stood ou
from the flatness, their thin branches like black latticewor
against the snow, while on the bare hillside boulders of dar
granite, the occasional outcrop, lay exposed by the wind. H
looked up: The sky was opaque with mist, the air fast losing i
sharpness.

The damned weather had been too good to last.

When he came level with the first hill he looked back. Ragn
had fallen ever farther behind.

In a fury of impatience he realized he would have to wai
for her, if only to tell her he was going on ahead and to giv
her directions to the hut.

While he waited he climbed a little way up the side of th
hill to make absolutely sure of his bearings in case the visibilit
should clamp down.

He glanced back the way they had come. The rolling land
scape was fast blending into a featureless expanse.

Something made him pause. He stood motionless like an animal scenting the wind.

He blinked to sharpen his focus. He thought he had seen something. Something that was moving.

He remained absolutely still, hardly breathing, his senses reaching out into the distance.

There. A small dark-gray dot, barely distinguishable from the mass of grayness surrounding it. He watched for several minutes. It *was* moving. He felt a leap of fear.

An animal?

Yet what sort of an animal traveled alone and didn't stop to scent the air; what sort of an animal was tall and thin and came inexorably forward with a jerky swaying movement.

A man.

Yet no one came up here in midwinter, no one except the Lapps. Yet this fast-moving figure was not a Lapp—was he?

He thought viciously: Who are you?

Whoever, he was coming their way, and along the same route. It wasn't too difficult to imagine that he was following their tracks.

Berg looked swiftly ahead, reexamining the lie of the land, then, with a jab of his poles, skied rapidly down to Ragna.

Hal stopped abruptly as the now-familiar nausea rose in his throat. The cold sweat came shortly after, followed a few agonizing moments later by the violent retching, which, since his stomach had long since been empty, squeezed his guts painfully. As soon as the unpleasant business was over he sat weakly back on his skis, pulling in great gulps of freezing air, waiting for the last of the shivering and faintness to pass.

He felt confused, cloudy, and it worried him. The tight vicious band of pain around his head could be ignored, the dry heaves were merely a nuisance, but losing his grip on reality was deeply disturbing, like being partially anesthetized, so that you were dimly aware of what was happening but unable to control it.

He pulled out his map and, frowning with concentration, tried to make sense of it. For the moment he couldn't think where he was. He backtracked mentally and realized that whole sections of the journey were a complete blank. He looked at his watch. Eleven. That should give him an idea of his distance.

He made a rough estimate, then looked around him, searching for landmarks. There was a hill, a distinct one, just ahead. On the map there were three, one after the other. He looked back and thought he saw one behind, but how far away he couldn't tell. His vision seemed to give him nothing but false readings.

He took a stab at a position and hoped it was right. He would have to check on it as he went along. When—if—he remembered. Would he remember? He wasn't at all certain. His mind was playing elusive tricks, grabbing thoughts then whisking them away again so that he couldn't pin down even the simplest thing.

He got wearily to his feet. His limbs felt very heavy, his brain so light it floated out of his head.

He scooped up some snow and rubbed it into his face. Wake up! *Wake up!*

He started off again, dropping his skis into the tracks he had followed all the way from the hut at the head of Kåfjord Valley. He didn't consider stopping, not while the going was good. Stopping would be tantamount to giving up, and giving up was the one thing you never did up here.

As he got back into his rhythm a thought hovered elusively in his mind. He tried to pin it down, but it kept fluttering away. Then, peering forward into the distance, the thought finally swooped in and settled.

The others. He hadn't caught sight of them yet.

He must go faster or he'd never catch up. Yes, that was it: he must go faster.

Lowering his head, screwing up his eyes with the effort, he pushed himself into an approximation of a run.

Rolf said: "Quick! Hurry!" then poled off rapidly, leaving Ragna to carry on as best she could.

Hurry! She could have killed him. What did he think she'd been doing all this time? God, if anyone wanted to hurry it was her! She thought of nothing but getting to a telephone—she clung to the idea as if to a lifeline.

And now he was saying hurry!

Something had made him impatient, something that had brought him down from the hillside in a rush, tight-lipped and pinched with tension. The weather maybe—she could see it was changing. That was all they needed—another storm. The thought was like torture.

Her skis back-slipped yet again. The back-sliding happened on almost every stride, wasting half of each forward thrust. Wax might help, yet the only stuff she'd managed to find was useless. Rolf, of course, had no such problem. His skis were an experimental design that had built-in fish scales along the sole that gripped automatically. *His* skis?—she almost choked. They had been Jan's.

Then there was the problem of her right binding. If she thrust forward too hard she walked straight off her ski. And even if she was careful not to push too hard, her boot came free every few minutes anyway. She'd tried to fix it, but it was impossible without a screwdriver.

The fatigue and the sheer discomfort of the journey were nothing compared to these frustrations, which drove her into rages of despair.

Rolf was poling farther and farther ahead. She thought: He's going to leave me behind.

But he came to a stop and she saw that he was waiting. Why? By this time she knew it wasn't likely to be out of the goodness of his heart. She struggled on, enduring the infuriating back-sliding, until she finally panted up to him. Before he could say anything, she sat down exhausted in the snow.

He reached for her arm and pulled her roughly to her feet. "I need you to go up that hill and look for the hut while I take a good look at the map."

A hut. The prospect of a short rest and some food was irresistible. She pulled her hood down from her mouth. "There's a hut?" she askd stupidly.

He gestured vaguely toward the map. She leaned over and got a glimpse of a small black dot in a large neutral expanse interspersed with the occasional blue-colored summer stream and numbers in black, showing the hill heights. She saw that the hut was well over halfway to the road.

Rolf pulled the map away. His eyes glittered harshly over the rim of his hood. "Go as far as those rocks there." He pointed to a dark outcrop some way up the gently rising slope. "You should be able to see it from there."

Another hurdle to be overcome. She nodded acquiescently. She certainly wasn't going to use up her energy arguing. With Rolf it was a waste of time.

Leaning down briefly to scoop up some snow and press it into her mouth, she pulled her hood up over her chin and started off. The surface soon turned from powder to hard crust ridged with icy furrows. Despite the gentleness of the slope her skis were soon back-sliding hopelessly and she had to sidestep.

She glanced back at Rolf. He was motionless, watching her.

The outcrop was much farther than it had looked. It took her a solid ten minutes to reach it. By the time she finally climbed onto it she was faint with weariness. She sat down and pressed more snow into her mouth. It didn't seem to do a lot for her thirst. She remembered Jan—or was it Hal?—telling her that it was bad to eat snow, but she couldn't remember why.

She looked for the hut and felt a quick disappointment. The weather was changing rapidly. A haze had rolled in, fading out the light and obscuring the landscape behind a soft veil of opaque mist. She could barely see the land just ahead, let alone a far-off hut.

She looked for Rolf to signal her lack of success.

He wasn't in sight.

Standing up, she looked right and left. No sign. She searched for a suggestion of shape or color, she examined every faint shadow, each wind-blown boulder and exposed rock . . .

He had vanished.

Her mouth went dry, she tried to keep calm. He couldn't have gone—she would have seen him.

Or would she have?

Even as she combed the slope for a sight of him, the mist seemed to close in around her, creeping down from the hill above, rising up from the snow below, becoming thicker, whiter, and more intensely cold, until the air itself seemed to freeze. Ice formed on her lashes and around her hood.

She looked for him and felt complete disgust.

It had been a trick. Of course it had been a trick! He'd sent her up here to give himself time to get away. And she'd gone like a lamb. Rolf must be laughing himself silly.

On the brink of tears, cursing under her breath, she leaned down and directed her rage at the troublesome binding, almost tearing it off in a vain and furious attempt to fix it. Her anger vented, she sank down into the snow, her shoulders sagged, she bowed her head.

After a time she pulled herself together. No point in feeling bitter or angry. Nothing had changed. She still had to get to a telephone. The only difference was that she was on her own. She only wished it didn't seem quite such a terrifying prospect.

She fastened the binding as well as she could, stood up determinedly, and brushed the snow briskly off her ski trousers. She faced the encroaching mist and, suppressing a tiny twinge of panic, tried to decide on her best plan of action. There was only one, she realized: to carry on into Finland. It was the shortest route and she shouldn't have any trouble finding her way—she'd have Rolf's tracks to guide her.

Filled with grim determination she thought: I'm going to get out of this if it bloody well kills me! And she felt absurdly heartened by her own bravado.

Fumbling with a mitten, she managed to get a bare hand into her pocket and find a bar of chocolate. Raw energy. She bit on it resolutely.

She paused in mid-bite.

In the mist below. Someone. But emerging from the north. From the way they had come.

Berg tensed and shifted position, ducking his head farther down behind the boulder. Moving cautiously, he peered around it.

There. A white figure, barely visible in the mist. But getting more distinct all the time.

Coming fast. Following in their tracks.

Who are you, you bastard?

A border guard? A soldier? Maybe the abandoned Land-Rover had been discovered. Maybe this was a rescue party that had been sent to save them! The thought was absurd, almost funny.

There was also the possibility that the man was completely innocent—a Lapp out hunting, or searching for his herd, or training for one of the spring endurance races that were held down south, hoping to win a prize and make his name . . .

And yet—Lapps didn't wear white, they wore reindeer skins and distinctive colors.

Who are you?

Berg pulled the rifle in to his shoulder, checked the magazine for the tenth time, and rested his gloved forefinger on the trigger.

Whatever the man's identity, he would shortly show himself for what he was. In about thirty yards he'd come to the point where the tracks stopped and turned sharply up the hill— Ragna's to continue upward, Berg's to loop back down to the boulder, although the man in white wouldn't be able to see that.

When he got to that point he would either pause momentarily and go straight on—an innocent hunter—or he would reveal himself as a pursuer.

The choice would be his, the choice whether to live or die.

Rolf, it could only be Rolf—*was* it Rolf? She stared uncomprehendingly: he must have backtracked, though God only knew how or why.

And his clothing— Rolf had been wearing a pale anorak and dark trousers. This figure was all in white.

It wasn't Rolf—it was someone else!

The figure was really shifting, his shoulders bent well forward, his body swaying from side to side as he threw his weight into his stride. At the same time his movements were strangely exaggerated, his head unusually low, as if he were tired.

He was showing no signs of slowing up, and she suddenly realized he was going to carry on past.

She shouted, but her voice was feeble in the heavy air.

It was possible he would pass without seeing her. Quickly, she set off down the slope on a convergent course, intending to shout again when she was a little closer.

Then, abruptly, the figure stopped, and in such haste that he almost tripped over his skis. Recovering his balance, he bent to examine the snow, then, looking wildly about him, slipped his rifle off his shoulder and into his hands in one deft movement. She guessed he had seen her tracks coming up the hill, for his head turned sharply toward her.

The rifle—the defensive pose—who was he? She decided she didn't terribly care. Stopping, she raised a pole and waved it frantically from side to side.

He saw her then; she could tell by the way he slowly lowered his rifle.

Skiing gently downhill she waved again, just to be sure.

An arm rose and waved tentatively back, as if he couldn't quite believe what he was seeing.

She called silently: Oh, I'm here all right! I'm here!

She ran into thick snow, it pulled at her feet, she flung out her arms to regain her balance.

When she looked up again a movement caught her eye. But it wasn't the waiting figure—he was still standing there. What, then? It took her a moment to find it: a dark object on the periphery, something that hadn't been there before.

She slowed momentarily and peered down through the frozen mist. Yes, to her right and just ahead of the man in white: a dark shape. It seemed to have appeared from nowhere.

It took her a moment to work out what it was. A head, arms: the top of a man's body, strangely crouched . . .

Suddenly she understood and the realization hit her like a punch in the stomach. She opened her mouth to scream, and this time it came out loud and strong, an agonized shout. She shouted again and again and thrust a pole in the direction of Rolf and begged the man in white to see.

But the figure in white stood immobile, puzzled, uncomprehending.

She thrust herself forward down the slope again. She screamed: "Look out! Look out!"

Then her binding came adrift and she pitched headlong into the snow.

Hal lowered his rifle and peered up the hill. Everything was hazy. He rubbed his good eye, but the blur didn't go away. It was the mist perhaps. He knew it was misty because he could see the general whiteness and the way his breath condensed and froze in front of his nose.

Another shout came floating over the air. High-pitched, feminine.

He listened in growing excitement.

When the shout came again, he knew.

Ragna.

A lump came into his throat and he had to swallow several times. He lifted an arm and waved. If only he could see her more clearly—

The shouts became shriller—almost like screams.

There she was—a small gray shape suspended in a gray sea of fog.

She was waving—or was she? He just couldn't tell. He rubbed his left eye again.

Yes, she was screaming and waving and . . . There was some meaning to all this, some significance to the noise and the strange movements. Scenting danger, he stiffened and looked about him.

Berg took long and careful aim.

This man was no innocent hunter. This man had been sent to find him. His purpose had been revealed the moment he'd reacted so violently and swung the rifle into his hands.

A pro. Suspecting an ambush.

How right he was!

But not a very smart pro. He was standing still, mesmerized by Ragna's screams and waves.

Just as Berg had hoped. Now he had all the time in the world.

Holding the rifle steady in his hands, Berg shifted his elbows slightly on the boulder, sighted down the barrel, and gently increased the pressure on the trigger.

Ragna fought her way hastily to her feet. As she looked down the hill two things happened, one immediately after the other. The man in white sagged forward and a shot rang out.

Ragna cried out.

The man in white sank slowly onto one knee. But he wasn't finished. He raised his rifle and aimed it in Rolf's direction.

"Get him!" Ragna shrieked. *"Get him!"*

A second shot rang out. Yes—from *his* rifle.

But he hadn't gotten Rolf. Rolf was still there, behind the
rock.

A third *crack!*

The man in white slowly toppled over.

Ragna let out a cry of anguish.

From behind the boulder Rolf stood up and began to plod
toward the prone figure.

Shaking with anger, Ragna reached for her lost ski and
rammed her foot into the loose binding. Digging her poles
deep into the snow she pushed off, and kept pushing and
pushing, swinging all her weight into the thrust of the poles,
willing herself forward. But slow, so slow!

At last the slope steepened a little and her skis found their
own momentum, and she suddenly didn't have to push anymore. She'd forgotten to pull her hood up and the frozen air
scorched painfully into her lungs and across her cheeks, like
fine broken glass. As the ground dropped away she went
faster still, wobbling dangerously on her loose ski, battling to
keep it running straight.

Rolf had gotten there. He was standing over the man in
white.

She hit a patch of soft snow and lost speed. She began to
pole again.

Rolf was picking up the other man's rifle. For a moment
Ragna thought he was going to point it at the man—maybe
use it—but he hoisted it onto his back and knelt beside the
immobile figure.

Almost there. Rolf became aware of her approach, for he
glanced over his shoulder.

The anger flowed over Ragna like a red-hot sea. "You bastard! You absolute bastard!" she screamed as she came up to
him. She swung a punch that glanced ineffectually off his
shoulder.

His kneeling body was masking the man in the snow. She
pushed at him viciously. "Get out of the way! *Get out!*"

Rolf yielded, getting slowly to his feet. "He's—extraordinary." His voice was heavy with something like admiration.

"Anyone else and . . ." He didn't finish but, straightening up looked nervously around him as if he'd suddenly remembered where he was. Then, without a word, he pushed past her and was gone.

Ragna looked down and saw the face of the man in the snow.

36

The darkness came early, infusing the fog with deep grays that ebbed and flowed and finally sucked the last whiteness from the snow.

Ragna increased her efforts, hacking at the heavy packed snow with a small tin cooking pan, then shoveling it clear, until at last she was satisfied. She had created a long hollow out of the deep drift that had accumulated on the downhill side of the boulder. The boulder itself formed the back wall of the shelter, a wall that receded toward its base, creating an overhang. With the loose snow from her diggings she had built snow walls on the two adjacent sides. Only the top and front of the shelter remained entirely open to the weather.

She unlooped Hal's survival bag from his rucksack. The bag seemed fairly waterproof, but she had the feeling it should have a groundsheet placed underneath it for added protection. She burrowed into the rucksack, but to her disappointment found only a thin lightweight tarpaulin which she'd already earmarked for the roof. Abandoning the idea, she arranged the bag in the hollow directly on the snow.

As she made her way back she had to peer closely at the snow to be sure she was retracing her outward tracks.

It was so dark she almost tripped over the huddled figure lying in the snow. He was so still—he seemed even more still than before. Half in dread, she bent down and put her face close to his. His breathing was shallow, his pulse faint but steady—he was unchanged. He'd been hit twice. The first wound, in the left hand, had been only too easy to see. Inside the remnants of his glove there was a frightful mess. Two fingers were little more than torn flesh and splintered bone—one finger was actually hanging by a thread. She'd done what she could, which was to bind the hand tightly with a makeshift bandage torn from spare clothing she had had in her rucksack; but it wasn't much, and she knew it.

The second wound she had found later, and immediately cursed herself for not having looked for it sooner. This one was in the back of his left shoulder and was bleeding profusely. She stuffed the rest of the vest inside his clothing next to the wound. It needed proper binding, but she dared not remove any of his clothing in this cold.

He had been unconscious throughout.

Now she must move him, and quickly—she could feel the chill spreading over his skin.

Moving a limp six-foot man of probably a hundred eighty pounds across twenty yards of snow was not going to be easy. She had an idea of how she might do it—but it was only an idea.

Hal was lying on his right side. She placed his skis side by side on the snow, parallel to his back, their tips by his head, then added her skis, one on either side of Hal's. She tied all the bindings firmly and tightly together in the center, so that the four skis resembled a narrow raft. Next she untied from her waist the length of thin rope she'd found attached to Hal's rucksack and, looping the rope around the tip of each ski, bound the tips tightly together. She left the ends of the rope loose in the snow.

This had taken a good fifteen minutes—her hands, clumsy and unresponsive with cold, were maddeningly slow.

Now to get him onto the ski-raft contraption. She pushed the ski-raft up to his back, then, straightening out his legs and shoulders, rolled him over. But even flat on his back he lay only half on the raft. She pulled his legs across, and an arm, then, trying not to touch the damaged shoulder, attempted to shift his body.

She heaved and strained, but one side of his body was deep in the snow so she had to lift his weight upward as well as across.

She moved herself around to the far side of his body and

tried from that angle. She gave a great shove. He moaned suddenly, a sound that was startlingly loud in the silence. She realized she must have hurt his injured shoulder.

She bent forward. "Hal?"

His breathing had changed; it was deepr, shorter. His hand moved and he groaned softly.

She pulled her hood down from her mouth. "Hal, can you hear me? Hal? I'm trying to move you. I need your help. Do you hear me?"

He groaned again, louder this time.

"I need your help," she repeated, more urgently.

There was a silence, he seemed to be listening, then he gasped what sounded like a yes. Had he really understood? She wasn't sure. "I need you to get onto the skis here. To lie on them, flat."

A pause, then his uninjured hand came out and patted the snow. She knew then that he had understood.

He lay still for several minutes until she thought he'd drifted off again. "Hal? Come on—you have to move!" He raised his head a little, then, his breath laboring, put his elbow across and attempted to lift his body upward. Slipping her hands under him, Ragna heaved. For a moment she thought they would do it, but with a sigh of pain he suddenly fell back into the snow, trapping her arms underneath him.

It was probably the shoulder; she should have warned him.

She extricated her arms. Feeling him rallying for another attempt, she said, "Wait!" and, going around to the other side, knelt down and dug her arms under his body. She counted aloud to three, he raised himself, she hoisted and pulled, and then, suddenly, he was almost on.

He was panting hard; it had taken a lot out of him. She hauled his legs farther across the ski-raft, then—carefully— his shoulders. "One more time," she said remorselessly. "Ready?"

"Ready."

She counted to three, they both heaved, and he was on.

Though he would never be completely on. The four skis were not wide enough for him and his shoulders spread over them onto the snow. But most of his body was supported, and that was more than she'd hoped for.

She bound him to the raft with the remainder of the rope, tying it under his arms, tightly around his waist and hips, and down onto the bindings. She ran out of rope and had to tie his ankles together with the cord from her hood.

A murmur came from Hal. She bent down to catch his words. He whispered: "Sorry . . . can't . . ."

"Quiet!" she said more sharply than she meant to. "Don't— there's nothing to be sorry about. Just—don't move!"

She suddenly realized she'd left no rope to pull him along with. What a fool! Drawing a deep beath, she untied him and did the job all over again, this time leading a loose rope tail up from the main bite around his waist.

Then, wrapping the rope tail around her hands, she tried to pull. Nothing happened. She put more weight into it, her boots sinking deeper into the snow. Suddenly the skis broke free, the raft jumped forward, and she fell sideways.

The raft had moved. She felt a small glimmer of hope.

Picking herself up, she pulled again. And again. After each pull she waded forward, braced the rope against her shoulder, and leaned her weight into the next pull. Hard progress—but progress. Sometimes the raft moved easily, sometimes it seemed to adhere to the snow—but it kept moving. Every so often she stopped and shone her torch on the ground to make sure she was still following the tracks to the boulder.

The distance was about twenty yards. She kept going fairly steadily until the last few yards. Then she met an upward slope.

She pulled and heaved but the raft refused to budge. She tried going to the back of the raft and pushing, but neither the ski ends nor Hal's feet offered enough resistance.

She sank into the snow, temporarily defeated, and tried to think. Returning to the front, she turned her back on the boulder and, doubling the rope around her waist, braced her feet against the snow and threw her weight backward.

Nothing. A moment of despair, then, fighting it off, she had another try. The raft shifted—an inch. She hauled again. Another inch.

Like a strong man in a tug-of-war, she leaned all her weight against the rope and won the ground with agonizing slowness. She leaned against the rope and hauled and panted and shifted her feet and braced herself and strained every muscle until she felt her veins bulge and her blood pound.

At last the raft moved more easily: the ground had leveled off. The boulder loomed darkly. She pulled her burden up to the mouth of the snow hollow. Then she fell back on the snow, panting hard, until she had regained her breath. Her hands, recently aching with cold, were now throbbing painfully as the blood surged vengefully back into them.

After a time she sat up again and untied the rope from around Hal's body.

"We're there," she said breathlessly in case he was listening.

"Well done." His voice, though rough, was surprisingly clear.

"Soon have you in the warm."

"Clever girl . . . Well done . . . Clever girl . . ."

His words, the gentleness of his tone, made tears leap to her eyes. She said unsteadily: "Your survival bag. It's all ready. Just beside you."

"My outers," he said. "Should . . . come . . . off."

She took his boots off, then his thin outer trousers. His anorak was much more difficult; she had to sit him up and try to get it over his head. He couldn't help much; he flopped against her, and her heart sank as she realized just how weak he was.

In the end she had to cut the anorak off with a knife. She then laid the anorak and trousers over the patch of snow between the raft and the survival bag so that when he slid across he wouldn't take any snow into the bag with him. It was important to be dry when you got into these things, she knew that.

She put the *finnesko* lined with sedge grass on his feet, then, pulling his good arm over her shoulders, she helped him sit up and slide his legs into the bag. This seemed to exhaust him completely and he leaned against her. She urged: "Almost there! Almost there!"

Panting hard, the blood pounding in her ears, she shifted him by degrees, calling a bright "One-two-three-UP!" as she lifted and pushed. At last he was sitting in the open mouth of the bag and, sensing that the journey was almost over, he made a last effort and helped to slide himself down into the bag.

"Warm in no time!" she said with false cheerfulness, zipping up the bag and pulling the hood over his head. He didn't reply.

She set to work on the rest of the shelter. She extended the snow wall across the front, so that Hal was now protected on all sides. Threading the rope through the eyes of the tarpaulin, she tied the thin canvas around the boulder and draped it down over the snow walls, building the snow up and over the edges of the canvas to anchor it down firmly. She left one small corner of the tarpaulin unfastened for an entrance.

This also took a long time.

When it was at last finished she squeezed into the shelter, next to Hal's feet, and pulled the rucksacks in after her. Shining the torch into Hal's she found a candle, and lit it.

The flame rose up, lighting the tarpaulin and gleaming rock face with flickering gold. She found the yellow light curiously reassuring.

She crawled up beside Hal. She had to steel herself to look at his face. Lightly she brushed her fingertips over the battered skin and around the wound on his cheek.

His eyes opened, but screwed up immediately as if the light were painful to him.

"I'll make a hot drink in a minute," she said. "And a hot meal. Then I'll have a proper go at that shoulder."

"Don't . . ." he said with an effort. "You must get going . . . while the weather holds."

"It's foggy. I can't go yet."

He frowned unhappily. "As soon as it clears, then."

She didn't reply. She was running her fingers onward, over the bruised eyes and the swollen nose. A bandage showed beneath his hood. She pushed the hood gently back and saw that the bandage was stained with old blood.

Brattdal. This terrible damage had been done at Brattdal.

For a moment she couldn't bring herself to ask the question that burned on her tongue. Finally, bracing herself for the answer she most dreaded to hear, she managed: "Kris, Hal. *Kris.* Is he—?"

Hal looked agitated, as if he should have remembered to tell her straightaway. "Safe," he breathed quickly. "With Sigrid. Safe. I took him myself."

Closing her eyes tightly, she dropped her head onto his chest and gave a deep sigh that was almost a sob. "Thank God," she murmured. "Thank God." And it was as if a great load had been lifted from her shoulders.

In a great upwelling of love and gratitude she looked into Hal's battered face and, pressing the palm of her hand against his cheek, whispered, "Oh, my dear. Oh, my dear." But relief soon gave way to despair.

Kris may be safe but Hal was half dead.

It was time to get to work. She found Hal's little Primus stove and, after some trouble with the primer, managed to light it. Taking the pan she had been using as a scoop, she filled it with snow and put it on the Primus to melt. Searching both rucksacks she selected a single can of meat stew, opened it, and placed it next to the stove.

Hal seemed to be sleeping. She decided to leave the bandaging of his wounds until after she'd gotten some hot food into him. In the meantime she took an inventory of their food stocks and divided it into two piles: a bare twelve hours' supply for herself, and the rest for Hal. Both were pitifully small. Realizing Hal probably wouldn't be able to cook, she rearranged the rations, leaving Hal most of the instantly edible food, like hard bread, cheese, biscuits, chocolate, and dried apricots. She reckoned it should be enough for three days. For herself she took a little dried fish and meat and some chocolate.

Melting down snow took time, mainly because several panfuls were needed to produce a few inches of warm water. But finally she had enough to pour into the single metal mug, with a soup cube dissolved in it. Emptying the can of stew into the pan to begin warming, she took the soup to Hal.

His eyes were still closed. "Dinner is served," she said.

He blinked several times as if getting his bearings all over again. Propping his head on her arm, she made him drink all the soup. "Main course soon," she said.

He lay back. Even in the warm candlelight he looked very pale.

She had to cajole him to eat the stew, and after a few mouthfuls he turned his head away. "Can't keep it down."

She insisted: "You must eat." But he wouldn't. Reluctantly, she ate the remainder herself.

"I'll have to see to your shoulder now," she said firmly. This time he didn't argue but let her open the survival bag and turn him onto his right side. As she loosened his clothing, pulling the layers out of his waistband, she found first a water flask, then a pistol.

Hal's eyelids fluttered. "You've found the gun?"

She held it up. He peered at it, narrowing his eyes. She realized he could hardly see it. Holding the weapon closer, she said: "Yes, the gun."

He seemed to recognize it at last. "The ammo's in . . . the anorak pocket. Take it."

Putting the pistol aside, she uncovered his shoulder. His inner clothing had soaked up a lot of blood. So too had the makeshift pad. She dabbed at the wound itself. It was seeping blood, but not so much as she'd feared. It looked as though it might stop altogether quite soon.

She stared curiously at the wound; she'd never seen a bullet hole before. It was strangely neat and inoffensive, a circle edged with a small rim of puckered bruised flesh. She examined the front of his shoulder—there was no other hole; the bullet was still inside his body.

Because she didn't know what else to do, she refolded the padding and, winding a long strip of the torn anorak material around his chest, bound it hard against the wound. Aware that he was getting very cold, she hastily pulled his clothing back into place and rezipped the bag.

She hesitated over the hand. It didn't appear to be bleeding too badly. Remembering the shattered fingers she decided against redressing it: she wouldn't know where to begin.

Hal slept again. She shone a torch out through the entrance of the shelter. The mist was as thick as ever, but whiter, sharper, bitten by cold so intense that the air itself seemed to be suspended in a deep frost.

She continued her preparations for the journey. Pulling her damaged ski inside the shelter, she painstakingly refixed the troublesome binding with the help of the spike and screwdriver on Hal's swiss knife. At the same time she melted pan after pan of snow until she had refilled Hal's flask.

Then she examined the map and tried to work out a position. A second hut was marked as clearly on Hal's map as it had been on Rolf's. But had Rolf been telling the truth when he said it was almost within sight? Or had he lied just to get her to hurry? She wouldn't be surprised if he'd lied; Rolf seemed to lie about most things.

She looked at possible routes. Heading back over the border was out: it would take longer, and even when she reached the Land-Rover, the car was unlikely to start and she'd be faced with a long journey down Kåfjord Valley. No, best to go on and find the road—but which way? She considered making straight for the border post, but ruled it out. It might look like a short cut, but there could be all sorts of obstacles in the way. Best to stick to the summer trail, such as it was, because it looked straightforward, with no hills and little chance of taking a wrong turn. Roughly nine miles to the south there was a lake. Once there the trail split, and she could head straight for the road.

When there was nothing more to be done, she extinguished the Primus stove and the candle and got into her sleeping bag and squeezed down next to Hal.

But Ragna couldn't sleep; the silence seemed to envelop her, the darkness to press in on her. The shelter was like a small boat in a vast sea of emptiness, totally encompassed by the rolling snow. Not a sound penetrated the tarpaulin, not a movement touched the air; the sense of isolation was overwhelming.

Yet there was something menacing about the deathly hush, as if there were some unimaginable thing outside, hovering just beyond the circle of darkness, waiting to pounce.

Hal moved his head and groaned. Extracting a hand from her sleeping bag, she felt for his cheek. It was still very cold. He didn't seem to have warmed up at all.

She remembered what one was meant to do in these circumstances. Unzipping her own bag, she unfastened his and crept in beside him, pulling her bag over the top. Hal sighed and muttered in his sleep. She pressed herself close against him, willing the heat of her body to spread into his.

Even after his skin began to return some warmth, she could not sleep. She thought instead of her life, and what a terrible mess she'd made of it. Again. *Again*. How was it possible to get it so wrong twice? When she'd met Jan she'd realized, hadn't she? Realized how shallow and superficial the old life had been. So how could she have been so blind as to be taken in by Rolf? Oh, he'd been attractive enough—but hadn't she learned that relationships with men like that were the loneliest of all? And how had she failed to see him for what he was? But she knew the answer to that. It was her own selfishness, her own determination to please herself and see only what it suited her to see. She'd just been running away, running away from the awfulness of Jan's death and the ridiculous guilt that went with not having been able to prevent it. Running away—to what? So-called freedom. Self-gratification.

She felt a surge of self-disgust. Never again! Never again. No more ruining other people's lives. No more selfishness.

And she'd make amends—oh, yes. To Kris. But most of all to Hal. She'd find her way out of this place if it killed her. She'd get help. The thought of failure was unbearable.

Finally, after what seemed a long time, she slipped into an exhausted sleep.

Much later she woke with a start. A sound—there had been a sound. From outside. What was it? The silence thundered in her ears. She strained to hear.

There!

A distant sound like—

Her heart hammered against her chest. It couldn't be—

It came again. Faint. Distant. Muffled. . . . Yet unmistakable. The howl of an animal.

A baying . . .

She gave a deep shudder and pressed herself closer to Hal. Trying not to listen yet unable to prevent herself, she braced herself, eyes closed, waiting for the awful sound to come again.

The silence stretched out. The sound did not come again.

She must have dozed, for she came to with a start, aware that quite some time had passed—maybe as much as an hour. She remained still, not wanting to move, not wanting to think about getting up to check the weather. But the darkness wasn't entirely dark. She looked up. Through a tiny gap between the tarpaulin and the rock she saw a single star.

Easing herself out of the bag she pushed back the corner of the canvas and looked out. A new world stretched before her: The fog had vanished; the night was hard and clear; a slight wind had sprung up.

She hesitated for one moment, remembering the chilling sound in the night. . . . But already it seemed distant, like a half-forgotten nightmare.

Without another thought, she hastily got herself ready. Relighting the candle, she packed her rucksack with a compass, map, one box of matches, her portion of the food, and two sticks of ski wax.

She placed Hal's food supply next to him within easy reach and made sure his water flask was in the bag where he would find it.

The gun—a revolver—lay where she'd left it. She examined it cautiously, then going to the shreds of Hal's anorak, she searched the pockets and emptied the ammunition into her own anorak. Picking up the gun again, she tried to see how you loaded and cocked it. She managed to break it open. All the chambers were full. She shut it again; it went home with a loud metallic click.

"Ragna . . ."

Her head spun around.

Hal's swollen eyes blinked at her over the edge of the survival bag. He seemed more awake—even a little better.

She smiled at him. "How do you feel?"

"Okay."

But, then, he would say that. She found the water flask and made him drink. He was very thirsty. She wished she'd melted more water.

"How is it?" he asked.

"Clear. And only a little wind."

"Watch out . . . for cloud . . . snow. Find shelter in good time."

She nodded.

"Got the revolver?" he asked.

She crawled up beside him. "Could you tell me exactly how to use it?"

He explained slowly, breathlessly, about the double action and how if you pulled on the trigger alone you had to put a lot of pressure on it, but if you first cocked the hammer back with your thumb the trigger pressure was considerably lighter. He told her it would kick quite a bit, and she should try to count the rounds so as not to run out at an awkward time.

"And . . . the ammo? You've got that?"

"Yes."

"Good." He closed his eyes for a moment, then reopened them. "Won't need to use it . . . but best to be safe."

She didn't tell him about the baying.

"One thing . . ." He frowned at some disturbing thought. "Don't go too quickly . . . whatever you do. Don't risk . . . catching Rolf."

"He'll be miles away by now."

He panted: "Can't be sure! Can't be sure! Please!" It seemed very important to him.

The risk of catching Rolf seemed very small compared to the risk of going too slowly and getting caught in another storm and not being able to get help. But she nodded firmly because she knew it would reassure him.

He wasn't fooled. His hand came out and felt for her arm. "Ragna, you must stay clear. You *must*. He . . . he'd do anything. . . . He'd kill you. D'you understand?" He peered at her for a moment, then added bitterly: "He killed Arne!"

She stared at him.

"Now do you understand? Say you understand."

She managed: "I understand."

And she did. After the initial shock it was surprisingly easy. Somehow killing seemed a natural extension of Rolf's character.

Poor Arne . . .

She shook herself free. She didn't want to leave without a look of unshakable confidence on her face; she wanted Hal to believe that she would bring help soon.

More than that. She wanted to leave Hal with . . . Her heart tightened.

She leaned forward and pressed her cheek against his battered face. "I love you," she said. "I love you with all my heart."

He was silent. When she pulled back she saw he had screwed his face up into a mild grimace. He gave a small exclamation of something between fondness and exasperation. Ragna . . ." And opening his eyes, he smiled faintly. "Just be careful."

"I will."

"Sure of the route?"

"Sure."

There was a silence. Impulsively she added: "I meant it."

"What?" But he knew.

"That I loved you."

"Tell me . . . when we're back in Tromsø."

"I will." She looked away. "Time to be off," she said brusquely.

"Yes."

"I've put food here—and the water flask's in there with you. And the matches are by the candle."

"Yes." He gave her an I'll-be-all-right look.

She pulled on her anorak. Then, fiddling with her gloves, she asked: "Tell me one thing, love, before I go. Tell me—what did Rolf have to do with Pasvik?"

He didn't answer at first. She stole a glance at him. He was frowning again.

"I need the truth, Hal," she prompted.

He narrowed his lips and turned his head to one side. After a time he seemed to come to a decision. Turning back, he said slowly and deliberately: "Rolf's . . . a spy. He leaked Pasvik to the Russians. Jan . . . Mattis . . . walked into a trap."

37

The police truck whined up the road in four-wheel drive and emerged from the thick mist that filled Kåfjord Valley into a clear starlit night.

It was Aslak who first spotted the car and pointed it out to the driver. They drew up beside it. It was impossible to see what color it was, for it was completely covered with thick frost which glittered and sparkled in the starlight. But Aslak recognized it. He told the police sergeant: "It's Ragna Johansen's."

They forced open the doors and looked inside, but there was nothing to be seen.

Two miles farther on they found the Land-Rover. That too was empty.

Soon afterward the condition of the road began to make the police driver decidedly nervous, and within sight of the hut by the lake he drew up and turned his vehicle around, ready to start straight back. Aslak and his cousin, Erkki Hetta, climbed out and, donning their skis and rucksacks, waved at the departing truck and started southward, pausing only to take a brief look inside the hut.

Aslak set the pace, a fast one. If Hal had been traveling at full speed Aslak knew they hadn't a hope of catching him, but if, as Aslak suspected, he had been slowed down by his injuries, if indeed he was in trouble, then they might just have a chance of finding him.

Aslak remembered the route they had traced on the map before Hal left, and it was this one that he followed.

It was three in the morning; the air was clear with only the

ightest wind. The temperature was very low, making the
now dry and powdery under their skis. Ideal. While it lasted.

hrane kept himself awake with strong black coffee and the
timulus of a growing bad temper. The army had finally mobi-
zed itself. A unit stationed near Skibotn had put up a road
lock on the Finland road, while another was hanging around
n Kåfjord, though what for, God only knew. It was all too
ttle too late. The crack mountain troops were cooling their
eels in Skibotn.

In the meantime, Ekeland had called from Oslo to report
hat things were moving very slowly on the diplomatic front.
The Finns wanted to know whether a warrant had been issued
or Berg, and if so, on what grounds. On receipt of the infor-
nation they would consider holding the man. But, they clearly
mplied, not before.

The Norwegian ministry of foreign affairs had subsequently
equested an official search for two other people believed to
e up on the plateau. This had confused the Finns consider-
bly—were these other people also wanted? Were they in
some way connected with the man Berg? Why had they gone
up onto the plateau in these conditions?

But despite having received few answers, the Finns had
agreed to mount an air search at first light, weather permit-
ting. It was a matter of pride that search and rescue were always offered immediately, without question.

They had also agreed to send a patrol up along the road
toward the Norwegian border, in case the subjects had made it
that far.

Ekeland asked if Thrane had any news from his end.
Thrane told him what little there was to report, carefully failing to mention that the two Lapps, Aslak Hetta and his companion, were on their way up onto the plateau. No point in
confusing the issue, not when Hetta had been planning to go
anyway.

Ekeland rang off. Thrane noticed he had made no apology
for having wrongly accused Starheim. In Thrane's absence he
was doubtless taking full credit for identifying Berg.

Thrane didn't awfully care. The important thing was that

something was being done at last. Yet he was haunted by th
fear that it wasn't enough.

He paced the room restlessly, then stopped to look at th
wall map for the fiftieth time, going over the route again an
again—the route that he would take if he were trying to ge
from Kåfjord to Finland. And not just to Finland—that wa
easy—but to safety.

From the top of Kåfjord Valley there was a natural trail tha
led over the border, through shallow valleys, along water
courses, heading south for some twenty-five miles until on
reached a small lake. Then there was a choice—to turn wes
and make straight for the road, which was only about eigh
miles away, or to carry on south until one hit the road at ;
more oblique angle, which was a distance of thirteen miles.

Thrane always chose the shorter route, mainly becaus
there was no advantage in the longer one. Neither brough
one out near any sort of civilization. Whichever Berg chose, h
would be forced to wait for some passing transport. Since th
Finns were patrolling the road, this might well result in hi
being held, if only for a short time.

On the other hand, Berg might be wary of the short route
It would bring him onto the road only a few miles south of th
very border post he'd tried so unsuccessfully to pass. He migh
guess there were patrols looking for him. He might keep ou
of sight of the road until he was many miles to the south. He
might . . . do anything.

Thrane paced to the window, to the desk, and back again,
fretting unhappily. The worst thing was being stuck here, jus
waiting for news, while everything was happening miles away.

Krog arrived with a sandwich, which looked almost as tired
as Thrane felt.

Thrane chewed on it moodily, hardly registering its flavor,
which was probably just as well.

He paused in mid-bite and shot a look at Krog. "Got a car?"

"Er—you want one? Our friends here can arrange one for
you, I'm sure."

"No, I mean *you*. Have you got a car?"

"Yes."

"Good." He stood up.

Krog said hurriedly: "When I say it's mine, it belongs to the
department."

"But I assume it hasn't got FO/S written all over it."

Krog blushed slightly. "No."

"In that case I'll have it off you, thanks."

"But—"

"You stay here and keep the shop. I'll keep in touch."

"Right."

"And if anyone phones, I've gone to Skibotn."

"And if the CO at Skibotn calls?"

"I've gone to Kåfjord."

Krog grinned. He'd gotten the idea.

Berg stopped impatiently for a deicing. With his gloved hand he scraped clusters of ice from the front of his headwarmer where his breath had frozen onto the wool, then rubbed at his eyelids, which were heavy with ice beads. Finally he checked his skis, which were gliding badly. No snow had accumulated on them: He decided the cold was the problem—it had made the snow hard and grainy.

He adjusted his hood. The night was alive with faint whispers of sound: vague cracklings and squeakings from the frozen bogs beneath, as if the very ground were expanding.

He set off again, relieved that the earth sounds were drowned by the squeak and crunch of his skis. He loathed having to stop—he hated the sound of stillness and the menace of an unchanging scene; he always felt that the snow was rising up around him, trying to swallow him up.

But being on his way—that exhilarated him. Because he knew now that nothing—and certainly not this godforsaken place—was going to beat him. It wasn't far to the lake, and there he would turn west and head straight for the road, no more than ten miles farther on. Twelve miles in all—four hours at the most.

His optimism was in stark contrast to his mood during the long hours in the fog-bound hut. The place had been empty of fuel and food. Using up almost the last of his stores, he'd eaten a half-frozen can of meat and a bar of chocolate which had been so hard he'd almost lost a tooth on it. For water he'd been forced to suck snow. Even wrapped in his sleeping bag the cold had been appalling and he'd hardly slept. And when he'd finally dozed into an uneasy sleep, it was only to find himself locked in a cell, no more than a few feet square, a cell where he was doomed to remain for years—which to him was forever. The sense of claustrophobia, of desperation, was overwhelming. But it was nothing compared to the curious emotion he felt when the dream allowed him to look out through the grilles and discover that his prison was not in Norway but in Russia.

When he'd finally awoken with a terrible start, it was to find that the fog had lifted and had probably been gone for some time. He'd cursed himself for wasting time.

But now he was on his way and going well, fueled by the certainty that he was going to make it. His only worry was what to do once he reached the road. Would they be looking for him? Would there be a reception committee? Presumably Hal had told someone—the Norwegian authorities. What Berg couldn't work out was how Hal had known where to find him. It was extraordinary. Perhaps the Land-Rover had been seen going up Kåfjord Valley. It was the only thing he could think of.

But even if the Norwegians were on to him, would the Finns agree to search for him? And if they managed to find him, would they hold him? A lot would depend on what the Norwegians had told the Finns they wanted him for.

If only he'd managed to talk to Niki. Niki would have fixed it.

If only he'd gotten the Land-Rover through that border post.

If only—yes, the real foul-up—if only he'd finished Hal off back at the island. Then he'd have been all right.

That's where a little kindness got you.

Well, Hal was dead now. Even if he hadn't been dead when Berg left, he would have been shortly after. No one could have survived a night in the open.

Berg checked his bearings. The lake should be coming up at any moment. He peered ahead. There was no moon, and the stars that had lured him from the hut had vanished. Nothing to worry about though—it was only a haze; there was no sign of the fog returning. Nevertheless, navigation was difficult: The snow was featureless and appeared to blend straight into the sky. He could just make out hills on either side, but it wasn't until the ground gently dropped away that he realized he was entering some sort of gully.

His skis lurched and rasped over rocky ground—a frozen brook probably. He guessed it must feed into the lake. His spirits rose even further.

He came up against a small boulder and moved around it. Then—

Aow-ooo!

An animal cry. Close.

The sound screamed at him, he started violently, the adrenaline leapt into his veins, his arms jerked into the air, he thrust his right arm back, grappling wildly for his rifle.

Then his ski slipped.

Fear grabbed at him.

He was *falling*!

He flailed his arms, clutching the air for something solid. He tried desperately to regain his footing.

But the ground wasn't there.

He was falling and there was nothing *there*.

He went backward, fast. The end of one of his skis caught on something and twisted around.

Then he hit the ground, his head jerked back, his skis were catapulted upward, almost yanking his legs out of their sockets, and one struck him hard in the face.

But he was on the ground—winded, stunned, but down. He was aware of enormous surprise and relief, and the next moment, of pain. His winded stomach was in spasm, his shoulder had taken a bad knock, his face was stinging—but that was all; his rucksack seemed to have taken most of the impact.

He sat up slowly, still very dazed, and took stock. Face—just a bruise, shoulder twisted and painful; then there was his neck—that had been whipped backward and was very stiff. Nothing else.

Lucky.

Rifle okay, which was just as well because he'd chucked Hal's away to save weight.

He gathered his wits and looked around. He saw now that he had fallen straight over a sheer drop of about fifteen feet. Reaching out, he touched long thick icicles.

What cursed luck. A bloody waterfall.

Then, as he regained his breath, he remembered—that sound. What had it been?

A fox? A wolverine or lynx—hell, a wolf?

But there was no sound now. Whatever it was had gone.

He levered himself weakly to his feet and checked himself over again. Okay.

The silence seemed alive. He felt the familiar panic closing in on him. Time to press on.

He set off. His right shoulder was very painful, almost impossible to move. Dragging his right pole uselessly, he put all his weight on his left.

It was only when he had fought his way through a dense patch of frosted brushwood and emerged onto clear snow that he realized there was something wrong with his right ski.

He bent down to examine it.

Split.

He swore aloud, long and viciously. The front section had split longitudinally, from the tip almost as far as his boot. When he lifted the ski one side sagged away. In a furious anger he ripped off the loose wood, roughly halving the original width, and started off again, plodding awkwardly but determinedly.

Nothing—*nothing*—was going to stop him from reaching that road.

Ragna realized she was going to make it. And the knowledge spurred her on.

It had been hard at the beginning. Her muscles had been painfully stiff, her legs as heavy as lead, and a couple of large blisters on her feet had burst and smarted with pain. She'd thought she'd never warm up. But slowly, slowly, she had come alive.

Now she was feeling good—not tired at all—and her limbs were moving fluidly: she felt as if she could go on forever.

It was amazing how the miles slipped by when you had the right wax and a binding that didn't flip off every few strides. She'd found the hut within an hour of leaving Hal. She'd also found Rolf's tracks leading away to the south.

She'd followed the tracks for a while, until the sky had clouded over and she could no longer see them. Now she was going by her own navigation. Every so often she stopped and checked the luminous hand of the compass and looked at her watch and worked out how far she had come. It gave her a strange thrill to realize how logical, how simple, all this navigation was—and how well she was doing it.

An extraordinary and rare confidence filled her. It sprang from pure determination: nothing and no one was going to prevent her from reaching that road. Not wolves—in fact she had stopped worrying about them a long time ago. They were frightened of men, weren't they? She'd read that often enough. They wouldn't harm her unless they had to.

And not Rolf—certainly not! *He* should fear *her*. Ah—for the chance to catch just a glimpse of him.

And yet . . .

Hal was right. An encounter would be disastrous. Rolf had killed Arne. Perhaps he'd killed others.

Would he kill her if he had to?

Probably. If she didn't kill him first. The thought gave her a savage satisfaction. She imagined the scene: she had a gun—a large one—and she held it steadily. He was standing in front of her, unarmed. Though he tried to stare her out, she held his gaze unwaveringly. He came toward her, smiling that glittering smile of his, saying those soft oh-so-reasonable words, thinking she'd never do it. . . . And she pulled the trigger. Just like that.

The next moment she saw the idea for what it was: ridiculous—she'd never be able to kill anyone—but also unworthy. She was merely allowing herself to be dragged down to Rolf's level. Nothing would ever bring Jan back. Certainly not more violence.

All the same, it was just as well Rolf was ahead and getting farther ahead all the time.

Just as well.

Another fifteen minutes passed. Her eyelids felt heavy and it took her a while to realize they were almost iced up. Without stopping she brushed the ice away. Her nose had lost feeling, her cheeks were smarting with cold, her feet throbbed dully. But nothing could be done; she must keep going. It couldn't be far to the lake. And then it was only eight miles to the road.

To her disappointment she began to feel tired. Just a little. Perhaps she had been going too fast after all.

Steady, steady.

The hills closed in, the ground fell slightly. She realized she was in some sort of narrow valley. The going got rough. She went very carefully, picking her way around the snow thatched stones and boulders. For one heart-stopping moment she almost stepped over a great ledge, but managed to pull herself back in time. When her pulse had stopped racing, she made her way to one side and carefully sidestepped down.

In the bottom of the gully she ran into stunted bushes, completely white with hoarfrost and invisible against the soft night-glow of the snow. They reared up in front of her, swiping at her face, catching at her clothes until she despaired of getting free.

But then the scrub was behind her and the snow was smooth and even once more.

She had reached the shores of the lake.

She made her calculations again—with the map this time—and there was no doubt.

West. Just eight miles.

Turning, getting her bearings, she settled into her stride, closing her mind to everything except the rhythm of her body, thinking only of the next step, and the one after that, and the one after that . . .

Did Hal think like this—taking each step as it came—when he had a long way to go? Yes, somehow she was certain this was exactly how he thought, and the idea warmed her.

An image of the lonely shelter in its vast expanse of emptiness flashed into her mind, and she pressed forward, the tiredness almost forgotten.

The interior of the smart new Volvo sedan was warm as toast. It was hard to believe it was minus thirty-five outside. Kari Valta glanced across at her husband. He was frowning slightly as he concentrated on his driving.

"Want a rest?" he asked.

"No, I'm all right for the moment."

She looked down at the map on her knees. Shining a penlight on it she remarked: "Only twenty minutes to the Norwegian border."

"We've made good time, then."

"Yes."

They had left their home in the suburbs of Helsinki at three the previous morning and had been traveling for twenty-four hours, with only the shortest of breaks to stretch their legs and put snow chains on the tires. The snow chains were a nuisance—they reduced speed and made a nasty drumming sound—but they prevented delay on the uncleared sections of the road. Generally, though, the snowplows had been doing a good job and, until they had reached this last section over the plateau, the roads had been fairly clear.

Mikko Valta asked: "Where's the next settlement?"

"According to this, there's an isolated house of some sort in about five minutes."

"We'll stop there, then."

"Yes."

"Unless you think we should press on."

"Oh, no." Kari rarely disagreed with her husband. That was why they made such a good team.

After a few minutes she checked the odometer. "Any moment now, on the left," she said.

Sure enough, the dark shape of a dwelling appeared. They slowed and stopped. The house, such as it was, was completely dark.

"No one at home," Mikko Valta observed.

"No."

"I'll go and check anyway."

"Yes."

He was back within two minutes. "Closed up," he said, and started off again.

"Nothing until the border now."

"Right."

She stared intently ahead, continuously scanning the area on either side of the headlights, not losing concentration for so much as a moment.

But there was nothing to see. After a time she glanced at the odometer. "Nearly at the border," she said.

"Tell me when, then."

"A little further." After a minute she said: "Now."

He pulled up and put on the hand brake. "Want to drive?"

"Sure." They changed places.

As soon as they were settled again she did a careful three-point turn—this was no time to get stuck in the soft snow at

the sides of the road—and set off back the way they had
come. "I'll keep our speed down."

"Yes."

He reached down to the floor. "Hungry?" he said.

"I am, rather."

He pulled a large plastic food box onto his knee and took
out some sandwiches, two apples, and two prewrapped pieces
of cake.

He replaced the box on the floor and, almost without thinking, ran a hand under his seat to check that the Luger P08 was
still clipped safely to the underside. It was.

Sitting up, he began to unwrap the sandwiches.

38

The road wasn't where it was supposed to be. Ragna couldn't believe it. And after all her careful calculations.

She stood, staring stupidly around her, longing to sink into the snow and get the weight of the rucksack off her back yet refusing to, knowing that the road must be so near.

It was eight in the morning, she'd been going for five hours, and according to the map she should be there. Yet in the clinging darkness she could see nothing but endless rolling snow. Worse, there was a hill ahead. Not a large one; in fact, it was probably no more than a slight bulge, but, tired as she was, it might as well have been a mountain.

Turning right to skirt the hill, she started off again at a heavy plod, slipping back into the numb mindlessness that had carried her forward for so long. Had it really been five hours? She'd lost all sense of time; when she looked at her watch the readings seemed to bear no relation to what was going on around her. Even her present vaguely defined misery seemed removed from her body, hardly to do with her at all.

A distant note—like a far-off insect—hovered in her ears. That too was unreal.

But it wasn't unreal. Suddenly she jumped awake and pulled her hood away from her ears.

A humming—an engine.

She looked about wildly.

Above the hill the dark sky glowed with light, whitening steadily until the rim of the hill became a hard black line. The light became intense, throwing up rays like the spokes of a wheel, then it was past, dimming rapidly. The engine sound rose, then fell away; the unseen vehicle had gone.

Ragna felt a momentary disappointment, then optimism—there'd be another car. The point was: she'd found the road!

Abandoning the circuitous route, she set herself straight at the slope.

An official vehicle, either police or army; it was impossible to tell.

Berg watched its taillights curve away into the darkness and realized: They were probably looking for *him*.

Well, at least he knew. At least he hadn't run into the road asking for a ride and gotten a nasty surprise.

Suddenly he felt very depressed. What had he done to deserve this unending run of foul luck? Hadn't he run circles around the precious Norwegians for years? Hadn't he outdone them at every turn?

And Niki. Jesus—hadn't he done enough for him? Why hadn't Niki protected him?

His anger mingled with a deeper tiredness. What he needed was a long rest. A nice holiday in the sun. The more he thought about it the more he fancied Australia.

Niki'd be arranging that now.

The thought cheered him.

All he had to do was get out of this place. Stop a civilian car, hijack it, or get into a house—there must be one somewhere—and use the phone . . .

He'd find a way. He always had.

In the meantime he huddled back into the snow and shifted his shoulder until the sharp pain eased. He closed his eyes. Sleep. Just for a while. Then he'd get on his way again.

South.

Ragna sank back into the snow at the roadside. It was unimaginable bliss to take the weight off her legs, to lean the heavy rucksack on the snow, not to have to make any more effort. She wouldn't stay long—an icy wind had sprung up and was swirling down the exposed road—but for a while, just a while . . .

Intending to have no more than a moment's rest she closed

her eyes and let her head drop forward, and immediately slipped into a light doze.

It was the creeping fingers of cold that eventually woke her, sucking at her body, drawing out the hard-won warmth. Rousing herself, she looked up. She realized she had been asleep for some minutes.

She peered about her, trying to take stock. The snow was lit by the first glimmerings of somber light and it was possible to make out the shapes of the hills, the line of the road, which stretched away into an empty distance in both directions.

How long before another car came?

It struck her that it might be a very long time. It was already nine. Suddenly she was furious with herself. How could she have let so much time pass! No good waiting. She must get going.

Pulling out the battered map she peered at it in the feeble light. One house was shown some miles to the south, but there was a strong possibility it was uninhabited at this time of year. To the north, however, was the border. That was most certainly inhabited. She remembered the three guards, and the one with the rifle, and the shots he'd fired; it all seemed a very long time ago.

She estimated the distance—ten miles. Another three hours, maybe less. She could hardly imagine keeping going that long. But she would, because she had to go somewhere, and it was the only place to go.

She pulled her last ration of chocolate out of her pocket and, breaking the rock-hard pieces off with her teeth, got wearily to her feet. She decided she'd go much faster without skis—the snow on the road was hard-packed and quite good for walking—so she left them at the roadside. Keeping her poles, she hoisted her rucksack higher on her back and, shivering in the vicious little wind, began the long trudge north.

It was uphill for as far as she could see, which was to a bend some half-mile away, but the gradient was slight. Nevertheless she divided the distance to the top of the hill into sections—halfway, three quarters—and concentrated on one milestone at a time.

Head down, eyes fixed a few yards ahead, she was aware of nothing but the panting of her breath, the scrunch of her boots on the snow, and the patter of tiny snow grains driven against her legs by the scurrying wind.

She didn't see the car. Not until it was well on its way down the hill. Then the lights caught her eye and she jerked her head upward.

For a moment she stared, not daring to believe what she was seeing.

Then she let out a joyful shriek and, moving into the center of the road, began to wave both poles frantically in the air, shouting wildly and ineffectually through the muffling layers of her hood.

The car approached, slowed, and drew to a halt.

Ragna went around to the driver's side and leaned down.

A woman wound down the window. In the seat next to her was a man. They both stared at her curiously.

Pulling the hood down from her mouth, Ragna said tearfully: "Oh, I'm so very glad to see you!"

"Where have you come from?" The woman spoke in Swedish, the language educated Finns used to communicate with other Scandinavians.

"I've been . . . I've been . . . I can't—" Ragna clamped her mouth shut and, mustering her Swedish, began again. "Please—*please*—could you take me to the nearest place that has a telephone—it's desperately urgent—someone needs help—I can't explain—"

The woman exchanged glances with the man.

Ragna hovered, expecting the woman to agree rapidly, to invite her in, to reach behind and throw open the rear door.

Instead the couple had a low-voiced discussion. Ragna couldn't believe it—how could the matter be in doubt? In this sort of wild country no one discussed whether to give help—it was given automatically and without question.

The woman turned back. "Who is this person who's in trouble?"

"You mean—you want his *name*?"

"Yes."

Ragna stared incredulously. "What difference does it make?" she shouted.

The woman's face was unyielding in the gray light. "We want to know."

Ragna threw her head back in disbelief. "His name is Starheim. Halvard Starheim! Now, are you going to help save his life or not?"

The woman looked back to the man. He muttered something then broke off suddenly and leaned forward in his seat, as if to take a better look at Ragna. Did he think she was a madwoman or something? Did he think she was going to—what? Her imagination failed. "For God's sake!" she cried.

The man's eyes were hidden in shadow but he was still leaning forward, staring hard. The woman too was staring—but past Ragna.

Past?

The tiniest suspicion darted into her mind.

She began to turn.

Something grabbed her.

She jumped violently and shrieked.

An arm had encircled her chest. Hard. The arm yanked her backward until her back was arched over her rucksack, her body pinned hard against the arm's owner.

Rolf's voice said in her ear: "Darling, I've been looking for you everywhere."

Berg smiled hard at the woman in the car. "Dreadful weather to be out, isn't it?"

The woman did not return his smile. Berg suddenly remembered his bruised eye—he probably looked a sight.

He said loudly to Ragna: "Darling, you really mustn't wander off like that. Really. I wasn't badly hurt at all. No need to get hysterical. It was only a fall." He cast an eye at the woman in the car. She was lapping it up all right. He said to her: "We were stranded, you know. The most ridiculous thing."

Berg sensed Ragna coming alive again, gathering herself to squawk. He moved his grip onto her arm, squeezed hard, and, wincing at the pain in his shoulder, drew the pistol out of his pocket and dug it hard into her ribs, whispering: *"One word . . ."*

She gave a slight gasp and became absolutely still.

"Well, can we have a lift?" Berg asked brightly.

The woman conversed with her companion. "Are you this man Starheim?" she asked.

Berg thought quickly. "Yes. I'm Starheim." And, pushing Ragna toward the rear door, he let go of her arm and tried the handle. It was locked. What were these people up to?

He leaned down at the open front window. "What's the problem?"

"We thought you might be someone else. We were looking for a friend."

They were *what*? Berg's patience was fast running out. He snapped: "Too bad! We're here and he's not!"

"His name is Harri."

"Well, you can—" Berg broke off and gaped at the woman. "Harri . . ." he repeated stupidly. Then in a wild upsurge of relief and joy he laughed, a wild crowing sort of a laugh. "Harri. *I'm* Harri!"

The woman looked a little dubious. "We have a mutual friend, then."

Berg realized: They wanted a name. There was only one name he could think of.

"Niki," he said.

It was the magic word. The woman smiled and, leaning back, unlocked the rear door.

Though Ragna was looking ahead, she registered nothing of the Volvo's progress over the long white road. She saw only the back of Rolf's head as he leaned forward to talk to the two in the front; she saw the thick blond hair, the hair she had thought so beautiful, the hair she had stroked. And she saw his hand clutching the pistol, the hand that had touched every part of her, made her body come alive, the hand that had killed Arne and shot Hal.

She couldn't take her eyes from that hand.

Rolf glanced back at her from time to time, keeping the pistol pointed in her direction. He glanced at her as if she weren't there.

It occurred to her that he was planning to kill her.

The man in the front said: "This is it."

They were approaching an unlit house set just back from the road. A deep dread gnawed at Ragna's stomach.

"It's empty," said the man. "I checked it earlier."

"Okay," Rolf said. "I won't be long."

"Can you manage?" said the woman to Rolf, glancing in Ragna's direction.

"I'll need help to get in."

"No trouble," said the man.

Rolf took a moment to slip his rucksack off his shoulders. Ragna noticed that he held his right arm oddly, as if he'd hurt it, and that he winced slightly as he moved. There was a heavy bruise on his face too, as though he'd been in some sort of accident.

"Open the door, Ragna." He gestured with the pistol.

She reached for the handle and maneuvered herself out, pulling her rucksack after her. Rolf got out, saying: "You wait just over there." She went and stood where he had indicated.

Keeping the pistol on her, Rolf waited as the man went around to the trunk and, opening it, removed a rope and some tools.

Rolf took the rope from him and, looping it over his shoulder, came up to Ragna.

She said: "Is that for me?"

"Yes. We can't possibly take you with us, you see." He gave her that slow smile, that intense look she knew so well—the one he used to charm people. She stared, trying to reconcile the smile with the Rolf who killed so easily.

She said: "You're not going to kill me, then?"

The smile changed into something colder. "No, of course not." He sounded offended.

"I suppose I should be grateful."

His lips narrowed, his eyes flashed with anger. "I've only done what I've had to do, Ragna."

"Oh?" She let the bitterness show in her voice. "You had to shoot Hal, did you?"

"Yes. It was him or me."

"And Jan?"

She'd caught him there; she saw the surprise in his face. He said in an injured voice: "I had nothing to do with it, Ragna! Hal always had that stupid idea it was me. Always. But it just isn't true." His eye had an open frank look; his voice invited confidence and trust.

"I see," she said. And she did. She saw that he was a compulsive and well-practiced liar.

The man came up, a crowbar in his hand, and Rolf gestured Ragna toward the house.

It was a small single-story building with boarded-up windows. The man went to work on the door with a crowbar. There was a splintering of wood and the door swung open.

Rolf indicated that Ragna should lead the way.

It was very dark inside. Someone switched on a torch. The beam sprang out and weaved around the walls, revealing a narrow passageway.

"I'll keep watch," said the man's voice. "Here." She realized he was handing the torch to Rolf.

Rolf shone the beam up the passage. "Go ahead," he said.

Ragna went forward. There were three doors at the end of the passage. Choosing the one that was already open, she turned left. Rolf's torch flashed into the room, revealing a table, two benches on either side, a tall cupboard.

Ragna went in and, lowering her rucksack onto the floor, turned to face Rolf.

"Make yourself comfortable," he said. "You might be here for some time." He shone the torch beam onto the walls and, finding a light switch, flicked it on and off several times. It didn't work.

"How long?" she asked quietly.

"Some hours. Maybe a day." He was hunting around the room.

"How will anyone know I'm here?"

"I'll phone." She'd heard that before—several times. The gnawing dread returned.

He gave a small exclamation of triumph and, going to the table, put down the torch and struck a match. He put the flame to a candle and a flickering yellow light filled the room. She realized he had put the pistol down to light the candle. Too late: he was already picking it up again.

She must think. She must *think*.

Slipping the rope coil off his shoulder he started to fiddle with it, but awkwardly, because of the pistol. His face was in shadow.

She had less than a minute. In a minute he would have her hands tied.

Panic clawed at her; she had to do something.

It was now or never.

Her heart thumped against her ribs.

Now.

Slowly, carefully, she bent down and reached for her rucksack. Her hand found one of the straps. She unhitched it. The clasp made a faint clinking sound.

His voice sprang out: "What are you doing?"

"My sleeping bag. You said to—"

"Wait!" He came up and waved her away. She backed off. "Anything in here?" he demanded. "Anything that shouldn't be here?"

"What do you mean?"

"A gun."

She was frozen into silence, her mouth moved soundlessly, she looked nervously toward the rucksack.

He read her face in the candlelight and gave an exclamation of fury. *"Christ, you—!"* Dropping onto one knee beside the rucksack, he began to pull at the second strap, saying viciously: "You don't know when you're well off, Ragna!" He gave a derisive laugh. "And you were going to reach for it, were you? My dear girl, I would have killed you in a second!"

He jerked at the strap with his free hand, but it wouldn't yield. He said in a cold rage: "Come and undo this!"

She couldn't move, her throat was dry, she wanted to scream. He *would* shoot her.

Then she thought of Hal and forced herself forward. She knelt down on Rolf's left, she undid the strap. Still kneeling, she straightened up.

Rolf started to pull things out of the bag.

The fear was so bad she had to bite her teeth together to prevent them from chattering.

He waved the pistol at her and she realized he wanted her to move away again.

She started to get to her feet, she slid her hand into her pocket, she gripped the bulky handle of the revolver, she began to pull it out. Rolf's head turned a little. She froze. But then he was bending over the rucksack, rummaging through it with his left hand. His gun hand sagged away, the pistol pointing at the floor.

She straightened up. She couldn't bring herself to pull the

revolver right out of her pocket. She felt ill; the blood roared in her ears. She tried to speak. Nothing happened. She croaked: "It's in the bottom."

"What?"

"The gun." She tightened her grip on the revolver.

He gave an exclamation of impatience and plunged his hand farther into the rucksack, twisting his crouching body slightly away from her.

She pulled the revolver out of her pocket. Now. Her senses screaming, her limbs shaking, she darted quickly behind him and, with both hands, thrust the revolver against the back of his neck.

He gave a violent start, jerked his head sideways, and began to twist his body and his gun arm around, trying to bring the pistol to bear over his left shoulder. His neck was slipping away; Ragna felt the barrel of the revolver losing contact. The fear stabbed at her. She followed his neck as it twisted, thrust her hands forward, found the neck again, and jabbed the revolver even harder into his flesh.

His body stopped twisting but his gun arm was still moving, whipping around. *Coming for her.*

She stepped farther behind him, keeping his body between her and the pistol.

"D-o-n't!" she screeched.

The arm, the pistol, were still coming.

"D-o-n't!"

He gave a sudden hiss of pain: The gun stopped coming. He grasped his shoulder and bowed his head, as if in agony.

Was he really hurt? Was it a trick?

There was a moment of silence, broken only by the panting of their breath. Ragna was shaking so badly it was all she could do to keep the gun pressed against his neck.

Slowly he twisted his head around again, trying to get a look at her. *Trying to work out how to grab her.* His bared teeth glinted in the light.

"Ragna . . ." he said softly.

She jabbed at his neck and cried: "D-o-n't, *don't, don't!*" Why didn't he shut up?

"Listen . . ."

She said: "I'll—I'll kill you—if—you—move."

"Ragna—"

"Don't—move or I'll do it."

"Ragna—you don't want to *kill* me."

"Don't move." She felt weak. What happened now? She didn't know what to do.

"My love, you'd regret it, you'd regret it terribly. It's me, remember? *Me*. Don't we mean something to each other? Weren't we good together? It was special for me, Ragna. Very." His voice was soft and low: The voice he used in bed.

She tried to shut the voice out, to think—to *think*.

"Ragna, remember the way we made love. It was good, wasn't it? Not something we could pretend about. Ragna, believe me, I wouldn't dream of harming you. I was only going to tie you up. It was going to be so simple. You'd have been found in a few hours. So why this, Ragna?"

"Stop! Get up! *No!* Stay there! *Don't move!*" She pressed the gun even harder against his neck. God, she was going to die of terror.

"But why all this?" Rolf asked reasonably. "What's the point?"

Ragna froze: a sound in the passage. The man! He was coming back to find out what was happening.

She knew Rolf had heard the sound too.

"Ragna," he went on carefully, as if explaining something to a child, "I'm going to stand up now, and I'm going to take your gun away and I'm going to tie you up—very gently—and then we'll be able to stick to the original plan, and no one'll come to any harm. Okay?"

He began to move.

She pushed the gun at his neck.

He kept moving.

More sounds from the passage. A voice calling: "All right?"

Ragna hissed: "Tell him it's all right!"

Rolf was getting slowly to his feet.

"Tell him!"

Rolf hesitated, then called: "All right."

"Don't be long!" The sound of retreating footsteps.

Rolf began to straighten up.

She kept the gun on his neck. She felt paralyzed, unable to decide what to do.

"Can't tie me up!" she declared.

He was standing up. "Won't be for long."

"Got to rescue Hal."

A pause. "Hal will be dead by now." He began to turn.

"No!"

He kept turning. *He'd grab her at any moment.*

She leapt backward—getting distance, *distance*—and pointed the gun at his chest, finger hard on the trigger. "Don't!" And this time her voice was a low growl.

He hesitated, then kept turning. In the flickering light she saw his gun hand coming around, she saw that beautiful ruthless face.

And then her uncertainty dropped away as if it had never existed. With a sense of being outside herself, of watching herself from far, far away, she squeezed the trigger.

Nothing. The trigger didn't move.

A moment of horror. She remembered—she must press much harder.

A sudden movement. Rolf. He'd realized. His arm—the pistol—was whipping up.

She squeezed with all her might.

The gun gave an almighty kick, an explosion filled the room, she was deafened.

She opened her eyes. Rolf was falling backward, backward. Gently, as though in slow motion, he crumpled onto the floor.

For a moment she couldn't move. She stared. Sounds encroached on her . . . small moans. It took her an instant to realize: It was she who was moaning. She moved forward a little way, stopped, moved again. Looked down. Stared.

The sense of unreality returned.

There was a red mess where Rolf's left eye had been. Blood spread across his nose and dribbled onto the floor.

She couldn't understand it: she'd aimed at his chest.

A sound from the passage.

The man.

Instantly alert again, she backed away into the shadows of the room.

"Hey!" the man's voice called. "Let's go! Come on! Let's go!"

Ha! She thought: Wrong person! Wrong person! It's me! It's *me*! I did it!

"Hey?" It was more of a question now. A squeak of boards: he was coming down the passage.

Ragna gripped the gun again. Then she remembered the double action, and finding the hammer, pulled it back with her thumb.

"Hey?" The voice was doubtful now. He began to appear around the door—an arm, a shoulder, finally a head. He paused, halfway in. He'd seen Rolf.

He looked down; he looked up; he saw her.

For a moment they stared at one another. Then, baring her teeth, she leveled the gun and squeezed.

His head vanished, the shot roared out.

When she opened her eyes he'd gone.

She ducked into the shadow of the tall cupboard, just in case the head popped back around the door. She thought: No one'll catch me now! No one! No one'll stop me now! And she raged with savage delight.

Silence. The rage began to die in her. Where was he? Her senses expanded.

A motor revving. The car. They were going.

Might be a trick. *Yes!* Couldn't fool her that easily! She laughed inwardly. She wasn't such a fool as to fall for that!

The motor revved to an even higher pitch, and drew away, fading rapidly.

Had they gone?

Then another sound. A second car. Idling.

The last of the rage ebbed out of her and she lowered the gun.

Thrane drove with the heat turned low. This was a severe form of punishment—he was half frozen—but it was the only sure way of keeping awake.

He'd seen nothing since leaving the border. He didn't know what he'd expected to find, but he couldn't help feeling rather disappointed. And now it was beginning to snow. That was all they needed! If it got any worse the Finns would have to call off their air search almost before it had begun.

He'd already passed the point he'd marked on the map, the point where he'd have joined the road if he'd been Berg. He'd slowed, had a good look around, and seen nothing. Now he

was five miles on and heading for the second mark on hi
map, the only other place he could imagine Berg joining th
road.

Coming over a slight rise he blinked and took notice.

A car, parked on the road with its taillights on. Next to ;
small dwelling. He peered through the wipers.

Travelers. But it might be worth having word with them
They might have seen something, you never knew.

They might even have picked up an extra passenger.

One could never be too careful. He slipped his Colt pisto
out of his jacket and onto the seat beside him.

The car was a Volvo, quite a new one by the look of it. It
engine was running. He drove up slowly, trying to get the
whole picture.

Someone was sitting in the driver's seat. The door of the
house appeared to be open.

Thrane drew to a halt some yards behind and looked at the
car's registration. Finnish. He memorized it.

The person in the car was agitated: a head kept peering
around, then the figure gesticulated urgently toward the passenger window, toward the house—

A man shot out of the house at a run. Thrane grabbed his
pistol and, opening the door, jumped out.

The man bolted into the car, and even before the door was
closed the car was spurting away in a cloud of snow.

Thrane stared after it, momentarily indecisive. To search
the house or to follow?

Thrane had never seen the running man before in his life.
He decided on the house.

He made his way through the falling snow, the Colt in his
hand.

A movement. He paused. A woman appeared in the doorway, a revolver dangling from her hand.

He blinked. Under all the heavy clothing it looked like—

It *was*. Ragna Johansen.

He hurried toward her.

She recognized him and a wild ragged grimace of a smile
spread across her face.

39

The area of high pressure was shifting at last, moving east over the Barents Sea. And as it moved the wind swung slowly around to the southeast. This brought a slight but welcome rise in the temperature—on the plateau, up five degrees to thirty below. But the shifting wind also brought something far less welcome: banks of snow-carrying cloud curving in from the Siberian plains. At first the snow came in a whisper, a thin veil of small flakes so light that they danced and swirled in the air. But gradually the flakes thickened, falling more resolutely, settling on the ground, covering the wind-razed surface of the plateau with a layer of soft snow.

And for once there was no howling gale to rip the snow away.

The visibility made an air search impossible. It was called off at ten that first morning.

At about the same time Aslak and Erkki Hetta reached the halfway mark of their journey and decided to press on quickly before the visibility deteriorated any further. They kept their eyes open for signs of life, of course, but the tracks they had been following had long since vanished under the quietly falling snow. From time to time one of them gave a loud cry, a high whoop, in case an answering shout should filter back through the whiteness.

But they saw, they heard, nothing, and as they hurried on through the empty land their hopes began to fall.

If the snow had eased a little, if the light had been a little clearer, they might have seen the marker, the two crossed skis

that Ragna had left standing in the snow beside the boulder
But the two Lapps passed some yards away and never saw
them.

Erkki gave one of his regular whoops a minute later, but
this, like all the calls before, went unanswered. Having no reason to suspect someone might be near, the Lapps did not repeat the call for some minutes, and by that time the boulder
was far behind them.

They sped on. After a few miles they came to the second
hut. In it they found an empty food can and a chocolate wrap-
per, which could well have been left recently—and could
equally well have been left some time before. The two men
could not decide.

Continuing their journey, they came to a gully then a lake.
Here they turned west, taking the shortest route to the road,
resigned to the likelihood that they would find no one, anxious to reach safety before a wind should whip up a blizzard
and force a halt.

In the increasing gloom they eventually found the road
more by accident than design, and began the weary plod back
toward the border. To their relief the Finnish military found
them half an hour later and gave them a lift as far as the
border post, where they sent a telephone report to Tromsø.
Four hours later they got a lift down to Skibotn.

It was about then that the wind came up, a heavy snow-
laden wind that sent the flakes streaking horizontally across
the landscape, blotting out everything, causing would-be res-
cuers to retreat to warmth and safety.

The two Lapps were the last people to venture onto the
plateau for four days.

Hal was woken by a combination of pain and raging thirst.

The thirst was the more urgent sensation. With his right
hand he felt about inside the survival bag for the water flask.
It wasn't there. He dimly remembered drinking from it before—how long ago? And what had he done with it? He had
no idea. With an effort he unfastened the top of the survival
bag and, pushing his hand out, searched the area near his
shoulder. His fingers touched the ice-cold flask. He grasped it.
The cap was hanging loose: he had left it unfastened. Even

before he tipped it up he knew from its weight that it was empty.

These maneuvers had tired him and, abandoning the flask, he closed his eyes again.

A drop of water fell on his face. Drips . . . He was vaguely aware that it was the drips that may have woken him.

Water. He had to do something about a drink.

Reaching behind his head he touched snow and, clawing some off, pressed it into his mouth. He repeated this several times: the chilling effect of the snow on his mouth and stomach was a lesser evil than the thirst.

He rested again—he was incredibly weak—and tried to think how long it had been since Ragna left. A day—two days—more? He had been drifting in and out of consciousness; it was impossible to tell. But from the thirst he guessed it might be as long as two days.

He had an overwhelming urge to sleep again, but resisted it. Reaching out, he touched the food, felt his way across it, and found the candle and matches. Gripping the matches in his teeth, he removed a match and struck it.

It went out immediately.

He tried again, more successfully this time, and, turning his head painfully, screwing his good eye up against the light, he put the lighted match to the candle. He held it there for several seconds before he realized he was nowhere near the candle wick. At the third attempt he made contact and the candle finally flamed.

This completely exhausted him and he was forced to rest again. He looked up at the dark rock just above his head. The surface was covered in ice. One icicle was dripping onto him. This had some significance, though for the moment he couldn't think what.

Ignoring the hum in his dead ear, he tried listening for sounds from outside, but nothing permeated the roof of the shelter.

Finally he roused himself and chewed at some dried fish. He soon gave it up: The stuff was hard as rock, and salty. The can of meat looked more inviting, but he couldn't have opened it if he'd tried. Heating anything was out of the question; the Primus would need pumping, priming, lighting, and he couldn't manage that. He settled on dried apricots—not quite as hard as the fish, and definitely not salty—as well as some glucose tablets.

As his senses slowly came to life he grappled with the significance of the icy rock. Finally he had it: no ventilation. No air was getting into the shelter. Which probably meant snow. Only a hermetic seal of snow could prevent the air from getting in.

He groped behind his head to the point where the tarpaulin met the rock and pushed his hand out through the gap. He touched snow, and more snow. He pulled the tarpaulin away from the rock side and agitated his hand, pulling in snow, until he felt a slight draft on his face.

He settled back, drawing in the cold sweet air.

Better, better.

But there was still the pain, a continuous and painful throbbing in his left hand. No other part of his body hurt, just the hand. As he chewed away at the apricots, he thought about the sort of pain it was and decided he should take a look at it.

However, the meal, such as it was, had worn him out again, and he allowed himself another rest before finally pulling his left hand gingerly out of the survival bag. He knew it must be in a bad way even before he unwound the stained bandage. He had to pull away the last layer bit by bit where it had stuck to the flesh beneath. Such flesh as there was. The first two fingers were a write-off, almost severed near the base. But that wasn't what caused his heart to sink quite so painfully. It was the sight of the swelling, the inflammation, the yellow pus: the rampant infection.

Bringing his hand close up to his eye, he examined the damage from every angle.

He thought about all sorts of things, like how long he might stay in his ice cave, and, if it was a very long time, how he would like to die. As he saw it, he had a choice between the quick agony of blood poisoning and the slow business of starvation.

He didn't know which was worse, but since one offered time and therefore hope and the other didn't, the choice was made.

Reaching for his rucksack he pulled it toward him and took out Aslak's hunting knife. He rubbed his thumb lightly over the blade. Sharp enough. He put the blade over the candle flame for some moments, let it cool, then, holding both hands up in front of his face, he positioned the blade carefully against the side of his first finger, below the damaged section.

Closing his eyes he began to saw the blade back and forth.

It took an instant for the pain to hit him. He gritted his teeth and kept sawing until the pain rose to a sweeping wave of agony and, crying out, he stopped.

Gasping, the sweat starting from his body, he peered at the hand. The first finger was almost off. Bracing himself he drew the knife sharply across and down once more, and it was done. He tossed the bloody remnant away.

Moaning quietly, he screwed up his eyes until the worst of the shaking and shivering had passed, then gathered himself for the rest of the job.

After roughly binding the first stump, which was bleeding profusely, he examined the second finger. This should be easier, since the bone was almost completely shot away. He decided to try to do it in one go. Bracing himself, grimacing in anticipation of the pain, he made one savage cut which was so unexpectedly easy that he had to pull up short to prevent the knife driving into his third and healthy finger.

He gasped and sobbed with pain, and almost slipped into unconsciousness. But he knew he had to make one more effort if the whole exercise wasn't to be in vain. First he squeezed the bleeding stumps to push out any remaining pus, then, fumbling in a pocket of the rucksack, he found the Primus fuel—paraffin—and dabbed some over the wounds. The stinging made tears come to his eyes.

Rebinding the hand tightly in the rough bandage, he refastened the survival bag, closed his eyes, and slipped into a dim half-world where the only reality was pain.

There was only one word for it: cruel. Five days. Five whole days of almost continuous snow. A search party had set off on the first day, but when conditions worsened it had soon returned. Since then—nothing.

For four days Thrane had waited at the Finnish command post, staring out into the gloom, watching the angry snow battering itself against the windows.

Now, on the fifth day, the strain was taking its toll. It was bad enough imagining what Starheim must be going through—even if he was still alive, which Thrane was beginning to doubt—but that was nothing compared to facing Ragna Johansen each day.

He'd never seen anyone disintegrate in front of his eyes before; he'd never imagined it could happen quite so fast. She was like a ghost, with dreadful staring eyes and sunken cheeks. That first day when the search party had returned she'd at least cried her eyes out. But now she just sat in a chair and stared. She wouldn't eat, she hardly slept, she spoke to no one unless she had to.

The only time she spoke to Thrane was when they yet again offered her a room at a nearby house, or when the doctor muttered about shock and hospital rest, but then it was only to grasp Thrane's arm and turn her large imploring eyes on him and beg him to make sure that they allowed her to stay.

He had done what he could and so far they had not insisted. But in view of her deteriorating physical condition he wasn't sure he could put them off much longer.

And then there was the questioning. The last time the Finnish security service had gently put some questions to her she'd completely forgotten what she was meant to say, had blurted out entirely the wrong thing, and had almost sunk herself and Thrane without trace. During the earlier interrogations she'd had it word-perfect, repeating the story just as Thrane had drummed it into her, recounting how the mysterious couple had taken her and Berg to the empty house and tied her up and shot Berg and driven off when they heard Thrane's car approach.

During his own interrogation Thrane had regretted not having seen the car's registration, but was under the impression it was Finnish. He didn't mention anything about the revolver, though he knew perfectly well where it was, which was carefully concealed in the seat of his car. Nor did he offer a motive for Berg's killing, though he did suggest that the mysterious couple most probably worked for the same people as Berg—the Soviets—and might therefore have had professional differences.

As an explanation of events it was workable, and certainly

he Finns had found no reason to doubt it—just as long as Ragna stuck to the right set of facts. He had reminded her of what would happen if the truth leaked out—her removal to Helsinki, long questioning, a possible judicial hearing—but he wasn't sure she was capable of taking it in. If they questioned her again he had the awful feeling she would tell them the truth.

And now it was the fifth day. And still they waited.

During the morning he avoided the room where he knew Ragna would be sitting. It was only after he'd been to the mess and picked at a meal and spent a good half hour on the phone to Oslo that he went to find her, bearing a plate of sandwiches in case he could persuade her to eat.

She was standing by the window. The moment she saw him she rushed up and fixed him with those enormous luminous eyes. "The snow," she said breathlessly, "it's stopping! It's stopping!"

He looked out the window. The sky was certainly brighter and, apart from a few desultory flakes floating in the air, the snow had ceased.

"Don't raise your hopes."

"But they'll go and look now—surely!" Her voice rose to a moan, her mouth trembled. Thrane realized she was finally at breaking point.

He grasped her arm and led her to a chair. "They'll certainly leave as soon as they can. You stay here. I'll go and find out what's happening."

"Let me come too."

He didn't argue—he had the feeling the slightest thing would finish her—but helped her back to her feet and led her to the operations room. The Finnish CO came out and said: "We're sending a helicopter. Takeoff shortly. There's room for both of you. And we'd certainly like you to come along, Mrs. Johansen, to help us pinpoint the spot."

She didn't speak. The tears streamed down her face.

Ragna sat behind the pilot and peered over his shoulder. The snow stretched out endlessly below, a vast gray desert under a heavy metallic sky. There was nothing to be seen at all—no hint of vegetation, no shadows, no suggestion of lakes or streams or gullies. Nothing.

The dread that gripped her heart grew into even more vicious forms. They would fly over him, they would hover over him, they would fail to find him! And in another hour or so it would be too dark and the helicopter would be forced to turn back—turn back without him.

The prospect was torture, unbearable, and, closing her eyes, she put up yet more desperate prayers.

Someone touched her arm. It was the navigator. He pointed downward then at his chart. Ragna craned forward, looked down, but saw nothing. The navigator passed the chart over and pointed at a tiny dot.

The second hut. They were over the hut!

She nodded stupidly and gratefully at the navigator. He tapped his watch and held up one finger. One minute, one minute to the estimated position, to the cross she had helped put on the chart. She exchanged glances with Thrane, who gave her a thumbs-up.

The helicopter reduced speed and began to descend. Ragna looked desperately out the window.

The snow came up to meet them. They hovered, went forward again, hovered, and finally descended onto the snow.

The two soldiers who'd been sitting in the rear of the machine helped her out and escorted her clear of the blades. She walked on, wading through the thick snow, trying to get her bearings, realizing with a growing sense of panic that she recognized nothing—*nothing*.

Thrane and the navigator joined her, waiting silently as she turned and turned again and finally looked at them in dumb helplessness.

Raising his voice above the helicopter's din, Thrane said: "Remember the snow's made it look entirely different!"

But this different?

The navigator shouted: "We're definitely on the trail as marked on the map. If we're off, it's only on a north-south axis. If you can work out whether we're north or south of the spot, then we can go back to the machine and take another hop."

She understood. She looked at the map and tried to identify

he slight hills, tried to make out whether she might have assed this way before Hal had been shot or after.

After. Her instincts told her after.

She pointed north.

They returned to the helicopter and made a short hop to he north.

They got out again and Ragna scanned the soft white land-cape once more.

There was a slight hill to the west of her and another to the north. Something about the one to the north made her pause. Could it be the one Rolf had sent her to climb? Might the rocky outcrop she'd reached be hidden under a slight hump halfway up?

The more she stared, the more hopeful she felt. Just as she was about to shout the news to Thrane, one of the soldiers signaled toward the north. Ragna lumbered through the snow toward him. "I think I can see something up there." He passed her his binoculars. She twiddled the focus and, follow-ing his directions, peered hard. A faint sticklike object. Very straight.

A ski. She hardly dared believe it.

No one spoke as they trooped back to the helicopter and climbed in. The machine revved, took off, and slowly ad-vanced. The navigator talked rapidly into his mouthpiece; the pilot nodded his head, looked down through his side window, nodded again, and lowered his machine once more.

They jumped out.

There, some ten yards in front of them, was a single ski standing upright in the snow.

Someone patted Ragna on the shoulder. It was Thrane.

They advanced. The soldiers had shovels in their hands. As they drew near, Ragna noticed that the second of the two crossed skis had almost completely fallen over. She mentally chastised herself for not having driven it deeper into the snow, then realized it didn't matter anymore.

Perhaps nothing mattered anymore.

They halted in front of the snow-covered mound that was the boulder. To Ragna's mind the white mound seemed to have transposed itself into an ice tomb, cold and still, and she hesitated, in the viselike grip of a terrible fear.

Then one of the soldiers leaned forward and swept some snow away with his glove, and she saw the fabric of the tarpaulin. Shaking off the fear, she joined the others, scraping at the snow, working feverishly until the tarpaulin was completely exposed.

It was Thrane who reached up and cut the thin rope holding the tarpaulin to the boulder. She stood back then. She stood back because she couldn't face the next few moments of uncertainty. She wanted Thrane to look, she wanted Thrane to establish the situation, she wanted him to turn to face her.

And then she'd know. She'd know by the look in his eyes.

They pulled the tarpaulin away. Thrane climbed in over the ice wall and stooped down. He stayed down a long time. He must have said something to the soldier, for the soldier nodded and hurried past Ragna.

Ragna could bear it no longer and stepped forward.

As she did so Thrane put his head up.

Then she knew.

The tears spilled down her cheeks. "He's—?"

"Just about. He managed a smile anyway." And then Thrane smiled too.

Epilogue

For eleven months of the year the house stands empty, the valley deserted. In the winters the west wind comes swooping over the island as fiercely as ever, disgorging snow that piles against the windows and doorways, snow that remains uncleared until the spring thaw.

No wood fires warm the cold house; no lights shine out over the valley. The vegetable garden has long since grown wild, died back, and been overgrown by tougher vegetation. The paddocks are empty, the barn unoccupied except for an old tractor which has seen better days.

But the trees! They are truly remarkable. Admittedly there are one or two gaps where the harsh winter of 1963 took its toll, but in the subsequent five years those that survived have flourished—by Arctic standards at least.

A grove of willows stands near the house; also a solitary lilac, which was long since given up for dead. Above, there is rowan, aspen, ash, and bird cherry, and higher still, pine and spruce which have finally grown tall enough to break some of the force of the wind.

But you have to come in summer to see the trees at their best. Then the sudden wealth of light and warmth causes the whole valley to burgeon with growth and color. In the shelter of the trees there is dwarf rhododendron and azalea, and on the more open slopes, purple and white heathers, and tiny white and pink Alpine flowers, even wild orchids. The lichens and mosses spring up, the grasses in the lower meadows grow tall, ready for the harvesting that will never come.

It is when the valley is at its most lush and beautiful that the eleven months' silence is finally broken. Then a boat motor close in to the shore and a party is ferried to the beach, complete with luggage and large quantities of stores.

Last year the party numbered four, but this year it's five. Young Jan is almost four months old.

Immediately after the party has landed, the valley is filled with noise—a great deal of it—as the two elder children streak off in search of adventure. Kris, a very grown-up ten, deigns to let his young sister, Elise, enter the boathouse and, though she's only four, allows her to help with the removal of the cover. She's not a lot of use, of course, but she tugs willingly and, once the cover is off, looks suitably impressed at the sight of *Lillebjørn*.

"Got no mast!" Elise remarks.

"Of course it has!" Kris scoffs. "It's lying down over there. There isn't room to put it up in here, is there?"

Elise studies the height of the roof and frowns. After a time she says: "Does it fall over?"

"Does what fall over?"

A pause. "The boat."

"What do you mean?"

Elise struggles with the effort of explaining this complex thing. "In the sea. Does"—she purses her lips—"does it get blowed over in the wind?"

"No!" Kris laughs. "Never!" He says it in the dismissive sort of way brothers reserve for younger sisters. "Hal and I sailed it in a gale once, in the middle of winter. And it didn't capsize then. Nowhere near it!"

Elise has heard this story before. As always she doesn't quite know what to make of it. Particularly when Kris has recently hinted that Daddy's missing fingers and his eye that can't see have something to do with the boat episode. Yet Mummy definitely told her that Daddy lost his fingers in an accident with a gun.

It's all rather mystifying and she's glad of the distraction of the shiny wood of the boat. She runs her finger over it and watches Kris as he sorts through the ropes in a knowledgeable manner.

A call sounds from outside and Elise scampers off to find

er mother sitting on the grass, the baby on her lap, sur-
ounded by luggage. "Oh, there you are," Ragna says, smiling.
he adds: "Daddy's gone to see if he can get the tractor
oing."

Elise vaguely remembers the tractor from last year and how
ery noisy and bumpy it was, and how frightened and thrilled
he was all at the same time. "Can I sit on your lap, Mamma?
n the tractor?"

"Mmm."

A movement catches Elise's eye, the bright fluttering of a
ny white butterfly, and, forgetting her fear of the tractor, she
uns off to investigate.

Ragna closed her eyes and let the sun beat against her face.
h, how she loved the summer! How she loved the days that
ever ended and the sun that never set. How she loved leav-
ng the south behind for these four precious weeks—leaving
he daily rush to get the baby fed and changed, and Elise
ressed, and Kris to school, and Hal off on one of his con-
ultancy jobs, or up to his study to write. Leaving that for—
eace. Up here there was no timetable, no hurry; with twenty-
our hours of continuous light the day just happened of its
wn accord.

She loved to see the children running free—dirty, of
ourse, and more than a little wild, but happy and, when they
weren't happy, tired and ready for bed. She loved to watch
Hal and Kris setting off on a fishing expedition in *Lillebjørn*, to
follow the white sails as they glided away across the gentle blue
water, to wait for their return and meet them at the shore and
admire the catch.

Ah, the peace, the peace.

Most of all, she loved the long evenings on the veranda after
the children were in bed, when she and Hal sat and talked, or
read, or listened to music floating out through the open windows of the living room.

Now and again they did none of these things, but sat in
silence, looking out over the mirror-calm water toward the
white-capped mountains. And then he would swing his arm
around her shoulders and she would reach for his hand and
squeeze it hard.

They never tried to forget what had happened—it woul have been quite impossible—and occasionally, when they fe the need, they talked about it. Then they always reminde each other—though reminders were hardly necessary—of a the good things that had come out of it: their new life, thre beautiful children, and, most of all, each other. Also, justice a sort. Yes: that was important too.

And Ragna would lean back on his shoulder and sneak look at him, at that face she knew so well, with its bent nos that had never gotten fixed and the scar on one cheek, an think how very lucky she was to have him.

But then there wasn't a day when she didn't think that.

A bird sang high in the sky above, a piercing song of suc sweetness that she looked up to search for it. The baby pulle at a button on her blouse and gurgled. The scent of flower: of grasses and soft abundance, rose up around her.

Ah, the peace, the peace.

The silence was shattered by the roar of the tractor's engin descending the valley.

Ragna gave an exclamation of pleasure and admiration He'd gotten it going! But after all these years she should hav known: he always did.

She stood up and called to the children. The tracto emerged over the brow of the hill and came down the track the trailer rattling in its wake.

Hal drew up and jumped out. "Where are my helpers then?" He grinned at the children.

As soon as the last bag was in, Hal helped Ragna up into th trailer with the baby and Elise, then climbed into the cab with Kris. As they bounced up the hill Kris whooped with joy, Elise clung to Ragna's trousers, and the baby fell asleep.

Once they reached the house it was quite a business to un load everything, find the food, get the perishables into the re frigerator—a luxury Ragna had installed—then feed the baby, put him down to nap, and prepare a meal for the rest of the family. By the time Ragna had gotten the food on the table, everyone had disappeared. She shrugged it off: situation normal.

But she had a good idea of where Hal would be.

She ran lightly down the veranda steps and walked around

the front of the old vegetable garden. There he was, ouching by the wall, pulling gently at the tall grass growing ver a small plot marked with stones. She didn't disturb him ntil he stood up.

"Hi," she called, strolling over.

He gestured toward the plot. "I'll have a go at this first thing the morning," he said. "And the sign too." He had a ooden marker in his hand, its inscription so faded that it was arely possible to make out the single word: BAMSE.

"Have we got any suitable paint?" she asked.

"I think so."

They walked back to the house.

"I thought we might go to Ringvassoy early next week," he aid.

"Yes."

Ringvassoy was the large island close by, where Arne was uried. Once a year they took flowers and tidied the grave and leaned the gravestone.

He asked: "And what about going to see Aslak? Have you lecided?"

"Yes." She looped her arm through his. "I won't bother. It's uch a way. And we can just as easily discuss things on the phone."

Undisguised relief came over Hal's face. He'd given her very encouragement in her continuing campaign for Lapp ights; he'd been proud when, despite losing the battle over he location of the Kåfjord installation, she'd won assurances hat the disturbance to the Lapps would be minimized. But, upportive though he was, he didn't like the campaign to impinge on their time together, especially here at Brattdal.

And he was right, she decided. Nothing must be allowed to nterfere with the peace, the perfect peace. She squeezed his arm, overcome by the wonderful prospect of having him and he children all to herself for a month.

They climbed the steps to the veranda and, pausing, looked out over the valley.

After a time she murmured gently: "There's a meal on the table."

He turned his head, a small frown of annoyance on his face,

the frown he always wore when someone spoke in his poor e
and he failed to hear.

She repeated it.

He nodded. "Where are the children?"

"Oh—vanished."

"Ha! Situation normal."

"Yes." And, catching his eye, she threw back her head an
laughed.

CLARE FRANCIS is no stranger to success. At thirteen, she was accepted by the Royal Ballet School. At seventeen, she entered London University, where she earned a degree in economics. After a brief, meteoric corporate career, she became famous as a sailor and adventurer, setting the trans-Atlantic speed record for a solo crossing by a woman. Her book about her sea adventures, *Come Hell or High Water*, was a #1 bestseller in England. Her first novel, *Night Sky*, spent ten weeks on the *New York Times* bestseller list, launching her in the U.S. as a top-ranking thriller writer. WOLF WINTER is her third novel.

TOP-SPEED THRILLERS WITH UNFORGETTABLE IMPACT FROM AVON BOOKS

TASS IS AUTHORIZED TO ANNOUNCE... Julian Semyor
70569-9/$4.50US/$5.95C

From Russia's bestselling author, the unique spy thriller that tells it fr
the other point of view.

DEEP LIE Stuart Woods 70266-5/$4.95US/$5.95C

The new Soviet-sub superthriller..."Almost too plausible...one of
most readable espionage novels since *The Hunt for the Red Octobe.*
Atlanta Journal & Constitution

RUN BEFORE THE WIND Stuart Woods
70507-9/$3.95US/$4.95C

"The book has everything—love, sex, violence, adventure, beaut
women and power-hungry men, terrorists and intrigue."
The Washington Po

COLD RAIN Vic Tapner 75483-5/$3.95US/$4.95C
A stunning thriller of cold-blooded espionage and desperate betray

MAJENDIE'S CAT Frank Fowlkes 70408-0/$3.9
Swindler against con man compete in a plan to bring the US to its kne
and wreak global economy for good!

THE GRAY EAGLES Duane Unkefer 70279-7/$4.5
Thirty-one years after WW II, the Luftwaffe seeks revenge...and o
more chance at glory.

THE FLYING CROSS Jack D. Hunter
75355-3/$3.95US/$4.95Ca

From the author of *The Blue Max*, a riveting, suspense-packed flyi
adventure in the war-torn skies over Europe.